D1387667

GREEN DRAGON, WHITE TIGER

ANNETTE MOTLEY

Macdonald

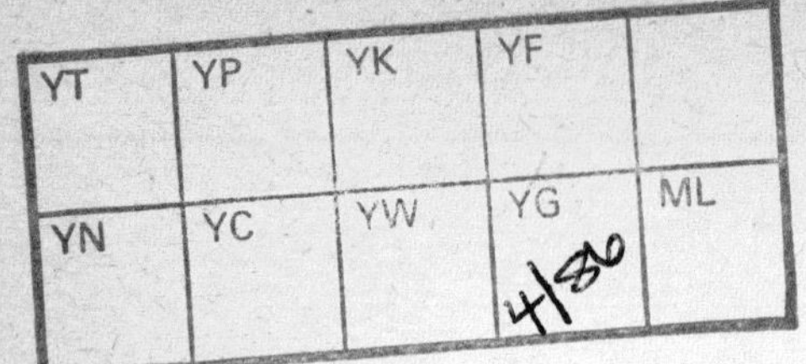

A Macdonald Book

First published in Great Britain in 1986
Macdonald & Co (Publishers) Ltd
London & Sydney

All characters in this publication are fictitious and any resemblance to real persons, living or dead, is purely coincidental.

British Library Cataloguing in Publication Data

Motley, Annette
Green dragon, white tiger.
I. Title
823′.914[F] PR6063.0842/

ISBN 0-356-10069-3

Photoset in North Wales by
Derek Doyle & Associates, Mold, Clwyd
Reproduced, printed and bound in Great Britain by
Hazell Watson & Viney Limited,
Member of the BPCC Group,
Aylesbury, Bucks

Macdonald & Co
London & Sydney
Maxwell House
74 Worship Street
London EC2A 2EN
A BPCC plc Company

The Prophecy

The astrologer was appalled.

The child turned in its nursemaid's arms and gave a shout of delight, grabbing at the shiny dragon pendant that hung from her neck. The girl chuckled and tried to loose the acquisitive little fingers, but they held on fast, both hands clutching the bright medallion.

Surely this was a sign that he was not mistaken?

The child's parents were waiting for his next words. The wind-scoured surfaces of the General's face showed no impatience but he was betrayed by the long grey vein that throbbed at his temple. His wife, Golden Willow, stood beside him, her silken sleeves folded across her breast, her graceful figure as tranquil as a pillar of jade. Only the extreme quality of her stillness told Yuan of her deep concern.

His apprehension subsided, giving way to excitement. In all his years of practice there had never been anything like this.

How should he tell them? He needed time. The occasion should have its dignity.

How would they take it? He had given them small cause for satisfaction so far.

The General had wanted no prediction for himself. He had enjoyed the friendship of two Emperors, and was now a duke, with the tax revenues of two thousand families, and the governor-general of the prefecture of Li Chou. He no longer had any need to question fate.

He had, however, been gratified to learn that Golden Willow was destined for wealth and contentment throughout her days, and that one of her children would bring her particular satisfaction. He had been less pleased to hear that this was unlikely to be their eldest daughter, Rose Bird, who would make the honourable marriage expected of her, but would later bring dishonour to her husband's name. Family pride had been further dashed by the news that, although the General's two young sons by his first wife would both enter the imperial service, they would never become first grade officials; their path to success was obscurely blocked by some greater force than that of their own destinies.

Each of these three children had been sent away in turn, and now only the youngest remained, the infant in boy's clothes who stared at Yuan out of strange green eyes above the captured dragon.

If only he could be absolutely certain. He felt the pressure of their waiting grow stronger. For good or ill, he must speak.

'The boy has a rare and remarkable appearance,' he began. He saw the little nursemaid simper and instantly he was sure. His expert eye retraced the delicate features which presented such an astounding revelation. Midway between a science and an art, his physiognomist's skill customarily showed him the broad outline of character and fate which would be filled in by the subject's horoscope. What he saw here had shocked him deeply.

'It would be helpful if you would put down the baby and let him walk about,' he said, marshalling his confidence. 'Oh, by all means let him keep the pendant, or he will screw up his face with tears and I shall not be able to observe him as closely as I must.'

The nurse smiled and did as he asked. The parents were silent. Yuan watched closely as the child staggered about the room before running to its mother, who bent to caress its dark head with a movement of pure grace. The proportions of the small body confirmed the conclusions formed from his examination of the bones of the head and the tiny, flowerlike face. According to the ethics of his profession, he must, of course tell them what he saw; but he would leave them an escape route, should they wish to take it.

What he was about to reveal was, after all, tantamount to treason.

'This child is marked and blessed by the rays of the sun,' he announced with the solemn mystery of his trade. 'This is the countenance of the dragon and of the phoenix – the sacred attributes of the great God-emperors of our history. You must realise that these are the characteristics of a person who will win great fame and wield unparalleled power.'

Pressed by the heightening of parental tension, he hurried on. 'I have yet to cast the horoscope, of course, but I am already perfectly certain –' He hesitated, aware of the enormity of what he must say, '– that if this child were a girl –' he looked quickly at the young nursemaid, who rewarded him with an instant blush,

'– there is no doubt whatsoever that she would one day become the ruler of the Empire.'

Golden Willow made a small sound. Then came a silence filled with the heartbeat of intense reaction.

'Your findings leave no room for any manner of doubt?' the General asked at last, quietly, but not without a measure of threat.

'I will stake my life upon them,' Yuan said simply. 'Indeed, I have already done so, in speaking to you so freely.'

'That is true,' the General allowed. He stroked his dark beard in deliberation.

'But is it not also true to say that the mandate of Heaven can never pass into the hands of a woman?'

Yuan bowed his head.

'Then we will not speak of this any further. There will be no horoscope cast. And you, astrologer, will never speak of it again, to anyone, no matter how exalted. Do I make myself clear?'

'It is understood, my lord.'

'Swear it!'

'I swear!'

The General turned appraising eyes upon the child's nurse, who stood goggling with one hand to her throat.

'And you, my girl – do you think you are capable of keeping your word, once you have given it?'

'Yes, Honourable Master. I swear!'

'For a lifetime?' His smile was kind. 'I believe women are fonder of telling secrets than of keeping them.'

'I have sworn.' The small chin went up. 'I will keep my word.'

'That is excellent.'

He knew he did not have to speak to his wife, who had taken the child in her arms and was holding it as though she would save it from an earthquake or a great fire.

'Then, now let us go and dine,' he said expansively, 'and leave the future in the gift of the Gods.'

They did so.

The astrologer did not again set eyes on the youngest child, concerning whose sex no one had spoken, but as he left the great house the next morning to begin his long journey to the capital, he said to himself with a strange exhilaration, 'If she can hold on to the Dragon Throne with as much determination as she held on to that bauble, her rule will be longer and stronger than any in our history!'

PART ONE
Spring Dreams

1

Spring dreams that went on
Well past dawn; and I felt
That all around me was the sound
Of birds singing; but really
The night was full of the noise
Of rain and wind; and now I wonder
How many blossoms have fallen.

(Meng Hao-jan, 689–740)

'He'll be here tomorrow! I can hardly believe it!'

Black Jade held out her arms in welcome to the sun. She was so happy that she wanted to sing aloud.

'Neither can I. It's the most wonderful thing that has ever happened to us!' Rose Bird waved away a bee from her peach-gold nose.

It was the season of plum blossom. The orchard hummed with the bees' song and the afternoon air was deliciously scented with honey. Among the dreaming trees small birds sang in hanging cages, their soft feathers as white as the prodigal drift of blossom, and their tiny claws gilded to match the hearts of the flowers.

Black Jade stood still and let the heady essences surround and seep into her until she seemed to swim in them, buoyed and floating on a sheer weight of scent.

'Come on, or we'll never be ready in time.' Rose Bird plucked at her sleeve, and slowly, half-drunk with the perfumed invasion of her senses, she led the way across the path of flat stones which allowed one to pass without injuring the fresh new blades of the grass. Winding between the trees, they soon reached the scarlet-painted pavilion where they loved to sit and gaze out over the gardens towards the stern longevity of the mountains. Old friends and guardians, these lifted their hawk-haunted indigo crags to form a protective phalanx far beyond the tall trees and the curving blue and green roofs of the Wu mansion.

While her sister hurried inside, Black Jade sat down contentedly on the pavilion steps and surveyed the familiar, beloved landscape. Slowly, possessively, her gaze stroked down from the mountains to the dusty golden bowl of the plain, ribboned by its bright tributary of the mighty Yellow River, and returned to the sunburned walls that kept her like a jewel in their strong casket. Within them, the various beautiful buildings were winningly disposed upon both banks of a narrow, discursive stream, the Hasty River. An ancestor with an artist's eye had widened one of its curves to form a pretty ornamental lake, where waterfowl led their chicks in and out of the floating lotuses and around the islands where they made their nests. There were several bridges across the river, as it wound among the gardens, conveniently dividing the apartments of the girls' father and of their other male relatives from those of the feminine members of the clan. One was never very far from the sight or sound of water, and in winter there was the sparkling pleasure of skating on the frozen lake.

But now it was spring, the time of year for feeling everything passionately. As she gazed at its beauty, Black Jade was filled with a deep and intense love for her home. Its unrivalled setting, just above the tree-line, overlooking the town to the east and the green and gold plain to the west, with the river to feed it, and the mountains to guard it, answered a need in her for the dramatic, the grandiose, the exceptional. It was simply the finest estate in Wen Shui, perhaps in the whole of Shansi province. The scene before her was especially glorious now, during the few days known as the period of Serene Clarity, when the sun smiled down from the mountains and the plum blossom was spread like white lace over the orchard.

This year Serene Clarity was more than usually auspicious. Tomorrow would bring inestimable honour to the Wu clan, who were already the acknowledged leaders in the province. It was the day when the Emperor himself would pay them a visit.

Black Jade sprang from her seat on the steps and did a small dance of joy which her stately mother would have considered unsuitable to the peaceful and harmonious surroundings.

'Just think!' she called to Rose Bird, who was, as usual, doing something useful, up on the veranda. 'Tomorrow the Son of Heaven will stand on this very spot! Like us, he will be ravished by the plum blossom. He will sit and eat in this very pavilion. His sacred hands will touch – at least I hope they will – the dishes we have spent so long preparing. Do you think he will like my

Hangchow ginger – or will it be too hot for him?'

'He'll love it,' said Rose Bird loyally. 'It looks so pretty, crystallised and coloured with lemon and rosewater. And he's sure to eat lots of the stone-honey cakes.' These were mouth-watering delicacies made from the juice of dried sugar-cane, shaped into little men and horses. Black Jade was very proud of them.

She stood up and paced in the longer grass beneath the wooden foundations of the pavilion. 'I can hardly bear this anticipation. It almost hurts. I wonder what he will be like? If he is even half the man Father says he is –'

'– Of course he is, probably twice the man! How can you doubt it? You have listened to all the stories, as often as I have.'

The stories. They had coloured their early childhood in vivid and exciting hues. First there had been the tales of the present Emperor's father, the High Ancestor, who had often visited here in the old days when the General had fought beside him to help him establish the dynasty. The girls had come to think of him much as they would of some elderly uncle whom they had never met. But his son, Li Shih-min the Magnificent – he was a very different proposition. His glorious achievements had already put him into the realm of myth, even in his own young lifetime. He was the people's hero – that, indeed, was the very meaning of his name – a figure of romance and chivalry to rival even the semi-divine rulers of the Empire's early history.

'I don't doubt it,' Black Jade cried, stretching out her hands as though she was already welcoming the paragon. 'I know he will be as handsome as the Yellow Emperor and as clever as the Monkey King.' He had to be, for at an age when most ambitious young men were seriously studying their classics, he had gathered and trained a military force that had unified the broken Empire by the power of a character that drew men towards him like a lodestone.

'Do you suppose he will speak to us – separately, I mean? Whatever would I say to him, if he did?' Rose Bird flushed, looking extremely pretty. At sixteen, she was old enough to weave romantic fantasies about the young hero.

'Oh, don't worry,' teased Black Jade. 'All you will have to do will be to bow in acquiescence. He will go to our honourable father, pale and shocked beneath the impact of your beauty, and beg him to allow you to become his concubine – or who knows, even a secondary wife? So enslaved will he be that he will sweep you on to his horse and carry you away with him when he leaves for Chang-an, impatient with the desire to make you his own!' she finished extravagantly.

'Don't be cruel, Jade!' Rose Bird was mortified by this more or less exact description of her private dream.

'I'm not. Really. I wouldn't be at all surprised if you were invited to enter the Inner Palace. The Emperor is very grateful to the General, and it is the accepted thing to reward his servants by giving positions to their sons and daughters. And I am sure,' she added warmly, 'that when he actually sees you, he *will* want you for his concubine. Though I would miss you, most terribly, if you went away.'

'You mustn't talk such nonsense,' said Rose Bird, scarlet and pleased. 'Now come in here and let's decide where everything is to be.'

'In a moment.'

Black Jade leaned on the crimson lacquered rail of the veranda, trying to make herself concentrate on their plans for the coming Feast of the Plum Blossom. Her own fantasies, which she now consciously repressed, revolved less around the Emperor than around the revolutionary career of his young sister, the legendary Princess Hero, who had thrown off the restraint and claustrophobia of the women's courts to ride at the head of her own cavalry and set out to conquer the capital at her brother's side. Black Jade had hoped that perhaps Lady Hero might, by some marvellous quirk of fate, accompany Shih-min on his present journey, but she had to admit that, since the Princess was now married and occupied with her husband and family far to the east of the province, her dream was less likely to be realised than was that of her sister.

She shook it from her and went through the delicate, open-carved doors to the pavilion platform. She had always loved the little building. The General himself had carved many of the lattice-work screens that made up its waist-high walls. It was an art to which he had always been partial, and all his children possessed intricate wooden toys, also of his loving workmanship.

Now his second wife's younger daughter cast a similarly artistic eye over the space that was to be transformed for tomorrow.

'I think we should leave most of it until the morning,' she decided. 'The blossom will be fresher if it is picked at dawn, and we can take the bird-cages at the same time. We can fetch the cushions, the shawls and the rugs today; this evening will do. It's the music I'm most concerned about. I've rehearsed the players several times, but it's by no means perfect.'

'It will be,' said Rose Bird with certain knowledge. 'Not even the Son of Heaven can be such a perfectionist as you are.'

This was so. It was why, in compliment to her talent for such things, their mother had placed her in charge of the organisation of the feast which the men of the clan would hold in the pavilion. Rose Bird would be her aide. They had always worked well together, for her sister was content to let her take the lead in their schemes, which suited her admirably. Rose Bird's taste was the more restrained, however, and she could be relied upon to scotch Black Jade's deplorable tendency towards exaggeration. She called her now, frowning slightly and dragging a piece of furniture.

'Haven't we a better dragon chair?' she asked. 'Part of one of the claws is missing at the back.'

Black Jade ran to help her, making a mental note to ask the maids to sweep and perfume the floor of the pavilion. She examined the vast ebony chair with the dragons writhing on its high back and crawling along the arm-rests.

'I think this is still the best. The upholstery is new, and besides, it's the one Shih-min's father used to sit in.'

'Hush, Black Jade! You know you must not speak the Emperor's name.'

'What can it matter? No one will know. I think it is a very foolish rule. The Son of Heaven must have a name, like anyone else. We call everyone else by their first names, even dukes – why not Shih-min?'

'I don't know. I only know we mustn't,' replied the law-abiding Rose Bird.

'I think,' said Black Jade after some consideration, 'that it is just another of those things that are meant to distance him from us, to make him seem a far greater creature than any mere man could be, like the laws about what colours he can wear and which way he is to face and what he must eat at certain times of the year.'

'But he *is* greater than any other man! He is more like one of the Gods. Of course he should be distant from us.'

Black Jade sniffed. 'Well, if I were Emperor, I should find it all very tedious. Nevertheless we had better get it right.' Her tone became businesslike. 'Now, according the Book of Rites we must place the dragon chair here, on the eastern side of the room, if we are to conform with the imperial orientation for springtime. I wonder if His Majesty *is* a strict observer of the *feng-shui*? I should imagine he'd find it more practical to choose which side of his palace he lives in according to the prevailing winds rather than the *Book of Rites*. What else? He won't wear green, as he should, because he is still in mourning for the Empress, but if he has something green about him, and asks only for lamb and sweetcorn, we shall know he does hold to the conventions. I hope he doesn't. What a waste of all our lovely sweetmeats! Now, where do you think we should put the musicians?'

'Not too near. They'll want to hear themselves talk at the table.'

'True. We'll put them among the trees, on the north side; the sound will travel gently from there. Have we thought of everything? We've worked out the colour schemes, and the food and wine are all arranged. The musicians have their orders.'

'I think that's all. Surely nothing can go wrong. These few days are under the rule of Jupiter, and the calendar says they are a time for "benevolence and the relaxation of authority". Isn't that lucky?'

Black Jade grimaced. The almanac also qualified Serene Clarity as a period of angry emotions. That, alas, would be nothing strange to the Wu household, whose lovely setting was not matched by inner harmony.

As if the thought had created its own image, the sound of male laughter gusted through the trees, and the girls saw their two half-brothers approaching, their faces alight with shared mischief.

They had evidently been hunting for their bows were slung over their padded jackets and their trousers, yellow with dust, were tucked into the deerskin boots that crushed their way through the new grass.

Yuan Shuang idly cracked his whip across a branch that lowered in front of him, causing a pale shower of petals. Then he stopped as if struck by something. He chuckled and seized his bow. Before the horrified eyes of his sisters he took aim carefully and accurately discharged the strong arrow that was made to pierce the hide of a deer through the narrow bars of a hanging cage, to break open the feathered breast of the white bird that sang there.

Both girls felt like bursting into aching tears. Black Jade caught hers back before they fell. 'You are a monster, Brother Fox!' she shouted. 'May you die in just such agony, and never return to the earth!'

Yuan Shuang raised a mocking eyebrow. 'I thought at least you might aplaud the shot,' he grumbled. 'It was an extremely skilful one. By the way,' he added vigorously, 'I hope you are about to be grateful to me, Little Sister. I have just exercised Snow Prince for you, since you hadn't bothered to do so yourself and my own horse is lame.'

Black Jade was now shaking with a double reaction. She glared at her brother with a passionate hatred.

'How *dared* you do such a thing?' she raged. 'He is *my* stallion, mine alone, and you are never to lay your filthy hands on him. I'd rather a leper rode him!' She loathed Shuang even more for his ability to reduce her to the child she thought she no longer was.

Triumphant, he grinned his satisfaction at her outburst.

'Listen to me, you imperious brat,' he ordered. 'You know perfectly well that the beast is too big for you. I find he suits me to perfection. In fact, I've a good mind to ask the General if I may have him. I'm sure he'll agree that the horse must have proper exercise. And I'm afraid he has a rather uncomfortable stomach, poor animal. You really can't have been keeping an eye on him.'

'What have you done to him?' she cried. 'He was all right yesterday.'

Shuang cocked his head at her with the foxy expression that had earned him the nickname by which the girls always addressed him. He had dosed the horse with cenna. He had been jealous of the splendid creature ever since the day that Black Jade had chosen him for her own. He *was* too big for her, but she had gained his confidence within a month and brought him to a perfect understanding of what she required of him.

'If any harm comes to him,' she said now, coming slowly down the pavilion steps and fixing her brother with a cold and curiously contained expression, 'I will cut you to pieces with your own knife.'

A splutter of manic laughter greeted her threat. It came from the other young man, Yuan Ching, known to herself and the still sniffing Rose Bird as Brother Hyena. As usual, they all ignored him.

Shuang fingered the hunting knife at his belt. 'Before you were able to do that, Little Demon, I should have stopped you, slapped you hard, then cut off your clothes with it, shred by shred until you had learned the meaning of maidenly modesty. You are an offensive little animal and I should enjoy your punishment.'

Rose Bird wailed, genuinely afraid of him.

'Talk like a dragon; act like a worm,' said Black Jade contemptuously. 'Never mind all that rubbish; I want to know what state my horse is in.'

Shuang tired of the game. 'I've shown him who's master, that's all.'

'One day we'll do the same for you,' Brother Hyena chimed in, looking her up and down in the slow, insulting manner he had developed recently. His narrowed eyes made her feel unclean.

Ching was a narrow young man in every way; his eyes, his shoulders, his hyena's face, his skinny frame, and above all, his shallow, imitative mind, the mere shadow of his brother's. Shuang had at least the virtues of florid good looks and his father's firm build and an astute and opportunist brain.

'You should be ashamed to speak to her like that,' said Rose Bird, finding her courage. She was always more shaken than her sister by their quarrels. Her voice trembled, but she went doggedly on. 'As for your despicable act just now – it was the most cruel and cowardly thing – it dishonours both yourself and the profession of archery. I am ashamed to be related to you, even by half!'

'Mind your own business, Rose Bird,' said Shuang nastily. 'Your mouth is better occupied in gulping up your idiotic tears. You are an amiable, boring girl whose body will be enough to excite some man to marry you, but lucid speech is not your competence.'

Rose Bird flinched at his rudeness. Black Jade, seeing that she was hurt, momentarily forgot Snow Prince.

'And what, I wonder, is *your* competence, Brother Fox? Or yours, Brother Hyena? Have we heard some mention of your entering His Majesty's service?' Her low voice purred. 'Then hadn't you better go and study your classics, so that you don't both fail the exam again and lose face for the whole clan?'

She was not being altogether fair. The brothers had already passed the difficult Civil Service exam at a respectable level, but if they were to graduate as *chin shih* scholars and qualify for high grade posts, they must be word-perfect in the five great classical books and be capable of writing an outstanding essay on any given subject. Shuang had very nearly passed last time they had made the attempt, though Ching's points had been low.

Her barb had found its mark. Shuang's look of fury satisfied her anger and the way he tightened his hand on his whip did not alarm her. He would never dare to use it on her.

Suddenly she wanted to waste no more time here. She was relieved to see her nurse, Welcome, hurrying across the path towards them. The young woman's face was set in the expectation of trouble. She had looked after Black Jade since the day she was born and loved her fiercely and protectively. She reached the steps and stood glaring at the discomfited brothers.

'You have no business here today, Young Masters. You should be with your tutor. Get along with you and leave the Young Mistresses to their duties.'

'I'd keep a civil tongue in your head if I were you,' said Shuang savagely, but he left them nevertheless, striding abruptly away with Ching loping behind him, still grinning idiotically. Welcome, unlike her mistresses, did not scruple to tell tales.

'Stay here with Welcome and tell her what we need for tomorrow.' Black Jade told her sister. 'I must go to the stables.'

Her brothers' boorish laughter followed her as she ran off. How she loathed them! If only Snow Prince had thrown the damnable Shuang and broken his insolent neck! She raced angrily through the innocent grass, leaving a wake of ravaged blades. Why did the General have to marry the boys' wretched mother first? She and Rose Bird had often speculated grimly on the character of that long-dead lady; her sons had certainly not received their heritage of jealousy and spite from their father.

Ever since she could remember, they had tormented their half-sisters, especially herself. She had grown up with an aggressive edge to her nature that was continually sharpened by their animosity. Their tricks and taunts were unceasing. Worse in Black Jade's eyes, they were scant in their duty towards her mother. They never quite dared to show her outright insolence; Golden Willow's stately and authoritative manner was too daunting for that. But from the early days of her marriage to their father they had slighted her, first with the stubborn speechlessness of children, later with a cool and studied politeness that hovered on the boundary of obvious indifference. Golden Willow rarely complained of them, knowing that to do so only increased the discord of the household. She was too wise to jeopardise her own relations with her husband for the sake of the temporary lull in hostilities that was all her interference could achieve. Neither did she please the boys by playing the wicked stepmother, but called to her aid the Confucian code that decreed that, after the age of ten, gently bred boys and girls should, in the main, keep apart.

The children themselves, absorbed in the fascinating tactics of partisan warfare, made nonsense of her efforts. They were developing their minds as much by the surprise and sabotage of each other as in their formal studies. Each also claimed the loyalties of half-a-dozen of the General's children by his concubines, eight boys and four girls, who made excellent infantry.

Black Jade brooded on her brothers as she made for the stables. So they saw themselves making their mark at court, did they? Imagined the Emperor would save them the trouble of resitting the exam? Well, so he might, if only as a favour to the General.

And if he did invite them to Chang-an? Perhaps Brother Fox might manage to acquit himself adequately. He had a certain vulpine intelligence that would serve him where he wished to go, into the prickly thickets of the law. Hyena-features, however, was no more than his brother's shadow, with all of Shuang's unpleasantness and none of his determination. Still, he only wanted to be a librarian; the lower grades shouldn't need much initiative. Hyena's classical studies were dogged enough and he had just about mastered enough characters to scrawl an unexceptional essay. But neither his abilities nor even Shuang's in any measure approached her own, and she knew it was this, rather than the older jealousies, that lay at the root of her dislike.

The General, once he had recognised in her the avid thirst for learning, had seen to it that her education matched that of his sons in every way. And when, during the last two years, she had begun to overtake them, he had provided her with special tuition. He did not, naturally, make any show of pride in her, but the boys, as they became young men, keenly felt the disgrace of being bested by a mere girl of thirteen.

The fact that Black Jade was now turning into a unique and arresting beauty was a further twist to the knife in their bellies. Their only relief was in fantasy. Shuang dreamed of ways of defeating her, from intellectual mastery to simply flogging her until her blood ran. Ching, whose nature was governed entirely by *yang*, had lately pleasured himself to sleep by imagining how he would rape her. He had once spied upon her naked body while she bathed, and now his lust for her developing ripeness overwhelmed him, despite the secret visits to the town's child prostitutes which he made with increasing regularity.

Though ignorant of its lurid private expressions, Black Jade sensed the growing violence of their hatred and longed to be released from its heaviness. She almost wished the Emperor *would* offer them the desired places at court then she would never have to suffer their obnoxious presence again.

Perhaps that would happen. But perhaps Rose Bird would be chosen too, and then she would be left without either the comfort of her best friend or the stimulus of her worst enemies.

Without noticing, she had reached the gateway to the stables. Now she was jerked out of her negative thoughts by a rich and affectionate chuckle. General Wu Shih-huo stood before her in the archway, his hands on his hips, his muscular bulk encased in the old army jerkin he wore for riding. The points of his fierce military moustache stood to attention as proudly as the wings of his starched cap. His eyes twinkled, as they usually did when they lit on Black Jade.

'*Amitabha*!' he growled. 'What is this evil little goblin doing in my path? You spoil your beauty, Second Daughter, with that hideous frown. Is anything wrong, or are you merely trying to frighten away some lesser demon?'

She shook her head, her face clearing, and bowed dutifully.

'Good morning, Honoured Father. No, nothing is wrong. I was just thinking.'

Whatever the provocation, one did not tell tales. The single aim in which the family was united was that of providing the General with an impression of undivided domestic felicity.

'Indeed? Then your thoughts will be more productive behind your normal face. What you need is a good gallop to get rid of those goblins. I was about to take a turn across the plain. D'you want to come with me?'

'Of course. I'd love it!' She beamed at him. Then her face fell. 'The only trouble is that – Snow Prince is tired,' she hesitated.

'Surely you've not been out already? There isn't a speck of dust about you.'

'No. I haven't. Shuang was riding him.'

Her father looked at her quizzically. 'You surprise me. I could have sworn you'd not let anyone else near that precious animal of yours.'

'I don't, usually; but Shuang's mare is lame. I'll tell you what, I'll take Sweet Briar, if you'll let me.' This was the General's second-string, a tough rough-haired mare bred by the Uighur Turks. He grunted agreement and the grooms fetched out the two mounts. Sweet Briar was personable enough, a tall roan, swift and reliable, but without the classic lines of the great stallion Wu-han, whose nostrils quivered eagerly at the sight of his master. He was a 'dragon-horse' like Snow Prince, with the long limbs, slender body and Roman nose that proclaimed his Arab ancestry, together with the muscle and staying power of the Mongolian tarpan that had married into it.

While the stablemen saddled up, Black Jade slipped into the stable to see if her favourite had come to any real harm. Snow Prince whickered plaintively from his stall when he caught wind of her, knowing he had been cheated of their time together by a second-rate and insensitive rider. He stamped his foot and nuzzled her cheek in forgiveness when she blew softly into his ear.

'I'm sorry. He shan't have you again, I promise,' she whispered, rubbing his smooth white coat. 'I'll bring you a sesame-seed cake later, just to make up.' She thought he seemed well enough, though the coat felt slightly damp, as though he had recently been rubbed down after sweating.

'Little Mistress? No need to worry. He was ridden a bit hard but he's fine now,' a cheerful voice assured her. It was Huan, the groom.

'Huan. You must never let Shuang – what's the matter? You've been hit. Did he do that?' There was a red weal on the boy's cheek.

Huan was her half-brother by the Lily Concubine and her sworn henchman. His passion for horses had earned him a place in the stables and Snow Prince was his especial care. He shook his head.

'Nothing to mention, Little Mistress. There's no damage to either of us. Young Master Fox gave our beauty a dose of something nasty, but I'm easily up to such tricks as that. I gave him a cure for it right away.'

'Huan, you are the best of brothers; I don't know what I'd do without you.' She clasped his shoulder for a second, making him flush to the roots of his glossy black topknot. He was a handsome boy, and resembled his father more closely than either of his legitimate sons. There had been a bond between the two of them since Huan had fished her out of the lake at the age of three, when she had decided to go swimming without the previous advantage of being taught to swim. He had been only a year older, but his mother, realising that he was going to be a particularly active child, had taken the precaution of throwing him into the lake when he was nine months old, and he swam like a fish.

'You should go now, Little Mistress; your honourable father is waiting.'

They ran out and found the General in the saddle and impatient to be off. Black Jade tucked her wide trousers into her soft leather boots, hitched up the skirt of her knee-length tunic and put her foot into Huan's clasped hands.

'Light as a lotus petal,' the boy grinned as she swung into the huge saddle. Sweet Briar was far too big for her, but she had ridden her often enough to feel sure of her.

'Tell me, do you know at what hour the Son of Heaven will arrive tomorrow?' Huan asked as he took the reins. He was too respectful to ask the General. The position of a concubine's child is somewhere between that of the wife's children and that of the servants. Huan never presumed upon his father's fondness for him.

'We're not sure, but we think it will be in the morning. His Majesty has only to ride from Taiyuan.' This was the provincial capital, some twenty-five miles away. 'But he may well go hunting first; we don't know. Don't worry, Huan, you'll be sure to see him. He's bound to visit the stables.'

The one thing everyone knew about Li Shih-min was that he had a passionate appreciation of fine horses. Black Jade threw a last smile to her half-brother and clattered after the General, leaving behind a cluster of indulgent faces. Even the ostlers and grooms were prepared to forgive the master for being so unconventional as to prefer the company of a mere second daughter, it being the general opinion among the household that this particular daughter was every bit as good as a son.

'Do you think the Son of Heaven will bring his "bayards" with him?' Black Jade demanded as she caught up with Wu Shih-huo and they rode through the gate, guarded by lucky stone lions, that led into the suave parkland watered by one of the General's irrigation schemes.

'Almost certainly – though none of them could equal their sires for spirit. Te-lei-piao is the one you would have coveted; white as silk cocoons.'

'The one he rode in the western campaign,' Black Jade nodded. 'At the touch of the whip he bounded into the air. His neighing filled the sky,' she quoted.

One of the children's favourite tales of the Emperor was how his six noble warhorses had carried him, often saving his life, through all the battles that had secured the dynasty. They had gone into battle with their manes bunched like the hair of wrestlers and with a matching endurance, their gleaming hides accepting arrows as tiles accept the rain. All had been killed beneath him and the Emperor had paid his debt to each of them in verse.

Black Jade and her father trotted companionably side by side without speaking, content simply to be together. Wu Shih-huo derived an unexpected share of life's pleasure from the company of this daughter whom he loved above his sons. Not for her beauty, though that was a miracle, surpassing even that of her mother, nor for her filial qualities, some of which were sketchy at best, but for the unique play of a mind that already had a reach as broad as his own, and for the uncompromising spirit that recognised no authority other than that of those who were fit to be her teachers.

Convention demanded that a young daughter remain secluded within her own apartments, occupied with her books, her religion and her domestic tasks; well, be damned to convention! He would not have Jade wasted away in the womens' quarters. He had spawned her – Heaven knew how – and he had a right to her company when he wanted it. He wanted it frequently. He played chess with her because she was an excellent player who often beat him; he discussed books with her because she always had something original to add to the deliberations of the scholars; he rode with her because she was a fine rider who truly respected her mount, and because, unlike most women and too many men, she knew when to hold her tongue.

He was not unaware of her faults. She was impatient, especially of those less intelligent than herself. She found it hard to control what could sometimes be a vicious temper – the whole household could recall the beating she gave the groom whom she had caught ill-treating her first pony. As for her relations with her brothers, the General saw more than his children supposed. He was well aware that his sons suffered at least equally with Jade, and suffered in their dignity, which was hard for young men. No, she was by no means perfect, his lovely and talented daughter. And yet, there was already that about her which drew men towards her, and women too. He was glad. To be well loved was the greatest gift of all. He hoped she would keep it all her life.

He often thought, lately, of the mariage to which he must one day lose her. He was at his wits' end where to look for a man who could match her and make her happy.

He had thought, too, of the prophecy of Yuan the astrologer. It would float to the surface of his mind when he least expected or welcomed it. He tried to allow it no conscious thought. He and Golden Willow had never discussed it after that first day; what would be, would be, they had agreed, and there was nothing to be gained from allowing themselves to speak, or think, treason. The prophecy was almost certainly mistaken; astrologers are not infallible, though they like to think they are. The General had consigned Yuan's words to a limbo of the mind, where they remained in abeyance, like ancestors starved of sacrifice.

They had reached the beginning of the true plain, arid, yellow, almost desert, where they habitually opened into a gallop. They did so now, as glad to be free of household and duty as were the horses to be free of the stable.

As they flew along, the roan pacing the stallion without effort as yet, Black Jade felt the burden of the morning's anger fall away. She was at one with the rhythm and motion of pounding hooves and fluid muscles, conscious of a harmony that sang far more seductively in her veins than that of pale blossom and green grass.

So much of her life was static, intellectual, domestic; it was good beyond belief to express herself physically, with total abandon to this headlong, urgent movement.

Wu Shih-ho, seeing the fierce grin of delight with which she rose in the saddle and crouched over her horse's neck, told himself, not for the first time, how much more easily he could see her riding into battle at his side than Shuang, who, although he must inherit his name and fortune, had the mind of a merchant rather than a leader of men, always adding up and taking stock, never showing enthusiasm or giving anything of himself. He knew what he wanted and what was his due, and would probably exert himself to get it, but there was nothing in him of the exultant joy in life that the General saw beside him now, the same that had fired his own existence for fifty God-given years.

Gradually he slackened the pace, knowing that the mare would soon tire; besides, to tell the truth, his own heart was beating an unusual tattoo. He must have drunk more wine than he had thought, last night.

Black Jade responded, slowing too, satisfied with her gallop. Her face was serene and happy as she gazed about her, complimenting the mountains on their magnificence, the plain on its immensity and her father, with her quick smile like the flash of a kingfisher, upon this precious hour of freedom. He returned the smile, baring his teeth as far back as the gap where a Hun's javelin had completed its trajectory, creasing the scar that covered it. He saw that the girl was pointing excitedly towards the north-east.

There was a sulphur cloud of dust about two miles distant, wide enough to signify a large caravan or a considerable party of riders. They stopped, shading their eyes as they tried to decide which it was.

'D'you think it could be the Emperor?' Black Jade bounced with hope.

'Not yet – but we'll go and see for ourselves.'

They moved off again, swiftly gaining speed. The dust cloud appeared larger and they could see now that it was actually moving towards them.

'Horsemen! Too fast for a caravan,' Wu Shih-huo bellowed. Black Jade brandished her whip in affirmation.

'Could it be Turks?' she shouted.

They were two hundred miles from the Great Wall but Tu-lu

Khan was reported to be making new border raids despite the treaties that the Emperor had forced upon him. The Turks were never quiet for long.

But the General shook his head. 'If they were coming as far down as this, they'd come in far larger numbers. Don't worry! Do you think I would let you ride to meet Turks?' Nevertheless he was prepared to turn at the sight of an unfriendly banner.

It was several minutes before they could make out the devices on the standards. Then Black Jade cried 'Dragons! Dozens of them! It *is* the Emperor!' She felt a surge of excitement. And she would see him before any of the others. How jealous her brothers would be!

They continued slowly, their decorous pace making her edgy. Left to herself she would simply have spurred off towards the cavalcade without an idea in her head of how to behave when she reached it.

The shapes of the approaching horsemen were now distinct. They were a sober band, coloured in browns and greys; about fifty in all, armed and carrying white banners bearing the Green Dragon. Many held falcons on their wrists and their hounds ran at their stirrups. Jade screwed up her eyes to try to separate the features of the tall man who rode at their head on the dazzling horse that might have been brother to Snow Prince.

He was lean and straight and his bearing would have proclaimed him the Emperor if the banners had not. A great Manchurian gyrfalcon, white as clouds, sat on his left forearm. He wore a silvered leather jacket over white robes. He was in mourning for his dead Empress, Pure Virtue, whom her mother had said he had loved dearly.

As they came closer, Black Jade saw a tanned and bearded face under a Tartar hat; he was still too far away for her to see him clearly when he threw up his hand to halt his party. He beckoned them to approach and they cantered towards him, Jade reining in to a respectful distance behind her father. Closer still, she saw Shih-min to be a vitally handsome young man with a curling black beard and moustaches, whose smile shone with pure pleasure.

When there were only a few paces between them, the General reined and made as if to dismount to perform his kowtow. The Emperor signalled him to remain in the saddle, calling cheerfully, 'Wu Shih-huo! You've come out to meet me! How did you know? Gods, but it's good to see you, old friend!'

His voice was deep, with the resonance of sounds in a forest. Black Jade could imagine him addressing an army drawn up in stillness. He trotted towards her father and clapped him on the back as casually as a brother. Then he glanced at the smaller figure behind the General, expecting to greet an eldest son.

He was unprepared for the face that he caught, equally unprepared, eating him up with greedy green eyes.

They were beautiful eyes, long, wide and black-fringed, their corners tilting lazily upward; they regarded him with a calculation he was not accustomed to see, as filled with interest as a leopard's which looked on its luncheon. The girl had evidently forgotten that she should not gaze at him directly. 'What impudence,' thought Shih-min. 'Magnificent though.' It occurred to him that she was probably the General's concubine and that this encounter was one of chance rather than purpose, interrupting their private time together. She was lovely enough, by all the Gods, but wasn't she a little young? Her shape was a woman's sure enough, but still very slight. Then the General held out a hand towards her.

'May I present, Your Majesty, my unworthy second daughter, Black Jade.'

Shih-min reproved himself, amused. He could see now, of course, that she was only a child; a child with a lovely face whose great green eyes were filled with the same vivid curiosity with which she would view a phoenix or a gryphon or any other fabulous creature who might, for her, inhabit the same bestiary as an Emperor.

Black Jade manoeuvred her mare closer with perfect control, then slid to the ground in a single graceful movement that culminated in a full kowtow, an arm's-length from his horse's nose.

'I am glad to make your acquaintance, Black Jade,' the Emperor said. His tone was kind and his continued appraisal seemed to please him. 'And although I am delighted that you do not in any way resemble your father physically, I hope to discover that you have inherited some of his excellent qualities.'

The General made a gruff noise of gratification, then was astonished to hear his daughter, who should have bowed and effaced herself as soon as possible, commit the impropriety of speaking directly to the Emperor.

'Truly, I hope so, Your Majesty. For as the Master, Confucius, said of himself, "He is the sort of man who is so interested in what occupies him that he even forgets to eat, and he is so full of joy that he forgets all worries and does not notice the onset of old age." '

Wu Shih-huo grimaced, embarrassed by her temerity and her compliments.

Shih-min, concealing his amusement at the latter part of the quotation – children think old age begins ten years later than their own – replied with suave courtesy, 'You use your classics well, Little Daughter, for did not the Master also say, "You may well be born with the good looks of Prince Chao of Sung, but you will find it difficult to escape unscathed by the world if you do not also possess the eloquence of the priest Tuo." '

It appeared he was testing her scholarship, for Prince Chao had been an infamous rake, while the priest Tuo was a man of great virtue who had used his eloquent gifts to persuade his feudal lord towards good works.

She thought for a moment. 'I would prefer to inherit the good looks of my lady mother, who is also virtuous, and although I do not presume to the eloquence of Father Tuo, neither do I expect to go through the world unscathed. Your Majesty,' she added, rather late.

Li Shih-min threw back his head and laughed. 'You have a rare cub here, Shih-huo. Are there more like her at home?'

'There are not,' asserted the General, uncertain whether he was annoyed or delighted by Black Jade's performance. Either way, it was time to put an end to it.

'Will you ride with us, sir, and let us go home? Then you may meet the rest of my family for yourself.'

The two men fell in together and were soon cheerfully discussing old times, and the times in between.

Behind them, riding next to a splendid courtier in black and silver, who announced himself, somewhat repressively, as the Archduke Chang-sun Wuchi, brother-in-law to the Emperor, Black Jade might have been heard, unrepressed, muttering yet another gem from the collected sayings of Confucius: 'Let us go home; let us go home. Our young men at home are wildly ambitious, and have great accomplishments for all to see; but they do not know how to *prune* themselves.'

'Nor indeed,' brooded the Archduke, who strongly disapproved of pert children, however pleasant to look at, 'do *you*, my prosy little peacock.'

Feeling the pall of his displeasure surround her with the dust, Black Jade had the sense to hold her tongue all the way back to the mansion.

2

The next morning was fine and warm and the decoration of the Scarlet Pavilion was accomplished to Black Jade's satisfaction. When they had finished, she and Rose Bird returned to their own apartments to get ready for the Emperor's formal audience for the family in the Hall of Fastidious Ceremony in the General's residence. The visitor had spent the remainder of yesterday in exclusively male company, apart from a courtesy call from Golden Willow, so that Rose Bird still had not set eyes upon him.

The girls had slid the painted screen doors between their rooms fully open. They and their maids moved in an aromatic atmosphere which breathed from two braziers burning incense of sandalwood and patchouli. Dressed only in trousers and undertunics of a silk as fine and iridescent as a dragonfly's wing, with their yard-long hair streaming, squeaky-clean, down their backs, they made a lot of commotion and very little progress as they swooped and twittered about, exchanging scent, combs, ornaments and advice.

'You still haven't told us how he *looks*,' complained Rose Bird, who had been enviously badgering her sister all morning, trying not to feel too much pique over her extreme good luck. It was she herself, after all, who had laid claim to Shih-min, even if only in dreams; but she was a little abashed by the presumption of the dreams, now that there was just the faintest possibility of their realisation.

'He said *you* had good looks; do you think he will like me as much?' she asked, without waiting for the answer to her previous question. Normally serene and easy-natured, she found this morning's tension hard to bear. She wandered restlessly about the room, pursued by her maid, Mayflower, who made random dashes at her hair with a comb laden with the gelid dressing known as *wu-mu.*

'He said Prince Chao of Sung had good looks,' her sister corrected her voice rising, muffled, from the chest where she kept her shoes. 'How do I know what he likes?' she asked, surfacing with a pair of satin gold slippers. 'You are more beautiful than I am. I expect he can see that as well as anyone else.'

Rose Bird wanted to believe this, but suspected it was untrue.

Her own beauty was soft and womanly; her face was gentle and sensual and glowed when she was happy; she had fine eyes, large, liquid and expressive, and a sweet mouth. But she did not consider that she was in any way unique. Not like her sister. There was something different, something very special, about Black Jade. It drew people to look at her, almost whether they wanted to or not. Their relatives and friends, the servants, even the brothers who so disliked her, all were drawn by the spell of her growing beauty. It was not simply the fineness of her features that arrested them, the graceful, ovoid head held at such a proud angle on the long 'phoenix' neck beneath its coronet of gleaming hair; the intelligent eyes with their hypnotic green gaze; the full, pouting lips that could suddenly become as firm as a man's. They were used to all these. They were drawn, more deeply, by a sense of the unusual and unidentifiable being who was developing before them, someone they could not comfortably categorise only as 'Second Daughter', whose sole worth lay in her marriageability.

But whatever her fascination, Rose Bird comforted herself that her sister *was* still only a child, despite the fact that she had begun to produce the monthly 'peach-flower fluid', and had put up her hair in the ceremony of *chi-chi*.

She sat down and picked up the mirror to reassure herself. She was looking very pretty. Her agitation lent an attractive rosy tint to her deep golden skin, enhancing the fashionable spot of crimson high on each cheekbone. She allowed Mayflower to slip her tunic over her shoulders and admired the effect of its soft blue-grey beneath her bright face.

'Here – let me paint your "yellow moon". I do it better than Mayflower,' offered Black Jade, picking up a tiny brush and a little pot of orpiment colour from a low table. 'As to the Emperor's looks,' she added, her tongue between her teeth in concentration, 'he looks like Father when he has just come in from hunting – shiny-eyed and crackling with energy – and very pleased with himself.'

'That still doesn't tell us much,' Rose Bird complained.

'Keep quiet, or your moon will be on your nose instead of your forehead.' Carefully, she filled in the tiny sickle she had drawn.

'Don't tease us, Little Mistress,' begged Welcome, folding back the gold sleeves of Black Jade's embroidered coat, ready for her to put on over the inner robe of cream silk. 'Your honoured father always makes out that His Majesty is like a young God. *Is* he a well-made man, or shall we be disappointed?'

'Welcome!' Mayflower was shocked. 'Disappointed? In the

Emperor!'

'The Son of Heaven is also the son of his mother, like other men,' said Welcome, unrepentant.

'Quite right!' Black Jade approved. 'Now pass me the lip-salve. Oh, very well!' she added as Rose Bird sighed with impatience. 'Yes, he is a handsome man. No, he isn't a God. And whether or not you will be disappointed depends upon what you expect. Now, let me be, all of you; you'll see for yourselves in half an hour.'

'The point is,' Rose Bird said wistfully, beseeching the mirror again, 'will *he* be disappointed?'

'He,' said Black Jade irritably, adding a black 'mouche' to the side of sister's mouth, 'is not expecting anything better than yet another boring provincial family who will endlessly kowtow and make fatuous speeches at him. He has, I think, a sense of humour; no doubt it serves him well on such occasions. Now, blue eyebrows? Or black?'

'Blue, it's softer.'

She painted two wisps of cobalt, like butterfly wings, springing from the point where the shaven brows had begun.

'Hurry up, Little Phoenix,' worried Welcome. 'You still have your own face to do, and your hair is so slippery after washing that I don't know how I'm going to pin it up.'

'I only take ten minutes, you know that.'

'Yes, but today is special.'

'So it is, but you may be sure there are still only twelve hours in it.'

Welcome clicked her tongue and held up the gold coat.

'Put this on, and never mind your nonsense!'

Black Jade sighed and did as she was told. Kneeling for the nurse to do her hair, she explained, 'I only meant, Elder Sister, that if a thing takes the time it takes, then that is the time it takes. Do you see?'

'No, I don't. Just keep still for a minute, will you?' As though to prove her charge's theory she deftly combed and wound her hair into two neat coils over her ears in less than two minutes.

'There! Now the shawl. Wear it just off the shoulders: it's more elegant. Now, a white camellia above the right-hand coil. Lovely! And the gold filigree across your forehead. Now you're finished. The prettiest thing I ever saw!'

'Except for *my* mistress,' said Mayflower loyally. 'I'll be surprised if today doesn't tell her fortune for her.'

'We'll see,' said Welcome quietly, smiling oddly at Jade who, unable to comprehend the meaning of her smile, began suddenly to catch her sister's nervousness.

The nurse watched them prepare to leave, fingering the dragon pendant she always wore at her neck.

When they left their apartments, the young women walked, rather self-consciously, through the greening gardens to their mother's house. Golden Willow greeted them in a soft peach silk tunic beneath a sleeveless over-robe in shimmering bronze brocade. Her dark hair was coiled inside a wreath of gold and pearls. They all told each other how lovely they looked, and then set off together towards the masculine apartments. These were reached by crossing the Bridge of Forgetfulness, which was so called because their honourable ancestor Wu Yang-li used regularly to cross it halfway and then forget why he was doing so. Below them the little river capered, chattering over the stones and falling suddenly still about the lilies. Golden Willow made them all pause for a moment to drink in its tranquillity. Then, after a last smiling touch to Black Jade's camellia and another to Rose Bird's quivering cheek, she led her daughters towards their father's house, which was the one nearest the bridge on the other side.

The Wu mansion was prevented by the landscape, with its rocky outcrops and tree-covered hillocks, from conforming exactly to the traditional pattern of a series of interconnecting dwellings and courtyards. Second Uncle, for example, observed a scenic bouldered grotto on the opposite side of his court, while Eldest Aunt was separated from the First, Third and Fourth Cousins by Pine Green Hill, a ridge topped by a grove of tall trees which were the home of a clan of noisy magpies. Even the conversational little river intruded itself at one point, sauntering confidently through Golden Willow's Hall of Contemplation so that a delightful water-garden had been created around it, greatly envied by the other ladies of the family.

Although the General was recognised as having brought the highest honour to the clan, his house was neither as large nor as imposing as the pagoda-shaped palace of Eldest Uncle, the patriarch of the family; but it was by no means modest. It was two storeys high, its slightly curving azure roof supported by pillars of rosewood carved with birds and beasts, its smooth perfection a memorial to Shih-huo's early days as a timber merchant; a somewhat eccentric start in life for the son of so distinguished a family of scholar-officials. The excellence of the timber also prevailed in the eaves, which, like the splendid many-layered doorways and the broad doors themselves, were lacquered in glossy crimson and decorated with plain and patterned tiles in the 'five colours' officially recognised by the court dyers; red, yellow, blue, black and purple. The steps before the main doors were guarded by phoenixes with their stone wings flying upward. Today these doors were open and members of the family were hurrying through them, the men filing to the right and the women to the left.

'Good day, Honourable Youngest Uncle, Honourable Aunt, Honourable Cousins,' chorused the two girls, trying not to stare too obviously at their relatives' new clothes.

'Good morning, Gracious Highness, Honourable Cousins,' the others replied, bending very low before Golden Willow.

'Don't turn round, or we'll have to greet half the clan,' muttered Black Jade. 'We can make do with nods and bows when we get inside.'

They passed through the doors and rounded the spirit screen into the courtyard to find themselves at the end of a long queue waiting to take places in the Hall of Fastidious Ceremony on the opposite side of the square. It occurred often to Black Jade that even the least intelligent of evil spirits, who for unfathomable reasons were believed incapable of walking other than in a straight line, *must* conceive the idea of cornering when they observed so many people doing it.

Almost the entire close family were present; four of the General's five brothers, with their wives, concubines and older children, plus *their* wives and accumulated dependants, numbering over two hundred persons; in addition to the General's four concubines and some of the higher stewards and local dignitaries who were also invited. The Emperor had made it clear that he wished to address the whole household. This was a signal honour and the crowning point of Wu Shin-huo's enviable career.

Inside the hall, which would hold five hundred comfortably, room had been found for two dozen ornamental trees and a score of aromatic censers, while the sexes were nominally divided by an exquisite gauze screen painted with the shimmering figures of peacocks and peonies. Coloured lanterns hung from the carved ceiling, more for their beauty than for any need of light, for the fretted bamboo windows allowed plenty of sunshine to trace their intricate patterns on the floor. There was a murmur of quiet conversation in the chamber, which was instantly hushed on the womens' side as Golden Willow and her daughters walked to their places in front of the platform where the Emperor would stand. Silent and graceful, with downcast eyes, they were a reproof to any who did not did not follow their example.

It seemed a long time to Black Jade before she heard the muffled tread of ceremonial shoes crossing the courtyard and noted the sudden hush of the men as the Emperor's entourage began to make its entrance through the doors at the sides of the dais.

Firstly several soldiers in crimson tunics posted themselves about the back and sides of the stage, then two rows of noblemen flanked them on the sides. These included her father and Eldest Uncle as well as her uncommunicative escort of yesterday, Archduke Chang-sun Wuchi. He was resplendent in layers of grey-threaded silk, the exact colour, she thought, of dead lizards, his stiff neck held in a high collar. She looked down hastily, but not before he had caught her critical gaze. That would earn her another black mark in his book, not that his opinion mattered to her; she did not like him – he behaved as though he had perpetual indigestion.

Now the drummers outside were beating a soft, arresting roll. Then came a deep commanding note from the gong near the doors and the silence in the hall became heavy and expectant. Everyone bent their backs in a low bow. There was a brief sibilance of silken garments and then further silence. Black Jade raised her chin and looked up through her lashes, as every well bred girl knew how to do, and so received her first sight of the Son of Heaven in his semi-divine aspect. This was such a shock to her that she forgot etiquette once again and stared openly, so great was the change in the figure who mounted the dais.

No one could have failed to take the man she had met yesterday for a great leader, or to accord him the deepest respect, but he had also been recognisable as a soldier, a hunter, a man among men and her father's comrade; capable even of capping quotations with a worthless girl-child. The refulgent image which confronted her now retained no trace of that everyday humanity. Robed in stiff white brocade encrusted with gold and silver dragons, and wearing a high barbarian hat ringed with gold medallions, the Emperor looked out over the crowd from a powdered mask from which all expression had been erased.

Another gong signalled them to straighten their backs. They were now permitted to contemplate, with awe and reverence, what it was to be an Emperor. The gilded idol that stood before them, its features blank and inscrutable, was nothing less than the living symbol of all terrestrial power; the deputy on earth of the Supreme Ancestor, by virtue of whose mandate he had become the father and ruler of his people; the Son of Heaven, whose name may be neither written nor spoken by any lesser man. As much reality resided in that shining, absent figure, Black Jade thought, as in the vast, dreaming sculptures of the Buddha in the temple in Wen Shui.

It seemed to her that she had stood for hours gazing in this suspended, half-worshipful state, seeing not the man but the ineffable thing that he represented, when at last the spell was broken by the Archduke who bowed towards the Emperor and stepped forward to speak.

'His Majesty wishes it to be known that there is no necessity for each and every one of you to approach and make the full kowtow. It will be satisfactory if you all make a simple obeisance in your places.'

He held up his bony, long-fingered hand and conducted them in the deepest of bows, foreheads touching the floor where it was physically possible. Black Jade sensed that he did not approve of this flouting of centuries of protocol, practical and time-saving though it was. As her brow hovered above the flagstones she felt her camellia wobble. She straightened with breathless care but the flower tumbled past her nose just as she raised her head. She saw that the Emperor had moved to the front of the dais. His expression was now more noticeably human; she realized that part of the change was simply that his eyes, which had stared so emptily into space, were now focused again. Indeed she thought for a second they fixed on *her* – the only one of her sex to be without cranial adornment in the whole nodding bed of flowers, feathers and jewelled concoctions before him. *Did* a brief smile warm his gaze, or was this her own fantasy?

The Emperor began to speak and became wholly a man again; no ordinary man, certainly, but neither a God nor a graven image. His speech was, she considered, blessedly brief and simple. She hated standing in crowds and she liked speeches only if they were amusing. The Son of Heaven thanked them all for their hospitality and duty, praised her father for his service, and concluded with two quotations from the *I Ching*, chosen for their suitability to the occasion.

When the Emperor had left everyone relaxed and began to talk. Black Jade and Rose Bird exchanged greetings and compliments with their neighbours.

'Pick up your camellia, my child, or it will be trampled underfoot,' was their mother's only comment before indicating that it was time for them to leave.

Black Jade absently speared her flower with a long hairpin, still pondering the ambiguities of the *I Ching*. She thought that one could probably make it mean almost anything one wished.

She considered, too, what she felt about the Emperor. Certainly he commanded her respect. He had displayed a subtle wit in addition to the heroic qualities she knew him to possess. She admired him for that, though it was what she might have expected. What she did not expect was the enormous personal magnetism of Li Shih-min. It had pierced through the cold, imperial mask of centuries of power and ceremony and had struck into the heart of every separate person in the chamber, including her own.

She found that she now felt very strange. She had lived through a new and exciting experience. Glimpses of a very different world from Wen Shui had opened to her. Why then, did she suddenly feel like crying?

By force of habit she paused on the Bridge of Forgetfulness, falling behind the others to brood over the glass-green water. Tears pricked at her eyelids. Without understanding them, she let them fall, to slip away on the stream and mingle with the current, to be carried away beneath her to Kuei Hiu, the black whirlpool that seethes in a bottomless pit in the Eastern Sea, where all the waters of the world unite.

She thought the tears probably had something to do with the blood that had flowed from her for the first time two weeks ago. Golden Willow had said she might feel a little moody from time to time. But then she had only suffered an insignificant pain, not this wretched, empty feeling – as though nothing in the world would ever happen to her again. Angrily she wiped her eyes, remembering where she was. Second Cousin was coming towards her, her round face full of gossip. Black Jade composed herself. Second Cousin was an unremarkable girl whose story would be written in a very few characters. Was her own to be a similar one? Of marriage and children and subservience to some dull man in Wen Shui? No! Her heart cried out that it was not possible. Somehow she could not feel that she was destined for such a commonplace existence. Nor could she imagine, at this moment, the probability of any other life for herself. The choice was not hers. All that she could do was to persevere. The lines of her future were hidden. Whatever they were, they would not reveal themselves until the time appointed by fate.

She smiled at Second Cousin and fell into step.

*

That evening, after doing flattering justice to the Plum Blossom Picnic, the Emperor was entertained in Golden Willow's Hall of Contemplation.

Wearing a long-haired Mongolian waistcoat over a simple white tunic and trousers, Li Shih-min lay back on his elbow on a pile of cushions, his long body completely relaxed and his eyes slitted with contentment. He resembled some self-indulgent Tartar chieftain. Once again the change in him was difficult to assimilate, a shock to expectation. His giant gyrfalcon, 'Army Commander', perched beside him half-asleep, trailing green jesses from a gilded rail.

Nearby, the General, never entirely at home indoors, did his best to look comfortable with the aid of an arm-rest and a stout bolster.

At a little distance, his two sons sat beneath a flowering cherry in the curve of the stream, amusing the company with war ballads from the northern borders. They accompanied themselves on a four-stringed lute and a small, lacquered wether-drum. They were delighted with their reception, for their guest had astonished them by joining in, contributing the rich bass that Wu Shih-huo remembered from a hundred camp-fires.

On the other side of the stream, prettily disposed upon a bank of green upholstery, Golden Willow and her daughters listened and applauded, each taking the covert opportunity to examine, in detail, the handsome features of their sovereign lord.

For Golden Willow, who had attended the court ten years ago for his coronation, Shih-min was the fulfilment of his early promise. He had been a youth of sixteen when he had persuaded his father, Li Yuan, then a provincial governor, to lead a successful revolt against the tyrannous misgovernment of the Sui Emperor, Yang-ti. The father had ascended the throne but it was his energetic younger son who, during seven years of bitter and complex clan warfare, destroyed all opposition and brought about a united Empire. Small wonder, then, that Heaven had given the mandate to the youthful conqueror rather than to his older brother, the Crown Prince, and had seen to it that Shih-min should escape when his brothers plotted against his life. Their father, Li Yuan, although a fine ruler in many ways, had been torn between his sons and was glad to give up the throne when it became clear, after Shih-min had killed his would-be murderers, that he was destined to be the next Emperor. Li Yuan had died soon after, and was known to posterity as the High Ancestor.

General Wu, although he had been loyal to Li Yuan, who had

given him his governorship, his dukedom and, not least, his patrician wife, a member of the deposed royal house of Sui, had fought mainly under Shih-min's command and had been openly approving of his bid for the throne.

Golden Willow veiled her eyes as she gazed at the superbly confident man who now held that throne in the absolute security that comes of the love of a nation. She had been married for five years at the time of the coronation. Rose Bird had been four and Black Jade a toddling baby. She had loved her husband and her life pleased her. She had found the hectic pleasures of the young court absurd and exaggerated. Its atmosphere had been unashamedly sensual, a foil for the virility of the charismatic young Emperor. He had done nothing to discourage its hothouse blooming; quite the reverse. Rumour had it that a quite amazing number of his 122 concubines were glossy with satisfaction, and Shih-min himself, with his feline tread and his speculative eye, seemed to confirm it with every gesture.

Great Heaven, that eye was upon her now! She had been looking at him so closely that she had not noticed her gaze was returned. She blushed with mortification, but he smiled and nodded at her, as though at an old friend with whom he shared a secret. Surely he could not be remembering that time when, not content with the perfumed ranks of his concubines, he had extended his purring sexual invitation to her? She raised her painted fan to cover the trace of her thought on her face. There had, of course, been no possibility of betraying her husband. Nevertheless – her lips curved despite herself – it was very pleasant to have been asked.

She returned the Emperor's smile sedately and turned her own attention to Rose Bird. Would her daughter now be asked to accept what she had been bound to refuse? It would be a great honour. And yet, if she were to choose for her child, she would rather wish her a marriage such as her own had been, to a fine man who loved her, than the narrow life, however luxurious, of a royal concubine, who was only one woman in over a hundred who must dedicate themselves to the wishes of a single male.

Rose Bird, who was unaware of her mother's thoughts and would have been shocked by some of them, was presently suffering, or enjoying – she was uncertain which – her first attack of pure physical desire. Like most girls, she had gleaned enough knowledge of the congress of man and woman to know exactly what it was she would like Shih-min to do with her, but never before had she felt it so insistently, and with precisely that part of her body which would be involved.

Her heart was thudding so that she was surprised no one had noticed it. Her throat was dry and she felt hot all over. She was also perfectly sure, as Golden Willow had been, that her thoughts were printed on her face. She touched a hand to her cheek as though to discover if this were so, and as she did so Shih-min turned towards her. He gave her a little smile, rather thoughtful, as if he *knew* what she was feeling. She was thrilled by the smile but at the same time she wished she could die.

Her discomfort increased as she felt a sudden pain in her ankle. Black Jade had kicked her beneath the spread of her skirt. She saw that her sister had her zither ready and she quickly reached for her own lute. Buddha Maitreya! Suppose she had failed to notice and they had begun without her!

Black Jade tapped out a rhythmic introduction on the sounding-board of her instrument. Golden Willow picked it up on her small, embroidered tabor, and their three voices mingled sweetly in the 'Song of the Plum Blossom', which Black Jade had written yesterday evening in an unaccustomed elegaic mood.

'As I sit with my lute in the orchard
A shower of petals blows across the grass.
Already? Is their season of loveliness so brief?
But no; it is only an intruding boy
Who spoils perfection with a careless hand.
He is making his way towards me.
How long, I wonder, will my own young beauty last?'

The melody was plaintive and delicate, descriptive of the innocence of maidenhood, while the underlying heartbeat of the drum suggested the shared fate of both innocence and spring blossom. It was a sophisticated composition and both words and music lingered on the spirit after the last questioning note was gone.

'Exquisite,' Shih-min said softly. 'How can I thank you for so much pleasure?'

Their voices were all musical, but the low, unexpectedly mellow tone of little Green-eyes had struck an answering note deep in his belly.

'Your pleasure is our thanks, Your Majesty,' Golden Willow murmured demurely, very pleased.

'The song was both beautiful and provocative. Tell me, where does it come from? I have not heard it before. Are the words by one of our court poets?'

'No, Majesty, they are the work of my presumptuous second daughter,' his hostess replied, more gratified than ever.

'Lady Black Jade – *you* wrote this?'

The Emperor was looking at her with real interest. And no one had ever addressed her as 'lady' before.

'I did, Your Majesty.'

'And the music, whose is that?'

'Mine also, Majesty.'

'Do you often write such things?'

'Quite often. I am fond of music.'

'I should like to hear more. You have great talent. There are many musicians in our academy at Chang-an who would be put to shame by such skill.'

'I am overwhelmed by Your Majesty's praise of my poor efforts,' Black Jade said politely, trying not to look immoderately pleased as she noted Shuang's sour face. Could he have realised that his rough gesture in the orchard had provided the inspiration for her song? And feared what more she might say?

At Shih-min's insistence she sang another song, alone this time. She chose the one she had written to thank her father for the gift of Snow Prince, a cheerful little ditty which she accompanied on her lute, cleverly graduating the rhythm from the walk to the trot and then to the full gallop, while Rose Bird paced her on the tabor, perfectly content for her sister to be the centre of attention and blissfully happy in the knowledge that the Emperor had noticed her own modest charms.

When the little song came to its breathless halt, Shih-min clapped his hands in admiration.

'Bravo, little Green-eyes! Your famous precursor, the Lady Pan Chao, was quite right to insist that girls too are worthy of education.'

'Thank you, Sir,' Black Jade replied, frowning slightly, 'but is it not a pity that she also thought their education should fit them only for absolute obedience to a husband to whom they must consider themselves greatly inferior?'

Suddenly everyone in the room felt as though there were a storm impending. Wu Shih-huo beetled his brows at his daughter and Golden Willow said sharply, 'That is enough, child! Be silent.'

'I apologise for my sister's insolence, Your Majesty,' intervened Shuang smoothly. 'Her head is turned by so much unaccustomed praise.'

Black Jade hung her head but her jaw was set stubbornly.

Seeing it, Shih-min waved away the family's embarrassment. The child was truly a revelation! Horsewoman, poet, musician, with a scholar's knowledge of the classics and the wit to make use of them; and now she appeared to wish to lecture him on the shortcomings of Confucian education.

'Do you then disagree with the precepts of Lady Pan?' he asked pleasantly, making it clear to them all that he wished to hear her opinions.

She knew she must choose her words carefully. Pan Chao had lived during the first century, the daughter of a famous author and the sister of a well-known historian. She had married at fourteen, but her husband had died young and she had then devoted herself to scholarship. She had become tutor to the Empress herself and her *Precepts for Women* was a classic treatise which, though it did champion equal elementary education for both sexes, was far from encouraging women in general to aspire to her own high level of learning. Indeed it presented the orthodox Confucian attitude towards women and their place in society. No right-thinking mother would be without it and every dutiful daughter knew it by heart. Black Jade loathed it from the bottom of her soul.

Golden Willow, who guessed what might be coming, prayed that, for once, her clever child would tone down the harsher notes of her criticism.

'I find many of the "precepts" admirable,' the girl began, leaning forward slightly as her thoughts began to take shape. Protocol was dismissed as the Emperor invited her to hold his gaze.

'To have respect for one's parents; to put others before oneself; to work hard; to cultivate a bond of respect with a husband; to seek harmony with his family – I have no quarrel with any of these. But the Lady Pan states, too, that a woman should look to four aspects of herself; her achievements, her speech, her appearance and her skills. As to her achievements, she need not be especially intelligent, only gentle, sedate, chaste and orderly in her attempts. Her speech need not be witty but she should choose her words carefully, uttering no unseemly phrases and avoiding unnecessary length. Her appearance need be neither handsome nor elegant as long as she is neat and clean. Her skills are to be the household ones of cooking, sewing, spinning and weaving – oh, and she must avoid, for some killjoy reason, all occasions for laughter or jest!' Here she paused for breath.

'And you condemn all this?' encouraged Shih-min, twisting a

lock of his beard round one finger.

'It seems so very *little* to ask of us,' she said simply, keeping the true extent of her resentment in check. 'Men are always required to do the best and highest of which they are capable; why not ask the same of a woman? Why should she not develop her intellect as well as a man may do? Why should she not speak as she finds, especially if she finds the truth? Why should she not dress as gaily or gorgeously as she pleases? And why should she not learn a hundred different skills? And if she's poor and must do all the household tasks herself, how much more does she need some other accomplishment, such as reading and calligraphy or music, to give her relief from her drudgery?'

When she had stopped talking, it seemed almost too quiet. Shih-min played with his beared a little longer, looking at her curiously, as if she were one of a rare species which he could not name. Her father, she saw with trepidation, was frowning.

'I think, Little Daughter,' the Emperor said at last, 'you ignore the fact that Lady Pan wrote her precepts for the average majority, not the gifted minority of women. She herself was a notable exception to the norm. There will always be such women; indeed, I think you will grow to be one yourself. But for every such exception there will be 9999 who are happy to take the "precepts" for their guide, to rule cheerfully over their households and leave all else to the men.'

'But what are the exceptions to *do* with their lives?' cried Black Jade, in an anguish which she scarcely understood. She felt, in that moment, as Shih-min rested those kind, dark eyes upon her, as if he might help her, and also as though she were on the brink of something momentous, something that might be achieved by her own behaviour, if only she knew how to behave. She had just spoken the way she did out of habitual frustration rather than good sense. No good could come out of disputing with the Emperor. She had not meant to do so. As so often happened, she had simply followed her nose into argument. She sighed, a lonely sound in the chamber where apprehension now rippled with the stream.

'Cheer up, little Green-eyes. We shall think of a solution to that problem,' Shih-min said softly. She saw that he smiled at her. His eyes were very gentle, and there *was* a promise in them. He nodded once towards her, like a conspirator, then turned away to question her brothers. There was a sensation in her head like the explosion when one bites too eagerly into a fiery-hot piece of ginger. She wanted to leap to her feet and run and dance.

Shih-min did not think her perverse. He liked her! He would give her his help. All was well again. Nothing was lost after all.

She gazed at the Emperor with adoration as he listened patiently to the desperate attempts of Shuang and Ching to reveal themselves as witty and talented enough to be invited to court without graduating. Shih-min had asked them what *they* thought a woman's place should be, and Shuang reeled off the doctrines of Confucius and Mencius, while Ching's critique was almost word for word the same as his brother's. When he had heard their glib recitations, Shih-min regarded them closely for a moment, then shifted to a more comfortable position.

'It is only those who ask questions who may expect to find answers,' he said. 'The sages were wise, I agree, but they did not live in our times. It is no insult to them that their ideas should be continually under review – rather than automatically accepted.' He turned now to Golden Willow, without giving the boys time to reply.

'And now I must thank you again for your delightful entertainment. I have greatly enjoyed myself.'

It was the sign that the evening was over.

The next morning the Emperor took his leave. He did not ask for Rose Bird as his concubine, nor did he invite either of thc General's sons to the capital.

Before he left he took Wu Shih-huo aside for a private farewell. They were friends who would not meet for a long time. Shih-min asked if there was anything he could do for the General or for his family.

Shih-huo knew that he might ask for the dreams of all his children to be realised and that Shih-min would do it gladly for his sake. But he also knew that his sons were unworthy of high places, and that if the Emperor had wanted Rose Bird he would have spoken for her.

'There is nothing,' he said. 'The Gods have been good to me. I already have everything I could wish for.'

'You are sure?' The Emperor hesitated, his arm about the General's broad shoulders. 'Then – there is something *you* might give me – if you will?'

'Of course.' His stomach sank. He knew. It would be the hardest thing of all to give.

But his Emperor was merciful. 'Not now. Not this year, but perhaps after a year or two, send me, old friend, your rare cub; when her green eyes are those of a woman.'

*

Golden Willow was surprised by her husband's news. It had not occurred to her that the Emperor had seen in their second daughter anything other than a precocious and argumentative child with a talent for music. She had spoken severely to Black Jade, citing her behaviour as egotistical, unwomanly and unacceptable. Her punishment was to remain in her quarters and write an essay on the general excellence of Pan Chao's precepts. She had not written very much and had been further immured until she learned to take her task seriously.

Her mother expressed her doubts to the General and was surprised when he told her, 'The Emperor sees what you do not – that the girl is outstanding. Therefore he offers her an outstanding opportunity.'

'I find this very odd. The only outstanding qualities she revealed to him were those of rudeness, arrogance and self-display. And you are not even angry with her!'

'I was, a little, that evening. But not any more. Black Jade is like a wild mare that is forced to live in a stable. His Majesty sees that and wishes to give her freedom.'

'Freedom? In the Inner Palace? It will scarcely be that.'

'I think the palace will have changed since the days of the Sui. My commander was never fond of unnecessary protocol. Black Jade will have educational opportunities far wider than we can provide. There is a freedom of the mind, too, you know. Give her a chance. She may yet turn out to be a second Pan Chao!'

When his wife had finished stating her reservations, she added, 'I thought he might ask for Rose Bird. She would have been far more suitable.'

'Surely, my wife, what is suitable is what the Emperor wishes?'

Golden Willow made a sound that would have been a sniff, were such a thing thinkable of her.

'One thing,' the General said, his tone deepening with concern, 'We will not tell Black Jade of her fortune; not yet. We will tell no one.'

They looked each other, sharing the reverberation of a previous, long-concealed prophecy. The General cleared his throat.

'Let her live out her childhood. There will be time enough to think of these things.'

'Very well. But you must allow me to do my best to smooth her rough edges.'

He smiled at her affectionately. 'Don't be *too* thorough about it! I imagine that, at court, she might have a use for a few protective spikes.'

'The way she is at the moment,' his wife replied with gloomy foreboding, 'it is the court that will require protection.'

Everyone was restless after the Emperor's departure. Rose Bird moped in her room, curled up on her bed with her hair down, greeting anyone who entered with a tragic expression indicating the death of all hope.

Black Jade, on the other hand, ranged about her circumscribed territory like the wild mare to which her father had likened her. Her main feeling was one of puzzlement.

Shih-min had seemed to promise *something* – though she didn't know what – but he had performed *nothing*. Had she been mistaken? He was not, she was sure, a man who made idle promises, even those signalled by the slightest smile of the eyes to an angry child. What was it he had made her feel in that shared second? So that, even now, with her hands and her future lying empty, she was aware of an unspecified hope, a richly tantalising sense of new possibilities.

When, at last, she identified the point touched by his golden needle, she became numbed and ceased her nervous wandering about her rooms. What Shih-min had made her feel was the sudden apprehension of her own worth, judged by universal standards rather than those of the Wu mansion. He had allowed her, during that tiny point of time when their eyes had met, to feel that she was, in some important manner that had nothing to do with position, or age, or gender, his match.

She finished her essay and went about her daily tasks with a renewed zest that was remarked by the whole household.

Golden Willow thanked her stars that at least *this* daughter did not need cheering back to life, and set her mind to the rehabilitation of Rose Bird.

She discussed this with her husband.

'It's obvious, isn't it?' declared the General. 'She's growing up; *grown* up in all but experience. She needs a husband.'

Golden Willow brightened. She put this consideration to Rose Bird, whose first reaction was to burst into tears.

'Well, think about it,' counselled her mother, looking distastefully at the streaming hair and the untidy kimono. 'And *do* smarten yourself up, my child. No sensible man would take you if he could see you now.'

When Golden Willow had left, Rose Bird washed her face and found Mayflower to do her hair. Then she went to look for Black Jade.

'What do you think?' she asked, after relating the news.

'What does that matter? What do *you* think?'

'I don't know. I hadn't even considered it.' Her eyes filled. 'I'd hoped – well, *you* know.'

'You must forget all that now,' said Black Jade briskly, aware of a certain dissembling in herself. 'You must expect to be married some day. Would you like it to be soon?'

'It depends, doesn't it, on the man? What would he be like? Do you think Honourable Father knows anyone even a *little* bit like the Emperor?'

'Ask him.'

'I couldn't.' Rose Bird blushed. She looked very pretty.

Black Jade sighed. 'No. You couldn't. Then I will.'

She did so as soon as the opportunity arose and reported back at once, slightly out of countenance. The General had laughed at her.

'He says the Son of Heaven is unique; but so, too, will be the man who marries you. And that he has nothing but your happiness and welfare at heart in this.'

Rose Bird cast down her lashes and looked demure, as though it were the General himself who stood before her. 'Then I must gratefully accept my honoured father's considerate choice.'

3

When Black Jade was to look back on her sister's wedding it was always to be under the shadow of the events that were to follow it.

The marriage itself was a triumph. The young man who was chosen for the honour of receiving the most sought-after bride in the province was Lord Ho-lan, an energetic careerist in the Board of Finance. By dint of some expert eavesdropping, Welcome was able to discover more about him than the few unrevealing facts that were considered suitable for an engaged girl to know.

'He's handsome,' she reported delightedly. 'A long face, rather aristocratic; slender – he's a regular sportsman – an excellent scholar and a patron of the arts. And he's *rich*, my little turtle! His servants say he doesn't drink to excess; nor does he visit the women of the tea-houses. You'll have to stop blushing, Rose Bird. You'll soon be a married woman!'

Rose Bird soon began to take an interest in Ho-lan. Her heart was captured at the moment when she learned that he wore his whiskers exactly like the Emperor's. She also liked his given name, Resolute Heart. She thought he sounded like a great paragon. Black Jade, though she did not say so, thought that since no one had mentioned his personality at all, he might well turn out to be a great bore.

On the day that Madame Ho-lan, the mother of the hopeful groom, came to make the customary inspection of her prospective daughter-in-law, Rose Bird made Black Jade promise that she would not speak unless spoken to, and that she would make replies that were dutiful rather than necessarily truthful.

'How ridiculous! If you are going to begin by being afraid of your mother-in-law, where do you think it will end? You should be very firm and show her who you are, right away.'

'That is not what Mother says. And if you are not going to behave yourself, I'll ask her to order you not to come in when we serve tea to Madam Ho-lan.'

'Oh, I'll behave – like a deaf mute, I promise.'

Luckily Madame Ho-lan proved to be a reasonable sort of woman with no especial interest in tormenting daughters-in-law. She liked Rose Bird at once for her pleasant and filial manner and her graceful way with the teacups. She also found charming the sweet smiles the girl kept for her stunningly attractive, but perhaps rather backward, little sister.

The match was made at once. A resplendent go-between, the groom's best-friend, arrived next morning with the scarlet envelope which contained the young man's precise hour and date of birth, which he ceremoniously exchanged for its twin, bearing those of Rose Bird. After the customary three days had elapsed without any contrary signs from the heavens, the two horoscopes were cast and an auspicious day chosen for the wedding.

Rose Bird shed the conventional tears very prettily when she was officially informed of the marriage and the occasion was then announced to the family and friends.

The date chosen was during the Little Heat, less than a month away, and the time passed very happily in a flurry of congratulatory calls and dressmakers' fittings.

There was also an interview with Golden Willow which Rose Bird repeated to Black Jade with flaming cheeks.

'Well, you knew all that! It's as I told you; just like horses.'

'No, there's more to it than that; much more. Mother gave me a book –'

'What book? Show me!'

'No, you're too young. She'll probably give you a copy when *you* get married.'

'That won't be for ages – three or four years. I might as well know what I'm in for now. Come on! Don't poke the poor frog if you don't wan't to see it jump!'

It took another fifteen minutes of persuasion before Black Jade held in her hands the fascinating pages of *The Plain Girl's Handbook of Sex*. It had the virtue of keeping her quiet for a very long time. She had always enjoyed physical exercise of any kind, and the book described an extraordinary range of shared gymnastics that would be interesting enough for their own sake, but were apparently all aimed at a single and specific incomprehensible moment of pleasure. It was, it seemed, absolutely necessary that the female partner should attain that moment every time she and her husband performed the activity; the man, however, gained strength and replenished his *yang*, not by a familiar attainment, but by holding back his seed (which *was* the same as a horse's) unless the date was a propitious one for the conception of a child. On the whole, she could see now, it was far more complex than anything Snow Prince might be expected to achieve.

'I can't imagine *you* doing anything so energetic,' she observed as she returned the manual to its owner.

'I expect you'll persuade Lord Ho-lan to stick to the "Close Union" and the "Unicorn's Horn" and leave complicated manoeuvres like "Reversed Flying Ducks" and "Jumping White Tiger" to his concubines. I wonder what it *feels* like.'

Rose Bird, who had experienced some premonitions about that, wisely kept them to herself.

Ten days before the wedding, the Bride's Feast was celebrated. Black Jade was rather pleased with the poem she wrote about it.

Moonlight blazes across the courtyard,
Jealous of the red lanterns in the cypress tree.
Laughter runs up and down among the tables
Echoing the music of the flutes.
Did you catch the whisper of silk
As a bold girl turns to look at the men's table?
She is trapped, as she deserves,

By the stalking eye of a stranger.
Who can blame them? It is a heady night.
There are drums in the music now; drums in the blood.
And here come the acrobats! How do they avoid the tables,
Tumbling among us like plums from plundered trees?
What a noise we are all making!
And soon there will be fireworks.
But first, the moment we've all been waiting for;
The bride is coming.
Here she is, hesitating in the lamplight,
Fire and roses beneath her veil. So beautiful –
I almost failed to recognise her,
Even though I know she is my beautiful sister.
It is because I look at her through tears.

Ten days later, red-veiled, painted, jewelled and dressed like a princess, escorted by drums and cymbals and children throwing flowers, Rose Bird was conveyed weeping from the house into a crimson-covered palanquin. This would lead the long procession of her goods and servants, eloquent of her wealth and status, down the thirty miles of road that would separate her from the halls of her childhood.

This time her tears were real, and they hurt her, for once she had entered the courtyards of her husband's house there would be little reason for her ever to leave them again. Or so, on that day, it was thought.

Black Jade was with her father when it happened.

They had ridden out across the plain that morning, scarcely two weeks after the wedding, into a beaten gold shield of a day, their gallop the more enjoyable for the memories it invoked of their meeting with Li Shih-min.

They thundered on, hot and happy, towards the point of that encounter, a shared but unspoken destination. They were still some distance away when the giant Wu-han seemed to miss his step and falter. The movement caught Black Jade's eye and she turned to see the General leaning down as though examining a loose stirrup. He pulled himself up at once and waved a hand to reassure her. They plunged on and the little break in the rhythm was forgotten as they raced for their objective, measuring the exact spot where they had met the Emperor by the distances between the two most prominent peaks of the mountains.

They reined in at approximately the same moment, exchanging

delighted glances at their agreement about the place.

'We should build a pavilion here, to mark the occasion,' suggested Black Jade.

'Very well. What shall we name it? "The Court of Imperial Welcome"?'

'No. I think His Majesty would prefer something more in keeping with his mood that day. How about "The Hunting Lodge of the Desert Generals"?'

Her father shook his head but supposed that she would have her way, though it was almost treasonable to include his worthless self in the same phrase as his Emperor.

'We shall paint it all in gold, so that it will appear like a mirage from the distance; and then, when they discover that it is real, and see its beauty, travellers will think they have entered the domain of the Yellow Emperor.'

'Ah, Second Daughter, your imagination takes you journeying as far as any traveller.'

'Is that a curse, or a blessing, do you think?'

'A blessing, surely, as long as imagination outstrips desire.'

She remained silent. She could not speak of her desires. They gazed up into the mountains, quiet for a time, letting the blue peace reach them.

Suddenly the General gave a little gasp, as if surprised.

'My father?'

He had clasped his hand over his chest. He looked at her in extreme puzzlement.

'What is wrong? Are you in pain?'

She manoeuvred Snow Prince closer to his side. He was very pale. She had never seen him so colourless, not even the time they had brought him home from the Wall on a covered pallet, wasted with fever and a thigh wound that would not heal.

He moved his head slightly as if to deny pain.

'How very strange,' he said wonderingly. Then he looked at her almost with apology, and with a half smile, wrapped the reins round his wrist and laid his head down on Wu-han's neck.

'Father! Please!' Black Jade reached out. It would be ill-mannered to touch him, but she needed his reassurance. She was afraid. His breathing came suddenly loud and harsh, as though he were snoring. Then, just as suddenly, it stopped.

'Merciful Kuan Yin! He must not be ill. He is never ill! Father! Honourable Father, please say something!'

Wu-han turned his head very gently, so as not to disturb his burden. As his melancholy brown eyes questioned her, Black Jade knew that the horse had understood more readily than she that his master would not speak again.

She pushed back her panic with a fury of impatience and, nudging Wu-han with her heel, turned both horses back towards the compound.

Slowly they brought the General home. The great-hearted animals sensed their owners' tragedy and walked, heads down, at a slow march.

It was the thirteenth hour before they reached the gates of the mansion. The grooms and stable-boys came out to meet them, alerted by their dreamlike motion.

There was a great dull silence, like that within a temple when a bronze gong has ceased to reverberate.

And then the wailing began.

The worst thing about their pity, she thought, as she was enfolded and suffocated by it during the hideous days that followed, was that there was no one, now, to whom she could ever have explained that what she suffered was not the choking depths of sorrow but the consuming furnace of impotent rage.

Alone in her room, she stormed at the Heavens.

'Why my father, you jealous Gods? Why him? You could have taken any of us. Why did you take him?'

And so, soon after the wedding feast, the rites of death took place. There would be forty-nine days of mourning before the burial, days when Black Jade must take her sister's place in comforting their mother, for Rose Bird would not return until the day of the funeral.

Golden Willow's mourning was intense and private. She remained in her chambers and did not allow either her family or the visiting troops of relatives to see the disgrace of a single tear beyond those publicly shed in ritual keening over the body of her husband.

Black Jade, who could bear neither her mother's crystalline control nor the weeping and hiccoughs of Welcome and the other servants, found some refuge in assisting Eldest Aunt to deal with all that must be done.

There was the provision of food for the hundreds of visitors who came to offer condolences; the ordering of white mourning robes for every member of the clan; the buying of quantities of incense for the services. There were arrangements to be made for 108 Buddhist monks from the Monastery of Heavenly Grace to sing the 'Litany of Great Compassion' in the Hall of the

Ancestors where the body would lie in state. This would win the forgiveness of their sins for the General and all the ancestors who had gone before him beyond the Yellow Springs. Every seventh day, the priests would perform the sacrifices of food and wine before the body.

They had dressed Wu Shih-huo in the magnificent gold-encrusted coat that had been made for him at the same time as the flawless rosewood coffin. Both had been created in haste. Another eight years should have passed before Shuang would have presented these things to his father upon his reaching his sixtieth year. But the sewing maids and the carpenter had put as much love and care into their work as though it had taken months instead of mere hours to complete. The coat seemed almost alive with the embroidered figures of horsemen which would have evoked the rich chuckle of its wearer, could he have seen it. The coffin was the most perfect selection of wood in the province, inlaid with pearl and jade, with hinges and handles of gold.

Despite the grandeur of the casket and the elegance of the robe, Golden Willow and her daughter were both adamant that, beneath the gold thread, the General should lie comfortably in his old leather jerkin.

'He would never forgive us if we let him go without it,' said Golden Willow, 'but Eldest Sister-in-law must not know. She would think he would lose face before the immortals.' Black Jade realised, with a hot rush behind her eyes, how much she loved her mother in that moment; though custom bound her life she would not let it overrule her love for the man who had, so often, gently put custom aside. If it had occasionally gained him critical comment while he lived, it had resulted in no diminution of respect now that he had left this life. Every day the Hall of Ancestors was packed with kneeling mourners in stark white who came to pray before the red-draped coffin where it rested on the bier behind the main altar.

On the first day, when they had brought him there, Black Jade was still wholly filled with the dark anger that would not let her accept this untimely death. The great hall had always been a place of mystery and faint, curious pleasure for her, its dim lamps and inextinguishable incense and the rows of ancestral tablets somehow reassuring, promising both peace and continuity.

But her father had not been ready for peace. He should have had many more miles to ride. The Gods had been jealous and she did not forgive them. She felt as though she were suffocating as she knelt among the clansmen in their white hempen robes, the men unshaven with their hair flowing loose and unwashed, the women unpainted, without jewels. The chanting of the priests who lined the walls, rudely colourful in their saffron gowns, seemed to her now a mocking parody of the bees' humming in the orchard, on that brilliant and hopeful day, such a brief time ago, when the whole world had been so brimful of life that it had seemed hardly vast enough to contain it all.

She watched with growing nausea as Shuang kowtowed three times before the portrait of the General which stood beside his wooden spirit tablet between the candles on the table before the bier.

The monks ceased their chanting and Shuang lit the candles and the incense. Then he took the bowls of food from the tray which one of the monks offered to him and placed them on the table.

He cried aloud, three times, 'Oh my father!' his clear voice reverberating among the stone pillars. Three times, again, he made the kowtow, touching his forehead to the floor. But what Black Jade heard in his cry was not filial sorrow for the death of his father, but ungodly joy in coming into his inheritance.

Wu Yuan Shuang was now the head of the General's household. She owed him all the duty and obedience she had previously owed her father. As she joined in the wailing of the women, her tears were as much for herself and her unknown future as for the dear spirit who, perhaps, could still hear her lament as he journeyed on his path towards his next incarnation.

'You should not have left me,' she accused inwardly. 'I still *need* you, my father.'

The astrologers and geomancers agreed that the forty-ninth day was well-aspected for the funeral, the hour of the Horse being the optimal time for the burial.

The ancestral burial ground of the Wu clan lay far up on the hillside behind the compound, where a clearing had been made among the pines. It was a place filled with the kind of silence whose depths only birdsong can sound. At the edge of the clearing, on a precipice which fell jaggedly away down to the rushing waters of the Hasty River, far below, stood the ancient Temple of Heaven's Threshold. This housed, as well as the saffron-clad monks who offered perpetual prayer for their departed souls, the earthly remains of generations of the clan. On the day of the funeral a mist hung about it, clammy and insistent. Its saturated whiteness lent a mourning garment to the graceful building and to the soaring pines, turning each separate needle into a fine black brushstroke upon a sky washed in white lead.

The procession that snaked its way back and forth up the hillside was headed by the Wu bannermen wearing the clan colours of scarlet and black, with mourning sashes of white silk. On the first and largest banner Wu Shi-huo's name and titles were written in clear black characters upon crimson brocade. Those which followed bore different motifs of flowers, birds, beasts or geometrical patterns, all in the two basic colours. Their bearers maintained as military a step as was possible upon the uneven path. After them walked Wu-han, caparisoned in scarlet, with trappings of jet; he was without a rider but behaved perfectly, keeping his step as steady and sure as when he had brought his master home for the last time. Behind the great horse, the Chief Steward carried a cushion bearing the General's sword. Others brought an ebony box containing his uniform and palace insignia. Then came his portrait and his spirit tablet which would be placed upon an altar in the temple.

The monks followed next in their two blocks of strong, solid colour, their lips moving in prayers that did not expect to be heard above the rumbling drums and shrilling trumpets of the musicians who walked some way behind, together with the porters of the gifts to Heaven, the sweepers of evil spirits with their long-handled brooms, and the dancing swordsmen who cut the mist into woolly ribbons with their flashing naked blades. This was to ward off inimical demons from the path of the scarlet-covered catafalque which was carried, with the utmost pride and pomp, by sixty-four satin-clad bearers.

The mourners followed the coffin, all the rich and noble of the province, the older men and the women in gaudy palanquins or bright sedans, escorted by their servants crashing gongs and cymbals or carrying ceremonial umbrellas. The young men took pride in negotiating the climb on horseback, forming a moving forest of pennants and streamers in the colours of five hundred households.

One of these, a heavy-jowled youth with a florid complexion, arrogantly forced his way to the front of the cavalcade, jostling all in his path until he was among the palanquins of the ladies of the house of Wu. He cast a choleric eye about until it fell on a particular bannerman, who stopped when he saw the rider and came to bow at his stirrup. Their conversation was brief. The horseman cantered swiftly to the front of the women's cortege, drawing alongside the sixth palanquin, a decorative affair in ebony, lacquered in gold and scarlet. He noted with satisfaction that the embroidered curtains were not quite closed.

Inside the jouncing vehicle, holding on to its sides and their own patience, were Black Jade and Rose Bird. The latter was lying back, her mood subdued. Her father's death had been a great shock to her and, thus far, her grief outweighed any pleasure she might have felt at seeing her home again so soon after her marriage.

Black Jade, chafing at the slowness of their bumpy and uncomfortable course, was keeping her temper by taking the opportunity to look about her. She had rarely been outside the compound, except on the rides with her father and upon a very few secret jaunts to the market with Welcome when she was small.

'You shouldn't,' Rose Bird reprimanded. 'Supposing someone saw you? This is hardly the time to lose face.'

'It's all right for you; you've travelled sixty miles recently. I've seen nothing but what can already be seen from Pine Green Hill; not that this is so very different. But I do like to look at the people.'

'You should have your mind on our father.'

'I have. But one's mind will hold more than one thing at once. besides – Honoured Father would not care. He believed it to be foolish that we girls should have to spend such secluded lives.'

'He never told *me* that.'

'No. Well, I suppose he didn't want to confuse you.'

'What do you mean? Why should I be confused, while you –'

'Hush! Look. There's a fellow there staring at us; well, trying to. At least I think he is.'

'Gods! Close the curtains at once!'

'He's tall and fat, and he has a face like a disgruntled pig. He's very richly dressed. He *is* trying to look in!'

Rose Bird swooped to close the curtains, securing them with one of her long silver hairpins.

'Now, will you behave?'

Black Jade shrugged and wriggled back onto her cushions. 'He wasn't much to look at, anyway. Just some vulgar toad, trying to see what *we're* like. Oh well, if you won't let me look out, you'll have to entertain me yourself. You haven't told me yet how you like being married.'

It took some time to persuade her sister that, unsuitable though this topic might be, it would serve to make their bruising ascent seem shorter.

They were soon deeply engrossed, and the inquisitive horseman was forgotten as Rose Bird shyly admitted to enjoying married life and all that this entailed. She refused to discuss the most intimate details, saving these at least for a more appropriate occasion, but she gave a lively description of the Ho-lan household, the likes and dislikes of her mother-in-law, the pleasant if unstimulating company of her sisters-in-law and the many presents by which her husband signified his satisfaction with her.

'Then you are content?' asked Black Jade.

'I believe so. Although I miss you all unbearably, I think, on the whole, I have been lucky. Marriage is a lottery. I might be said to have won.'

'I am so glad for you. I have missed you too, and could hardly bear to think you were not happy.'

Now they had arrived at the summit and could stretch their cramped limbs before entering the temple. The space before it was noisy with people and crowded with abandoned sedans and servants holding horses. They went inside, and the cool, scented darkness, solemn with the presence of the Buddha imaged many times over in wood and stone, rapt and mysterious in the light of a thousand candles, restored the dignity of the day.

When they were all assembled, Shuang and Ching entered and carried the portrait and spirit tablet of Wu Shih-huo to their place upon the altar.

Shuang kowtowed to the tablet, then declaimed in his clear, cold voice, 'It is I who should die, for my sins are many and great. Heaven has given me the hardest penance of all, in taking, instead, the life of my father. I, his eldest son, my brother and all his family shed bitter tears for him now.' He recited the long list of the General's good deeds and virtues and ended with the dedication of the mourners to perpetuate his sacrifices.

As he finished his speech the monks again took up the prayers they had chanted almost ceaselessly since the hour of death. Now followed the ritual sacrifice, the burning at the altar of the funeral gifts; of food, wine and money; of personal possessions such as Shih-huo's riding whip and his favourite chess set, the lute he had played, and the papier maché images of everything that he would need for the life of his spiritual soul, the *hun*, for its new existence in the Western Heaven; and also to ensure that the animal soul, the *p'o*, would rest peacefully in the grave, slowly fading with the body's decay, and would not roam the earth as a famished ghost, a *kuei*, an enemy to living men. Black Jade wept as the flames consumed the little horses, the soldiers, the paper palace and the ranks of diminutive servants. She was glad they had remembered the leather jerkin.

For the rest of that day, as the wake proceeded with its noise and its fireworks and the endless chanting of the monks, it was Rose Bird who lent her strength to her sister as she threatened at last to give way to grief. The reversal of their roles was satisfying to both of them.

During the few days that they were able to spend together they otherwise fell into their old relationship. Rose Bird was staying in her own rooms, while her husband slept in the General's residence, now Shuang's. So happy were the two girls to be in each other's company that, as time went on, they had to be reproved at last for thoughtless laughter, and threatened with separation. But the parting came soon enough, and this time it would be a very long one, as far as either girl could see.

As she stood at the Ceremonial Gate to wave away the last of Rose Bird's departing train, Black Jade was swamped by the sudden returning sense of her double bereavement.

For nearly a week she kept to her room, wretched and listless, feeling as though she hadn't a friend in the world except Welcome, who constantly tried to raise her spirits with kind words and favourite titbits.

'Take heart, Little Phoenix! The celestial Kuan Yin will take pity on you shortly, and things will get better, you'll see.' Then, hesitantly, guiltily prey to the forbidden memory of a prophecy in which she could not quite disbelieve, she said, 'I'm sure Heaven has something wonderful in store for you.'

'Nothing good will *ever* happen to me,' was the gloomy reply.

The next day she became even more certain of this.

She felt that she must, at all costs, get away from the sad confines of her rooms and her misery. She had not been riding since the General's death. Now ten weeks had passed and she thought that probably no one would try to stop her if she were to take Snow Prince for a quiet canter.

She would take Huan as her escort. He had been exercising the horse all this time and would make as good company as anyone in the future. He would know how to be quiet and let her seek her father's spirit where, she knew, she would be most likely to find it, out in the open spaces that they both loved so much.

When she reached the stables, Huan came running out to meet her. He kowtowed, then lifted a face full of bad news.

'What is it, Huan?'

'It's your honourable brother, Little Ancestress; he has taken

Snow Prince for himself and has given orders that no one else is to ride him.'

Black Jade was blank with shock. Then she realised wearily that she was not surprised. This was what was to be expected of the mean-spirited Fox. For a moment she savoured the idea of killing him; of taking his own dragon-handled sword and running him through with it. Then she laughed at herself, though without mirth.

'Thank you, Huan. Don't worry. It's not your fault. Just look after Snow Prince as best you can.'

She could not even bear to stroke the stallion's loving, curious nose, not today. She turned on her heel and went at once to seek an interview with the most powerful person in the compound. She knew her rights and was determined to be given them.

Eldest Uncle might, at this time, be expected to be found in the suite of rooms known as his study. These comprised a library, a sleeping chamber and a room reserved for receiving guests.

Taking Welcome, who preceded her to dispose of any male servants who might be in her path, Black Jade marched into the receiving court and sent in her request.

The maid returned at once to say that unfortunately the patriarch was away in the capital, on clan business, and would not be back until the end of the week.

Patience was not a quality Black Jade had ever bothered to develop and she fared badly now.

'Why don't you ask your lady mother to intercede?' suggested Welcome. 'Your honourable brother, piss take him, could hardly refuse a request from her.'

'I wish I was certain of that,' said Black Jade. 'Anyway, I don't want to bring my troubles to her at present. She mourns my father deeply and should not be distressed about anything else. I'll just have to wait until Uncle returns.'

The waiting, which she discovered unhappily to be almost a full-time occupation, was interrupted in the early evening by a mysterious summons to the General's house.

'What can it be? It's not like the Fox to send for me.'

Welcome wagged a finger, presaging some piece of country wisdom. 'The duck never found out how to get chicks by turning her face to the drake.'

Black Jade took her point and wrapped herself in a shawl, then they both set out across the Bridge of Forgetfulness. At her father's house, some maids were waiting to escort her inside. They took her to the General's small reception room, a comfortable chamber lined with books and swords. Her brother Shuang was sprawled on the raised *kang* at the back of the room, grinning like a monkey. Beside him, she realised with an inward jolt, was the pig-faced young man who had tried to pry into her palanquin at the funeral. A wine jar, three cups and several dishes of food stood between them.

Behind her, Welcome gave a hiss of disapproval. It was unforgivably ill-mannered of Shuang to allow his sister to be seen by a man who was not a member of the family.

'Come away at once, Young Mistress. Someone has made a mistake,' the nurse said coldly, looking her master firmly in the eye. 'This is a house of mourning.'

'Hold your tongue, you damned interfering bitch, and get outside until you're wanted.' Shuang's voice was thick and slurred.

Welcome stood her ground, pulling at Black Jade's sleeve.

'By Heaven, I'll have you whipped, half-naked, and then turned out of doors!'

'Please leave us, Welcome. I shan't be long,' Black Jade said quickly. She would die if Welcome were taken from her too.

'That's more like it,' approved Shuang with a crooked rictus. Welcome pattered away, chuntering to herself.

'Now, Younger Sister, won't you sit down and take a cup of wine with us? You need not object to the presence of my friend Roly Chun.' He sniggered. 'He is a very *close* friend, whom I hope will become even closer.'

The young man nodded, his piggy eyes openly examining her.

'Oh, sweet, merciful Buddha, no!' she thought. 'Not yet. And not, for the love of Heaven, not *this*!'

Roly shambled to his feet and bowed. She almost expected him to grunt as he said, 'It is most charming to meet the celebrated young Lady Wu. Rumour has not been untruthful, only too sparing in her praise.'

Black Jade did not move or speak.

'I said *sit*, Little Sister, and drink with us,' Shuang insisted in a bullying tone. 'And later, perhaps you might entertain us with one of your songs.'

She knew she must be careful; she did not want to lose Welcome. She seated herself on a rosewood stool at some distance from the *kang*.

'Allow me,' said Pig-face, pouring wine into the third cup to do her honour.

There should have been a female servant present to pass her the cup, but since there was not, she must accept it from him. She managed to do so without touching his hands, noticing that even these resembled half a catty of pork sausages, pink and shiny, their skin stretched taut about the full flesh.

If Shuang thought he was going to marry her to this repulsive creature, he had better first think in what style he would like his coffin!

'I did not expect to meet a guest. We have mourned our father for only ten weeks,' she said neutrally. Convention dictated that there should be no extensive entertainment during the three years of mourning, especially in the first year.

'But, as you will soon realise, Roly here is a very special guest,' said Shuang with a private leer for the youth. It had not occurred to him that Black Jade had guessed his intentions.

'Oh, why is that?' she asked innocently, loathing him.

'All in good time,' Shuang replied.

His visitor had the grace to blush at this point, if grace could be the result of such an extensive inflammation of porcine cheeks, jowls and flabby neck. To cover his confusion he suddenly thrust his pork sausages towards her again, wrapped around a small dish of sweetmeats.

'Do try one, Honoured Lady. I picked out every one myself.'

'Very wise.' She fixed him with the eye of a serpent. 'After all, one would not wish to buy a pig in a poke.'

She ate the sweet, which tasted of dust, drank half a cup of the sweet rice wine and then said firmly, 'It has been kind of you to think of me, Elder Brother, but now I must leave you. I have to join my honourable mother in her prayers.'

Shuang could hardly insist on keeping her, in these circumstances. When, unwillingly, they let her go, she was aching with repressed anger. All she wanted to do was to take Snow Prince and gallop off on to the plain, faster and faster, taking nothing with her and never coming back. She would go to the border, over the Wall, and join a tribe of the Huns, who were said to admire Chinese girls. At any rate they would treat her as well as her brother did. She managed to repress herself further, however, and went home, instead, to write out a petition and complaint to the patriarch. No doubt Shuang thought she would keep quiet to save face; but face was all very well when one had got one's life into some sort of order; it scarcely mattered when every bit of it was falling apart.

After that, she did join Golden Willow in her prayers, finding comfort and some measure of rest in her tranquil presence.

The rest of that week was an agony of waiting and fuming, with dreadful shouting nightmares in which unutterable things from the *Plain Girl's Manual* were done to her by a hideous, snorting creature in a pig's mask, with trotters for hands.

At last Eldest Uncle returned. Welcome dashed to tell Black Jade the moment she heard of his arrival. They were patient for just one more day while the patriarch unpacked and made his necessary dispositions, and then Black Jade, looking her prettiest, tidiest and, very purposefully, her *youngest*, answered his long-awaited summons.

To her surprise, the interview was apparently to be held in Eldest Uncle's grandest reception room, the one whose walls were covered with cerulean blue brocade and hung with exquisitely painted scenes from the legendary life of the Yellow Emperor. The clan children all loved to look at these, but hardly ever had the chance to do so as they rarely attended any function in the chamber.

Black Jade was intrigued to find about fifty of the household maids flanking the steps as she ran up them with Welcome at her heels.

'Something important must be happening. I wonder what?'

'Follow your nose and you'll find out,' muttered her nurse, equally curious.

When they came into the hall, they saw not only Eldest Uncle, seated in his favourite high-backed chair, but also all the other uncles on his right, and on his left Golden Willow and all the aunts.

Black Jade quickly scoured her conscience but found it clean.

The patriarch smiled at her and she relaxed, reassured. Then he did something extraordinary.

He left his great chair and walked towards her. Within six paces of her he dropped to the ground in the most perfect kowtow, knocking his brow three times on the floor before her.

Bewildered, she looked to her mother for some sign as to what had come over him. But Golden Willow merely smiled and nodded.

'Please get up, Honourable Eldest Uncle. It is only I, your unworthy second niece. It is I who should kowtow.'

Eldest Uncle rose, still smiling.

'One far greater than this insignificant servant of Heaven has found you worthy, my niece. You have brought outstanding honour to the whole clan.'

She caught her breath, uncertainty and knowledge clashing like cymbals in her spinning head.

'Hurry, Uncle,' she thought. 'Say it quickly, for I cannot wait another second.'

But the patriarch was enjoying the protraction of his news. Golden Willow was the only one who had shared the secret until this moment.

'I know that none of you will be able to guess what this great honour can be,' he suggested, beaming at the row of his siblings, all of whom were trying not to look as astonished and curious as they were.

Black Jade looked at him in agony, assailed by the ruffian fear that this might merely be the precursor of an announcement that she was to be married off to two hundred catties of pork chops. But if this were the case, surely her mother would have warned her? She had no right *not* to tell her. How could she be so cruel? And where was Shuang? Why was he not here to enjoy his victory?

She was at least to learn the answer to that immediately.

'Forgive me, my niece; your brothers should also be here to add their congratulations. I can only assume that my message has gone astray. I will keep you in suspense no longer.'

He stopped and beamed again at the row of bland faces, each revealing nothing of the strain of concealing a ravenous interest. When every eye was upon him, and Black Jade's stomach was churning like a water-wheel, he produced a scroll from his sleeve. It was tied and sealed in bright yellow, the imperial colour.

At the sight of those seals the nightmares receded and she found that she was now unusually composed. She clasped her hands and let them hang loosely before her, covered by her sleeves. She looked demurely at Eldest Uncle as he prepared to read to them the Emperor's edict.

The patriarch spoke clearly and steadily for about two minutes. It was only when he had finished that she realised that she had heard not a single word of it. But when he bowed again, and then they all kowtowed to her, every one of them, even her mother, she began to know for certain that Shih-min had kept his promise.

She had been invited to enter the palace.

They all rose and crowded round her and their blessings fell upon her as softly as the petals of the plum blossom. Those who knew her best began to weep, knowing that they were unlikely to see her again.

When they had all left, still marvelling, Black Jade walked with Golden Willow across the Bridge of Forgetfulness.

Halfway across they paused and leaned on the parapet, letting their eyes follow the slow ripple of the water among the lilies.

'I will miss you, my daughter,' Golden Willow said quietly.

Black Jade saw that, now that they were alone, her mother's eyes were shining with tears.

Deeply touched, she attempted to comfort her. 'The honour to the clan will more than compensate for the loss of one unharmonious child,' she said gently. 'It is I who will be lonely, far away among strangers. My home here is all I have known. It is part of me and I love it. But I do have a restless nature,' she grinned suddenly. 'I shall probably find enough mischief to occupy me at court.'

Golden Willow smiled. 'I don't doubt that. I sometimes think you were a monkey in a previous incarnation.' Then she voiced her fears.

'The honour is great, I know. But what disturbs me is that you will be only one among so many. His Majesty has numerous consorts who have already given him several sons. How are you to distinguish yourself when so many are ahead of you? At best you may become the mother of one of the Emperor's youngest and least important sons; at worst you may be ignored altogether. And *that*, my wayward daughter, would by no means suit your temperament. And then,' she finished wistfully, 'you are so very young, to go so far away from us.'

If her mother were to continue long in this vein, Black Jade would soon be in tears herself. She did not want that.

'I am to be admitted to the presence of the Son of Heaven,' she said proudly, lifting her chin. 'How could such a wonderful thing lead to unhappiness? You know him; you know how he cared for my honourable father, how kind he was to all of us when he was here. Can you doubt that I will be well cared for in his palace? There is no need to weep; this is a time to be glad! If I were to remain here, what would happen to me? Shuang would marry me off to some repulsive friend of his and I'd be locked up in the womens' court until I died! At least I will see something of *life* at court!'

Golden Willow touched her daughter's smooth cheek. 'There is something in that,' she sighed. 'Nevertheless, you are the child of my heart and the house will be without music when you are gone.'

For a moment it seemed that she had more to say, but she shook her head and dismissed Black Jade with a kindness that was near to pity. She had wanted to tell the child of the prophecy concerning her, now that she was to approach so near the seat of power. But a stronger instinct, coupled with an uncomfortable and incomprehensible foreboding, prevented her.

4

Over my bed the moonlight streams
Making it look like frost-covered
Ground; lifting my head I see
The brightness, then dropping it,
I am filled with thoughts of home.

(Li Po, 701–762)

The journey to the capital was a frustrating experience for Black Jade. To travel over four hundred miles, through rugged mountain gorges and defiles and along the rutted ochre roads of the plains, through country long guessed at and desired from the pavilions of home; to hear the roar of the mighty Yellow River as their path came close to its rock-filled course, or the mingled sounds of men and animals when they passed the tents of another caravan, or even the nightly singing, beneath the stars, of the soldiers who were her escort – to know all these from the claustrophobic seclusion of the dusty palanquin, from which she should descend only when no man was looking her way, drove her to make feverish plans for escape. She and Snow Prince, who was safe in the hands of Huan somewhere behind, would pursue the tantalising train of one of the passing merchants, whose foreign voices, fine horses and jingling, frosty-faced camels offered one unbearable invitation after another.

Welcome, who intended that her mistress should reach Chang-an within the expected ten days, and without having thrown over too many of the proprieties, was unsympathetic. Every evening she argued Jade out of dressing as a boy and taking to horseback, if only to exercise her protesting body.

'It would be unthinkable in a royal consort! You must have a demon in you to torment me like this.'

'No one would notice. I'd be careful.'

'Don't fool yourself, Little Mistress. Everyone would notice. They watch you as though you were a strange planet. They hope to see *you* as much as you hope to see the world! Well, neither must be satisfied and that's that. You must be content to look through the curtains, and they to know you are behind them.'

There was no persuading Welcome, and cooped up as she was, Black Jade could do nothing without her assistance; so she settled down resentfully to suffer the agonies of impatience all the way through the Land Between the Passes that led to Chang-an.

In the end it was the cold that helped her. Despite her well-padded clothing, her circulation rebelled against her inaction and attacked her with pins and needles and numbness in the legs. Welcome relented at last and permitted her, swathed and veiled to ward off masculine eyes, to walk alongside the palanquin for half an hour each morning and evening.

It was during one of her evening walks that they caught up with another caravan, apparently also on its way to the capital.

'Who is it? Some merchant?' Black Jade asked.

Welcome was eager. 'I'm not sure; but one of the soldiers says he saw dragon flags. It might be some imperial official.'

'Why don't you go and see,' said Black Jade casually. Curiosity had always been her nurse's weakness. 'I'd like to know if it's anyone important.'

Welcome hesitated. She longed to go, but was not sure how far she should trust her mistress.

'Oh, go on,' urged Black Jade. 'We'll be making camp for the night, any minute now. They're slowing down already. Why not see what you can find out?'

'Well – after I've seen you get back into the palanquin.'

Black Jade climbed back into her prison, complaining bitterly. It seemed to satisfy Welcome, who pinned the curtains together with a final motion and went off to investigate their neighbours.

Black Jade soon accomplished the gymnastic feat of changing into her riding clothes inside the palanquin. Then, with her hair in a topknot and a scarf tied round it in the manner of any poor lad who worked for his living, she slipped past the Wu guards, who were too busy setting up tents to notice her escape, and made for the back of the caravan where she would find Huan looking after the horses.

'Little Mistress!' the boy gave Jade his monkey's grin. 'I have often tried to see you, to tell you Snow Prince is well and eats like a pig – but Welcome is as fierce as a whole regiment of guards!'

'I know.' She returned his smile. 'She was brought up with seven brothers, and by all accounts she ruled them all like the Goddess of the Western Heaven.'

Huan chuckled. 'I never knew that.'

'She was the eighth child. Her parents were unusual in badly wanting a girl. So – when she arrived at last, they called her

Welcome and spoiled her dreadfully from that day on, including allowing her to bully her brothers. The trouble is,' Black Jade sighed, 'that now the only person she has to bully is me. And since I shall feel the rough edge of her tongue later, I must make the best of my small freedom. Will you saddle Snow Prince for me? I want to explore the hills for a while.'

The boy frowned. 'You won't go alone? This is dangerous country.'

'You may come with me – if you don't mind the consequences.'

She thought that Snow Prince would be the one to betray her, so loud were his delighted whinnies when he saw her; but the soldiers and servants were preoccupied with the evening camp drill and no one noticed the two figures on horseback as they trotted off up a twisting path that led up into the mountains.

Very soon they were able to look down on the two camps spread along the valley below, close to the river. Already they looked like terracotta toys into which some God had amused himself by breathing life.

They stood on a green bluff which marked the end of the easy part of their path. Above them it became steeper and narrower as it plunged up a defile between overhanging cliffs.

'Are you sure you want to go this way, Little Mistress? It would not be a good place for a horse's foot to slip.'

'When have you ever known Snow Prince to slip? Or Bannerman either?' She looked at Huan's sturdy mount, her father's present to him shortly before his death.

'Very well. Will you lead or shall I?'

'I will!' She turned Snow Prince and urged him up the path, letting him finding his own pace as he picked his way among the stones and boulders. On either side the cliffs rose sheer above them, studded with twisted trees and bushes whose hold seemed wildly improbable.

'Mistress,' Huan called from behind, 'I have not thanked you properly for asking that I might come with you to the palace.'

'Don't thank me. I wouldn't have gone without you, and Welcome of course. I had to have a friend or two with me; besides, my horse needs you!'

'That is true,' he conceded, 'but you have my thanks nevertheless. Tell me, are you glad to be entering the palace – or would you have preferred to stay at home with the clan?'

'Very glad,' she shouted. 'I should have been lonely at Wen Shui with my father gone, and Rose Bird. And anyway, I think myself lucky to be offered such a change in my life. It happens to so few.'

'Then Buddha be thanked! I too consider myself very lucky.'

The trail became more difficult now. They fell silent, concentrating on its intricacies. Soon it became wider again and Black Jade saw that it broadened considerably just ahead into a sort of small grassy plateau ringed by rock. She had hardly time to take in a rough idea of the place before a sixth sense forced her to look to her right. What she saw then was imprinted upon her senses as colours are laid upon silk. Everything seemed to happen very slowly, each movement drawn out longer than was realistically possible, stretched into some new dimension of time; it was almost as though she were an observer, rather than the incredibly swift follower of an instinct that hurled her into action without thought or fear.

Beneath a jut of overhanging rock, his face just beginning to register her approach, stood a young man a few years her senior; he was leaning against the flank of his horse, which was nuzzling the grass. Above them on the rock, crouched to leap, its yellow eyes still calculating which one should die, was that striped and awesome overlord of the mountains, a large and muscular tiger.

Snow Prince crashed into the browsing horse's side just as the great beast launched itself from above. The impact was sickening, both horse and man tumbling across the grass to shocked safety while the tiger finished its spring in bewilderment, clawing at thin air, and landed with its teeth gritted around a few white hairs from Snow Prince's tail.

Black Jade had nowhere to go; the path had simply stopped. Snow Prince whirled before he smashed into hard rock and stood trembling and transfixed as the tiger shook himself and stared at them both. Behind him Huan was sliding from his saddle, his hunting knife in his hand.

'No!' screamed Black Jade, knowing that way was certain suicide.

'Keep back!' yelled a voice from her left and she turned, dragging on her struggling stallion's reins, to see the winded stranger poised like an athlete, about to heave a jagged piece of rock at the snarling cat.

Before she had drawn breath the projectile had found its mark. There was a howl of pain from the tiger and it turned and fled, blood pouring from a wound above its eye. Huan flattened himself and the shivering Bannerman against the cliff-side as it bounded past and disappeared down the path, around a bend and out of their sight.

The three tremulous humans relaxed and their horses reacted by urinating in unison.

Black Jade found that her legs were made of cloth and had

difficulty in dismounting. Huan raced towards her but the stranger reached her first. She placed her foot in his cupped hands and allowed him to help her to the ground. When she had steadied herself she found that he was kneeling before her, gazing into her face with a passionate admiration.

'You have saved my life,' he panted. 'There is no way I can repay such an enormous debt. I have never seen such courage, though it defeats me, Exceptional Young Master, why you should take such a risk for one so worthless.'

'I didn't think,' said Black Jade truthfully. 'Anyway, it worked rather well. But you are the one who really saved the day. If you had not flung that stone the cat would have had one of us for his dinner.'

The young man surprised her with laughter. She gestured him back to his feet, studying his face as he rose. It was clear-featured and mobile, with the large eyes and slanting brows of the races north of the Great Wall. He had a pointed chin and a wide, soft mouth. He reminded her of a faun. She thought she would probably like him. He could not be more than three or four years older than herself.

He bowed, accepting her scrutiny, returning it with more circumspection. 'My name is Chinghiz,' he said. 'I serve the Emperor and am at present among the escort of one of the ladies of the imperial family. I was exercising her favourite mare when we so fortuitously met. So you see, I have more than one life to thank you for. My Lady would have been heartbroken if any harm had come to Sherpah.'

As Black Jade considered the finer points of the handsome roan who was now sufficiently recovered to be rubbing noses with Snow Prince, Huan moved closer and bowed respectfully to Chinghiz.

'My humble apologies, worthy sir,' he said, 'but you should be aware that despite appearances you are addressing the Lady Wu Chao, daughter of the Ancestor General Wu Shih-huo, imperial duke and governor of Li Chou.' Chao was Black Jade's formal name.

'*Amitabha*!' cried the young man, gazing frankly into her face. He struck the side of his head with a long, sensitive hand.

'I should have realised – I of all people! Your voice, though sweet, is deceptively low. But I am a fool! How could such an exquisite face belong to a boy?' He made another graceful bow.

'Why "above all people"?' asked Black Jade, curious.

He smiled. His smile was charming. 'Because it is my honour to hold a post in the Inner Palace. I spend most of my days among women; I am disconcerted to find myself suddenly incapable of recognising one.' In fact he had thought, if he could be said to have had time for thought, that she was somebody's page, chosen as such boys often are for his beauty.

'The Inner Palace,' she replied, pleased. 'That is where I am going.' She blushed.

'My mistress is to be one of the imperial consorts,' said Huan proudly. It was not something he should have mentioned in front of her, but his years in the stables had relieved him of any manners he did not normally need.

'That does not surprise me,' said their new acquaintance softly. 'Forgive me, Lady Wu, but I have seldom seen such beauty as yours.'

Black Jade disliked all such remarks. She wished that people would forget what she looked like and learn who she was.

She changed the subject to one she preferred.

'That is a splendid mare you have; whom does she belong to?'

'She is the prized possession of Lady Hero, the Emperor's sister – a present from His Majesty.'

'The Lady Hero!' Black Jade was thrilled. That she should so close to the woman who had been her childhood's heroine!

'Tell me,' she went on impulsively, encouraged by the faun's admiring smile, 'would it be possible – could you arrange for me to meet Lady Hero? I should like it better than anything.'

Chinghiz beamed. 'Nothing could be simpler. She will be *demanding* to meet you when I tell her what you have done. Why don't you go back now? I think the horses have recovered. You and your – companion – are invited to supper with her ladyship, instead of us all feeding the tiger!'

Their laughter was a mixture of camaraderie and sheer relief.

'I'm sorry,' Black Jade said, 'I should have introduced Huan. He is my groom, but he is also my half-brother, and that is how I think of him. We are friends.'

Huan flushed scarlet with pleasure and Chinghiz clapped him on the back. 'You are very lucky in your friends.'

'What about the tiger?' Black Jade wondered next. 'You don't suppose it will be waiting for us, to ambush us on the path?'

Chinghiz shook his head. 'No. We are too many for it. One careless man and a horse was one thing. Three people and three horses are something it would never contemplate.'

This proved to be true, though each of them was privately nervous until they had regained the valley floor.

Chinghiz left them there and spurred off to find his mistress and inform her of his escape. He would return for them in an hour and escort them to Lady Hero's tent.

'Go and put on anything you have which is good and not too creased,' Black Jade instructed Huan. 'There's no point in both of us eating tongue pie before our dinner.'

Huan obeyed her thankfully. He had seen Welcome's unwelcome side too often to want more of it.

When her mistress approached she was waiting with one hand on her hip like a cheated market-wife.

'Where have you been, you wicked piece of mischief?' she cried, well aware that she was making Black Jade lose face before the guards and servants. 'For all we knew you might have been kidnapped – or eaten by tigers!'

She was astonished and offended by Black Jade's peal of laughter. 'I very nearly was!' she said cheerfully.

'And how *dared* you go about like that, got up as a shameless boy?' the nurse continued, her pleasant face red with anger. 'If your honourable mother could see you now, she would have you whipped until you couldn't sit down.'

Black Jade caught the tail end of a grin on a soldier's lips and decided enough was enough.

'Welcome,' she said in tones of icy command, 'You overstep the kindness we have shown you. If you cannot show respect to the house of Wu, you are at liberty to go back to your village. I shall willingly give you an escort.'

The high colour was bleached from Welcome's face and her guileless eyes filled instantly with tears. Sniffing, she bowed before her young mistress, evidently ashamed.

'I beg your merciful pardon, Little Mistress. This insignificant worm will earnestly try to please you in future, if only you will let her her remain in the light of your presence.'

'Oh, don't be so foolish!' said Black Jade, embarrassed by her own excursion into imperiousness. 'Go and look for my best dress, if you please. I am going to supper with Lady Hero.'

Welcome gave a single squawk of surprise and rushed to do as she was told. During the hour that followed she ably demonstrated her indispensability by organising a warm bath in a canvas bucket, washing Black Jade's hair and steaming the creases out of the most attractive of her white mourning dresses. When Chinghiz arrived to collect her, precisely on time, he was stunned by the change in her. The slender boy with the beautiful face had become a ravishing young woman whose body flowed like water in its swooning silks, whose blue-black coronet of hair made her the Queen of the Night, whose face, if it had been beautiful before, now transcended all that he had ever known of beauty, gleaming in the softly falling darkness like the candle that he had lit to guide her way. He found her intoxicating. He was drunk with her as he uttered the courtly compliments that could never begin to approach the truth. Black Jade sensed something of his admiration, though not all, and was pleased. She was glad that she looked well. She wanted to make a good impression on Lady Hero. Chinghiz himself, she thought, now looked rather splendid. He was in a tunic and breeches of red and gold shot silk with an extraordinary turban, twisted in the Indian style, surmounted by a cockade of bright blue feathers. They were, she noted, a match for his eyes, which, unusually, were also a bright and extremely attractive shade of aquamarine. She thought he was probably the most handsome young man she had ever seen. She wondered if he were married. The thought annoyed her; she was becoming as simple-minded as Rose Bird.

The tent where the Emperor's favourite sister entertained her guests proved to be a vast pavilion striped in green and white. Dragon banners flew from every upright post, beginning to stream nicely in the brisk little wind that generally got up in these early winter evenings. There was also a device which Black Jade coveted, the scarlet figure of a woman on horseback, holding up a sword. The woman she would meet was a great princess who had ridden to victory in battle. Like her brother, she was the stuff of legends. What would she be like?

Chinghiz gave their names to the green and white guards at the curtained entrance to the tent. With Huan walking proudly behind them they made their entrance into a warm pool of light and sound. There were torches everywhere, bright flambeaux and soft candles, and there seemed to be at least a hundred people, some seated at long, low tables, others reclining on piles of cushions in the centre of the floor. There were musicians somewhere, plucking lazy strings, but most of the noise was simply that of energetic conversation. A deep layer of perfumed incense hung above the company.

Chinghiz steered Black Jade among the tables until they reached a section of the pavilion which stood back from the rest beneath an inner canopy of rose-coloured gauze. Here, behind a marble table heaped with beautifully arranged fruit and flowers, stood several rosewood chairs, deep and tall. Black Jade looked at the occupant of the central one of these and knew that she had found her legend.

The woman whose eyes met hers with pleasant curiosity was

perhaps thirty-five years of age, with a strong-boned beauty that owed as much to experience and the custom of command as it did to her actual features. Her eyes were as black and bright as those of a hunting falcon, and her nose also put one in mind of that noble bird. Her mouth was very red and smiled encouragingly. She held out a long, welcoming arm, a cacophony of bracelets.

'I am very happy to make your acquaintance, Wu Chao. No, let us have no ceremony. Come and sit next to me and tell me what on earth possessed you to hurl yourself at a ravening tiger in order to save that valueless morsel of vanity at your side.'

Hero's voice made a warm mockery of her words and Chinghiz looked unutterably pleased by them. He bowed and seated himself on a tambour with the air of one who expects to be entertained.

Black Jade took the chair next to her idol, who laid an indigo sleeve across her gold one.

'My dear, you are quite the loveliest thing I have ever seen; my brother, as always, is a very lucky man.'

'It is I who have had good fortune, to be chosen by the Emperor,' Black Jade said dutifully, thinking that she would gladly exchange whatever beauty she had if only she could look like *that.*

Lady Hero patted her hand. Her own was loaded with rings.

'Well, let us hope so,' she said vigorously. 'I have already heard that you do not suffer fools gladly. I'm afraid the Inner Palace is full of fools; positively stuffed with them. I should not have thought it the place for you, but the Emperor assures me you will be able to develop your abilities beyond those of gossiping, dressing up and cramming your mouth with Turkish Delight. I shall demand an account of him myself, every so often, to make sure that this is so. I promise you that, Wu Chao.'

'Excuse me, Highness –'

'Yes, child? What is it?'

'It is nothing; at least nothing of consequence.' She felt herself blush annoying. 'It is only that I am not called Wu Chao. Chao was my given name – but its meaning, as you know, is Brightness; and I – well, I was such an ill-tempered baby that my father decided to call me Black Jade instead; black for my temper, but jade because he still held me precious.'

Hero laughed, a delicious, gurgling sound. 'I like it. It suits you far better than Brightness; somehow that, like so many of our names and nicknames, is a little too much to live up to.' She held out her ringed fingers in a hopeless gesture. 'Take my own, for example. Because of it I was forced to take to my horse and do things which no sensible woman would ever have considered doing! Just as well that I succeeded, or I should have had to have been renamed like you. And now, Black Jade, you are to tell me *all* about the tiger!'

'I'm sure there is nothing that Master Chinghiz –'

'That elegant streak of silk? He has told me nothing that was not garbled, exaggerated and probably quite wrong. You see, *he* is one of those unfortunate people who has spent too much of his time in the Inner Palace.'

'To my great sorrow, Intelligent Mistress,' grinned Chinghiz, looking not the least bit sorrowful.

'A confirmed liar; you should have let the tiger have him, poor hungry animal. A little touched by winter sunlight, were you?'

Black Jade laughed. 'No. I don't know why I did it. It all happened far too quickly for thought. There seemed to be nothing else one *could* do.'

'Except turn and ride away,' said Chinghiz quietly. 'As many would have done. Even seasoned soldiers are afraid of tigers.'

'Perhaps,' said Jade seriously, 'I did not have the sense to be afraid. I think that was probably the case.'

Hero clapped her hands. 'Buddha be praised for sending us an honest woman! Black Jade, I can see why your father held you precious. I've not yet seen the dark side of your nature, but I doubt if it diminishes your value. Dear girl, I should like to make you a gift – for although others might think me a fool to set any store by the dizzy exquisite whose life you saved, I am in fact very fond of him, for he has an inspired hand with the lute and can make one laugh when one needs to. And he is also very pretty, don't you think so?'

'Most attractive,' mumbled Black Jade, determined not to blush again. Behind her, she knew, Huan was grinning broadly.

'Well, what can I give you, my Tiger Tamer? Jewels? Here, your hands are bare.' She swept an amethyst from her little finger and slid it on to Black Jade's second one. 'I'll not give you emeralds, to match your wonderful eyes; I am sure my brother will want to do that.' She considered, her head on one side. 'How old are you, my dear?'

'Nearly fourteen.'

'So young? I had thought you at least sixteen. Well, in that case, you may have to wait a while for your emeralds. What else would you like – silks, a horse?'

'No. Thank you, Highness. At least – perhaps –'

'Yes?'

'What I should like more than anything in the world is simply more *freedom.* I cannot bear being fastened up in that suffocating palanquin!'

'Great Heaven, I should think not! That means of travel is for the infirm and the timid. I'm sure you would prefer to ride, with me?'

'Oh yes! Indeed I would!' It was a dream come true.

'Then I shall arrange it. We shall ride together into Chang-an, and I shall personally introduce you to the *other* Tiger of Shansi.'

This, Black Jade knew, was the affectionate name by which the young Emperor was known all over the eight provinces.

It was on an evening of red and gold skies and strange warm winds that Black Jade had her first sight of Chang-an. She reined in beside the Princess, who had rarely allowed her to leave her presence during the last days of their journey. She knew that she had made a friend for life, and a very powerful one at that, but Lady Hero would not stay for long in the capital; she had an impatient husband and vast estate waiting for her near Taiyuan, where she and the Emperor had been born. Nor did Black Jade expect to see much more of her, now that the palace would claim her; their stations, however the Princess might belittle the fact, were very far apart.

Her parents had described Chang-an to her many times, so she had a certain idea what to expect. Nevertheless she caught her breath when she saw the six-mile spread of the great northern wall of the city, rising before her at a distance of half a mile across the undulating plain which had lain at the foot of their descent from the mountains.

The imperial city of the Tang dynasty covered thirty square miles of walled splendour and housed over a million citizens. Many of these were foreigners. The fame and the fear of the conquering Emperors had brought first embassies and later settlers; Turks, Uighurs, Tocharians, Sogdians, Arabs, Persians, Hindus; all of whom mingled their blood, their strange tongues and their distinctive costumes in the markets and bazaars, the taverns and the temples of this rich, proud heart of China.

Black Jade stared at the roofs, domes and minarets which rose beyond the wall. Immediately behind it, she knew, lay the vast pleasaunce of the imperial park, accounting for half the area of the city. She asked Hero to point out which buildings belonged to the Inner Palace, where she would live. She could herself easily identify the soaring, gilded roofs of the Ta Ming Palace, the

Emperor's exotic new residence, completed four years ago.

'Follow a line directly to the south-east of that. Do you see? All those little pagodas and cupolas? That is the Forbidden City, with the Inner Palace at its centre.'

Black Jade shivered. The Forbidden City, the Great Within, the Inner Palace – the small kernel of concealment from the world where she would spend the rest of her days on earth.

'What is it, Immortal Child? You have gone quite pale.'

'It's nothing. It's just that I cannot yet come to terms with the idea that anything is forever.'

Hero smiled wryly. 'I shouldn't let it torment you. I have found that, in practice, nothing ever *is*!'

They rode on and Black Jade lapsed into silence, apprehensive in spite of her companion's words. She stared at the great walls that seemed to grow taller as they approached. How the Chinese man loved to build such walls. It was part of his temperament. He built them around his cities and his houses; around his women; and most of all around his inmost thoughts. There was no 'within' as mysterious as that of the Chinese mind, Black Jade considered as she watched the walls that would shortly enclose her. She pictured each of the million or more citizens, all going about their daily business with their destinies locked within them. Walls within walls. Very soon she would become another such one amongst them. Could she ever learn to bear the number and extent of those intimidating walls?

The Princess's caravan would enter the city before the Wu party, as a matter of protocol. Lady Hero said a warm farewell to her young protégée.

'As soon as it can be arranged, when you have had a little time to settle down, I will present you to His Majesty. There now, don't look so woebegone. You already have two good friends in the palace – and I am giving you Chinghiz for your own – at least my brother is doing so, though he doesn't know it yet!'

Black Jade's heart raced. 'For my own?' she repeated stupidly.

'Of course! You must have a steward, must you not, for your new household? Every royal consort has one.'

Soon she was gone in a cloud of dust, leaving Black Jade to say her own farewells to her escort of soldiers, who would go back to Wen Shui after resting for a day or two. She and her tiny train were transferred to the care of a squad of palace bearers and outriders. Chinghiz was nowhere to be seen, so Jade judged that he had gone ahead with his abdicating mistress.

Convention insisted that she get back into her palanquin, but this did not annoy her; she had enjoyed a great deal of freedom during the exciting ride among the hills and passes. Night was falling as they entered the archway into the great park. Shortly beyond the gate they crossed the River Wei which had come down, like themselves, from the mountains of Honan, its waters yellowed by the dust of the loess.

For six or seven miles they traversed the royal demesne, through gardens enchanted by the rising moon, where tall trees and magnificent buildings – temples, palaces, pavilions – stood etched in its dim, dramatic glow while unseen flowers released their scents, and startled animals – deer perhaps – scudded away from the cavalcade.

They had entered the city by the back gate and would have immediate access to the Inner Palace. They approached it beneath the three-tiered tower of the famous north gate, the Hsúan-wu, which Shih-min had stormed when he took the throne in the teeth of his brothers' treachery. Now it was guarded by the likenesses of the two generals who had aided him that day – cheerful witnesses to the reward of loyalty, and, thought Jade as she peered between the curtains at the bulbous, cranky faces, to the imperial sense of humour.

She was a little disappointed with their back-door arrival as she had looked forward to seeing something of the great halls of audience and the ceremonial courts of the public parts of the palace; though, as Welcome reminded her, she could have seen very little through slitted curtains in fading light. What she did see, as her bearers trotted through the narrow, high-walled streets of the Forbidden City, with their ornate, roofed doorways flanked by lion-dogs or phoenixes, seemed very similar to her native Wen Shui. She prepared, on the strength of this, to be unimpressed when they turned in through one of the doors.

When eventually the sedan was set down and the despised curtains withdrawn, Black Jade stepped out into a moonlit garden courtyard, perhaps a quarter of an acre in size. There was the scent of winter jasmine. Fountains leaped above a lotus-filled pool and the beds were filled with shrubs beneath the stark outlines of trees that would blossom in the spring. She had time for only a brief impression before she realised that someone was bowing towards her from the top of a flight of shallow steps which led up to a veranda and an open, light-filled doorway. The light struck at a more revealing angle and she saw that it was Chinghiz, smiling and looking mightily pleased with himself.

He ran down the steps past a fine pair of life-size gilded

leopards and threw himself triumphantly at her feet.

'Mistress Black Jade! You have saved my worthless life, and only if I may spend the rest of it in your service can it have any justification! If you will permit me, Honoured Mistress, I will be your loyal servant all my days.'

'How very dramatic. You do these things so nicely.' She smiled her appreciation. 'If these are your orders, I shall be delighted to have you with me. If you are sure?' she added doubtfully, for he seemed to her far too grand a young man to be anyone's servant, especially that of one of the most junior entrants to the palace.

'Quite sure.' His teeth showed white in the moonlight. He held out his arms extravagantly. 'Welcome a hundred thousand times, Courageous Lady, to Green Fragrance Court.'

'What a pretty name,' murmured Welcome, who wanted her nurseling to like her new home; she would then fret less for the old one.

They followed Chinghiz up the steps and into the house. They were in a broad reception area with warm, wood-block floors and an elaborately painted ceiling. There were silk pictures on the pale gold walls and the room was furnished with low tables and screens and many green plants. 'Would you like to rest after your journey, my lady, or shall I introduce the other members of your household?' Chinghiz asked, offering her a cushioned bamboo chair.

'I should like to meet everyone, please. And perhaps we could have something to eat? I am not tired, but I am quite incredibly hungry.'

The young man clapped his hands and a door to the left of the hall swung open almost at once to allow the entry of four girls, dressed in the Wu colours of scarlet and black, wearing paper poppies in their hair. They carried a teapoy and several dishes of food, which they took, after bowing in unison to Black Jade, through to an inner chamber at the back of the house. Following them, Jade found this to be a chamber of great charm. It was furnished with a wide, stone *kang*, well-stocked with burning wood and covered with thick carpets and cushions in soft, delicate colours, while the body of the room contained three tables of varying size and several comfortable seats. There were shelves filled with books and scrolls, leaf-filled vases and pieces of jade, and a steatite tripod burned benzoin incense before a carved niche which held a golden image of Kuan Yin, the Goddess of Mercy and especial patron of women. There were more porcelain vases, filled with rushes, on the floor, and everywhere stood carefully tended plants and vines. In one corner there was a miniature garden, with a tiny bridge over a ridiculous little stream and a dwarf-sized winter-flowering cherry in full bloom. Black Jade almost wept; it was a miniature of Golden Willow's Hall of Contemplation.

The maids set out the food on one of the tables and, encouraged by the pleasure in their new mistress's lovely face, lined up, smiling shyly, to be presented by Chinghiz.

'This is Silver Bell,' a pretty girl with a perfect oval face who flushed as she curtseyed.

'Second Singer,' who looked as though she was intelligent.

'Here is Yarrow.' This one was tall and strong, older than the others. Her smile was reassuring rather than shy.

'Lastly, Sweetmeat.' A calm, almond-faced beauty who whispered her welcome in the soft accents of Soochow.

These four, together with Welcome and Chinghiz, would be Black Jade's companions, day and night, for as long as she remained in the palace.

She introduced Welcome and told them, 'I am delighted to meet you all. I know that I shall have a great deal to learn about the ways of the palace, and I'm sure you will help me. Please divide your duties as you please. If I wish to change anything I can do so later. As I am so used to having Welcome attend me personally, I should prefer her to continue to dress me and do my hair.'

There was murmured acquiescence and a rumble from Welcome, who had not even dreamed of being superceded. The girls moved about, serving food and putting things away. It was as if a flock of gay doves was in the house. Welcome wondered how long it would be before their youthful high spirits got the better of them and they were laughing and singing about the place as she was sure they normally did. They seemed a pleasant quartet, especially the older one, Yarrow. Perhaps she would be able to make a friend of her. Welcome was twenty-eight and had given up the hope of marriage to stay with Black Jade, so that any opportunities for friendship were valuable to her. Her devotion to her mistress was complete, but there was enough common sense in her character to prevent that love from becoming an obsession.

She wondered, as she watched the handsome Chinghiz tempting Black Jade with delicious morsels of food arranged like tiny works of art, and saw how his blue eyes glittered as he watched her, whether he too would be able to strike that balance. She very much hoped so, for the boy's own sake. His role would be a very difficult one if he should truly make Jade his reason for living. She spoke to him with unusual gentleness as he brought her a filled plate.

Black Jade herself would not have noticed if he had flung her food at her in a bucket, so ravenous was her hunger. She demolished two dishes of fried prawns, one of devilled chicken breasts, half a bowl of polished rice and three orange pancakes while the young man amused her with descriptions of the palace and some of its inhabitants. His voice was soft and musical and soon she realised with a start that it had nearly sent her to sleep. Perhaps, after all, she was tired.

Chinghiz laughed softly. 'Lady Jade, I am sorry. You must be exhausted. I'll leave you now. I have my own apartment, very near. I will come again tomorrow when you are awake.'

'Thank you, Chinghiz. You have been very kind. I – I'm so happy that you are to stay with me.' Once again, she hoped she was not betrayed by hot colour. She knew he should not make her pulse race like this. But he was so very handsome, and such an excellent companion. She had never had such a feeling about a young man. It troubled her. It was not appropriate.

After he had left them and Welcome had deftly stripped her and rolled her into the warm, carved bed in the small chamber to the right of the garden room, she said sleepily, curling up, 'What a charming young man that is. But I can't understand why he is able to become my steward, just like that. Surely he is too well-born to be a servant? Shouldn't he be some sort of courtier or official instead?'

Welcome bent over her and tucked the goose-feather quilt around her shoulders. A look of intense compassion crossed her face. She touched Black Jade's cheek in gentle sympathy. What a child she was still. How little she knew of the world.

'You must realise, Little Mistress,' she said with infinite kindness, 'that your Chinghiz is one of the palace eunuchs.'

Black Jade felt her whole body burst into flame.

'Oh. Yes. Of course,' she mumbled, deep in the quilt. 'Well then – that's all right, isn't it?'

'Yes, little dumpling. That's all right.'

Left alone, Black Jade cried herself to sleep. There had been no eunuchs in the Wu mansion.

Next morning she found herself forced to give even deeper consideration to the condition to which all the male servants of the Inner Palace must be reduced.

When Chinghiz returned, his morning smile even more dazzling than his green tunic sewn with blue and silver beads, he was as attractive and as seemingly carefree as ever. Somehow she had expected him to be different. She looked at him shyly. Was it she who felt differently? She supposed she must. If she had begun to feel a foolish and forbidden tenderness for this engaging young man, she knew now that it was twice as foolish as before, and forbidden not only by the law of the Emperor but also by that of nature.

She had spent a miserable night and had awoken to further sadness. Trying to comfort herself she had fixed on the undeniable fact that she and Chinghiz could still be friends. She could keep him near her for as long as she wished. She knew now that the palace rules would not have permitted her to do so unless he were – as he was. Perhaps this was better than losing him altogether.

'Lady Jade?' His soft voice was puzzled. 'Is something wrong? Have you slept badly?'

'Oh, perhaps not very well. Only because it was the first night,' she assured him, smiling brilliantly.

He brought her mint tea to refresh her. He thought that she had looked at him strangely as he bade her good morning. Some sadness in her had struck straight to his heart. That heart was already wounded in a manner he had always hoped to escape. It had been bruised before, by a select string of ladies culminating in the Princess Hero, but never before had it suffered serious damage. There were those who imagined that one of his kind was unable to experience either romantic love or sexual desire; for some, he believed, that was true; but for a great many it was not. It was both his curse and his salvation to be one of those who could, and did, know both. He would, of course, keep this tragic, treasured fact from his brave and beautiful mistress. It was his burden, and he would bear it singing.

When Black Jade seemed more cheerful he put a question to her that took her mind off her own aching emotions.

'The officials need to know what are your wishes in connection with Huan, your half-brother.'

'How do you mean?' asked Jade, who had rediscovered last night's appetite under her steward's expert coaxing. She licked omelette off her fingers.

Chinghiz lowered his faun's eyelashes. 'They wish to know if he is to serve outside, in the palace, or if you would prefer him to join you in Green Fragrance Court.'

She looked down, knowing at once what he was telling her.

'If he comes into the court, he must be –'

'– made a eunuch? Yes.'

She pretended to ponder, to get through the difficult moment. Poor Huan! What a payment that would be for his years of devotion to her and to Snow Prince. He had been so thrilled about coming to Chang-an. He had been the only gift she had wanted when Eldest Uncle had wished to please her. She moved about the room, trying not to look too closely at Chinghiz. What did it mean to be a eunuch? She would certainly never have guessed that he was one. He was tall, slender and well-muscled, and although the chest revealed by the V of his tunic was covered in medallions rather than hair, he had a very luxurious topknot, which was also decorated with beads and chains, rather than hidden under the conventional cap. His wide eyes were bright and clear and his skin had a sheen that many a girl might envy. He was high-spirited and very positive. In fact he seemed altogether a most contented person. Would Huan be like this, if they castrated him?'

She fixed Chinghiz with a candid eye.

'Would you recommend it?' she asked directly.

The boy gave his soft laugh, careful that it should not be bitter.

'I have known nothing else. My parents mutilated me when I was a child, so that I could be presented to the palace.' He would say no more of himself. 'But I think your brother's pleasures are not those of the inner courts.'

'No. He likes to be outdoors, and with the horses.'

'Then he must not become a eunuch. Anyway, he is too old. The operation would be very painful, and he might not recover. If you agree, I will suggest that he is sent to work in the imperial stables. That should make him happy.'

'Very happy. As long as I may see him sometimes.'

'Of course you may. I shall see to it myself.' And he would do so, even though it was strictly against the rules for a lady of the Inner Palace to have commerce of any kind with a male; a brother, he felt, should be an exception.

Later in the day Chinghiz told her what her own status would be.

'Because you are so young, and because your honourable father, the ancestor, was not of noble birth, although possessing every virtue, you are to be placed in the fifth grade of concubine. You will therefore be known as the Elegant Lady Wu.'

'Welcome will try to see that I live up to that. What are the other ranks and titles?'

'Above you, in the first grade, are the four chief consorts. They are known as the Noble, the Pure, the Virtuous and the Excellent consorts. In the second grade are nine ladies whose titles express their own qualities – such as Luminous Demeanour or Cultivated Beauty; then there are three lower grades, the Beauties, the Accomplished Ones and the Elegants, twenty-seven in all. Beneath these are another twenty-seven who are simply handmaidens. The noble ancestress, the Empress, was of course above them all, and only her sons may claim the succession.'

Black Jade made a face. 'I see now why my honoured mother did not see my position as hopeful. If one begins three-quarters of the way down the scale, one has a long climb ahead. Not that I expect to be doing any climbing.'

Suddenly she felt lonely and ill at ease. What on earth was she doing here, so far away from home?

'I don't know *what* I am expected to do; I've no idea.'

He saw her insecurity and hastened to dispel it.

'Don't worry, my mistress. Everything will be explained to you in its own time. For the moment you need do nothing except try, if you can, to be happy. I will always be your shield and your ally. I have known the palace since I was three years old. I know all its ways, its virtues and its vices. I shall try to keep you comfortable, contented and well-informed.'

A small smile rewarded him. She was thinking, sadly and ridiculously If only you were the Emperor, how easy everything might be.

'You are very good to me, Chinghiz.'

'There is no question of goodness. I have told you how it is. You have saved my life; it is yours. The better I serve you, the greater is my reward.'

She did not quite know what to do with such firmly stated devotion. She was already aware that she had the power to inspire such emotion, but neither Welcome nor Huan, for example, had ever put it so forthrightly into words.

'You have great beauty,' he continued, covering her hesitation. 'Beauty means a great deal to me. I have made it my creed, almost my morality. I have consciously developed my aesthetic sense in place of that which I cannot develop.' It hurt him to speak to her like this, but it was a hurt he must master, and immediately. 'Don't mistake me; I have seen that you also possess an unusually good mind, and more than that, an unusually strong will. Because of these, you will rise here at court. And I, in my fashion, will rise with you. I ask only to remain near you. If I had the good luck to own an exquisite vase from the Han dynasty, I should want to look at it several times a day.'

'And now you own me instead?' Black Jade was amused.

'In a manner of speaking, my lady. But you, of course, have your small foot set on my neck, and may crush it at a second's whim.'

'Luckily I am not given to whims. But I *would* like to see something of the palace grounds, if that can be arranged.'

She did not want to discuss her possible career at court. It was too soon. Time enough when she had got her bearings. Realising this, Chinghiz was glad to be able to turn the conversation to Lady Hero, who had sent a message that she would show Black Jade the imperial park, that afternoon at the hour of the Monkey.

it was at the end of her second week in the palace that Jade received her first summons from the Emperor. She was to be presented to him, informally, at a small audience in a chamber not far from her apartments. For the first time since the General had died, she would be permitted to put off her mourning.

Chinghiz made as much fuss as though she were getting married that morning, casting one set of bright garments after another on to the floor of the little room she used as a wardrobe, until it resembled the fabulous Garden of the Dragon King, with every outsize bloom flattened in the storm of his wrath.

When Black Jade and the maids began to giggle and regress to the schoolroom, he swooped decisively upon an almost transparent gown of peach silk and threw it at her, his slanted brows bolted crossly together.

'Here. Put this on. They *all* choose scarlet. At least you'll be different. And kindly stop laughing. It may not appear so to you, Little Mistress, but this is a serious moment in your life!'

'Why not red? It is the colour of joy, and brings good luck to its wearer. *And* it is one of the Wu colours.'

Chinghiz sniffed. 'It also makes a louder statement than its wearer, in most cases. The maids will wear your colours.'

He wanted nothing to detract from the impact of the unique face. The pale apricot would complement her golden skin. She would wear nothing but the simple gown, and the gold net scarf and loose trousers that went with it. Perhaps a single flower in her hair? No, not a flower; a tiny leaf spray, to catch the astounding colour of her eyes.

'No jewels? I shall look like a pauper.'

'The Emperor is aware of your fortune. You have no need to display it upon your back like a huckster's camel!'

Welcome was hovering nearby, her nose well out of joint.

'Do hurry up, Master Chinghiz. I want to dress my little phoenix's hair,' she said stiffly.

'Please do not trouble, Miss Welcome. I shall dress the hair myself today.'

Welcome spat. 'Mistress! Tell this importunate person to leave us. I never heard anything like it!'

Black Jade groaned. Their rivalry had been inevitable, but it was wearing.

'Both of you will please remember the courtesies. Welcome will do my hair. My usual simple style will do very well. Chinghiz, I would be grateful if you would fetch my filigree butterfly from the jade box on the ebony table. I shall wear it on my sleeve.'

Her servitor departed, with a toss of his topknot. But he had to admit the brooch was a nice touch.

in the small chamber known as the Hall of Sparkling Wit, which he often used to entertain his concubines, Li Shih-min was enjoying a temporary respite from a difficult morning.

He had left his ministers in the council chamber, to harry the next problem without him while he refreshed himself with a cup of wine in the company of a dozen of his youngest consorts. The Archduke, wearing his dead-lizard robes, was with him; as an imperial relative he was one of the few men permitted to enter the Inner Palace. He poured the wine and distributed avuncular smiles to the girls, who giggled and fluttered at him from their seats about his brother-in-law.

Shih-min drank gratefully, the heaviness of the last hour lifting from his spirit. One of his most thankless tasks, in the pulling together of the slack-reined empire his father had left him, was the discouragement of corruption, especially in high places. He had invented an administrative machinery that would run the state as smoothly as a water-clock – if only he could find men as trustworthy as the machine.

He had reduced a bureaucracy swollen with the glut of his father's enobled supporters, and had set a constant check on local government by dividing the country into ten inspection circuits, travelled by imperial commissioners.

He had tried to temper the hothouse atmosphere of the court by ensuring that provincial appointments, poorly esteemed in the previous reign, should recover their cachet.

But, although he personally selected all candidates for the Empire's 358 prefectures, and took learned advice on the appointment of magistrates and other county officials, the bribery continued.

Today he had sentenced two corrupt magistrates to penal exile, advising them to reflect, should they feel unjustly singled out, that only six years ago their penalty might have been the amputation of their feet.

The revision of the law was one of Shih-min's main interests. Disposed towards a humanitarian leniency, he had abolished the ancient punishments with their crudity and cruelty, so that now even a man convicted of treason or murder could be executed only after three appeals to the throne.

This business of the magistrates was depressing. He had hand-picked both men himself. He sighed deeply, wondering what it was that made men so greedy when they were already so well provided.

He felt a butterfly touch on his sleeve. An impish face deplored his brown mood.

'If Your Majesty continues to look so gloomy, we shall all feel that we are useless donkeys, unsuitable to be your companions!'

It was Precious Cloud, a recent acquisition from Soochow. She was soft and round and full of laughter and was already known to everyone as 'Dumpling'. He had enjoyed her twice in the last fortnight. This favour made her deliciously bold in front of her sisters. He gave her his cup to sip from, so that they would all know he was not displeased.

'We are all anxious to meet the new consort,' Dumpling said, showing a double row of dimples as she wiped the silver cup on her handkerchief before handing it back. Shih-min indicated that she should consider it a present and turned to acknowledge a signal from an extensive gentleman, magnificently robed in fuschia and magenta, who stood near the door. This was Lord Shen, the Chief Eunuch, whose power was almost as extensive as his person, and whose presence, as High Steward and councillor to the entire harem, would lend all that was necessary of formality to this occasion.

There was a rustle of interest and twelve pairs of critical eyes were fixed on the doors.

They opened and Lady Hero glided in, glittering with her usual array of jewels and looking as if she had just got the better of someone, which she probably had. Behind her were a couple of very uncastrated guardsmen, and behind *them* came Black Jade, with her maids and Chinghiz in attendance.

'Ah, Maitreya!' thought Shih-min, hearing the soft sighs around him. So he had not over-estimated the angry child with the challenging green eyes. Her remembered face was flawless, less rounded than when he had last seen it, the fine bones beginning to take prominence. She was much taller. They grew so quickly at that age. He had seen it in his own daughters, of whom he had many, as well as fourteen sons. Would he get another child by this perfect flower who now lay stretched on the ground in submission to his right to do so? The thought was very tempting. Her gauzy robe revealed a shape that would equal the face in beauty – but not yet. He had forgotten how young she was. Her questioning mind had already outgrown her developing body when they met. His sister had reported that this had not changed, so far as she could tell. The girl was still more interested in horses than in men. Well, he would leave her for a while. He did not take children into his bed. He had taken her into the palace early because he had seen how it was between her and the half-brother who was her father's heir.

'Good day, Younger Sister,' he said amiably. Dumpling had vacated her seat for Hero.

'Good morning, Your Majesty. May I present to you my young friend, Lady Wu, whom of course you have already met?'

'You are very welcome amongst us, Black Jade,' Shih-min said kindly, lifting his hand to tell her to rise. 'I hope it does not distress you too much to leave your home at such a time. I was saddened to hear of your father's death.'

'Your Majesty is very kind.' She dared to smile shyly. As she did there was another faint sigh among the concubines.

'Great Heaven, child, how lovely you are,' Shih-min declared, with an answering smile that included them all. 'We shall have to call you "Beauty" so that we shall know what our new standard is to be.'

Black Jade was embarrassed. This was exaggeration. She was already tired of the fuss about her looks. She lowered her head in a rather repressive little bow, saying nothing.

'Take care! I should not like you to lose your leaf-spray; it is very becoming.' So was her obvious modesty.

So he *had* noticed her, that day in her father's hall. Behind her she heard Chinghiz emit a small sound of gratification. He had won his point about the leaves. She hoped he wasn't going to become a tyrant about her appearance. All this emphasis on exteriors seemed to her excessive. One looked as one looked. Every girl in this room was beautiful, as doubtless was every woman in the palace. Surely it was doing her no favour to single her out among them. She made a quick reconnaisance of the assembled faces and found, to her relief, that they were friendly and indulgent. All except one.

From behind the Emperor's chair, Archduke Chang-sun Wuchi surveyed her with neutral appraisal. She did not think that good looks played an important part in *his* estimates of his fellow beings. It was a pity that they would dislike each other; he was obviously very influential.

Shih-min chatted to her for several more minutes, asking whether everything had been done for her comfort and what interests she might be helped to pursue. 'I'm afraid we can't allow you to go on a tiger hunt, but there are excellent music teachers here, should you feel you have anything to learn.'

'Why not?' Lady Hero had been tapping her feet. She disliked idle conversation, and the giggling of the concubines always made her want to wring their silly necks.

'Why not what?' asked her brother inelegantly.

'A tiger hunt? I should enjoy that and so would my poor soldiers; they are sadly unused these days. We could teach Black Jade how to spear the beasts; then she would be ready, the next time she encountered one.'

'If she happened to have her spear with her,' said Shih-min reasonably. 'But I think not, Little Sister. Black Jadc is to become one of the chief ornaments of my court, not a mighty hunter. All women are not like you.'

'This one is,' said Hero flatly. 'And one day you will recall that I said so. You must not lock her up in the courtyards. She is used to having the whole of Shansi to roam in.' This was by no means true, but if it persuaded the Emperor to relax some of the irksome restrictions that already surrounded her comings and goings, Jade would be grateful for the lie.

'Well then, you must not neglect your exercise,' he said understandingly. 'You may ride at any time when your duties permit it. The imperial park is at your disposal provided you are suitably accompanied.'

Black Jade expressed her thanks and the interview was over.

It was not until she had returned to Green Fragrance Court that she began to take stock of it.

'He treated me like a father,' she told Welcome.

'Of course. The Emperor is the father of his people. And now he takes our beloved ancestor your father's place as your guardian.'

'But I am supposed to be a concubine.' Jade was faintly querulous.

Welcome chuckled. 'There is a great deal of time before you, Little Egret, and many things to fill it. The Emperor will take you into his bed when the time, and you, are ripe.'

Black Jade sniffed, uncertain whether to be relieved or offended.

'Answer me this, Beauty Wu,' said Chinghiz, still thoroughly pleased with himself and with her. 'Have you any wish to enter His Majesty's bed? Do you desire his body?'

Her scarlet colour answered him. 'Certainly not! You shouldn't talk of such things. And don't call me Beauty!'

'It is what others will call you.' He was even happier now. She could never want him, but as yet she did not even want the Emperor, which meant that she was completely his for some time to come.

'Not to my face; I'll see to that. Anyway it's an order. You forget yourself,' she added primly.

Chinghiz apologised in Turkish, Arabic and Hindustani, to Jade's unwilling amusement and considerable envy. Later he brought her a pair of rose and blue singing birds in a filigree cage, to make up for his bad manners.

After this he was gone for some time and could not be found when she wanted to play chess with him. Deciding to read instead, she was soon deep in the *Book of Songs*, travelling homeward to her favourite verses. It was the ragged old copy the General had given her when she was five. A few tears dropped on it, now and then, when she came to the lines he had especially loved.

Her reading was interrupted by the arrival of Lady Hero, dressed in kingfisher trousers and an orange shirt, with her hair tucked under a gold net cap.

'Don't get up. You look so comfortable, curled up like a little cat. I can't stay long. I have come, alas, to say goodbye.'

Black Jade was astonished at her own sense of desolation.

'I didn't think it would be so soon. I'm sorry. I shall miss you,' she said shyly.

'I shall miss you too, child. You are the first female I have heard to speak common sense since my mother went to her ancestors. But I have made my brother promise to send reports of you, as I said I would. And you will write to me in Taiyuan? And tell me all the scandal that Shih-min is too proud to describe!'

'Of course I will write – but I don't hear very much in the way of scandal.'

'You will.' Hero grimaced. 'It's early days yet. Wait until you make friends with that gaggle of powdered little monkeys you met this morning. You'll hear nothing else!' She came closer in a waft of cedarwood and bent to rub her cheek against Jade's.

'For a hairpin I'd demand to take you with me – but I know I'd be refused. Keep up your courage, Black Jade. You will find many more tigers in your path. Concentrate upon growing strong enough to overcome them all. Chinghiz will help you. He will polish you until you glow!'

'If I let him!'

A long blue fingernail tapped her uplifted nose. 'If you have the sense I credit you with, you will let him. Now!' Hero whirled and strode for the open doors. 'I detest maudlin farewells, and I could easily take part in one now. So – we shall meet again, my young friend, and in the meantime I look forward to your letters.'

She was gone before Black Jade had uncoiled and run to the door. She watched as the lithe figure ran lightly down the steps and across the court. With a sense of deep anticlimax she returned to her chair and sat with her book open on her lap, staring at nothing.

Chinghiz found her in this lacklustre position when he returned. He made her a delicious herb tisane, served with the thin orange biscuits she loved, and offered on a celadon tray.

'It is hard to lose the company of a friend,' he observed, 'but very pleasant to reflect upon our good fortune in ever having encountered such a friend.'

She sat up straighter then.

'Have a biscuit,' she smiled. 'You are right, of course.'

5

One afternoon Black Jade was disturbed by a lot of noise on the other side of her courtyard. Yarrow, sent to investigate, reported that they were to have a neighbour.

'It is the Elegant Consort, Precious Cloud, Mistress. She hopes you will call when she has finished unpacking.'

Black Jade did so, taking an ivory inlaid make-up box as a housewarming present, though she regretted the loss of her privacy.

She recognised the sweet-faced, plump girl who had sat near the Emperor at her presentation.

They completed the courtesies and Precious Cloud offered tea and the invitation to call her Dumpling.

'Lord Shen has moved me next to you because I am relatively new here myself and can probably be of assistance to you in some ways. I am glad, because before I was near Lady Hope, who is very solemn and serious, and *you* look as if you might be fun.'

Her voice was low and liquid, bubbling up into frequent laughter that came as naturally as her breath. She had no idea that the serious Lady Hope had found this the most irritating sound in the world and had begged the Chief Eunuch to remove Dumpling before she did her some mischief; nor that Chinghiz had requested her presence in Green Fragrance Court on the grounds that a little of her frivolity and sophistication in certain matters might be a useful influence upon his mistress.

'It is kind of you to say so,' Jade replied, 'though you'll find that I too am serious about some things.'

'What sort of things?' Dumpling passed a box of sweets.

'I like to do the things I do as *well* as I can. Music, for example, or poetry.'

'You write poetry? How marvellous. I have no head for words. And my fingers are an insult to the strings of any instrument – but I do love to sing.'

'What else do you enjoy?'

'Oh, I don't know.' Dumpling wriggled as she tried to think. 'I suppose my main interest is in other people's business, to tell the truth. I try not to *spread* gossip, but I do manage to *hear* most of it. Everyone realises I have no particular ambition, beyond being contented and trying not to get *too* fat – so people are not threatened by me, and they tell me things.'

'My mother said the palace would be riddled with intrigue, but she didn't say what sort.'

'Well, with 122 women locked up for the pleasure of only one man, there is bound to be a good deal of a struggle for position – *and* a certain number of illicit affairs.'

'However do they manage that? Don't the eunuchs stop them?' The eunuchs were the palace police; if they discovered a consort to be having sexual relations with any man other than the Emperor, the penalty was death.

'The eunuchs are mostly very greedy. If a girl is rich enough, she can have all the lovers she wants. The eunuchs will even smuggle them in for her. But she must be careful; if one of the other women is jealous of her, she might report her to Lord Shen. Unless one is very brave it is safer to fall in love with one's own sex.'

Black Jade sighed. It was evident that intimate relations of various kinds would be the main ingredient of Dumpling's conversation. She liked the girl's gaiety and ingenuousness however, and thought she could probably bear her as a neighbour if they did not see too much of each other. She asked her where she had been born, and they spent some time making comparisons between Soochow and Wen Sui, the soft south and the harsh north, the suave city and the territory of the tiger.

They soon realised that their temperaments were as opposed as the climates of their birthplaces, and both were satisfied that the *yin* and *yang* inherent in this situation made it likely that they would become good friends.

When she judged that they had reached the right degree of cosiness, Dumpling asked delicately, 'Beauty Wu, have you been wrapped in the quilt yet?'

'Whatever do you mean?'

Dumpling flushed and wriggled again. 'When you are summoned to the bed of the Emperor, you are first stripped naked by Lord Shen and wrapped in a quilt. Then another eunuch carries you on his back to the bedchamber. It is an old custom to ensure that no woman can conceal a weapon about her and attack the Son of Heaven at a time of weakness.'

'Why should she wish to?'

'Not every girl comes here willingly. And imperial history shows countless intrigues between, for instance, a concubine and the heir to the throne. It is a sensible precaution, I think. It only happens the first time, now. This Son of Heaven is less careful than his ancestors.'

'He probably finds the whole thing ridiculous.'

'He didn't say so.'

Black Jade digested the information contained in this remark. 'What about you? Didn't you find it undignified?'

Dumpling gurgled. 'No. I found it all rather delicious! But I would prefer His Majesty to have undressed me rather than Lord Shen; his hands are clammy and he looks you over in just the same way as you have seen him look over a bale of cloth or the carcass of a pig.'

Black Jade could well imagine it. She did not look forward to the experience. Lord Shen, with his dominant height and bulk and his dryly penetrating eye, struck her as a repellent figure.

'Of course, one forgets everything when one is with the Emperor,' Dumpling continued, her voice collecting nectar. 'I can't *tell* you how wonderful it is!'

'I expect you'll find words.' Black Jade was curious, just as she had been about Rose Bird's marital experiences.

'Well, first he gave me a robe to wear, which seemed a bit pointless when I'd just been peeled like a lychee; then he just *talked* to me for a while, asking me about my home and my interests and so forth – just as you have been doing. He gave me wine and sweetmeats, and it seemed, oh, ages, until he laid me down on his bed and we began the clouds and the rain.'

'Were you nervous?'

'No. I had longed for it since I first saw him. He is so unbelievably handsome! Isn't it the same with you?'

'Go on.'

'Well – he was very gentle, and yet completely in command of what we did. He showed me how I might pleasure him without any need for words. We did the Unicorn's Horn and the Winding Dragon and Fluttering Butterflies – and I *think* it was the Goat Facing a Tree!'

Black Jade recognised three of the numerous versions of the sexual act recommended in the *Plain Girl's Manual.*

'How very energetic,' she admired.

Dumpling sighed and moved her hips reminiscently. 'His Majesty is a tiger, a white tiger! You'll see. He has sent for me twice already. I can hardly bear to wait and see if he will want me again. I am hoping for next Tuesday. It is my best day for conception.'

'Yes, but does the Emperor know that?'

'In a manner of speaking. Such matters are all written down in Lord Shen's Red Book.'

'What matters?'

'The dates of every consort's 'peach-flower fluid' and the nights she spends with His Majesty. If a girl conceives, the Emperor must be certain that the child is his.'

'So he is aware of these "affairs" that go on?'

Dumpling gave this some thought. 'He is not aware of the actuality, but he is aware of the possibility. Thus the Red Book. Besides, if there were no such book, Lord Shen would have invented it. He adores details and statistics. Your maid must remember to tell him if you are ever irregular.'

Black Jade gravely relayed this piece of information to Welcome.

'Old Man Heaven!' chuckled the nurse. 'We won't worry about that just yet. You get on with your studies and leave that side of things to me.'

'Am I never to become a proper concubine, then? Dumpling isn't much older than me, and she –'

'– is *very* well-developed for her age. Now listen to me. the Son of Heaven isn't interested in unawakened girls; he wants grown women who will enjoy the congress as much as he does.'

Black Jade shrugged, feeling unspoken relief. Her curiosity on the subject of 'congress' was not yet a physical thing. True, she had been disturbed by Chinghiz's blue eyes, but she did not lie awake and long for what she did not know, and anyway could not have. She was surprised and disappointed, when she got to know more of her companions, at how much of their talk circled about their encounters, or lack of them, with Shih-min. All of them possessed at least one handbook of sexual behaviour, and they held frequent discussions, punctuated by blushes and giggles, of the relative merits of *The Plain Girl, The Dark Girl* or *The Chosen Girl* as opposed to the robust and unequivocal prose of the *Amatory Arts* of Tung-hsuan which was favoured by Lord Shen.

These volumes were a necessary part of her studies and she tried to read them seriously. She found, after an early period of raucous amusement, that they were simply boring, so she put them away for the day when she would be 'awakened' as Welcome put it.

If she could not enjoy the harem conversation, Black Jade soon discovered other ways in which she could amuse her companions. Her gift for music and poetry was much admired. So was her talent for inventing new word-games or forfeit games, and for endless, cliff-hanging storytelling. She did not put herself forward unduly, but it soon became obvious that, when the girls in her grade were at a loss for entertainment, it was the new arrival who would provide it. In the daytime, when they had exhausted their rather nominal palace duties, she encouraged them to rediscover the use of their perfumed but largely unexercised bodies. They went out into the park, under the delighted eyes of several of the younger eunuchs, and played football and a game which Jade had played in Wen Shui, involving a circular course and a bat and ball. It was a strenuous addition to their customary *Tai chi chuan* movements, which were beautiful in their slow deliberation but did little to use up youthful energies.

In the evening, more healthily tired than they had been since they entered the palace, the girls would sing and demonstrate to each other the dances of their particular birthplace. It was Black Jade who decided that they should turn their accomplishments into an organised showcase and ask if they might perform before the Emperor. She even agreed to be the one to ask permission of Lord Shen, of whom every girl was in considerable awe. Jade was high in his favour, which meant that she had, just once, received from him the accolade of a single, carefully measured smile. This was because, when he had set her the usual examination by which he was able to judge his protégées' mental abilities, she produced the most brilliant papers he had seen since those of the dead Empress – perhaps more so, if he were to be honest.

Permission obtained, the young concubines began to hold nightly rehearsals for their performance, which was to be a programme of singing, balletic dance and a brief drama which wasn't yet written but would tell the story of the Weaving Maid and her lover the Herdsmen, whose tragic romance culminates in their turning into star-gods with the charge of watching over all human affections.

It was during one of these rehearsals that an event occurred that was to cause scandal to reverberate throughout the palace city like the thousand wind-chimes of a Taoist shrine.

The rehearsals took part in Green Fragrance Court, partly because everyone seemed to congregate there, now that Black Jade and Dumpling lived there, partly because the broad terrace at the top of the northern steps acted as an ideal stage once they had denuded it of Chinghiz's lovingly arranged garden of potted plants. Behind this was a twisting path leading to an archway through to another court, unoccupied. Beyond that was the gateway to the imperial park, to which Lord Shen held the key. The girls had to ask him for it every time they wished to go into the park.

As the weeks had passed the performers had reached a high standard of excellence, and Black Jade considered, in her role as impresario, that they had nearly acquired enough polish to present themselves to the Emperor. One more week of practice should do it.

That night things were going quite well. The singers and musicians sounded as though they had already become immortals; the dancers were certain and smooth in their movements; the play was almost word-perfect and the acting good. There were, however, some difficulties; the Turkish Harem Troupe, one of the most daring offerings, were admirably sensual once they had thrown off their dark cotton *chadors* to reveal their graceful bodies in rosy net trousers and a few rows of bells – but they moved like constipated elephants, their directrice told them, while they still had them on.

Having decided that they must get it right tonight, Black Jade worked the unfortunate girls like the said elephants, becoming even more critical. They seemed to be more lumpish and inelegant every time they danced. She couldn't understand it.

'What's wrong with them?' she appealed to the rest of the cast. 'It's as though they were wrapped in carpet, not cotton. Oh well, we may as well leave it. It won't improve tonight. But tomorrow, it must perfect,' she finished threateningly.

'Please, just let us complete the dance, called one of the muffled elephants, rather hoarsely. Jade wondered if she had kept them too long outside. The night air was still chilly, even in early spring.

She nodded. She didn't want to dampen enthusiasm.

The dark shapes bowled about like drunken tops; they *should* have been whirling like temple maypoles. It was horrible. They would never do for Shih-min. He would simply laugh at them.

She was about to clap her hands and put a stop to the unlovely performance when the dancers began to fling off their *chadors*. Perhaps now they would improve.

It took her two full eyeblinks and the gasp of excited horror from behind her, to realize that what she was looking at was not two rows of Turkish delight with breasts bobbing with bells, but two rows of smug, grinning, strongly muscled and half-naked men!

'*Amitabha*! Who are you?'

One of them strode insolently forward – was therc a slight halt in his step? He stood at the front of the stage, smiling derisively, his hands on his hips. He looked vaguely familiar. Like the dancing girls, he and his companions wore loose, diaphanous trousers and not much else.

'Fame is evidently a poor thing in the palace. Tell me, how do you like our rendering of your dance?'

'Not at all,' Black Jade replied before her mind had begun to function again. 'It was insufferably clumsy.' Even as she spoke she saw the grinning mouth twist into something less pleasant, and realised that she was speaking to Li Cheng Chien, the Emperor's oldest son and Crown Prince of the Empire. Lame since birth, he had been hopelessly spoiled by his mother and had grown up doing very much as he pleased. Rumour had it that some of the things which pleased him were very odd indeed. Yarrow had once said that he had loved to dress up in the Empress's robes and had limped wildly about the courtyards at the head of a gang of naked little boys. He was insolent to his tutors and impatient of his duties. The latest gossip was his preference for all thing Turkish. Thus, Jade supposed, his present appearance.

'You surprise me, mistress. I thought we made rather charming young ladies. What is wrong? A little too much paint and powder? The occasional over-muscular leg? The unfortunate hair upon some of our chests? You must forgive that; some of us actually *are* Turks. You must admit that –'

'– Your Highness will forgive me – but you have no right to be here. It would cause endless trouble if you were discovered. You have had your joke at our expense. I congratulate you on its speed and dexterity. Now, if you will return the young ladies you have – removed, we will go our separate ways.'

The Prince regarded her thoughtfully. 'And who are you who so confidently give orders to your betters?'

Seeing the Prince begin to frown, she introduced herself and performed a perfunctory kowtow. She did not feel afraid of him, though she sensed that he would like her to be.

'Ah yes. I have heard of you. You are the girl who makes full-grown tigers turn tail. Do you, I wonder, accomplish this merely by the use of your tongue?' He sounded genuinely interested.

'No,' she snapped. 'I reserve that for royal imbeciles who are foolhardy enough to indulge in adventures which, in the past, have been known to signal their death-warrant.'

He laughed. 'My honourable father is no such tyrant. He knows I don't covet his women.' He raised one brow and grinned at the young man next to him, a slight figure with an enviably tiny waist. 'I have, as you must know, several consorts of my own.'

'Nevertheless, this escapade will hardly please His Majesty. You must leave at once,' Black Jade said firmly. Behind her she could feel the round eyes of her friends, almost popping out of their painted heads. They probably expected her to be executed on the spot. She was not sure she didn't expect it herself.

'We will leave when it pleases me,' the Prince drawled, beginning to be annoyed with her. 'First we invite you to join us in the dance. Our presence will invigorate it considerably.'

She could not prevent the impropriety of a shared dance, therefore she would see that it was as well-organised as possible, and as brief as she dared to make it. She nodded to both dancers and musicians and the slow, sinuous notes of the flute began to coil about the heartbeat rhythm of the drums.

'You! I want you for my partner!' the Prince cried.

Black Jade joined him with a sigh. After all, she had written the music and planned the choreography; also she was undoubtedly the best dancer amongst them, so she might as well enjoy the experience. She began to move, swaying her hips and throwing back her head in the provocative manner she had seen long ago in Wen Shui, when a troupe of travelling entertainers had lodged in the Wu mansion.

The Prince matched her undulating motion, surprisingly graceful, his disability scarcely noticeable as he responded dreamily to the mounting music. They moved together in warily appreciative silence for a time, then suddenly the young man swooped and caught her in his arms; holding her in a painful grip, he thrust his face into hers and attempted to give her her first kiss. There was a concerted gasp of horror from the concubines. Any man who defiled an imperial consort with his touch had condemned himself to death, should the Emperor wish it.

'Don't struggle so, damn you, little tiger-demon! Great Heaven, you still haven't any idea what it's all about, have you? Who would have thought it, with a body like that? A virgin!'

His roar of dismissive laughter sliced through the tentative pleasure even the girls had started to feel as they danced.

Just as he reached for her again, someone came swiftly up the steps and bowed before him, a tall figure, stern in indigo robes. It was Chinghiz, carrying a greater weight of implicit authority than his mistress would have thought possible.

'Your Highness,' he said, his voice carrying without difficulty to every pair of ears, 'I have to tell you that the Lord Shen is waiting to speak with you. You will find him in his library.'

The dancers had stopped, one by one, and stood awkwardly about, sensing that the fun was over. As Cheng Chien stared at the steward, the girls ran instinctively into a bunch at the side of the stage, while their erstwhile partners, still grinning like half-shamed schoolboys, looked towards their leader. The musicians faltered and came to a halt.

'Since when, you insignificant animal,' spat the Crown Prince, 'has the Imperial Heir taken orders from Lord Shen?'

'I am also empowered to say,' continued Chinghiz neutrally, 'that you are to consider it your extreme good fortune that your forthcoming interview is with Lord Shen rather than your illustrious father.' His balanced, reasonable tone made the boy's choice quite clear.

Cheng Chien was spoiled and mischievous, but he was not quite a fool. He turned his back on the fascinated Jade, nodded curtly to Chinghiz, then limped towards the archway which would lead him to the imperial park. His muscular maidens, their paint beginning to run after their exertions, fell in behind him, sadly aware of looking ridiculous. The Prince himself, oddly enough, did not. His costume suited him extraordinarily well, especially when he turned and flashed his kohl-lined eyes and tossed his unbound swathe of black hair in contemptuous farewell – the actor's timeless salute to an audience which does not know how to appreciate him.

'Chinghiz!' The concubines clustered round him, admiring him with soft, caressing eyes.

'I *had* wondered where you might be,' said Black Jade, almost accusingly. Had she? Well, if not, she should have done.

'I saw what was happening some time ago,' he reassured her. 'It was obvious that I could do nothing, alone, to stop it. The question was – whom to tell? I decided Lord Shen was my best answer.'

'Why?' asked Black Jade. 'Why not the Emperor?'

'Because that would have been too extreme. Anything could have resulted, from the Prince losing his lunatic head to *you* all being sent home in disgrace.'

'How dreadful!' Dumpling voiced it for them all. 'Our clans would lose face before the whole Empire. We'd each be locked away in shame, and never heard of again.'

'I understand,' said Black Jade. 'Also, if you tell Lord Shen you give him no more power over us than he already possesses. In fact, our behaviour is to a great extent *his* responsibility – so he is probably very grateful to you for telling him and no one else?'

'He is. And he will be even more grateful, and will show his gratitude to all of you, if you will each promise *not* to speak of this episode to anyone who is not present here.' His blue eyes claimed the separate word of each girl. There was a warm flutter of agreement and the names of the Buddha and of Kuan Yin were taken many times, not, it is to be hoped, in vain.

When the others had all returned to their own apartments, under the hawk-eyes of their personal eunuchs, who had come to collect them promptly on the single hour of the Pig, Black Jade settled down to discuss matters with Chinghiz.

'First – tell me how you managed to give us all such a tremendous impression of authority! I have never seen you like that. How did you do it?'

'Little Mistress, I am deeply hurt! Do you suppose it was simply some charlatan's trick, rather than the true jade in my character?' His faun's eyes were large and innocent.

'Yes, I do,' she stated certainly.

'Good! You are learning. It was partly a matter of dress, partly of *address*. You will have observed this rather severe indigo robe. An abbot might wear it. Very different from my usual affinity with the rainbow. I keep it for grave occasions. All I needed then was Lord Shen's blessing, a back like a guardsman's spear and that detached and aristocratic manner, which I borrowed from the Archduke.'

'It was the best performance of the evening,' she allowed.

'Thank you. But don't forget, Little Huntress, that the point of any dramatic persona is to become so close to it that it eventually becomes part of oneself. I was merely rehearsing this evening, but one day I shall *be* that commanding figure. Do you see?'

'Will you teach me?' she said simply.

'All I can. But when you have grown up, just a little, there will not be very much I can teach you. These things are chiefly a matter of instinct – and you have as much of that as I have.'

'What sort of instinct?'

'For the right moment, the right word; for character and motive. When to be kind and when not. For what you can and can't get away with.'

She nodded. Then, rather than relating his words to herself, she said, 'Do you think the Crown Prince has any of these instincts?'

'No, I don't,' said Chinghiz sombrely. 'He is governed entirely by self-will. I am not even sure that he is quite sane.'

'Then why is he the heir? The Emperor may choose any of his sons.'

'He is young. He may change.'

'Let us hope so. If he can't rule himself, how can he rule the Empire? Surely Heaven will not grant him the mandate?'

'There are some who would agree with you. No doubt you have heard of the rivalry between the Prince and his brother, Prince Tai?'

'Dumpling mentioned something like that. She thinks Prince Tai is a prig; too clever, too charming and much too fond of himself.'

'There is something in the description, but he is also very much respected at court, especially among the ministers.'

'So he will have plenty of support should he wish to challenge his brother's position?'

'That is so. But Tai is the son of a concubine; Cheng Chien is the son of the Empress and has the right to succeed.'

'Do you know Prince Tai?'

'I have met him on several occasions.'

'Do you think he would make a good Emperor?'

'He would be preferable to the Turkish Maiden. But you need not concern yourself with that. The Son of Heaven, as you will, will live for ten thousand years.'

'All the same,' Black Jade said softly, 'it would be more than sad if such a magnificent man should not have an heir he could be proud of.'

Chinghiz was pleased to hear her speak like this; it was the way in which her thoughts should be tending. But it also touched the shadow over his heart; she so rarely mentioned the Emperor.

The activities of the Crown Prince went from bad to worse. The harem was delighted. Under the guise of an intelligent interest in court politics they kept the eunuchs running back and forth with his latest eccentricities.

'He will have nothing to do with anything Chinese,' reported Dumpling, who was usually first with the news. 'He says we are over-civilized and have a lot to learn from the simplicity of nomadic life. He is proud of the Tartar blood of his ever-so-great-grandmother and will sacrifice only to her spirit tablet. None of his other ancestors receive his prayers.'

'I saw him yesterday, during my morning ride,' Jade told them. 'He was still dressed as a Turk; a male this time. He wore those baggy trousers and a shaggy waistcoat and was waving a great scimitar as he raced across the park. He quite frightened the deer.'

'Didn't he frighten you?' several girls asked.

'No. Why should he? He can do nothing to any of us. We belong to the Emperor.'

That was true, but the concubines, on the whole, enjoyed being frightened. It made them feel as if they were taking part in the great world outside the walls of the Inner Palace.

'Have you heard what he does to *his* concubines?' asked Gentle Orchid, the daughter of one of the councillors. She was a tall, slender girl with an attractive, fine-boned face and a low voice that always had a catch in it. They turned towards her eagerly, while Welcome refilled their teacups to prolong expectation.

Gentle Orchid lowered her lashes. 'I have heard,' she whispered, 'that the Turk likes to – pretend that they are boys.' She covered her lips with her sleeve. Jade wondered what she meant.

'I've heard worse than that,' offered Welcome, who had established her own sources of information, not to be outdone by Chinghiz.

The flower-like heads swivelled towards her.

'I got it from one of his harem maids. He makes his consorts pretend that they are *mares*! He makes them stand naked, straight-limbed on all fours, while he does his business with them from behind. If they should fall to their knees, he horsewhips them.'

There was a concerted shriek of prurient horror from the girls who plied their fans vigorously to cover their scandalous pleasure.

Black Jade was slightly impatient. 'There are stranger things than that in the *Amatory Arts*,' she said airily. 'Though I must say, the whipping is cruel.'

'Just think what he might have done to *us* – if Chinghiz had not saved us that night,' whispered Gentle Orchid.

'Oh, by all means think of it – if that's what you want to do,' replied Black Jade with unusual ill-humour. 'As for me, I think I will go for a ride.'

There were times when she found the company of her peers nothing short of unbearable.

Prince Cheng Chien had now turned Turk completely. He dressed only in the Turkish style, ate only Turkish food, and chose only Turks for his companions. Since most of these were prisoners of war who worked in the imperial stables, his choice was not popular among the young noblemen at court, who began to gather about his brother Prince Tai in a recognisable faction. This did not appear to bother Cheng Chien, who took to living in a tent made of animal skins which he had set up in the grounds of the Heir's Palace. There he spent his time riding bareback and listening to Turkish music. Attended by his breeched and turbaned cohort, he feasted nightly upon whole, spitted sheep, carved with the end of his sword. He insisted that his title was now Cheng Khan.

If he was then slightly mad, an event occurred which was to fill him with further numbers of unstable demons.

During Black Jade's frequent riding expeditions she had kept up her close friendship with her half-brother Huan, who was in his element in the royal stables and still considered Snow Prince the first of his responsibilities. He was not permitted to ride with her, but he was always waiting for her when she came to the stable court at the hour of the Dragon, while most people were waking to their morning tea.

This morning the stables seemed unusually busy. The grooms stood talking in excited groups with soldiers of the imperial guard, who were present in larger numbers than Black Jade had ever seen before. She pulled down her veil over her face and sent Chinghiz to see what the fuss was about.

He soon returned with Huan, who led Snow Prince. As they crossed the yard one of the officers clapped the boy on the shoulder.

'Good morning, Little Mistress,' Huan beamed. 'Such goings-on!'

'So I gather – but what are they?' Black Jade gave Snow Prince the sesame cake she always saved for him.

The officer, who wore a purple plume in his cap and the two belts and varied insignia of a general, had followed after Huan.

'Young man, I have something for you,' he called as he came closer. 'It is less than you deserve, but I think it will please you.'

Huan swallowed and dropped into a kowtow. Before he could speak, the General had realised the sex of Snow Prince's owner.

'I do beg your pardon. I had no idea a lady was present. Well, Wu Huan, will you not present me?'

Huan appeared quite overcome. But he struggled to his feet and bowed again. 'This is the Lady Wu Chao, Your Highness, known as the Elegant Consort Black Jade.'

'I am Prince Tai,' the officer told her, bending slightly in his turn, an unnecessary courtesty from one so august. 'Has your groom yet had time to tell you of his bravery?'

'No,' she replied, curious. 'What has he done, Highness?'

Huan seemed to be trying to screw himself into the ground beside her; he had always been ridiculously modest.

Prince Tai resembled neither his father nor his brother. He was tall, elegant and very assured. His face was noble rather than handsome, and there was something a shade too polished in his manner; it was intended to charm, she felt, rather than being naturally charming.

'My dear Lady Wu, you must hear at once. Huan has captured a Turkish prisoner as he tried to escape. He is the Khan's brother and we don't want to lose him!'

'I am so proud of you my brother, so proud!' cried Black Jade delightedly.

'Your brother? I had not realised. Then it is not so surprising. He shares the blood of the tiger-tamer.' His smile did not disarm her. She wished the episode of the tiger to be forgotten. She was tired of it. Did everyone in the place know about it?

'He shares the blood of our honourable father, Wu Shih-huo,' she said firmly. 'And he has brought honour to it.'

'It was nothing. I enjoyed the chase,' said Huan truthfully, his tongue released at last. 'But the Turk will die in the market-place. I am sorry for that, despite what he did.'

'Never be sorry for an enemy,' said Prince Tai firmly. 'Do not consider that you have lost this man his life, rather that you have done a service to the Son of Heaven. If the Turk had been spared he might have tried again – and succeeded.'

Huan tried to look as though he were comforted.

'So end all Turks,' the Prince said coldly. Black Jade suspected that he might have one particular 'Turk' in mind.

'And now let me give you His Majesty's thanks,' Tai continued, brightening. He snapped his fingers and a groom led a fine bay out of the Emperor's private stable. Black Jade recognised it as having been bred from one of the original 'dragon-horses' whose exploits had enlivened their childhood.

'Take the reins,' Tai said to the open-mouthed Huan. 'He's for you.'

Thrilled beyond the possibility of speech, the boy dropped to his knees beside the shining chestnut flank. Tai waved a hand in acknowledgement of the thanks he could not express.

'Lady Wu – it has been a pleasure to meet you. Your beauty puts the wakening sun to shame,' he said neatly, by way of farewell. Then he strode off across the court, a fine figure in his well-cut uniform.

'He's very young to be a general,' said Black Jade doubtfully.

'He's only a parade general,' said Huan. 'It's an honorary rank, because he is the Emperor's son.'

'You sound as though you don't like him,' she challenged.

'I don't, not really.' Huan scratched his head. 'I can never quite make out why not.'

'It is because he is a man who wants the world to love him, rather than a man who loves the world.'

She repeated this discovery to Chinghiz, who chuckled and told her that her instincts were coming along nicely.

As a result of this, Cheng Khan's behaviour deteriorated still further and people began to talk openly about a change in the succession. Prince Tai was very much seen about the court, dispensing pleasantries and favours. His opinion of his brother was obvious to everyone. Whenever the two met, which was seldom, Tai was the first to hurry away as if from some infection.

'Why doesn't the Emperor put an end to Cheng Khan's antics?' Black Jade asked Chinghiz, at a loss to understand how Shih-min could accept such prolonged indignities.

'Think of your history books,' the steward advised. 'The succession has always been a matter of the utmost delicacy. Intrigue and treachery have often surrounded it. This Son of Heaven gained the mandate after a conspiracy of brother against brother. He does not wish to see the same trouble repeated in his own reign.'

'Then why doesn't he act? Why let Cheng Khan make such a fool of himself?'

'No, His Majesty is right to wait. If trouble threatens, you can sometimes evade it by ignoring it – or at least put it off for a very long time. During that time, things might change; Cheng Khan might improve – or even die.'

'I'm sure Prince Tai hopes so. How strange it all is. I didn't expect it to be like this. There is so much emotion of one sort and another crowded into this palace, that even though it is so immense, sometimes it seems as small and stifling as a single room in summer.'

As the months passed the charged atmosphere did not improve. Cheng Khan continued to be outrageous, his madness erupting from time to time in a conflagration that covered the lower slopes of the hierarchy in a thick lava of scandalised reaction. There were raids on the homes of innocent subjects; there were bloody mock-battles in the imperial park; there were further indignities to concubines. There was the night the 'Khan' half-killed a high-born officer of the guard who had tried to remonstrate with him about his excesses.

Black Jade, while horrified at the Prince's lack of humanity, found that his sins at least provided peaks of interest in a life that she was beginning to find somewhat dull in its repetitive pattern.

Her days were filled with study and duty. The duties were not heavy. It was her responsibility, shared with Dumpling and four more Elegants, to look after the apartments of the dead Empress, making sure that they were kept fresh and habitable. As it appeared unlikely that the Emperor would ever remarry, the exercise seemed pointless and rather sad.

Yet it was when she held in her hand the rich fabrics that draped the Empress's great bed that Black Jade experienced the only sensation that she had ever received of there being any reason at all for her presence in the palace.

It was a strange feeling, part physical, part psychic, and wholly defiant of analysis. She could describe it to herself only as a sense of certainty, like a premonition that one *knows* will prove itself true. Whatever it was, she was grateful for its reassurance. She was beginning to feel that she was lying fallow.

Today she decided she would write to Lady Hero. Their correspondence had so far been sparse but very satisfying. Black Jade had done her best to describe her daily life with humour and detachment, and Hero had replied, much as she spoke, in a continual torrent of amusing ideas and forthright opinions.

She would take her paper and her brushes to the Empress's room. She would not be disturbed there at this hour of the afternoon, and Green Fragrance Court was ringing with the voices of the maids and some domestic dispute between Welcome and Chinghiz which she was anxious to avoid having to solve.

The dead Pure Virtue's rooms were decorated in pale pastels which added to their air of gentle sadness. The woman who had chosen them had been, she had heard, of a mild and sunny disposition, soft, feminine and unfailingly kind. Something of the tranquillity of such a nature remained in the soft hangings and the faded rose, blue and grey that had pleased her. Jade looked forward to her hour of complete peace. Unlike her companions, who were afraid of ghosts, she felt very much at home there.

With her green writing-paper and brushes in the pocket of her sleeve and her new inkstone wrapped in a scarf, she slipped into the apartments by a side door and made her way slowly to the bedchamber. She had a fancy to use the pretty rosewood desk that stood at the east window. Her soft silk shoes made no sound on the bamboo floors.

Even had they done so, it is doubtful that the occupants of the Empress's bedroom would have noticed it. They were intensely engaged in what they were doing.

Quite what it *was* that they were doing was not at first clear to Black Jade as she pushed open the light screen doors and saw the two writhing figures on the bed.

They did not hear her; they would not have heard an earthquake. Both were naked, their bodies moving rhythmically among the strewn silks, deep golden-brown and a lighter gold beneath, mingling with the rose and blue.

Jade stood transfixed, all eyes; no breath, no capability of motion. She watched the even tension and relaxation of the muscles along the hard male back, the knotted thrust of the buttocks, heard the gasps of extremity and enjoyment. The slender, paler, splayed legs beneath quivered, the toes digging into the coverlet. They were very small toes.

She had read enough to know what she was watching. It was

'Reversed Flying Ducks', if she was not mistaken. But who could the man and woman be who would take such a flagrant risk? She would go. She did not want to be party to anyone's secret. Just as she turned to leave there was a cry, as if of agony, from the bed. Looking back, she saw the man roll over and throw himself heavily on to his back. It was the Crown Prince, Cheng Khan.

It was not his identity that brought back the horror that had originally turned her to stone. It was the other, his companion in the act of copulation. It was a child, perhaps twelve or thirteen – a lithe, golden, grinning child. A boy.

She could not stop crying. She didn't know why. There seemed no reason for it; she just couldn't stop. Welcome had rocked her, holding her as she had when she was an inconsolable little girl, but it had not stopped the flood of tears. Nor had the soft, insistent voice of Chinghiz, telling her that it was all right, that what she had seen was not going to alter her life, or her mind, and that it didn't really matter.

Eventually he had recourse to strong rice wine instead of words. This seemed to have very nearly the desired effect. Sobs were reduced to hiccoughs and the stream of precious coloured paper handkerchiefs could be lessened.

'But – I didn't know – none of the books said,' she began, only to break down again in shame.

'Little Mistress, Little Flower,' wheedled Chinghiz, 'You sound as though you felt it was *you* who were at fault. No shame attaches to you simply because you had the misfortune to witness one of Cheng Khan's less attractive facets.'

'I *feel* as though it does!' she cried, outraged. 'I feel dirty all over.'

'Then why don't you have a bath?' asked Chinghiz practically.

'It wouldn't make any difference,' sniffed Jade. She thought about it. Clear, clean, warm water, in that comfortable tub with the dolphins round the rim. 'Well, perhaps I will.'

While the water was being heated she managed to stop crying at last, though she still looked so woebegone that Welcome wondered whether to look for the old toy dragon that she used to take to bed with her, a battered old thing, loved half to death.

Chinghiz had different ideas. 'What has happened today is something that will continue to happen, in various parts of the world, from now until the Last Reincarnation,' he said gently. 'It is not usual; and in our society it is not acceptable. That is why you have never heard of it. But in other societies, that of ancient

Greece for example, it was not only acceptable but considered a rather stylish relationship. All the great philosophers of that land, I am told, had their male lovers.'

'Ugh! Don't talk about it. It makes me feel sick.'

'You must not be childish about this. You are no longer a child. You have had a shock, yes; but it has not harmed you. You have learned something about human nature that you did not know before. You should look on it as an advance.'

'How can you be so – so cold about things?'

'I am not cold. It is just that I have learned nothing new today. I am trying to help you assimilate the shock, that's all.'

'You mean that you *knew* about – about Cheng Khan –'

'Yes, I knew.'

'Then why didn't you tell the Emperor? How could you let that filthy creature go on –'

Chinghiz sighed. 'I believe most women feel this way. It is a pity, I think. After all, no one is hurt by the practice. And if it is what two people want –'

'Don't be disgusting! Is my water ready?' She would hear no more.

'Yes. Where do you want it?'

'In the wardrobe room.'

Two stout eunuchs entered, carrying the tub, half-full of steaming water. They staggered into the wardrobe room and set it down, begging some honey cakes from the maids before they left. Eunuchs have notoriously sweet teeth. Welcome and Second Singer added cold water until it was the temperature Black Jade liked. then she took off her robe and trousers and stepped in.

'We'll perfume it with nothing but flower essences. Then you'll feel really pure,' said Chinghiz. Jade had the suspicion that he was laughing at her. He rained scented oils and rose-petals over her shoulders until he had made her laugh too.

The tub was waist-high and generously built; it would hold two if so required. Black Jade sat with her knees bent and let Chinghiz rub her all over with a sponge for which some diver had risked his life in far-off waters. He had earned this privilege by doing it better than any of the maids. Welcome disapproved of this, though she did not say so because that would mean explaining why she felt that way. She hovered for a few moments, unwilling to leave them alone, but the room was too small and too crowded with chests, clothing, stools, make-up boxes, jewellery boxes and the bath itself to hold another adult comfortably. Muttering to herself about ordering some tea, she left them in peace.

Chinghiz scrubbed and stroked until Jade announced herself sufficiently purified. Then she rose from the tub with the liquid grace of a water goddess.

'Well, what are you waiting for? Give me the towel.'

Chinghiz unwrapped the big cotton towel from its hot stone but did not transfer it to his mistress. Instead he stood gazing at her as a holy man might contemplate his shrine.

'What's the matter? Have I got a mosquito bite?' Black Jade tried to examine those parts she could not normally see.

'Don't do that; you look like a cat trying to wash its behind!'

'Don't be so rude! And give me that towel!'

'In a moment. Are you quite warm?'

'Yes, but I –'

'Then come with me.' Before she could protest he had thrown the towel around her and lifted her out of the tub. He did not put her down but carried her over to the long bronze mirror near the latticed window.

'There now. What do you see?' He removed the towel.

'Myself, you idiot! What game are you inventing now?'

'It is called taking stock of one's assets. You never look at yourself properly, from head to foot. It's time you did.'

'What is the point?' She glared at the highly polished version of herself that shone before her.

'Because if you were to take note of certain things, you might begin to think of yourself as a woman and not as an ignorant child. It is high time.'

She looked resentful. 'You say that because I disliked what I saw today. Thinking as a woman would make no difference. I shall never accept that perverted –' she sought for a word – 'congress.'

He smiled affectionately. 'It is nothing to do with that – though I admit the incident has made me realise that you are sadly in need of certain tuition.'

'I've been reading the books. What more do I need?'

'Those manuals!' he scoffed. 'They are about as descriptive of human needs and pleasures as are geometers' drawings of the God-inhabited heavens!'

'Then why do I have to read them?'

He changed his imagery. 'Well, it is useful, when travelling in unexplored country, to be equipped with a map.'

'Is my body a map?' She squinted down its length. The way it curved in and out was rather pleasant, she thought.

'It is a map of the citadels of your own pleasure.'

'Where are they, these citadels?' She already had far more than a suspicion where they were, but she felt like teasing him.

'Show me. Show me on the map.'

Chinghiz trembled. He knew her well enough to know what she was doing. He stood for a moment, still, while a wave of desire and physical pain rolled up and over him. Surviving it, he stepped behind her and cupped her beautiful breasts in his hands. He nipped their golden-brown tips. 'Here,' he said, caressing them into life. 'And here.' He moved his hands lower.

Black Jade gave a surprised little gasp. It was also one of pleasure.

'What now?' she asked, wide-eyed, as he moved away from her. Her body was singing all over. It was a wonderful sensation.

'Now,' grinned Chinghiz, master of himself again, 'I give you the towel!'

6

Cheng Khan and his little dancing-boy continued to be careless. It was only a matter of time before some self-seeker carried the tale to the Emperor. Shih-min, appalled by such evidence of his son's weakness, had the boy, just thirteen, instantly executed.

Once more Black Jade wept on his account. Her tears, at least, were more adult than the previous ones. They sprang as much from anger as from sorrow.

'I never thought he could be so unjust!' she cried. 'It is so cowardly – to punish a child for the sins of a man.'

Chinghiz did not tell her that the child in question had probably been a party to such sins since he was five years old.

'I think he expected this to break Cheng Khan's spirit. I don't know if he has succeeded. The Khan is hysterical with grief; he has locked himself into his palace and swears never again to speak to his father.'

The morning after this unfortunate denouement, Black Jade rode out early, giving the slip to Chinghiz, and brooded upon a new awareness of the precariousness of life in the palace. It was a far less pleasant place than she had imagined from the seclusion of Green Fragrance Court. This morning she wished, for the first time in the four years that she had been here, that she had never come to Chang-an.

'Snow Prince,' she murmured into the laid-back ears in front of her, 'if only you were a real "dragon-horse"! You could fly right up over those beastly walls and take me back home.'

Snow Prince, rather than showing any willingness to accommodate her, suddenly slowed up. His reason was excellent; there was a sizeable party of horsemen in their path. Black Jade saw that the tall central figure was the Emperor.

What should she do? They must have seen her. She had come so far towards them in her introspective flight that she could hardly back off now. It was a grave misconduct, however, for her to approach any man in the palace, let alone His Majesty himself. Nor should she have been out unchaperoned.

She sat foolishly, paralysed by the dilemma. The courtiers seemed to be examining a riderless horse, held by a groom. Perhaps, after all, they might not notice if she went quietly away. She turned Snow Prince's head. Just then Shih-min glanced in her direction. At once a guard rode over to her. Sheepishly she followed him.

'It is Beauty Wu, isn't it?' smiled Shih-min. He was uncertain because of the thick veil she wore.

'Yes, Your Majesty.' She thought he looked tired. The usual bright flame of his energy burned low. It served him right if he hadn't slept, she thought, after killing that child,

'I am sorry to have found myself in Your Majesty's path. I'm afraid I was not looking where I was going.'

'Never mind. I am pleased to see you.' She was surprised to be reminded how attractive his voice was. 'I recall you to be something of a horsewoman. Tell me what you think of this creature.'

The stallion was dappled grey, powerfully and poetically built; and to judge from the gleam in his eye and the swish of his tail, in a state of high ill-temper.

'A fine animal as to his looks. What is his nature?'

'Much as I see you suspect. We have been here two hours, trying to master him. He has even thrown your half-brother. Poor Huan has gone off to bathe his bruises. I'd like to try him myself, but I can see he aims to do the same to me. You are a mountain rider; what do you suggest?'

She knew he was merely being charming so that she should not be shamed before his companions. She was about to murmur some courteous nothing and excuse herself when she caught the sardonic eyes of the Archduke upon her. Suddenly she wanted to show his Insufferable Superiority that she was not to be discounted. She thought again of the dead boy.

'An ill-natured horse is like an ill-natured boy. He can be controlled. For this you need three things – a whip, an iron baton, and a dagger. If the whip does not subdue him, you should beat him with the iron. If that does not persuade him, then you should cut your losses and use the dagger to slit his throat.'

She regretted her temerity the instant she had spoken. The hiss among the courtiers told her that they had understood her meaning. She thought she had probably committed some kind of treason. What would be the punishment for a seventeen-year-old, unused concubine who dared to tell the Emperor how he should treat his errant son?

The Archduke's expression was a study in consternation. At least she had that satisfaction.

'Don't you feel that would be a little excessive, even unkind?' Shih-min was regarding her with what seemed to be wary amusement. She wished she might remove the veil, so that he might see her regret. She now felt oddly sorry for him. He was transparently careworn. She cursed Cheng Khan before replying gently, 'I did not intend unkindness. I love the beasts dearly. But when one of them is possessed by demons, what else can one do?'

'One might give him time.'

'The measure of such time soon makes itself clear.'

'Or I might set him free, to live as he pleases.'

'That would undoubtedly be a kindness, my lord,' she agreed doubtfully. Perhaps also wise – in the case of the horse.

A horse cannot study revenge.

All day Black Jade waited apprehensively in Green Fragrance Court, hourly expecting some sign of royal disapproval. Even Chinghiz had been perturbed when she had told him how she had spoken.

'My lady only answered His Majesty's questions,' defended Welcome. 'What fault can they find with that?' She was truculent.

'They will find whatever they wish. I'm afraid such expressions of opinion, however disguised, can do our mistress no good.'

For once he proved to be wrong. Not that this distressed him at all; indeed he exulted in it. For, late in the afternoon, there did come a message from the Imperial Palace; the Elegant Consort Black Jade was to go that night to the Emperor's bed.

Shaking with nerves and determined not to show it, Black Jade explained to her assembled friends and household, all of whom were at a pitch of excitement that made her own butterfly stomach seem insignificant, how pointless it was to dress her in her new peach-red robe and turn her hair into a living representation of the basket-weaver's art. The Emperor would never see the robe, and the hair would soon replace it as the only covering for her modesty. Her reasoning only provoked ribald jests, however, and she ceased to protest.

'Here, you may borrow my ambergris perfume. The Emperor said it reminded him of warm rocks in the sun.' Dumpling, who had visited the royal couch many times, regarded herself as an authority on Shih-min's tastes.

'You are kind,' Jade smiled, 'but I'd like to wear my own sandalwood. We don't want His Majesty to confuse the two of us.'

Their laughter released her tension and the butterflies were still. She was ready to go. 'Chinghiz. Am I as you would want me?'

He stood at the door, his arms folded, an odd quietness about him. 'Very much as I would want you.' There was a silver glitter in his eyes.

She clasped his hands. 'I am glad. I want you to be proud of me.'

She took leave of them amid a shower of good wishes and last-minute advice. She thought then of Rose Bird, leaving their home for ever, to live and pillow with a man she had never seen. Perhaps, after all, there were some advantages to palace life. She had not only seen the man who would take her virginity tonight; she almost thought that, despite the fact that he was the Son of Heaven, she already knew him a little.

She stood before Lord Shen without blinking. The immense eunuch did not, naturally, look at her face as he unclothed her, unless the probing of her ears and nostrils for poison-pills counted as doing so. He did stare at her breasts in an unnecessary fashion. He then asked her to stand with her legs apart while he ascertained that she was indeed a virgin. His hands were, as Dumpling had said, clammy. She disliked this procedure very much, although she could see that it was perfectly reasonable. The Chief Eunuch completed his work by ordering her to remove every single golden hairpin and let Welcome's triumphant coiffure fall to premature destruction.

Lord Shen then bowed to her and clapped his hands. Another large eunuch appeared, carrying the famous quilt. This was scarlet with gold embroidery and Black Jade was relieved to be wrapped in its silk cocoon. The man picked her up and slung her across his shoulder like a rolled carpet. She felt somewhat foolish as she stiffened to make his task easier.

She was startled to see, as they passed through a doorway, an excellent likeness, of Cheng Khan's dead tutor painted on the wood. Dumpling had not mentioned that. She must have been too excited each time to notice it.

The Emperor's bedchamber was furnished with surprising simplicity. Shih-min himself was sitting with his feet up on a long sofa, with a bundle of papers on his lap. He wore a loose gown in the Arab style, open almost to his waist. He seemed rested and refreshed since the morning.

When Jade was deposited in front of him he swung round to welcome her, pouring wine while her porter deftly removed the quilt and replaced it with a thin rose-coloured robe.

When they were alone he said, 'You're frowning. Don't you approve of our ancient palace protocol?'

He touched her shoulder, pressing her lightly towards the sofa. His touch astonished her; it was as though she were suddenly pierced by golden needles.

'I see the necessity,' she said, recovering herself, 'but it makes me feel belittled, and therefore resentful, rather than –'

'Rather than inducing any notion of desire. I understand. However, the custom is designed to prevent future disasters as well as possible present ones. By her enforced nakedness and her passage like a bale of goods upon the eunuch's back, the concubine is reminded of her position here in the palace, and will, it is hoped, consider carefully before supposing that she can alter that position by the application of her wiles to the Emperor. You are the first, for many years, to make known her feelings on the subject.' His eyes teased her.

He settled into the high back of the sofa, as relaxed as a full-fed panther, and, Jade sensed, every bit as mischievous.

'Am I therefore to be trusted least of all?' she enquired, sitting bolt upright and taking the cup he offered her.

'I'll tell you that when I've experienced the quality of your wiles.'

Black Jade was not sure she wanted to be teased just at the moment. It seemed that Shih-min was *still* treating her like a father. And yet when she saw, and felt, how he looked at her, she knew she no longer had that refuge.

Whether or not she wanted a refuge was another question. As always, what she chiefly wanted – and in this case, as in so many others, could not have – was the inestimable liberty of making her own choice.

'Why is the portrait of the old minister on the door?' she asked, displaying no wiliness whatever in her blatant change of topic.

'Long ago my sleep was plagued by demons. We painted two of my fiercest generals on the main doors, but the demons were clever and went round the back. I thought my old tutor was the one to see them off. He used to put the fear of Heaven into me!'

'And did he? See them off?'

'He did. I normally sleep like a baby.'

She flinched inwardly, thinking that tonight he would not soon seek sleep. She drained her cup quickly, hoping to find confidence at the bottom of it. Shih-min refilled it politely.

'That is a fine horse you were riding,' he said warmly, aware of her nervousness. 'I'd like to breed from him. May I?'

'I will give him to Your Majesty with pleasure,' she offered dutifully, her heart racing.

He smiled. 'Do you think I would be so thoughtless as to take him? No. I'll be just as happy with a couple of colts.'

His look softened. 'You are one of the few women I've seen who cut a good figure on horseback. My sister is the same. In that you do resemble her; she was right. It is an accomplishment I love to see.'

Black Jade's face was suddenly alight. He did not understand the change, but was drawn by it.

'Perhaps you should keep your given name. Chao; Pure Brightness. At this moment it suits you remarkably well. And they tell me that your illumination extends, as I knew it must, to the things of the mind. I so well recall the child who challenged me over Pan Chao. And now you are a scholar to equal her.' He held her eyes levelly. 'And one who would challenge me upon the conduct of my son.'

She looked down, afraid. 'It was importunate.'

'But you make no apology?'

He was not angry. She took a chance. 'No. I spoke as I did because I remember the conduct of Your Majesty's brothers.'

His eyes narrowed. 'Never think that *I* do not,' he said softly. 'And now, Black Jade, unless it is your intention to lecture me all night, perhaps you might find other ways of amusing me?'

He faced her and she was forced to look at him. She thought him fiercely beautiful. The slanting lines of his face seemed all bent towards her in curious concentration. She was pierced upon his gaze as a silken blind is pierced by light. She had the sensation of being unable to move; unable, even, to desire what he did not desire. There was no possibility of choice. For a second her spirit rebelled. And then, beneath the sardonic and critical gaze of that spirit, her body took over her government.

Shih-min slowly put out his hand, as if to a tentative animal. He sensed more vitality, more will and determination to be her own woman in this girl than in any he had known. Her femininity was as different from that of others as was the domestic lap-cat from the tigress. She would, he sensed, make him the most splendid match. His desire was already thrusting upward, impatient of the delay.

The years of control easily mastered it.

He took her hand. 'Your beauty may be greater or less than that of others,' he murmured. 'What concerns me is that I find it uniquely to my taste. We are opposites, you and I, Jade. You are blunt where I have learned to be subtle; you are without experience where I am expert; you are full of the pride of youth where I am hollow with the knowledge of age, and –' he disengaged the cup that she still gripped like a lifeline – 'you are very probably drunk whereas I am sober; no bad thing in our present circumstances.'

She giggled, surprising herself. He seized upon the momentary lightness to kiss her, very quickly, before she knew it. Her lips tasted first of wine and then of her own sweetness. He lingered, knowing it was more than likely to be her first experience.

When he raised his head he found her green eyes blazing, wide open, into his, filled with a deliciously startled novelty.

'You like kissing, then? A good beginning.'

She did not reply, being breathless, and he bent to her again.

The kissing went on for a very long time, until Black Jade had learned that to kiss is to put down a strange upside-down seed, whose speed of growth is incredible, which sends its roots straight to the womb and its shivering leaves and blatant flowers to every furthest part of the body, its flourishing was marvellous to her and she rejoiced in its discovery.

Slowly, and with exquisite tact and patience, Shih-min revealed to his young concubine what no manuals of copulation could reveal, the pleasure that none of them could describe, and the sense of glory that came in its triumphant wake.

He had loved many women in his life, but he had never lost his wonder at the beauty and intricacy of the human body, and could communicate it whole-heartedly to the girl it was his privilege to deflower.

Once he had shown Black Jade that to have breasts which swelled to his touch, with soft tips which stood erect, to have secret, rosy openings which issued liquid invitations, was more miraculous than any shaman's magic, her innocent pride in these things became a further incentive to his own desire.

When at last he spread her upon his broad bed and entered her, he knew that her welcome was as absolute as that desire. He knew too that he would find it impossible to conserve his seed as he should, reserving it only for the chosen days of conception. He didn't care. This wonderfully responsive girl made him feel as young again as she was herself. When he heard her laugh aloud in jubilant happiness as he filled her with aspiring members of his clan, he found himself answering her in the same exultant strain.

Later, when Black Jade had washed them both, admiring the lean hardness of his long brown body, they leaned back on the pillows in extreme contentment. Lazily, he questioned her about her days in Shansi. Himself a native of Taiyuan, where his father had been Duke of T'ang, he still yearned for the clean, sharp forms of the mountains, treasuring a boyhood spent among the weathered border troops. He pictured for her his delight in the hunting that had gone on for days at a time, and the eternal challenge of the Turks in their neighbouring fortresses in the Mongolian steppes. The very air had been sweeter there – or was it *then*?

She brought it all back to him, this wild and willing girl, with her free thoughts and her sharp mind and her beautiful, already hungry body.

Black Jade responded spasmodically, still convalescing from the shock of the new. She decided, as she watched the broad soundboard of his chest vibrate to the rich, inviting resonance of his voice, that she now wished to do very little else in life other than endlessly to repeat this evening's ecstatic activities.

Her wish was granted, at any rate, on two further occasions during the course of the night that followed. When, at dawn, she awoke to the knowledge of bliss and prepared to kiss her sleeping lover and return to Green Fragrance Court as she had been taught, Shih-min woke instantly like the seasoned soldier he was, and took her thirstily in his arms again – a thing he had not done for a very long time.

That day he sent her emeralds.

That night he sent for her again.

7

Black Jade found that love was just as hazardous an experience as she had read that it was. She knew that it *was* love, the rare, the difficult thing, and not the mere combination of lust and romance that was the common emotion of the harem, because of the ferocious and ineluctable possessiveness that overwhelmed her from the very beginning of their union.

She wanted to be with Shih-min every minute of the night and day. She resented every moment he spent away from her, every slightest affair of state or court. Her thoughts were daggers in the breasts of other girls with whom he occasionally passed the night, and she felt the blade turn still more sharply in her own. She wished with all her heart and soul that he were not the Emperor, so that she might be the first with him, as he was with her.

She said nothing of this terrible feeling, not even to Welcome or to Chinghiz. With Dumpling she pretended delight when the girl was once sent for in her place. Her place. For it *was* her place. At his side; in his bed; in his heart. She was his, by his right and by her father's gift before he died – but he was also hers, by no right except that it *was* right. Because they were perfect together in understanding and because there was love between them, no less in him than in her.

She knew that he loved her; how could she not know it when he told her with his eyes, with the tone of his voice, with the worship of his intoxicating body? Sometimes, on the giddiest heights, she wondered if he would make her his Empress. (Chinghiz, she knew, would wonder far more energetically.) But he never suggested it. He did not even offer her the petty promotions of the harem. Perhaps he no longer thought of her as one of its members. At any rate, such matters did not appear to concern him and, in truth, scarcely mattered to her either. He gave her his love and his time; she could ask for nothing more. She did not even want, particularly, the jewels he brought her, though she wore them for his sake. Jewels could show little value when matched against the precious moments of their time together.

At first he sent for her often. His duties to his other consorts were seriously neglected. He allowed her to know that when he did choose another woman it was out of duty, that his desire was only for her.

For over a year they were very happy. Black Jade had a triumphant sense that every aspect of her life until now had been bent towards this; all her learning and her skills, everything she was. She wanted to extract the essence of herself and turn it, by some as yet undiscovered magic, into a scented oil that she might rub over every inch of her beloved's body, until she was part of the sanctuary of his being and he could not be rid of her ever. She told him of this and the eroticism of it aroused him so swiftly that he took her, quickly and violently, upon the edge of the *kang* in her apartment, with the sound of the maids' laughter buffeting them gently from the next room. This was by no means the only occasion when Shih-min forgot his dignity as Emperor and was willingly carried away on the crescendo of his wanting flesh. In the mornings he would rise early and meet her in the park. They would ride quickly towards the river without speaking, dismounting as soon as they were sufficiently concealed from all possible interruption, and he would lay her on his silken robe upon the ground, thrusting into her and being received with an urgency which suggested that they would have behaved no differently had the palace been ablaze behind them. During the ride back he would be as carefree as the boy he had been before he had any thought of thrones.

And then, as suddenly as it had come to them, all innocence and carelessness was taken away.

Shih-min had promised to visit her in the afternoon, as has become his habit. It was obvious as soon as she saw him that all was not well. She shooed away her servants and brought him ginseng tea herself. As she offered the cup, for the first time his answering caress was absent, almost automatic. She felt herself cut off, shut out from him. There was an overwhelming moment of panic. She overcame it, wondering how to bring him back to her. Instinctively she knew that she should not use her body for the purpose; that was not what his first need was, not today. There had never been any barrier in their talk with one another so she simply laid her hand on his and said with all the kindness of which she was capable, 'Something is troubling you; what is it, my dear lord?'

He sighed. 'I apologize. I've been trying to shake it off. I don't want to bring you my cares. I have ministers enough for the purpose.'

She stroked his sleeve. 'I *want* you to bring them to me. It is very important to me. Ministers, I hope, are rather less than lovers.'

He smiled wearily. 'They are certainly different. Since you wish to know – one of my sons has been planning revolt.'

'Prince Cheng!' she said quickly.

He frowned. 'No. It's Prince Chi, the governor of Chi Nan Fu. I thought, when I sent him there, he would grow up a little; he was always a light-minded boy.'

It was the custom for imperial princes to gain experience of government in the provinces.

'Chi Nan Fu is five hundred miles away! How did he hope to cause a revolution from there?'

'The boy has declared a revolt and proclaimed himself the sole authority in his province. The citizens remained loyal, however, and I've despatched the Great Wall to deal with the rebel army.' This was his most famous general who had gained his sobriquet when acting as a bastion against the Turks.

'I expect news of his success at any hour.' His eyes were dull. 'But success can only mean that a son will be brought to me in chains. It is the worst kind of disloyalty, Jade, passing that of women. It is certainly the most painful.' He gripped her arms with sudden strength. 'Don't let's talk of it any more. I need to think of something else – or better, not to think at all. I am tired. More than I had thought.'

She gave what comfort she could, but sadness weighted his response. They made love quietly and a little desperately. Afterwards he sank more deeply beneath his depression and left her sooner than usual. Alone, Black Jade herself went down into wretchedness because, after all, there had been nothing her love could do to help him.

Black Jade did not see Shih-min for two weeks. She spent the time nervously feeding new doubts and fears, and biting the heads off members of the household.

When at last he stormed in one evening, his whole body outraged with anger, everyone scattered before the dismissive sweep of his arm, leaving Black Jade to give three cups of wine and no words until he had drained them, staring darkly over the rim of the cup into the immediate and evidently hideous past.

She had heard rumours, but she waited for him to speak. He sat for some time, his eyes unfocused on space like an old man remembering, before dragging words from himself with infinite weariness.

'My son was forced to surrender to his own garrison; the army was faithful, as it has always been.'

'Then it is over? And you have many other sons who love you.'

He sighed, bitter as lime. 'When princes fall, they seldom go down alone; others are entangled in their traces. It is worse than we thought. One of the men we arrested in Chi Nan Fu has also confessed to an involvement which will not surprise you; he was engaged by Prince Cheng to murder his brother Prince Tai.'

'Oh, my dear!' She could not bear his hurt.

'It seems he blamed Tai for the discovery of that unfortunate affair with that boy I had executed. He may be right in that; I don't know. Also, he feared my anger would cause me to make Tai heir in his place.' He stopped, his fingers working on the stem of his cup. 'He planned, together with one of my half-brothers who has always envied me, to take the throne. The Gods alone know what troops he thought he would use! Any one of my guards would have torn him limb from limb if they had discovered his plans. It would all have come out, anyway. Treachery breeds treachery. He had no hope.'

Black Jade murmured wordlessly and went to take him into her arms.

'You are not surprised,' he said bleakly.

'No.' She swallowed. 'Are you?'

He spread his hands, a gesture of futility.

'Perhaps I shouldn't be; but yes, damn him! I hadn't thought there was so much of evil in him.'

'What will you do?'

'I won't put him to death,' he said harshly. 'That is what they all want, the Archduke, Old Integrity and the rest. But I will not lift my hand in blood against my own sons.' He shook the idea from him. 'I shall take time. It was a wide conspiracy. There are many accused. Some will die, no doubt, but I will show mercy where I can.'

Rebellion was a capital crime. It was punishable by death, not only for the leaders, but also for every member of their families, from old women to helpless babes. Relatives by marriage or of the maternal line were banished for life. Black Jade could sympathise with Shih-min's desire to be merciful.

She said nothing, but came to stand behind his chair and smooth his knotted temples with comprehending hands. Once more she wished with savage hopelessness that he were nothing greater in this world than simply her loving husband.

A few days later Black Jade was sitting upon the stone sill of the fountain in Green Fragrance Court. She had her sleeves pinned back and was disentangling the new spring shoots of duckweed from her prized blue lotuses.

Her mood was dreamy and disconnected. She had very few

thoughts these days. Her whole being was occupied in waiting; waiting for Shih-min to find time to come to her. It acted upon her like a soporific, otherwise she would not be able to bear it.

So now, half asleep, she tugged patiently at the fronds of weed, her mind a great white blank with the dark silhouette of her lover printed upon it. She had told everyone she wanted to be alone for a while, and they had respected her wish.

She was momentarily annoyed, therefore, when she heard swiftly running feet approaching through the empty upper courtyard next door. It seemed that she was to have an unwanted visitor.

A male voice cried roughly, 'Stop!' and the footsteps ceased.

'Oh, please,' implored another voice, much younger, 'Don't –'

'Don't do what, eh, you miserable little piece of monkey-shit? Don't wring your skinny neck? Can you give me one good reason why not?'

This was a voice she recognised, though its bullying, contemptuous tone was very different from the unctuous charm that had informed it when she had heard it in the stableyard. Without a doubt, it was Prince Tai. But who was the other, his young victim?

'You are wrong! You can't seriously think I had anything to do with it! Why should I?' There was desperation in the unsteady cry. 'It wouldn't make sense!'

'Would it not?' the Prince continued, a silky torment replacing the bombast. 'I think it makes excellent sense. You know very well that the Archduke and Old Integrity are urging father to make you the heir instead of me! You joined the Khan's plot because you knew he was as mad as a speared boar, and no one would believe him if he said he'd included such a useless little fart-arse as you in his interesting schemes for the future!'

'No, I didn't. I knew nothing about it! Why should he tell me? He never has anything to do with me. Please, I beg you to believe me – ouch! Let go! You're hurting me!'

'I will do more than hurt you if I hear any more of this plan to make you Crown Prince. You may mewl and puke and swear you are not a traitor –' an unpleasant smile seemed to hang in the air with these words – 'but it will do you no good at all. I shall simply hand over the evidence to the contrary.'

'What evidence?' There was genuine puzzlement mixed with the fear. 'There can't *be* any evidence. None of it's *true*!'

'So you may say,' came the sardonic reply, 'But you will find a great many virtuous men will say otherwise. And don't think you can escape the consequences. Our father is far too lenient in such matters, but *my* idea of justice is swift and sharp!'

A sob followed.

'Remember, little game bird – swift and sharp!' The hateful mocking voice receded and Black Jade heard the pad of his boots as the Prince left the courtyard.

When she was quite sure he was gone she ran up the steps and through the overgrown archway. A boy of fifteen or sixteen was sitting forlornly on the steps of a ruined cupola. Honeysuckle trailed around him, touching him here and there as if in sympathy. His head was in his hands and his shoulders were shaking.

'My lord,' she said, very gently.

He flinched and looked up, fear dying in his eyes as he saw that she meant him no harm. He was a handsome boy; beautiful some would have said. His fine features were familiar to her. She smiled. She was becoming accustomed to seeing echoes of Shih-min in the numerous faces of his children. Which of the younger princes was this?

'I'm sorry – I –' He was at a loss.

'Don't worry. He will not come back. I'm afraid I overhead your conversation. I live in the next court. I am Lady Wu.'

He smiled nervously. 'I know who you are. Everyone does.' To his heightened senses her beauty seemed to give off a power, like scent. Even in his distress, he envied his father. She could not be so very much older than himself.

He collected himself and rose to bow. 'My name is Li Chih – but most people call me Pheasant.'

Ah, the game-bird, she thought. 'What an attractive name. How did you come by it?'

He was embarrassed. 'My mother, the Empress, gave it to me. When I was a child I used to enjoy dressing up. I was always trailing about in robes that were too long for me, like a pheasant's tail, my mother said. The name just stuck.'

'Well, if I am to call you Pheasant, you must call me Black Jade. She told him, in turn, how that name had come about.

'And now, why don't you come into Green Fragrance Court with me and we'll have some nice cool sherbert? And my nurse has made some absolutely delicious honey-cakes.'

'I don't want to put you to any trouble.' He longed to accept.

'No trouble. It's nice to have a visitor. I don't have so many as I used to.' It was true; her friends called less often now that she was marked out for the Emperor. He found the noisy crowd of young concubines too ebullient for his recent sombre mood.

Jade led the boy down the steps and across the blue tiles of her courtyard. He still looked nervously behind him until they had entered the house.

'My mother loved this court,' he said wistfully as he accepted the sparkling sherbert from a blushing Sweetmeat, who was surprised that so old a boy should still be visiting the Inner Palace.

'One of her ladies lived here. I played here often.'

'I wish I'd had the honour to have known Her Majesty,' Black Jade said quietly. 'She was a most well-beloved lady.'

'Yes. I too loved her dearly. She was – she was my friend.' He stopped, unhappily contemplating the motherless present.

She offered him a honey-cake, moist and sweetly scented.

'It must have been hard for you to lose her. And your brothers – it would seem that they have not been your friends?'

'No. At least – especially not Tai. He has always thought me – well, beneath his contempt. It is because I prefer the quiet things of life; music, painting, poetry. I am not very interested in politics, or war, or even in sport, apart from archery.'

'I am fond of archery too,' she smiled. 'My father taught me when I was very small. He made me a special little bow. I have it still, on the wall in my bedchamber.'

Pheasant felt a warm sensation at the thought of her bedchamber.

'Perhaps we might have a contest,' he said shyly, 'if you would consider such an unworthy challenger as myself.'

'I should like that,' she said firmly. 'You must not think yourself unworthy, just because your brothers have mistreated you.'

She rose to refill his cup. Then she knelt before him with the same sympathy she had so often lately shown to his father. It was strange how alike they were to look at, and yet not one single expression had crossed Pheasant's softer and more refined features that had ever touched the stern and sensual face of her lover.

'You must not allow Prince Tai to distress you,' she said, speaking softly as if to a child. 'I promise you everything will be all right. You are going to stay here with me until your father comes – I am expecting him – and then we will tell him everything that has happened here.'

His eyes filled with tears. 'You are so kind. I don't know how to thank you. But won't my father believe Tai?'

'No,' she said very firmly. 'He will believe you, and he will believe me – because we will be speaking only the truth.'

'Tai wants to kill me!' the boy said with sudden hysteria. 'He will if he can! He's right about the Archduke wanting to make me the Heir Apparent. But I don't want to be! I *never* want to be Emperor. And Tai wants to so much! Why can't they just accept him? Buddha knows how glad I would be!'

'Hush. You mustn't upset yourself like this. Here, take these tissues and wipe away those tears. Nothing bad is going to happen to you. I have promised.'

He was very young for his age, she thought as she coaxed him into a semblance of normality. He had stayed in the inner courts with his mother far longer than was usual for a boy, and was now having difficulty adjusting to the man's world outside. She soon discovered that he was almost as afraid of Shih-min as he was of his brothers; but the fear was equalled by an adoring admiration in his father's case, so that he calmed down and listened avidly as she began to tell him stories of the Emperor's boyhood; of the time he had been stung half to death stealing honey from a Taiyuan neighbour's bees, or the time he had netted a leopard and brought it home in triumph, only to keep it awhile for its beauty and then set it free. Listening, the boy soon forgot to leave one ear cocked towards the door, and the frozen, white look gradually left his face.

He even asked Black Jade, shyly, to tell him something about herself. She gave a lively account of her own rivalry with her brothers and some of the amusing schemes by which she and Rose Bird had got the better of them. She also spoke of her love of books and music, of her rides with her father, and of the General's friendship with Shih-min. When she paused for breath the young Prince came and sat next to her on her floor cushion and told her with ingenuous simplicity, 'Black Jade, I should like you to be my friend, if you will, just as your father was a friend to mine.'

She was touched both by his sincerity and by his obvious need. She did not think he had made many true friends, in his secluded life, as yet. She reached out and took his hand.

'We are friends already,' she said warmly. 'That is what we have been doing this last hour – making friends.'

If her words thrilled him, the touch of her hand both did and did not, for it meant that she was thinking of him only as a child. Well-mannered young ladies did not make contact with the flesh of a man who was not a close relative. Although, of course, she must often touch his father. And more.

He flushed as he thought of what more must take place between his father and this, the most beautiful girl he had ever seen, and surely also the kindest. Something dark shivered in him which he was too inexperienced to recognise as sexual jealousy.

When, shortly after, Shih-min came in – in the first good humour Black Jade had seen him in for days – it was she who had to speak of the boy's trouble. Pheasant became tongue-tied, unable, as he had feared, to cause his father's displeasure.

The Emperor lifted a hand, as she quietly completed her revelation, as though to ward off speeding arrows. He closed his eyes and breathed, just once, very deeply, then opened them again on to yet another livid tile in the pattern of disillusion that the Gods were laying for him.

'They will kill me,' he said with wondering agony. 'Three of my sons – all would bring me down like a hind at the kill. How many more, I wonder, are waiting to divide the prey? Dogs and jackals! They are not worth my clemency. Let alone my tears,' he finished fiercely, turning his face from them and biting down on his sorrow.

'I tell you they will kill me!' he cried again. 'Perhaps I may even save them the trouble. What reason to stay in a world where so many of my own blood wish me dead?'

Black Jade was afraid for him then. She could not support such a change in him. Part of her almost despised him for it; that such a martial man, so great a hero and so skilled a leader, could be brought so low by the intrigues of a litter of spoiled boys. She would have killed them all for him if she could, with her bare hands and gladly. She ran to him and wrapped her arms about him, trying to give him her strength that suddenly seemed great in the face of his weakness.

'You must not speak like that,' she said hotly. 'It is not the way to think. Your enemies stand before you, each one accounted for. You have only to dispose of them as you wish. And if they are the sons of your body – well then, isn't it as well that you've found them out before their presumption had indeed brought you to your death? And you might consider,' she went on robustly, 'the ways in which you must have failed with them – so that they could have grown up to become rogues and traitors!'

She should have been appalled at her own presumption. Pheasant, listening, shrank into his cushion, certain that the heavens would fall about their ears. But all was well. Black Jade had judged her moment. She and Shih-min were too close now for him to insult her with conventional rebuffs. Besides, she was right, and he knew it.

He held her tightly, his lips in her hair. She felt the deep, despondent beat of his heart above her breast. He kept her close, drinking in her love and her strength.

At last he looked over her shoulder into the wide, confused eyes of his son and let her go, recovering himself as he smiled reassuringly at the boy.

'Well, Pheasant – the Archduke wants to give you the heir's crown; what have you say to that?'

'I – I'd rather not,' stuttered Pheasant, cheeks ablaze.

'No?' Shih-min laughed shortly. 'I can't say I blame you. You would open yourself to a life of lonely, difficult decisions – made as you dodge between the assassin's dagger and the poisoner's potion. Neither do I think you have the aptitude for it. However, you are the son of the Empress, you are young, and you are uncorrupted. You can be taught, and you may grow into it, in time. I should like you to try. Let us all hope you may succeed.'

He clapped the boy on the shoulder, not as an equal, but rather as he might calm a skittish mare who feared breaking-in.

'Come with me,' he invited, with something of the old, careless ring in his tone. 'Let us, you and I, go and try to put our ravaged house in order.'

Black Jade would never forget the irony in his face as he left the room, nor the desperate look of appeal that his son threw to her as, unwillingly, he followed him.

The House of Li was indeed put in order.

Shih-min stubbornly maintained his refusal to countenance the execution of any one of his sons. Their punishment was exile and degradation.

Cheng Khan, whose accusation of his brother Tai had, after all, been justified, was stripped to the rank of commoner and sent to a frontier town in Szechuan province, where his life would lack all further comfort or respect.

Prince Tai, whose evil was considered the lesser, was banished to Hupei province, his status reduced to that of a petty lordling and with the weight of his disgrace like a yoke about his neck.

The foolish young ex-governor of Chi Nan Fu was likewise imprisoned, far from the capital. The Emperor's half-brother was, as custom allowed, invited to take his own life, a consideration granted to members of the imperial family. His relatives were not, however, penalised. This clemency was repeated amongst the families of the minor conspirators, who themselves were all beheaded in the market-place of Chang-an as an object lesson to the innocent populace.

When the blood had been sluiced from the stones of the square, colourful tents and curious sideshows mushroomed overnight, and in the morning the festivities began which would mark the investiture of the new Crown Prince.

As he walked beneath a far greater weight than that of his magnificent crown, Pheasant's eyes raced hither and thither about the coronation chamber until they found the quiet green ones they were so feverishly seeking. His relief when they did so was so evident that Black Jade, after a smiling nod of encouragement, drew herself up and lifted her chin with a superb arrogance worthy of Shih-min at his most regal.

The boy saw what was her purpose and tried his best to imitate her as he left the hall to be greeted by the cheering courtiers. He walked tall and counterfeited a confident hauteur – just as though he knew himself to be, in every inch of his shrinking flesh, a proud and puissant prince of the T'ang, and the unassailable future ruler of the Empire.

The succession may have been settled but the Emperor's mind was not. His son's betrayal had aroused a wild sorrow in Shih-min that would allow him no rest. On many nights Black Jade held him, sleepless, in her arms, waking at dawn to find that she too had betrayed him in finding her own sleep so easily. Very often they would pass the night together without making love. The aptitude for joy had departed from Shih-min, and although Jade used every instinct to woo its return, it would not come. Those nights when he did not visit her or send for her became more frequent, and his days, she knew, were heavy with the sense of failure. To offset the gloom that surrounded them she found herself looking forward to the visits of the young Crown Prince, who now seemed to take for granted her close and personal interest in his fortunes. He brought her each new experience of his altered days, laying it at her feet like a friendly pup.

They had given him a consort, the Lady Paulownia, a member of the powerful Wang clan of Taiyuan, who were related to the T'ang imperial house. Pheasant hoped he might grow fond of her. Although he found her somewhat reserved, this had the effect of lessening his own shyness.

'And already she seems devoted to me. She is so dignified. It is unusual in a girl of her age. She is always grave and good, and though she does not talk very much she says what she thinks when she does, even if it is not always what others want to hear.'

'And you admire her outspokenness?' asked Black Jade a little enviously. She herself was having to learn, unwillingly, to temper her speech, lest her volatile spirits cause any further distress to the

Emperor.

'Yes, I do. I think she rather disapproves of our life here at court. She does seem to look down her nose a little. She is very religious and has, I think, absolutely no frivolity in her.' He spoke resignedly, as if a little frivolity would have been welcome.

'I expect,' he sighed lightly, 'that they thought she would be another good influence on me.' The Prince was now surrounded by a whole admonition of advisors, including the Archduke, Old Integrity and the formidable general known as the Great Wall.

'And is she also attractive, your little paragon?'

'She has beauty. But she is as cool as snow. She is not nearly so lovely as you,' he added impulsively. Then, more daringly, 'No one is.'

Black Jade attempted a look of motherly concern. 'Thank you, Your Highness; but you will find your ideas of beauty change almost as frequently as the things you like to eat.'

His smile was impish. 'Don't try to sound so elderly and experienced. I know you are only a little older than I am.'

'Nonetheless, what I say is true. And you should keep your compliments for your consort,' she advised. 'Perhaps they will have the effect of reducing her gravity.'

'I doubt it. She takes everything I say and do very seriously. But I was wondering if, perhaps –' he employed a winning note.

'Well, go on!'

'I'd be endlessly careful if *you* would be a little kind to Lady Paulownia. I'm sure you could make her feel more at home in no time; she has no friends in the palace, and will make none unless someone like you takes her in hand.'

Jade hesitated. The girl did not sound likely to be good company. But Pheasant was staring up at her in that intense way he had, with his father's warm, slightly moist dark eyes. She enjoyed pleasing him; it was such an easy thing to do. She had become very fond of him during the past few weeks and she wanted to see him as happy as possible. The more content he was, the more confidence he would gain, and eventually, 'after 10,000 years' (the accepted euphemism meaning after the Emperor's death), the more effective would be his rule.

She sent Chinghiz across the park to the Heir's Palace to invite Paulownia to take tea with her.

The girl was tall and thin. She held her back very straight and her chin high, but her eyes were cast downward and appeared to inform her of little of her surroundings that was not immediately under her undeniably aristocratic nose. She was, as Pheasant said, beautiful in a cool way, and had the abstract, disconnected air that one sees in a temple novice or a dedicated scholar.

She thanked Black Jade for her welcome, then sat down calmly to be entertained. There was in her demeanour a suggestion that it was she, if any, who was conferring a favour by her presence. She was here, indeed, only because Pheasant had desired it. She did not think it suitable that a Crown Princess and a daughter of the Wang should go calling upon a concubine of the Fifth Grade, even if she were the current favourite of the Emperor. Black Jade sensed this and began to wonder if what Pheasant had taken for reserve was better described as simple arrogance. She persevered for the Prince's sake, doing her best to show a willingness for friendship.

Their conversation progressed like a lame bird, full of false starts and odd little hops, with a basic limp caused by Lady Wang's unsociable habit of saying nothing when there was nothing to say. Jade soon became both bored and irritated, but she was determined to bring her visitor out of herself. With uncharacteristic patience she set topic after topic in flight, only to have each one flop at her feet, exhausted almost before it had tried its wings.

'You must find life here in the palace very different from your days at home in Taiyuan?' she persevered resolutely.

'It is different, of course.' The voice was low and non-committal.

'I found that I missed our clear mountain air a great deal at first. I imagine you have the same experience?'

'Not really.'

'Well, certainly, if one must live in a city, the palace is designed, above all, to make one forget this; we have so much space here and such abiding peace that one would scarcely think we inhabited the capital of the modern world.'

Paulownia inclined her head.

Yarrow and Sweetmeat, quick to observe a pause, came forward to offer delicate cakes. The guest waved them away without a glance at either girl.

Black Jade produced a bright tone. 'It occurred to me that you might like to make the acquaintance of some of the other ladies of our age? I would be delighted to invite a group of them here to meet you.'

'That would be very kind,' said Paulownia without enthusiasm.

'Then you must tell me,' Jade said nicely, curbing a sudden

impulse to fling her tea bowl into the composed lap, 'what are your tastes in music and whether there is anything with which we can especially tempt you to eat.

Unable to take a cake while her visitor refrained, she was now suffering pangs of hunger as well as annoyance.

'I am fond of all good music. As for food, it is not one of my preoccupations.' Her voice was without colour yet she somehow managed to make Black Jade feel both presumptuous and greedy.

'I can see I shall have to be careful,' she said drily. 'You know what Confucius said about the music of King Wu's court.'

'The Master said that it was perfectly beautiful but not perfectly good,' Paulownia quoted, adding politely, 'But I am sure your musicians will play only that which is both.'

Black Jade took this compliment as the sign of a very slight thaw.

'You are charming,' she said, 'but do you not think such a judgement a little foolish? Surely an evil man may write a good tune as well as a virtuous one?'

Paulownia looked serious. 'Such an unworthy scholar as myself cannot find the Master's opinion to be foolish.' Neither she implied, should her hostess. 'Indeed, as always, he is perfectly right. A man's character is revealed in everything he does, whether he is a musician or a minister, a peasant or a prince.'

'I disagree. A piece of music, a turn of strategy, or even a ploughed furrow may be good or bad examples of their art, but they cannot in themselves display the moral character of the man who made them.'

'And if a song were to glorify drunkenness?'

'As many do. I should judge the song and not the singer.'

'Then perhaps indeed I have cause to fear the music of Lady Wu.'

But a thin smile had appeared beneath the well-bred nose. Black Jade had unknowingly touched the Princess's weakness. Paulownia was both learned and intelligent and like most people who have these qualities, she loved to argue. And since in Black Jade she intuited her own opposite in every way, she had found the perfect partner in discussion.

Quite soon they were talking so energetically that she had rescued her hostess from starvation by eating three cakes without noticing.

Despite this hopeful precedent the party which Black Jade held to welcome her new acquaintance was not a success.

The apartments were beautifully decorated with branches of the freckled purple fingers of paulownia blossom; the food was delectable; the four maids played what was undoubtedly the music of Shun upon their lutes and low-pitched pipes; the guests had been carefully selected from among the most serious of the concubines, with the addition of Dumpling for light relief; their conversation sparkled with gratifying ease and they plainly enjoyed themselves – all, that is, except for the guest of honour.

Paulownia was simply no good in company. Her shyness overwhelmed her and she became a living monument of rock and frost. No kind questioning could reach her, no compliment evoke a response. She stood all afternoon in a corner of the room, refusing to circulate and clutching her tea-bowl in stiff hands. Occasionally she rewarded an intrepid inquisitor with a brief word, or more often a curt nod, but she would give nothing more, not even when Black Jade came and stood next to her and chattered like a magpie, drawing in everyone around them in a determined discussion of the recent events in Korea, a subject which must concern them all, not the least Paulownia herself.

Last year the Korean king had been assassinated and replaced by a ruthlessly efficient dictator, Ch'uan Kai-Su-Wen, who now controlled a puppet monarch of his own choice. Korea was, in theory, a vassal of the Empire, but this relationship had lapsed into one of normal diplomatic exchange. Now, however, her dictator had invaded the small kingdom of Silla, on the south-eastern seaboard of the Korean peninsula, which was also a Chinese vassal. He had closed the roads to the north, thus cutting off communication with China, but messengers had escaped by sea and had arrived at the T'ang court with an appeal for military aid.

Li Shih-min had decided to prove to Silla's aggressor that no tributary of the Empire should ask for his help in vain.

'All I want to know,' said Dumpling with a languishing look, 'Is whether the war will take the Emperor from us. For Heaven's sake, Black Jade – if you *know*, tell us! Don't waste words on boring ships and dreary soldiers.'

'I wish I knew,' sighed Black Jade sombrely. 'He talks of his plans and strategies like a boy with his terracotta armies, but he still hasn't decided whether he will lead our forces. All the ministers seem to be against it.'

'Let's hope they convince him,' Dumpling pouted.

'I don't agree,' said Black Jade, her voice rising. 'The council doesn't want him to go to Korea because the last Sui Emperor tried and failed to bring it to submission. It shows precious little faith in Shih-min. They seem to forget he has already brought the Empire itself into subjection. It should be well within his compass to put down one petty tyrant!' She was scornful of the over-solicitude of the politicians.

'But surely you don't *wish* the Son of Heaven to leave us?' Glad Lotus raised plucked eyebrows. 'My father, Great Wall, is quite capable of reducing the armies to dust – and as for the tyrant, he will bring back his head in a basket!'

'Don't be so disgusting!' yelped Dumpling.

'The Emperor's place is at the head of his armies,' stated Black Jade. She believed this. She was a soldier's daughter too. If Shih-min had even once encouraged her to discuss the matter, she would have told him that she welcomed his determination and would send him on his way with pride. She would not tell him, ever, how little she could bear the thought of his leaving her. She knew how much he needed this war.

Gentle Orchid was speaking kindly to Lady Paulownia. 'If the Emperor does march out, will he take the Crown Prince with him? It would be so sad for you, when you have been his consort for such a short time.'

Paulownia's eyes widened. She stared dumbly at Gentle Orchid, evidently deeply distressed.

'I'm afraid I can't tell you,' she said at last. She turned to Black Jade and made a hurried bow. 'I am so sorry – it has been delightful, yes, delightful, but I can't –'

She fled the room, leaving an embarrassed and sympathetic silence behind her.

'I don't believe it had occurred to her at all. Poor thing!' said Dumpling.

'Oh, they won't bother to take Pheasant along,' said Glad Lotus contemptuously. 'Even papier maché soldiers would be more use than him!'

'Don't be so unkind.' Black Jade was quick to defend her protégé. 'He has other virtues.'

'What are they, then.'

'He is pleasant, amusing and good to his friends. He enjoys life and is no one's enemy. He is kind and gentle. If he has shown no interest in warfare as yet, it is too soon to say that he will never do so. He would do anything to make his father proud of him. If he does go to Korea, you can be sure he'll do his best to earn credit. But you can't expect a boy of his unassuming temperament to turn into a great martial commander like the Emperor or your father.'

'Don't be angry. I didn't know you were so fond of him.' Glad Lotus was half teasing.

'I'm not angry. I don't want this war to happen any more than Lady Paulownia does.' Black Jade smiled at them all. 'Come on, let's play forfeits and forget about it at least until it *does* happen.'

When she learned for certain that Shih-min would lead the troops, there was no way to prevail over the shocking pain of the knowledge, even though she understood how important his leadership was to him.

It was more than the pride of a prince in being the foremost into battle. Day by day, as the troops mustered and the ships slid down their slipways, she watched her lover slough off the thick, unhealthy skin of disillusion and depression in which his sons' treason had enveloped him. He would stride into her rooms, his eyes bright with interest after a day's conference with his generals, reminding her of that first time she had set eyes on him, glowing with pleasure in the chase and her father's welcome, as they came together at that same spot where Wu Shih-huo had died.

He would swing her up and kiss her, his mouth tasting of outdoor things, the muscles of his arms like iron, ready to make love three times over, as he had been in their first ecstatic weeks.

Black Jade gloried in the change in him, and threw herself into the battle plans with an enthusiasm to match his own. She surprised him with her intimate knowledge of many of his old campaigns.

'You are more like your father's son that his daughter. You know as much about those early days as I do myself!'

'They were my bedtime stories, that's why. I don't think I realised, at the time, that they were all *true*. You were a legend to me then, riding out beneath your dragon banners, so young and bold and brave that I used to cry myself to sleep because I too had not ridden beside you.'

He kissed her softly. 'There will be no tears this time, will there? You will cheer me forward like the bright champion you are?'

'Yes, I will,' she answered seriously, forcing him to look into her face. 'But first, I will ask you this – only once. But I beg you to consider it. Will you take me to Korea? I would cause you no regrets, and you might find my company welcome at the end of the day. My father said he sometimes longed for the sight of a woman's face that was not one of the enemy and wreathed in tears.'

Shih-min was quiet, giving her the consideration she had asked for and deserved.

'I would like to take you,' he said at last. 'But I can't. It wouldn't be fair to my officers. Only the common soldier is permitted his camp follower. Generals must be more strict with themselves.'

'That hardly seems to be the right way around,' she smiled, giving no sign of her intense disappointment. She had thought he might take her; she knew he loved her enough to need her.

'No, perhaps it isn't,' he said tenderly. 'And yet, a general is unlikely to be killed; a common soldier very likely; so we shouldn't grudge him his small amount of comfort.'

'Very well. I shall not. I shall only grudge the length of time it takes you to reach a victory.'

'Spoken like a trooper! Oh, how I wish I might have you as my lieutenant! I can just hear you swearing at my batman and trouncing the captains at cards. And you would make the camp-fire music sound like the Consort of Immortals. Gods! But I'm going to miss you! I didn't know I could ever miss a woman so much!'

'You have not left me quite yet,' she said silkily, winding herself about him and letting her weight fall against him with the luxurious heaviness of desire.

'No, indeed,' he muttered, kissing her. 'But I must. Tomorrow.' He waited, afraid of tears from her because he could weep himself. There were none. He blessed her courage. By Heaven, she was more than worthy of an Emperor of the T'ang!

'Your skin smells of peaches,' he said, licking it.

'Chinghiz. He slices them into my bath.'

'An artist. But your taste is all your own.'

The familiar joyful ache began in her loins. She stepped away from him and untied the ribbons of her loose blue robe. It slid to the floor. She waited, no longer careless of her beauty, now that it brought him so much pleasure. He gazed at her, trying to do so intellectually, as an aesthete, knowing that he would only see her like this in his mind's eye for – how long? He did not know. For a fraction of a minute he succeeded. Then she made some small movement and he fell upon her, pulling her towards him with a foretaste of his coming starvation.

'I want to give you a child tonight,' he said harshly, in the words of all departing soldiers.

She felt herself turn to liquid mercury between his knowing fingers.

'Then let us make sure,' she said with only the faintest husky tremor, 'that this will be a night we shall remember.'

8

Paulownia was copying the Emperor's proclamation in a calligraphy whose pure strokes took the breath away. It helped her, she said, to forget how much she was missing Pheasant. When she had finished, the yellow silk scroll would hang on the wall of her chamber, a public statement of the compassion and magnanimity of the Son of Heaven to his enemies, even in the guise of a conqueror.

The proclamation represented the epitome of Confucian idealism as applied to the art of war: the welfare of the people as the only basis of good government. Black Jade, asked to admire these noble sentiments, gave an elderly little smile.

'The Emperor must always tell us what we wish to hear. If he does not mention the normal territorial ambition of an invader, it is because he is not yet certain of success. If he does not say that it is in our interest to maintain a divided Korea, so that Ch'uan does not develop his own taste for conquest any further, it is because it sounds better to say that we go to the rescue of the innocent.'

'Black Jade! That is at best cynical, at worst treasonable!'

'No, only realistic.'

'You accuse the Son of Heaven of hypocrisy.'

'Not at all. Merely diplomacy. In the end it is the result of this war that will be remembered, not the motives for waging it; should we not succeed it is as well if those motives are known to have been benevolent.'

Paulownia looked at her in wondering fascination.

'You are such a warm-natured person. How can you be so cold? Is it clarity that informs it – or plain misjudgement?'

Black Jade laughed. 'Neither. You forget how well I know my Emperor. Conquest is in his blood. But he is also a good man and he means what he has said in that edict. It is just that I like to keep in mind those things that are beneath the surface as well as those that are easily seen. Now, tell me, what do you hear from Pheasant?'

Paulownia brightened.

'He says that he is cold and tired and bored, that he misses us all dreadfully, and that if this is what it is like to be Regent, how much more insupportable it must be to be Emperor. He is joking, but only a little, I think.'

Pheasant had been left in Ting Chou, the northern city from which the army had begun its march to the border. His appointment as Regent was a nominal one, in case of the unlikely death of his father, but he was beginning to learn, under the tutelage of several guardians, the basic machinery of the administration of an empire. To Black Jade he wrote, 'Look after my dearest consort for me, and try to lend her some of your laughter.'

She also heard, rarely, from Shih-min. His letters were rather like military despatches, and she felt the spirit of her father very near to her as she scanned the racy, exuberant descriptions of his march across the border of Southern Manchuria in the wake of his 'Great Wall' and 60,000 troops.

The Gods were on his side. There was a resounding victory, with 20,000 Koreans dead on the field. 'How can it be otherwise', he wrote, 'when I am in command of my armies?'

It was the exultant cry of the boy who had first longed to be a general, half boastful, half simple truth, for there was no doubt that the presence of their legendary leader had inspired his troops to superhuman efforts.

'I will come home to you soon, my love,' his last letter had said. 'Soon I will know how it is to lie in your arms again.'

But that was not how it was to be. The stubborn and impregnable city of An Shih Cheng was determined to stand siege and recoup the lost honour of Korea.

Now the Gods who controlled the elements turned fickle. First the Dragon of the North Wind, and then his fellow demons of the cold, the rain and, at last, the snow, conspired to defeat the invader. Men cannot fight among frozen rocks in lancing rain or blizzards that provide an invisible cloak for native troops. The severity of the winter eroded the crops and pastures so that there was food for neither troops nor animals.

The Emperor was too good a general not to know when he was beaten. He had wasted three useless month on the siege. His last sight of An Shih Cheng was that of its garrison waving an ironic farewell as he marched away from its indomitable walls.

Black Jade received no more letters after that discouragement. She had to get her news from Paulownia, to whom Pheasant relayed his father's increasingly terse bulletins, or from Chinghiz, whose sources were, as usual, many and various.

The war wound down in a slow anticlimax. The winter

punished the imperial armies more rigorously than ever the Koreans had done; frostbite, dysentery and hunger haunted their ragged camps.

When she heard that Shih-min himself was ill, suffering a disease of the stomach that had not been strong since his brothers' attempt to poison him so many years ago, Black Jade was beside herself with worry.

'For the Gods' sake, why don't they bring him home?' she demanded of anyone who would listen. Have patience, they told her; they *are* bringing him home. Fifteen hundred miles is a very long way.

In the palace there was brave talk of the successes of the war – the cities annexed, the prisoners taken, the willing exodus of 70,000 Koreans to China, glad to settle out of reach of their dictator's extortions. But what Black Jade felt most deeply was what she knew Shih-min must feel – the failure to penetrate the main southern capital of Korea and the greater failure to prevent the continued rule of the regicide. No one could blame him for this. Not even an Emperor is master of the elements.

But neither, she knew, would he gain the measure of praise for which he had longed, the unalloyed recognition of a great campaign and a great commander which would have wiped the slate clean of the haunting shame of his son's conspiracies. There would still be a bitterness underlying the unavoidable celebrations with which Chang-an would greet its hero's return.

Black Jade had come to respect Paulownia during their shared separation from the men they loved. If she could not give her the easy affection she gave to the sunny and uncomplicated Dumpling, she could admire her for her determination to make a success of her relationship with her hesitant prince, and also for the seriousness with which she regarded her own life and the lives of others, even in the fermenting atmosphere of the Inner Palace. There was much to be gained from the differences in their natures and attitudes, and each was wise enough to learn from the other.

When Paulownia said to her hesitantly, when they learned that both Shih-min and Pheasant would soon be returned to the court, 'He will be very much altered, your Emperor – perhaps even towards you,' she took the words as gravely as they were given. It was something for which she must prepare herself.

And yet, when the shouting in the streets had died down and the ministers had heard the best of the tales of blood and guile, and they had let him rest at last and refresh himself, and think how he could adjust to being nothing more than an Emperor again, when for a few short months he had been almost a hero, his impatient mistress found that she was not, after all her efforts, prepared to meet the man who came to her at long last, and kissed her brow instead of her lips, and sat looking at her from the distance of a high-backed chair, his slender fingers tapping upon the head of the dragon carved into the arm.

He was so much thinner, and older. He looked ill, which was bad, and immeasurably distant, which was so much worse.

'Have you been well, my dear?'

She wanted to ask him why he mouthed such a polite nothing at her. He knew very well how she had been. Her letters had told him very frequently. She also wanted to say how sad she was that she had no son to show him on his return; even a daughter would have filled the aching gap that seemed to yawn between them for no reason, or for many reasons, but not one of them of her own making.

'I have been well. But the lack of you has been a great sorrow to me.' She would have gone down on her knees and laid her head in his lap, but his courteous nod paralysed the impulse.

Dear Buddha, was this how it was going to be between them?

She saw at once that, whatever there was to be done, it must be she who would do it. Shih-min was simply devoid of resources. He seemed hardly to know how to speak to her, sitting there so insubstantial-seeming beneath his heavy wine-coloured robe; he was a shell within a shell. He looked at her as though he were bone weary. He might just now have walked off the battlefield.

'What now then?' he said colourlessly. 'Have you no questions for me? No lust for the deeds of brave men and braver beasts?'

She shook her head. 'No questions, my lord.'

She began to feel the bitterness that consumed him. She thought she would give her life to lift it from him.

She stood, ignoring the distance in his eyes, and stretched out her hand.

'You are not comfortable there. You have a great need of rest. Come with me into the next room where you can lie and drink a little wine and perhaps sleep for a time. Or I could read to you, if you would prefer it.'

A look of immense relief was her reward; he had not the energy to conceal it. For the first time, he smiled; very faintly, but it was a smile.

'Thank you, Jade. I believe I would like that above all. Just to hear your soft voice flowing over me. I thought of that, sometimes, when I sat in my damp bivuouac.'

She knew what had been the reason, now, for his detachment. He had known that he would not have the desire for the clouds and rain; being unable to approach her in the manner which she might well expect, he could not come near her in any other way. She made quite sure that her pity did not show in her demeanour as she gave swift orders to the girls to make the bed ready, then to leave them a flask of rather rich wine, and go elsewhere.

She just had time to relieve him of the weight of his outer robe, before he fell on to her bed with a groan of welcome, murmured some grateful incomprehensibility and was immediately asleep.

She thought how the last few hours must have tired him, as he tried to bear himself like the conqueror they all expected, thinking all the time that he had been the loser, one whose proud promises now hung about him on the walls of his palaces, in mockery of all he had set out to accomplish.

Once again she was despairingly aware of how little human love can do in the face of a man's karma. She bent over him, feeling herself filled with a youth and strength that were of no use to her, since they could not help him. She resented every new line upon his beloved face; the threads of puzzlement on the brow, the deep grooves of disappointment beneath the curving moustaches which were no longer soft, but harsh and streaked with grey like his beard. She hated the pallor that had replaced the sheen of health on his cheek. She loathed the disease that ate away his energy and reduced the tautness of muscle and resilience of tissue.

It had not been worth it; not for half a conquest, not even had the whole of Korea made the kowtow of submission.

But these were a woman's thoughts, and he would not thank her for them. She drew her hand, just once, softly across the familiar surfaces of his sleeping face, and then she picked up her book of verse and began to read aloud, very quietly. He would not hear her, but perhaps some sense of the love and calm she wished to bring him would penetrate the clouds and dreams about him now.

She read on steadily until her throat was sore. After an hour she gave it up and asked Welcome to make her some rose-hip cordial to soothe it. Then she sat on the veranda with her book unopened in her lap, regretting what could not be altered and apprehensively trying to gauge the future. After a further three hours Chinghiz blew in, returning from a visit to the bazaars.

'Look here, mistress!' he called importantly, running up the steps. 'I've managed to get you some dried seal's testicles. If the

Emperor is half as debilitated as they say he is, you must put it in his food whenever you can!'

'Chinghiz! How can you be so irresponsible? For all you know, the filthy stuff may be poisonous!'

'Not at all, my dear girl!' Shih-min appeared, tying the strings of his robe and grinning sardonically. He looked rested, but sleep had known no alchemy to put back the fullness in his cheek or the glow of confident selfhood in his eye. He looked at Chinghiz with indulgent amusement.

'I believe your seal's balls are a most efficacious aphrodisiac. They also have the power to exorcize demons, and some say their decoction prevents one from copulating with ghosts in one's dreams – most unseemly behaviour! It will also ward off the attentions of fox-spirits, though I must say I've always found the thought of those, rather attractive. You would make a very pretty fox-spirit yourself, Beauty Wu, with your little pointed chin and your clever eyes. And let us not forget your long silky brush.'

He came near to Jade and stroked her hair. His touch flamed in her and she leaned against him in silent thanksgiving that he was no longer a stranger.

'Now, Chinghiz,' he said, holding her close, 'What is your opinion? Do I take your potion, ensuring that the clouds and rain are the fiercest and brightest we have ever known – and if I should not, will Black Jade turn into a vixen and disappear with my immortal soul in her mouth?'

'Your Majesty is making fun of me,' complained Chinghiz with pretended petulance. 'All will be well. You may take the medicine with every confidence. And in *my* part of the country fox-spirits bring only good fortune to those who love them.'

'Indeed? How convenient. Then I await your potion with the utmost impatience.'

Chinghiz bowed and withdrew to brew his mixture while his Emperor dissolved into laughter behind him.

'I suppose that now I *have* to consume the horrible stuff?' he moaned, drawing Jade with him into the bedchamber.

'Certainly. He'll be very hurt if you don't – as I will be if you don't kiss me this very second!'

When Chinghiz returned a little later, with a pleased expression and a cup of wine turned the colour of old, bad blood, he found his mistress naked in Shih-min's arms.

He tasted, then proferred the cup. The Emperor sipped obediently.

'Ugh! I knew it would be disgusting!' He handed the cup to

Black Jade.

'Coward! O Maitreya, you are right! Just – leave it on the table, Chinghiz, where we can reach it. You may go now.'

The eunuch obeyed, not without his characteristic sniff of disdain for those less wise than himself.

'Perhaps he is not so ill as they say,' he pondered as, his expression still pleased, he went to spread the glad tidings about the courts; the Son of Heaven had come to the Little Ancestress almost as soon as he had returned to the palace. It would not hurt her growing reputation for this to be known.

As for his private emotions, these were now well within his control. Soon, he intended his ambition for her to cloak them absolutely.

Despite his continuing delight in Black Jade, it soon became clear to her that Shih-min was a much changed man.

His illness steadily worsened, draining his energy and replacing it with a nervous restlessness that would not let him sleep.

Remedies were sought all over the Empire. Each one was found to contain more unlikely ingredients than the last, and none of them did any good.

With the failure in Korea eating at his self-esteem, even as the disease fed on his bowels, the Emperor developed an obsessive interest in the reputation of the T'ang beyond its borders. He spent many hours closeted with the envoys of the Indian states and the Khans of the Turkish tribes.

His confidence was somewhat restored by the successful promotion of the revolt of the Uighur Turks against their greedy overlords, the Sarinda. This campaign, master-minded by Shih-min and carried out by the Great Wall, increased imperial prestige so much that Chang-an was inundated with ambassadors eager for goodwill and trade, some of them from lands so far distant that even their names were unknown in the Middle Kingdom.

Black Jade was particularly fascinated by the northern barbarians; they came from frozen fastnesses where the days are short and the nights long; they were big, broad, fair-skinned men with round blue eyes and red-gold hair and beards, like demons. They wore horned helmets and drank fiercely. They were a sea-going nation with a tendency to pillage and piracy. Like all barbarians, their language was grotesque and ugly, and when written was clumsy and wasteful, using countless numbers of unnecessary characters, joined in ridiculous rows. It was impossible to teach them the good sense of having one set of characters to signify several different things, depending on the pitch of the voice, in the Chinese fashion. They seemed incapable of becoming civilised.

However, all such visitors were royally treated and sent home laden with valuable gifts. They were also given honorary ranks in the army of the T'ang, which, although its great leader presently dwelled upon its one recent failure, was to the outlanders an all-conquering machine of terrifying efficiency.

None of the foreigners were able to suggest any guaranteed cure for the Emperor's sickness. The hopes of the court were raised, however, when their own Ambassador Wang returned from India.

Wang Hsuan-Tse had been collecting the imperial tribute from the Indian vassal states. He had brought gold, slaves and numerous articles of artistic or religious value; and one rather special old man.

Narayanasvamin was tiny, bent, and wrinkled like a tortoise, as fragile as a butterfly cut out of eggshell. He was famous in India as a druggist and apothecary and he claimed – indeed he *looked* – to be two hundred years of age. He owed his years, he said, to the magical elixir that he had distilled after decades of trial and error, and which he now felt confident in offering to the sick Emperor – the Elixir of Immortality.

The will to believe in such things is strong, especially in the very sick; nevertheless Black Jade was astonished and horrified when Shih-min, the most rational of men, who had laughed with her over Chinghiz's foolish potion, shut himself up for hours with the venerable alchemist and gave every appearance of taking him seriously.

Secure in the royal patronage, the ancient settled in a comfortable house near the palace gates to spend the remainder of his immortality making up pretty little bottles for the ladies and gentlemen of the court.

To distract her from her disapproval of the little Indian, Shih-min made Black Jade a gift of one of Wang's more delicate spoils. It was a sensitively carved image of the Bodhisattva Maitreya, who waits in the Western Heaven for his incarnation as a Buddha, when all manner of ills will flee the world; meanwhile he exercises compassionate influence over the affairs of men in his half-human, half-immortal state as the Buddha-who-is-yet-to-come. He had been a favourite deity of the General's and Black Jade was very pleased to have him in her small pantheon. She prayed to him daily, as she did before the figure of Kuan Yin in her anteroom. Her prayers, she hoped, were more likely to help Shih-min than the vaunted elixir of life.

For a time, happily, it seemed that one or other of them did succeed; the Emperor enjoyed a remission of his illness and the palace was restored to its former gaiety. Black Jade continued her prayers, this time in thanksgiving, and devoted every other hour to devising schemes to amuse her love during his convalescence.

One of these was the production of a spectacular performance by a troop of magnificent temple dancers whom she had discovered among the Indian captives. Thus saved from slavery among the feverish southern swamps populated by murderous aboriginals and ravenous crocodiles, they gave their utmost. With all the silks and brocades of the subcontinent at her command, together with limitless financial resources, Black Jade discovered herself to be an impresario of considerable stature. All her old friends clamoured to help, and the imperial academy of music offered its services.

The performance was faultless. As she sat in the warm darkness next to Shih-min, and felt his eyes turn continually back to her from the whirling swirl of fast and furious colour on the stage, she felt that her life could have nothing more to offer. She loved and she was loved. He was well, and he was with her, and nothing else mattered.

That night the clouds and rain were very good. Shih-min's strength was almost what it had been when they first met.

The leaden months of war and disillusion fell away from him and he felt a resurgence of his early exultation in the perfect matching of their bodies. At first it was a mating of the eyes alone. They travelled each other's expectant nakedness with a greedy worship, dark and golden limbs illumined in candlelight. His first touch upon her breast drew a wild, demanding cry from her. He delayed a little, prolonged the exquisite ache of desire. Her thighs quivered; her face gleamed white against the black waterfall of hair. He plunged into her and at last they merged and flowed like the meeting of two great rivers after long separate journeys down from parched mountains. Their shared relief at the renewal made them both weep and as she stroked the tears from his cheeks with her loving hand, Black Jade trembled with a sense of the terrifying vulnerability of human strength.

'I am living through an hour of perfect happiness,' she told him seriously when the journey was done and they floated at peace, far out to sea. 'It is something I always think of when we are together like this, but never more than tonight.' His body was folded around her like great warm wings.

'To recognise happiness is almost as great a gift as the joy itself,' Shih-min said. 'How you have grown up, little Green-eyes.'

'You sound sad when you say that.'

He smiled. 'Do I? Then it is foolish of me. The happiness is also mine.'

He leaned over her and kissed her deeply, glorying in the miracle of her response. His face was fierce with love as he came into her again, and there was no further possibility of awareness of the hour, or of the moment, or of anything other than a pleasure as strong as pain, and almost indistinguishable from it.

Next morning, she received congratulations on her Indian dancers from so many courtiers that she could not keep count of their notes and visits. Even the Archduke unbent so far as to send her a brief billet. From Shih-min himself she had a tiny gilded image of the Indian god Shiva, who was known as the Lord of the Dance. She placed him thoughtfully in her bedchamber, where he could offer no barbaric offence to Kuan Yin or Maitreya.

It was a few days after this triumph that the Emperor suddenly became gravely ill. There had been no warning. It was as though his life force had been spent along with his great enjoyment, and now that the dance was over, he could not summon the strength to rise again.

Black Jade was devastated by the swiftness of the change. She managed to conceal her fears when she visited his bedside, behaving with a matter-of-fact acceptance of his relapse that she hoped might reassure him.

'It is often like this,' she said certainly. 'You recovered too quickly for your strength. Now you must do so again, but slowly.'

With his permission she dismissed his servants. As she poured some of the clear soup they had left into a bowl, she felt his eyes follow her movements. He said suddenly, as though the subject had occupied him, 'What a damnable thing prophecy can be!'

She carried the bowl carefully over to him, then sat down near to him on the bed while he should drink it. He sniffed appreciatively and took a few sips. She was glad to see signs of appetite.

'Prophecy?' she asked. 'How, damnable?'

'Well, when I was young, there was a prophecy that carried me towards victory as surely as my horse did.'

She nodded. Everyone knew that it had been foretold that the house of Li would rule the Empire.

'But the Gods are inconsistent. Yesterday I heard of a

prediction that would deprive me of all I have won! Have you heard nothing of it? The whole court must be alive with it by now.'

She smiled. 'I went to pray in Kan Yeh Convent yesterday – and Chinghiz is making his annual retreat in the White Horse Monastery, or I'm sure I should have heard.'

'Your Chinghiz will gnash his teeth when he hears what his long ears have missed – especially when he learns of the *name* mentioned in this disturbing prophecy.'

'Indeed? Why is that? And they are not long; they are pointed and rather pretty.'

'Oh, not another word against your paragon! But you should be equally interested. The prediction says that after three generations of the T'ang dynasty it will be replaced by that of a woman! A woman who ranks as a prince, and whose name, Little Tigress, is Wu!'

For a moment Black Jade felt her heart give a great lurch, almost as if he had accused her of some crime.

Shih-min was grinning at her in triumph at having surprised her.

'How extraordinary,' she said wonderingly, quite recovered from the odd reaction. 'The mandate has never come to a woman. It is most unlikely, even impossible, that it ever could. What do you think is the source of such a rumour? Whom can it serve?'

His eyes slanted with a mischief she was delighted to see.

'Is that all you can say? Don't you wonder whether it is your exquisite self who is meant by it? After all, you are well-known enough at court now to have some sort of reputation among the people.'

'Wu is a common name,' she said serenely. 'And I am no prince. As for my future 'dynasty' – I have no children.'

'You may have them, some day.' He smiled, a little sadly.

Pain shot through her. He did not believe he would live.

'Indeed, I hope so,' she said delicately. She bent to kiss him and he leaned his face against her cool silken shoulder.

'May Heaven grant it,' he prayed.

She must put sorrow to flight.

'There has only been one generation of the T'ang,' she said quickly, 'except for yourself.'

'True. This unlikely lady is not destined to make her killing until poor Pheasant has ruled. I only hope she may not snatch the throne from him in one of his more abstracted moments. The boy has not the stature for the work he must do. I will do all I can for him – but I fear for his future.'

This was a familiar subject, and one that always distressed him.

'But what will you do to curb this prophecy?' she asked brightly. 'Surely it is treason for such a thing to run freely on gossiping tongues?'

'One can hardly tear out the tongues of half one's population. No, we shall just have to hope it dies a natural death, like so many of these rumours.'

This hope was not to be realised. The prediction had got a firm hold in the countryside near Chang-an and was speeding outward in all eight directions.

Happily for Black Jade, who soon began to fancy that the court was indeed looking at her askance, the unwelcome fortune found its subject at a far remove from either herself or her family.

Shih-min came to her very late one night, half drunk and in a state of some excitement. Feeling much better lately, he had been feasting some of his generals. As the wine had flowed and the talk turned away from shared battles towards more frivolous subjects, he had happened to ask them all what had been their familiar names in childhood, the name which for every Chinese precedes the 'polite' one he is given at puberty.

'Well, at the end of the table, there was seated a general named Wu. When I asked for his milk-name he looked dreadfully embarrassed. I could see he didn't want to tell me. No wonder! His name had been "Wu Niang".'

'Fifth Girl!' exclaimed Black Jade. 'How ridiculous!'

'Just what I said. What sort of girl was he, such a manly and courageous fellow? He told me his mother had called him so because he had been sickly at birth and she wished to fool the Gods so that they would not take him from her.'

'I asked him then if he had heard of the prophecy,' Shih-min continued, frowning. 'He said not, but he looked uneasy. He wouldn't meet my eye after that. I don't like it. I think I'll have him transferred somewhere out of harm's way, to be on the safe side.'

'What harm could he do, even if he thought the prediction referred to himself? Here, in the palace, surrounded by the guard?'

'Oh, nothing probably. But his presence will cause more talk; now they can say there *is* a "woman" named Wu in existence. He's better off out of the way.' He smiled. 'That is, if he's not a beloved relation of yours.'

'No relation. But poor man! Just because some mischievous soothsayer has made up some nonsense.'

Shortly afterwards she was to regret her sympathy.

General Wu, smarting under his unjust removal to a frontier post unlikely to further his career, soon began to take a deep interest in the still-circulating prophecy. After consulting a Taoist priest known for his psychic powers, he became certain that it was indeed himself who was indicated as the next Emperor but one. Since he was already a man in his prime, he did not take to the idea of waiting for the demise of both Shih-min and his son; so he set about raising a force which would overthrow the Emperor and enable him to take his place.

Naturally, Shih-min had not sent him so far out of the way without several pairs of eyes trained upon him. His conspiracy was reported when it was just ripe enough, and General Wu's career came to a sudden and dishonourable end.

One morning Shih-min came to Green Fragrance Court straight from hunting. He was a little out of breath but his eyes glowed with something like his old fervour. When he spoke Black Jade realised this came of anger rather than health.

'This is too much! Do you know where I have just found that damnable rigmarole written up? On the remedy stone in one of the villages!' There were set up in public places, carved with a list of common ailments and their cures. 'I had it torn down, to relieve a case of terminal stupidity! By all the Gods, I've had more than enough of this nonsense. It is because they think my illness makes me weak that they dare to show such insolence.'

'I don't think it's that,' said Black Jade thoughtfully. 'I think it is more likely that they are fearful and want reassurance. You give them that by going about as you do, showing them that the illness has not conquered you. If they lose their Emperor, they lose their God. That village will have raised a loyal proclamation in place of that stone by now.'

She would make quite sure that it did so; Chinghiz would be her agent.

Although, on that occasion, she managed to allay Shih-min's misgivings, she knew that he was correct in his assumption that his sickness was the cause of unrest among the people. Not only was their once invicible, indestructible hero betraying signs of normal human physical decay, but also many of their other great leaders, the generals and ministers who had supported him in his rule, were coming to the end of their lives. Such deaths leave room for burgeoning ambitions, as well as for the prophecies which are their compost.

Perhaps Shih-min had recognised this, for he decided to lay the matter to rest, once and for all.

'I hope you don't mind, Black Jade,' he told her next afternoon. 'I have asked the Grand Astrologer to visit me here. I don't want our consultation to be known about the palace. See to it that your people don't talk. I'd like you to be a witness, if you will. It's as well to have someone – and I trust you as I would trust the Archduke, though I hope you won't lecture me afterwards as I know my brother-in-law would.'

She ignored this reference; she was still on very guarded terms with the Archduke, who disliked her continual proximity to Shih-min.

'The astrologer is welcome. I admit to a certain curiosity.'

She called Welcome and gave instructions about refreshments for the visitor, together with a stern admonition on discretion. Welcome promised the Emperor's favourite prawn and sesame biscuits and made a mental note to listen at the door.

When the astrologer arrived, half an hour later, it was Welcome who waited with Chinghiz on the veranda to greet him. As the tall figure in the long blue-grey gown crossed the courtyard, she felt the hair rise at the base of her chignon.

He was much changed, much older, but it was he. It was the man who had entered the Wu mansion when her Little Mistress was a child in her arms and who had turned their small, safe world upside down with his monstrous, wonderful prediction. She had been forbidden to speak of it and she had never done so. Often she had longed to tell Black Jade, but had realised that would only place a great burden upon her. There was no need for her to know. If that unspeakable fate were indeed to be hers, it would be so whether she knew it or not.

Welcome bowed very low as Yuan Tien-kang passed into the house. He scarcely looked at her. She did not think he could possibly recognise her. She had been a girl of fifteen; now she was a mature woman, and besides, who noticed servants? There was satisfaction in her smile as she watched him go into the room where the Emperor sat with Black Jade. He too, was due for a shock.

Yuan Tien-kang was older than his Emperor. His grey hairs suited him and his years sat lightly upon his sparse frame. Those who wished to compliment him remarked on his similarity to the known likenesses of Confucius.

His kowtows effected, he turned to thank Lady Wu for her

hospitality. It would have been a great disappointment to Welcome to know that he was not suffering from shock, but rather from the glow of satisfied expectation. Naturally, he had kept himself informed as to the fortunes of the daughter of Wu Shih-huo. He would have been very surprised, having himself read her those fortunes, if he had *not* discovered her, at some point, to be in the palace.

She was all that he had known she must be, he thought, as he listened gravely to his Emperor's questions concerning the newly resurgent Wu prophecy. How calmly she sat, attentive to their conversation and their needs, passing wine and biscuits with her own slender and steady hands. Had they ever told her, he wondered. Surely not. If they had, she could not maintain such tranquillity. At this moment she reminded him very much of her lovely mother, although of course the daughter was infinitely more beautiful; glorious, a triumph of the Gods.

'What I really wish to know,' Shih-min finished after detailing several instances of the prophecy which he had lately come across, 'is whether you can tell me if there is any truth in this wayward prediction.'

Yuan was quiet for a moment. He had known this hour must come. He had not looked forward to it. This was so often the case for a man in his profession. Even when one has reached the ultimate position, as he had done, one was by no means immune to the dangers; perhaps indeed one was more susceptible to them, since one dealt continually with the very great.

He had kept his faith with General Wu. He had not spoken. But the heavens may be interpreted by any who can read them. The prophecy had surfaced without his aid.

He finished his biscuit and wiped his fingers on the tissue which Black Jade had handed him with a sweet smile. She let him see her loveliness, her femininity, he thought, but her power, if she were indeed aware of it herself, she kept hidden.

'Naturally the story has concerned me, Your Majesty. I have already considered both the portents in the heavens and those on earth. There are those who say that the recent appearance of the planet Venus during daylight hours indicates the ascendancy of a woman; but I do not think that, in this case, we can deduce an event so far in the future.'

'Excellent!Then I need not –'

'– If Your Majesty will permit?'

'Of course. Continue.'

'From my own examination of the signs it is obvious to me that this prophecy *is* a genuine one. Indeed I am now making it myself, here and now, in Your Majesty's presence. The person in question is already living in the palace and is one of Your Majesty's household. In no more than forty years from now this person *will* rule the Empire, and will all but exterminate the House of T'ang. All portents show that this cannot be avoided.'

Shih-min stared before him, a heavy silence settling round him. His loneliness was almost tangible. Black Jade wanted to reach out to him but knew, at this time, she must not.

Eventually he said dully, 'And how if I seek out every possible person who might become this usurper? And kill them, every one?'

In other circumstances Yuan might have smiled. It is the custom of humanity to believe that fate can be tricked.

'The decree of Heaven cannot be set aside by men. If you were to exterminate every Wu in the Empire, nevertheless the one destined to rule would escape the massacre, while countless innocents would be slaughtered.'

'You are right, Yuan Tien-kang. It was an unworthy thought.' Shih-min was ashamed. He was also afraid.

'You say my dynasty is to die out? The House of T'ang to be reduced to nothing?'

'Almost to nothing. There is hope in that "almost".'

'What hope? Will my seed overcome the usurper at last? Or have I given life to nearly forty sons in vain?'

'I'm afraid I cannot see so far. Your Majesty must forgive me. I wish I might be the bearer of happier news.'

'You are forgiven,' said Shih-min ironically. 'Please leave us now. And if you should learn more –'

Yuan bowed and withdrew.

Outside, in the cool air of the pretty courtyard, he found he was streaming with sweat. He felt the interview had taken twenty years from his life, which left him with only borrowed time. Knowing what he did about the nature of the transcendent beauty who had sat so imperturbably through his revelation of her destiny, he thought that, on the whole, he would be thankful.

Her nature? Or merely her deeds? But surely these must be one and the same? A man's character is witnessed by his deeds. A woman's too. He shuddered.

He heard light steps and she was beside him.

He turned. Her face was full of gentle colour.

'Tell me, Yuan Tien-kang,' she said imploringly, 'has it never occurred that your readings of the heavens have been mistaken?'

He saw how deeply she suffered. She was hardly more than a girl as yet, and she truly loved the Emperor.

He sighed, hating to kill hope. 'I have rarely been mistaken, Lady Wu, and never in a matter of such gravity.'

She looked at him sadly. 'I would give my life to prevent the fulfilment of this fate.'

He smiled, carefully avoiding irony. 'I'm afraid that would not be possible.'

She bowed her head and stood still for a time, as though she might be praying. He wanted to help her.

'Honoured Lady, although it might seem to us now that there is nothing but darkness in this foretelling, it is entirely possible that there may also be a great deal of good in it. We foresee only events, not the reasons for them. The reasons may be very good ones, and offer the salvation of hope.'

She raised her head. 'Thank you, astrologer. I hope you may be right. It is difficult, at present, to be concerned with anything other than the immediate future. Forty years is – a lifetime.' He grimaced. Forty years ago he had been a boy; it was not so long.

'You will certainly grow in courage, Lady Wu,' he told her. The ring of assurance in his voice gave her an odd comfort.

'I must go back to His Majesty,' she said softly.

She has a lovely voice, he thought. Had he expected to find such a wealth of charm and freshness in her? Not, he was sure, to the extent that it was present. He could not begin to imagine this utterly captivating girl carrying out the actions he had seen in his heavenly mirror.

'Was there something you wanted to say to me, Honourable Master?'

'No. No, nothing.'

They exchanged grave bows and Black Jade went back into the house.

She thought that he had looked at her with pity.

When Yuan Tien-kang was safely out of the way, Chinghiz took out a bottle of the very special plum spirit that he kept for holidays and feasts. It was strong, fiery and vastly inebriating. He found Welcome, taking a well-earned rest in the servants' court at the back of the house, with her shoulders fitted comfortably into the split trunk of the great mulberry tree at the centre of the little garden. He sat down beside her and offered her some.

'Master Chinghiz!' Welcome was pleasantly surpised. The eunuch generally looked down his nose at her. 'I don't know that I –'

'Go on. It will give you an appetite.'

An appetite was the last thing she needed. Welcome was already twice the woman she had been in Wen Shui. But she did love spirits, especially plum brandy.

'Well then – if you are having some yourself –'

Later, much later, when the bottle was more than half empty, the steward said solicitously, 'I could not help noticing, Mistress Welcome – forgive me; it is really none of my business – but I happened to see that Master Yuan's visit caused you a certain amount of disturbance.'

Welcome floated down from the top of the mulberry tree where she had been enjoying a novel sensation of weightlessness.

'Not at all,' she enunciated with effortful clarity. 'Why sh'd you thin susha thingas that?'

'My dear lady,' Chinghiz said, his voice as warm and thrilling as his brandy. 'The last thing I would wish to do is to pry – but it perturbed me to see you so distressed. You went quite white, you know. As though the astrologer were a hungry ghost.'

Welcome struggled into a more dignified position. She couldn't defend herself from this wily Tartar if she were slumped in her seat like a sack of millet.

'You must've been mish – mis – taken,' she said stubbornly.

Chinghiz shook his head; tiny bells jingled. 'I think not,' he said. 'I think something is worrying you quite dreadfully. You would feel so much better if you were to share the burden.'

Welcome compressed her full lips; they quivered slightly.

'You know,' he whispered passionately, 'that all I care about in this life is the happiness and welfare of our Little Mistress.'

Welcome felt herself slipping; he was stronger than she. They both knew that.

He pressed her, his blue eyes outrageously concerned.

'It may well be that it could be – safer – for Black Jade, if I were to share the secret.'

Her round, kind face puckered with alarm. 'I don't know what you can mean by that. There *is* no secret.'

Chinghiz didn't know either, as a matter of fact; he was working by instinct as he always did.

'Think about it,' he said ominously. 'But not for too long.'

He rose as if to leave her. Welcome suddenly felt bereft of a friend. The blessing of the brandy seemed about to turn its frequent trick of bringing depression in its wake.

'No. Don't go. I – yes, there is something. There always has been.' Her eyes were dark with the knowledge she had carried for so long. 'I should not tell you, perhaps. Indeed I have sworn I would not. But – perhaps you are right. Perhaps someone else should know; someone who loves her too –'

He veiled his eyes beneath the long, demure lashes.

'Indeed that is so. I think you are very wise, Honourable Mistress. I am deeply touched that you should wish to confide in me.'

She was not sure how it had come to be that way round, but it seemed to be the right thing to do, after all. She would feel nothing but relief when she had told him.

'Here – take another little sip or two – just to oil the voice,' her new ally said helpfully.

'Thank you.' She smiled and drank.

Then she wiped her lips on her handkerchief and began to talk.

9

Whether or not the astrologer's revelations were to blame, Shih-min soon became seriously ill again. His appetite left him and the resulting curtailment of his diet left him continually tired. He could no longer take pleasure in hunting or archery, or any other strenuous sport. He could no longer stay up half the night feasting. He could no longer enjoy the clouds and rain.

Black Jade was with him constantly. If she could not be his concubine, she would be his nurse. She devoted her whole strength to him, feeding it to him with every mouthful of rice or soup.

At the beginning of summer, when the heat haze begin to lie above the city like a floating scarf, she persuaded him to retire to his favourite residence, the Kingfisher Blue Palace, in the cool foothills of the Nan Shan mountains, twenty miles south of the capital.

Knowing that he must now have only a short time left to him, Shih-min planned his summer with ruthless efficiency. There was a great deal to be done.

His main concern was for the future of the administration under the inexperienced hand of Pheasant. He took the boy and his solemn consort with him, as well as the man who would be his son's best counsellor, the Archduke Chang-sun Wuchi. For his own spiritual comfort, and equally for his amusement, he also invited an old friend, the scholar-monk Hsuan-tsang, whose breadth of mind was equalled only by the unusual extent of his travels and the girth of his person.

From a fabled journey across the mountains ranges of Turkestan to Persian Samarkand, then on into India through the passes of Afghanistan, Hsuan-tsang had brought back a priceless treasure in religious books, collections of sutras, and carved and jewelled images and relics of the Buddha Gautama.

On the blue-tiled veranda that faced the sunlit mountain slopes, Hsuan-tsang was trying to persusade Shih-min to give up taking the Indian chemist's elixir of life.

'I am certain it is doing Your Majesty no good. It may be doing much harm. I have detected both mercury and cinnabar in its concoction, and both are poisonous.'

Shih-min smiled at him indulgently from the daybed where he relaxed in a half-sitting position, Black Jade beside him on a small stool.

'I am not yet dead,' he observed dryly, 'so how can you tell whether it is doing me good? If I were to stop taking it today and die tomorrow, you would look very silly, my friend. As for poison, I thought medicine was based on the administering of such substances in the correct quantity. As far as I know, no one has died of Narayanasvamin's elixir as yet.'

'Probably no one else who is taking it has a chronic disease of the stomach,' said the monk shortly. His Emperor was trying his patience.

'Please let us not discuss it any more. You may give me a dose of that painkiller you made up. It seems to work better than most things. Is it your own, or one of Sun Szu-miao's?'

The great Taoist physician Sun Szu-miao lived a dedicated and reclusive life writing commentaries upon the works of the Lao-Tse and other masters of the religion and doing original research into the use of drugs and medicine. He was well-known for his collection of remedies in three hundred scrolls, entitled *Recipes Worth a Thousand Metal Coins.* He had also completed the first Chinese treatise on opthalmology. Hsuan-tsang had been his disciple for a number of years, often leaving his own monastery to work with the old man upon some project.

'This is my own. It's main ingredient is opium – but not to the point of addiction or poison,' he added grimly. 'As for the elixir – why cling so strongly to a sick body, when you may expect to be reincarnated in a healthy one; especially since, as Emperor, you will certainly return to earth as a Bodhisattva, and attain *nirvana* very soon?'

'Does it surprise you that I have no wish to die?' asked Shih-min with brows raised.

'Have you not? I thought you had,' the monk said cheerily. 'Otherwise you would not keep swallowing that infernal potion!'

'Confound you!' Shih-min was beaten. 'Throw the stuff away if you like! At least I'll be spared this wrangling every day.' He smiled at Black Jade, who was hiding her hurt at the talk of dying.

'What d'*you* think, Little Fox? Will I die tomorrow, without the Indian's magic?'

'I don't think so,' she said calmly. 'I have more confidence in Master Hsuan-tsang. He may not be two hundred years old, but he *does* look very much healthier than that shrivelled little Indian.'

The Emperor laughed. Hsuan's rubicund good health was almost an embarrassment to him; he looked like a very large schoolboy whose mother fed him too well.

At this point the Archduke was ushered in, his severe face brightening at the sight of Shih-min's amusement.

'I'm glad to see Your Majesty so cheerful. I think you will be even more so, shortly. I have made my report upon the matter of General Li Shih-Chi.'

Shih-min sat up intently.

'You should hear this, Hsuan; I have set my old friend a test.'

'How so?' the monk asked innocently. 'Don't you trust him?'

'Absolutely. I am, perhaps, trying to show him that he can trust himself.'

Black Jade, who knew that this subtle scheme had originated with Wuchi, studiously avoided his over-shrewd eye.

'As even a man of peace like yourself must know,' Shih-min said dryly, 'the Great Wall is now the most powerful and influential military commander in the Empire. It has been known in the past for such men to rise up and overcome a ruling prince –' he hesitated, his head cocked. Everyone smiled except Wuchi. For, of course, this was how Shih-min's father had come by his throne and the mandate.

'If that prince is as young and as inexperienced as my son, there is an added temptation. I have therefore asked Chang-Sun Wuchi to order Li Shih-Chi to a provincial post. And I have told my son that, if the General leaves without question or delay, he is to recall him after my demise and give him back his command of the armies. Tell us, Wuchi, what did he say, my trusted Great Wall?'

'I am pleased to report that the General left the city as soon as he received the appointment; he did not even return to his own house first, but sent orders for his household to follow him.'

An expression of boyish pleasure crossed the Emperor's drained features. 'I am so glad. I knew it, of course.'

Black Jade, who knew how he now feared betrayal, even in most unlikely places, rejoiced in the old General's probity.

'I'm not sure I quite understand,' said Hsuan-tsang, his genial face like a puzzled baby's. 'What sort of a test was this? Simply of his obedience? What does that tell you?'

Shih-min shook his head. 'No. It's like this; the Great Wall knows I am dying. Ah, now Little Fox, none of that! You are too brave for that. If he is content, when he is now at the head of the army, to leave the capital, one may assume that he harbours no disloyal ambitions; if he had demured or delayed, we would have been forced to believe that he has only awaiting my death before initiating an army coup. I feel damnably weary, all of a sudden, right now. Just leave me alone with Black Jade, if you will be so kind. We will discuss other matters later.'

She tried not to feel panic. These periods of sudden desperate tiredness were becoming more and more frequent. They sapped his strength to a terrible degree, and yet he would not leave off the work he had set himself to do. She helped him as much as she could, acting as his secretary, taking notes, running erands, keeping the court physicians at bay, even copying out in her own exquisite hand the book he was writing for Pheasant, the *Ti-fan*, the 'Plan for an Emperor'.

Hsuan-tsang left at once, after setting light to a taper of the aromatic camphor that eased his master's breathing. Wuchi started to leave, then turned and said, 'Perhaps Lady Wu would like to rest and eat now. I would be glad to attend you in her place.'

Shih-min smiled faintly. 'No. I want her with me. Thank you all the same, old friend.'

The minister nodded and strode off. It was by no means the first time that he had tried to take Jade's place; it was quite clear to her that he felt that *she* had taken the one that belonged to him. He was Shih-min's oldest and closest friend, the companion of his youth and the brother of his dead Empress. It was natural, she told herself, that he should resent her usurpation of his time and his affections.

Nevertheless, she wished that he did not dislike her quite so much; in her present weakness, it made her feel threatened.

'Sit close to me, sweet,' Shih-min said drowsily. 'I want to feel you near me. You're so lovely. I wish –'

He had drifted into sleep. She bent over him as she had learned to do recently, her heart dull and sick, to make quite sure that it was only sleep that had claimed him.

She stretched and leaned against the edge of his couch, breathing the pure, sharp tang of the 'dragon-brain' aromatic, the crystalline substance that Hsuang-tsang had discovered, which comes from the wood of the camphor tree in the far jungle country of Borneo. Sailors called it 'dragon-brain' because anything distant and precious was apt to be given the characteristics of dragons, the most magical and mythical creatures within their superstitious knowledge. Whatever it was, it certainly cleared the head.

Not that she wished it to be clear. She did not like what she was forced to see when her mind was fresh. Shih-min might talk of dying, every day, as he did, but she had not accepted it, not yet. So unrealistic had she become that she almost wondered, now, as the fumes wreathed through her sinuses, whether he had been wise to cease taking the Indian's elixir.

She was rescued from such negative meanderings by the soft entrance of Pheasant. She put her finger to her lips to warn him to be quiet.

'How is my father?' he whispered, looking with deep concern at the Emperor's sleeping figure.

'Tired. Too tired. He does too much. We'll go inside; we mustn't talk here.'

She waved to one of the imperial guards, who were on duty further down the veranda, to come closer and watch over his master.

Inside the pleasant studio chamber where Shih-min held small audiences, did his writing, ate and slept, Pheasant drew up a couch for Jade and took a floor cushion for himself.

'I am glad he has you with him. You make him happy. It is very easy to see that.'

'If only I could make him *live*!' she said fiercely.

'Perhaps you have; who knows? He might have gone much sooner, if you had not been here.'

'Pheasant, don't talk foolishly. His disease has it's own timetable. And it is approaching the end of it,' she finished squarely, her face set. Then, to the Prince's dismay, she laid her head upon the end of the couch and burst into furious, heartbroken sobbing.

At once she tried to control it, lest she wake Shih-min. Pheasant rose and closed the screen doors.

'Please don't! You don't know what it does to me to see you like this; you, above all people. You see, I have come to rely on you. I think of you as someone who is always strong. Please, dearest Black Jade – don't let me be wrong.'

She sat up, wiping her eyes on her sleeve.

'I'm sorry. I don't often let myself go. It's just that – sometimes I begin to realise, to make *real* for myself, just how it will be to live without him. I can't face it; not for myself; certainly not for you. All strength has its limits, Pheasant. You must not expect too much of people.'

'I don't. Not of you,' he said warmly. 'You have been magnificent. I've watched you. You have seemed so happy; just as my father is happy. It is like – like a bolt of kindly lightning – that shoots between you, forging a bond that others see only for a second, but *you* know is always there.'

She called up a smile. She would try to have finished with tears.

'You put it very poetically. I shall remember your words.'

He looked shy. 'That is kind. But then you are always kind.' He gazed urgently into her face. 'Oh Jade, I shall need that kindness even more when – when –' He did not need to finish.

She shivered, staring at the tormented, beautiful face which he held up to her like a cup ready to receive water. He wanted too much of her. She was not the one who must be his chief comforter.

She broke the thread of tension between them, groping for words which would deflect but not hurt him.

'You never bring Paulownia here,' she said evenly. 'Why not? I'm sure your father would like to see you together.'

Pheasant shrugged, disappointed.

'She came a few times, at first,' he said rather sulkily, 'But she could never think of anything to say to him. And his jokes made her uncomfortable.' He brightened. 'Perhaps it would be better if she came when you were here? You are the only one who knows how to draw her out.'

'Very well,' she sighed. Sometimes she wished, more than others, that the boy's mother had not died. 'By all means, if that is what you would like. Tomorrow. And now, I am so tired. I don't know why –'

'Of course.' He was solicitous. 'Dearest Jade, you look worn out. I'll leave you now. Go back to my father. He'll want to see you beside him when he wakes.'

She nodded, bone weary with the knowledge of his need of her. Go back to your consort, she thought; she is the one upon whom you should place your reliance.

She went out on to the veranda and sat beside Shih-min. At first she watched his sleeping face, trying to remember how it was when she had used to do so before; when she had always known that he would wake, refreshed and filled with joy in the new day that their last night's love had made. It had always been her luxury, as it is with a mother and her child, to watch him sleeping and know him to be hers. Now, it was an agony to her. How many more times would she see him wake? And what would she do when the sorrowful purpose of her watchfulness was accomplished, and he did not wake again?

On the loveliest day of the summer, the Emperor had them take his day-bed out into the gardens. They placed it beneath a peepul fig, the divine *bodhi* tree of India, under whose shade the Buddha entered *nirvana.* It was very tall and its wide, flat, dark green leaves gave shade from the heat to a colony of small, bright-eyed, black and white monkeys, as well as to Shih-min and Black Jade, upon whom they occasionally cast down an unripe fig or a broken piece of branch.

The whole of the small court was outside that day, which Shih-min had declared an unofficial holiday. He felt so well, he said, that he wanted everyone to enjoy the perfection of the palace and the glorious weather as he intended to do.

The tree stood upon a little mound, so that they could view the countryside in all the eight directions. The Emperor, one of whose titles is He Who Looks South, was positioned so that he might do just that, with the verdant slopes and the intricate, rocky heights of the mountains before him. Jade, who was sitting on cushions at his side, was able to look beyond him to where her companions from the Inner Palace were boating on the ornamental lake; their purpose was to collect the pink and white flowers of the floating lotuses with which to decorate the palace. The sound of their singing challenged that of the myriads of birds which piped and fluted among the trees, together with little clouds of laughter when someone's sleeves fell into the water.

The Archduke had been disposed to join Shih-min, but Hsuan-tsang had carried him off to belabour his unwilling ears on the subject of gardening and could be relied upon to wear him out.

Shih-min did indeed look so much better this afternoon that Black Jade began to allow herself to hope again. There was a bronze tinge in his skin and the harsh lines of his face had relaxed, making him appear more youthful than he had done since before the Korean war.

He asked her to read to him from the *Book of Songs*, choosing one of her own favourites. She picked 'The Ballad of Mu-lan', a story which she had loved ever since she could remember. It tells of a young girl who rides to battle in her father's place, so that he may remain at home to bring up her younger brothers.

Shih-min caught the little sigh that followed as Black Jade finished reciting. She had not once looked at the book.

'It was my sister's favourite too – but of course, you would know that. Do you still long so much to do a man's work, little Green-eyes? As you did when you were twelve years old?'

She shook her head, ashamed to be swept by old, forgotten longings in present circumstances.

'The Lady Hero is one of the few women who have turned their childhood dreams into reality.' She smiled at the memory of that quicksilver mind and body, and the friendship for which she would always be grateful. She had written to Hero, who would soon be here.

He took her hand and kissed its fingers. 'Have I caged you, after all, when I thought to give you some measure of freedom? Perhaps I should have left you to ride wild across your yellow plain?'

'No. No, how can you say so?' She was penitent at once. '*You* are my life now, and I could have wished for nothing else, how can you think so? I was looking back to childhood things, that's all. Dreams and fantasies, nothing more.'

He bent towards her and they exchanged a long kiss. As always, his touch had the power to excite her to the peak of desire. She looked at him, a half-question in her eyes; it had been so long now since they had enjoyed the clouds and rain. Today he seemed so much stronger.

But he released her gently and gazed beyond her for a moment towards the blue gables and scarlet-painted pillars of the palace. The faint tintinnabulation of bells came to them through the trees behind them; the girls had hung them in the branches of the pines and the cassia. An oriole flashed golden from the leaves above their heads, its harsh cat-like cry sentencing some tiny, gauze-winged thing to death. Rarely seen, its hidden music had teased them since their arrival in its territory.

'Did you see it? That's good fortune. It must mean you will soon recover!'

Shih-min pulled down his mouth at her, his way of signifying gentle disapproval. 'I hear enough nonsense from my physicians; I don't want to hear it from you. You are normally above such play-acting. Now listen to me, love. What will you do – after ten thousand years, as they say? How will you spend your life? I want you to think about it.'

She gave him a tormented look. 'Well, *I* don't want to think about it. How can you *know* you will not get well? You have been better every day since you stopped taking that Indian elixir.'

'Think so if you wish; it will make no difference. I am disappointed in you, my tigress.'

Her spirits plummeted. He was right; she was being childish, perhaps even cruel.

'I'm sorry. Forgive me. It was only my love that made me foolish; that, and the lovely day, and the flush in your cheek – and the oriole.' The Gods should not tempt us so, she thought.

He stroked her hair. 'No talk of forgiveness. If I won't let you hope, it is only to prevent hope in myself. Now tell me that you will make the life that you want for yourself. I couldn't bear to think of you wasting away in a convent. You are only twenty-four. You must marry, have children, become a woman of affairs. You were meant for a full life, not to be hidden in a bundle of dusty robes.'

She met his questioning look. 'I have thought of this. And I wish to enter the convent with the others.'

It was the custom that all the imperial consorts should take the veil upon the death of the Emperor, although some might be given permission to return to their homes and begin a new life.

Her eyes were filling with tears. 'Please, don't let us speak of this any longer. It is a beautiful day; we are making it ugly.'

'Very well.' He grinned at her. 'Do stop it; you look like an ill-treated fawn. Soon you will be writing one of those interminable poems about wet sleeves and moonlight. There's only one thing I need to say to you, really. It is this; I want you to promise me that you will do your best to be a mentor to Pheasant, when he is Emperor. He'll make a poor fist at it, probably. He likes you; he trusts you; and he's going to need you. He is my son, the part of me that will remain with you. So then – wring your sleeves for a time, if you must, though I won't thank you for it – but then, come out into the world again and help my son to be the ruler I'd like him to be.' He touched her cheek. 'This isn't a request, Little Fox; it's a command.'

She got up and made the kowtow. She could give him no other answer.

'I must say,' Shih-min observed, seeing her shut-in little face, 'I wish I might be reincarnated very quickly, and in the palace, so that I might see the woman you are going to become. I shall miss that. It is one of my chief regrets.'

'If you have your way,' she grumbled, 'it seems I shall become an interfering old busybody who tries to tell the Emperor his business. I should imagine his ministers might have something to say about that! The Archduke will be the first!'

'Oh, I am sure you will be a match for Wuchi,' said Shih-min cheerfully. 'You have the advantage of possessing a sense of humour. Not that you display much evidence of it at the moment. If you don't improve I shall have to send for little fat Dumpling to make me laugh.'

Black Jade tried to smile, but the day held too many changes.

Shih-min signalled to the servants who waited further down the slope beside tables heaped with food and drink. Loaded trays were brought and he scanned them carefully.

'Ah – just what you will like – golden peaches cooled in silver ice; the peaches from Samarkand, and the ice from the mountains before us.' He selected one for her and the servant sliced it neatly, retaining its shape about the stone, then presented it to her in a blue jade dish which also contained the bloom of a white peony.

She forced away her unhappiness and looked greedy to please him, feeding him every alternate slice.

'Let me taste you now,' he demanded, when the fruit was finished. They sucked the delicious juice from each other's lips, and found when it was finished that they wanted something more.

'Shall we go inside?' she asked vibrantly, feeling the swell of her breasts beneath his hands.

'No. I shall send everyone else inside,' he said. 'There are times when it is enjoyable to be an Emperor; one can get away with such unreasonable behaviour.'

He gave the order and the vast gardens cleared as if by magic, the sound of faintly disgruntled or scandalised voices gradually leaving the field to the chattering of the monkeys and the concert of the birds.

Shih-min rose and took off Black Jade's clothes, laying her naked on the day-bed in a nest of silks. He courted her welcoming body as carefully as he had done upon the first occasion he had made love to her, with the exquisite courtesy of the true lover, whose sensuality is very great, but never greater than his affection.

The clouds and rain were strong and beautiful and she knew that he was purposely giving her this hour to remember when there should be no more like it to follow.

She made this thought a stranger, did not allow it to follow her into the private territory they shared together. She would not give him the memory of a weak and weeping woman. If she must soon lose him, she would not lose a single moment of the joy she could give him. In love she had never been less than his equal, her passion and her mood the instinctive complement of his. She played upon his body with sensitive fingers, an accompaniment to his own delicacy. She traced the scars of battle upon his breast and his thighs, the fine mapwork of muscle outlined on his pelvis which allow it to fit so snugly into hers. She stroked the strange, metamorphic organ which had given her so much pleasure, smiling as women do when it stretched blindly into life. Suddenly, urgently, she wanted him inside her. She rose and sat astride him, sinking down upon him with a gasp of achievement as she closed on his hardness. When, soon, she felt the warm flush of liquid on her thighs, she thought with a yearning intensity that such a bountiful source of *yin* must surely give him back his strength. Surely it could not be true that he was going to die?

As if he read her heart he grinned and turned their bodies in a swift half-circle so that he was the one astride, laughing down at her, banishing the darkness again with the boy's mischief she loved in him. She laughed with him, proud of his courage eager to match it. They moved together in a glittering of locked eyes and laughter, brave and beautiful and perfect in love.

They lay afterwards interlaced on the couch, gazing lazily up at the dark leaves and the cloudless sky, serenaded by the oriole and its companions and reminded, from time to time of their vulnerable humanity by the well-aimed missiles of the monkeys.

'It seems you were right after all,' Shih-min murmured before they both lapsed into a contented drowsiness. 'The yellow bird did bring us luck.'

She smiled and pressed herself more closely to him.

After a time he said, 'We have loved each other well, you and I. It has been a great blessing.'

She laid her hand gently over his heart. She dared not trust herself to reply.

Shih-min died that evening at twilight. Black Jade was reading to him from the *Lotus Sutra.* She could not say at what precise moment he had left her, for she was accustomed to read, every night, until he slept. Her voice, he had once said, was like a melody made out of opium.

When she saw how it was, she laid down the book and covered

his body with her own, in a passionate attempt to warm him back into life.

There! Surely his heart was still beating?

But no. It was her own, dully and pointlessly continuing to measure an existence that no longer had any purpose.

She lay there for a long time, cradling Shih-min's face in her hands, stroking his hair, his cheek, his shuttered eyes; kissing his lips that had at last grown cold to her touch.

Her great loneliness had begun.

Later, when she had told them, she began to learn that the passion of loneliness was to be, for her, a luxury she was denied.

Pheasant soon entered the chamber and threw himself, sobbing, on his father's body. He was as incoherent with anguish as if he had had no expectation of the death, as wounded as an abandoned child. Ministers and courtiers stood round in wooden embarrassment as he threw away the dignity of the heir to the Dragon Throne and writhed upon the bed as though he had inherited Shih-min's finished torment.

Black Jade, white and wide-eyed with pain, touched his shoulder, gently pulling him back. He shook her off and redoubled his heaving sobs.

'Perhaps, Honourable Gentlemen, you would leave us for a few minutes? I am sure the Crown Prince will soon recover himself.'

They demurred, but Hsuan-tsang came to her rescue, clearing the room in seconds with his gentle insistence.

Black Jade looked at Pheasant with tired pity. The boy seemed to have travelled almost as far as his father, so extreme was the abandonment of his grief. Almost she envied him the ability to give it such a strength of outward expression. She wondered wearily whether she ought to slap him to stop his hysterical weeping. As though he caught her thought, Pheasant suddenly reduced the level of his gasping breaths, subsiding slowly into intermittent sniffling and hiccoughs.

'Good. That's better. It will have done you good to weep. But you must try to recover yourself now. I know it is not what you would wish to think of at this time – but there is the question of your face before the ministers. They will, of course, have sympathy with your grief, but they will only appreciate your demonstrating it at what they will regard as the appropriate time – during the funeral rites.'

Pheasant sat up, calmed by her low, affectionate tones.

'Of course, you are right,' he said shakily. 'I apologise. It was the behaviour of a child. I will also make my apologies to the ministers –'

'Oh, I don't think there is any need to do that. Your sorrow will be understood. And, dear Pheasant – you will soon be the Emperor,' she said very gently. 'The Son of Heaven does not apologise to his ministers.'

The boy's face whitened. 'Emperor.' He quavered on the word. 'Yes. I suppose I am.' He laughed, an unnerved and unhappy sound.

'You won't believe me, but – you see – I had forgotten that. I knew my father was probably going to – but it wasn't the same as – when it actually *happened* –'

He stared at her with such misery that her heart went out to him. Without realising it she held out her arms. With a deep cry he came to her and flung himself into them.

They sat there, beside the body of the father and the lover, the Prince wrapped in Jade's compassionate embrace, until Chang-sun Wuchi returned to see if his young master had recovered from his deplorable lapse from self-control.

Black Jade met his eyes over the boy's hunched shoulder. They were filled with a livid contempt.

Jade met the Prince again, just once, across Shih-min's coffin, where it lay in state in the incense-scented Hall of the White Tiger.

She had been praying there for some time when Pheasant came in to pay his own respects. They stood for a moment in silence, their heads bowed, when Pheasant hesitantly spoke.

'They tell me you are to enter Kan Yeh with the others.'

She nodded. 'I leave tomorrow.'

He cleared his throat. 'I wish you would not.'

'I'm afraid there is no other possibility. I wish to go; out of respect for your father, and because there is nothing for me here any more.'

The boy lifted his chin. 'My father told me, very soon before he died, that you would probably go there – but that you would return to court whenever I might ask you.' His look begged her.

'That is true. I made him that promise.'

'Then stay,' he said urgently. 'I need you *now*.' He came to her side of the coffin and seized her hand.

She freed herself. 'That is nonsense. And most unsuitable. Your Highness forgets that I am – was – your father's consort. There can be no possibility of my remaining at court.'

'But if I order you to? I shall soon be Emperor.'

'Then you should not begin your reign by flouting convention.

Your ministers will be offended.'

'I don't see why.'

Her voice rose slightly. 'Then I will tell you. I don't suppose you will have heard what is being said in the palace?'

'What do you mean?'

She looked at him sadly. 'The Archduke, having seen my attempt to comfort you just after your father had died, has spread it about the court that you intend to take me for your concubine, now that he is gone. Do you see now why I must leave?'

Pheasant gasped. 'How can this be – how do you know of this?'

'There are people who made it their business to tell me.'

'But it is such wicked nonsense! It is –' he stopped, reddening.

'Yes. But you see I must go to the convent?'

'Very well.' He was forlorn. 'But I shall soon send for you.'

'Give me a year.' She found she was imploring him. 'At least a year.'

'I will try,' he said, smiling shakily. 'But I do not know what I am to do without you.'

'You will be your father's son,' she said softly, touching his hair.

He let her go then, as he would let her go to Kan Yeh.

But he would be the Emperor. He would let her go, as was right and seemly; but he could bring her back whenever he liked.

10

Summer days, winter nights –
Year after year of them must pass
Till I go to him where he dwells.
Winter nights, summer days –
Year after year of them must pass
Till I go to his home.

(from 'Young Widow's Song', *The Book of Songs*)

Black Jade was working in the summerhouse. She had made it her own in the winter months, when its wide views and the sense of space they gave her recompensed her for the hours she must spend in the narrow confines of her cell. It had been cold, certainly, but she had wrapped up well and had set her feet on a firebox beneath her desk, with another smaller one in her lap, and had applied herself vigorously to the copying of the Mahayana sutras that Hsuan-tsang had prescribed as an antidote to the desolation that had claimed her soon after her arrival at Kan Yeh.

Now, with the hard-won acquisition of some semblance of peace of mind, she was able to look back with equanimity on those early weeks of misery and emptiness.

None of the women from the Inner Palace had genuinely wished to enter the convent. It was a mischance that they had not expected, the Emperor having died while still in his forties. Even the older ones among them had looked forward confidently to some twenty years or more in the palace. During the first weeks there was a great deal of coming and going of letters and messengers while many of the unwilling novices attempted to escape and go back to their homes. A few were successful, others not; some of the more contemplative ones settled down into the routine of work and prayer without apparent difficulty. To Black Jade, at first it simply did not matter where she was; Kan Yeh was, as were all other shelters, a place where Shih-min was not. No longer bound by the need to make a show of composure before the court, or of courage for the young Prince, she lapsed into a condition approaching that of shock. She felt nothing; there was only a great numbness at the core of which, faintly throbbing, was the knowledge of unendurable pain.

This first stage revealed itself to have been a merciful one when she entered the second, in which she became fully aware of her loss and was able, at last, to cast herself down into the deep pit of black grief that had been waiting for her. The discipline of her life fell apart and her mind became the habitation of broken, circling apprehensions and hurts; coherent thought was beyond her. The regime of the convent meant nothing to her. Her days and nights ran into each other without appreciable difference.

She wanted Shih-min.

Without him she did not exist.

The Reverend Mother could do nothing with her. Lady Wu did not eat, nor take care of her appearance, nor did she attend services or prayers. She did no work, she spoke to no one and she did not open any of the pile of letters that had come for her.

The Abbess was a kindly, bread-shaped woman, admirably suited to her vocation, both for her dedication and compassion and for her deep interest in everyone's business as well as the state of their souls. She had made enquiries as to who among the novices were Black Jade's friends and had set them in league to entice her out of her self-imposed isolation. It had not worked. Even the loving and patient Dumpling could not break the unseen cage of glass that protected her friend from reality. But she did have an idea as to the one person who might be able to do better.

When Hsuan-tsang learned that Lady Wu seemed intent on loosening all ties with the sensate world, without having established any noticeable relationship with the spiritual one, he descended upon her like a benevolent landslide. Books, wine, food, musical instruments, aromatics and more books tumbled in his wake, in the arms of a number of his own young novices from his monastery of Hung-fu.

'Work is the salvation of sorrow!' he bellowed, pouring wine and forcing her to eat as though she were a starving chick. 'It is far more important that the world should receive my sutras than that you should waste your time in this life in selfish and inconsiderate moping. Your Emperor would have been ashamed of you! Here – pig's crackling – scrumptious! Now then – you'll be working on the great *Yogacara-bhumi*. It's the most exciting of all, the very reason for my journey to India. If there's anything you don't understand, I shall be keeping an eye on you from time to time. And I'll send you one of my lads, now and then, to make sure you're not starving yourself. A sick body does poor work – and I don't want any mistakes!'

He had offered her no choice and, since some part of her which was still sensible agreed with every word he said, Jade obediently started eating, bathing and deploring her shaven head, and got down to the task he had set her.

She did not notice exactly when the transition began from complete lack of interest in life to a burgeoning fascination with the texts she was copying. She woke up one morning to find that she was glad to do so, that she no longer awoke to the knowledge of a sadness that was too heavy to bear. She had carried the burden of her father's death; now she would carry that of her lover's.

She did not expect to meet the equal of either man during her present incarnation, but she had been blessed with their presence as a brief gift from Heaven, and they would set the standard of what a man should be, throughout her time to come. And one day, they would surely all meet again, either in the Western Heaven or in some later life – just as surely as they must have met in a previous existence, to have loved each other so dearly in this one.

Her friends began to find that, although she did not recover her gaiety, they were welcome when they called on her, and the Abbess was gratified when she started to attend the services in the temple, especially when she heard how greatly Jade's pure voice added to the beauty of the singing. She opened, at last, her chestful of letters, and answered, first, the one from Lady Hero which ordered her to 'leave the convent as soon as possible – you were not born to turn your back on life, but to celebrate it!'

She spent most of her time in the summerhouse, however, where there was an unspoken rule that no one should intrude. There had come to be an exception to that rule, though nobody was sure quite how it had happened.

Every week, an attractive boy with a look of oddly adult humour about his wide brown eyes brought her figs from Shantung, or ginger wine, or the latest music from court. He also brought from her taskmaster a new supply of the best hempen paper from Szechwan. When she had finished, her scrolls would go to join the 200,000 others in the library of the Son of Heaven.

One day this errand-boy, Meng Shen, appeared at the summerhouse behind a large bunch of unknown greenery with bright emerald leaves and pale stalks.

'Spinach,' he said proudly. 'A transplant from the palace gardens. It comes from Nepal. You'll like it; it's different. I don't know yet, but I think it's very good for you.'

He gave her solemn instructions for the cooking of the interesting vegetable, warning that most of its bulk would disappear. It tasted, he said, a little like iron.

It soon transpired that the boy was engaged in the development of a scientific attitude to dietary matters. Although a Taoist, he scorned the uses made by some of the priests of such dubious substances as the bezoar stone, a concretion from the gall-bladder of an ox, or the verdigris scraped from an old copper roof, which they regarded as strong medicines. Shen considered that one's health had a great deal to do with what one ate, and that remedies should not contain any substance that is not normally ingested in food or drink.

'You are very full of ideas for someone of your age,' approved Black Jade, who found his enthusiasm congenial, remembering her own early thirst for knowledge.

'Only because I have had the best of teachers; Sun Szu-miao has let me study under him, and now Hsuan-tsang also.'

'Do you want to become a physician, then?'

'That is my ambition. I work very hard. I was wondering – you may think me insolent, but if one doesn't ask, one cannot receive. It is this; my mind is quite good, I think, but my calligraphy is horrible. Hsuan-tsang says it reminds him of worm-casts. So I thought – I have seen your own beautiful work – when you are not too busy, if you could perhaps give me a few lessons? I learn very quickly,' he finished hopefully.

And so, because it was good to have someone ask something of her again, Black Jade became his teacher.

Today, as she sat at her desk, looking out at the full-blooming June loveliness of the garden, she was expecting Shen to come running up the path that twisted among the peonies at any moment, for she knew he had a new recipe to show her.

When the interruption came, it was not the boy but the Lady Abbess herself, in a state of unusual fluster.

'Lady Wu! Great news! Gracious, I'm out of breath! You are to have a visitor. The Empress herself intends to honour you. Today! Hurry! You must make ready for her!'

Paulownia. Her quiet and contained companion of the war days was now the Empress, and had been so for nearly a year. They had exchanged a few brief notes in the past months, courtesies without content or character. But now she was to receive a personal visit. It was unlike Paulownia to make a move in another's direction; she must, therefore, have a serious purpose in coming to the convent.

The Abbess had hurried off to see that the Receiving Hall was spotless and the flowers and candles fresh, and that all her protégées presented themselves at their best. Black Jade, following slowly, felt an unwarranted weight holding back her steps. She could make nothing of this, so she ignored it, concentrating upon making the most of her cleanest grey habit and combing the short cap of hair that framed her face like the petals of the lotus.

The Receiving Hall was upon the opposite side of the cloistered court from the temple of the Heavenly Ancestors, where perpetual prayer was offered both for and to the departed Emperor. The sound of the drums, bells and gongs that punctuated the chanting provided a pleasant, continuous background to the entertainment of visitors and offerants to the convent shrine. When this was counterpointed by a murmurous clamour from the direction of the main gates, Black Jade knew that her visitor had arrived.

She reached the great roofed gate of the compound just in time to see the arrival of the imperial carriage, an imposing vehicle painted yellow and writhing with gilded dragons. With her usual dislike of having too many people around her, the Empress Wang had brought only four attendants, all of whom she dismissed at once into the care of the Abbess, saying that she wished to be alone and undisturbed with Lady Wu.

Jade led her into the smaller, informal anteroom of the Receiving Hall, and seated her on a couch among baskets of roses and lilies.

'Forgive my presumption, Your Majesty, but our voices would fly about like bats in the great chamber; we shall be much more comfortable here.'

'Black Jade, you are far too thin,' the Empress said, frowning and ignoring the pleasantries. 'I thought Hsuan-tsang was making sure you ate properly.'

'I do, I assure you,' smiled Black Jade. 'It is just that, taking so little exercise, I have a small appetite.' Lately she had begun to miss her rides in the imperial park.

'Nevertheless, you are to eat more.' Paulownia was now accustomed to having her orders obeyed. 'And you must let your hair grow. It's quite pretty, in an odd sort of way, but it is not womanly.'

'That hardly matters, since I am a nun,' Jade replied gently.

'You will let it grow,' repeated the Empress firmly.

The nun bowed her head.

She waited for Paulownia to give her reasons for her visit.

'I want you to return to the palace as soon as possible,' she said, her eyes cast downward in her unrevealing manner.

Black Jade felt a flutter of panic.

'But I have no wish to return. I have taken my vows and my life is here, in the convent.'

Not yet, sweet, merciful Kuan Yin. It is too soon, too soon.

'And if the Emperor wished you to leave? You have promised that you will give him your support and counsel.'

'I do not intend to break the promise I made to His Majesty's father; but surely, as a religious, I will be better equipped to give my poor counsel than as a lady of the court?'

'Nonsense! My dear Jade, you might one day make an indomitable Abbess – but you would never make a contented one. You know it as well as I. Your place is in the palace.'

If only I might go home, Black Jade thought, as she had before, home to Wen Shui, to my beloved mountains and the plain.

'I need you.'

The bald remark startled her.

'In what way, Your Highness?'

Paulownia seemed to crumple suddenly, as if her stiff white

gown had been holding her up and could do so no longer.

'Pheasant – the Emperor – has changed since you last saw him. He is no longer an uncertain boy who needs reassurance. In some ways he has become a man; although he has not, necessarily, grown up.'

She hesitated. She found it very difficult to speak her intimate thoughts, even to this warm-hearted girl to whom she had given as much friendship as there was in her solitary nature.

'Pheasant is trying to rule as his father would have done – but he is not his father. He has not his wisdom and cannot have his experience. Among the councillors whom Shih-min could so easily control, he is like a feather, blown on their breath. He knows they have no reason to respect him. I see how he suffers, and I – I sorrow for him.'

Black Jade saw that she would soon be in tears. There was more, she knew. Novices were not supposed to take an interest in court gossip, but Chinghiz and Welcome had relayed most of it during their monthly visits.

'You did not come to me,' she suggested delicately, 'simply to speak of His Majesty's inexperience.'

'No.' Paulownia flushed. 'Our relations,' she said awkwardly, 'are no longer harmonious. I have always loved my husband dearly, though perhaps I am not so – well-attuned – to the clouds and rain as he could wish – and as others are. It used to seem, though, as if he returned my affection.' She paused wistfully.

'I am quite sure that he did,' said Black Jade warmly.

'It is not so now.' The Empress steadied her voice and her resolution. 'As you know, His Majesty has taken several consorts since he reached manhood. He showed little interest in any of them after we married – until this year, soon after you left. Then he met Bright Virtue. She is beautiful and accomplished and enjoys the ways of society. She is nobly born and he has made her the Pure Concubine. He – my husband spends many of his nights with her.'

She sounded so miserable that Black Jade longed to comfort her.

'You are the Empress,' she murmured. 'There will always be concubines; but you are his wife and the first lady of the Empire.'

'I may be,' said Paulownia bitterly, 'but Bright Virtue has given him something that I have not been able to give. She has a son.'

Black Jade nodded. The Empress's childlessness had been the subject of Kan Yeh's prayers on many occasions. The Emperor's eldest son, fathered upon a low-grade consort, had been adopted as his heir until those prayers should be answered.

'Is Bright Virtue an ambitious woman?' asked Black Jade. If so, she might try to influence Pheasant to raise her son as Crown Prince, or even to depose Paulownia as being incapable of bearing a child. Such things had been known.

Paulownia met her eyes. 'Yes. I think she is very ambitious. She is also vain and frivolous; a poor companion for an easily influenced young ruler.'

'How do you feel I might help you?'

'It is hard for me to say this, but I know my husband has always had a special – fondness – for you. He used to listen to you, to follow your advice. I hope he may do so still. I know that you care for him, for his father's sake. I do not care how you do it, but I beg you to return to court and do your utmost to recall him to his duty.'

'I am sorry that you are grieving this way. If I can use any influence I may have with the Emperor to help you, I will; but I do not wish to leave Kan Yeh. Not yet. Not for some time.'

'Then how can you help?'

'Next month we hold the services of remembrance upon the anniversary of the death of the Grand Ancestor.' Her voice trembled; convention had taken Shih-min even further away from her. When an Emperor died his name was changed. Shih-min would be known to posterity as Taitsung, the Grand Ancestor.

'The Emperor will be invited to pay his respects to the spirit of his father. If he accepts the invitation, I will make an occasion to speak with him.'

'Is that all you will promise?'

'It is all I can promise at the moment. Perhaps, in a few months –'

The Empress smiled. 'You know it would not be seemly for me to *order* you to leave. I shall not do so. But be sure that the Son of Heaven will be present here on his father's anniversary.'

Black Jade bowed very low.

The ceremony had been very beautiful. Black Jade had stood among the rows of nuns in the incense-clouded temple, opposite the tall portrait of Shih-min which stood on a table before the altar of Heaven. Hoping that his spirit might hear her, she spoke to him with her heart.

'I shall not pray for your soul today. I have prayed for that every night and morning since you left me. I know that this is the day, above all, when I should do so, but, forgive me, beloved, there are matters in *this* life which must be attended to. You know that your son will ask me to return to the palace, and to that life for which you said I was intended. I will go, because you wished it, and – it may be – because it is ordained so. Perhaps, by now, you know *everything* that has been ordained. If this is the case, perhaps it is I who should seek your prayers, to all the Gods, both for the future of your son, who did not want to be the Emperor, and for my insignificant self, who has no wish to be taken out of this pleasant grave and returned to the centre of the world. O my dear, can my love still reach you with my words? I hope it may, for I cannot hold it back.'

The scent of amber and benzoin sent her into a reverie which was far from concerned with sacred matters, as she stared at his bold and noble face, fancying that the painted features came alive in the flickering of the candles. The lips seemed to curve in the private smile of amusement and admiration that he had kept only for her. She closed her eyes and felt his touch upon her, and her body and mind were ravished by his nearness.

The singing stopped. The service was over. Black Jade opened her eyes and knew herself alone. The portrait gazed, unseeing, into the shadows of the carved pillars, lifeless and one-dimensional. It was not even a very good likeness.

With apprehension, and a sense of excitement which she tried to overcome, she came out into the sunlight of the wide, cloistered court. She knew that the Emperor would be waiting for her. She had not been able to see him from her place in the temple, and would not, in any case, have looked his way. These last few hours had been wholly his father's.

A year was very short. It had not been enough.

Pheasant was standing in a group of courtiers, with his eyes fixed upon the doors of the temple. As Black Jade came down the steps he went forward to meet her. The courtiers murmured and spoke behind their fans.

The Emperor reached the bottom of the steps before his father's mistress. He put out a hand to halt her, so that she stood just above him. He bowed before her with consummate grace, and spoke so that only she could hear.

'You know why I have come. I have given you your year. Now I beg you, most sincerely, not as the Emperor, but as your true friend, to return to lighten our hearts in the palace.'

It was the speech he had prepared, but now that he was in her presence it seemed a tawdry thing. In no way did it express how she overwhelmed him, standing there in her simple gown, her head and back bent gracefully in obeisance, which was all the homage she could perform since he had kept her on the steps and thus prevented her kowtow. He had not expected this great swimming of the senses as her quiet gaze encompassed him. He had remembered her beauty, but had not known how deep and sudden would be her power over him.

Without being aware of it, he reached up his hand to her.

Fastening his eyes on hers, he let them tell her what was happening to him.

As she watched him fall in love with her, Black Jade turned cold with dismay. This was not how it ought to be. Indeed, it must not be. Then reason returned and she quickly collected herself. This was nothing; Pheasant was still the impressionable boy he had always been, despite his twenty-four years and the ceremony that now surrounded him.

She came slowly down the three remaining steps and stood facing him.

'I had forgotten,' she said gently, reminding him who she was, 'how very much Your Majesty resembles his father.'

Pheasant scarcely heard her words. Because he could not help himself, he touched her hand for an instant. There was a hiss of indrawn breath among his attendants. It was the first sign of the scandal that would surely follow. But he did not care.

He was the Emperor.

'Come with us now,' he begged, his brown eyes moist with longing. 'We will send for everything later.'

She met his ardent gaze very calmly. 'If I am to do that,' she said, 'there are certain conditions I would like to impose. You must remember that it is not my choice to leave Kan Yeh.'

He smiled, with a wisp of Shih-min's irony. 'Conditions? For your Emperor?'

'Yes indeed. They are these. Firstly, I should like Lady Precious Cloud to return to the palace with me. She is unsuited to convent life, and I would be grateful for the support of her friendship.' Dumpling loathed the cloister; she would be thrilled beyond measure.

'By all means.'

'Also, I should like my honourable mother, Lady Golden Willow, and my sister, Lady Rose Bird, to pay me a long visit in the palace. My sister was widowed recently and I know she longs to see her family again.' The sad news had come a month ago.

'I am sure their visit will give pleasure to all of us at court. Is there anything else I may do for you?'

'That is all, Your Majesty.' Her tranquil gaze distanced him from her, but he smiled, delighted. So little to pay, for so much.

'It will be pleasant to visit you again, in Green Fragrance Court. You will find everything as you left it. Your steward has kept it impeccably.' He did not tell her how in the early days, before he had known Bright Virtue, he had often gone there, to sit in her little garden room, trying to catch the lingering breath of her perfume. He had not known then that he loved her.

Bright Virtue. She had beauty and was talented both in the ways of the court and of the bedchamber. She had taught him a great deal and he was grateful to her. He would always treat her as was fitting to the Pure Concubine and the mother of his son.

'Paulownia will be delighted that you are to return,' he said, noticing now that Black Jade was thinner than he recalled. It touched him, almost to tears. 'She has been begging me to "rescue" you, as she put it. She has missed you, I believe, almost as much as I have done. Dear Jade.'

'Your Majesties do me too much honour,' Black Jade replied courteously. 'And now – if you will allow me a little time to change my clothes –'

The Abbess bustled forward to offer hospitality to the Emperor.

As she put off her nun's habit, Black Jade was forced to admit to herself that she would find it almost as simple a matter to put off her vows. She knew she had never had a true vocation. She had used the convent as a means to have time to herself; as a place to grieve, to think, to grow. She had thought no further than that, had not feared the unknown future because she had not yet begun to contemplate it. She had found peace, but it was not the peace of spiritual dedication; rather that of the mind that is left undisturbed by the normal demands of human relations.

No, she would not find her karma in the convent.

Would she, then, find it in the court? And if so, what would be her future role? What place was there for the favourite concubine of a dead Emperor? Certainly she must not expect to claim the leading position that had once been hers.

She looked about her at the grey walls of her cell. She would miss its simplicity. She would also miss Meng Shen, she thought, as she put on the lavender half-mourning robe that Chinghiz had sent her. It was improbable that they would meet again, but a bond had been forged and she would try to keep a watch on his future career.

As she unwillingly prepared herself to face her new life among the ghosts of the old, she thought of the charming, enthusiastic boy as her last link with the innocence of her own youth.

PART TWO
Summer Flowering

11

A moon rising white
Is the beauty of my lovely one.
Ah, the tenderness, the grace!
Trouble consumes me.

A moon rising bright
Is the fairness of my lovely one.
Ah, the gentle softness!
Trouble torments me.

A moon rising in splendour
Is the beauty of my lovely one.
Ah, the delicate yielding!
Trouble confounds me.

(*The Book of Songs*)

Coming home to Green Fragrance Court was a joyful occasion. The members of Black Jade's small household were waiting in the courtyard to greet her when she stepped out of her palanquin. Welcome and the four maids were weeping cheerfully into their prettiest sleeves, while Chinghiz, in an iridescent kaftan whose colours shifted like the flitting of gauzy wings, appeared to be in the grip of several emotions, chief of which was triumph.

He cast himself, with evident pleasure, at her feet. It was a courtesy he performed with particular grace.

'Beloved Mistress,' he apostrophised from the blue tiles, his robe spread like a peacock's tail, 'only tell us that you are truly happy to be with us again, and we shall ask nothing more of

Heaven for nine thousand years!'

Laughter caught in her throat where already tears were threatening.

'Oh my Chinghiz,' she said gratefully, 'You don't know how good it is to hear such nonsense again!' She signalled him to rise and impulsively held out her arms towards them all.

'Yes! Yes, my dear friends, I am very happy to be with you again – I have so often thought of you here in my little house, and missed you sadly in my daily life.'

'Honourable Mistress, live forever!' chorused the posy of maids, delighted with the compliment. They bent their slender necks like blown grasses as she passed between the guardian leopards, who were wearing scarlet bows in her honour, and ran up the steps into the green and white welcome of the house.

The sense of homecoming was overwhelming; she had not expected to be so deeply moved. Green Fragrance Court had been dearer to her than she had realised. And since all her friends had remained in Kan Yeh except the deliriously grateful Dumpling, she supposed it might now become almost as peaceful a sanctuary as the convent had been.

'Perhaps my life will not be so very different from what it has been for the past year,' she suggested to Chinghiz when, her unpacking finished, they were drinking piquant 'Dragon-leaf' tea in the anteroom, surrounded by a jungle of exotic plants which the steward had coaxed to extravagant growth.

His blue eyes regarded her thoughtfully. 'I should not count upon such a quiet life, if I were you, Exquisite Mistress.'

'Why not? The favourite concubine of the Grand Ancestor is of little interest to the court. And despite Paulownia's hopes, the Emperor himself will scarcely have a great deal of time to visit old friends.'

Chinghiz laid down his cup. 'Are you trying to convince me of this – or yourself?'

She felt an odd sense of danger. 'Why should I have to convince either of us? What are you saying, Chinghiz?'

'I am saying', he offered sweetly, 'that the Son of Heaven did not take you from Kan Yeh merely to have you create your own cloister in this courtyard.'

'No. He will wish to see me from time to time. He feels he can trust me, wants my advice. He is still very young. He misses his father.' Her voice shook a little and recovered. 'What he really wants is the reassurance he gains from the knowledge of my closeness to his father. I am a link with Shih-min, that is all.'

'Do you really believe that?' The caressing voice was very low.

She looked up, suspicious. His eyes were hidden beneath their ridiculously long lashes.

'Why should you think otherwise? It was the Grand Ancestor's own wish, as you know very well.'

Treading eggshells, he continued. 'I regret the damage, if any, to your delicate sensibilities, but the talk at court is not of your use to the Emperor as counsel and confidante – but of his intention to take you into his bed. Bets,' he added laconically, 'are being placed as to how long it will be before he does.'

'I see.' She remained, he noted with pride, expressionless.

'Better you should hear it from me than from behind the fan of some "well-wisher".'

'Infinitely. You are most considerate. Have you any other little pleasantries, or shall we pass the time in throwing knives at each other?'

'I am sorry; but you should be aware of your position. The knives will be thrown; rumour will follow your every move and translate it into scandal.'

'And is there anyone in particular who adds fuel to such rumour?'

'You mean the Archduke? Hard to prove. He's very circumspect.'

'I can believe that. However, you may suppose you have now armed me against my enemies, and we will go on to do the work for which I have been recalled.'

Her dry tone assured him that she wished to hear no more of rumour. Well, he had done his duty; it would do her no harm to think about it. And anyway, the future was not in her hands.

'You will help me, won't you, Chinghiz?' she appealed then, her brisk manner deserting her. 'His Majesty needs real friendship if he is to gain the goodwill and respect of the council; which he *must* do, if he is ever to rule as his father ruled. At present, inevitably, it is the Archduke and Old Integrity who govern the Empire, backed by the Great Wall and the army.'

'More or less. The Emperor attends the council, but they say he rarely speaks, having no confidence in his opinions.'

'He probably *has* no opinions, as yet.'

'Precisely. He tries to win their approval in other ways. He spends very little, for instance; rarely goes on expensive hunting expeditions or throws lavish feasts and entertainments. But somehow he cannot gain the stature he needs in their eyes. It is sad to see, especially as the Empress has already won the confidence of all the senior ministers, without any effort.'

'I'm not surprised. Paulownia is a serious and intelligent girl.'

'Unfortunately, hers is the not the greatest influence on His Majesty.'

Black Jade held out her empty cup. 'No. I should like to meet Lady Bright Virtue. You know her; does she present a real threat?'

'She is the kind of woman who has done so in the Empire's past. Vain, greedy, ambitious – charming too, particularly if one is inexperienced in recognising a well-polished veneer.' He admired his fingernails, which were a startling turquoise.

Black Jade sighed. 'Poor Paulownia. And poor Pheasant too. You do truly wish to help them, don't you, Chinghiz?'

Her sudden demand took him off-balance, as she had intended. Her questioning gaze was limpid with innocence.

'Naturally I will do whatever you wish, in all things,' he answered quietly.

'Good. It is only that you used to speak, once, of being ambitious – for yourself – and for me. I was just hoping that you had not considered that this might be the appropriate time for such ambition.'

'Certainly not,' said Chinghiz virtuously.

'Then we must do all we can to help the Empress.'

'Indeed yes. And His Majesty must be helped to establish himself in his council's goodwill.'

Black Jade stared into the past. 'Ah, Chinghiz,' she said sombrely, 'How much has changed. Can you imagine anyone daring to speak of Shih-min as we have spoken of his son?'

His blue eyes flashed. 'No, mistress, I can't – and like you, I am more than sorry. This will be a difficult reign.'

They held each other's eyes, conscious now of the deep, instinctive bond that existed between them, for which both, in their different ways, were grateful.

'I wonder,' said Jade softly, caught in his blue hypnotic gaze, 'what you and I were to each other once, in a former incarnation?' Then, realising the strangeness of her words, 'I mean, sometimes I feel as though you might have been my brother, or –' She left the rest unspoken, shrugging, with a helpless little smile.

A dark blue flame gleamed and was gone; he slid his eyes from hers with a calculated laziness.

'Who knows?' he said lightly. 'Perhaps it was on your account that I committed the sins for which I am now making a more than adequate recompense. For you – with you –?'

There was silence. She knew she should have reprimanded him, but it would not have been honest.

In tacit agreement, they let the moment lapse.

There must be no more such moments, Chinghiz swore to himself. They were a heady luxury which he could not afford. But his heart, which he was training to be passive and obedient, gave a great leap of unruly joy.

'We must be very careful,' he said next with businesslike energy. 'The Archduke is a very powerful man.'

'We will be careful –' She grinned. 'But even the Archduke can hardly object to my attempting to draw the Emperor closer to his wife.'

'That is not how he will view what you'll be doing.'

'Never mind, my Chinghiz. You and I will be secure in the knowledge of our unshakeable virtue.'

Her loving servant returned, with some pain, her sweet, conspiratorial smile. It hurt him not to be able to reveal the whole of his mind to her; but ever since his memorable conversation with Welcome and the bottle of plum brandy, he had known that he could not do so again for some time.

Black Jade did her best to bury her awareness both of rumour and of the expression on the young Emperor's face as she had descended the steps of Kan Yeh. It was difficult, since both were regularly repeated. She told herself that rumour (and the Archduke) was simply taking a mean advantage of a boy who did not yet understand his own emotions. What Pheasant felt for her was merely a residue of the puppy love he had given her while his father lived. If everyone was sensible about it, it would go away, as such juvenile passions always did.

She set an example by ignoring it herself, and by being careful never to be alone with Pheasant. She intended to woo him back to his marital duty not by the use of personal stratagems, but by social ones.

Firstly she insisted that Paulownia forsake the company of the older and more aristocratic ladies she preferred.

'They may be pillars of moral rectitude, practically on the threshold of *nirvana* – but they are also entirely lacking in any kind of style, vivacity or physical attraction. I am not surprised that Pheasant avoids them; they are dull, dull, inexcusably dull! Confucius,' she added treacherously, 'says you can tell a man's character by the friends he keeps.'

'But I *like* them. I'm comfortable with them,' grieved Paulownia.

'Old boots are always comfortable, but the time comes when we have to throw them away,' her mentor insisted.

In place of the mortally offended old boots, Black Jade cultivated a vibrant collection of dancing shoes. With the aid of Chinghiz and Welcome, who seemed to know everyone in the palace, she gathered the brightest of the new young consorts and courtiers into the Empress's spacious villa. They brought with them their music, their laughter, their flair and their insatiable passion for enjoyment. Paulownia hated them.

The invitations always went out under the Empress's signature, but try as she might to make the unsociable girl the centre of each little occasion, so that her husband might see her thus favourably lit, it was about her own warm candle that the young people circled. They found Lady Wu enchanting; so lovely and welcoming, and so *interested* in them all – no wonder, they whispered, that His Majesty was, well, *you* know –

Her consolation lay in the fact that Pheasant did, at least, come regularly to these gatherings, and seemed to enjoy them. She was less pleased to discover that he was as eager for her own conversation as for that of his wife. He would sit dutifully beside Paulownia for the first half of a concert or a soirée, but somehow he would always find his way to Jade's side soon after.

'You are going to have to try harder,' the vexed go-between told the Empress privately. 'Polite conversation simply isn't enough! Why can't you just relax and be yourself with Pheasant, as you used to?'

'Because I know *he* doesn't feel as he used to,' replied Paulownia miserably. 'And anyway, you know how difficult I find it to behave naturally in front of so many people. It just makes me feel old and sensible. I'm afraid I was *born* old and sensible.'

'You'll be old soon enough! Don't you ever want to simply to enjoy a few things? There was splendid music yesterday – didn't you take pleasure in that?'

'Yes – but everyone was laughing and talking all the way through. I wanted to send them all packing.'

Black Jade despaired. But she knew she must not.

'You will just have to learn to pretend,' she said directly. 'Pheasant is a normal, pleasure-loving young man with all the appetites one would expect of him – and the power to satisfy them all ten thousand times over. Why should he choose the company of a cool, stand-offish girl who can't enjoy herself, when he has so many others at his command? Paulownia, you must become more realistic, or we shall not succeed.'

'I'm sure you're right, Black Jade, but I am as I am – and it is not in my nature to dissemble.'

Black Jade groaned.

'Pheasant would not be deceived if I were to change,' the young Empress added sadly. 'He knows me too well.'

'I suppose there's something in that.' Jade had a more delicate matter to discuss. 'Tell me, if you will, how is it between you otherwise? What about the clouds and rain?'

Paulownia became desolate. 'He does not visit me any more often; perhaps about twice a month, on my days of conception.'

'Then you will have to attempt to seduce him.'

Paulownia frowned. 'I am the Empress. I leave seduction to such women as Bright Virtue.'

'Very well. If you do that, you will certainly lose him. Oh, my dear friend, don't look like that. I don't say such things to be cruel, but only to try to shake you into some sort of comprehension of how things are.'

'I wish,' said Paulownia dully, 'that they had let me stay in Taiyuan. I wanted to enter the convent, you know. It's ironic, isn't it? You are so glad to be free of Kan Yeh, while I, who wear the Phoenix Crown, would fly there tomorrow if I could.'

'I'm sorry, Paulownia,' Jade said gently. 'So very sorry.'

'You see – I don't really enjoy the clouds and rain – or at least, not as I understand others do. I want to please Pheasant, because I truly love him – but I have never experienced the joyful abandon of which you have spoken; I think I never will. So you see, it is difficult for me to think in terms of "seduction".' She ended with a shy, forlorn smile.

Black Jade coaxed her with kindness until her dark mood had lifted, but, as she later reported to Chinghiz, she could think of no other way, other than that of nature, to bring the estranged pair together.

'These are early days,' the steward reminded her. 'We must continue as we are; the Emperor finds it pleasant to visit Lady Paulownia's apartments when you are there to bring them alive. Perhaps you should invite Their Majesties here together. Perhaps the lady will relax more if she is not the hostess.' He was smugly conscious of a different motive behind the innocent suggestion.

Jade determined to act on this advice. Soon, it seemed as though she had never left Green Fragrance Court. The faces were different, but the laughter and the gaiety were just as they had been, with the daring addition of a deeper note, for, now that she moved in the highest imperial circle, the company of a few carefully chosen young men was permitted, as long as the party was scrupulously chaperoned by the eunuchs. Pheasant felt more at ease with such friends about him.

One afternoon a small crowd had gathered to play at charades in Black Jade's courtyard. The Emperor arrived in obvious good form, laughing and talking with a tall girl who walked beside him.

'Maitreya! It's Bright Virtue. I'd better send a message to the Empress. Or should we let them meet?' Chinghiz cocked a malicious eye.

'Of course not! Don't be so unkind. And hurry with that message!'

Black Jade went forward to welcome Pheasant.

So this was Bright Virtue. Beautiful certainly, but with the closed look of those who gaze too long into the mirror. A fine-boned, deceptively fragile face that would rarely express the truth of ambition; a slender, full-breasted body wrapped in the very latest style, a tight little silk top and jacket, embroidered with birds, and a matching skirt in thinner silk, daringly showing half an inch of golden flesh at the waist. Her shape was pleasing but not poetic, Black Jade decided, recognising her own beauty to be superior and wondering why this should satisfy her; she was usually above such idiotic vanity. Perhaps it was because, even before Pheasant had made his slightly smug introductions, she had decided that she did not like Bright Virtue.

As she curtsied faultlessly, both hands placed neatly upon her right hip, to the girl who so far outranked her, she wondered fleetingly just what rank she herself *did* hold, now that she was not actively a fifth-grade concubine. No one seemed to have thought about it, not even the protocol-conscious Archduke.

The Pure Concubine inclined her head, not very far.

'I am delighted to make the acquaintance of Lady Wu. I have heard that all the pleasure in the palace is to be found in her courtyard.' She looked about, by no means vaguely, Jade noted; she would know exactly who was, and who was not, here.

'Tell me,' the visitor asked pleasantly, when she had chosen a seat between the Emperor and her hostess and been given grape wine in a translucent jadite cup, 'don't you find it rather taxing, all this entertaining? I should have thought it the last manner in which an avowed nun would wish to spend her time.'

'Not at all.' Black Jade was equally pleasant. 'I have left the convent for ever, Lady Virtue.'

The Pure Concubine drew violet brows towards each other. 'I see. Then you have – how does one put it – broken your vows?'

'One may put it like that. They were the vows of a novice, which may be annulled in certain circumstances. I did not take the final vows – or I should not be here.'

Pheasant was both amused and bemused. He thought he quite enjoyed the fact that these two so evidently disliked each other; but he was not absolutely sure.

'We are all eternally grateful that you had *not* taken the final steps,' he said firmly, passing her a Damascus fig which Chinghiz had peeled for him. Bright Virtue gritted her teeth.

Feeling the air about him begin to crackle, the Emperor suggested that they get on with the charades. It was a game he enjoyed; it was considered novel and daring.

They decided to begin by miming the characteristics of various deities. Black Jade invited the Pure Concubine to begin.

Bright Virtue's choice was a simple one. She rose and went over to the fig tree in the north-west corner of the court; she sat down beneath it in the lotus position and looked hard and solemnly into space. She was, everyone recognised, contemplating infinity.

'She's the Buddha Gautama!' shouted a young exquisite in puce.

'Wait! It isn't finished,' he was advised.

Bright Virtue now passed an expression of intense ecstacy across her delicate features, rather as one might a face flannel. Then she rose and walked, trancelike, as if on wheels, towards the steps to the 'stage' of mischievous repute. She began gracefully to ascend and then something seemed to strike her – on the left ear, judging by the way she cupped it in both hands. Then, with a look of intense longing (or profound stomach-ache), she turned back towards the admiring audience and slowly began to descend.

'It's Kuan Yin,' they all howled, delighted to have been given such an easy one. Indeed it was; nothing less than Kuan Yin, the supreme representation of compassionate womanhood, the Goddess who, at the moment of attaining her own *nirvana*, had heard the concerted cry of suffering humanity and turned back to give it hope, vowing to postpone her own deification until every living creature had reached her own sublime height of consciousness. An easy choice; also a presumptuous one.

'Let's have Lady Wu next!' cried the puce person.

'Yes, Black Jade!' they all agreed. 'Not too easy, this time!'

It seemed that Lady Wu, too, would make use of the natural stage at the top of the north steps. She ran up to it quickly and lightly, in a dancing parody of human movement. Halfway, she turned and pounced on the trailing end of her skirt, then skipped to the top where she arrived with a jubilant leap. Then she scratched herself thoughtfully and strode about as if new to the place, poking this and that and occasionally pulling her ears.

The audience were delighted. They loved her for forsaking dignity in the cause of comedy, a gift that very few women possessed.

'She's an animal!' Lord Puce discovered.

'Anyone can see *that*, ninny! But which animal?'

'A – a cat!' the young dandy hazarded. 'She washed behind her ears. She's a cat goddess!'

'*Is* there a cat goddess?' somebody wondered.

'There's got to be! There's one for everything else!'

'Is he right, Black Jade? Is that what you are?' There was a helpful chorus of miaowing and tomcat howls.

'No. I'm afraid not,' Jade regretted, grinning in what really was a recognisably catlike fashion. 'You should have let me finish.'

'Go on, then.'

'No! No – he has to pay the forfeit first!' It was Dumpling's voice which insisted. She rather liked the young man in puce, and was happy to draw herself to his attention in this way.

'It's the rule! If someone guesses wrongly they pay up at once.'

'Oh, all right. Give him a forfeit, Black Jade!'

'Not me. I think His Majesty should give the forfeits.'

It was, naturally, a popular choice. Pheasant thought hard. He wanted to please them, and make them sit up a little. Dispensing with the usual invitations to sing or tell jokes or recite Confucius backwards, he fixed the young lord, who was now wafting himself with a plum and magenta fan, with a mock-funereal eye and growled, 'Tell us, immediately, what is the most exquisitely hideous death you have ever heard of?'

The concubines squealed rewardingly, while it was Lord Puce's turn to scratch behind his ear.

'Well? You've had enough time to think!'

'Certainly, sir.' The lordling shook out his staggering sleeves and prepared to enjoy himself. 'It was in Turkestan that it took place – as well know, the Turks are a horribly cruel race. It was in the harem of the terrible Tulu Khan; two of his concubines had been found guilty of adultery. What he did to them was unspeakable.'

'No it wasn't! You can tell us!' shouted a wag at the back.

'Oh dear! I hope it won't be *too* revolting,' lied a consort, big-eyed.

Lord Puce sank his voice to a throaty whisper. They all leaned forward to catch every nasty syllable.

'What Tulu Khan did was this – he had the naughty ladies stripped to their adulterous skins. Then he had the executioners cut off their hands and feet –' a scream of horror went up – 'and then, so that their torment should last as long as possible, he had them put into a vat of fermenting ale.' His audience looked blank, except Chinghiz, who had already heard of the case.

'Their wounds were cauterised by the chemicals – so they would live for several hours, slowly, very slowly, bleeding to death.'

'Ugh! That is simply disgusting. What a foul idea!'

Black Jade agreed with that.

'Does anybody,' she asked in a small voice, 'want me to finish my charade?'

Everyone did, chiefly to get over the unpleasantness of the forfeit.

Eventually, after she had scampered up and down several times on five roughly parallel paths, stamping her feet and swishing her silken tail, looking trapped and cross, Bright Virtue called out, in a tone that made swingeing allowances for lesser minds. 'It is obvious. She is the Monkey King, who cannot get out of Buddha's hand. How well you personify a monkey, Lady Wu!'

They were still clapping both performance and guesswork when the Empress arrived.

Paulownia came down the steps, flanked by only two attendants, holding her white mourning robe out of Jade's energetic dust.

'I'm sorry to be so late, Black Jade. I was –' she stopped short.

She had seen Bright Virtue.

Although it was considered only civilised behaviour on the part of any primary wife, Empress or peasant, to live in harmony with her husband's other consorts, Paulownia was finding it extremely difficult in the case of the Pure Concubine. She therefore avoided her company except on compulsory ceremonial occasions, and expected her few friends to act accordingly.

Now she stood transfixed on the steps as though by a javelin, and stared at Black Jade as though she were the one who had thrown it.

'Oh Buddha!' muttered Pheasant uneasily. 'That's torn it!'

'You'd better take her away,' murmured Jade *sotto voce*.

'I will – *if* I can come back later, alone,' he whispered warmly.

'I shan't be here,' she countered. 'Out to dinner.'

Aloud she said brightly, 'We are all so sorry that Your Majesty cannot stay with us a little longer. But, when the Archduke calls –'

There was a grumble of dour appreciation of archducal peremptoriness and the bright group parted its ranks to allow majesty to pass. Pheasant and Paulownia met at the foot of the steps and exchanged slightly stiff courtesies. The Pure Concubine bowed three times to the Empress, but also wounded her with a small, superior smile. She might have to prostrate herself in public, but in private, everyone knew who held the winning hand. At least, they had up to now. She hoped that hand had not changed. She had not cared for the way the Emperor looked at Black Jade. She understood there had been rumours; but then there were always rumours.

She leaned, muskily, to offer an invitation to her lover.

Pheasant, uninvited elsewhere, accepted with anticipated pleasure.

As they left, Paulownia made for Black Jade and swept her into the house where she confronted her with anger and distress.

'I would never have expected this of you! It is the very cruellest thing you could do, to bring me face to face with her, in front of all those grinnings apes and peacocks! I thought you were my friend!'

'You didn't get my message,' said Jade flatly. 'I told you not to come here, and I told you why.'

'Oh.' Paulownia's sails collapsed. 'Then what was she doing here, in any case?' she asked querulously. 'What have you to do with her?'

'Nothing really. She came with the Emperor.' Jade was unemotional. 'On the other hand – do you, I wonder, ever read Sun Tzu?'

'The military strategist? Why should I?'

'Because one needs strategy for all of life, not just on the battlefield. Anyway, one of Sun Tzu's basic maxims – almost too basic to mention – is "Know your enemy". I think that is something you might consider.'

'I see,' said the Empress huffily. 'You were getting to know her.'

'The opportunity was there.'

'And do you now know her?' A weak attempt at sarcasm.

'Better than you, Paulownia.'

'You didn't – *like* her, did you, Jade?' A sad little question.

'No, I didn't. But she wasn't trying to make me like her. Or, who knows, I might have done. Unlike you, she is a perfect dissembler.'

Paulownia did not learn to dissemble, either in bed or out of it. Pheasant did begin to see rather less of Bright Virtue however. This brought little comfort to his Empress, and less to Black Jade, for he spent the time that had once belonged to the Pure Concubine, the afternoons at any rate, in Green Fragrance Court.

Now the hub of the new young wheel at court, her pretty rooms were no longer a sanctuary but a trap, and one she had unwittingly made for herself.

At first Pheasant did no more than call, uninvited, to drink tea with her. Often a friend or two would be there, and sometimes he brought others with him. They would read poetry or listen to music.

Occasionally, he came alone. These were the dangerous times. On the surface, he treated her much as he had always done, though he had acquired a new assurance that sat well on him and was very attractive. He was affable, pleasant and affectionate. Their talk ranged from his difficulties with the ministers to the latest acquisitions of the stables or the new stringed instruments from India.

But always, behind the easy conversation and the warm glances, there was a sense of waiting.

Black Jade did her best to ignore it. She spent as much time as she could with Paulownia, though increasingly conscious of the odd girl's dislike of her new companions, who did not, after all, do anything to bring Pheasant to her side.

Soon, when Jade called, she would find the Empress deep in some religious argument with her old friends, and often with the nuns from Kan Yeh. It was evident, from her enraptured face, that this was the pastime she preferred.

'Go back to your parakeet's cage,' she told Black Jade serenely, 'and try to keep Pheasant out of mischief. I am really so much happier where I am.'

Jade did as she was told, with much misgiving.

And then one night everything changed.

'A message has come from the Emperor,' Chinghiz told her with a face cut out of granite.

She stretched lazily on the warm *kang* and offered him a dried apricot. 'What does he say?'

'He wishes you to visit him.'

'Oh, when?'

'Now.'

'I see. Do you think –?'

'I don't know.' His heart was behaving strangely, uncomfortably. 'What will you wear?' he enquired cheerfully, ignoring it.

'I can't be bothered to change. He'll have to take me as I am.'

He wished she had chosen her words differently. 'No,' he

insisted gently. 'You will wear the cream gown with the pink lotuses. That grey is too drab.'

'I *am* still in mourning.' In fact it was only half-mourning, as she was not a member of the imperial family.

'Will you come with me?' she asked, as she changed obediently. It was not an order.

'Naturally I will – and Welcome too.'

It was a late autumn evening, crisply chill. The palace was a living network of shadows, where restless spirits moved, punctuated by blessed pools of candlelight or flares. As the three of them flitted across the gardens in the moonlight, Black Jade felt those unseen presences as never before. As a rule she did not much concern herself with the spirit world, since it, in turn, had never reached out to her – not even when she had called on her dead with an aching heart. But tonight she sensed the excitement of other minds, close to her in the dark. Were they benign or inimical? Did they seek to harm her, or to warn her? Welcome evidently felt their presence too, for she hurried them along urgently, muttering prayers and imprecations, making as much noise as she could in the hope of scaring them away.

'Don't worry,' Chinghiz reassured them. 'We are in a garden; it will be filled with flower-spirits, all well-disposed to us.'

Welcome grunted. 'What about the devils that descend on a place where wickedness has happened? Plenty of that in a palace! We must mind they don't try to trip us. I knew a man, once, whose neck was broken that way!'

They were glad to arrive amid the bright glow of the Ta Ming Palace, Shih-min's personal indulgence in architectural fantasy. Its carved and gilded roofs and pillars stretched upward in a rainbow urge to bridge the space between man and Heaven, which was, of course, the preoccupation of its main inhabitant. By night, in the flame of torches, its curved and cupolaed splendour had a surreal, insubstantial quality, as though it were only a paper facade with emptiness behind it.

Proving the untruth of this fancy, Black Jade was welcomed by maidservants, who took her attendants into their quarters while an imposing eunuch – not, she was relieved to see, Lord Shen – led her to the Emperor's chambers.

Pheasant was standing before an unshuttered window, looking out into the dusky gardens. The room was furnished informally with sofas, many books, and a desk covered with scrolls and papers, which proclaimed it his study.

Black Jade waited until he turned around.

'No.' He held up his hand. 'You are not to kowtow. This is not to be an occasion for protocol. If it were,' he added very deliberately, his eyes wide with suppressed excitement, 'I should have had you brought to me rolled in a quilt.'

There was a pool of enormity which was also silence.

'Well, Jade – have you nothing to say?'

He was, she realised, very nervous. He was having difficulty in keeping his hands in their easy pose at his sides.

She had nothing to say, but she must say something.

'I remember,' she began, her voice low, 'that when your father sent for me in that way, he explained to me that the device of the quilt was designed to show me exactly what was my place in the palace.'

She raised her eyes to his, intending him to consider now what that place had been. He returned her clear look without embarrassment. He knew what he was going to say.

'While he lived, my father loved you. You brought him great joy, and I am glad of it. But my father is dead,' he said gently, pausing as though to emphasise the finality of this.

'And I am living – and in some ways, it seems, I am very like my father.' He smiled, almost with mischief. 'I want you, Black Jade, just as he did. You know it, don't you? I believe you have known it for quite some time – so please, let's have no more pretence between us –'

'It *wasn't* –' she began, but his raised hand forbade her.

'No more aimless afternoons, talking of this and that and nothing in particular. No more ebullient parties designed to show Paulownia to me in a more desirable mould than the Gods have cast her. And please, dearest Jade – no more talking down to me as you do, as though I were your son as well as my father's.'

'Please stop. It isn't right to –' Her throat was dry.

'Be quiet. You are just two years older than me. You are transcendently beautiful, rarely gifted, and extraordinarily exciting – especially when you are trying not to be. You are what I want. You are what I have wanted for an *unbearable* length of time.' His smile was beatific. 'I do not have to bear it any longer. I am the Emperor.' He paused again.

'I have been patient, to honour the properties. I even allowed you your refuge in Kan Yeh. But that is in the past. All of it, Black Jade. Including my father.'

She flinched. That had been brutal.

And yet, at the same time, she felt the first flicker of appreciation for him that was not mixed with the sympathy which had always been, yes, more than a little maternal in its tenderness. And he was right; she had tried to keep it so.

He was waiting for her to give him her answer.

There could be only two possible resolutions to their interview. Either she would refuse him, and be forced by her position to immure herself in the convent for the rest of her life, or she would become his mistress.

She did not want to go back to the convent. She wanted to live; as fully as fate might offer. At this moment, she was aware, it was offering a great deal.

She said calmly, her expression simply pleasant. 'You must know what they will say of such a relationship. They will call it incest.'

He would match her *sang-froid*. 'Possibly, but I will deal with such suggestions when they occur. It doesn't matter what the court thinks, and the people will believe anything I tell them.'

She stared at him, amazed at the change which had taken place under her ignorant nose.

'Can you so easily contemplate taking your father's concubine? Don't you feel any shame? Doesn't the thought disturb you?'

'I have told you. What is past doesn't concern me. But as for my father, he asked you, did he not, to remain at my side? Do you seriously think he had not considered the probability that you would become more to me than that unlikely hybrid, a female counsellor?'

She was startled. It had never occurred to her, but it was just possible that it was true. Shih-min had wanted her to have children. Was this what he had envisaged? And if so, had it been some sort of betrayal – or an immense generosity of spirit?

'I have consulted an astrologer,' Pheasant continued cheerfully. 'Both the turtle shell and the millet stalks assured him that you and I were fated to unite our destinies.'

'Truly?' She supposed that made it faintly more respectable.

'He consulted the *I Ching* and threw the hexagram *chi-chi*, which expresses the perfect harmony of sexual union. Can you doubt, now, that you and I will bring each other great happiness?'

He was holding out his hand to her.

'Now, come here to me, and let me show you how it will be.'

Very slowly she closed the space between them, knowing that these few steps defined the future direction of her life. She trembled.

When she stood before him gravely, he took her gently by the shoulders and brought her even closer. There was affection, but also a steady determination in his eyes – those same eyes, darkly liquid, that were his father's – as he looked down at her.

'Good. Now I shall take you to my bed, and we shall discover, quite clearly, that you are neither my surrogate mother nor my father's widow – but only *mine*! This night, and forever.'

He bent to kiss her. She felt a small shock at the firm insistence of his lips as they moved to soften the stiffness of her own. He put his arms about her and his warmth encircled her like an animal's. He smelled of musk and roses.

His kisses probed gently, even teasingly, at first, but soon became harder as, beneath their continued insistence, she began to respond, her mouth opening to his tongue.

All the lore of sexuality dwelt on the importance of sufficiently arousing one's female partner, so that her valuable secretions would flow freely and replenish her lover's virility. Pheasant had prepared himself for this moment with research and practice, and was determined that Black Jade would be so thoroughly aroused that all her doubts would be swept away on the tide of passion. Partly because he wished their consummation to be a stupendously memorable one, and partly because he judged that it was the only way in which he could compete with Shih-min's ghost, he would use all that he had read, and done, all that Bright Virtue had taught him, to bring her body to the point of utter subjection to his own.

Rather than wooing her with soft words and gentle caresses, he began with what he considered would be a salutary shock. Transferring one of his caressing hands to her breast beneath the opening of her robe, he used the other to place one of hers upon the hard upward thrust of his erection.

'That, my dark orchid, is what will unite us from now on; not the withered memory of any shared past.'

He searched her face. Satisfied with what he found there – half-scandalised amazement and a nectarine blush – he led her by the hand into the next room where the imperial couch lay waiting.

She followed him in a chaos of sensation and emotion, intrigued and aroused, despite herself, by the change she found in him.

They reached the bed and he pulled her to him, bending her backward in a kiss that informed her of his need, and intention, to dominate her. Then he placed her, seated, upon the side of the bed and opened her robe. Pulling it down from her shoulders, he knelt and took her breasts in his hands, courting their dark amber tips while he stared, drugged with excitement, into her eyes. He brought his head down and began to suck, and also, quite gently, to bite. Looking up, he caught her gleam of pleasure and grinned wickedly, thus banishing, his look told her, any notion of their further playing at mother and son.

He lifted his head from her breast as a man rises from a battlefield, overjoyed and drunk with surprise to find that he is, after all, winning.

He touched her nipples again, drawn to their rosy erectness. Then he bent suddenly and thrust his hand roughly between her legs. He held her for a moment, panting, then got to his feet, his eyes lit with a feral pleasure.

'Stand up now. I want to see you naked.'

He pulled at the cloth about her hips.

She resisted the desire to slap him and made as if to pull up her robe.

'No. Stand up and let it drop.'

Raging, yet caught up with him in his original campaign, she did as he wished. He gazed at her face and at her breasts, then pointed to the cord that fastened her silk trousers. She untied them, her eyes on his, and let them fall. She stood naked before him in the pool of settling silk.

Pheasant remained still for a moment, in almost abstract contemplation of the beauty he had coveted for so long. She was even more exquisite than he had dreamed. To look at her like this caused him a pleasure that had its roots in pain.

He made a small sound of content, then came and lifted her on to the bed where she lay gazing up at him, her green eyes glinting like those of an irritated tigress.

He took off his own robe and knelt beside her, bending to kiss her once, long and deeply. Then he lay down with her and began to trace, with his hand, the contours of her body, getting to know it as a blind man might learn the geography of a room, blessing the Gods who had given him what no blind man could possess – the extraordinary sight of all her golden beauty stretched before him like a new tributary to his Empire.

Black Jade lay consciously trying to assimilate her emotions. There was her constant bane, her resentment at the lack of any element of choice in her fate. There was the knowledge of Shih-min, of the love that was no longer present and could not be repeated, never, in this life, and the sadness and longing that accompanied this knowledge. But there was also the disturbing sensation of Pheasant's hands upon her skin, his intent stroking of every part of her body, as though he claimed it, inch by cherished inch, for his own. She intuited a need in him for *possession*, one that had never troubled his father. Shih-min had wanted more to give than to have. But she must not think of that now. It would take his son a long time to learn, as all intelligent men must learn, that to enjoy rights over a woman's body is by no means to own any part of her intrinsic self. Not even if one is the Emperor.

'What are you thinking?' he demanded suddenly, his fingers circling, weighted with feathers, below her navel.

'I shall not tell you.'

'Then you shall have no more time to think!' He threw her a smile of pure exhilaration, then swooped to kiss her, biting her lips. As his hard and beautifully made body pressed down upon her she was sluiced by a wave of desire that was undeniable. As he felt the small tremor go through her, he gave a cry of triumph and kissed her more deeply.

'You see?' he said happily.

He glowed with the satisfaction of a small boy who has caught the fish he has played all morning. He made her want to laugh; and it was this that was her undoing. The laughter inside her loosened her resistance so that she suddenly realised how much he had aroused her; how her skin loved his carefully orchestrated worship; how harmoniously their two perfect young bodies complemented each other.

'My beauty,' he murmured, his hand sliding down the black waterfall of hair. 'My incomparable girl.'

She tried not to smile.

'I would rather you did not talk to me as if I were one of your horses.'

He saw her amusement as she twitched her hair from his grasp, and knew that her words represented his victory. And so, first pausing to look at her again in sheer brilliant happiness, he took her and opened her for himself like a miraculous New Year present, and entered into the possession of all his life's joy and pain.

12

'Oh, Chinghiz, what shall I do?'

'Continue as you are; you are doing remarkably well.'

'No, no. What can I say to her? How shall I tell her? I would give anything not to have hurt her this way.'

'Anything?' The slanted brows flew up in the radiant, sardonic face. 'Would you give up the Emperor? Return to Kan Yeh?'

'You are cruel. No, I would not. Will not.'

'Well, then, you should certainly go to the Empress. If you do not inform her of your new status, you can be certain someone else will; and that would be even less kind.'

Despising herself, Black Jade left for Paulownia's villa.

'All things must have their balance,' murmured Chinghiz, not very helpfully, behind her as they walked. 'Last night the joy; this morning the pain. Buddha be praised!'

'And you, my friend, may be damned!' declared his mistress, stiffening her step.

'You can wait outside,' she told him when they reached the pale pink marble palace. 'It will punish you for untimely mockery.'

'Better to laugh than to cry,' he offered sententiously, settling his serpentine length against a convenient pillar, at home as a vine.

'I will wait to carry away your charred remains – but remember, however affected you may be by Her Majesty's suffering – the Monkey King cannot escape from Buddha's hand!'

She averted her eyes from such insolence and went inside.

Paulownia was surprised. She was only up to her second bowl of morning tea.

'Black Jade, how nice. Will you have mint, or lemon and rosehip?'

'No tea, thank you. And it isn't – won't be – at all nice, I'm afraid. Paulownia, I have come to tell you something.' She swallowed hard. 'Only, I have no idea in the world how I'm going to do it.'

The Empress considered her friend's demeanour.

'You are certainly very pale. Sit down and tell me, slowly, what is the matter. Surely it can't be as bad as that?' She tried to remember if anyone was seriously ill. No one close, certainly.

Black Jade accepted the seat; her legs were dissolving. She scrabbled wildly in her disordered mind for words. There weren't any. 'Eighteen hells and damnation!' she cried, despairing. 'I have never been in a situation I have liked less!'

Paulownia frowned, beginning to realise that it was serious.

'Perhaps I could alter that, if I knew what it was,' she suggested quietly.

'It is hard to tell you,' Black Jade muttered. 'I am ashamed.'

Paulownia looked surprised. She waited.

Black Jade took a single very deep breath and looked the

Empress straight in the eye. 'Pheasant sent for me last night.' She seemed to be gabbling. 'I stayed with him till dawn.'

At first Paulownia didn't accept it. Her heart offered her a specious excuse; they had simply been talking; Pheasant had kept her all night, talking, telling her his troubles. Then she looked again at Black Jade's miserable face. No, it wouldn't do.

'I suppose I know what you are telling me,' she said slowly, 'but for some reason it is hard for me to get hold of it. You are saying that Pheasant has –'

'– Yes. The clouds and rain. Yes.'

Horror dawned in Paulownia's eyes. 'But you were *his father's* consort! It can't be true! You can't have done such a thing! It would be an abomination!'

Black Jade looked wretched. 'But we did,' she whispered. Then she thought of Chinghiz and became firm with herself.

'It would be dishonest if I were to offer you apologies. They would mean nothing. The Emperor intends to make me his consort.'

'And you will allow this?' Paulownia was incredulous.

'He is the Emperor.' She paused. 'And I do not wish to go back to the convent.'

'Ah!' Triumphant contempt. 'So that is why!'

Black Jade shook her head. 'Not really. At least, I don't think so. You must forgive me; I am still more than a little confused myself.'

'Forgive you!' Paulownia seized on the word; it seemed to her to have a dreadful enormity. 'That is something I will never do!'

'No,' Jade agreed sadly. 'I don't suppose you will. It has all gone wrong. I should have been able to stop it. I thought I had.'

Paulownia's mind was racing. 'Did you? Did you even try? Perhaps I should have listened when they told me to beware of you. Isn't this what you have wanted? Isn't it *why* you left the convent?'

'No! That, at least, is unfair.' Hurt stabbed her. 'But I can't *make* you believe me. Oh, Paulownia, I cannot bear to be the one to cause you such distress.'

Paulownia rose and placed her tea-bowl carefully on a small lacquered stand.

'Perhaps not. But one cannot have everything, can one?' she said lightly and venomously. Then she left the room.

Outside, Black Jade found that Chinghiz, who was absent, had summoned a sedan. For once she climbed willingly into the musty depths and gratefully closed the curtains.

*

'I suppose I should have expected this.'

Green Fragrance Court was overflowing with would-be visitors.

'They all have their fortunes to make. You are the rising star.'

'I suppose the Archduke isn't there?'

'Not quite. I believe he pays *his* morning calls on the Empress.'

'Ah, well, as that lady so rightly observed, one cannot have everything. Is there anyone of interest here?'

'It's hard to say. They are mostly so young. There's Hsuan-tsang, of course; he's here with a pile of sutras; I expect he wants our maids to help with the copying.'

Black Jade laughed. 'Oh, I must see *him*. How like him not to be one of the Righteously Shocked!'

'And how like him to bring the sutras – as the price of his continued friendship,' suggested her cynical steward.

But Hsuan-tsang brought with him more than sutras. When he bowled into her anteroom like a friendly typhoon he was followed, with considerably less force but far greater subtlety, by an elegant man in several tones of blue satin, whose height and general prepossession commanded the eye.

'May I present to you,' the monk beamed after his own short, fat bow, 'the new President of the Board of Rites, Lion Guard, Lord Hsü.'

Black Jade became alert. She had heard of the man who had waged a successful campaign against the Archduke's chosen candidate to become chief of one of the six great administrative boards that governed the Empire.

'You are welcome, Lion Guard.' She was consciously charming. 'My congratulations on your appointment.'

He released a sophisticated smile. 'You have forestalled me, Gracious Consort. I have, of course, come to offer my own felicitations.'

Pheasant, in response to the sibilant hiss of 'incest' which was inevitably snaking about the passages of the palace, had raised her to the rank of consort of the second grade, with the title of 'Luminous Demeanour'. This demanded a public respect which would give her some protection from the execration of the older and more powerful members of the court.

The ebullient monk had brought her a valuable gift; if she could draw this man to her side, she would have even greater protection.

'Thank you. Your visit sets the seal on the honour done to me by His Majesty. But are you sure,' she added with beguiling candour, 'that it will bring equal honour to you? I should not like the Board of Rites, the guardian of our moral and religious duties, to lay itself open to criticism.'

Lion Guard smiled, sincerely this time. 'Lady Wu, I admire your honesty, and am grateful for your concern. But I think my Board, since it now includes myself, is proof against the bad eggs of the ignorant.' He turned to his rotund companion.

'Hsuan-tsang has been my friend since childhood. He did me the honour to be busy on my behalf – and I owe him a great deal. I am fortunate to have such a champion. And when he confided to me, Exquisite Consort, that he was also inclined to be your champion, I begged him for the honour of meeting you.'

'You are kind. But you need not,' she said smoothly, 'have waited until this auspicious time to introduce yourself.'

He knew she was telling him his acquaintance would have been even more valuable had he offered it *before* her own promotion.

'Ah, Delectable Lady,' Lion Guard said sadly, 'if only I had dared to presume. But then, you see,' his shrewd gaze became disarming as he held out empty hands, '– I had absolutely nothing to offer you.'

Her smile appreciated him. 'You are too modest. Any friend of Hsuan-tsang is always welcome here. What is it, I wonder, that you will offer me now?'

The elegant lord fell upon his knees in a blue wave of satin and looked into her face with a calculation which he allowed to be seen.

'I think,' he said seriously, 'that I may well offer you a lifetime's devotion.'

She raised amused brows. 'A large gift: you are wise to give it further consideration before making the offer final.'

Hsuan-tsang laughed aloud. 'Take no notice, Little Daughter! He's a born politician; he can't let his right sleeve know what he has up the left one. He's a good fellow for all that – even if he is almost as fond of fashion as he is of politics.'

'I had noticed the ensemble,' Black Jade grinned. 'It is rather as though he had laid the ocean at my feet. I have always wanted to see it, ever since I was a baby.'

Lion Guard, who was not without vanity, looked pleased. Before he left, he gave her an enamel sash-pin in gold and sapphires. He took it from his left sleeve. She might have thought he had only just decided that he was, in fact, going to give it to her, had it not been in the shape of the dancing figure of the

Monkey King. Her little charade was now famous, as was its aftermath.

'When the young minister had left, she looked affectionately at Hsuan-tsang, who was seeing how many of her crystallised fruits he could eat without stopping.

'Thank you, old friend; you are a father to your little daughter.'

'I'm glad you liked him,' the monk said, chewing. 'Now, about these sutras. I brought twenty scrolls, just to start with –'

'I have two things to ask of you,' said Black Jade softly. She lay at Pheasant's side in the vast imperial bed. They had just finished the Reversed Mandarin Ducks, which had been highly satisfactory.

'M'm. Don't have to ask. You can have anything you like.' Pheasant nuzzled further into her shoulder, averse to getting up and performing his extra-connubial duties.

'Never jump into a well until you know there's water in it.'

'Welcome! Where does she get them all?'

'From a farm in Shansi. She's a woman of the people. Anyway, the first thing I want is an easy one – you promised when I left the convent that my mother and sister could visit us.'

'Of course. I'm longing to meet them. Is your sister as lovely as you?'

'Lovelier. The other thing, I'm afraid, is not quite so simple – and also none of my business. However, it does concern me. Pheasant, I know how many nights you have spent with me – but will you tell me how many you have spent with Paulownia since –'

'– since you made me so ecstatically happy? Oh come on, Jade, what do you expect? She's furious with me. She wouldn't receive me if I did go to her.'

'Have you *sent* for her?'

'Of course not. One does not send for the Empress.'

'She may be the Empress, but, as I know she will be thinking almost hour by hour, she is not the mother of your heir. Doesn't that bother you at all? Don't you *want* an heir?'

'I have one. A charming boy.'

'You are being foolish. And can't you see – it will be much easier for me, for *us*, if you have a son by Paulownia. Then the Awful Old Men can't accuse me of threatening the throne with my un-blue blood and my evil ambition.'

'Is that what they say? How unkind!' He raised himself slothfully and fitted his body over hers.

'You know it is. Please, be sensible –'

'Open your legs.'

'Only if you promise to spend tonight with Paulownia.'

'You are my concubine. I may do with you as I wish. Open your legs.'

'One day,' she said, accommodating him, 'you will *have* to grow up!'

'Not,' he wriggled, 'for Ten Thousand Years.'

Since her unique position at court had established her as something of a law unto herself, Black Jade took advantage of it to exempt herself from some of the more tiresome conventions.

One of these dictated that a woman who had entered the palace should never, unless under extreme circumstances, leave it. But when Golden Willow and the widowed Rose Bird took a small, pretty house in the eastern quarter of Chang-an, she became their regular visitor. Cloaked and veiled in layers of silk and secrecy, she travelled with Welcome in her black and scarlet palanquin, looking out through the curtains with the longing of a captive bird for the wild. Her curiosity, she noticed, was generously repaid by the citizens, who stared at the stylish little equipage in admiring conjecture.

Today she hardly bothered to look out at the crowded streets and bazaars, not even at the Market of Green Creation, where Welcome offered to stop and bargain for the exotic shrubs which were coming in for spring planting. She was already wearing a flower, and one that carried a very special message.

The afternoon was warm and soft. She found her mother and sister sitting on stools in the courtyard, beneath the green spread of the plum tree that reminded them of home. Both were embroidering bright gowns for Rose Bird's two children, an attractive boy of three whose laughter filled the court as he rode his wooden horse over the mosaic tiles, and the baby girl, Lotus Bud, who had been born, sadly, after a malarial fever had deprived her of a father.

Golden Willow was the first to look up, with a welcoming wave.

'How nice to see you, Second Daughter. You look very pretty.'

Black Jade smoothed a crease from her turquoise robe and casually readjusted the day-lily she wore in her violet sash.

Rose Bird caught the careless gesture and her eyes widened.

'That is a very early bloom,' she said, looking carefully at her sister. 'Wherever did you get it?'

'From the imperial hothouse.' She could not keep from smiling.

'Mother! Is it possible? Black Jade, you must tell us at once, and don't stand there grinning in that maddening way!'

'I expect Black Jade will speak when you give her the chance,' Golden Willow said calmly, though even she peered at her second daughter with a trace of ignoble curiosity.

'It is true, Honoured Mother. I want you to be the first to know that I am With Happiness. At last! I have so longed for a baby. And I'm sure it is a boy. I need no lilies to bring me luck. Here, you may have it; put it in water.' She held out the son-inducing flower to Rose Bird.

'Thank you. Though I, unhappily, will have no more children, boys or girls. But I am so happy for you, Black Jade.'

She held out her arms and Jade went to kiss her, sad that so much beauty should be wasted in early mourning. Rose Bird was at her zenith, her soft, womanly curves and colours a reproach to the sad white gown she wore.

'You must marry again. I shall make sure of it,' she promised, hugging her fiercely.

'Oh no! I can't!' said Rose Bird involuntarily. 'That is – I still think of Resolute Heart.' She blushed, as she had always done when attention wa drawn to her.

Black Jade transferred her embrace to her mother. These two were very close now. Jade had deeply feared their first meeting, certain that Golden Willow would regard her liaison with Pheasant as immoral and an insult to all the ancestors concerned. She had been inexpressibly relieved when, after she had haltingly raised the issue, the redoubtable lady had stopped her short with the words, 'There is no need to distress yourself on my account. Better to reflect on the wise words of the Old Philosopher –

> "As the soft yielding of water cleaves obstinate stone,
> So to yield with life solves the insoluble."

Yield to your karma, dearest child; you cannot alter it.'

Black Jade had been very surprised; but then, she could not know that Golden Willow, having observed her daughter's career with interest and misgiving, had begun to think new thoughts about the early prophecy of Yuan Tien-kang. Like Welcome and like Chinghiz, she did not intend to tell Jade about it because she did not want to add to the burden her daughter was already beginning to carry.

Now she held the girl close for a moment, happy that she would soon be a grandmother for the third time.

Jade laid her cheek against one as smooth and soft as her own. The intervening years since she had left Wen Shui had dealt most kindly with Golden Willow; only her back was perhaps a little straighter, to counteract the insolence of time.

'Have you told the Emperor your good news?' she asked, thinking privately that although Black Jade had become astonishingly mature over the years, the Lord of Ten Thousand Years himself was still scarcely more than a spoiled boy. Luckily, it was their mothers who attended to the needs of children.

'I shall tell him tonight; he will be delighted.'

'And the Empress,' said Rose Bird mischievously, 'will be furious.'

'That is no matter for mockery,' said Golden Willow quickly. 'It seems it is Her Majesty's unhappy fate to be barren; she will indeed feel this very deeply – and may take steps to bring about Jade's downfall. You must be very circumspect from now on, Second Daughter, and give no cause for any adverse comment. Until now, you have been Paulownia's rival only in the Emperor's affections; if you should have a son, she will see him as a rival for the succession.'

'Perhaps he will be,' hazarded Rose Bird. 'Pheasant might depose Paulownia and raise you in her place.' Her eyes shone.

'You are never to say that again,' said Black Jade coolly. 'Your words were, for your information, treasonable.'

Rose Bird was abashed. Her sister continued severely.

'It is unlikely that His Majesty would ever degrade Lady Paulownia. She is a member of one of the most powerful clans. The Wang extend influence over half the northern territories, and have always intermarried with the imperial family. Even should the Son of Heaven choose to disregard these things, his ministers would not permit him to put her away. And certainly I have no desire to be the cause of any such upheaval.'

'All right; I was only considering,' said Rose Bird. 'And as for the Empress's planning your downfall – your friend Dumpling told me something very interesting yesterday.'

Black Jade groaned. In her sister, Dumpling had at last found the ideal receptacle for every drop of gossip she could collect.

'Apparently Paulownia gave a private audience to – guess who?'

'The Hare in the Moon,' said Jade, unenchanted.

'To the Pure Concubine!' revealed Rose Bird triumphantly. 'They spent two whole hours together; can you imagine?'

'The mind limps,' admitted Jade. 'But, on reflection, it's not so surprising. Bright Virtue will have sought the interview because she hoped to persuade Paulownia that they were now two of a kind, deceived and supplanted by this unworthy person. And Paulownia, when she had listened for a while to the stream of clever compliments and professions of interest in abstruse sutras that I'm sure Bright Virtue produced, would begin to melt; she needs a friend, to replace me. Perhaps she has found one.'

'I hope not. That would be two great clans lined up against you.'

'Not forgetting the Archduke.'

'Oh, does that matter so much? His family belonged to the old Empress.'

'They are also related to Paulownia. And, what is more important, Pheasant is afraid of him.'

'Can you do something about that?'

'I am trying. I make Wuchi the constant butt of my arrows of airy wit; but as far as Pheasant is concerned the bull's-eye is sacrosanct. The Archduke is his inheritance; it is not funny.'

'I heard something else from Dumpling,' Rose Bird suddenly remembered, bored with the Archduke. 'Excuse me, Mother; it isn't very pleasant –'

'Oh, don't mind me; I am learning a great deal.' Golden Willow was thankful, not for the first time, that she had insisted on living away from the palace, which she regarded much in the same light as the city dunghill.

'Well, the latest anti-Jade story is that some man swears he interrupted her – having the clouds and rain with Pheasant, when he was Crown Prince! In the room next door to the one where Shih-min was dying! He said she had solicited the Prince while he was making use of a urinal. I'm sorry,' she finished, crimson, 'but it's so revolting that I thought you should know.'

Golden Willow shuddered.

'I agree. She should. It is time, my child, to build up your defences. You are your father's daughter; it should not give you any difficulty.'

Jade, who had shown no particular emotion over the slander, was surprised by her gentle mother's practicality.

'Powerful forces are gathering against you,' the tranquil voice continued. 'Consider what your future would be if they were to succeed in your overthrow.' Prophecy was all very well, but it was also sensible to secure insurance.

'The convent? Exile? Even death, if Paulownia were seriously to seek it. But I can't believe –'

'Nevertheless, it is wiser to raise one's protective wall and let the enemy occupy himself in looking for chinks, than to allow him to wander freely about one's inner courts.'

'You sound just like Father,' Black Jade smiled. 'But don't worry, I am aware of my position. I do have my friends, as well as enemies, and some of them are quite powerful.' She told them of Lion Guard's visit and of Hsuan-tsang's increasing influence among the senior Buddhist churchmen; also of the growing group of younger ministers and officials who were flocking to her standard and being well-rewarded by the Emperor for doing so. Even Wuchi could not oversee every appointment he made, every gift of silks or string of cash.

'And best of all,' she beamed, 'is the fact that Lady Hero seems to feel no anger at what has happened since Shih-min died. "Life", she writes, "is full of surprises; and the most surprising are the ones we deal to ourselves. Be happy, Black Jade, and celebrate life!' "

'She has a rare understanding, that lady,' Golden Willow approved, 'And a great gift for friendship. And, like all those who admire your intelligence and talent, she probably feels that, unlike Bright Virtue, your influence on Pheasant is all to the good.'

Rose Bird now excused herself to feed the baby, and her mother took the opportunity to ask the question she had long wished to ask. Laying her fine hand on the turquoise knee, she said shyly, 'Does the Son of Heaven bring you happiness, truly?'

Black Jade touched the bright flame of her lily. 'This is my happiness. And yes, Mother, there is love between us.'

She would not try to explain the nature of that love. It was nothing like that which she had shared with Shih-min; could only have shared with Shih-min. For his son she felt a deep affection which would always be partly protective. She could not forget, in the arms of the man, the boy who had once clung to her in sorrow.

The clouds and rain were different too; there was ebullient lust, melting tenderness, and a strong element of battle in their congress. His obsession with her grew stronger with every tumultuous act of union. He had tried to explain that obsession once, and in that explanation she had recognised the true springs of the power she had over him.

'It is as though, because you took his seed, you still carry my father within you,' he had said wonderingly. 'You are imbued with his magic, his potency – and when we lie together in the clouds and the rain, you give that magic and that potency to me.'

She sincerely wished that it might be so.

*

The midwife held up an untidy dangle of something that looked a bit like raw meat, but which turned, upon being slapped, into a squalling human infant.

'What is it?' gasped Black Jade, trying to lift a head that was full of boulders.

'A boy, Highness!' the midwife carolled. 'A great, big, beautiful boy! A little prince!'

'I can believe he is big,' the newly delivered mother responded. She placed an experimental hand on her stomach. It didn't seem much flatter, considering. She was very sore. She wanted to sleep. She realised, as she drifted into a vaguely painful haze, that she was crying. How silly, she thought, when I am so ridiculously happy. A boy! I've given Pheasant a boy!

As she floated into her well-deserved slumber the midwife handed the naked, squirming and still vociferous bundle through the curtains of the bed-screen and into the hands of the physician, who checked it for any irregularities. Finding none except unusually splendid size, he smiled, murmured the conventional blessings and went off to drink the young prince's health, thankful that he did not have to risk the blame for any deformation or unsightly birthmark.

When Black Jade awoke, astonishingly alert and jubilantly pleased with herself, she found the room to be a riot of scarlet ribbons and children's toys. The curtains were drawn back, the air was fresh and lightly scented with something green.

She began to struggle upwards, the signal for a fluttering feminine foray with Welcome in the lead, which gained her a clean nightgown, two stout pillows behind her back and a red-clad, red-faced bundle to hold.

'Great Buddha! Is he *supposed* to be as big as this?'

'Of course, if he likes,' said Welcome, who had seen several births during her very early years on the farm.

'He's absolutely beautiful,' breathed the proud mother, gazing love-struck into the third generation of large and liquid brown eyes.

'Just look at those lashes – and he has fingers and everything. He *has* got everything?' she added, beginning to unwrap the scarlet parcel. When she had assured herself that he had, she allowed Sweetmeat, who adored babies, to wrap it up again.

Hearing that she was awake, Pheasant arrived to examine his latest accomplishment. He looked very young and ludicrously proud as he held the fat, glowing cushion of flesh and furnishings.

'He looks just like you – or is it me?' he grinned, kissing her.

'Either way, he is utterly magnificent. Shall we call him that? Magnificent Li; he's bound to grow up to deserve it!'

'Oh, no question!' Black Jade was perfectly serious. 'But don't you think, something a little bit less overwhelming for his milk-name?'

'Oh, you must choose that. Anything you like. Magnificent Li,' he repeated exultantly. 'Black Jade, you are miraculous!'

'Well, you did have something to do with it,' she allowed, 'though I think the presumptuous size is probably the fault of his grandfathers. I'll think about a milk-name. It'll come on its own.'

It did. To her everlasting pride and pleasure, it was Welcome who named the thumping child, whose welfare she soon made her own province, pointing out, with some logic, that Black Jade knew nothing about babies.

'Who's a bold little tiger, then?' she crooned as the infant prince grabbed at her shapely, milkless breast with hungry hands.

'Bold Tiger! I like that; it suits him,' his mother decided. 'It will do very nicely while he's waiting to grow into Magnificent.'

During the week after the birth, Pheasant showered Black Jade with jewels to such a prodigal extent that one day she sat up in bed with them all displayed around her on the golden coverlet, herself decked in an emerald tiara, diamond eardrops and two knucklesful of sharp and spiky self-defence.

'You see that you must stop!' she laughed as he swept the glittering collection aside and took her in his arms. 'Mind the tiara! It's caught in my hair.'

'I see nothing of the kind. Give them away if you don't want them. But keep the hairpin. It's the start of a collection.'

'Of course! How many shall I have? A lucky three, or six?'

The golden hairpin was a husband's traditional demonstration of gratitude for becoming a father.

'Why not nine? Even luckier.'

'My dear, think of the noise!'

Towards the end of the second week their idyll was rudely interrupted. The Archduke and his confrères were insisting that the Emperor give his attention to a certain unpleasant affair of state.

Pheasant, toppled from the peak of paternal pride into a sudden cold depth of misery, brought his trouble to Jade's brightly coloured nursery in Dumpling's old rooms.

'I wish you'd agree to move into the palace,' he murmured abstractedly, knocking into a set of wind-chimes carved like animals.

'I like it here,' she replied with mechanical contentment. She noticed his expression. 'Is something wrong?'

'The Archduke wants me to execute my sister.'

She sighed. 'Welcome, will you take the baby for some fresh air? I don't think this is going to be fit for his ears. He's too young to hear about violence.'

Welcome departed with her charge, now more recognisably a member of the human race, and a very handsome one at that.

Recently, to the horror and titillation of the court, the Archduke had uncovered a conspiracy among the old supporters of the exiled Prince Tai, who had once so terrified his brother. Tai had disconcerted them by dying, but his banner had been taken up by the Emperor's half-sister, a woman of uncomfortably strident nature, whom Pheasant never saw if he could help it. Her rather loosely planned coup also involved several of Shih-min's sons-in-law and even one of his father's. The vigilant Wuchi had rounded up all the conspirators and tidied them into jail, where they now awaited the Emperor's mercy.

'How can I do it?' Pheasant said dolefully. 'She *is* my sister, even if I can't stand to be in the same room with her. My father wouldn't have done it.'

Black Jade forbore to remark that if his father hadn't allowed Prince Tai to go on living, he couldn't also have gone on plotting. What Pheasant wanted from her now was a running repair to his confidence, damaged in the morning's wrangle with the council.

She pondered how to give it, while also giving her own opinion. She gave him a good, solid hug to start with.

'The sad thing is, my poor love, that there is really only one answer. It may be personally horrible to you, but the Archduke is right – he often is, unfortunately – you have to execute them, every one. You must take a strong line, now, at the outset, or your reign will be plagued with such plots.'

'Not you too!' He released the anger he had kept leashed in the council chamber. 'Only the barbarian kills his own family. How can someone so new to motherhood harbour such vicious notions?'

'Perhaps because I would like to see Bold Tiger grow up in safety, and not as a subject for the whims of any usurping sisters or aunts or brothers-in-law!'

'This plot would never have succeeded; it isn't important.'

'No; but it *is* important that you show courage in executing justice.'

'Courage! What's courageous about killing helpless prisoners?'

'Doesn't it take a certain special kind of courage? A dispassionate putting aside of self and selfish ties, in order to execute justice upon one's own family, as upon any other in the Empire?'

He looked wretched. 'I don't know. I didn't expect you to say this.'

'It is only what your ministers have already said,' she urged gently.

Resentment crept in. 'Well, all I can say is, I'm glad this didn't happen while you were carrying our child. If he had sensed such cruelty in you, he might have been born a monster.'

'Never fear!' she flashed, impatient now. 'I ate only rose petals, drank only water from the sacred springs and looked only upon the image of the All-Compassionate thoughout the entire pregnancy! Pheasant, Bold Tiger will be what we make him – not the reflection of ancient and foolish superstitions.'

His eyes filled with self-pitying tears. 'Don't let's quarrel, Jade. I can't bear it if you are against me too.'

'I'm not against you,' she said reasonably. 'How could you think so? I am only anxious that you should decide, now, at the beginning, to make wisdom your weapon; it will save you a great deal of hardship later.'

She knelt before the couch where he sat and placed her hands on his.

'Don't be angry with me,' she pleaded, smiling. 'Of *course* I find it horrible that you must sentence your relatives to death; but I must confess I find it far more horrible that *they* should have wished to steal your throne, perhaps even to murder you.'

She sniffed, now also threatened with tears. Ashamed, Pheasant raised her to sit beside him and held her close to console her.

'I'm sorry, my dearest love. I shouldn't have spoken to you like that. It's just that I hate this business so much. Come on, let's go and find our son, and forget all this monstrousness until tomorrow.'

They kissed and were very kind to each other for the rest of the day, which they spent playing with Magnificent Bold Tiger and indulging in the gentle caresses which, for another two months, would have to take the place of the clouds and rain – though both doubted whether they would be able to abstain for so long. Such rules were laid down by celibate philosophers, not lovers, and bore little relation to the realities of life.

The next morning the impatient Archduke was gratified to learn that the Emperor consented to the decree of execution for every one of his prisoners. Those who were members of the imperial clan would, of course, be permitted to make use of the yellow silken cord which he would send to them.

While Pleasant thus discovered the beginning of wisdom for a ruler of the larger part of the known world, Black Jade sat in her anteroom, staring gloomily at a territorially ambitious plantain which was obscuring her bookshelves.

'Two weeks ago I took part in the miracle of birth,' she announced heavily. 'Yesterday I was instrumental in ending several people's lives. I don't like myself very much.'

Chinghiz, thus addressed, applied himself to the problem.

'The Emperor could not make up his mind. The court was in session; a verdict was necessary. You know you did the right thing.'

'Being right does not necessarily mean being in any way pleasant.' She sighed. 'That, I suppose, is what I was trying to show Pheasant. It was memory that nudged my elbow. You remember that day, too, don't you – when Shih-min was nearly sliced in little pieces by the antics of his beastly, treacherous children? "They will *kill* me," he said. I can still hear the anguish in his voice. Oh, Chinghiz, Pheasant hasn't one tenth of Shih-min's strength! How will the world deal with him if *I* don't try to give him the courage and certainty he will need? Even the courage to be cruel, as he was today?'

'Golden Phoenix, your own words are your justification. Do you also need the encouragement of another's fortitude? If you do, whatever I have of that quality is at your disposal. And my first counsel is not to distress yourself unduly. Like the Son of Heaven, for you too it is a question of getting accustomed.'

'To killing people? I hope I may never do that. Bring me a mirror,' she added, with sudden misgiving.

She stared into the heavy silver-backed bronze, looking for some change that ought to show in her eyes. There was nothing; only the evidence of a sleepless night.

Chinghiz, gazing into the pretty toy from behind her, thought that she had the look of someone whom the world has wounded. He tried, very hard, not to let himself feel pity. She was young and strong, in heart, mind and body. Like the young Emperor, she had had to make a beginning. She had made a good one. he would make sure the Archduke knew to whom he owed the new-found imperial strength of purpose.

*

The pain of his half-sister's manner of leaving the world soon abated for Pheasant. He had no wish to dwell on unpleasantness. He looked to Black Jade to banish the shadows from him, and because he was so willing to believe in her power to do so, it was a simple enough task.

In the late mornings she listened to his account of his meetings with the ministers and gave him the benefit of her own and Chinghiz's advice. In the afternoons and evenings she filled his life with education and pleasure, devoting herself to the task with spectacular energy and success.

At night, she welcomed him into her arms and body with increasing delight, for he returned her ready giving of herself with an aptitude that was turning them both into accomplished voluptuaries, and lavished upon her an affection whose steady growth was obvious to everyone in the Palace City.

When, a year after the birth of Bold Tiger, she gave him a second son, Young Tiger (until he should grow into the name of Glorious), Pheasant's pride in Black Jade determined him to create for her the title of Queen Consort. The Archduke and Old Integrity were so firmly against such a precedent, however, and Jade herself so cheerfully indifferent, that he abandoned the idea for the present.

It occurred to Black Jade that, since her life seemed to have settled into a reliable pattern which she might expect to maintain for some time, she might make an attempt, after so long, at a reconciliation with Paulownia.

The two opposing factions which surrounded herself and the Empress were still growing, and would go on growing as long as there was an emergent group of young and ambitious officials on one side and a strong entrenchment of elder statesmen on the other. The alignments were, of course, perfectly natural. They scarcely needed the daily fuel of rumour and falsehood to keep their fires alive.

Black Jade thought, however, that perhaps by now the intelligent Paulownia would have come to accept what she could not change, and might even welcome a new relationship with herself; not the old friendship, that was too much to expect; but at least a decent respect that would put the mischief-makers out of business.

She suggested this to Pheasant one afternoon when they were visiting the imperial zoo with the babies and their nurses, all of them supervised by the broad, protective bulk of Welcome.

Pheasant looked doubtful. He stopped in front of an enclosure containing a splendid lion sent in tribute by the Afghans; he shared the generous landscape of carefully arranged rocks and desert plain with two lithe consorts, one of whom had recently give birth to twins. Bold Tiger urged his nurse closer to the bamboo bars and set up an energetic one-way conversation with the animals.

'Oh dear – that doesn't sound at all like Chinese! I do hope he isn't going to turn into a barbarian,' his father grinned.

'How rude! He's a brilliant speaker. Look, the beast is obviously benefiting from his excellent advice.' The lion had turned its back and begun to wash its generative parts.

'But, Paulownia – I don't know, Jade. She has never once mentioned you when I've been with her, not in two years. On the few occasions when I have, when our sons were born for example, she simply pretended not to hear. But by all means try, if you wish; you can only gain virtue by it.'

They had passed to the picturesque gorge constructed for the black bears, presents from Indian friends of Hsuan-tsang. They had been much publicised as ferocious carnivores which had relished the flesh of lion, man and white elephant before intrepid tribesmen had lured them into a honey-trap. Now they stood up drolly on drunken hindlegs, indicating with lolling pink tongues and the absurd suggestion of smiles that they would be quite content with less exotic fare, if only someone would throw them something.

'They seem almost tame,' Pheasant said, taking a leg of lamb from their keeper and tossing it accurately to the smallest bear.

'You could probably even teach them to dance; they would make a sensational climax to your next concert.'

'They're really rather sweet,' she agreed, watching Welcome swoop to detach small fingers from the bars. 'I suppose there's more rumour than truth in most evil reputations.' She was thinking, hopefully, of Paulownia. Pheasant did not know it, but Chinghiz had information that the Empress had actually been tempted to think of poisoning the girl she now considered her greatest rival, just after the birth of Young Tiger. The temptress had been, in defiance of her title, the Pure Concubine. Neither Chinghiz nor Jade herself were at all inclined to believe this, but it had been the determining factor in her decision to seek an interview. She did not know how she hoped to achieve it, but she wanted to make the fabrication of such rumours impossible in the future.

Having adopted this positive attitude, she was unsurprised

when the Empress agreed to see her.

'Look out for her mother,' Pheasant warned lugubriously. 'She's a Tartar, beady-eyed, bearded and barbarous!'

Black Jade was received in a small, formal chamber whose walls were hung with ice-blue damask and improving texts in stark black. Its only furniture was a number of severe indoor trees, several blue and white vases and three high-backed ebony thrones; Paulownia, in a robe of imperial yellow which flowed round her feet, occupied the central one of these. She was flanked on one side by the graceful figure of the Pure Concubine, radiating virtue, and on the other by a woman of middle years and important carriage whose clothing was so stiff with jewels and embroidery that she simulated the temple images of Kuan Yin, festooned with the offerings of grateful votaries. Here, any resemblance to that compassionate deity ended, for this was the formidable Lady Osier, Duchess of Wei, the Tartaric mother-in-law. Black Jade had not met her, but she was reputed as overbearing, snobbish and single-mindedly ambitious for her daughter's complete reconciliation with the Emperor. Rumour also named her as a witch; she was known to have dealings with Taoist shamans of dark denomination.

Black Jade, having noted the company, stood before the doors and waited to be summoned forward. Nothing was said. The three glittering figures might have been carved into their chairs.

Seeing how it was, she prostrated herself, according to strict protocol, in the full kowtow. She rose and came forward a little. At this point the Empress might wave away any insistence on the two further prostrations dictated by custom.

Paulownia made no such gesture.

Black Jade therefore stretched herself out again, hugging the floor like a carpet. This was not an auspicious beginning.

A third time. She tried not to resent it. It was the Empress's right. It was not even necessarily unfriendly; Paulownia had always been a stickler for the conventions.

Jade rose for the last time and stood at the prescribed distance from the Phoenix Throne.

The Empress regarded her frigidly. 'You requested an interview. For what reason?'

'I wished to pay my duty to Your Majesty.'

'Some time ago it was made clear to you, Lady Wu, that I did not wish to have you in my presence. Have you any reason to think that my wishes might have changed?'

There was a rustle of sleeves as Bright Virtue put her fan over her lips to conceal her amusement.

Black Jade looked tranquilly into Paulownia's face. There were changes since she had last seen her so closely. Her expression of abstracted pride had become one of conscious arrogance, concealing, she thought, a deep unhappiness.

'I had hoped that after so many seasons Your Graciousness might be disposed to recall our former amiable relations,' she said gently. 'It seems to me that our separate friends are making no good use of the space that exists between us.'

'You are insolent. Do you set yourself on a level with me?'

Black Jade bowed humbly. 'Indeed not, Highness. I wanted only to state for myself that I am by no means your enemy, as rumour and malice might have you believe.'

There was an implosive noise from Lady Osier, whose doggy face was set in grim disapproval.

The Empress stared hard at Black Jade. For an instant there may have been a softening in the clouded grey eyes; then they resumed their downward direction, their heavy lids as concealing as the Pure Concubine's painted fan.

'I have nothing to say to you, Lady Wu,' said Paulownia colourlessly at last. 'You may go, as soon as you please.'

If only I could speak to her alone, Jade thought. She is still the same person. She has been deeply hurt, and to a great extent I am responsible for that hurt. I would like to do what I can to mend it, to show her that things could not have been otherwise; that if Pheasant had not loved me, he would not therefore have loved her the better. She is the victim of self-deception; and others are helping her to maintain it, when they should be assisting her to overcome it.

She moved forward slightly, catching a glint of malice from Bright Virtue.

'Your Majesty,' she said urgently, 'before I leave I would like to beg the favour of another interview, a private one. What I wish to say is for your ears alone.' The matter of the poison must be discussed, for both their sakes.

Paulownia drew herself up angrily. 'You insult my honoured mother with your unworthy words! How dare you comment on the fact that I choose to have friends about me when the jackal comes to call?'

The Duchess, who had been silent far longer than suited her, rapped her long vermilion fingernails on the arm of her chair.

'My illustrious daughter has ordered you out of this room. Do you want to be dragged away by the guard, and flung into a dungeon for the disobedient whore you are?'

A firework flashed in Black Jade's skull. She smiled calmly. 'I must remind the Lady Osier that I enjoy the Emperor's protection.'

'You have no need to remind us,' Paulownia cried with sudden shrillness, halfway out of her seat. 'Do you think I do not remember it every day? You have his protection! You have his love! You have his children! And what have I? What is left of the feast for me? I am the Empress. And I have nothing. Nothing!'

She subsided into tears, turning away in shame and pressing her brow painfully into the carved wood of the throne. Jade moved as if to go to her, but Lady Osier barred her way, her chin bristling with malevolence.

'Get out of her sight!' she hissed, her scarlet mouth very near to her victim's ear. 'And I would counsel you to walk warily, wherever you may go, for you have offended the Gods – and you may expect their punishment to be terrible.'

In that instant Jade believed everything she had heard of Lady Osier. She felt contaminated by the heavy, scented breath that touched her cheek. She could accomplish nothing while this inimical creature was present.

She stepped back and bowed once towards the crumpled bundle on the Phoenix Throne.

'It is as you wish, Your Majesty. I am leaving now.'

She walked as quickly as she could, with the sense of being pursued by something vile. She realised unhappily that she had made matters far worse by this morning's work. She had not even begun to get near to the strongly fortified cell that was the frightened and despairing self of Paulownia. And in being the unwitting author of her public tears, she had committed the unforgivable sin of causing the Empress to lose face.

Saddened, she collected Welcome, who was waiting for her outside in the tree-lined square. Her set face was a clear signal that questions were not in order.

Welcome rolled home behind her mistress, looking unexpectedly philosophical and thinking private thoughts about some people whose toffee-noses were soon going to be rubbed in the dust.

At the hour of the Monkey on an autumn afternoon, Black Jade sat with her small maternal family on the veranda of Green Fragrance Court, keeping a watchful eye on Bold Tiger who was clambering with two-year-old determination on to the back of one of the gilded leopards that guarded the short flight of steps to the courtyard. Young Tiger lay milkily asleep in his rush basket, his tiny fingers curling round the ear of his favourite toy, a dragon, bright green with red silk wattles, made for him by his sweet-smelling aunt, Rose Bird.

That young lady was presently roaming restlessly about the garden, teasing a plant here and there, supposedly busy cutting out dead growth. Her mind was not on her work. Nor was it on the relentless chatter of her small daughter, Lotus Bud, who was following her with a basket for the cuttings.

'Hon'ble Mother, you are not liss'ning to me,' complained the bright treble. A hand pulled at Rose Bird's sky-blue skirt.

'Tie your sash. You will take cold. It isn't summer now,' her mother said abstractedly. She was not looking at the child but up at the veranda where Golden Willow stood at a portable table employing her perfectionist's calligraphy in some correspondence for the 'Lotus Sect', the Buddhist group of which she was an enthusiastic patron.

'See, Little Pigeon, these tiny four-leaved ones are weeds. Let's see how many you can find before tea. All by yourself.'

Lotus Bud nodded, sensing that she was not going to engage her mother's attention. Rose Bird straightened and went purposefully up the steps without noticing Bold Tiger's grin of achievement. She looked tense.

'Honoured Mother, there is something I have to say to you. You also, Black Jade, if you will.'

Golden Willow rinsed her brush and laid it carefully in its porcelain tray. She cleaned the inkstone with tissue and placed jade weights upon the corners of her paper so that it should not warp while the ink was drying.

'Very well, Elder Daughter. What is your trouble?'

Rose Bird smiled ruefully. 'Is it so obvious – that it is trouble?'

'Let us say that, this afternoon, you have mislaid your repose.'

'And for a very long time, perhaps. O Mother, I have been very foolish.'

Black Jade's instinct leaped to its conclusion as her sister knelt at Golden Willow's feet and bowed her head.

'Look up, my child, and speak without fear.'

Rose Bird took a deep breath. 'You will remember that, after Resolute Heart went to his ancestors, his second cousin called many times to pay his respects to the body?

'Indeed I do. A familial and dutiful young man. What of it?'

Rose Bird sighed. Black Jade, understanding, sorrowed that she had not shared her troubled heart, so far away.

'He – Quiet Spirit – he came again, after the funeral. He came often. I was allowed to spend time with him, since he shared my love of music, and is a most respected member of the family, one of the clan leaders, renowned for his scholarship.' She faltered, blushing like an afflicted peony.

Golden Willow's kohl-black brows moved delicately towards each other. 'So you have told me before.'

'We – he and I – we found we had much in common. His company was very congenial to me. He did a great deal to comfort my distress. I was very lonely without my husband,' she finished in a whisper.

'That is natural and as it should be,' said Golden Willow automatically. The echo of a prophecy had once again entered her mind.

Rose Bird took another breath. 'I did not think I should see Quiet Spirit again. But then, last year, he came to Chang-an to attend the court. He holds a position in the imperial library. I did not tell you, Mother, but he called on me one day while you were at the Lotus Temple. He has done so many times since.' She looked up shamefacedly to judge her mother's expression. Nothing could be deduced from it.

'Continue, please.'

'Well, at first we simply talked, and played the lute a little, as we had in Taiyuan. But then, we began to know what we felt for each other – an affection that was more than that between friends. Oh, Mother, must I go on?'

'I'm afraid you must.'

She will bring dishonour to her husband's name, the echo said.

'Then, it is this. We are lovers. I love Quiet Spirit. And I am carrying his child.'

Black Jade did not wait for their mother's reaction but took Rose Bird at once in her arms. Her sister was weeping now.

'Hush. Hush, now. It is over. You have told us. No one will judge you. You are no better or worse than I am.'

She looked at Golden Willow above Rose Bird's bent head, challenging her generosity, knowing the truth of her words. She also marvelled at the uncharacteristic secrecy that had prevented her sister from telling her of her forbidden love.

Golden Willow seated herself in a woven cane chair and looked sadly and thoughtfully across the courtyard where a few leaves were beginning to blow in the fresh breeze that was rising.

'Come here, Precious Mouse,' she said, using Rose Bird's

milk-name. 'It is not the end of the universe.' She smiled. 'Indeed, it is another new beginning. You will have to be very courageous. You know that, don't you? You will not be able to keep your child. You must bear it and then it must leave you. It will be hard for you, but there is no alternative.'

Rose Bird knelt at her side. She laid her head in the narrow lap.

'I understand. I know it must be so. I am so sorry, Mother.'

Golden Willow shook her head. 'It is karma.'

It may well be karma, thought Black Jade, but it isn't necessarily the end of it.

'Tell me,' she said, now feeling free to speak, 'is Quiet Spirit already married?'

'He has a wife, a secondary consort, and two concubines,' said Rose Bird dully.

'And is there no room for you also, in such a rich household?'

'Certainly not! It would be most unsuitable!' declared Golden Willow firmly. 'There has already been quite enough unconventional behaviour. We will keep this knowledge among ourselves.'

A flicker of hope had lit and died in Rose Bird's eyes.

'Forgive me,' said Jade, saddened too. 'I only thought that a marriage might be best thing, or even to be a concubine.'

'The daughters of General Wu do not become concubines,' said his widow sternly. 'Not, that is, in normal circumstances,' she added, fixing her second daughter with a quelling gaze.

'No, please – let's talk about something else,' begged Rose Bird.

Black Jade felt responsible for a change of subject. She could in fact, alter only its direction, towards herself.

'Well, as it happens I also have some news – rather similar in nature. I too am going to have another child at the end of winter.' She covertly examined Rose Bird's face for traces of justifiable bitterness, but found none. They hugged each other and Rose Bird said shakily, 'At least we shall be able to share our discomforts for a while. I'm so glad for you, Jade.'

Golden Willow, with the exquisite tact of a Sui princess, managed to reconcile the different aspects of the situation in her own mind, though her heart was very sore for Rose Bird, whose child must go to adoptive parents whom she would never meet, while Black Jade's would be acclaimed as a member of the imperial clan of Li.

They never found out how it had happened, who had eavesdropped and where or when, but somehow, as the months passed, the word became current that the sister of the Concubine of Luminous

Demeanour was carrying a fatherless child.

Because Pheasant was often seen to visit the little house in the suburbs, not always in the company of Black Jade, it began to be said that he had desired the young widow as he had desired her sister, and that now both carried his children.

The friends of the Empress saw that this became accredited truth. No criticism (naturally!) attached to the Emperor, but it was agreed in certain circles that the women of the Wu clan were of a loose and carnal disposition, and that it was a matter of political expediency to make an end of their influence on the young monarch.

13

Rose Bird was delivered of a boy at the beginning of the Season of Rain Water. The child was taken away and adopted immediately, as her mother had promised. Rose Bird was depressed for a time afterwards, and it was difficult to persuade her to come back to the palace after the birth. Only when Jade's confinement was due did she apparently throw off her mourning and reappear in Green Fragrance Court, a little pale still and rather thinner than suited her, but doing her best to act like her old self.

Black Jade's child, to her great delight, was a daughter. She had longed for a girl, there being little danger of the lofty imperial roof being lowered, as the popular saying would have it, by the birth of a worthless female.

The baby was an especially pretty one, with a grace of her own from birth. In her mother's opinion she outshone her brothers for both looks and intelligence; for her eyes, green as the pool in the courtyard where she would one day play, seemed already to focus upon the world with a grave curiosity. She fed and slept without any fuss and seemed only to cry for the pleasure of trying her voice.

Pheasant was at his wits' end as to what he should give Black Jade for her birth gift. She had forbidden him jewels after he had inundated her with another shower of them when Young Tiger had been born. Bolts of silk, since they were the commonest currency of the rich, were out of the question. In the end her love of animals had come to her rescue.

After he had picked up his sleeping daughter and kissed her pink bud of a nose, he gave the scented bolster to Welcome, who was overjoyed to have a baby to nurse again, and clapped his hands as a signal to someone outside the green doors.

Jade wriggled further up her pillows, curious to see what would appear.

The door slid back to reveal the resplendent figure of Chinghiz, dressed in an outlandish costume of beads and brocade in the black and glowing scarlet of the Wu clan. Beside him, sitting very straight and self-conscious in a collar of rubies that must have cost a sultan's ransom, was a young black panther, its ears pricked to attention. As Chinghiz stalked into the room it followed him close at heel, stepping lightly and soundlessly on its broad pads.

'We have had her trained. She is perfectly tame,' said Pheasant. 'We must have guessed you would give me a girl.'

At this point the baby awoke with a fierce caterwaul, her very first, which the panther answered with a sharp miaul.

'Well, she is a very handsome beast,' said Black Jade philosophically. 'And she already seems to understand my daughter. I suppose she is house-trained?' There had lately been several problems with puppies and kittens brought in by animal-mad Bold Tiger.

'She is as perfect a lady as our daughter will be.'

Pheasant bent to kiss her again. Jade took his hand, pulling him closer. 'You don't mind that this one is a girl?'

He brushed her lips, licking the salt of her struggles from them. 'I wanted a girl. I shall load her with the jewels you will not let me give you.'

'I shall allow you to do nothing of the kind. I dislike spoiled children. She shall have a good Confucian upbringing, and learn to despise the shows of affluence.'

'Sublime Enchantress, you know you may do with her, as with her father, anything you wish.'

He left her then, to sleep.

Later, towards evening, she swam slowly back to reality after the satisfying slumber that follows a birth. There was, she realised almost at once, an unusual bustle in the outer chamber. It must have been the noise that had woken her. Welcome slid open the door narrowly and ran to her side.

'Oh, good! You're awake, Little Mistress. You'll never guess!

The Gods have taken a holiday today, they're in such a good mood! The Empress is outside! She has come to visit you, to congratulate you, she says, on the birth of the little Princess.'

'*Amitabha*! Paulownia! I can't believe it. Well, what have you done – kept her waiting on the threshold? Ask her in, for Heaven's sake! Is the baby awake?'

Welcome went to see. 'Yes. She's just stirring, bless her! I'll just put her in that little pink robe your honoured mother made for her. Don't worry. Chinghiz is looking after the Empress. He's showing her the panther.'

There was time to tidy Jade a little, to freshen her face with rosewater and wrap her in a new apricot jacket, before Paulownia made a hesitant entrance, stopping just inside the threshold.

'Lady Wu. Is it permitted that I should enter?'

Black Jade smiled like the sun. 'It is welcomed as a tremendous and signal honour. You bring me a great gift in your presence.'

The Empress returned the smile with a hasty one of her own before dropping her gaze to its comfortable floor level. Her cheeks were pink with something other than rouge, indicating unusual excitement.

'I have decided that you were right; we should not allow evil tongues to keep us apart. And truly,' she added with an odd abruptness, 'I miss your intelligent company.'

'Your Highness is much too kind,' murmured Jade happily.

'Not at all. I have brought a toy for the baby. May I see her? I am told you have a girl.'

'She is in her cradle. I will ask Welcome to get her up for you.'

'No. Do not trouble Welcome; I may have no children, but I think I know as well as any woman how to hold one.'

She came around to the other side of the bed and leaned over the cradle, dangling her gift, a set of tiny silver bells in the shape of drooping flower-heads, above its wide-eyed occupant. Jade heard a note of comment from the baby, and then Paulownia had lifted her out of her nest, studying her little face with a grave concentration.

'She is charming. She has your beautiful eyes.'

'She is delicious. I could eat her. Will you give her to me, or do you want to hold her a little longer?'

'Oh, let me keep her for a while. We shall walk about the chamber together and look at all its new and amazing sights.'

This was a side of Paulownia that Black Jade had never seen. She thought once again how misfortunate it was that she could have no babies of her own. Her sympathy was very deep, for she herself had found a joy and fulfilment in motherhood that she had not expected to find, never having thought of herself as a maternal creature. This baby, above all, perhaps because she too was female, had instantly engaged her heart so that she still felt the umbilical tie, responding to her with a love as physical as that she shared with the child's father.

She lay back and watched lazily as the Empress walked about the room, directing the infant's gaze at plants or vases, and the view of the wintering courtyard outside the gauze-covered windows. Paulownia began to sing softly to her charge, making a cradle of her thin arms, so that very soon the child was sleeping again. Jade, too, had begun, without noticing, to feel drowsy, and she was suddenly subject to one of those disconcerting jerks which often disrupt this pleasant state.

'Oh, I'm sorry. I didn't mean to go to sleep. How very rude of me!'

Paulownia had put the baby back in the cradle and was standing beside the bed, looking down at her. For a moment her eyes seemed blank, but she smiled as Jade spoke, and shook her head.

'No, indeed. You should be asleep, both of you. It was selfish of me to come here at this time. But I wanted you to know that I no longer bear you a grudge.'

'I am very glad,' Black Jade said simply.

'Then, I will leave you now. Your daughter is beautiful. Even the Gods must envy you. Sleep now. I will come again.'

She slipped out of the room and Jade heard a brief, vague murmur in the anteroom as she left the court. Then she slid down the soft slope into sleep.

When she awoke again, Pheasant was bending over her, his face transparent with love.

'You are so beautiful when you are asleep; so vulnerable. It makes me want to be with you always, so that I can protect you from dreams brought by evil spirits.'

He tenderly stroked back the hair that had fallen over her cheek.

'I am never subject to those,' she said calmly, perfectly awake, 'unless I have eaten too much. Now, please bring me our daughter, so that I can see if she has grown even more adorable while I slept.'

'Let me kiss you first, before I lose all chance of securing your attention. M'm! You smell like a temple garden.'

During their embrace Welcome arrived, smiling broadly, with the purpose of making Jade look more respectable.

'Now, sit up and let me get a comb through this magpie's nest,' she ordered. 'I don't know how it manages to get like this; I plait it tight enough to begin with.'

Jade sat up and suffered her ministrations. The Emperor, realising that his private moment was over, strolled towards the cradle to pick up his daughter.

'She's still fast asleep. She's turned over on her stomach and has her little fist in her mouth. Come along, my sweeting; it's time to greet the world again!'

He lifted the child carefully and held her up, gazing into her face. She seemed strangely somnolent, making no movement, her eyes still shut. Her skin was smooth; he missed its comical array of puckers and dimples. She was sound asleep, even now. He shook her, very gently. The small head lolled.

'Oh, Great Heaven!'

'What?' Black Jade cried sharply, catching his note of alarm. 'What's the matter?'

'I don't know. Something's – here, Welcome, you take her. I can't get her to wake up.'

Welcome snatched the child. One look was enough. She sank to the floor with the still bundle in her arms, moaning softly.

'Gods, will you *tell* me!' screamed Black Jade, struggling to get out of bed.

'It's no use, Little Mistress –' Welcome held up a face seamed with sorrow. 'Our little one has gone to her ancestors.'

'She can't have! Give her to me!' Jade was hysterical with fear. She shook her as Pheasant had done, calling to her in an agony of disbelief. The Emperor, not knowing what to do, sat down helplessly on the bed, his head in his hands.

The cries brought the servants running and the room was soon smothering in their lamentations. It was Chinghiz, his face tense, who knelt in front of the distracted Black Jade and made sure that the baby was, indeed, dead.

'Please! Control yourselves!' he ordered the keening women. 'Your behaviour can only add to the grief of the Emperor and Lady Wu.' Used to obedience, the maids quietened, sobs and sniffs breaking through now and again.

Chinghiz knelt again beside Black Jade. He longed to take her in his arms, to give her what comfort he could. But that, alas, was not his right.

'Dearest lady,' he said tenderly, 'if you will, give her to me.'

With his life's most gentle gesture he rose and took the tiny corpse from her despairing grasp. At first she tried to cling to it, but soon let go – with a wrench, it seemed to her, that tore her very womb apart. Her eyes pleaded with him, begging him again that it might not be true. He shook his head, minutely, and turned away. She broke into a silent storm of weeping.

The Emperor still sat with his long fingers pressing against his forehead. Chinghiz touched his shoulder. He looked up, then nodded, only half aware of what was meant.

Chinghiz looked once, sorrowfully, at the tiny, shut face, then wrapped the child in one of her shawls, and carried her out of the room.

Pheasant recovered himself sufficiently to lift the shuddering Black Jade and bring her back to the bed.

'I'll look after her now, Majesty,' whispered Welcome, subduing her own grief with a necessary effort. 'I'll give her something to make her sleep. It's all anyone can do. She is not strong enough for this. Oh, sir – how can it have happened?'

'I don't know.' Pheasant was numbly despondent. 'She was a healthy little girl. I just don't know.'

An opium draught was brought and he managed to induce Black Jade to drink it. He would never forget the pain in her eyes as she sank beneath its heavy waves.

In the anteroom Chinghiz was waiting for him.

'We must ask ourselves – *you* must ask yourself – if you will pardon me, Majesty, how indeed could this have occurred.'

'How can we know?' asked Pheasant wearily. 'The Gods have taken her back, that is all, before her soul was properly at home in her body.'

'I have made enquiries, sir,' Chinghiz continued relentlessly. 'It seems that the last person who is known to have handled the child was the Empress.'

'Paulownia?' The Emperor was clearly astonished.

'She came to congratulate the Little Mistress on the birth. I believe she said she – wished to make amends for the rift in their friendship. That is what I was told.' He had in fact listened to every word spoken by the Empress; his concept of his duty to Black Jade was exact and all-encompassing.

'I would never have expected her to come here,' Pheasant wondered, his emotions too raw for him to notice he was confiding in a servant.

'No,' said Chinghiz with measured neutrality. 'That is what everyone is saying. That it was a – very sudden – change of heart.'

The Emperor stared at the young Tartar, the pain-tilled soil of his mind accepting, and allowing to germinate, the seeds of suspicion that were being sown.

'Be very careful,' he whispered.

'I know,' agreed Chinghiz, his beautiful voice still level. 'What people will soon be saying – is very high treason.'

Black Jade awoke into hell.

Her baby was dead. That sweet, soft life of her life was gone.

It was not possible, but it had happened. During that brief period when her tired body had taken its rest, a time when the maids were tiptoeing in and out of the room, secure in the certainty that her little daughter was asleep, the small soul had already gone back to the Limbo which, for the first thirty days of its life, it would never completely have left. Without those thirty days to measure the first full year of her life, so joyfully begun in the womb, it was as though the tiny spirit had never existed.

She groaned, fighting off the opium. She didn't want to wake up, but knew she must. She had to face her loss.

Chinghiz was in the room, close to her. She sensed his love, his urgency to bring her back.

'Little Mistress, drink this. It will do you good.' She groped for the bowl which he held steady for her. It was sweet rice wine, fiery and pungent; it seared her throat but it also cleared her head.

'Mistress, please listen to me very carefully.' He would give her no time for the tears that were brimming her eyes in mute, automatic misery. 'What I am going to tell you is the truth, beyond all hope of doubt. It was the Empress who murdered the little one. Do you understand?'

'No!' He suffered with the agony in her cry.

'Murder! No!' she moaned again. She pushed herself up on her elbow. 'How can you say this? What do you know?'

He sighed. If only he could spare her this, at least. 'I had long ago made arrangements of a domestic nature within the Empress's household. My source is impeccable. It is *known*, not suspected, that Lady Paulownia has considerably hardened in her feelings towards you. Only a few days ago she expressed the wish to her mother – forgive me, Bright Phoenix – the wish that you might die in childbirth.'

'Kuan Yin have mercy!'

'So you must see that it is not only possible, but almost certain that it was she who put an end to the baby's life – though how she found the opportunity – I myself was close by, and other servants too, all loyal to the bone; at least I have managed to watch *them* well enough to be sure,' he finished, in savage self-scourging. He had been so close, and yet had not prevented the death. He would never forgive himself.

'Don't; it was not your fault.' Even in her agony, she felt the pull of their closeness, could not let him suffer pointless guilt.

She dragged her hand over her eyes, trying to think.

'Then – what do the doctors say? Don't *they* know how she –?'

'They say they are unable to tell,' he replied with unveiled contempt. 'They say she *could* have been stifled, but that again, infants do die mysteriously in their cradles. Not one would be responsible for making a diagnosis; they are afraid for their skins.'

'Of course,' she said, not really listening.

'Paulownia,' she began again, weeping. 'I can't seem to be able to believe it, though I suppose I must trust in what you say. But she, when she was here – she held the baby so tenderly; she sang to her so lovingly – oh Gods, how could anyone hide so cold a heart as that?' She was sobbing now. Forbidden to comfort her with his touch, Chinghiz caressed her with his soft, velvet voice.

'Beautiful Orchid, listen to me. This is the worst you will have to suffer; this; here, now. If you can get through these few terrible minutes, you will become invincible. The world will not touch you. Take courage, Black Jade. You have the strength. You will always have it. You know it.'

Did she? She thought she had never felt so weak.

'Oh, Chinghiz –' her voice broke. 'I lack the courage even to face another day. I almost wish that I too –'

'Enough of that!' He forced contempt and callousness into voice. 'The Empress is your implacable enemy! She has murdered your newborn child,' he said with cruel clarity. 'How will you answer her? With tears – or with justice?'

'Get out! Leave me alone!' she cried, glaring at him. He saw her anger and was satisfied.

'Send me Welcome, and get out of my sight!'

Her loving servant bowed and removed himself. Outside the door, he smiled.

The Emperor reluctantly came to agree with Chinghiz. When he next visited Black Jade he was sombrely convinced that Paulownia could well have killed their little daughter.

'At first the idea seemed impossible,' he told her. 'But then I began to think back a little. I saw a side of her that you never did, I think. It was while you were in the convent. She was so desperately jealous of Bright Virtue! One night, I remember especially; she was beside herself with rage. There was a black storm of tears – quite unlike her normal behaviour. She begged me on her knees not to go to Bright Virtue that night. I was astonished – I'd never seen her lose control. It frightened me; she was always so cool and correct, seemed so far apart from mundane emotions.' Troubled and bewildered, he suddenly seized Black Jade's hands and held them against his cheeks.

'Was she ever like that again – when you and I –?'

'No. Then, she simply withdrew from me. Except, of course, to perform her monthly duty, though even then I never felt she was really *there*, with me.' He shuddered. 'It was a strange experience. She still hoped against hope that she might conceive, but there was no pleasure in it for either of us. In the end, I had to give it up, although I have still paid her a courtesy visit every month, her and that evil-minded old woman –'

'But do you think,' Jade broke in, 'that she is capable of – murder?' She had spoken the word. She had avoided it until now.

'I am beginning to think,' he said slowly, 'that she might be a little mad.'

'Mad?' She shook her head. 'I don't believe that. Although it would certainly be a kinder thought than the one we presently entertain. Kindness, however, is not our aim – we need to discover the truth. It might be hard. Paulownia has powerful friends to protect her.'

Pheasant squared his shoulders. 'Whether or not she is guilty – and if she is, the torments of all eighteen hells are not too painful for her – the suspicion of it will rend the court in two. Harmony is destroyed. We can't go on like this.'

He leaned over and took her very tenderly by the arms, kissing her slowly and with reverence.

'Black Jade, you are the only woman I want beside me. You are the mother of my sons. I love you more than life. I have thought about this for a long time, and last night I lay awake thinking about it. Now, I have made my decision; I want to make you my Empress. Bold Tiger will be the Crown Prince. Order will return.'

She caught her breath, new life striking within her like a flint despite her weariness and desolation.

'You are sure?' Her eyes searched him, green as glass.

'Very sure.' He smiled tremulously and touched her hair. 'We will have to struggle for it, at first, but it will be worth it.'

'I know. All the Awful Old Men. They dislike me so.'

'Then they must learn that it will be their duty to love you.'

'Your father chose them. They served him well,' she allowed.

'If my father were here now, he would tell me to do just what I intend to do. I'm certain of it.'

Black Jade was by no means so certain, but she did not say so. Shih-min had also chosen Paulownia. He had respected her clan and its influence, and he had approved of her steady integrity even if he had not found her personally attractive. It was doubtful that he would have given credit to her guilt.

Did she herself give it credit, she pondered when Pheasant reluctantly left her for a council meeting?

She consulted her own memories of the tall cool girl whom she had been asked to look after during her early months in the palace. The proud demeanour, the few words, the icy reservation of self. The other girls had disliked her, in general, and she herself had never felt really close to her, despite those depressing days they had shared during the Korean war. Even then she had been kept at a distance, less than others perhaps – but at a distance all the same. A cold nature then, which found human contact difficult. But a murderess?

The thought was suddenly too much for her and she was crying again, great heaving sobs that said she *was* beginning to believe it. The baby was dead. And Paulownia had said she wished that Black Jade might die. She could not have hoped to kill the mother with impunity, but a baby was so tiny and defenceless; sleeping, trusting in the new world she had entered. It would have been so easy, so pitifully easy.

And yet, later, when she had begged Jade to leave Kan Yeh, and after – surely she had then regarded her with friendship? True, she had loathed the sociable life which Jade had created for her, but she had seemed to become fond of her, to rely upon her, to seek and willingly accept her advice. Surely, oh surely, there was a time when they had been friends?

She carried her doubts to Chinghiz when he came to comb her hair.

'There is simply no one else who could have done it,' he said relentlessly, drawing the ivory comb down the yard-long fall, released from its plait.

'Consider,' he said, trying a new tack, 'the lightning changes in Lady Paulownia's attitude to the Pure Concubine. There you have hatred and jealousy apparently becoming a form of affection – they're together a great deal now – why then, in such an unpredictable nature, shouldn't the reverse also be true? If she cared for you once, she detests your very name today. Face it.

There is no alternative.'

He had stopped combing and was bending all the considerable influence of his blue, feral stare upon her. She sensed that he wanted to shake her, to hurt her if necessary, anything to force her into the reality that waited for her.

'I'd like to sleep again, for a little while,' she told him softly. 'Afterwards, perhaps I will get up. Will you choose something for me to wear?'

He left her, sensing some change in her, or at least the will towards it.

Alone, Black Jade forced herself to contemplate the evil thing once more, and the woman who could have done it. Reliving it, she fell again into despair. Its depths were fathoms deep and she went down into them alone.

When she returned, it was with the sense of someone who has been newly abandoned, weak but whole, by the demons whose work it is to harrow the mind into insanity. With a clarity that astounded her, she knew she had come to a resolve. She was certain, now, in her heart and head, that Paulownia had indeed killed her little daughter.

She would not cease to mourn; that small soul had entered deeply into her own. But one day she would have another daughter; and perhaps the Gods would relent and allow the reincarnation of the life that been so brief.

As for Paulownia herself, she was no longer to be thought of as a woman, but as a dangerous predator to be hunted down. Her punishment was required by Heaven, and it would be very great. Black Jade would take her crown, her respect and, at last, if it were granted to her, her life.

When Chinghiz returned, carrying a pale grey robe, she tossed it aside, her eyes blazing with a light he had not seen before.

'Bring me the colours of my clan,' she ordered, thrilling him with the new, as yet undefined, fire and flash of her spirit. 'Scarlet and black. The colours of Wu. The colours of war!'

'He wants to make her the Empress,' revealed Chinghiz to Welcome, offering her the spirit of celebration in the form of her previous downfall. 'What do you think of that!'

'Glory be to Heaven! It's all going to come true!'

'So let us hope. But this,' he reminded her, 'is only the beginning. The Phoenix Throne is not the Dragon Throne, and as yet she has secured neither.'

Welcome tippled a little, gasping as the burning white liquid whipped down her throat to meet the tumult of excitement below.

'Shall we – you, shall you tell the Little Mistress, then? Now that it all means something?' She gasped again with the effort of forcing words up a red-hot funnel.

The steward looked at her sternly, wondering if he ought not to have given her the brandy. 'No,' he said, with all the chill authority he could command. 'I will not. And nor, my dear Welcome, will you. If you do, believe me, the words you use will be the last you speak. We have a very nasty way with the tongue-cutting scissors, in my part of the world.'

Welcome was afraid. She giggled, but it turned into a hiccough.

'All right! There's no need to be like that. I won't say anything, though may I never be reincarnated if I see why not!'

'Because this is not the time,' said Chinghiz slowly and clearly, wishing the Gods had installed a higher intellect in his fellow-conspirator. 'We will tell Black Jade the truth of the prophecy when she has great need of its impetus; when it will drive her forward to things which she would otherwise fail to accomplish. She has another impetus at present – perhaps the strongest known to fallible humanity. Do you know what it is, Mistress Welcome?' He finished on a note of irony that concealed his regret.

'Oh yes, I know. I'm not quite so stupid as you think, Master Chinghiz. Revenge. That's what keeps the Little Mistress going now. I wish it were anything else.'

He filled her cup and lifted it in a conspirator's toast.

'We must do what we can with what we have,' he said lightly.

The war had to be fought with guerilla tactics. It was no use considering an all-out attack on the Empress. For one thing, she had too many partisans in high places; for another, although Black Jade might think, and even the Emperor might think, that she was guilty, it was quite another matter to prove it.

'We could have her tortured, you and I, privately,' Jade suggested to Chinghiz in frustration.

'Not so. She would accuse you, even if she, in that event, were the one without proof.' He was very clear. 'If you are to take the place of the Empress, your opposers must not be able to say you have treated her with anything but scrupulous fairness.'

Pheasant, when applied to, agreed with this.

'What we must do,' he determined, 'is to break down the opposition. My wishes, after all, must surely count for something, even in the mule-minded ranks of my father's ministers.'

They began with the cornerstone of that opposition, the Archduke himself, Chang-sun Wuchi.

Pheasant did not anticipate an easy task. These first moves were designed to hoist the standard of his intentions rather than in real hope of an early victory.

He proposed to his uncle-in-law that he should pay him the signal courtesy of a visit to his home. Such a rare event would be written down in the official history of the reign, heaping honour upon the clan of Chang-sun.

The Archduke prepared to entertain his nephew with the requisite prodigality, despite a certain cynical self-questioning as to the reason for the feast.

When his royal guest arrived with Lady Wu beside him, that question was resolved. Wuchi noted that the Son of Heaven showed her extreme consideration, bending to catch her every word as she stepped down from her palanquin, which flaunted the imperial colours. The appalling woman had her wretched pet with her, the young female panther that had become part of her shadow, moving when she did, quiet when she was still, its clear green gaze as much to be trusted as her own.

Smiling, he went forward to welcome them.

'Your Majesty. My poor roof is raised to Heaven by the honour.'

'No need to be so formal, Uncle. I would prefer you to look on this as a family occasion. I believe you are acquainted with Lady Wu?'

Wuchi bowed stiffly. 'For many years, though our encounters have been all too brief. Her beauty illumines us all.'

'Your Highness is far too generous.' Black Jade rested both hands lightly on her left hip and bent gracefully at the knee, her expression demure and respectful. The panther yawned and stuck out a hind leg for a casual lick.

'I hope you do not mind Mao-yu; she is usually very well-behaved.' Her lovely eyes teased him with a different meaning.

'She is a beautiful animal, very picturesque; but I'm sure we have no need to fear her.' He met her, recalling an impudent child.

'Only if you cross her, which would be unwise and unnecessary, as she is very easy to please.'

Content that they understood each other, they exchanged another bow and the party moved on to the superb pavilion that Wuchi had constructed in the grounds of his mansion. It was built from the green and white marble found in the hills south of the capital, and was designed as a well-heated winter imitation of the summerhouse of a Turkish pasha. Its octagonal walls were so finely carved as to seem like ivory, patterned into the shapes of the leaves and flowers that surrounded it, so that it became a perfect example of the harmony between man and nature.

The food which was served them now was as finely wrought as their setting; Wuchi's chefs were objects of constant seduction by his peers. Jade ate sparingly, though praising the food to her hostess, the Archduchess, a slightly plump, reflective woman of middle age who projected an atmosphere of calm pleasure which she was far from feeling. Beneath her sociable talk Jade recognised an outrage at her own presence which equalled her husband's.

The conversation circled in a civilised manner about the smaller affairs of the court and the activities of the Archduke's family. When it languished a little, the Emperor produced his surprise for his uncle.

'I've decided it's time I did something for those three boys of yours,' he said expansively, waving his hand towards the Chang-sun heirs, seated below the courtiers on the men's side of the table. They tried not to prick up their ears; Pheasant's voice was melodious and he had inherited his father's ability to reach the back of a hall.

'Your Majesty is magnanimous, but it is quite unnecessary,' said Wuchi firmly, knowing that, in this case, a favour was expected for a favour. 'My sons are unworthy of your notice. They are unintelligent and lazy, and deserve nothing.' This was quite untrue, but the Archduke was cornered. His sons, embarrassed but still hopeful, engaged their neighbours in strenuous conversation, leaving the matter to Heaven.

Shortly, each one was called and told that he had been awarded a promotion on the strength of his exceptional merit; one became a chief librarian and the others rose within the State Department. They were very grateful.

The wine flowed liberally in celebration of the young men's achievement, and then it was time for more surprises. Black Jade watched with concealed amusement as Pheasant gave the signal for the ceremonial procession through Wuchi's manicured lawns of ten carts, pulled by thoroughbred horses and loaded with gold, silks and jewels shipped from every port in the world from Baghdad to Nagasaki.

Despairing, the minister expressed his unbounded gratitude, followed swiftly by his iron determination not to accept such largesse.

‘I have done nothing to merit such splendid gifts. It would shame me before my peers to give in to your heavenly generosity.’

‘Well, well, Uncle. Let us leave it for now, shall we? The things are here; they have no other home.’ Pheasant grinned with a fine appreciation of the archducal discomfort. Now he knows what it is like to wriggle for a change, he thought cheerfully. He was enjoying himself.

Musicians and dancers were brought to cover further embarrassment. They performed a dance-pantomime called ‘The Peacock King’, in which hundreds of thousands of bird’s feathers were sacrificed to decorate the nakedness of the Indian dancers who had been sent in tribute to the ‘Instruction Quarter’ in the city. They were accompanied by drums and flutes which, happily, made conversation impossible.

When they had done, the Archduke’s fortunate sons gave a spirited rendering of ‘Crushing the Barbarians’ as a sign of their gratitude. This, since there were only three of them, was quieter.

‘What excellent young men they are,’ said Pheasant admiringly. ‘You must be very proud, Uncle, to have such sons.’ He sighed and looked painfully into the middle distance. ‘It would set my own mind at rest if my poor Empress might give me just such a fine set of boys as my cousins are.’ The second sigh came from the depths of his soul. ‘But I’m afraid that will never happen. The Gods condemn Lady Paulownia to unhappy infertility.’

‘But the boy you adopted is a good child. I am always hearing tales of his intelligence and progress,’ said Wuchi quickly.

‘He may be a paragon,’ countered Pheasant smoothly, ‘but he is neither the highest in birth nor the closest to my heart.’ He hesitated, delicately. ‘As you know, Lady Wu has given me two splendid boys –’

‘Forgive me, sir; you will think me rude, but my wife is trying to attract your gracious attention.’

The Archduchess came forward, urbanely on cue, to beg the honour of presenting some of her relatives.

The sticky moment over, Wuchi was careful to present no similar opportunity to his nephew. The rest of the evening progressed gently into drunkenness while the hordes of guests and clansmen surrounded their Emperor with loving attentions. The three sons, unable to credit so much good luck on one night, were deputed to entertain the outrageously beautiful and charming Lady Wu.

Black Jade went home with her ears burning with compliments and her sleeves full of hastily scribbled poems to her eyebrows;

but she had not moved a single step nearer to the Phoenix Throne.

Next morning the ten cartloads of gifts trundled back into the sumpter yard of the palace. Pheasant received a polite note from Wuchi saying that he had kept one bolt of silk, in order not to seem ungrateful.

Pheasant sulked and boyishly kicked the edge of his chair.

The Luminous Demeanour of his concubine remained optimistically bright. 'We have been a little too obvious, that's all. The Archduke is a subtle man. He doesn't respond to the normal methods. He needs exceptionally careful handling. I have a suggestion to make.'

'We send him to govern Outer Mongolia?'

'Is it ours? I didn't know. No, let us put Chang-sun Wuchi in the gentle hands of my lady mother.'

But even Golden Willow, despite courtesy, piety and undoubted social and personal attractions, was unable, after several pleasant afternoons of good music and stimulating conversation, to move the cornerstone by the hundredth part of an inch.

It was not until towards the end of the summer that the Gods put a possible weapon into Black Jade's hands, a long summer spent at the Kingfisher Blue Palace, where they had tried, with the aid of its blossom and beauty, its picnics and expeditions, the laughter of children and the unending solace of the clouds and rain, to erase the unhappy memories of winter.

Black Jade, almost herself again, though with a new and permanent edge to her nature that would, if tried, prove deadly, had taken up her old habit of riding early in the morning, accompanied by Chinghiz. Pheasant shunned early rising whenever he could.

Today they had reached the banks of a river, some dozen miles from the palace. They left their horses to enjoy the lush watered grass and sat down to hypnotise themselves by staring into the slow golden current, thick as treacle with loess dust from the mountains, and feel themselves part of its flow.

After a period of mutually consenting silence, Jade became aware that her companion was having difficult in achieving the selfless tranquillity recommended by the Taoists in such surroundings.

'Very well. What is it? I can *hear* you thinking.'

Chinghiz smiled and tossed a stone into the water. 'You are right. I have some news for you. Interesting. Useful. But rather disturbing. I did not wish to dispel the peace of the morning.'

'You already have. Go on.'

'Thank you. First, I want you to promise not to be afraid. I can assure you that no harm will be allowed to come of this.'

'Afraid?' she asked irritably. 'Please don't be so mysterious.'

'I'm sorry. But it is a serious matter. It is this; the Empress and her mother, whose reputation you know, have been practising sorcery against you.'

She controlled her alarm. 'How do you know?'

'I was told by one of our friends who attends Lady Paulownia.' 'Our friends' were a growing number. Black Jade herself knew few of her steward's web of spies, but he had assured her it covered every necessary area of the Palace City.

'They had made a doll to look like you. My informant found it under the Empress's bed.'

Black Jade shivered. She did not subscribe to all the ancient beliefs of her uniformly superstitious nation, the charms, the repulsive cures, the old wives' tales, the rules and taboos that surrounded the smallest natural or man-made object; but sorcery came into an altogether different category. Whether it was the potent mixture of alchemy and spiritualism practised by the priests, or the malevolent mumbling of half-mad old women in villages across the Empire, there was no question as to its power to harm. That was why it was a capital crime.

Despite Chinghiz's assurance, she was afraid.

He saw it and repeated his comfort. 'We know it now. We are armed.'

'Armed? Against demons? What arms do we employ, I wonder? Do we recite the *Book of Rites* in reverse? Or shoo them away with a flywhisk? What precautions can we take against magic? We can hardly find a taster for it, as we do for poison – or a strong guard, as we have against assassins!'

'Little Mistress, the sorcery has not worked. You are well. You are here. You are healthily angry.'

'At the moment!' she flashed. 'How about tomorrow? I don't want to be found with my neck broken like Welcome's old acquaintance!'

'Like who?'

'It doesn't matter. Take me back to the palace. I've lost my taste for Taoist tranquillity.'

When she was shown the obscene little image, wearing what was unmistakably one of her latest robes, with the great iron nail driven up between its splayed wooden legs, Black Jade wanted to be sick.

She controlled herself and demanded, instead, to know what Paulownia had said when she had been accused.

She had claimed, reported the captain of the guard, a handsome man who was much taken with Lady Wu's unfailingly pleasant manner towards himself and his men, that the image must have been placed in her room to incriminate her. She had suggested that possibly Lady Wu herself might have had a hand in this.

'Sacred Kuan Ti!' cried Black Jade, relieving her feelings later, in the company of the equally angry Pheasant. 'Is there to be no end to this? Is she to be allowed to murder and enchant until she has turned the whole court into a nineteenth hell? Why is she still free? Why is she not chained in a dungeon, as she would be if she were anyone else?'

Pheasant sighed. He was unhappy and confounded. He had spoken with Paulownia. She had cried. It had unnerved him – not, of course, that he had believed her pleas of innocence, though he did think that her old beldame of a mother was probably at the root of it all.

'I've sent Lady Osier away. She is exiled from Chang-an,' he offered Jade, aware that it was not enough.

'That's madness,' she shouted. 'Do you think you can stop sorcery by sending it away? It's like religion and poetry – you can do it anywhere!' She slumped on the *kang*, despairing of any sense in the world.

Pheasant looked at her helplessly, at a loss how to help her.

'It's the same as before,' he said despondently. 'There's no proof. If Paulownia *says* the doll was put in her room, we have no way of proving otherwise. I can hardly send *her* away; I've already had several stiff petitions complaining of my treatment of the Duchess. The old witch!' he finished savagely.

'I suppose,' he began again, apologetic and hesitant, 'there's no possibility that Paulownia *did* have nothing to do with it, that it was all Lady Osier's work?'

In the calmness of spent rage, Black Jade conceded the merest possibility. 'But that makes no difference, does it,' she said softly, 'to the fact that our child was killed?'

To demonstrate the hardening of his intentions towards Black Jade, the Emperor invented another new title for her; 'Imperial Consort', which would outrank the first grade of concubines. The expected gale arose among the ministers, and several windy petitions landed on Pheasant's desk. Jade, her thoughts on the future, noted their signatures.

'Give it up,' she advised him cheerfully. 'You've given them their chance to be graceful; why waste time over a lesser step, when you have already decided to take a greater one?'

'Good!' Pheasant brightened. 'Then, when I *do* make you Empress, everyone who opposed me now will be worried about his job. Serve them right; they should remember, sometimes, what they have to lose.'

During the next month, he further signified his discontent with Paulownia by removing her maternal uncle, her chief mentor and the leader of the Wang clan, from his lofty government post, and despatching him quietly to a minor prefecture in Szechwan. There were few complaints, as it was assumed he shared the accepted obloquy of Lady Osier, whose departure had inspired sighs of relief; while no one except those close to Black Jade believed her daughter a witch, it was unimaginable that *she* was not.

Pheasant came looking for Jade one afternoon while she was playing with her children in the courtyard. The boys were trying to catch little lacquered cut-out fish in the pool around the fountain, scooping at the water with excited treble squeals and getting it over everything in sight.

Avoiding the puddles, the Emperor stopped the admire the view his beloved presented, seated on the lip of the pool with her green trousers rolled to the knees and her hair in a dripping plait over her shoulder. He managed to kiss her without getting wet, almost deflected from his purpose as her lashes flirted with his cheek.

'I have here two petitions which are rather interesting,' he said in a briskly assumed council manner. 'This one is from my uncle, demanding that I transfer one Li-I-fu – he's a member of the Secretariat – to some beastly muddy province; and *this* one,' he dangled it by its scarlet ribbons, 'is from the same Li-I-fu, begging me humbly to *remove the Empress and replace her with you*! There? What do you think of that?'

She wrung out her plait and thought about it.

'I think,' she decided, grabbing Bold Tiger by the scruff as he tried to climb into the pool, 'that the same Li-I-fu must feel he has something to gain by such a petition – and that this is a sign that things are beginning to move our way. What will you do?' She chuckled. 'You can hardly grant his wishes overnight like the Wishing Fairy.'

'If only I could. But this is the real beginning. I talked to Li this morning. He's very intelligent, the sort who's sharp enough to cut himself. Apparently he's known as Dagger Smile about the court. It suits him; wait till you see him – teeth like a basking crocodile, and dripping with suave man-of-the-worldliness. I didn't like him exactly, but I could see he'd be useful. He's well-respected in his bureau.'

'So you will refuse his transfer.'

'I have. And I've confirmed his original rank – but I think it might be a salutary slap in the face for my uncle if I also promote him to a vice-presidency.'

Black Jade smiled at him over her son's spiky wet head.

'It will be the first time you have acted without the minister's approval. The palace will be humming with it! It will also,' she said thoughtfully, 'probably have the effect of bringing some of our more backward supporters out in the open. Lord Hsu, for instance; I think I can persuade him to begin campaigning for me – now that he sees you are willing to make a real stand.'

'Excellent. The tide is turning. It is time to take on the concerted Awfulness of the Old Men!'

''Certid awfooness!' squeaked Young Tiger, joining in the general ebullience and scrambling, sopping wet, on to his progenitor's knee, to the detriment of the imperial yellow silk.

'It is certainly high time I began to let them know, especially my uncle and Old Integrity, that it is I who am the Son of Heaven,' Pheasant continued, on a high cloud of self-confidence.

'They will be disturbed, I'm sure,' Black Jade agreed slowly, 'but that does not necessarily mean that they will yield, not yet. They've been accustomed to having their own way for too long. You must prepare for a fight.'

'I look forward to it!' declared Pheasant, tossing Young Tiger into the air and only just catching him.

'I wonder sometimes,' said Jade affectionately, through the resulting mayhem, 'if Your Imperial Majesty will ever grow up.'

His answer was to swoop on the pool and set the little boys roaring by scooping several bright fish in a single predatory trawl.

'There they are,' he cried, 'high and dry! Let's see – I think this angry-looking red fellow must be my uncle, don't you?'

The Emperor had summoned his four senior minister to a private meeting in the small Hall of Wise Counsel.

They gathered in the anteroom. The Archduke was first to arrive, fashionable in his red boots and astrakhan hat. He also wore a peremptory look, as though he wished to get this business over, whatever it was, and return to more important matters.

Old Integrity followed, puffing, at his heels. He was a little, pussyfooting man with bright eyes in a tiny, bald skull, who rubbed his hands together constantly within his silver-grey sleeves with a faint sound like muted cymbals.

Lord Yu came after him, a quiet industrious scholar who shared with Old Integrity the office of Vice-President of the State Department, and never said boo to a goose.

The last to arrive was the magnificently built General Li Shih, the Great Wall, his head shaved like a Tartar brigand's his restless stride indicating that, in spirit, he was still a soldier. He was no longer Commander-in-Chief of the Armies; that rank was now held by the Archduke, as a counterbalance to the General's extreme popularity among the military; he was now the Controller of Works. None knew better than he, who had marched along so many miles of them, the state of repair of the imperial highways.

They greeted each other. Old Integrity said with the little, nervous cough which often prefaced his remarks, 'His Majesty wishes to depose the Empress and will now ask for our support. I assume we can reach agreement here and now?' He shook his fragile head. 'Pheasant is no longer the amenable boy he was. His present mood is unpredictable. If we oppose him, the consequences may be very bad for us.'

'Nonsense,' muttered Wuchi, frowning nonetheless.

'We shall see,' the little man nodded. 'But I'm afraid matters are all too clear to me. I owe everything I have to the late Emperor. How shall I face him in the Western Heaven if I have betrayed his trust?'

'You're right, Old Friend,' the Archduke said crisply. 'We mustn't give in to the boy's first romantic whim. How about you, General?'

The Great Wall studied him thoughtfully for a moment. Then he appeared to reach a conclusion.

'What I say is,' he smiled wrily, 'that I find myself suddenly very unwell. An inconvenient recurrence of a constitutional kind. I shall not attend this meeting. Gentlemen, good day.'

He bowed, turned and marched away, leaving them in no doubt that he was not prepared to oppose the Emperor.

They exchanged grim looks and entered the council hall.

The Emperor, calm-faced, was seated on the Dragon Throne. He held the jade sceptre and wore the imperial insignia. There were four chairs placed to his left but he did not invite his ministers to sit.

Stretching out the sceptre he fixed his eyes on the central figure of Old Integrity and said coldly, 'The Empress has no sons. The Concubine of Luminous Demeanour has two sons. I wish to make her the Empress. What have you to say?'

Old Integrity gave his scratch of a cough. 'The Empress Paulownia comes from an illustrious family, and was the Grand Ancestor your father's choice. I have not heard that she is guilty of any crime. How, therefore, can you set her aside? It grieves me to disagree with the Lord of Ten Thousand Years.'

Pheasant glared at his old tutor. His challenge was clear; if Paulownia was accused of murder, or of sorcery, let her be brought to trial. The wily little turtle knew very well that there was no risk of that, not without a single solid item of proof.

'Your opinion is of no assistance to me,' he said shortly. 'Has anyone else anything to say?'

His uncle stepped forward, and bowed. 'I can say nothing that would be of greater assistance.'

'Then you had better go; all of you. I suggest you think carefully over this matter. I have made my wishes clear. You may come back tomorrow, and we will discuss them again.'

The next morning Pheasant, still riding on a wave of euphoria swollen by the younger courtiers' enthusiasm towards Black Jade, suggested it might be fun to play a trick on his recalcitrant Awful Old Men. He would have a large, decorative screen set up behind the Dragon Throne, and Jade should hide behind it and listen to their conference, which he optimistically intended to be the last on the subject.

It seemed a harmless, if schoolboyish prank, and she concealed herself, giggling, to please him.

As before, Old Integrity was the spokesman. Today, he tried a different attack.

'If Your Majesty insists on changing your Empress,' he began reasonably, 'I would like to suggest that you make your choice from among the ladies of noble birth. Lady Wu, while of a good and loyal clan, is not an aristocrat.'

'She is my choice,' said Pheasant repressively.

'A choice I cannot approve.' Again the irritating cough. 'Lady Wu was formerly the concubine of the late Emperor. Everyone knows that; it cannot be lacquered over. By now it is possible that the entire Empire is aware of it. History,' he puffed sternly, 'will call you to account if you raise her so high.'

Amitabha, thought Black Jade, I'm afraid this is *not* what poor Pheasant intended me to hear!

The little man grated on. 'Your Majesty must reconsider his wishes. Think what your reputation will be as an Emperor who takes his father's used woman into his bed.'

'How dare you?' Pheasant's pure rage seemed to present them with the very ghost of his father. 'Is this the way you speak of the mother of my sons?'

Old Integrity was abashed. Wheezing and scratching, he came to the steps of the throne and laid down his official wand upon them, placing his official cap neatly over it. He kowtowed three times with evident difficulty. He was not a well man.

'Your Majesty,' he implored, 'be so gracious as to allow me to return to my house in the country, to live out my old age in your father's memory. I cannot betray it here, for the sake of a foolish boy and his unimportant amours.'

'Will someone please remove this dolt from my sight!' ordered Pheasant, trying to control his anger and humiliation.

'Why not remove him altogether from the earth?' came a sudden hollow voice from behind the screen. Black Jade, determined both to lift the unhappy mood for the beleaguered Pheasant and to give the Awful Old Men a fright, was gratified by the result. The Archduke, who had stood sneering down his nose during his colleague's performance, jumped halfway out of his smart red boots and lost his astrakhan hat altogether. A moan of shock and distress was heard from Old Integrity, as he was hurried, then carried out of the room by two straight-faced members of the household guard. Lord Yu, whose presence anywhere was that of a cipher, studied the floor and shook gently.

Furious, Wuchi took up the offensive, ignoring the interruption with fine contempt and addressing his nephew as though he were something nasty in the meat-market.

'The minister whom you have chosen to dismiss was entrusted with your father's Will. Even if Your Majesty considers him at fault, that trust protects him from punishment.'

'Is that all you have to say?' asked Pheasant, meeting the glacial eye with the accumulated dislike of twenty-five years of repression.

'That is all.'

'Then you will leave. Your opinion is of no account.'

With the shallowest possible bow, the Archduke obeyed. Lord Yu, behind him, did his best to look like his shadow.

'Oh dear,' said Black Jade comically, emerging from her hiding-place. 'That isn't exactly how you wrote the scene, is it, my darling?'

'I'm not sure I feel like laughing,' he said shakily, falling into her arms. 'But if *you* can, I'm sure I should. You are full of surprises, my sweet love. Any other woman would be rolling on the floor in fury.'

'It's funny you should say that,' she whispered, holding him closer, 'because, if you were to get rid of all these guards, standing about like indoor conifers – there is a *very* sensual pile of rugs behind that screen. Shall I show it to you?'

When Pheasant discovered that the Great Wall had been loath to take his uncle's part against him, he determined to try to bring the ironclad warrior out on his side.

The General wielded tremendous influence. Of all statesmen, he was the best known and the best loved among the people – the citizens, the artisans and farmers whose lands and livelihoods he had marched to protect. Despite the Archduke's higher rank, it was he who, in any crisis, would command the loyalty of the armies. If he could be persuaded to support Black Jade's cause, the opinions of his colleagues would hold far less sway. Like Wuchi, he had been one of the founding fathers of the dynasty. If he could be seen to tolerate change, a great many people would tell themselves that they could do the same.

The Great Wall was summoned to a private audience. There had been a number of such audiences lately, especially among the junior ministers and leading young noblemen. The General thought he knew what to expect. He also knew what he would say. His loyalty was to the Emperor, the son of his father; not to Lady Paulownia or her ambitious clan.

After fifteen minutes of wine and pleasantries, during which the Great Wall sat stolidly uncontributing, like his namesake, Pheasant solicited his opinion upon the matter in hand. He made it clear that he wanted a direct answer. He was also honest enough to point out that Old Integrity's decision, as the living reliquary of Shih-min's Will, was of paramount importance to most people.

The General nodded. 'He is an upright and conscientious minister; but surely, what you have here is purely a family question? A private matter. No? Personally, I see no real necessity for Your Majesty to ask the opinion of outsiders.'

Pheasant had to sit on his hands to stop them from clapping. He had won! No one could stop him now!

'By all the Buddhas, you're right!' he cried jubilantly. 'I shall seek no further advice outside my family. You, of course, General, are a member of that family, and your ideas on the matter are very valuable to me.' He referred to the fact that Shih-min had conferred the supreme honour, the use of the imperial surname of Li, upon the great soldier who had helped him to gain his Empire.

'My uncle, the Archduke,' grinned the grateful Emperor, 'is happily related only by marriage.'

When the Great Wall left his triumphant young ruler, he strode across the broad square to the Hall of the White Tiger, to pray for a time before the spirit tablet of his old commander. There was not much of that great heart in this son of his, he reflected. The boy was charming, but he lacked strength and had not yet found his vocation as an Emperor. The same could not be said, on the other hand, for the exquisite Lady Wu. She was an intelligent woman, and Shih-min himself had been her tutor. She might do very well as Empress. She could hardly do worse, in any event, than Lady Paulownia, who seemed to have no idea at all how to communicate with the rest of the human race. He had noted that, where Black Jade was popular, she was very popular indeed. He himself had warmed to her on the few occasions they had met. And Shih-min had loved her very dearly. That, in itself, was enough to elicit his own good opinion. Having decided to give her at least his tacit support, he bade an affectionate farewell to his favourite ancestor and stamped off to discuss the affair with Lord Hsu; as President of the Board of Rites, he was Lady Wu's most influential partisan.

It was Lord Hsu who, next morning, awakened the palace with the announcement, on behalf of the Emperor, that since the meanest peasant did not have to ask for his neighbour's opinion when he had raised a good harvest and could afford a new wife, the Son of Heaven did not intend to do so either. At the same time the despairing Old Integrity was demoted and condemned to end his days as a provincial governor-general. This, on the whole, was felt to be rather extreme, but the Emperor was adamant; an example must be made, in case anyone else thought he could address the Lord of Ten Thousand Years like a scolding old nanny.

On the morning of Pheasant's interview with the Great Wall, Black Jade had also received visitors. As both were uncastrated males of high degree, convention dictated that Lord Shen should also be present. But as Jade had no desire for him to witness what promised to be a very interesting conversation, she gave him her gracious leave to depart, saying firmly that her lady mother, who happened to be with her, would be an adequate chaperone. Lord Shen knew better than to comment. He made her his best kowtow, loaded with sequins and obsequiousness, as he withdrew.

'I regard him as the weather-vane of my fortunes,' she remarked to Golden Willow with a smile. 'It appears that I am set fair for the future.'

'He certainly carries the sun upon his back.' Her mother raised delicately disapproving brows at the Chief Eunuch's magnificence.

'Paste!' advised Chinghiz contemptuously, swimming through the room on some errand of his own. 'All that jangles isn't jade!' He was looking inordinately pleased with himself. He had reason. Yesterday his mistress had given him an emerald riviere which she said was far too vulgar to wear. He had had it broken up and sold to a jeweller in the city; he now possessed, as Black Jade had intended, the foundations of a fortune. Their eyes met, in mutual gratitude, as he passed.

Very soon, he ushered in the gentlemen callers.

They were Hsuan-tsang, who had recently become an abbot, and his old friend Lord Hsu, Lion Guard.

'Ah, you're fatter! Excellent,' cried the Abbot, advancing on Jady without any bothersome bowing and scraping, and handing her a plump package. 'A gift from a friend of yours. He wouldn't let me get away without it.'

A tear in the rather unruly parcel revealed a dark green, leafy substance. 'I know who it's from!' She tore at the clumsy wrapping, her face full of amusement. A bundle of spinach appeared.

'Dear Meng Shen! How is he? He has not been to see me since I left the convent. I still remember his bright eyes and his non-stop questions.'

'He's doing very well,' the Abbot replied. 'We seem to be making a physician of him; a good one too. There's something else; it's probably wrapped up in the spinach – horrible stuff, can't stand it myself – it is a more elegant gift than one might at first expect, I assure you.'

Jade untied the cool green bundle and a small phial dropped out.

'Oh Heaven! I hope he hasn't found another elixir of immortality!'

'Open it, Illustrious Lady,' encouraged Lord Hsu, draping his tall figure over the arm of a sofa.

'The stopper is gummed. will you do it for me?'

The elegant minister reached for the bottle and chipped away the gum arabic, sacrificing his long, marine-blue nails to beauty in need. They matched exactly, she noticed, the silk lining of his chestnut brocade overgown. He held the phial to his nose and inhaled extravagantly.

'*Avalokitsara*!' he cried, kissing his fingers. 'But this is a masterpiece! The very breath of Kuan Yin! Take it, Incomparable Consort – you will never use any other. It was created for you. It expresses perfectly both your exorbitant beauty and your serene subtlety.'

Lord Hsu swiftly plucked a curved petal from one of Jade's camellia plants, poured a few drops of the essence into it, and handed it to her with a flourish of his blue and tan sleeve.

The room already breathed with the aspiration of the aromatic candle that counted the hours, and with everyone's chosen perfume, Chinghiz striking the highest note with his 'Dreams of a Thousand Nights'. Even so, the bitter-sweet redolence drifted about her nostrils in a cloud that seemed to settle around her as though it had found its home. She could not name any of its hundred fragrances, but dreamily accepted that they would be a part of her aura from this day forward, as necessary to her as certain music or the verses of the poets she loved.

'Please thank Meng Shen for his gift,' she said gently to the Abbot, who was sniffing the air as he did when faced with appetising fish, but with less enjoyment. 'And tell him there is nothing I could treasure more than this. Ask him if he will continue to make it for me. And perhaps you will discover for me what it would give him most pleasure to receive in return? And now, my lords, perhaps one of you will tell me why you have so kindly given up your valuable time to bring me a young man's gift?'

The Abbot grinned. 'I hope you are not becoming a cynic, Little Daughter! However, as you suggest, we do have another charge.' The grin was wiped clear. 'You will recall the disgraceful affair of Lady Osier? Well, it seems that her dismissal was not sufficient to discourage the powers of evil in the Inner Palace.'

'No?' Black Jade waited. Golden Willow held her breath.

'In the absence of her mother, the Empress has found another tutor in wickedness. It has been discovered that she and the Pure Concubine were working together to poison the Emperor.'

Golden Willow gave a small cry of horror. Black Jade, to Hsuan-tsang's surprise, seemed still to be waiting.

'Doesn't this distress you?' he enquired, puzzled.

'If it is the truth, it is most distressing; but is it the truth?' she asked bluntly. 'I am sure that Paulownia has sought my own death by sorcery, and there is an obvious reason why she should – but why, in the name of Gautama, should she want to destroy the Emperor, whom she loves, who is still her husband?'

The Abbot stared stolidly in front of him while Lion Guard cleared his throat and whistled softly.

'I had feared you might ask that,' the minister admitted.

'And the answer?'

'Is that the poison was, indeed, intended for you. But that there is a feeling among the ministers – those of us, that is, who have your best interests at heart – that it would sound a great deal better in an imperial edict if we were to say it was the Emperor who was threatened.'

'An edict?'

'It is to be issued very shortly. The Lady Paulownia will be accused and demoted. She will then be imprisoned. Following this, there will be a petition from the court as a whole, asking that a new Empress should be appointed.'

Golden Willow looked at her daughter. The lovely face was expressionless. It was hard to believe her the same ecstatic child whose every experience had once been brushed upon those sculptured features, joy flitting after sorrow like summer rain after cloud.

Black Jade slowly inclined her head towards Hsuan-tsang, holding his eyes steadily. 'And do you approve of this, my father?'

'I do,' he said forthrightly. 'It is time that harmony was restored to this court. We have certain proof – there are witnesses in her household who will swear that the Empress has committed a crime. It does not matter to us what we may call it; but it *will* matter to the people, who worship the Son of Heaven at humble altars throughout the Middle Kingdom. They are not, as yet, aware of the talents of the consort Black Jade – although I make no doubt that this will soon change,' he added with a twinkle.

'And you, Minister? You are satisfied with the morality of this plan?'

Lord Hsu threw up his hands in a flash of silk lightning.

'Honoured Lady – what can I say?' he demanded with a winning smile. 'One is a politician. One simply does what one must, to accomplish that which must become fact.'

Black Jade looked at him gravely. 'I shall remember that phrase. I may wish to make use of it in the future.'

The future seemed suddenly much nearer.

14

The period between the eighth and the twenty-third days of the tenth month is known as the Cold Dew. Its premonition of winter fell chill upon the heart of the Empress Paulownia when she read the edict which charged her with having plotted to poison the Son of Heaven and degraded her to the status of a commoner. Her family would share her shame, stripped of all rank and title and exiled to the pestilent swamps of Ling-nan. The Pure Concubine, her aide in crime, would share her punishment.

As the impervious guard escorted the two young women through the dank passages which led to two bare rooms on the dark side of the palace, Paulownia tried to exercise the paramount virtue of filial piety and avoid blaming her mother for their sad case.

It had never been her own wish to use sorcery against her rival. And if that had not been discovered, no one would have suspected the poison. Even that had been Bright Virtue's idea. But she had not prevented it, and was therefore guilty of a great crime, even if it was not the one of which she was accused. She understood the reason for that accusation and did not hold it against her husband.

Indeed, Pheasant had been kind to her. She might live imprisoned for the rest of her days, but she still had her life. Perhaps, after many years of prayer and contrition, the Gods would allow her to make reparation through her reincarnation as some loathsome, crawling thing, or one of the poorest of the diseased and suffering poor.

Bright Virtue, whose reaction to her disgusting accommodation was to consider which of the guards might prove to be the least impervious, suffered from no such self-scourging. Her single regret was that Black Jade still lived and prospered, and that her foolishness in trusting the members of Paulownia's household had led her to overlook the insidious machinations of that devil-brained creature, Chinghiz.

She had no intention, if there were any way in which it could be escaped, of spending the remainder of her young life in a dripping cell.

She thought that, after a certain time had elapsed, there might be a way.

*

At the last dawn of the Cold Dew the denizens of the market-place were edified, once they had woken up and dragged out without his trousers the man who could read, by a second imperial decree.

It made known to them the virtues and talents of the Elegant Concubine Wu Chao, known as Black Jade, whose illustrious lineage and many-jewelled intelligence had recommended her to the late heroic Emperor as lady-in-waiting to his Empress, Pure Virtue. In this position, she had so far won the goodwill and respect of her superiors that the Son of Heaven, in approbation of her unique qualities, had bestowed her upon his son, the present Emperor, with honour to both young people. It was only fitting therefore, the edict concluded neatly, that she should now become their Empress.

Breath was drawn. Murmurs hummed. Someone laughed, a little off-key. Copious mucus released troublesome demons.

'Won't she be a bit long in the tooth for the Tiger's Cub? Or did she serve Pure Virtue from her cradle?'

'One *had* heard that she served His Majesty's father, rather than his mother.' Silence and more demons released.

'I remember her own father, General Wu.' An old soldier steered them away from lese-majesty. 'My brother was with him, up on the Wall. The General gave him a pair of boots once; he'd actually noticed the ones on his feet were falling to bits.'

'Wonder what his daughter's like? We'd be lucky if we ever saw even the toe of one of her boots.'

'What does it matter to us what she's like? She's the Empress, that's what she's like.'

'She won't be old; she'll be young, and a beauty,' said the man who could read, authoritatively. 'What would the young Emperor want with anything else?'

'Quite right!' Bursting with self-importance, a palace guard averted his nose from those whose behaviour he was set to supervise. 'She's as ripe as two melons and as sweet as dumplings.'

They attacked his ears with questions and defeated his nose. He answered all the queries that pertained to the present reign.

At a more civilised hour, in a packed and perfumed chamber in the Palace of Golden Bells, the same edict was read out to a court swollen with curiosity and redolent of the superior sweat of those who were wondering if they had not better change their allegiance if they wished to prosper.

Unlike their inferiors of the market-place, they were aware of every discrepancy in what they heard. But although it provided them with a positive banquet of toothsome gossip, not one of them would challenge it. They did not wish to follow the unfortunate Old Integrity into exile. If they were admirers of Black Jade, they threw their fans in the air and cheered. If they were not, many did the same. As their Empress, the upstart concubine would wield a great deal of lethal power.

The day of Black Jade's coronation dawned with pure clarity in the sort of cold that hangs in the air like the note of a huntsman's horn. Wrapped in her quilt, her veins racing with an excitement that would not let her sleep, she crept from her bed and went out into the courtyard. She wanted to meet the morning alone.

She had spent her last night in Green Fragrance Court. Pheasant had been a little hurt by her wish to remain there, but had been glad to let her do so; a few hours were a small gift and he understood the need to be alone, to gather strength for a great occasion.

She sat in her favourite spot, on the edge of the fountain, shivering a little in the sharp air. Her breath curled about her head and she amused herself for a moment, watching it. Then she dipped her fingers in the icy water, enticing the hardy fish, who nibbled at them and flicked away, disappointed. There was not a single thought in her head and yet it seemed filled with noise, as though many thousands of voices were speaking to her from a long way off. She didn't want to hear what they said. She didn't want to think. She consciously pushed away thought. She wanted this last brief period of perfect peace. She loved Green Fragrance Court. She would leave a part of herself here, the pattern of her growing into womanhood, even as she had left the pattern of her childhood among the hills and plains of Shansi.

Today she would again become someone different; different from her past self and from every other woman. She would be above and beyond them all. She would be the first lady of the Empire, and therefore of the world, for every ruler must bow before the Emperor of the Middle Kingdom.

Today she would be given power. She was not yet fully aware of what that might mean. What she did know was that Pheasant would refuse her nothing. But then, she had not yet asked for anything above the level of small favours for friends or relatives. Now, she would have no need to ask for such unimportant things;

she would have the power to grant them in her own right. She would hold the jade seal of the Empress, its unquestioned authority second only to that of her husband.

Suddenly she stood up and held out her arms, breathing in with all her strength, so that the cold purity filled her lungs and her stomach; there was exhilaration in every pulse as she held the breath deep within her until she felt her heart knocking at her ribs. She was taking it all into herself, everything that would come to her today; today, tomorrow and forever.

At last, tingling and aware in every nerve, she let the air leave her body, exhaling on a wave of happiness, hearing herself call out joyously to any who were awake to hear her, the one word of committed affirmation – 'Yes!'

When it was time to eat, she could not, and only sipped tea.

'Very well,' declared Welcome shortly. 'Spoil the whole performance with a belly that gurgles like a peasant's donkey!'

Black Jade obediently forced down her breakfast, without any idea what she was eating.

When her mother and Rose Bird arrived to help her dress, she had gained enough command over her nerves to display her usual calm amusement and acceptance of other people's bustle. The house was already seething with noise and activity, with Chinghiz in a state of near hysteria because the imperial tiara had not yet been delivered, and the maids squealing in counterpoint. The hubbub reached its crescendo when the steward tripped over the comfortably snoozing Mao-yu and had his ankle severely nipped.

'That animal will have to go! It should be in the zoo, not in a civilized home! Go on – get out of here, you obnoxious beast, or I'll take a revenge you won't like!'

There was no danger of this; Chinghiz adored the panther for her beauty and would shortly spend a precious half-hour grooming her to lustrous perfection so that she would be an adequate foil for her mistress. She was to wear a new collar of gold and pearls to match the Empress's crown.

Golden Willow and Rose Bird had brought their own festive dress to change into, and their maids to help them do it. Very soon the noise in the house was such that Mao-yu might have been forgiven for thinking that she was indeed in the zoo, especially as all the pets of Green Fragrance Court, the monkeys, the parakeets and doves, the cats, the Tartar hunting dogs, joined in amiably with the humans, getting in everyone's way and shrieking, yowling and babbling with transferred excitement.

In a relatively quiet corner, secluded from the chaos by Welcome's effective erection of several bamboo screens, she and Chinghiz began to construct the image of an Empress.

First there were the fine silken undergarments, white shot with gold, to cover the peach and pearl perfection of the body which each one regarded with such different emotions. Then there was the attention to toe and fingernails, which were painted with powdered gold. Their owner was forbidden to move during the brief battle which followed, as to whether or not the stiff, formal gown, the *wei-yi*, worn by the Empress upon state occasions, should go on before her face was painted.

'If this one is ruined, there isn't another,' Jade pointed out.

'When have I ever caused a single drop of pigment or dusting of powder to fall upon a gown of yours?' demanded Chinghiz with exaggerated umbrage.

'Well, I don't want you to do my face. I'll do it myself.'

Her servitor fetched a swift sigh of pique. 'I *had* thought I had pleased you well enough, Exalted Mistress, to deserve –'

'Oh Chinghiz, kindly spare me the dramatics. I want to present my own face because it is the one I shall show to the people and I want it to *be* my own, not a temple mask.'

Welcome, rounding the screen with a bowl of *wu-mu* for her hair, smiled with dimpling reminiscence. 'You were just the same on the day that you were first to appear before the late Emperor, may Heaven soon reincarnate His Magnificence; insisting on doing everything yourself.' Good taste had never been Welcome's forte. 'Now then, am I to do your hair, or will you take charge of that too?'

Black Jade smiled, shaking an errant memory out of her head.

'No, I should like you to do that, please; in my usual simple style. The headdress will be more than enough ornament.'

'I am not quite an idiot, even if I don't possess the rarified aesthetic sense of Master Chinghiz.' Despite their private collusion, the old rivalry still erupted at times of stress.

The hair was dressed, in simple wings across Jade's temples with a plaited coronet that would fit inside the tall headdress that was the Phoenix Crown. Then she chased her servants away while she carefully coloured the face that the people – her people – would see today. She had decided to show them the humanity which she shared with them, rather than appearing to seek any part of the semi-divine aspect of the Emperor. She used her usual pale powder, not the lead-based paint that created the dead-white mask of imperial pomp. She added a single dark blue mouche where her smile would dimple, leaving out the crescent moon on the forehead which would soon be dripping with pearls, and colouring her cheeks in a softer and more natural manner than the stark red patches of fashion.

'You might as well go with a naked face,' Chinghiz grumbled when he saw her, but she could see that really he approved. He would always place diplomacy before all considerations, and he recognised that this was Black Jade's diplomatic face.

'They will welcome you like a sister,' he said. As they had been allowed to welcome no other.

He and Welcome now lifted the heavy *wei-yi* over her head. It fell to the floor in stiffened rods, its deep blue colour striking echoes from her coiled hair. As many of her gowns would be, it was embroidered with flying phoenixes, so cleverly that one would swear their rainbow wings were feathers; *Feng*, the phoenix, being the female counterpart of *Kung*, the dragon, the male symbol which belongs to the Emperor.

It is the edict of her husband which raises an Empress to her unparalleled rank, and not the placing of a diadem upon her brow as is the custom among certain barbarian nations. It was Chinghiz therefore, his sapphire stare striking sparks from her emerald one as he held it out to her, who placed the Phoenix Crown upon her piled hair. Although it was tall, it was very light, for the gold was finely wrought and the pearls weighed almost as little as the tears to which they are often compared.

On this day there would be no tears, unless they were of joy. These Black Jade saw all around her as she gathered her attendants for the procession to the Hall of Supreme Harmony where she would be inaugurated as the Empress with the charming title, chosen by the Son of Heaven, of Wu Tse Tien – the Image of Heaven.

There was one last hug from Welcome as they prepared to leave. Then the sobbing nurse stood back beside Chinghiz, now burning like a furnace in scarlet and black and cloth of gold. She touched the dragon pendant that she wore sleeping and waking.

'Should I give it to her, now that the prophecy is coming true?' she whispered, profaning his magnificence with tears and a patchouli scent which he considered mortally vulgar.

'No,' he replied so softly that only she could hear. 'That is not for today. It depicts a dragon, not a phoenix.'

Welcome gave an odd little shiver, which she put down to the entry of a mischievous dust turtle into her throat, then nodded obediently and put the medallion under her robe.

*

The ceremony in the Hall of Supreme Harmony was a model of dignity and brevity. Before the assembled ranks of statesmen, their splendid robes of office partially obscured by mountains of flowers and smoked by energetic braziers, the Great Wall – Archduke, General and Chief Minister, as well as the idol of every man of fighting age in the Empire – presented the grave, incandescent beauty that was their new Empress with the jade box which contained her seal. With this act the court was advised of the legitimacy of her position as well as her power to employ it.

After this Lord Yu, the only remaining Vice-President of the State Department, was rewarded for his silence upon certain occasions with the honour of handing her the letters patent.

She was then hung about with the plaques and seals which identified her rank and privileges, and led up the steps to the Phoenix Throne, placed on the dais next to a proud and smiling Pheasant. Once seated, she returned his smile and listened with becoming modesty as her champion Lion Guard, thrilling in blue and silver, read out the imperial scroll which lauded her many excellences. Black Jade was thankful when it was finished, and they might leave the hall and pass on to the next of the day's ceremonies.

Breaking all precedent, which was a thing she expected to do rather frequently, she would present herself to the entire court, from the highest minister to the lowest secretary, so that each one could see her face to face.

The venue she had chosen for this innovation, on the practical grounds of there being enough space, and the dramatic one of its being a superb stage setting, was the balcony of the great tower of the Su I Gate, whose turreted height guarded the way to the harem quarters in the Inner Palace.

The courtiers were already assembled in a chattering mass of clashing silks and scented flesh, in the square beneath the gate-tower, as the newly accepted Empress drove through them in her blue and gold carriage with its scarlet wheels and waving coronet of 'phoenix' plumes. She was preceded by her horse guards and followed by innumerable bearers of ceremonial banners, and singing priests and swingers of pungent censers. Dragons and phoenixes were everywhere, writhing and curling in every colour and material known to man. As Black Jade looked out between her deep blue curtains, pulled well back so that the crowd could see her, she remembered with a pang the small angry girl who had said to the man she would one day love with her heart's blood, 'Why should a woman not go as gorgeously as she pleases?' Well, today she was going as gorgeously as ever she would.

She smiled, holding the memory, and those nearest to her were ravished by the depth of sadness in the smile, unable to know that her next thought had been that she would gladly go in rags for the rest of her life – if it might gain her a single hour of the presence of that man and that love.

But then, 'I must never look back. Never again,' she told herself firmly, so that those who had secured the enviable places near the gateway, although equally ravished, were impressed by the resolute and cheerful demeanour of the Empress, as well as by her astounding beauty, for which, despite rumour, those who had never seen her had not been prepared.

She reached the gate and quickly climbed the tower, emerging on the balcony above the field of moving faces which became still, wave after wave, as they caught sight of her glittering figure. Almost at once they were silent.

She would have liked to speak to them, to tell them that she too was one of them, that she understood their hearts and minds, their ambitions and their fears, that she intended to be their good guardian, as the Emperor was, that they had nothing to fear from her and everything to gain. Public speech, however, was a proscription she did not dare to break. It was, after all, only her first day as Empress, and she felt she was doing enough to flout the conventions by which most of her subjects lived.

She stood close to the rail, smiling down at those who looked up. Here and there she caught and held a gaze and felt the trembling birth of adoration.

She raised her arms and held them wide for a moment, as she had done that day at dawn, once more affirming her gladness in her fate. The crowd gave a great roar of approbation, reaching and ricochetting from the azure lid of the sky. Before it had died, their Empress, with a consummate appreciation of fine timing, had gone.

The coach now carried her swiftly through the cheering ranks and down the wide, lined boulevards of the Palace City until it reached the eastern gate, where, instead of wheeling back towards the Inner Palace, as everyone had expected, it raced straight through and out, unchallenged, unheard-of and definitely un-imperial, into the crammed and clamorous streets of Chang-an.

Here, as within the palaces, everyone was celebrating, wearing his best and drinking as much as he could; or wearing her best and trying to stop him. When they realised, as though ducked in a sudden cold shower, who was among them, they milled about the multicoloured coach like feeding pigeons, clambering over each other to get near, impeding her progress, crying out blessings and compliments, making her laugh aloud with their pleasure. No one dared to touch her, though a man had only to reach out, it seemed, to lay his hand upon the living, laughing lips, or to take the slender, gilded fingers in his own. That smile, those open, gesturing hands, and that fabulous face would remain with them long after they had spent and forgotten the shower of silver that had fallen about her as she moved between them. She was the first Empress in their long history to offer herself to them, and they accepted the gift with a boundless joy and trust.

The coach carried Jade swiftly back to the palace where she would attend another unheard-of event in the prettiest of the receiving courts. Here she entertained the wives of all the officials serving at court, and also the ladies of all the foreign ambassadors, to an elegant reception with wine, delicate foods and fine music. It was an occasion for every woman to be seen at her best, to walk about and talk to her friends, and if she were among the lucky ones, to have the opportunity of conversation with the Empress. It was the kind of gathering Black Jade had always managed to perfection, and even she herself was able to relax and ignore the stiffness of her robe as she gathered all her old friends about her and drank a cup of wine with them. When she had rested for a while she asked for several ladies to be presented to her and talked to them seriously about their children or their husbands or their especial talents that had just been whispered in her ear by the omniscient Dumpling. She knew that, in this room, she was laying as strong a foundation for her good reputation as she had done at the Su I Gate. Again she was surrounded by approbation like a cloud as the women made known their gratitude for her thoughtfulness in offering them a special claim on her time on such a propitious day.

'I believe they really like me,' she whispered to Rose Bird as the wife of a court censor (grade seven) went away beaming with pleasure at the interest the Empress had shown in her worthy but undistinguished line of ancestors.

'Well, of course they do,' her sister replied. 'You are extremely likeable – especially when you are determined to be.'

'All the same, I don't think I shall do this too often. My jaw aches from smiling!'

Nevertheless she employed it once again in a short speech to the company, for there was no prohibition against her addressing women. She said simply that she wished to be their good elder sister, and that they should bring their needs and their concerns to her; they would always find a sympathetic ear. She thanked them for the support they had given her on this, the greatest day of her life, and for the pleasure of their company. Then she left them to talk about her for as long as they pleased.

The early evening was to be dedicated to rest, for the coronation feast which was to follow would last long into the night. Black Jade fell gratefully upon her new bed in the Empress's Palace and instantly slept the deep and satisfied sleep of those who have done their duty.

It seemed hours later when she was awakened by a movement at her side. Pheasant was bending over her.

'Today you were magnificent,' he said, his eyes worshipping. 'With you beside me, I feel that there is nothing I could not accomplish. You have made me completely happy. I thank you for it from the depths of my heart.'

'My only wish is to give you my help in everything you do,' she said softly. 'And now that you have made your beautiful speech, for which I also thank you – there is room for you in this bed; so much room that I feel lonely without you.'

'You shall never be without me again.'

'Never? Your other consorts will hardly approve.'

'I have no need of other consorts,' he said ardently, pulling her towards him, delighted to find her naked beneath the quilts. 'Your love is more than enough for one man; it is all I want, all I will ever need. Only love me, my wife, and we will make legends together. They will speak of me as they speak now of my father, and they will tell tales of your beauty and your inspiration until the last reincarnation.'

His happiness and confidence blazed about her as he began to arouse her to a pitch that matched the supreme heights of the day. As he reared triumphantly over her in the final moment of consummation, his face was so radiant with newfound strength and purpose that she saw it, in that transcendent second, as that of Shih-min, and came shuddering and weeping to a pinnacle of ecstacy which was beyond anything she had previously experienced with this son who wanted so much to become his father.

Only when it was over, and he nestled into the relaxed curves of her renewed and lightened body, saying lazily, 'My beautiful girl;

tell me that you love me. I want to hear you say it,' did she know him for himself.

Shih-min had never asked for her love. He had always known it was his. But Pheasant, after all their time together, remained in the position of a suppliant. It seemed he could never quite accept that she was truly his; he must always look up to her, worship her, be grateful for her love. She did not blame him for it; how could she? Rather, she pitied him, and pity was not among the emotions she wished to feel for her lover. But it was not always there, indeed not even often, and tonight hardly at all. She was a fool to have felt that slight irritation, that sense of condescension, because he had shown humility in his love. Humility was a quality she did not possess. It was something she might do well to cultivate, though she did not think it would flourish in her inhospitable soil.

She turned to watch Pheasant as he slept. There was an expression of pure contentment on his face. His skin glowed, his lips were parted, still smiling at the day that had passed. All his gladness had been for her. Her eyes filled. Swept by tenderness, she put her lips to his cheek, still as soft as a boy's. He was right. There was nothing they might not accomplish together. She would make him the best Empress that the kingdom had ever known. She would dedicate herself to him and to the people. She would help him and protect him, and try to grow within herself the authority and the will towards right that he trusted her to have.

As for herself – she must take what help she could find, in books, in history, in the memory of Shih-min, and among the increasing numbers of her friends.

15

Chinghiz was pottering about the room, doing self-imposed, unnecessary tasks with the air of dedicated deliberation that meant he had something unpleasant to say and was waiting for a ripe moment to say it.

'If you water that poor narcissus once more, it will drown,' his mistress observed. 'I wish you would settle to something elsewhere. Your mind is buzzing; it makes me uncomfortable.'

'It is concern for your comfort that causes it to buzz.'

Black Jade sighed and put down the summary she was making

of Lord Hsu's brilliant and exhaustive volume of dynastic history.

'Very well. What are you worrying about now?'

The eunuch abandoned his watering jar and faced her, hands folded in his sleeves.

'There is a rumour,' he invited, his faun's eyes solemn.

'The walls of the palace are hung with rumours; which of the ten thousand has set up the irritation?'

'It is not pleasant. I have heard it said that it was not the ex-Empress who killed the little Princess, but you yourself.' He ignored her indrawn breath and finished quickly, 'You are accused of smothering the child in order to discredit the lady Paulownia with the blame.'

She thought she would be sick.

Chinghiz saw her face whiten and hurried to bring her strong rice wine. She waved it away and he saw that it was rage, not distress, that filled her throat.

'Who are they that say so?' she whispered, not trusting her voice.

'The usual people – though all would deny it, of course. It seems that your coronation has not had the effect of sending your enemies to ground. Rather the opposite. I imagine they find your interest in matters of state rather alarming.'

'I am very glad of it,' she replied, her voice still low but in her control. 'They do well to be alarmed. Tell me, is there no way to tear out the tongue that first spoke this foulness?'

Chinghiz shook his head sympathetically. 'I think not. I heard of it from a servant who had it from a lower servant who will say he got it from another such, and so on. But my mistress knows who are her enemies.'

'Indeed. And they evidently think me as powerless as Empress as I was as a concubine.'

He applauded the tight hardening of her tone. If he could, he would slay every one of the those enemies, from the Archduke to the tattling kitchen sluts who carried his poison. One day, perhaps, it might even come to that. On the other hand, perhaps it would not prove necessary; he had recently seen the sense of power begin to awake in her. On the day of her crowning it had worked in her like the most potent wine or the strongest of passions. She would want more.

There was a scratching at the door. It was Silver Bell, flustered, her pretty face red with embarrassment.

'Please – I must speak to our mistress.' Since they had all moved to the palace the maids no longer ran in and out as they had done in Green Fragrance Court.

'Come in,' Black Jade called wearily. If the girl had brought her some new problem, at least she would have some slight respite from the hideousness she had just heard.

Silver Bell bowed shyly. 'Your Highness – I don't know if it is my business to say this, but I thought you would want to know.'

The Empress encouraged her with a small movement of her fingers.

The maid cleared her throat nervously. 'This morning I met with – an acquaintance – a relative,' she enlarged hastily, 'who is a member of the imperial guard. He had just come off duty patrolling the northern parts of the palace. He told me that, as he had passed a certain chamber, one which has sealed windows and heavy locks on its doors, he saw His Majesty the Emperor come out of it, looking, he said, very upset. Later he asked the guard on duty there what was inside. Little Mistress – Your Highness – it was the chamber where the Lady Paulownia and the Pure Concubine are imprisoned.'

'Dear Gods!' Black Jade did not know that she spoke. This news was heavier even than the other. What had possesed Pheasant to visit those women? What possible purpose could he have with the murderess of his child? Her own would-be destroyers? All at once her stomach seemed to rise into her chest, suffocating her. She gasped. A yawning gulf was opening before her into which was tumbling all her hard-won security and certainty. She must *know* what he had meant by it. She must know at once!

'Thank you, Silver Bell. You have done what was right. You may return to your duties. Chinghiz – please discover where I may find the Emperor. Right away.'

Chinghiz, who had installed an information network that ran through the palaces with the speed and smoothness of mercury, was able to tell her in ten minutes. The Son of Heaven was in the royal mews. One of his hawks was sick and he had gone to inspect its progress.

Black Jade flung a shawl around her shoulders without waiting for anyone to bring her quilted coat.

'Come with me,' she ordered Chinghiz abruptly.

'Mistress – His Majesty will surely call upon you very soon,' he murmured. She would lose face by a precipitate confrontation which would reveal the strength of her anger.

'Do as I tell you,' she said coldly. 'And bring Mao-yu. She needs exercise.'

She needed to have the wild creature with her. Tamed and controllable as she was, today there was a sympathetic solace in her company; her instincts, like Jade's own, were only sheathed in good behaviour as were the claws in the velvet fur. There was in the beautiful cat, and now in herself, the permanent possibility of sudden and shocking mayhem.

When they reached the great, tree-lined mews of the palace, Pheasant was still in earnest conference with the Chief Austringer. It was his favourite golden eagle which was ailing; its plumage was dull and it had lost all desire for the hunt.

The Emperor looked rather like some exotic, noble bird himself, wrapped in his ermine coat, with a Tartar cap, glistening with rubies, covering his bound and braided hair.

Black Jade strode between the long lines of tethered hawks, each one a hunter, most of them asleep at this time on their perches.

Chinghiz, who had been drawing some interesting comparisons between the beady black and yellow eyes which flanked them and the implacable green glare of his mistress, drew in Mao-yu's lead and melted into the shadows of the mews as she approached the Emperor.

Pheasant looked up, his eyes full of concern for his patient.

'Please dismiss your keeper. I wish to speak to you,' Black Jade said evenly. She had made no curtsey. The austringer took note of this, although Pheasant, surprised by her abrupt appearance, did not.

'My dear. What is the matter? You look most disturbed.'

'Small wonder, when my husband sees fit to consort with the murderer of my child and the witch who tried to poison me!'

Pheasant uttered something between a laugh and a gasp. How, in the name of all devils, did she know that? He had rarely seen her angry. He did not like it; she looked somehow – alien to him. His first instinct was to deny the visit, but he supposed there to be little point in that; it was obvious that someone had spread the news. He should have thought of that.

'There is nothing in this to trouble you,' he said as firmly as he could, in the light of that glassy gaze of hers.

'You think not? When my husband, who has sworn unimaginable love to me, by day and by night, commits the one act that could cause me the greatest possible amount of pain?'

'Oh, surely not! I had no intention – you must *know* I never thought to distress you. It was simply that –'

'Yes? I can hardly wait to know what *was* your intention. You must have had a transcendently important reason, certainly, to honour those executioners with your presence.'

His heart sank, weighted with guilt. She would like his reason for going as little as she had liked his going.

He drew himself up as she had once taught him to do.

'I do not believe I am required to explain my activities to you. What right have you to question me?'

'The right of the mother of your dead child. I wish to know – and you *will* tell me – what brought you to the door of that woman and her filthy accomplice?'

He sighed. He had best get it over with.

'Bright Virtue sent me a message. She sold her last jewel to the jailor for its delivery.' He hesitated, cowed by the look on her face. 'She wanted to make a confession, to throw herself on my mercy.' He did not say how greatly that desperate appeal had moved him. Even in those unsalubrious conditions, Bright Virtue was a lovely and sensual woman. Her tears had almost unmanned him.

'She deeply regrets what she has done – no, please, let me finish! It is important. She said that the sorcery had been all Lady Osier's doing, that Paulownia had opposed it; and that the poison had been her own idea. She had not told Paulownia until it was too late to put a stop to the scheme. So you see –'

'What do I see?' Her contempt scorched through the rags of his pity. 'That you are so weak that she has made you believe what she wishes you to believe.' Suddenly she groaned and dropped her face in her hand. 'Now indeed they have bewitched you,' she whispered. Her anger was draining away, defeated by his unpredictable turning away from the truth.

'I don't know,' he said wretchedly. 'I am no longer sure. It was horrible to see them in that place – they had no fire, no warm bedding or comfort. Their food is not worth eating, and they have had no air or exercise since they entered those rooms. I confess it freely – I was sorry for them. They are both women whom I have – been close to, in the past.'

'You remind me of that? Now?'

He did not know what to do. She looked as though she hated him.

'They were locked into one small room,' he gabbled. 'The door was barred and the window reduced to a tiny aperture to receive their meagre food. There is no light other than one small square of daylight, high up in the roof. They were thin; ill. Paulownia has a bad cough. It was because of that, too, that Bright Virtue had written to me. She is prepared to go on suffering, if she must, but she begs that her mistress should go free. Black Jade, if you could only see Paulownia – she makes no great protestations, only says quietly that it is my belief in her guilt which most distresses her. And Bright Virtue is unshakeable in her own statement. I don't know. In those circumstances, when they have so little left to lose – it sounded to me like the truth.'

Black Jade stared at him. Her gaze was a sword.

'What they have left to lose,' she said with quiet purpose, 'is that which they took from my child, and would have taken from me.'

She left him then, with no more courtesy than she had greeted him. Chinghiz slid after her, a shadow shadowed in turn by the slender animal he held close to his heels, their every step strained by her captive desire to claw, crunch and consume the wary, watching occupant of each perch she passed.

On the steps of the Emperor's Palace, Black Jade suddenly swung round. A change was in her face.

'Do you know where Paulownia is kept?'

Naturally, he had made it his business to know.

'Then take me there.' He saw that she must go.

They walked for twenty minutes through the walled alleys and open squares of the Palace City. The women's prison was in a remote northern part of the Inner Palace, a place of dust, vermin and running damp, unused and forgotten.

The guards, startled for the second time that day, were playing *Go* in a room they had made comfortable at the end of the dank passage. They stumbled up, bowing and mumbling apologies, and shamefacedly let the brilliant figure of the Empress into the gloomy cell. It was, as one said to the other afterwards, as though a fire had been lit in that chill twilight.

Black Jade took Mao-yu's lead from Chinghiz.

'Wait outside,' she told him. She wanted no witness to this interview. An enemy is as intimate as a friend.

The air in the room was stale and smelled of damp. The two women, as astonished as the guards, stood frozen before her.

Then Paulownia bent in the kowtow and Bright Virtue straightened quickly, though shaking, perhaps with cold, after a perfunctory bow.

'Move into the light, where I can see you.'

They shuffled stiffly into the grey beam from the high window. Both had altered; Paulownia, always thin, now seemed scarcely to inhabit the layers of summer clothing which hung from her sharpened shoulderblades. Bright Virtue was also thinner, but she had once been plumply voluptuous and now, though colourless, was still in reasonable health.

Black Jade examined them carefully. She was looking at the woman who had murdered her helpless baby, the little creature whose loss she would never learn to bear, and who had wanted her own death; and at the ambitious minion who had aided and encouraged her. She remembered their haughty demeanour on the day she had begged an audience to try to repair her friendship with Paulownia. Bright Virtue had laughed at her behind her fan.

'Your Highness –' Paulownia's greeting caught in her raw throat.

Black Jade ignored it.

'You have had the insolence to address yourselves to His Majesty.' Her voice was calm in their ears.

'You are convicted felons and have no such right. Your lies, and your attempt to gain the Emperor's sympathy for your very just predicament, are deserving of further punishment. I shall see that it occurs.'

'It is you who have no such right!' Bright Virtue was virulent with loathing she did not bother to conceal. 'The law allows an accused person to appeal three times to the Emperor before he is condemned. We have had no trial. We may write what we please!'

Black Jade had not yet understood the strength of the Pure Concubine; she realised that she saw it now. In other circumstances she might even have admired it.

'You have admitted to sorcery,' her cool voice continued, cutting the dark. 'And you have been saved from the indignity of a trial, for which you should be grateful to His Majesty. You are guilty; both of you. You deserve death.'

Bright Virtue stepped forward. An aura of hatred replaced the perfumes she lacked. Mao-yu growled, deep in her throat, and strained at her leash. Black Jade vanquished a rogue impulse to let her go free. It would be so easy; one lethal spring and the hatred would be gone forever.

'I feel no guilt,' the Pure Concubine said proudly, seeking her visitor's eyes in the gloom. 'I acted only in the interests of the true Empress, and the harmony of the court and the kingdom. It is you, Lady Wu, who are the destruction of our peace. My only wish is that I had not failed!'

'No! Please, you must not say such things –' Paulownia spoke, her breathing laboured, rasping into a cough. 'Your Highness, you must not listen to her. She is often repentant, believe me. We have done you a great wrong. Indeed, now I can hardly think it was myself who could have considered such evil actions.'

She reached out a hand towards Black Jade, pleading. 'I can only say that, in some way, it was *not* myself. I was distracted by grief – in losing my husband's love I had lost everything, and to you. I do not excuse myself,' she added urgently, 'except in one circumstance – and here I beg you, in the name of merciful Kuan Yin, in the name of our beloved Emperor himself, to believe me. It was not I who killed your child. I am incapable of such an inhuman crime. I felt love for the baby. I sorrowed deeply for her death. Tell me, Black Jade; say to me that you believe this. Then I will go to my grave with peace in my heart.'

Black Jade waited for her coughing to subside; it had punctuated all of the intense little speech.

'I do not believe you,' she said simply. 'There was no one else who could have done what you did. Your further crimes only prove it. You are lying. Like your companion, you hope to gain the Emperor's sympathy because you know him to be soft-hearted. But he is not the fool you think him; he will not listen to you.'

Paulownia tried to search the white face before her. Then she bent her head. 'It is not so,' was all she said.

'Gods! But Pheasant *is* a fool!' cried Bright Virtue in fury. 'He listens to you, and the Empire may go to perdition while he does so! Only be careful! He may not always listen. You will grow older, and your beauty less bright. There will be another like you to take your place. There was a time when he said to *me* that to be in my bed was to have his bones and marrow melt in intoxication; he would have given me anything I asked. But I wanted nothing –'

'Liar! You wanted to be Empress.'

Bright Virtue laughed without mirth. But it was true. Paulownia had been right, once, to fear her. But now Paulownia was her only friend, and her sole possibility of escape from this living grave was for Paulownia to touch the Emperor's heart, as her enemy had guessed. Black Jade understood her too well; she was, perhaps, of the same kind. She did not, however, give up her attempt

'The past is the past,' she said impatiently. 'What concerns me now, though you call me a hundred times a liar, is that my mistress should suffer no longer. She is innocent. Why do you doubt it, when even I, who would have more to gain by loading her with blame, affirm her innocence before Heaven and earth?'

'You say this because you hope to creep out under her banner, if she should be released,' Black Jade said accurately. 'And of course, it appears becoming to plead for her. You could hardly do so for yourself, when you have admitted to treason.'

'Do not harden your heart, Black Jade,' begged Paulownia, now kneeling on the cold earthen floor. 'You may have need of gentleness yourself, one day.'

'That may be, but gentleness is not appropriate here.' How she despised this cloak of righteous suffering that the she-wolf had stolen. It sickened her. The whole dreadful business sickened her. It was time for it to be over and done with. She saw, perhaps she had always known, that there was only one way. She stepped back, trembling a little, because of what she must say.

'In return for my innocent daughter's life,' she told Paulownia, 'I take yours. You are both guilty of too much evil. You will die today.'

Paulownia bent her head, saying nothing. Bright Virtue, wild with vanished hope, cried out, 'Then I curse you with every curse known to magic and mankind! You can kill me, but my strong spirit will never rest until it has brought you to ruin!' Her glistening eyes fell on Mao-yu, sitting slit-eyed and erect beside her executioner.

'I shall return to you in the body of a cat, and I shall tear out your pitiless heart, and no human agency can save you from it! Oh, but I am glad – how it makes my blood sing – that your child is dead! May every child you conceive be blasted in the womb!'

She had intended that they should die decently, but now it was not so. The rage in her throat was choking her; and with it rose the image of a death that was just for such a woman, an image of helplessness and humiliation that had hung in her mind, unwelcome, because of its pure power to appal.

Upon a wave of dreadful euphoria she shouted for the guards.

Your prisoners are sentenced to death,' she said breathlessly, her heart pounding. 'You will carry out the sentence at once.' The large man paled before such fury. 'You will begin with one hundred strokes of the whip –' She could not quite yet pronounce the other. '– And then –' She tried to control the tremor. She could not. Somewhere she heard a woman cry out, softly. 'Then you will cut off their hands and feet –' The cries were double, lowing, an agony. '– and toss them into one of the vats in the brewery. Let their bones and marrow melt for as long as they may, intoxicated –' She ran from the room, tears falling unnoticed down her face.

Outside, men stood obedient as wooden cattle, their hard faces puzzled. They bowed as she stumbled past them, one unsteadily.

Chinghiz materialised from the wall and took the panther's

leash from her sweating hand. He said nothing as he shepherded her through the descending evening. Nor did she speak.

The enormity lay between them, changing its shape even as they walked, damming all talk, all coherent thought.

In the darkening gardens the spirits surrounded them.

She sat in her room, waiting for him to come to her, Mao-yu crouched beside her. In other rooms, Chinghiz came and went, keeping the servants out of her way.

It was a long time, four hours, before he came at last. It was the vintners who had spoken. The guards had not dared.

He stood at the door, his eyes wide as though he had awoken from a nightmare. Her punishment began.

'Say it isn't true. By all the Gods, tell me *it isn't true*!'

'It is true.'

He leaned against the frame, panting. He seemed ill.

'I had sent them food and clothing,' he said irrelevantly. Then, 'But why with such cruelty? Such savagery?'

She shouted. 'It was your child too!'

'She may have been innocent! I think she *was* innocent! Oh Jade, what have you done?'

She screamed at him now. 'Justice! Justice! Justice! *You* would not have done it!'

He turned his face to the wall, one hand to his eyes. He was shaking, weeping. He could not look at her.

'Don't you see? It had to be done. Not only because they were guilty, but because as long as Paulownia lived there would have been those who would work in the dark against me, against you, against our innocent children.'

He shook his head. 'No, no; it was no reason to –'

'– It was every reason. Would you rather that I should have died?'

He continued to weep, turned away from her, clasping at the cold wall, comfortless.

She had one appeal. 'They have put it about that it was I – *I* – who killed our daughter, in order to lay suspicion upon Paulownia. Can you begin to imagine how I felt when I heard that? Well, they will not dare to speak so of me again. They will not dare!' Couldn't he hear how she was desolate?

He turned then, his face distorted with tears and hurt.

'Is that what they say? At this moment, I could almost believe it,' he said bitterly. 'You have done far more than you know today. I no longer know who you are.'

She stretched out her hand, terrified by his words. But he shook his head violently and ran from the room, from her; from what she had done; from what she had become.

When he had gone, she curled on her bed and at last allowed herself to weep.

Nearby, Chinghiz listened to her agony. He would not put upon her the added burden of his company.

Later, he found her sleeping. He covered her softly with furs and rugs, looking down at her with pride and pity.

She woke at dawn. He sent away the maids and went in to her. She was sitting on the edge of her bed, small and stiff amid the tortured luxury of satin quilts.

He hesitated, but she accepted his presence as she did that of the air about her.

'Chinghiz, am I a monster? No, listen. I have been reading, in the histories. You must know of the Empress Lu, who did what I have done – only she treated her rivals to additional injuries to the eyes, and to the ears.' Her voice rose. 'Then she had them made dumb, using poison, and thrown into a pigsty for the amusement of the court. And there was the consort Chao-sin –' a sob escaped her – 'who had fifteen women killed, each more unspeakably mutilated than the last. Monsters. Have I become one of these?' She wrapped her arms about herself and rocked back and forth, gasping and weeping.

Surely, just once, just now, it would be permitted to touch her?

He reached and took her by the shoulders, hushing her as he would a little child, holding her fast between loving hands. He shook her very gently.

'Softly, little bird; you will harm yourself. Listen to me. These women you speak of – they were monstrous, yes; because it was their pleasure to inflict pain for sport. You did no such ignoble thing.'

Her sobs had ceased. She faced him through a veil of silent tears.

'How can you know?'

'I was there. The circumstance is very different.'

She made a movement that recalled to him a bird he had seen, with clipped wings, trying to fly.

'I hardly know myself, why I did it,' she said, low and ashamed.

He rose and began to put the bed to rights, treating her much as part of the furnishings. Then he threw open the door and called out for tea.

'You will be more comfortable in the study,' he said, giving her an authoritative arm to help her rise. 'Where, perhaps, we might try to discover your reasons; I think that is what you most need.'

She allowed him to wrap her in, a loose gown and place her on her favourite couch near a south-facing window overlooking the gardens. She drank her tea and let him talk.

'It is true,' he began, for it must be said, 'that you might have shown mercy, might have offered them the axe or the silken cord –'

'– I would have done,' she said swiftly. 'If she had not –'

'If the Pure Concubine had not said what she did. If she had not cursed you and exulted over the death of your child. What you must do now is to relive that moment; then, perhaps, you can be free of it. What did you feel, Black Jade, when she taunted you as she did? Don't fear it; let it come.'

Trusting him, she cast herself back into that cell filled with hatred and despair.

'It was Bright Virtue, yes; but beneath the sound of her curses I could feel the stubborn, lying meekness of my child's murderess. What happened to me was strange; I couldn't control it; suddenly I had the freedom – my hatred could feed on its fuel. It roused and blazed like a pure, clear fire; my soul seemed to rise, consumed in its fury. I felt, for that moment, incandescent, purified. It was a healing fire, not a destructive one. Can you begin to understand?'

He nodded gravely. 'Vengeance allied with the knowledge of justice can be a glorious emotion.'

'But the fire died,' she said bitterly. 'In its ashes, I no longer feel glorious. Only ashamed. My hatred is for myself now.'

'Ah. That is where you are wrong, where you must use reason, and not emotion. You have learned what power can do; now you must learn to apply it without the excess of feeling.'

'It is too late,' she said wretchedly.

'It was only the first test. And you were greatly provoked. You must not let pity or regret persuade you that you were less than justified. They had to die. What you have to do now is to find a way to be able to take the responsibility for their deaths.'

Her tears, he saw, had ceased. She was beginning to think again. If he could snare her bright intellect, he could bring her back to herself.

'The reason for these deaths,' he said firmly, 'is unimpaired by their harshness. It was just that they should die; that will be accepted by all who know their crimes. You must remember that this was not a mere act of private vengeance. You are the

Empress, and your actions demonstrate your personal power; they are therefore political acts.'

'It seems,' she said, shakily but with a wisp of irony, 'rather a dire demonstration with which to begin.'

'Is it? I'm not so sure. If you had been a man, and had dealt with your enemies in such a fashion, the court would have accepted your severity. You have made it known, to the court, to your friends, to your enemies – and to the Son of Heaven – that you are the Empress; that you know how to use the power of your position; that there is no longer a place in the world for those who seek to harm you; and that those who do so may expect a similar end to that of those two women. So you see, little mare, all in all, you have done well.'

'Little mare?' She raised her brows.

'I apologise. Among my people, it is a term of – appreciation.' He would never tell her how much more it was.

She was considering his argument.

'There is a great deal of good sense in what you say. But the fact remains that privately I have a very human need for forgiveness.'

'Forgiveness? From the Emperor. If he will try to understand what has happened, there will be no need for forgiveness.'

'He cannot bear the sight of me,' she said miserably. 'That is all that matters to me. How can your rational explanations deal with that?'

For three days and nights Pheasant refused to see Black Jade. The whispering among the court of her adversaries rose to a muted howl of triumph.

During that period news was brought that Paulownia and Bright Virtue had completed their agony and attained the mercy of death. Their bodies, according to custom, had been cut to pieces and decapitated.

Black Jade, shut up in her chambers, fought hard to conquer the horror that engulfed her each time she allowed herself to consider the overwhelming cruelty of their suffering.

Chinghiz repeated his arguments, reasonably, kindly, lovingly. It was no use. She needed Pheasant to forgive her, and to put his arms around her again. It was the first time she had ever needed him in such a way. And he had fled from her door.

In the end, her servant took pity on her and gave her a stupefying draught of opium and myrrh.

'Sleep is what you need. Drink it, and leave us for a time. It will take you wherever you wish most to go.'

'I wish, more than I would have thought possible, that I could drink it and leave you forever.' Her eyes sought him.

'I did not think you lacked courage,' he said coldly. 'There are some things that it is not fitting that you should ask of me, nor would it be fitting that I should grant them.' He watched her, silent, as she drank down the potion, then took the cup and left the room.

He had decided to visit the Emperor. He too, was in need of rational explanations.

She was dreaming of Wen Shui. It was plum blossom time and she was seated beneath one of the flowering trees in the orchard. Her mother stood a little way off with her back turned. Black Jade called to her twice, but she would not turn around. The blossom was drifting down upon them. Golden Willow shook it off and began to walk away without looking at her daughter. She tried to rise, to run after her, but found that she had not the power. The pale petals fell upon her faster now; she felt their weight. It was as though they were made of metal, not flower flesh. Again she tried to get up, calling after her mother, but the blossom pelted her, bruising her, pushing her back, down, heaping itself upon her body with the gravity of earth. She could not breathe.

She awoke, gasping, clawing at her chest. As she came into the darkness, her flailing hands met the warmth of fur. Green eyes searched hers, wide, then narrowed, a pinpoint of scarlet at their centre.

Mao-yu was crouched along the length of her body. She rose up screaming, waiting for the clench and the spring to her throat. She could see only blackness now, in the muffled void of the curtained bed. Her mind was already beginning to accept the pain.

Then the curtains were flung back and Welcome was holding her.

'There, my little bird, my lovely. You've had a dream, that's all. It's all right now. It's all over.'

'Where is she?'

She was shaking, her heart thundering like a runaway horse. Welcome stroked her back.

'Who? There's no one here. You're safe here with me.'

'Mao-yu. I *felt* her –'

She looked about her fearfully. The light of Welcome's taper revealed only the familiar shapes of plants and furniture. She heard the maids whispering at the door.

'She *was* here. It was Mao-yu. She was – sitting on my chest. I couldn't breath –'

'You were dreaming. You must have been. Master Chinghiz would never have allowed that cat to get in here.'

'But she was here! She was!'

'Well, I'll go and see what –'

'– NO! Don't leave me!'

'Hush, my bird. All right.' She raised her voice. 'Will one of you girls fetch Master Chinghiz, quickly?'

The screams had already woken the steward, who like his mistress had been unusually in need of sleep and had therefore reacted slowly to the cries. Now he burst into the anteroom, tying up his undertrousers, his eyes searching on all sides for danger. The knot of murmuring women in the doorway reassured him that nothing grave had occurred, but he felt deeply his own failure to be the first at Jade's side.

'Little Mistress?' he said anxiously. 'Are you ill?' She looked dreadful. He must send for a doctor.

'Mao-yu. Where did she go?' Her eyes roamed the shadows.

'I'm sorry?'

'The cat. Is she tied up or not?' Welcome asked, shaking her head.

'She's locked in her quarters, on a long leash, as always.' He was puzzled.

'Will you make sure of that? Our mistress thinks she saw her in here, a minute ago.'

'She was sitting on my chest,' Jade repeated with brooding horror.

One of the maids had made soothing camomile tea and Welcome persuaded her to drink it. She managed only a few sips before Chinghiz returned, looking more cheerful, to report that Mao-yu was safely in her quarters and fast asleep. The guards in that area were awake and vigilant and had sworn that the animal had not been let out since Chinghiz himself had fed her and left her to sleep.

Black Jade's instant reaction to this news was to bury her face in Welcome's breast, shaking as though fevered.

The nurse waved him away, the maids too. 'Leave her to me. I'll stay with her for the rest of the night.'

When they had gone, Jade raised an ashen face to her oldest friend. 'Welcome,' she whispered, 'if it was not Mao-yu, it must have Bright Virtue. She swore that she would come to me in the shape of a cat. She means to kill me. Oh, what can I do? It was she; I know it!' It was pure panic.

Welcome hugged her closer. This was a serious matter. Spirits had been known to cause the death of the living, but only if they were stronger than their chosen victims.

'It may be so. And it may be, too, that it was only a dream. Time will tell.'

She shuddered. 'I don't think I could bear it – again.'

'Nonsense! What, you, not bear the foolish tricks of a contemptible ghost? I had thought better of you than that. You must ask your own illustrious ancestors to help you get the better of that one!'

'I will. I will. I will give them titles and rich offerings. You are right. I must fight her. It is just that, for now, I am confounded by the fear. I do not think I have ever truly felt fear before. I am not sure how to deal with it.'

'You'll beat it, don't worry. And now, you must try to sleep again. Your eyelids are almost closing, no matter how much you protest you're afraid. I'll be here beside you. I'll keep the light burning till morning. There'll be no more visitors tonight!'

Fear, whatever other fee it exacts, takes a great deal of energy. Black Jade found it amazingly easy to lie down again and let her eyes close as they wished. Her last waking thought was not of Bright Virtue but of wholesome amusement at the determinedly pugnacious expression on her nurse's face, as, single-handed, she prepared to take on the powers of darkness and of death, sitting bolt upright at the foot of the bed with an embroidery needle for her sole protection.

Something, some faint sound, or perhaps only premonition, caused Jade to wake just before dawn. Strained grey light penetrated the curtains. Welcome had fallen asleep across the foot of the bed; she was snoring slightly, her mouth open. But that had not been what had awoken her.

Already she knew that there was someone else in the room.

'Chinghiz! Is that you?'

There was no reply. She felt her hair begin to rise. She peered through the swathed silk of the curtains; she could make out nothing in the gloom.

She was wrong, foolish; there was no one there. It was last night's leftover fear that had tricked her.

What she needed was light. Welcome's candle had burned down, but there was a taper and a tinder box upon the wide shelf at the head of the bed. With fingers that trembled irritatingly she managed to get it alight, all the time feeling that she was being watched and waited for. She made a sound of annoyance, wanting to hear her own voice. In a moment she would wake Welcome. It was idiotic to sit here shivering for no reason, when a little commonplace human contact would put everything to rights. She shuffled to the edge of the bed and prepared to fling back the curtains, conscious, as she had always been as a child, of leaving a safe, warm and protected world for an unknown territory.

What was that?

It had been very slight, but it had been a sound. Tiny, insignificant, like the fall of a single drop of water.

Grasping her candle, she threw the curtain aside. A deep, terrible howl filled the morning. It came from her own throat.

They stood waiting for her across the room, their faces livid above their blood-soaked robes. They held out empty sleeves towards her, the ends of them dripping, dripping – There were pools of darkness beneath them. They looked at her mournfully, accusing her. They came towards her, their dreadful arms outstretched.

She threw herself backwards, still surrounded by that hideous howling. They followed, their faces close. The taint of blood hung acrid in the air. She felt the sodden cloth begin to wrap her in a foul embrace. She tore at it, struggling for her life in a paroxysm of fear, weeping and panting with terror.

Then she reeled back, her hand to her cheek where a forceful slap had cracked across it. She knelt, half-stunned, recognising Welcome, white and determined, one hand still raised to fend her off.

Weeping, she collapsed into the nurse's arms.

Welcome held her for a long time, stroking her wild hair and speaking softly to her, as she had used to do in the nursery after some childish crisis. Black Jade quietened beneath the reassuring touch, her sobs subsiding and her breathing easier. Then suddenly she started up again, her eyes frantically searching.

There was nothing. They had gone.

After a time, she was able to speak of what she had seen.

Later, Welcome held a private discussion with Chinghiz. They decided the Emperor must be told of the night's business before he learned it from less sympathetic tongues.

Chinghiz set off again for the Palace of Golden Bells.

Pheasant had always been a little in awe of the steward, whose intelligence overwhelmed him and whose bearing now held an authority which even an Emperor might envy. His evening had been permeated by the man's insidious arguments appealing to the cause of justice and harmony, and speaking of the real sorrow felt by Black Jade. He had resisted them, called them specious and mistaken, but they had done their work, and his mind was now open to doubt.

When his subtle interlocutor returned, at such an early hour and with such a grave face, he was at once disposed to fear worse news than he received. In pure gratitude that it was not so, he agreed to come at once to his wife's apartments. Truth to tell, beyond all rational disputation, he had simply been unable to prevent himself from missing her. A love so deeply dependent as his could not be killed in an instant, however greatly he might believe he wished it. He had dismissed the steward's reasoned pleading, but he could not dismiss Black Jade's need.

When he entered the bedroom and saw her crouched in Welcome's arms, worn out with tears and terror, his love rose up in him as strongly as ever, and with the new and piquant addition of a sense of compassion, a desire to protect, which formerly had not been necessary.

He nodded to Welcome and gently took her place. Black Jade fell into his embrace like a half-dead thing, her weeping starting afresh.

'No, no. We will have no more of this. It is bad for you.'

'They are dead. But they have come back. And it has made you hate me.'

He touched her tormented face. 'I tried, perhaps; but it seems that I cannot.' She looked so young, so defenceless, more like a child that has disappointed its parents than a woman who has committed an ineradicable crime of violence.

Surely, Pheasant concluded, with uncharacteristic irony, it was better to think ill of the dead, if they were not among one's own immediate ancestors, than of those who were living and whom one loved? He had not been prepared for what Black Jade done, but he understood now, through Chinghiz and from the desperate face that he now held close to his heart, that she herself had been equally unprepared.

If she were given back these last few days of time's repeating wheel she would act differently, he thought. The tenderness she had longed for welled up in him, and he gave her all the comfort he had held back.

'I shall never leave you alone for a single night,' he swore to her. 'I will make myself your refuge. These unhappy ghosts will not come near you while I am with you.'

*

Black Jade and Rose Bird were waiting for Golden Willow. At first, Jade had not dared to send for either her mother or her sister; she feared their horror, and worse, their contempt. But today Rose Bird had appeared with her festoons of children and nursemaids in their usual clamorous fashion, had greeted the Empress with warm affection and announced that Golden Willow would join them presently. The children were despatched to the zoo, a favourite treat.

'They say those dreadful women are haunting you; is it true?' Rose Bird asked fiercely when they were alone.

The indignation in her sweet face flooded Jade with relief. Her eyes filled. She cried easily now.

'Little pigeon!' Rose Bird engulfed her in silk and scent. 'You mustn't let them distress you so. What can they do? They are only dead things. They have no poison in their fangs.'

'It isn't that. I thought you would condemn me.'

Rose Bird's reply was immediate. After her initial shock and revulsion, she had thought hard and worked her way to a conclusion.

'Never believe that. The wicked woman who killed your poor baby, who would have killed you, deserved to die a thousand times. As for Bright Virtue, she was well caught in her own filthy web. You must try to keep them out of your mind; then they will lose their power to come back to you.'

'You think so?' said Jade gratefully. 'It won't be easy. The way they died –'

'– was kinder than many. You could have had them flayed slowly, or cut into little pieces, day by day.'

'Nonetheless, I will be hated for it.'

'Only by a few. And only because you, a woman, took the execution of justice into your own hands. It shocks their sense of fitness. It is not Confucian. But tell me, have you done nothing to try to rid yourself of these importunate ghosts? There are rites of exorcism; have you called a priest?'

Her sister made a wry mouth. 'We have tried everything. Abbot Hsuan-tsang himself performed the rites. The morning after the ceremony I turned a corner, and there they were, just as before! Rose Bird, their appearance is so horrible! They are just as they must have been when they died – without hands or feet, dripping wine and blood from sodden, dark-stained robes.' Her voice was rising; she caught and controlled it. 'I am trying to win over them.

I have begged the Wu ancestors to intercede for me with the Queen Mother of the Western Heaven. I long to ask help from Shih-min. But it was he who chose Paulownia to be Empress, and I can't be sure that, despite his love for me, he does not disapprove of everything I have done since he left us. That is a burden which does not, and will not lighten. But yes –' she forced a more cheerful note – 'we have done what we can. Pheasant prays for me, and has the rites performed continuously. He never leaves me at night, though sometimes they come while he sleeps and I lie awake.' She smiled regretfully. 'Because Bright Virtue threatened to destroy me in the guise of a cat, I have had all my sweet felines banished from the palace. Even Mao-yu is only permitted to be with me at a distance, securely leashed. I miss her sadly; poor beast, how can she understand? I have even had the Emperor change the names of the two women to Lady Snake and Lady Vulture; many believe he has the power, as the intermediary between earth and Heaven, to alter their spirit form to whatever name he may given them. Should either of these ill-omened creatures appear in the palace, they will be instantly killed. And then, of course, I must not forget Welcome's immortal remedy!'

'What is that?'

'Hawk shit.'

'Ugh! You have to eat it?'

'She puts it in my night-time drink. Luckily, I can hardly detect it. Anyway, Welcome swears by its powers.'

'Well, who knows? Though I think it more likely to keep you awake. But, Little Sister, this hideousness must leave you soon. I have never heard of such visitations continuing for long.'

She did not say that she *had* heard of cases where the victim had succumbed and died, his heart torn out by the supernatural tormentor. She was afraid for Black Jade, but she would not show it.

'And you have Pheasant's loving support; that must give you hope.'

'That is true. I had feared his anger, his horror – as I feared yours. But we are closer, now, than ever. I am glad. I need it. But there is something else that worries me. All this is taking its toll of Pheasant. The hauntings, the difficulties of my position, the daily concerns of court and council – lately it has all seemed too much for him. He has been unusually tired. He seems to have no energy, any more, for hunting or his beloved archery. It is all he can do to perform the ancestral rites and consult with the ministers. He is pale, prefers to be inactive, yet he says he feels well enough, apart from the tiredness. He won't allow the physicians to examine him because he says he is not ill.'

'You must persuade him. And make him save his strength. It is difficult, I know. I used to feel so *useless* when my own husband was so ill – but he had the wasting disease,' she said quickly, 'and the Emperor has nothing like that, I'm sure. He is just exhausted with your troubles and from working too hard.'

'I hope so. I pray it is so. I only wish he did not have this extra burden of the new action in Korea. It looks as though we shall soon have a full-scale war on our hands.'

It was then that Chinghiz announced Golden Willow.

Black Jade shot a look of agonised apprehension at her sister. How would her mother greet her, the child who had departed so very far from her compassionate teaching?

Golden Willow entered, displayed her customary calm which was echoed in a cool ensemble of sky-blue and white. Bending like a lily she performed the three formal kowtows which convention demanded before the Empress.

'You are most welcome, Lady Mother,' Black Jade said nervously.

'I am glad to see you at last, my child.' The dark eyes surveyed her with concern. 'I had heard that you were not sleeping. I have brought you a tisane of my own concoction. The recipe is a very old Taoist one. I have great hope that it may give you rest.'

Black Jade stood still, longing to embrace the achingly familiar figure, but afraid of repudiation.

Golden Willow would not let her suffer. 'Come here, then, and let me kiss you. It is quite long since we last met. I have been distressed for you.'

She went thankfully into a warm, welcoming cloud of carnation essence. Her mother kissed her cheek, then held her gaze for a little while, letting her daughter understand that she knew all that there was to know. She did not, however, propose to discuss it, either now or at any time in the future. That too was implicit in her clear grey eyes.

'Mother,' murmured the Empress, her voice a mere whisper, 'Can you ever forgive me?'

'There is no question of forgiveness.' Her firm tone warned Black Jade that she was coming too close to the boundary that had just been set. 'You should not dwell too much upon what is past, Second Daughter. Your duty, all of it, is to the future. There, child, you have my blessing, of course you do; as always.'

As Black Jade, suddenly deliriously happy, fell into her arms, she responded with all her wealth of careful affection, determined that this cursed, blessed and favourite child should never guess how bitter a course she had had to follow, in aching thought and heartfelt prayer, before she could school herself to accept and assimilate what she now so bravely described as the past.

16

Her strength renewed, Black Jade set herself to win back the love her recent action would have lost her in some circles, though not, as Chinghiz had guessed, in the more sophisticated echelons of the court.

There was also a renaissance in her relations with her husband. Pheasant, as though trying to make up for those three black days when he had let it be known that he could not bear to see her, was now constantly at Jade's side, letting the whole world observe his loving care of her.

If it was muttered in doorways that she had bewitched him, it was cried delightedly in daylit courts that he had fallen in love with her all over again.

It was far from being the doting Pheasant's fault if, sometimes, in the full face of that sunlight or in the dark depths of a sleepless night, she could still hear the halting resonance of his voice, speaking harshly against her – 'Is that what they say? At this moment, I could almost believe it.'

They were words which he had forgotten, and would certainly withdraw in horror were she to remind him of them, but they had established, unknown to either of them, a thread of separation between them, insensibly fine, but as strong as the spider's filament. They drew close and it was covered, but nonetheless it was there.

In order to provide a new talking point for the court, the thoughtful Lion Guard chose this time to suggest that, now that Lady Wu was Empress, it was unsuitable that the adopted son of a concubine should continue as Crown Prince. The Emperor agreed and Bold Tiger became heir to the Empire.

Shortly after this confirmation of her status Black Jade found to her joy that she was pregnant again. The news bound her even more closely to Pheasant, and very often the business of government got short shrift as they whiled away dreaming hours in the gilded depths of the Ta Ming, making poetry, love and music.

'If only Heaven sends us a girl this time! It would be as though the horrors that have passed had never happened. We would have our baby daughter again and the world would begin afresh! And I am sure that if I do have a girl, those unhappy spirits would leave me forever and continue their journey beyond the Yellow Springs.'

'Then a girl it must be!' declared Pheasant. 'She will resemble you in every way, a tiny, perfect mirror of your beauty. What shall you name her?'

'I will call her Taiping – the restoration of tranquillity. It will be a wonderfully good omen for the future.'

The pregnancy was an easy one. Black Jade felt well and strong and full of energy, which she applied chiefly to preventing her husband from wasting his own depleted resources. He was still far from well, although he complained of no specific discomfort and would see no other physican than Abbot Hsuan-tsang, who asked several diagnostic questions but came to no conclusion. As her pregnancy proceeded, Jade suspected rightly that he was relieved to let their lovemaking lapse. He seemed happy just to lie beside her, stroking her into sleep. Suspicion was confirmed when, rather than seeking the comfort of his other concubines, the Emperor redefined their duties as those of 'Assistants of the Imperial Virtue', an innovation which caused hysteria in the harem, a cauldron of gossip in the courts, and a selfish satisfaction in Jade's protective heart.

To relieve him of further strain, she encouraged him to avoid the council chamber and to work gently, instead, upon the essay he was writing upon the responsibility of rule. They worked together in the scholastic peace of the imperial library, where she continued her own studies in political history, determined to extract the lessons of the past in the interests of the future.

She kept herself as busy as her condition permitted; the more exhausted she was when she slept, the less likely it proved that the spirits would visit her. As for the daylight hours, she found the best method of keeping them at bay was to fill her mind with other things.

When the nine months were over, both she and Pheasant looked forward to the birth. It would set the seal upon their hopeful efforts towards happiness.

The lying-in chamber roistered with ribbons and bells and clambered with winter-flowering plants. Black Jade had never felt so well and so exuberant. The maids took her mood and ran about singing. She held court in the huge bed, her visitors lined up across its foot, couched on a rampart of cushions larger than her own satin bastion. They drank tea and tattled and nibbled at an inexhaustible wealth of tasty titbits. Rose Bird played her lute and Dumpling's round and raucous laughter rioted about the walls like a flight of fat, imprisoned ducks.

The child who came, with understandable speed, to enjoy this encouraging welcome, was perfectly formed, lusty-voiced, deep orange, and unequivocally male.

Black Jade was inconsolable. Her happiness dropped from her like a detected disguise. Nothing anyone could say would convince her that Heaven was not displeased with her.

She had not been forgiven for her cruelty.

That night the dead shades of her victims crowded close to her bed, their faces hideous with sly satisfaction.

A month after the birth of Prince Li Che, known as Loud Tiger for deafeningly obvious reasons, Black Jade decided that the only way to escape her supernatural visitors was to put a wide physical distance between them. Ghosts were known to frequent a particular area. They might well follow her about the palaces they had known, but they would not have the power to leave the environs in which they had lived.

'Beloved, I want you to move the court to Loyang.'

'Gods and dragons! When?'

'Now. As soon as we can be ready.'

'My precious girl – have you any idea of the organisation involved? The expense, the sheer physical difficulty of shifting hundreds of people and their goods and encumbrances over two hundred miles in the middle of winter?'

'Your father did it; on three separate occasions.' This was no time for delicacy. 'It is customary for the Emperor to spend some time in the eastern capital.'

'Certainly. After due consideration and planning. But –'

'I don't ask only for myself. There are other sufficient reasons, should the ministers ask for them. I have been talking about it to Lion Guard.' She had marshalled her forces with care; she intended to have a runaway victory.

Pheasant looked apprehensive; the intention was all too clear.

'Most important is the fact of the bad harvest; since Chang-an is notoriously difficult to supply, it would save a great deal of money, and relieve the poverty in this area, if the court were to leave for a time.'

This was true. The capital was ill-situated, on an infertile plain subject to the twin devils of flood and drought, and cut off by the formidable San Men Rapids from the canal system which augmented the country's natural waterways; it was indeed difficult, and expensive, to supply.

'If we had only had the idea some time ago,' Pheasant said doubtfully, 'it would have been possible. But we can't simply leave now. We need months of preparation.'

'In my experience what can be done in months can probably be done in weeks. A month.' She held his eye. 'I want to leave in a month. Or perhaps,' she added quietly, sadly, 'you would allow me to go alone. I promise you, I can bear it here no longer.' Her voice broke. This was nothing but the truth.

'My dearest!' Sympathy shook him into acceptance. There was a crumbling sensation in his chest, alien fingers working under his ribs. He took his breath slowly.

'I know how you – I am so sorry, Jade. Perhaps, yes, something might be arranged – a small retinue, just at first. I could not let you go from me, though. I cannot be without you.'

'No. I know. Nor I without you. I should not have said that. It is only that I *must* get away from them. You understand.'

He touched her hand, saying nothing.

She remembered what Lion Guard had said. Wise words.

'There is another reason why we should leave Chang-an. It has become the focus of too much influence, too many ambitious clans. All those who have helped to build the Empire, and have claimed their rewards in office. That is at it should be, but not all of them agree with you on certain matters – and my own position is still disputed amongst them. What better way to show them that they are out of harmony with the times than simply to move the centre of power out of their orbit?'

It was incontravertible good sense. He admitted as much.

'Then – we may go?' Her gratitude was glorious, if premature. What could he could do? He could not destroy such relief, such hope.

'We will go. I want you to be happy. It is decided,' he said. He held out his arms for his reward.

It was the first time Black Jade had travelled a distance of more than a few miles in the nineteen years since she had left Shansi. During every minute of the week they took to reach Loyang she lived upon a peak of exhilaration that caught the breath of everyone who came near her.

At first they went by water. The excited court, over a thousand eager people, had packed its bags and boxes and crammed them, with itself and its servants, into the series of barges which would carry them along the canal which by-passed the shallow, silting River Wei as far as its confluence with the Yellow River at Hua-chou.

By day they moved between banks carved from the bones of the tens of thousands of long-dead men who had hewn them out. The dragon-prowed, silk-furnished vessels cut swiftly through the territory of the water demons, propelled by the oarsmen; bent and brown, their knotted tendons tortured into unnatural curves, half-naked to winter's approach, they sang as they pulled, their deep strokes timed to the rhythm of the helmsman as he called out the chant;

> 'Heave away! Heave away! Hey, hey, hey!
> A hard wind blows; my body's cold.
> Hey, hey hey!
> You and I, chained together
> Will push this boat to Hua-chou.
>
> Heave away! Heave away! Hey, hey, hey!
> Come on, come on, move your oar!
> Hey hey hey!
> Flying forward, all together
> Carry the great ones to Hua-chou.'

Black Jade, wrapped in a wolfskin, banished cold, courtiers and convention; she would not conceal herself behind a severing screen, but walked the deck among her people, or stood at the rail, her sleeve touching her husband's, living only through her eyes.

On either side there lay the plain, a starving landscape of harvested millet fields with only a few poor dwellings and scattered, scarecrow figures to fill it. Beyond the plain rose the mountains, in rows of ragged crests like the scales of some gigantic, sprawling, mythical beast; demon and guardian, feared and worshipped, each peak housed tutelary Gods and devils.

By day there were the mountains; by night there were the stars. Camped in tents of brocade and the warm skins of animals, the court made music for Heaven; for Shang-ti who is the supreme power and cannot be imagined or envisaged; for the Moon Goddess, who is the errant wife of Yi the Excellent Archer, who used her magical skill to shoot down nine of the ten flaming suns that once troubled the earth. Yi had travelled to the Western Heaven, where the Queen Mother had given him the precious Herb of Immortality. His wife had stolen it and fled to the moon; they could see her now, quite plainly, drifting in her dress of changing gauze against the dark clarity of the sky, shaped like a hare, or, as the boatmen preferred it, a toad.

They sang too, for the Weaver Maid, while Black Jade, with her children cuddled into her cloak, told them her story.

'Look there – do you see her where she lives, on the far side of the River of Stars? She is so lovely, poor Princess. Once she lived happily with her husband, the Cowherd, in a rich valley, but her father, the mighty Shang-ti, became angry with them because they were so much in love that they neglected their duties; the loom was idle, the flocks straying. He sent a magpie to them with a message, condemning them to a separation; they must meet, from that day, only once every month. Well, the magpie, alas, was a forgetful bird, and he foolishly got the message wrong – he told them that they could meet only once a year! And so it has been. But the silly magpies have done their best to make up for the mistake; they have joined together to make a bridge in the sky – there, that great, untidy arch – so that the Weaver Maid can cross over to see her husband.'

The solemn little faces gazed upward. It hung above them on the end of their mother's fingertips, a fretted network of brightness flung across the heavens as though a careless Tartar had kicked over a pail of mare's milk.

At dawn, as the courtiers experimentally stretched creaking limbs and shook out crushed robes, the boatmen had already forgotten the terrors of the night and were busily attending to the demands of the river deities, who shared their breakfast of roast meat and oranges, and were also treated to an astonishment of firecrackers, by grace of the Imperial Entertainments Officer.

It was when they reached the Yellow River that propitiation began in mortal earnest. At the point of the confluence stood the shrine of the most fearful of all the water Gods, as temperamental and unpredictable as he was powerful, that mighty demon, the Count of the Yellow River.

At the shrine the court shed offerings with the alacrity of young lovers shedding their clothes. Jade rings, gold pins, pieces of silk embroidered by departed grandmothers, coins, cash, bottles of the very best brandy – nothing was too good for the Count of the River. If they gave him less than the best, he might revert to the demands he had made in older days, when the most beautiful girl available was chosen to be his bride; arrayed in matchless finery, jewelled and scented, spotlessly virgin, she was laid upon her marriage bed, which was then pushed out upon the passionate current; it was never very long before the eager Count claimed his consummation.

Now, however, the moody nobleman was content with a counterfeit, and it was thought that the charming little boat, carved and studded with jewels, which was launched by the Empress herself, would be sure to guarantee a safe passage.

It was so. They reached Hua-chou without incident and there disembarked to be entertained in fitting style by its citizens. That such style would leave many of the citizens penniless and many more starving was thought to be compensated for by an amnesty for the coming year's taxes. That the court had consumed almost the entire harvest and most of the fattened beasts along the viparian areas was not considered. The peasants would manage somehow. They always did; or else they died.

The court continued their journey by land. To the populace it was as though a flight of locust-gods had passed over them, half plague, half blessing, leaving them stricken and exalted. Although in a few weeks they would be too weak to bend and kiss the earth where it had fallen, they had set their unworthy eyes upon the Emperor's shadow – a fulfilment to last them the rest of their days (which for many of them were now few), and a legend to leave their descendants.

As they approached Loyang the border of patient and marvelling peasant faces was replaced by a more well-to-do and cosmopolitan species as the citizens gave themselves a holiday and flooded out to welcome the Emperor whom Heaven had so suddenly returned to them. They lined the route in their thousands, having half-killed each other in the race for a good viewpoint. They were ecstatic, quite drunk with delight, roaring and cheering their approval of the dusty calvacade. They threw flowers, they played drums and pipes, they even served tea to the grateful travellers, threatening to overwhelm them with their goodwill long before they reached the impressively towered southern gate by which the Son of Heaven must enter the city.

Loyang was divided into three walled complexes like Chang-an. The Palace City lay to the north with the government buildings to the south of it. The main township clustered about these in an untidy horseshoe of temples, monasteries, public amenities and housing of every degree. There were wide, tree-lined boulevards with an air of southern languor about them, where the mansions and palaces of the very rich stood behind secretive walls fronted by magnificently gaudy gates. There were great expanses of parkland, ornamented with lakes and a profusion of wildlife. There were shops and warehouses, offices, schools and hospitals, fine restaurants and tea-houses. The humming street life centered around the unrivalled southern market, whose very name was enough to make the mouth water; 120 bazaars overflowed with the juiciest fruits, the most exquisite flowers, the most exceptional ceramics, the dearest of damasks, the most fluid of crepes, the subtlest of perfumes and the most flattering of tinctures for the palette or the complexion. There was everything the greedy heart could desire, in street after narrow, excitable street of expensive perfection.

Wishing both to see and be seen, Black Jade, on entering the city, pulled back the curtains of her yellow palanquin and also the veil of her broad-brimmed feathered hat. She instructed her guards to walk at a distance of two yards from herself and one from each other so that no one's view should be interrupted.

The citizens, she noted, were prosperous, attractive and exceedingly well-mannered. They fell to the stones of the streets like grass mown down by a scythe in the swathe of her passing, their vibrant silks bleeding into the dust. She saw that they nonetheless managed to look at her face, and having looked, were suddenly translated, their careful manners abandoned for smiles of delight. Her returning smile constituted an outrage to imperial propriety; she was very glad that she had her beauty to offer them.

Welcome, travelling just behind with her mulberry curtains drawn tight together like disapproving lips, noticed only that the noise and stink were very like those of Chang-an – the endless hubbub of humans and animals supervised by the bells and the drums of the temples, and the warm mixture of spices, cooking, frost, and honest and dishonest sweat, punctuated at certain corners by the pungent stench of the public cloacae, where excrement was collected to manure the fields. Her scandalised ears had soon told her what her little mistress was up to. She made a mental note to give Black Jade a good talking-to, Empress or no Empress. She also detected that they were going to be extraordinarily popular here.

When Their Majesties reached the Palace City, their reactions were much the same as had been the citizens' to the imperial countenance. The buildings that rose about them now were of an unparalleled splendour. Standing proudly amongst regiments of animal and vegetable statuary, their layered and many-coloured roofs rearing towards the clouds, glittering with gold and mica, each one seemed more outstanding than the last; it was as though a divine and profligate hand had flung a mountain of silver at the feet of a number of eccentric and talented architects and told them to build as they pleased, and to give themselves plenty of space to do it in. Therefore, although there might be, perhaps, a palace masquerading as a simple Tibetan lamasery, apart from the fact that it was built entirely of white marble and jade, next door to a pavilion that had been painted, belled and turreted like a Canton brothel, these did not conflict, being screened from each other by a merciful grove of mulberry trees.

The Imperial Palace did not disappoint them; it outdid all the rest. Individually styled to represent the extreme and often decadent taste of the Sui Emperor Yang-ti, who had rebuilt the entire city with an extravagance that had ruined his exchequer and broken the backs of thousands of his subjects, it was as decorative as a peacock's tail. Black Jade explored it with a great deal of amusement and a growing liking. She had always been fond of show. Here, there writhed more dragons, flustered more phoenixes, leaped more leopards and meddled more monkeys than in any given space she had ever seen. It was gaudy, brilliant, spectacular in scale and concept. It was just what they needed.

As they walked through the painted halls and silken chambers, studied the statuary in the courts and gardens, conned the calligraphy on the hanging scrolls, raised their brows at too much magnificence, controlled their smiles at too little shame, Jade and Pheasant became very happy.

When at long last they were alone for their first night together in the chamber they had chosen, one which rested quietly in shades of terracotta spiked with autumn white, she swam up from their first embrace wearing an expression of dawning mischief.

'I know I am safe now,' she said, and amazed herself by making a joke of it. 'Paulownia will never join us here. She could not bear to set foot in such a place, dead or alive!'

Pheasant's answering smile was a little nervous, but time, to their vast relief and content, proved her to be right.

With that great burden removed from her, Black Jade began to blossom. She was filled with new energy and enthusiasms. She personally surpervised the toning down of the palace to her own level of éclat; she gave audiences to ministers and local noblemen and scholars; she gave concerts and fêtes for their wives and held competitions for their children. She was seen boating on the lakes, and later skating on them. She was heard, by a chosen few, to sing, and her verses were quoted in the bazaars. She changed the names of everything to bring good luck, and she changed the rhythm of daily life, making it swifter and sweeter and a hundred times more exciting, using nothing but her own personal magic. She was determined to remove all care from her husband and to prove to any who still doubted it that she was more than worthy to be his helpmeet.

The small chamber was hung with green silk of every shade from malachite to milk-opal. It was strung, almost imperceptibly, with fine netting, and Black Jade was feeding the swooping flights of tropical birds who lived and sang in its gentle cage.

Chinghiz watched her, dwelling upon the cooing curve of her soft lips and the slender gift of her outstretched hand, upon all the loveliness that was his for this half-moment before he must break her peace.

'Lord Hsu is in the anteroom, with another gentleman.'

She turned. 'Something in your voice, and in that wide, innocent gaze, tells me I am about to learn why you have been so damnably busy and secretive lately.'

He returned her smile. 'Perhaps.'

The visitors entered. She was always pleased to see the elegant President of the Board of Rites; she liked and trusted him and enjoyed his delicate wit.

Of the man who followed him in she was not so sure. A large, well-made man in middle life, with sensual features – the lips moist and red, the eyes as glossy as a stallion's – this was Li-I-fu, more commonly known as 'The Leopard', and to his enemies as 'Dagger Smile', a man of singular character and subterranean ways, and one to whom she owed a considerable favour.

It had been repaid, for they had made him a chief minister a year ago when he had sent in his audacious petition begging that Black Jade be made Empress. He had been the first to dare to strike so deeply into the heart of imperial custom as to condone Pheasant's 'incest' and to challenge the insulted vengeance of Paulownia's aristocratic clan. He had since worked assiduously for her advantage; and also for his own.

Always flamboyant, disdaining the quiet, dark hues customary for ministers, today he wore peacock blue with flashes of magenta and a capful of brilliant tail-feathers.

Eyeing these, his Empress acknowledged his bow. 'Oh dear, I

do hope my poor birds will not feel threatened!'

'Ah, no. My preference is for larger game.' His eyes wicked, he twirled before her, and she saw that, in insouciant acceptance of his nickname, a leopard stretched its embroidered length from the back of his muscular neck to the hem of his robe.

She turned to Lion Guard and asked what business had brought him to her.

'An unfortunate one, I'm afraid. We knew, of course, that we had brought a certain number of trouble-makers with us from Chang-an.' The policy had been to keep the more influential of these under close surveillance, and to leave the small fry behind in the capital. 'We did not, however, expect them to be quite so busy, or so well-organised, for that matter.'

Sensing some threat, Black Jade looked automatically for Chinghiz. She found him behind her shoulder, listening impassively.

Lion Guard sketched the problem swiftly. 'The information came through Leopard's agency. There is a conspiracy, at a high level, to depose His Majesty and put the ex-Crown Prince on the throne.'

She showed no surprise, only the wish to listen.

'The presidents of both the Chancellery and the Secretariat are involved.' Both men had been opposed to her impartial appointment.

'You will recall that these lords were eager for the recall and reinstatement of Old Integrity? Well, it appears that the old incorrigible is equally capable in exile. It was a mistake to make him a military governor. The garrison he commands was to be the nucleus of a revolt. Later, the ministers I have mentioned would have set matters in motion in Chang-an, in His Majesty's absence.'

Black Jade tried not to be swamped by dismay.

'Would they have found it so easy? I can believe that border garrisons become dissatisfied and may perhaps be suborned, but those near to Chang-an are all fiercely loyal.'

'It would depend,' suggested Lion Guard, 'from whom their orders came.'

'The Archduke?' she breathed. Wuchi was still the commander of the Armies. 'Is there any evidence –?'

'No. None whatsoever,' her champion regretted. 'But it is a possibility to bear in mind. The adopted boy was his especial interest; the plan was drawn up by his closest friends.'

'How was it discovered?' the Empress asked.

Lion Guard coughed and exchanged a glance with his feral companion.

'They were foolish enough,' the Leopard said suavely, 'to commit themselves to paper. A message, from the Chancellor to Old Integrity, which friends of mine intercepted; quite incontravertible proof. I am very sorry. Men in such high office. I am ashamed.'

He looked ashamed. Both of them did. They stood in poses of weary dignity, their heads bowed for their fallen colleagues.

A suspicion tickled her. 'Was the message in the Chancellor's hand?'

The Leopard considered, judging his leeway.

'Alas, no, not his own hand,' he said at last. 'A secretary, a mere minion. Regrettable, I know, but –' he lifted his hands.

Black Jade did not at once reply. Lion Guard was deepening his study of the birds. Even Chinghiz, for once, was not looking her way.

Eventually she nodded, her expression the model for a Buddha.

'It was good of you to inform me of this. I will speak to the Emperor. I will not mention the name of his uncle Wuchi; it does not, at present, seem appropriate. Meanwhile, I am sure I may rely upon you both to do everything you deem necessary to correct this unfortunate situation?'

'It will be our privilege, Intelligent Highness.'

'Tell me why you brought them to me,' she demanded of Chinghiz when they had gone. 'To me, rather, than the Emperor?'

She held out her hand for the dish of bird-food and he followed her closely, holding it as she took handfuls and offered them through the netting.

The fluttering and swooping softly percussioned his answer.

'If you, in return, will tell me why you gave those two their head – and what you expect to come of it.'

'I make no bargains.'

'No?' His brows slanted. 'I rather thought you had just done so. I brought our friends to you,' he continued hastily, as an emerald spear raked his face, 'because – well, I might say it was because His Majesty is fatigued today and I wished to save him further pressure –'

'But that would not be the truth.'

'No. Let us by all means have truth. I did it because I wanted to see how you would handle it.'

The impudence was staggering, or would have been, had it

come from anyone else. But she had long since allowed him to become his own law. She would not, now, complain of it.

'I see. And have I passed the test?'

'Admirably. First grade. *Chin shih.*'

'Thank you. And why, might one ask, was one being tested?'

He hung fate in the balance. Should he tell her now? No, it was still too soon, perhaps by weeks, by months, or even years.

He smiled, guileless as a sparrow. 'Forgive me. It was a mischievous suggestion. But it has seemed to me that, given the Emperor's nature, and your own, and the distressing fact of His Majesty's frequent periods of lassitude, you will find yourself doing more and more of his work. It also seemed that this time we are spending in Loyang provides you with both the space and the time in which to make experiments.'

She let the last of the grain run from her hands. The birds flew upon it, piping like choirboys, pecking and shouldering.

'Experiments in what? In government, or in assorted underhand methods of ridding myself of my detractors?'

'They are often the same thing. As you perfectly understand. You have just proved it, I believe?'

Grudgingly, she accepted the lure. 'If you insist. I accept that there was probably a plot. I accept that it was discovered by those who uphold me, and was engineered by those who would depose me; most convenient, like the written evidence which has stuck so stickily to the paws of the sly Leopard.'

'And your expectation is?'

'That the two plotting presidents will be removed to the usual penitential and pestilential governorships – their clans might grumble if anything worse happened to them – and we shall reward our watchful servitors with the offer of the conspirators' old jobs, if they want them. And Old Integrity,' she added thoughtfully, 'had better go even further out of harm's way, beyond the Wall, if necessary, the wicked old man!'

'It would be wise. And?'

'And the watch which must by now almost have doubled the staff the Archduke thought he owned, will soon treble it.'

He grinned. She was having difficulty in maintaining in acid tone.

'And I shall have proved myself fit to occupy the Phoenix Throne and sit at the right hand of the Lord of Ten Thousand Years, who has been deprived of considerably fewer of them than he would have been if allowed to trouble himself with such trifling matters as the defection of half his cabinet and the treasonable intent of the single most powerful man in the kingdom!'

'I bow to your excellent grasp of the situation.'

She flung the bird's dish at his head.

Since it merely glanced off his gold-padded shoulder, she saw no reason to apologise when everything of which they had spoken came to pass. Pheasant, somewhat bemused by the swiftness of his ministers' decisions, and briefly surprised by their claim to Black Jade's authority, was glad, on the whole, that the trouble had been solved with such apparent ease; these things could turn very nasty if the leading clans became involved. He appreciated the despatch and certainty of his new Chancellor, Lion Guard, whom he admired as a gifted historian, and of the new fellow, with his amusing nicknames, who seemed to have such a sure nose for evildoing.

He was a little doubtful at first about the transfer of his childhood's mentor, Old Integrity, to a foetid outpost in Nan-chao, but he soon saw its necessity. When a pathetic letter came from the old man, pleading his innocence and long loyalty to three Emperors, Black Jade, who dealt with his correspondence more often than her husband, did not show it to him; it would, she decided, have been too painful for him. She herself had been touched by the old rascal's protestations and had been forced to remind herself, lest she weaken, that he was one of her most implacable enemies.

They stayed for a year in Loyang. Although she realised that the Emperor must return to the seat of government, she regretted leaving the gracious city, which she had taken for her own. She had been happy there, charmed by the warmth of its people, the flamboyance of its architecture, the gentler idylls of its lakes and pleasances. She had worked hard – even Chinghiz could not complain that she was not doing her best to learn how to be an Empress. But she had also had time to play with her children in the sunlit courtyards, and to find again the innocent companionship she had first shared with Pheasant.

She had returned to Chang-an eaten up with apprehension, expecting to be greeted by the evil ghosts from whom she had escaped. But she found the palaces swept clean, with sweet air running through them, scented with flowers and grass, and the only things which waited for her around their thousand corners were the skittering litters of kittens which had been let in to vanquish the rats. She closed her mind, then, to the host of unwelcome memories, of death and suspicion and the murder of a tiny child; and she hoped, though she never spoke of it, that Pheasant did the same. She recognised, and was grateful for, the fact that a far stronger woman had returned to the scenes of her early triumphs and tragedies than the confused and fearful one who had left them.

She had gone as the concubine whom the Emperor had raised; she had come back the Empress, secure in her own authority.

On the fifth day of the fifth month, thanks to a man who had died nearly four hundred years ago, the Empire was on uproarious holiday.

It was the day of the dragon-boat races.

This time it was going to be even more stupendous than usual. The royal family were going to join in. The Emperor, who, they said, had not been quite himself lately, was going to show his loving people that he was in robust health and had graciously consented to judge the races. The Empress, whom they had not seen since she had shown them her lovely face at her inauguration, was going to show it to them again, and it was rumoured that they might also see the pride of little princes.

In the palaces, as in the city, everyone was in a panic of preparation, treading on his neighbour, tearing his costume, spilling pots of paint and calling on his ancestors.

Black Jade, who was ready before anyone else, had taken Loud Tiger into the nearest courtyard to try to calm him down. He was still unmelodiously vociferous, the excitement being too much for his eighteen-month-old powers of self-expression.

She had just got him interested in a large dragonfly when Chinghiz emerged, dizzily splendid in his best scarlet and black, with a white turban and a gold-dipped egret's feather or two.

Loud Tiger at once transferred his interest to these. Chinghiz absent-mindedly stood him on a wall so that he could reach and destroy them more easily.

'Someone,' he remarked with finely calculated nonchalance, 'is trying to kill you.'

Her heart skipped a beat. She lifted one violet-tinted brow.

'Indeed? How very inconvenient of them. Am I to be allowed to enjoy the races first? Or must I leave incontinently, without my breakfast?'

'It was the breakfast,' he said, more solemnly, 'that was trying to kill you. Your taster has just died.'

'Oh.' She was sickened. 'I am so sorry. Will you –?'

'His family will benefit more from his loss than his life.'

'I know, but –'

'It is one of the evils in the balance, for an Empress.'

'People die because of me. I know; it is necessary. But that doesn't make it any easier to accept.'

'I'm sorry. I wouldn't have told you. You have quite lost your festival face. On the other hand, a public holiday provides excellent cover for all sorts of misdeeds. You must be on your guard, every minute of the day. I am not sure, even, that you should go ahead with your plans.'

Her chin went up. 'Nothing,' she said firmly, 'would make me change them. What can happen to me in a dragon-boat?' She grinned shakily. 'I can swim. We all swim like fishes – except the infant here, whose style is more like a frog's.'

Hearing himself referred to, Loud Tiger fell neatly off his wall. Chinghiz caught him by his bright blue trouser-seat, gave it a light spank for misplaced showmanship, and returned him to his mother. He showed them his tonsils in an incipient yell, and then, catching Black Jade's eye, thought better of it and turned it into an accommodating smile.

'But you will take care?' the steward insisted. 'They will certainly try again. They will have other agents.'

She nodded. 'Of course. Who, do you think?' she asked wistfully.

'That is what we shall have to discover. The kitchen, of course, will spend its day being grilled at its own hearth.'

'How unfortunate for the innocent,' she sympathised.

'More so, let us fervently hope, for the guilty.'

Loud Tiger blew him a bubble.

The banks of the Wei were as crowded as a millet-field. Courtiers and citizens stood shoulder to silk and cotton shoulder, laughing, quarrelling and expelling demons at a disgusting rate. The less sophisticated wore variegated approximations of dragonhood, and the rest simply slew each other with expense. There had been some solid attempts at organisation, the reserving of places, the buildings of stands and barriers, but for the most part this had been undermined by exuberance, so that, for example, the Archduke's Duchess found herself sharing her many-pennanted box with a one-eyed butcher from the bazaar, who grinned and bowed like a mechanical scythe when addressed, but absolutely would not budge, even when her preoccupied husband joined her.

Somehow, the Emperor's party wrestled its way through his

subjects, making a bold dash from the comparative sanity behind the north gate of the imperial park, and careering at a smart trot in four coaches and seven fat palanquins which arrived very much the worse for wear. The cheering hurt their ears.

They fell out upon the red carpet that denoted their portion of the river-bank, and distributed themselves, their children and their servants on the seating provided. Behind them, the crowd roared and hooted and tried to throw away its arms and legs.

Chinghiz, adhering to his mistress like Buddha's loincloth, deployed his protective phalanx with swift, swivelling eye-contact. He was beginning to sweat, he noticed fastidiously, beneath his costly carapace. He returned bows in a thousand directions and cursed all public holidays with silent linguistic invention.

They were lining up for the first, the most important, race.

'Long ago in the Chou Dynasty, in the time of the warring states,' Black Jade had told her small listeners, 'there lived a good, wise minister called Chu Yuan. He was a poet and a sage, and he tried to make his Prince govern well and be kind to his people; but the Prince listened to evil councillors instead, and the country suffered. Jealous enemies drove Chu Yuan away from the court, and he lived the life of a wandering traveller, writing about the ills he saw, so that everyone would know what was wrong with the government. At last, when the state had become so wicked that he did not want to live any longer in such a place, he showed people how he felt by jumping into the river and drowning himself. It is that courage which we celebrate in the dragon-boats. We go to search for his body, and to feed the water demons, so that they will not harm it.'

'He couldn't swim!' Bold Tiger had stated, not without contempt.

'I'll tell you again, next year,' his mother had smiled. One of these years, he would understand; it would be soon enough.

Now the gilded and feathered representatives of the Four Great Surnames (eleven first families, in fact) were lined in ragged order in their long and narrow boats, dragon-prowed and scaly-painted, coloured like parakeets and shivering with the eagerness of their noble crews, their long necks craning for the start.

There was one boat that was not yet full; its brilliant double strand of beautiful young men were already preening themselves over their oars, but it lacked its captain. It was a particularly pretty vessel, its saurian head and sides covered entirely with flowers, real ones in scarlet and silk ones in shimmering black.

The spectators held their communal breath.

Then they let it out in one glorious shout as five figures, two adult, two under-age and one an encumbrance, marched firmly towards the flowery craft.

'I wish I had thought to put wool in my ears,' remarked Black Jade to Chinghiz as he handed her into her rocking commission, his other arm clutching Loud Tiger like a grappling iron.

She wore no hat, only an absurd little cap like those of her sons, skewered into her yard-long plait. Her robe and trousers were poppy-red, and the boys were in green, yellow and blue. They intended to be seen.

The citizens of Chang-an appreciated her care for their eyesight, though many of them showed a disconcerting tendency to weep. Their beautiful Empress had come among them again; she was going to race before them like one of themselves; and she had brought out all her little Tigers for them to see. Poor integrity-ridden Chu Yuan was long forgotten. It was 'Wu Chao! Image of Heaven! Black Jade!' that they cried in their thousands, all the louder if they couldn't even see her. They loved her. They worshipped her. They would have died for her!

Chinghiz had thoughtfully produced three lengths of strong twine, which he attached to the stout belt of each small Tiger, tying the other ends in a secure and seamanlike fashion to the oarsmen's bench. 'Now, let them swim if they dare,' he muttered into his collar.

The race, of course, was a put up job. It had to be if the Empress's boat was to stay in the lead and allow the squirming myriads populating the banks to see her properly. Happily that part of the river was not wide and their view was more than satisfactory, except for the moments when the young hopefuls in the other boats drew ahead occasionally, just for the look of the thing.

They were racing from the grand jetty to the Serenely Smiling Bridge; this owed its charming appellation to a series of toothy protuberances on the underside of its arch, whose reflection, in unkind truth, smacked more of the idiot than the sage. As it leered cheerfully nearer, Chinghiz ripped the banks with a blue gaze like a hail of needles, while the two rows of idling dandies who sat between the rowers, presumably for decorative purposes, did their best to emulate his scrutiny.

He had thought of the bridge; his watchmen were posted along its crowded curve, their eyes skinned, peeled and quartered.

One cannot, however, watch every man in a crowd of several thousands. As they drew near to the grinning arch, the lucky ones above roared and screamed, whistled and stamped their encouragement; they waved flags and shook streamers and made appalling noises on all sorts of windy instruments. In the leading boat, the little Tigers jumped up and down, their faces scarlet, their lungs bursting. Black Jade, who wished they could have made a fair race of it, was nevertheless leaning forward, her eyes shining.

Soon they would rush under the bridge. She looked up to wave and smile at its crammed and cacaphonous roof, and, too late, Chinghiz's instinct took his eye to the man with the blow-whistle. He watched in slow-seeming despair as the blue and yellow paper unrolled and released its note and its poisoned dart.

'Mama!' raged Loud Tiger in the same split second. Her head spun. He was not overboard, as she had feared, only tangled in his rope and bawling like a bull-calf.

'Row!' bellowed Chinghiz.

They shot under the bridge.

On the other side, Black Jade found herself crowded by congratulatory young men. It was pleasant, but claustrophobic.

'Excuse me,' said Chinghiz with, she thought, a grim pleasure.

He leaned behind her and extracted the slender, death-dealing dart from her dense pigtail.

Their eyes met as he showed it to her.

'You feel I am over-decorated?' she enquired solicitously. 'Ah well, I expect you are right; it probably didn't suit me.'

'Yes. I was right,' he said quietly. 'I was also only lucky; not omnipotent, omniscient or gifted with a thousand eyes. I think, if you have seen quite enough of your ravished and lethal people, Your Highness had better make for home.'

It took her all afternoon to soothe him. By the time he had hurried her back to the palace, lined up and questioned all the servants, scoured every dish in the kitchen and personally eaten half her innocent dinner, his nerves had begun to string themselves more or less into line.

But he was not happy. To calm him further, she let him accompany her on the gentle walk she usually took, on these balmy summer evenings, with Mao-yu.

'It is all very well, this scourging of your sensibilities,' she complained, as he went over her escape for the tenth time, 'But it is I whose delicate brains were nearly skewered and served in the Turkish style, not you. *I* am not making a fuss.'

'Headsman's humour does not appeal to me, just at this

moment,' he replied sourly, tugging the panther away from something she thought smelled nice in the shrubbery.

'No? Well, having a border of bored swordsmen dragging at my skirts doesn't much appeal to me.' She turned and indicated a bashful group of her black and red guards who were having difficulty with her stop and start method of taking the air.

'You must have protection,' Chinghiz said curtly. 'I should have thought today had proved that, at least, to your satisfaction.'

She sighed. 'But does it have to breathe so heavily, and wear such thumping great boots?'

He strode ahead, still more annoyed with himself than with her.

Because she thought he needed the release of tension, it was a long walk, in and out of several broad courtyards, through the pleasantest of the gardens and once around the smallest lake in the park. They made numerous stops to see how various pet plants of Jade's were surviving. They were all in blatant good health, which somehow depressed the steward.

In the park, they let Mao-yu off her lead, so that she could stretch her magnificent limbs in a stunning fifty-mile-an-hour run, and then lured her back with raisin cakes, for which she had an unfeline passion.

'Did I tell you, they have found her a mate at last?' Black Jade asked. 'He was sent from India. He's exceptionally beautiful; black, like Mao-yu, but with a curious grey pattern along his backbone, almost like the marks on a dragon-horse. I'm glad we waited. He is really worthy of her.'

'I'm sure she is delighted,' he said, his eyes flickering about the darkening bushes as they returned to the garden of her own palace. 'What will you name him?'

She was close enough for him to see her sudden flush.

'The zoo-keeper's had already done so,' she said, off-hand. 'They called him Shih-min.'

'Ah,' he said, thinking sad, private thoughts about worthiness. And mating.

In a rosy sunset with tasteful blue-grey edges, the gardeners were watering the roses and camellias and peonies and daisies and lilies and lilac and the lingering blossoms of spring. In the distance the city and the countryside were still rowing the river, searching for the never-to-be-found body of the disillusioned poet. They were consoling themselves with constellations of fireworks which made the sunset and the sky light up like a maddened and magical noon.

'Oh look! My little trollius is doing well here. I wasn't sure if it would. I moved it from –'

This time there was no sixth sense in Chinghiz as the gardener turned, grinning, from the clump of yellow, open-faced flowers he was weeding. But he saw the flash of the knife and without hesitation, almost without thought, he had let go the great cat and given her the single word of command that he had taught her.

Black Jade looked up aghast as the animal went for the killer's throat, his vicious, slim-bladed dagger falling harmlessly into the earth. Growling deeply with a pleasure she had not known to exist, Mao-yu sank her teeth into the fresh, living flesh.

Not wishing to lose his witness, Chinghiz, attempted to haul her off, getting severely clawed for his pains. Other gardeners raced up and also did what they could, but the throat lay open and pulsing blood. They all stared down, disgusted, fascinated, horrified.

Black Jade, unsteady as she had not been in the dragon-boat, reached for and held on to Chinghiz's arm.

'You saved my life,' she said. Her eyes were filled with reality.

Even now, her touch sent him to join the firecrackers in the heavens. 'It is a debt I have wanted to repay for a great number of years,' he said, and there was pain and deep love in his voice. She recognised both, but answered, as he would wish, only his words.

'It is discharged,' she said gravely. 'But how can I thank you?' She managed the lick of a smile. 'I can hardly offer you my life's loyal service, as you did to me, so long ago.'

He stood still, treasuring the trembling warmth of her hand. 'You may allow me,' he said with reverence as well as the faint humour to which she was encouraging him, 'to renew the lease of that service. After today, I realise that it is a thing one should do on a weekly basis, at the very least!'

She let him turn her away from the blood and the fireworks, and the baulked and angry panther, and lead her, her small hand still in his possession, back to the palace.

'For how long,' Black Jade asked him later, as they sat playing chess by candle-light, 'has my poor, exquisite animal been a potential man-eater?'

'Oh, since she was trained to walk at your side, or run at your stirrup, or keep quiet and clean in the house.'

'I see. You evidently expected today to come.'

He shrugged. 'It seemed a sensible precaution.'

'But won't she start to attack indiscriminately, now that she has tasted human blood?'

'I can't answer that. I wish I could. I hope not.'

'I wouldn't like Mao-yu to be sacrificed for me.'

'It would be the preferable alternative.'

She put her arm about the cat's sleek shoulders as she sat purring, her claws licked clean of blood and precisely aligned.

17

There were, happily, no further obvious attempts on Black Jade's life. Not that this was her chief concern, for her husband's weak and listless condition had returned to worry her more seriously. She persuaded him at last to consult with the College of Physicians, but although he spent hours answering their questions and having all twenty-seven of his pulses read, they still could find nothing specifically wrong with him. It was even suggested that his malaise was one of the spirit rather than the body, brought on, perhaps, by the terrible weight of the burden an Emperor must bear. They insisted, at any rate, that he should attend the council only on alternate days. Black Jade made his days as tranquil as she could, deflecting or herself dealing with all inessential business, and surrounding him with her own affection and the laughter of his children.

The Emperor and Empress were taking the spring air in the imperial park, followed at a proper distance by the three small Tigers and a host of nurses, servants and bodyguards. It was the loveliest time of the year in Chang-an. The sky was the blue of a northern barbarian's eye, and a frisky wind drove woolly clouds across it like a flock of sheep harried by a zealous dog. Black Jade made some remark to that effect. Pheasant seemed not to hear. He walked abstractedly, his eyes on the ground, ignoring antic nature.

'Beloved you are not with me. Is it the sickness?' Yesterday he had complained of a shooting pain in his arm.

'No. It is something worse.' He looked at her, she thought, a little guardedly. 'You will no doubt have heard. Lion Guard has accused my uncle Wuchi of treason.'

Her surprise was genuine. 'No. He has said nothing to me.'

'It is quite ridiculous.' Pheasant's face was flushed. 'Some of the librarians have formed a club of some kind – a literary study club. Lion Guard will have it that it is a cover for a dangerous and illegal secret society, and that Wuchi is at the head of some far-fetched plot to do away with all our loyal ministers and declare martial law. I told him he was out of his mind.' He was very angry.

She took her time. She understood why Lion Guard had not told her; he had known that she would have to face this unhappy moment, and had felt that she could, at least, not be blamed for what she did not know.

'Lord Hsu,' she said softly, 'is not usually taken in by nonsense.'

Pheasant made a furious gesture. 'My uncle and I may have had our disagreements, but he is a man of high integrity, and I would swear on my last breath to his loyalty to the throne!'

'What does Lion Guard say, exactly?'

'That he was investigating the so-called "secret society" when the librarian who was the chief witness attempted suicide. He did this, it is alleged, to prevent himself from breaking down under interrogation and implicating his leader – whom Lion Guard claims to be Wuchi. When I declared my utter contempt for anything so preposterous, he had the insolence to remind me of my late half-sister's attempt on the throne – and of other similar plots and stratagems, down through the dynasties – hoping, he said, to show me that no Emperor should be fool enough to trust his relatives!'

Black Jade said nothing, thinking of the brothers and the sons of Shih-min, and of how Pheasant himself had come by his throne. Certainly an Emperor would be a fool to trust his relatives; Lion Guard was right; he had, however, evidently been a little too thrusting for his soft-natured sovereign.

'I ordered Lord Hsu to make a further investigation. I urged him to think most carefully before repeating his accusation.' Pheasant sighed. Such threatening storms made him feel horribly alone.

'What do *you* think?' he begged his wife. 'I know you dislike the Archduke, and with reason; but do you think him capable of this?'

Of this, and perhaps of more, she thought grimly.

'I believe I do. If he thought he had reason enough. He would never seek to depose you, but he might feel that his wisdom was greater than yours – and with the army behind him –'

'Oh, I don't know. I don't know!' repeated Pheasant wretchedly.

'Then we shall have to wait until we have learned more.'

They did not have long to wait. That evening Lion Guard asked for an interview. Black Jade was present.

The minister was brief.

'I regret, Your Majesty. I know how painful this must be. Last night the librarian confessed to assisting Archduke Chang-sun Wuchi in his plan to take over the government. He claims that you have forfeited the mandate by your appointment of the Empress, your deposition of the ex-Crown Prince, and your refusal to listen to wise counsel.'

The Emperor was ashen. 'I can't believe this! Why should he wish to do such a thing? He was my father's man. He is already second in the Empire; he has everything he could wish for. He has been steadfast for so long. How can he have changed to this extent?'

'The librarian has said that the Archduke had been fearful for his position, perhaps, ultimately, for his life, since the enthronement of the Empress, whom he considers his enemy. The conviction of his friends, the two exiled presidents, and the further exile of Old Integrity persuaded him that he must study how to protect himself and the Empire.'

Pheasant looked as if he were going to weep.

'My investigation was – most thorough,' Lion Guard continued, his tone tinged with sympathy. 'There is, I'm afraid, no possibility of error. It is my duty to ask that Chang-sun Wuchi be arrested and brought before the tribunal.'

Black Jade moved closer to her husband. She would say nothing. It was not her place to speak; besides, there was no need. Lion Guard had the situation well under control. For a moment she wondered, as she had wondered on a previous occasion, whether his accusations were true, or whether they were the product of a vast political sham – to save her, and to save the throne, perhaps, in the last resort – but a sham nonetheless, and one which would bring down a man who might be innocent. Might be. Or might not.

It did not matter. This much she had learned during the hard lessons of the past few years. She must be content to be saved.

Wuchi was her last great enemy. She remembered the first time she had seen him, riding behind Shih-min to her father's house. He had disliked her even then. It was a pity. She had often thought so. He was a man of unique talents and unparalleled experience.

He would be missed when they sent him into exile. But there, at least, he could finish his book, his history of the man who had made him, and had begun to make her – Li Shih-min, whose death had been the beginning of all these present troubles.

She watched Pheasant's tragic face as he listened to Lion Guard's seamless arguments, and a familiar wave of pity and warmth washed over her. His dear, dead father had been right; he was not born to be an Emperor. The harsh decisions of justice and diplomacy were alien to his gentleness.

She would have to be especially kind to him during the days that would follow.

It was thanks to the discredit of the Archduke that Black Jade was soon to have the wish of her heart; at the beginning of winter, in the season of Frost Descending, they left Chang-an again for Loyang.

After Wuchi's disgrace and the accompanying fall of his entire family, sons, brothers, uncles, all brought down, Pheasant suffered a new and debilitating crisis of confidence.

'I am quite alone now,' he cried to Black Jade. 'All those great men my father knew – gone into exile and degradation. It is as though the very pillars of the Empire are crumbling.'

When he heard later that Wuchi, harried by interrogators intent on wrenching every last detail of evidence from him, had taken his own life, he was overcome with a terrible foreboding.

'He was innocent; I know he was,' he whispered, hollow-eyed.

'But surely, this suicide proves his guilt?' She was gentle with him, but she could see he did not believe her.

'Hold me!' he cried suddenly. 'Hold me fast. I need your strength. I do not think I can carry on much longer.'

'This will pass, my love.' She stroked his damp hair. 'You have been under a great strain, but it will pass.'

'You are all my joy, and all my help,' he said, burying his face in her breast.

He became convinced that he was unworthy of the mandate of Heaven, even as his uncle had declared.

'The mandate belongs only to the man whose wisdom and virtue entitle him to stand as Heaven's deputy on earth. If I am that man, why have so many of my highest ministers seen fit to conspire against me?'

She reassured him as best she could. But even she could not dismiss his greatest fear – that those dead and exiled statesmen had been right, and that he had been wrong to put away Paulownia and raise Black Jade against their wishes.

He must not think so, for it was done and could not be undone; and she was the heart of his life, his love, his bright phoenix. And yet he could not help weeping for his uncle, whom he had loved and feared for as long as he could remember; and for Old Integrity, that brave, strong critic whose ascerbic tongue had flayed him through his first attempts to read and write, and would not be heard again, for the old man had died in his cold exile, his stout heart broken by his Emperor's loss of trust.

When Black Jade tentatively suggested that they should return to Loyang, where they had been happy, he agreed at once, fleeing reverberations of his own unwilling justice as she had once fled her departed ghosts.

'In Loyang you can rest, and try to forget. You are not without help. There will be new ministers to guide you, a generation who will owe their fortunes to you, not to your father. And there is still the Abbot; you are fond of him – and Lion Guard; he may be getting older, but his loyalty and ability are unflagging. And, if you don't object, I would like to recall the Leopard. I know he is mischievous, but it is as well to have a little mischief in one's armoury – and he does seem to get results.'

'Anyone you like.' He waved an accommodating wrist. 'I trust in your judgement.' For one thing, trusting her judgement saved him the energy he would have expended in exercising his own. If only he did not feel so physically weak for so much of the time. He wished they would find out what his sickness was. Or perhaps, in Loyang, it would cure itself. He had felt better there, before. Black Jade had been right to persuade him; it would be good for them both.

'I will make it official this time. We will leave Bold Tiger in Chang-an, as my Regent.'

She laughed, rather wistfully. 'Poor little boy. The title will be too large for him; he is only six years old.'

'He will grow into it,' Pheasant replied. 'He will have to, one day, poor little devil!'

Although both his parents and his little brothers missed Bold Tiger sadly, there was a decided improvement in the quality of their life in the eastern capital. There was so much to do and to plan if they were to make it a fully administrative centre, with branches of all six state departments, a new university and a properly stocked and staffed library. The graceful city burgeoned under their busy hands, and the atmosphere was one of creativity and purpose.

Pheasant felt considerably better, and the court offered grateful prayers to the ancestors.

Seeing the colour come back into his cheeks, Black Jade devised a scheme to keep it there. They would go, slowly and pleasantly, upon a court progress. So few of his people had seen their young Emperor outside of the two capitals.

They planned a grand tour of the province of Shansi, where they would visit the ancestral home of the imperial family, the Li, in Taiyuan, and also that of the Wu clan, in Black Jade's beloved Wen Shui.

They set off in springtime when the wild magnificence of the landscape was at the height of its beauty.

It is a country to which poets and painters have paid homage since the invention of the brush; the sovereign territory of the Lame Dragon of the North, and of his lieutenants, the leopard and the tiger; where the mountains soar ten thousand feet and the river depths are a hundred fathoms. The hawthorn hangs upon unreachable crags; the white poppy sleeps in secret plateaux. The air crowds into astonished lungs, sharp, clean and singing. Today you are ringed by winter-frozen peaks; tomorrow you ride on the wind across a green and gold valley as wide and open as fate.

For Black Jade, at one with her dragon-horse as she outstripped all but the best of the cavalry, flying towards Wen Shui, it was a return to the best of herself; to childhood and innocence, and to that tantalising and deluding notion, first nurtured in her there, the idea of personal freedom.

The whole clan had converged upon their ancestral mansion for the imperial visit. So too, had old friends, among them, to Jade's unbounded joy, the Lady Hero, at the head of a shimmering train spiked with swords and gems. Golden Willow and Rose Bird had returned beforehand to help prepare the welcome.

So too had Black Jade's half-brothers, Shuang and Ching, with their wives and families. Both now worked in government departments in Taiyuan. Black Jade liked Brother Fox and Brother Hyena no better than she had as a child, but that need not signify. She would have only the most tenuous, necessary relations with them.

All went well in this respect until the feast which Golden Willow gave to mark her daughter's homecoming. It was also her way of offering graceful thanks for the recent honour she had received. She was now the Lady of Jung, among the highest rank of the nobility, with an extensive income and property of her own.

The banquet took place in the Hall of Contemplation.

Gentle sunlight washed through fretted bamboo windows wreathed in pink and white blossom, and played glittering games with the sportive little stream, across which an independent girl-child had once challenged an Emperor.

The inner circle of the clan sat at tables ranged on either side of it, their eagerness to exchange news almost negating their interest in such delicacies as stewed badger, peppered pigeons, seethed yellow heron or roasted black crane in blueberry sauce.

Chopsticks lay idle while tongues clattered, and the wine circled as swiftly as the gossip.

Eldest Uncle, with his brothers and their wives, presided at the table honoured by the Emperor. Across the stream, Black Jade, with her mother and sister, entertained Lady Hero and did her best to be polite to her half-brothers.

Although their correspondence through the years had necessarily been sporadic, she and Hero had remained close, and now, as with all good friends, it was as though they had parted only yesterday – apart, that is, from the inordinate amount of news they had to exchange.

'Won't you, really, come to court?' Jade was cajoling, her hand caressing Hero's, weighted with jewels as she remembered.

'One day, one day, I promise – but I can hardly leave at present. The Turks are almost at our gates every seventh day, and my husband is never at home to look after his estates; someone has to do it.' She shrugged with a rich metallic jingle. 'And then, what would I do? I – without my hills and my horses and my fine young men to ride beside me?'

'Don't! You can't think how jealous I am!'

The jingling hand turned and squeezed hers. 'I know. I know. But you are here now, my dear. We will have some time together, in peace. Oh damn! I believe your unprepossessing brother is trying to catch your eye. I must say, I find the relationship hard to credit – with either of them.' She sniffed and glared hard down the table.

'I too,' murmured Black Jade, avoiding the seeking eye. 'They haven't changed. They've kept their early promise.'

It was so. Shuang was handsome, assured, his cold gaze always assessing the main chance. Ching was slippery-tongued and wet-lipped; just now he was feasting chiefly upon the women in the company, not least upon Jade herself. She recalled the days when she had suffered his lascivious look without recognising it for what it was. She knew it now and found it disgusting.

Catching her gleam of distaste, Ching offered her an oily smile, then raised his cup and stood to toast her.

'Exquisite and intelligent Empress, may you live forever,' he intoned formally. She nodded coldly.

Golden Willow, seated opposite her stepson, was precipitated by his words into one of those sudden, rare, luminous realisations of the passing moment.

'The Empress,' she said with a wondering sweetness. 'Your sister is truly the Empress. The miracle has happened.' A recollection like a pain showed her the face of the astrologer who had hardly dared to name that miracle, and more. She felt proud and humble. She saw that the sweet and sour achieved no culinary balance in Ching's envious features, and she could not resist the urge gently to tease him.

'Remember, Yuan Ching, how things used to be between you children? Well, what do you think of the General's second daughter now?'

The hyena eyes narrowed. 'You speak of my father. You do well. For it was my father who achieved this family's position in the world; aren't we in danger of forgetting that?'

She regarded him calmly, seeing his jealousy, his hatred.

'The father of my daughters brought me an incomparable happiness, and great riches,' she said firmly. 'But he did not have it in his gift to make me the Lady of Jung.'

Ching tasted bitterness. What right had she to such a title? His tongue, acrid, ran away with him.

'It is fitting that those who perform a service to the Emperor should be rewarded. It is *not* fitting that such rewards should be gained merely through – family connections.'

He was still the resentful boy who had blamed her for taking his dead mother's place.

'You don't, then, see your honourable father in the light of a family connection?' she enquired with tender sarcasm.

'My father earned his success with long and hard service,' Ching retorted venomously. 'You can hardly equate the work of helping to build an empire with the behaviour of a woman who opens her legs for the son when she has scarcely buried the father!'

Golden Willow did not gasp at his coarseness. Neither did she comment upon it. She merely rose without fuss and asked a servant to move her seat next to that of Rose Bird.

Black Jade, deeply engaged with Lady Hero, nevertheless noted the change and asked her mother about it later.

Golden Willow repeated a less offensive version of Brother Hyena's insolence, and saw her daughter too revert to the old grudges of childhood.

'The contemptible little vulture! Why does he think he can get away with such disrespect? I promise you he will pay for it. He is a great fool to show so little fear of the Emperor's displeasure. Or of mine.'

Her mother shook her head. 'He is nothing – a little wind, whining through a crack. Ignore him. He cannot harm us. It is only rather sad that the happiness of others should twist like a knife in his belly.'

Next morning Black Jade got up very early. She and Hero planned to go riding, alone, a difficult thing to arrange with two cohorts of guards and servants surrounding them.

Welcome, who had drunk deeply the night before, was still snoring, open-mouthed, when Jade crept past. Even Chinghiz, in his usual catlike drowse on the *kang* in the anteroom, failed for once to catch her muted tread.

In the stables, where she and Hero met, grinning, and grasped hands, a couple of sleepy grooms pushed fists into their eyes, unable to believe that this was the Empress – dressed in a faded archer's jacket and worn trousers tucked into old boots. They saddled Little Dragon, the youngest son of Snow Prince, whom he resembled almost exactly, and brought out Hero's fierce Arab.

As they rode through the tiered, red-painted gateway that opened on her old road to freedom, Black Jade was ambushed by a furious attack of longing for her father. She could almost persuade herself that he was with them now, riding the great stallion, Wu-han, wearing the old coat that they had buried him in, and grinning, his scar crooked, at the morning before them.

If she turned, would she see him? Would he nod and smile at her in slow appreciation, as he had used to when she beat him at chess or wrote a passable essay? In a passion of wishing, she did turn.

There was nothing, of course. Why should there be? Only unquiet spirits had any need to return to earth; the General had Wu-han to ride across the bright plains of Paradise. What reason had he to come back to Wen Shui?

Nevertheless, 'We were happy here, weren't we, my father?' she whispered, just in case he might somehow hear.

Without thinking, she followed the old course of their rides together, trotting easily with Hero pacing her, her eyes on the castellated crags of the mountains, their indigo heights satisfying, as they always had, her instinct towards inhuman splendour, with their hard, enduring strength that was impervious to challenge. They were the mansions of the Gods. They fed her spirit.

Where the true plain began, its grasses shooting, a sharp, irrigated green, its dusty track gilded by the pale early sunshine, she caught Hero's eye and they urged the horses into a gallop.

An exhilaration, almost an ecstacy, took her as she felt herself once more become part of the beating hooves, the forward urge, the supreme harmony of horse and human in the broad landscape.

She felt as though she owned the world!

And at the same time she was nothing – a tiny, indecipherable figure in a painting of vast distances; a pinpoint of perspective, otherwise without meaning. She relished the thought, loving its purity. How glorious it was to be home!

After a time she instinctively slackened their pace. Hero looked a question and she called, 'We are near the place where I first met Shih-min. My father and I stopped here and watched his banners come towards us in a cloud of dust like gold!'

Hero waved acknowledgement.

A little further, and they reined at the spot where Black Jade and Wu Shih-huo had planned their monument to that historic encounter.

'It was to have been a gilded pavilion – a miraculous mirage for travellers – floating on the sands like a golden ship! But it was not to be. The day of its conception was the day of my father's death.' She was quiet for a moment, and Hero, understanding, did not speak.

He had been so close to her then. Had the General foreseen, she wondered now, that the man he revered would become close to her in his turn?

They stayed for a time in the imaginary pavilion, without talking, their minds resting upon those two who had been so dear to them both. There was no pain any more, Black Jade thought sadly, only a consciousness that part of her was missing, and would not be replaced.

At last she raised her head. 'We should go back,' she sighed. This morning she was to hold a reception for the women of the clan.

As they rode back, more slowly than they had come, the Empress set her gaze and her mind upon the roofs and trees of the Wu mansion and those who lived there, the places and people of her childhood. From quite far off she could see the feather tops of Pine Green Hill, and the upper layer of Eldest Uncle's pagoda-roofed residence, flashing a brilliant vermilion greeting. How proud he had been, how delighted by the visit. How pleased and honoured all of them were. She had expected that they might have had reservations, having packed her off to the harem of one Emperor and seen her return the wife of his son; but if that were so, they did not let her see it; all the uncles, aunts and cousins, once, twice, three times removed, who had crowded home to see her triumph.

Some of them were riding towards her even now, she realised, as a cloud of dust materialised ahead. They had come to meet her, thinking it unmannerly to leave her without an escort.

'Our precious hour of peace is over,' she said ruefully. It would have to last her for a very long time.

Hero reined close and reached to touch her arm. 'I am glad that we have had it,' she said. 'We did not speak much, but now I know you even better than I did from your letters.'

Black Jade stopped the rush of tears with an act of will. She would never have to tell his sister how she had felt about Shih-min, and how she felt about his son; she knew already.

When the small party of riders drew nearer, they saw that it was six of her black and scarlet guards, led 'Oh Maitreya! My brother Fox! The Gods, to underline the passing of a private hour, have sent me the man I have the least desire to see!'

Her brother forged ahead and wheeled to wish them good day, bowing deeply from the saddle.

'Good morning, Eldest Half-brother! Why so hot on our trail?'

'Am I not welcome, Highness?' With a twisted grin for Hero.

'I am merely curious. You do nothing, as I recall, without reason; and certainly never for simple pleasure.'

He withered the spring with another smile, calculating whether or not to be blunt in Lady Hero's company. He decided in favour of it.

'I wished to speak to you in some privacy.'

'You may do so now, since you evidently think it a matter of some urgency.' Her tone relayed her annoyance.

'That depends how you look at it. I agree that there are people who might find the lowly position of the Empress's nearest relatives a matter of consequence; but others, obviously, do not.'

His clever eyes challenged her. Hero he ignored.

So that was it. 'Very well, Brother Fox, tell me your grievance. Is your work in the Board of Revenues not to your taste?'

'It has been satisfactory. But I am capable of higher things.'

'Indeed?' She would give him no help.

He was angry. She was looking at him in the old, superior way he remembered only too well. And unquestionably, she now was his superior. He loathed her for it, but he would wrest what he could from her. He controlled the loathing.

'I am not alone in my opinion. The clan is with me in thinking it time that you shared something of your good fortune with your brothers. It is unacceptable that Golden Willow should become the Lady of Jung, while Ching and I remain merely gentleman scholars.'

'What do you want?'

He could not tell what she thought; her face was closed to him.

'My father was given a dukedom.' Hero caught her underlip in her teeth.

'Our father was a victorious general.' Jade's eyes glinted. 'And an outstanding administrator. What have you accomplished, to lay claim to what he was given?'

He stared into her contemptuous little face; she was drawn up like a cat about to spit. He laughed. She had changed so little.

'As much as you, and more,' he said easily. 'I have used my brain and my talents in the Emperor's service.'

Not my harlot's body, you impudent little whore.

But she heard what was unspoken; it sang so loud in his head.

'Very well, brother,' she said softly, smiling with a pleasure long deferred. 'I will give you your just deserts.'

'What is that?' Should he trust her? He still could not read her.

She signalled to Hero and they began to ride away from him.

'You will know tomorrow; the Emperor will send you his decree.'

Pheasant was at a loss to understand why, after so long, she still felt so strongly about her unimportant half-brothers. But for the sake of peace, and the continuation of her almost childlike pleasure in their visit, he agreed to do what she asked.

'The Emperor decrees that Wu Yuan Shuang and Wu Yuan Ching, by virtue of their loyal service to His Majesty, should be granted the following appointments as a reward of their worth – they were two very minor posts in a distant and unfashionable part of the Empire.

'There now,' murmured Black Jade, with a dry, deceptively mild smile. 'No one can complain, after this, that the Empress does not treat her relations with absolute impartiality with regard to honour and degree.'

Somewhere, there was the sigh of a prophecy coming nearer to fulfilment.

18

In the autumn after the visit to Wen Shui the Emperor suffered a stroke. It happened while he was taking part in an archery contest. He had drawn the bow, aiming at the bull's-eye. Archery meant more than mere skill in shooting. The bowman must think of the target as the delineation of his own character; to hit the bull's-eye denoted the character of the perfect prince. As each archer fitted his arrow to the string he must ask himself how nearly he approached this ideal of integrity.

Pheasant, who felt himself to be far from perfect at this point in his life, had raised his bow with trepidation. He fitted his arrow and waited for the bell to sound its release. It came. He loosed the arrow and it seemed that he had also loosened something inside himself, in his chest, or his belly, perhaps even in his head; he was not sure. There was a flight of birds inside him, struggling to be free. They were turning the world with the black flapping of their wings. He saw the sky, wheeling above his head. Then he saw nothing. He was in a warm red darkness. He could not sec it but he sensed that it was red; he did not think he could breathe, but then he probably did not need to. Somewhere there were pinpoints of light. Then they all went out.

'My love – can you hear me? Can you speak?' Black Jade bent over the bed. Behind her the physicians conferred, their white beards touching in a closed circle of esoteric knowledge. Her husband's eyelids had fluttered once or twice and there had been some feeble movement of his left hand.

He moaned and made a croaking sound.

'Yes, my dearest, what is it? Try to tell me.'

Pheasant cleared his throat and his eyes opened again. This time they stayed open.

'Where are you?' he asked. His voice quavered like a frightened child's.

'I'm here. Right beside you.' She took his hand.

'Oh!' It was a cry of distress. 'I can't – Jade, I can't *see* you!'

Tears sprang glistening down his pale cheeks. She saw that his eyes were indeed sightless.

'Abbot!' she called. 'Quickly!'

Hsuan-tsang was instantly beside her. She did not yet trust the other doctors fully. They were greatly experienced and excellent scholars, she knew, but Hsuan-tsang was a dear friend and she could more easily draw comfort from him.

'It is quite often the case,' he reassured her. 'It is more than likely to be a temporary blindness. As to the paralysis –'

'Paralysis!' They had not told her of that.

'Now you are not to distress yourself; this is also a common symptom after such a seizure. It too is likely to be temporary.'

She wanted to sink down on the edge of the bed. She could not do this in the presence of the doctors; they had been scandalised enough by her unscreened presence in the sickroom. She straightened her backbone and asked what questions she could think of, conscious of her limited knowledge of medicine.

She stepped back and the white beards converged on the bed. Their muttering and head-shaking obscured Pheasant from her for perhaps twenty minutes, while the good Abbot moved to and fro as a go-between.

'They wish,' he told her, 'to let a little blood from His Majesty's head. He has a very painful headache and this will relieve it. It will also perhaps help to clear his sight.'

'Are they mad?' she cried. She had heard of blood-letting, but never from the head, the noblest and most essential part of man! Only the most contemptible of criminals were forced to shed that blood, and that in the most dishonourable death known to justice – decapitation! To ask that the Emperor, the very fount and head of his people, should lose even a drop in that fashion was impious and treasonable.

'Compassionate Highness –' Hsuan-tsang's voice soothed like aromatic balm. '– It has proved to be an excellent method. I know it is hard to accept, but I honestly do advise you to do so. The Son of Heaven is suffering great pain.' Black Jade strode to the bedside, dispersing doctors like cotton bolls in a high wind.

'Beloved,' she whispered. 'How is it? Is the pain very bad?'

'Yes,' he replied. 'My head hurts so I can't think; and my eyes. Oh, what if I should be blind forever? And not to move. I can't move my hand – this one; or the foot. I can't *feel* them! Oh Jade – make them cure me! I must get better, I cannot live like this.' He was weeping again, tears of impotence and shame.

She could not bear this. Those weeping, sightless eyes tore at her breast. She felt her throat contract. She must not break down in front of the physicians.

The moment was over. She had made up her mind.

'Very well. Let the bleeding commence. But remember, your reputations depend on the result.' What she really meant, as they knew very well, was that their lives depended on it, for if the Emperor should die from their ministrations, they would die too, every one. She had no real need to remind them, only to show herself steadfast in strength.

The bleeding seemed to take a very long time. Black Jade waited in the next room until Hsuan-tsang came to give her the news.

'It is remarkable!' His broad face beamed. 'The headache is lessening and already the eyes have cleared somewhat. We may give thanks to merciful Kuan Yin.'

The flood of relief was such that she seemed to feel it streaming from her like sweat.

'How is he? May I speak to him?'

'Well, just for a moment. He will sleep now, for a long time. But he is much recovered. It is a good augury.'

When she leaned over Pheasant once more, she saw with delight that he recognised her.

'Sleep now, my beloved,' she said softly. 'Soon you will be well again. Only you must rest now and regain your strength.'

'Not for long,' he said indistinctly. There was something wrong with the left side of his mouth; it remained straight while the rest moved in speech. 'So much to do – I can't be ill. The – Emperor can't be ill –'

She smoothed his forehead, corrugating with the effort to talk.

'I will take care of everything. You must not worry. I am here.' He gave a twisted smile of gratitude and soon drifted into sleep. She remained at his side for a while, trying to think what this might mean to her, to them all.

After a while, Hsuan-tsang came to her again.

'He is still very ill,' she said. It was a question.

The Abbot thought for a moment. 'I have seen very many such cases. Sometimes there is a complete recovery. Sometimes it is incomplete. Most frequently there is a pattern of recovery and relapse. I'm afraid I can't tell you yet which will be the case with His Majesty.'

'I see.'

A great weight was descending upon her. She felt dulled, stupid, too tired to take it on her shoulders.

'We shall just have to wait and hope,' the Abbot said, in the words of comforters down the ages. 'I need not tell you, Little Daughter, that you will have the utmost support that your loving friends can provide during this stressful time.'

'I know. And I thank you.'

Her gravity unravelled the edges of the rotund churchman's implacable cheerfulness. He had always loved her for her gaiety, and for the darting wit that lit it into brilliance; he did not like to see her sad. Privately, he promised her wheels and wheels of expensive, scented prayer.

She would need the help of her friends. The great weight would not go away. It was the weight of the Empire, and Pheasant, she accepted, could no longer support it. In truth, he had never supported it alone, as his father had done.

During the long weeks, then months, of his illness, which soon assumed the tantalising pattern of recovery and relapse of which Hsuan-tsang had warned her, Black Jade was forced to reconsider her position as Empress. She realised now that she had given it no long, conscious analysis, had only accepted it and its power with a glad, though not greedy, committal of her mind and heart.

Now she saw clearly, for the first time, the other face of power, the set and enduring profile of responsibility. With, at first, a passionate reluctance, she began to let the weight of the Empire settle upon her shoulders.

In return for her own determination, she found, to her surprise and deepening pleasure, that the weight was not, after all, such a universal labour as she had expected; it was rather more like that of a heavy, ceremonial cloak, which one carries with some difficulty, it is true, but with dignity and pride.

As the days passed, it began to seem as though she had been born to the work of an Emperor.

She had summoned the council. She received them seated behind a latticed screen upon the dais that held the Dragon Throne.

The list of items for discussion was lengthy. She had already taken sound advice, in private, from Lion Guard, and the Leopard had given her several pieces of scabrous information with which to flay those officials who might be expected to question her absolute authority.

They stood in a deferential circle facing the concealing screen, and were newly reminded, deprived of the sight of her, of the darkly delicious tones of their mistress's voice.

'This morning, gentlemen, I would like your opinions on the subject of the imperial examinations. It has been His Majesty's aim, as you know, to ensure that any scholar who shows merit shall have the opportunity to advance himself, no matter how poor. Some years ago we opened our special schools for the study of mathematics, for languages, and for the translation of manuscripts, reserved only for the sons of the less fortunate. Sadly, we found ourselves with so many well-qualified young men that we had to close down those schools two years ago. Today I should like you to consider reopening them.'

There was a murmur of interest.

'His Majesty and I have discussed a plan whereby the schools would be run by the departments which would eventually employ their graduates. This would mean that numbers could be controlled, and curricula could be set to the departments' own standards.'

She paused, inviting them to speak. A younger man she scarcely knew stepped forward, a member of the Board of Rites.

'Honoured Empress, forgive me – but might it not be said, if we do this, that we are breeding professional bureaucrats, rather than the pure scholars who have been the mainstay of the Empire?'

'That,' she told him dryly, 'would be the whole point of the colleges; we simply wish to train men for the work they will do.'

'I understand, Your Highness.' The man stepped back, unconvinced.

Lion Guard swished fragrantly forward, flicking his bold junior with a well-aimed fan as he passed. 'I would only say that we would all wish to compliment Your Majesties on the simple virtue of the plan.'

'Thank you. The Emperor will be delighted.'

The reopening of the schools had, in fact, been Black Jade's own idea. She hoped that the sheer good sense of it would overcome the doubts of the purists. It was no great matter if it did not; Lion Guard and the Leopard could be relied upon to carry it through.

Anyway, the next item on her agenda would cause them a far worse bellyache. It always did. It was money. The exchequer needed a great deal of it, just at the moment, and it was not getting it.

The vast and economically various Empire was taxed according to the Register of Households. Every adult male who owned or occupied land owed his dues in grain, cloth and labour service. This should have been a simple system to operate, given the immense web of the Civil Service that was there to support it. Human frailty being what it is, however, although the number of households numbered something near to 9,000,000, only

3,800,000 appeared on the register.

This was unacceptable, to say the least of it; especially when the Emperor was engaged on an extensive building programme.

Black Jade began with a notable harangue of the Board of Finance.

'Many of our troubles spring from the appalling failure of local prefects to register the population in full. This is something of which both the present and previous Emperors have frequently complained. When they have done so, there has been a small improvement – but never a lasting one. And, while I understand that nobody *wants* to pay taxes, I must insist that the Board begins to take its responsibilities far more seriously. There is also the matter of the coinage; it appears that the populace is counterfeiting it almost as fast as you can mint it! You will recall that His Majesty attempted to rectify this by buying back the counterfeit cash at a discount; this method was not a success, apart from proving the government to have a sense of humour. It is therefore time we considered substantially stiffer penalties for counterfeiters –'

Several members of the Board, she noticed through her lattice, appeared rather taken aback at being addressed so forthrightly. They had not expected a woman, even the Empress, to pay such close attention to the vulgar matter of money.

'I hardly have to remind you,' she continued, rubbing their fastidious noses in it, 'of the pressing need for revenue. The war in Korea is now in its fourth year of unproductive border engagements. While these may occupy thousands of enemy troops, they do not bring us any closer to victory. Gentlemen, I am the daughter of a general, as His Majesty is the son of a greater one; and we say to you that it is time to change our tactics.'

Before this meeting, she had argued for hours with the Great Wall, once more the commander of his beloved armies. Groaning, he had advised her to leave military strategy to the War Office. She had retorted that they had already done that for too long. He had wistfully hoped that she was not about to upset too many of his colleagues.

She had done her best not to do so. She had held private discussions with Lord Luck, the War Minister in his chambers at the Board of War. She had studied again the manuals of Sun Tzu and Wu Shih-huo's own treatise on warfare, and had retraced the history of Shih-min's ill-fated Korean campaign.

She had re-read his letters, as well as the military reports; those precious scrolls which had kept him close to her across the waste of miles.

'Let me give you a great victory,' she whispered to his interested spirit, which seemed very near when she looked again at his clear, bold calligraphy. 'It will make up for what you did not accomplish; and it will prove to the world that you left behind you a most apt pupil.' She did not, at that moment, recall that Shih-min had also left behind a son. It was not relevant.

She had worked hard, and taken good advice. Now her strategy was prepared. She would, of course, present it in the Emperor's name.

Now she sat, in an ordered litter of notes and maps, peering through her screen at the bland-faced men who waited, with nervous courtesy, for her to open the subject of the war.

Suddenly the foolish lattice enraged her. There was enough of obscurity between them without this damned Confucian blanket! On a clearsighted impulse she swept up her papers and issued forth to confront her ministers, deploying her smile and her beauty as assurers of her welcome.

Some were aghast; others bewildered. All were perturbed except Lion Guard, whose transcendental calm did not alter, and the Leopard, the faint relaxation of whose handsome features permitted a twitch of the whisker.

They did not know how to take it. The Empress should not show herself to them. It was immodest. It was against the nice, safe rules of protocol which bolstered their upright lives.

'That's better,' beamed Black Jade, gathering in their dismal faces with apparent pleasure. 'Now I can see you all, and we can look at the maps together, around a table. Far more efficient, I'm sure you agree?'

How could they not, when she was looking at them with such approving green eyes, and speaking to them in a voice that was like syrup running over precious stones?

In case there should be a single, ungracious dissenter, the reliable Lion Guard added his contribution.

'Your Highness's condescension is most gratefully appreciated. Your presence illuminates our poor board. It is clear that Your Highness will do her utmost to take the place of the Son of Heaven, without consideration of her own comfort or modesty.'

They hadn't thought of that; but since he put it that way – shyly they began to answer her smiles. And she, now that they were gentled, began to pull them towards her.

She talked of the war, careful to praise the troops and the

generals, and addressing the War Lords with proper womanly deference. She talked in matter-of-fact terms about Shih-min's ambition to put down the Korean tyrant, and of his son's natural desire to see it fulfilled.

She spoke to them quietly, persuasively, and it was a discourse, not a lecture. She questioned them and they answered her with courtesy and, very soon, with respect. They were stunned. They had not expected her to discuss war with them on equal terms, let alone to stand in for the Emperor in its direction.

Her plan for the invasion of Korea was simple, soldierly and classic; they would cross the sea as they had before, and would crush Silla's southern aggressor, Paekche, in a well-organised pincer movement, before joining with the Sillan army to attack Koguryo, which had been kept heavily engaged on the northern borders.

They got down to details. Those who doubted her good sense because she was a woman soon changed their attitudes when they saw that the Great Wall and Lord Luck treated her as one of themselves. They could not fault her. By the end of that long day, none of them wanted to.

Once, as she bent with them over the great map, she was shaken by a sudden realisation which made her tremble – the awesome fact of the unparalleled immensity of the Empire. A wave of nausea followed, as the unwanted moment of clarity expanded to show her the vastness of the responsibility she had accepted. Inwardly she reeled, her mind a field of white noise, of pure, clear panic; but like those of her ministers, her lovely face, well-schooled, revealed nothing but the determination to succeed.

When she staggered out of the council chamber at the end of that day, looking bruised about the eyes and gulping air like a landed carp, Chinghiz, who had not been with her, enquired solicitously about the ministers' reactions.

'There was a passable satisfaction in it,' she told them, bathing cheerfully in the blue balm of his gaze. 'They thought I hadn't the wits of a tin whistle; and now they know better.'

Time passed. Pheasant did not improve.

Black Jade began to find the burden heavier. She spent her daylight hours in musky chambers, pouring over maps and ledgers, or in conference with this or that official. Her reward was their growing confidence in her and her own knowledge of her intelligence and efficiency.

But if she had her rewards she also had, devastatingly

undeserved, her punishment.

Pheasant's illness made him increasingly weak. He became querulous. Furious at his own debility, he began to resent his enforced absence from the Dragon Throne. His early, almost tearful gratitude to Black Jade fell away, and far from feeling relief that she was there to take his place he began to accuse her of neglecting him; even, in their private moments, of failing to love him.

'But it is because I love you that I work for you,' she would say, his white face on the pillow accusing her own blooming health.

He would shake his head. 'No, Jade. You do the work because you love to do it. Because it fulfills you. As I can no longer do.'

'No, no. It isn't so.' Her frown was compassionate. 'Don't torment yourself. You only think such things because you are ill.'

But she recognised the kernel of truth in his words.

It was not that she didn't love him; but she hated his weakness, the loss of manhood and purpose that made him unable to be either a husband or an emperor. She felt this to be a cruelty in herself, but she could not help it; he was not like her; he did not fight the disease as she would have done, pitching her whole mind and soul against it until the poor, wretched body was defeated. And if he suffered, so now did she.

Her solution to their problem should perhaps have been to spend more time with him, but there *was* no more. She enlisted, therefore, the gentle aid of her sister. Pheasant had always been especially fond of Rose Bird, and her little daughter Lotus Bud was his favourite niece. They both moved into the palace, where Rose Bird could give her brother-in-law the loving attention for which Black Jade had so little room in the crowded calendar of her days.

It soon proved to have been a very good move. Pheasant found the young Duchess's soft, domesticated presence healing to his bruised emotions. She would sit beside him for as long as he wanted. She talked with him – about pleasant, inconsequential matters – never bothering him with the tangled skeins of government which Black Jade so inconsiderately brought him. No; soft-spoken, sweet-natured Rose Bird was a natural nurse. They gossiped and sang together like the old friends they were, and played cards and board games with Lotus Bud, who at eleven revealed her inheritance of all her mother's tranquil beauty.

One afternoon, as he lay on a day-bed, listening to Lotus Bud reading from the *Book of Songs* and watching the winter light play upon Rose Bird's face as she concentrated on a difficult bit of the coat she was sewing for him – in light, warm lambswool, far less of a burden than his imperial robes – the doors slid swiftly open and Black Jade came in like an exhilarating shower into an over-heated greenhouse. Her eyes sparkled and her step tapped; she was all motion, eagerness and pleasure.

He quelled a groan at the wreckage of his peace and held out his hands towards her.

'You look very pleased with yourself, my dear. What is it?'

'Paekche has surrendered its capital! The King and his family are our hostages. The entire Kingdom is ours! I wanted to be the first to tell you.'

He remembered how long it had taken her to persuade him to attack by sea, with the memory of his father's failure at his heels.

'So – you were right, after all. And I am delighted. You deserve your victory. Come and kiss me; you look so pretty.'

She did so, her heart full.

'It *is* wonderful,' she exulted. 'And now, with our feet firmly planted in the south, we can go on to claim the whole peninsula for the T'ang!'

He demanded detail, which she gave expertly. It was a tremendous victory; he wished, with sudden passion, that he had been able to lead the troops himself.

'Yes. Yes,' he murmured. 'I must send congratulations to the generals, and do something about a bonus for the men –'

He sat up and swung his feet to the floor. He stood up too quickly and felt dizzy and sick. Black Jade put her arm round him and made him sit down again.

'Curse this damnable, rotten disease! I'm no more use than a child of two!' Tears of impotence stung him.

'But you're getting better and stronger every day,' came Rose Bird's reassuring voice. 'Anyone feels faint if he leaps up as you did just now. But no wonder you did – what marvellous news!'

As always, she knew instinctively how to steady him. He smiled gratefully at her.

'A great day for the T'ang. We must give thanks to the ancestors.'

'So you will authorise a further advance?' demanded Black Jade, thinking ahead. 'What if we repeat the pincer attack – one advance to the north, across the Liao River; others from the new bases in – oh, I'm sorry! I'm hurrying you. Snatching away the sweets of victory before you've had time to sink your teeth into them. Forgive me?'

She looked bewitching. How could he not forgive her? She had taken the victory he had longed for above all others and was pouring it into his hands like a stream of new-minted coins. How bright her eyes were, how exciting her excitement! As soon as Rose Bird left them he would make himself the master of that excitement. He had not been able to enjoy the clouds and rain recently. He had been too weak, or she had been too busy. But now he felt his passion rising with a fresh urgency.

'It's time you remembered you are a woman,' he told her later, only half-humorously, as he undressed her.

Her eyes swam at him, surprised. 'Have I seemed to forget?'

As he entertained himself, and her, with one or two unstressful positions he had found in some ancient books he had been looking at, Black Jade considered, with some irony, a detachment which she did not want, and the beginning of sexual pain, how simply a man might satisfy himself that he was a man.

For herself, if she had truly forgotten that she was a woman, it was because she was coming to understand how very much more she might become.

Pheasant's period of brightness was short-lived. Black Jade was entrusted with an increasingly great part of the business of the state, as he cared less and less to exercise his own judgment. Ostensibly his go-between, the decisions she carried to the council were more frequently her own, arrived at far more quickly than he could manage; one of the dangers of his illness was the slowing of his mind to match the lessening of the demands made upon him. Black Jade saw this, but Pheasant defeated her efforts to overcome it.

'It's all very fine for you,' he would say, grudgingly. 'You have the constitution of a water buffalo.' And he would turn fretfully into his pillows, and refuse to look at the report or the speech that she had brought him.

However, after quite a long period, perhaps eighteen months, Jade could tell from his increasing vigour that he was regaining his strength. He began to appear in the council chamber again, though he kept her beside him, preferring not to act alone after such a long reliance on her advice. As there were still days when he was afflicted with the dizziness, the blurred vision and the various aches and pains associated with his disease, this seemed to everyone a sensible arrangement.

A smaller chair was placed beside the Dragon Throne; ministers could be confident that this, at least, would always be occupied. On the day that this first happened, Chinghiz, shedding his carefully nurtured dignity as an actor sheds one disguise to reveal another, rehearsed an unlived boyhood on his native steppes in a wild, lithe, inventive dance of exultation. The maids were scandalised.

Not everyone in the Empire was as delighted. Nor was it to be expected. The adherents of the Wang clan, naturally, and most of those who bore the Four Great Surnames, were mortified by Black Jade's elevation. They stayed away from court, unless ordered to be present, and presumably grumbled, perhaps even plotted, among their exclusive selves.

Although their dislike was hardly at the forefront of her mind, Jade was aware of it; it was a constant reminder that Empresses could fall. But then she had always known that – she had felled one herself. She did not think she had very much to fear. As long as her conduct was irreproachable and she had the support of Lion Guard and his colleagues, all should be well.

To her blank amazement, for she had not been thinking of such things, she suddenly found – or rather was dryly informed by Welcome who had been more observant – that she was pregnant. She was greatly taken aback.

'But I don't,' she wailed, 'have *time* to have a baby!'

'Then you'll just have to *make* time!' Welcome said grimly. 'Babies are more important than Empires, and it's high time you looked *that* fact in the face and spat on it!'

Between them, she and Chinghiz made sure that the Little Mistress suffered daily periods of enforced rest, and Pheasant, as proud of his prowess as though it had been his first-begotten child, fussed and fluttered about her in an even more maddening fashion.

'I want to celebrate this baby,' he said cheerfully one day. 'We have been blessed this year. We shall give thanks to the ancestors for this child, and for my own recovery. Then we'll have a family party. We haven't had a proper feast for months.'

'I'm not sure I *feel* like celebrating,' grumbled Black Jade.

Nonetheless, a few evenings later, she found herself, in a resplendent gown of iridescent blue and green, with her face painted to match by a determined Chinghiz, seated next to Pheasant at a long table in a splendid but intimate chamber in her own palace, known as the Painted Hall.

Young Tiger was sitting self-consciously next to his brother, trying hard not to wriggle, and to behave like a Confucian gentleman. He specially wanted to make a good impression today because he was in the company of his two chosen heroes, Abbot

Hsuan-tsang and his cousin Sage Path, who was nearly grown up and alarmingly sophisticated. He followed the talk that was tossed back and forth between the candles, hoping that it might somehow land in his lap.

'Hey! Elder Brother! Pass me the wild duck.' A sticky fist dug into his ribs. Loud Tiger was rocking dangerously on his stool, one arm reprehensibly under the table. His face, his brother noted, was red and greasy already, and they had hardly started on the meats.

'Your plate's full of sugar crabs; don't be a greedy pig!'

'She doesn't like them; the shells hurt her mouth.'

'Oh Buddha! You've got Mao-yu under there! They'll lather you if they find out. We're supposed to be being polite.'

He passed the wild duck. The conversation evaded him for some time after that, as both boys perfected their performance of impeccable table manners, punctuated by a steady stream of swift and secret arm movements.

Mao-yu had just presented her handsome mate with what was probably her last litter of lacquer-and-liquorice cubs. Realising that she was in for a sustained treat, she absented herself carefully and quickly, an unseen deepening of the shadows, and returned before her benefactors had had time to notice.

Young Tiger now shot a surprised foot backwards, impelled by the shock of a cold nose between his thighs and hot claws up and down his new trousers. On his other side, the admired Sage Path delivered a look of amused curiosity.

'Gods! She's fetched the cubs!' imparted Loud Tiger, as quietly as nature permitted. 'Keep feeding them, as much as you can, or they'll make a fuss and give us away!'

'What do you mean – us?' hissed Young Tiger, deprived of his first chance to be at one with the adults. But he began at once to shovel food indiscriminately into the hot, wet guzzling little masks at the ragged ends of his fingertips. His red tunic became unspeakable round the edges.

'I say – they haven't half made a mess under here,' said his brother's voice, muffled and doleful, from beneath the board.

'Get up you fool!' he said savagely. 'There's nothing you can do about it. You should've thought of that before!'

'What, in the name of seventy-seven devils,' drawled the satin-clad figure of Sage Path on his right, 'is going on down there? I will accept that you are able to kick, even that you occasionally set your teeth in a tasty trouser-leg – but I will *not* believe that you are so slavishly appreciative of my excellences as to lick my hand until it is nearly raw!'

'Oh! I'm really sorry, Sage Path!' He had more pride than to blame his brother, but promised himself to make up for that, later.

'Don't mention it. Just get them to *stop* it!'

Sage Path, who had never done anything in the slightest bit likely to earn him his hopeful name, was beginning to enjoy what had been rather a dull family dinner. He was accustomed to entertaining evenings.

Happily for the three permanently occupied conspirators, the talk gathered speed for a while, and there was little attempt to include the junior end of the table. Loud Tiger, who was now underneath it with an adult panther, three small panthers and a dangerous assortment of legs, was engaged in an ingenious attempt to lash all the cats together, and then to the table-leg, with his own and his brother's new sashes, which he tore in two under cover of the Abbot's gigantic laughter.

When he emerged, grunting and triumphant, his father was speaking to Rose Bird, his soft looks divided between her and a blushing Lotus Bud.

'Now, tell me how this young lady is progressing with her music. She played to me very sweetly the other day.'

'I wasn't sure if you really liked it,' said Lotus Bud with a delicious daring. 'After all, you *did* go to sleep!'

Pheasant laughed. He loved to be teased by the pretty child.

'I thought it was a lullaby,' he said gravely.

'Well, it *was* rather slow,' conceded Lotus Bud. 'But I'm not very good at the fast ones yet; my lips get all dry and knotted, and nothing comes out of the flute but air.'

'Dear child, the slow ones are charming. I much prefer them. And now let me hear from your brother. What is your latest escapade, my boy? I hear you're becoming quite the dandy, and breaking hearts in every quarter?'

To his dismay both Rose Bird and her son flushed a startling crimson. Fascinated, Young Tiger held his breath.

'Sage Path is at a rather foolish stage, just at present,' Rose Bird said hastily. She had not discussed the embarrassment with his uncle, but she would have thought that even Pheasant must have heard of his recent undignified fall from grace, which was to get not one but two of her maids with child.

'I only wish,' she went on bravely, 'that he would pay more attention to his tutors and give less time to – frivolousness.' She finished on a rather high note, and made a grab for her wine-cup.

Pheasant suddenly recalled what it was he had heard about his nephew. He wanted to laugh, but did his avuncular duty instead.

'I am disappointed to hear you say so,' he said, shaking his head. 'The Empire needs men of serious intent to serve her, not wastrels. I hope to hear better of you, boy.'

Sage Path rose and bowed, sensibly saying nothing.

But before the conversation could continue, they were interrupted by a sudden whoop which accompanied the precipitate disappearance of Young Tiger. From beneath the table came awful growls and squeaks and the heavy, littered board, with its fruits, crystallised and fresh, its silver dishes of nuts and sweets, its climbing fantasies of marzipan and whipped sugar, its glass and its porcelain, its xylophone of chopsticks and its flamboyant trees of the best Szechwan candles, began unsteadily to walk away from them down the room, its heavy brocade covering drooping askew like the cloth on a drunken man's camel.

Loud Tiger had joined his brother at the first lurch. They crawled, weaving, among the disgusting debris of the feline feast, slipping and sliding in indescribable substances; the little panthers were not housetrained, and were very excited. In front of them the four shiny rumps strained unevenly above sixteen slithery paws as they enjoyed the novel game of cart and harness. The table veered off to the left, reflecting Mao-yu's superior pull.

'You should've left one cub free; it might've been more even,' counselled Young Tiger, rather tardily.

'I'm *trying* to free them, turtle-brain!' Loud Tiger was puffing. 'Only this knot won't come undone. Have you got a knife?'

'I'll get one off the table.' He emerged, filthy, into the rumbling hum of adult outrage.

Sensing the end of her adventure, Mao-yu put on a sudden, mad, gay spurt. The table raced happily into the bottom left-hand corner of the beautiful, tranquil room and turned on its side in a paroxysm of bamboo exhibitionism. Everything fell off.

'What did you want to do that for?' demanded the fouled and exasperated Young Tiger, standing revealed in gravied and excretory glory in the middle of the hall. 'I'd just got the knife!'

Pursued by a hubbub of vengeful expostulation, which he ignored for the time being in the cause of practicality, he slid to the scene of disaster and viewed the damage. The panthers, still bound to their chariot, were struggling energetically in their blue and green traces. Loud Tiger was not to be seen, but there was vocal evidence of his continued existence under the thick folds of betrayed brocade. Pausing only to consider the amazing elastic properties of a good silk sash, Young Tiger proceeded to cut free the heaving pile of black fur, taking care to avoid the sharp bits.

Afterwards he wondered if he had done the right thing. Released, the cubs, encouraged by their mother, who should have known better, began to run riot about the room. Someone had been kind enough to arrange this pleasurable experience for them, and they certainly were not going to appear ungrateful. They raced towards the approaching phalanx of diners, dressed in their best clothes, who were doubtless coming to make much of them, as they did every day. Intoxicated by total freedom, they leaped to lick the kindly faces, placing their peccant and besmirched paws upon silken fronts and soft-clad thighs. Pandemonium prevailed.

'*Don't* try to explain just now,' Black Jade dared her sons as they stood before her, stinking, their mouths beginning to open. 'I don't think any of us could bear to hear.' She pointed to the door.

Slowly, their heads hanging, the young Tigers slunk away.

As it was not yet late and Black Jade did not want the celebration to break up on a note of destruction, she sent everyone off to change into clean clothes and invited them back to another chamber to finish the evening in peace.

The room was small, scented and quietly furnished, darkened so that their new silks bloomed under the false suns of softly golden lanterns. Candles had been banished, as had all talk of cats or boys.

There was exquisite music, offered by Black Jade's small consort, the best in the Empire of All That Is Under Heaven. There was choice wine, garnet-coloured in the deep, cloudy glasses. They suspended their tired emotions and let themselves be ministered to with all the grace that their hostess could command.

After a while, Lotus Bud and her formidably subdued brother were asked if they would offer a song.

'It is a slow one,' Lotus Bud reassured them as she took up her flute. Sage Path would be the singer and would also carry the rhythm on the small lap-drum borrowed from a musician.

They sang softly, in close, accustomed harmony, the pure, sweet lyric called 'Watching the Moon in Brahman Land'. Black Jade became dreamily contemplative as she looked at the two beautiful faces bent over the music, and listened to the young man's fine, true tenor, tempting the maiden to leave her chamber and watch the moon with her lover.

'This is just as we used to be,' said Rose Bird softly when the song was over. 'It is my sweetest memory of our father's house – the two of us singing with our mother, and the dear General trying not to show how impatient he was to be back out in the stables, or with the men in the barracks. I really believe Sage Path has inherited *your* lovely voice. He sings far better than poor Lotus Bud. I'm glad she is fond of her flute; it lets her off the singing. Though I wish –' she broke off suddenly, an uncertain look crossing her face.

'Yes? What do you wish?' asked Black Jade gently. 'Rose Bird, what is it? Are you ill?'

Her sister was clasping her hands over her stomach; pain and surprise twisted her features.

'It's nothing, I'm sure. Probably indigestion.' She waved a hand. 'Don't think of it. It will go away. Please, children, be little immortals and sing "The Monkey King" for me?'

They sang again, and after that Sage Path was asked to dance for them. He was a graceful and accomplished performer, much in demand among the jeunesse dorée of the court. Hsuan-tsang himself took over the little drum to pound out the fierce martial beat of the strange tribal dance from north of the Wall, full of astounding leaps and alarming cries, with which the Tartars heated their blood for an attack on their neighbours.

Rose Bird, though she listened with an appearance of concentration, did not feel any better. The pain in her belly continued to shock her with its intermittent onslaughts as though an enemy stabbed her from inside. At last she could bear it no longer and quietly excused herself, saying she really had drunk a little too much and, if they didn't mind, would go to bed and try to sleep it off.

Black Jade, who had not liked her heightened colour and her set face, shortly followed her to her room. She found her sister groaning and twisting on the bed, all pretence of indigestion dropped.

'Gods! It hurst so much. I can hardly stand it. Oh, Jade – what can it be?'

Black Jade's reply was to send a maid for the Abbot, who came instantly; he was already perturbed by the Duchess's evident distress.

'Can you tell what is wrong?' Jade was impatient. 'Could it have been the fish? No one else liked the sauce. She ate quite a lot of it.'

The Abbot felt for each of nine pulses in Rose Bird's wrist.

'It's possible,' he said. He looked grim. 'I must examine the abdomen. If you would find a curtain –'

'Never mind that! She looks very ill. Hurry, please.'

His examination was brief and thorough. When he

straightened, his gravity told Black Jade more than she wished to know.

'You must send, now, to my laboratory.' He was scribbling with charcoal on a notepad. 'Give this to the messenger. He must hurry.'

A man left at once.

Black Jade bent close to her sister's tormented face. 'Easy, my love. You will be well soon. The Abbot will give you something to take away the pain. Is it very bad, my poor girl?'

'Quite bad. I'm sorry to be such a nuisance.' Her hand closed convulsively on Black Jade's. 'We were having such a lovely time together. We should have these family occasions more often. It is good for us all – especially you,' her voice ran on feverishly, as though it alone could keep the pain at bay. 'You are working far too hard, you know. It cannot be necessary. Pheasant needs you; and it is important that you do not miss your children's growing up.' A wisp of smile touched the recollection of those children. 'Promise me – you'll try to spend more time with them?'

'Yes. Yes, of course I will.' Distressed beyond measure at the sight of such pain, she would have promised anything.

'Pheasant,' Rose Bird repeated. 'He loves you so much. But he does not completely understand you. If only you would make time for him to do so. He is so much better; soon he will be in command again – of himself, of the Empire. But I think he sometimes feels that you are just as happy on your own –'

'My dear – try to be quiet, and to sleep, if you can. It would be best for you. You must not worry about me; I am perfectly all right. And so is Pheasant. We are both very grateful to you.'

Rose Bird smiled clearly. 'For nothing. It is I who am grateful, to feel that I am so much needed. But listen, Black Jade – it is Sage Path who worries me most. He is not growing into the man he should be. He goes through life without respect, without being affected by what he does. It is my own fault; it must be. I have spoiled him. I have loved him too much. His father cannot be pleased with either of us, as he watches with the ancestors.'

Black Jade soaked a tissue in rosewater and drew it over the creased and feverish brow. 'Your son is very young. He is flexing his wings,' she comforted. 'We will see that he learns to fly straight. Oh, *where* is that fellow with the draught?'

'Two minutes more,' said the Abbot. His face was still grave, though he smiled encouragingly at Rose Bird.

Her lips moved as though answering his smile. Then she arched her back and cried out in agony as the knife went through her more viciously than ever. White pain seared up and over her. Her breath was caught and trapped somewhere where she could not get to it. She felt her whole body shuddering like some inexplicable engine that was nothing to do with her. She tried to cry out again but heard nothing. She could see nothing either.

There was nothing.

She fell back upon the bed, her breathing stertorous and harried. The harsh sound became a rattle and then, as Black Jade met the Abbot's eyes in terrified denial, with a shocking suddenness it ceased.

19

The whole court was surprised by grief. They had loved the gentle Duchess better than they knew. Her children raged and wept, the two little princes with them. They mourned, with a sure instinct that would not yet come to the adults; not only for a beloved mother and loving aunt, but for the warm, unselfish heart whose care had been that they should all be joined, each to each, not only as the working units of an imperial household, every one with his own daunting task, but as a true family.

Rose Bird had made them remember to think of each other, to care for each other when they were inclined to scant care. She had strung them like unwitting beads upon the slender strand of her affection so that they were unconsciously held in a familial circle that would otherwise have existed only upon such rare, happy occasions as the one which had preceded her death.

Now that skein had broken. The beads still kept their circle, held together by the tension of mourning; but in the children, in Young Tiger and in Lotus Bud especially, there was a sense that they soon might scatter and lose each other in the vastness of the palace, of imperial duty and of life.

Black Jade lay on her bed, half her world of love fallen away. She was ill. They had feared she might miscarry, but the child in her womb, unthought-of, unwanted, still lived and thrived. Irrationally she wished she might have given its life for her sister's.

She had known at once, with a terrible clear certainty, at the moment of Rose Bird's death, just how much she had lost; known that she had taken her as much for granted, and counted her as necessary, as the ground beneath her feet.

That ground gone, she swayed in a fearful dark void, calling into it for the Gods to relent and send back her help and comfort. The Gods – when they struck at her struck deep and true.

Pheasant had tried to comfort her, but it had not been possible; he was himself in great need of comfort. They did not find it easy to share their grief, each feeling that they had lost more than the other could understand. They mourned apart, keeping to their separate palaces.

But today Pheasant had come into her room in his white clothes, looking like a man defeated in some cataclysmic battle, paler and more despairing than he had been a week ago when Rose Bird had died.

'You look more ill than I am supposed to be,' she greeted him wanly. 'You must look after yourself; you must not have a relapse.'

'It doesn't matter. I'm all right.' His voice was dull. For some reason it annoyed her. His posture seemed to claim all suffering for himself, as though only he were affected by grief.

'Have you visited the temple?' she asked neutrally. Rose Bird would lie for forty-seven days in the Buddhist temple where she had worshipped.

'Yes.'

'Does she – how does she look?' The Abbot would not yet allow Black Jade to leave the palace to pay her respects to the catafalque.

'Beautiful. Very peaceful. And alive,' he finished bitterly. He was staring at her very hard, his eyes grey and troubled, like distant bad weather.

'I shall go there tomorrow. I am quite well enough. There's no need for me to stay in bed – what *is* it, Pheasant?' Her irritation surfaced of its own volition. 'You look very strange. Are you sure you're not ill again?'

'No. Not ill. Just – oh, Jade, I'm sorry – but you must tell me! You must say there is no truth in it!'

She frowned, weary. He was babbling. 'No truth in what, for goodness' sake? You make no sense.' But beneath her impatience she had caught an old echo that chilled her suddenly.

'Surely, someone must have told you – your precious Chinghiz, for example – what is being said?'

'I have heard nothing.' She spoke slowly and a little loudly, as though to a deaf person. 'Please explain what you mean.'

He took a run at it, blunderingly, afraid of her, afraid of what he meant.

'They are saying – it was Lion Guard who told me; he thinks it was put about by the Wang faction, though he cannot prove it –' He stopped, stared at her again, gulped air and set off once more, his eyes begging her not to blame him. 'It is rumoured that you – that you had Rose Bird poisoned –' Her little cry arrested him, then he went on doggedly, '– because you were jealous of – of my affection for her. I know I have spent a great deal of time in her company,' he ended miserably.

It was Jade's turn to stare. She simply did not believe it. He must be raving. His grief had turned his mind.

'Don't you see – I must know.'

He was actually pleading with her, preposterously, blasphemously craving for her denial! Belief tumbled into her, hot and furious.

'You foul thing! Get out of my sight!'

Pheasant cringed, but he hung on. 'It's not that I believe it – honestly – it's just that – after Paulownia, I have to hear you say it. I'm sorry. I know it is unforgivable.'

'You pathetic fool!' Contempt released her anger. 'Which is it to be? Am I guilty of the most hideous crime you could name – or is it an unforgivable insult to suggest it? Which? You will have to choose, won't you?' She flung her words at him, her eyes swords, her hair a tempest tossed by her fury. 'How dare you bring your wretched, misbegotten rumours in here and tax me with their parentage! If it's rumour you want, what about that other piece of dog's vomit? The one that says *you* fathered Rose Bird's bastard child? Did I ever ask you if *that* was true? It could well have been – if the way you used to look at her was any witness to your feelings for her!'

It was grossly unfair, but she was badly hurt.

Her shrieking had brought Welcome running from the next room.

'Sweet Kuan Yin, what's the trouble? I've never heard such a row!'

'Get out! No one called you!'

After one scandalised look the nurse retreated, silenced.

'And you!' Black Jade rounded on her husband. 'You can go too! I don't want to see you. I cannot bear you in my presence!'

'My dear,' he pleaded. 'I was only – Gods! Black Jade, don't you see how I *suffer* through all this?'

She laughed, a sad and hollow sound. 'Then enjoy your suffering! It appears to be your greatest talent. And now *leave* me! Or I swear I will drop this accursed child of yours, here and now, before your eyes!' She clutched at her belly, whose swelling was in turbulent motion.

Pheasant was shocked into clarity. The anguished clamour that had beaten in his head since he had heard the dreadful story now diminished; and he began to see that he had been horribly wrong.

It was an appalling failure of judgement. She would never forgive him. And she would be right; it did not admit of forgiveness.

He moved towards her, his hands supplicating.

'Get out!' she screamed. 'Get out! Get out! Get out!'

After the funeral they returned to Chang-an. Once again the Emperor attempted to cure sorrow by turning his back on it. Surely, after a time, in new surroundings, with new cares, Black Jade would begin to forgive him.

He offered to build her a new palace; it would be the most graceful dwelling the Empire had ever known.

To his surprise and joy she agreed. She began to build it – the Penglai, the Palace of the Immortals. She would bear her child there, and make a new beginning. To Pheasant, who soon found himself utterly excluded from the plans she made for it, she gave no explanation of her acceptance of his gift.

There were a very few who understood it; Chinghiz, Welcome, her four faithful maids, and Golden Willow, in whose compassionate lap she laid her broken and fearful heart.

For her ghosts had come back to haunt her. Their grey faces waited on her waking bedside, their dripping robes hovered in corners – all the stale, hopeless panoply of the restless dead.

'It is your unhappiness that calls to them,' Chinghiz told her, his face a blue-studded mask of regret. 'My sweet mistress,' he added, with a passion whose seriousness cut deep into her own grief, 'if I were whole, I would give my manhood over again, ten thousand times, if it could make you know happiness!'

'My dearest friend,' she said, raising a face swimming in tears, 'You have never lost your manhood. Never. Others, perhaps, but not you.'

He savoured the bitter recompense of this.

Pheasant, deprived of his wife's comfort, nevertheless recovered from his illness sufficiently to return to the council chamber. He could not yet do without Jade's assistance; he found it easier to concentrate if she were present. Also, the only way she would consent to meet him now was in the company of the ministers, or, at official ceremonies, of the courtiers.

He dared not visit her bed. She would not visit his. She did not speak to him if she could avoid it.

But every day, she sat beside him as they debated with the ministers.

She had noted a new face amongst these, one which, had she been less hurt, less angry, less harshly enclosed in her own thorny cage of pride, she might have taken for a sign, slight but telling, of a change in the Emperor's dependence upon her. The zealous Leopard, whom she had recalled from exile and who was dedicated, with Lion Guard, to making every man of moment in the palace hers, had harried the biddable Love Learning from his post in the Secretariat; he had discovered the harmless man to have concealed a hunting accident in which his son had inadvertently killed someone. The moral Leopard was disconcerted, therefore, to find, when he put forward the name of his candidate for the replacement, that it was refused. The Emperor had, it seemed, a man of his own in mind.

His name was Lord Shang. His qualifications were impeccable. He was a respected scholar and a court favourite among the poets. He was also a strong adherent of the Wang clan, and had served as tutor to the ex-Crown Prince, the adopted son of Paulownia. Black Jade viewed his appointment sombrely, but it did not occur to her to see it as a warning.

Chinghiz, who did, said nothing about it; he had no wish to add to the burden of her troubles. He noticed that the Emperor soon became very fond of Lord Shang, and was often seen to solicit his advice.

Despite the workload she soon piled up for herself – overseeing the building of the Penglai; the construction in the city; the long debates in the War Office; the overhaul and administration of the examination system; the new schools and hospitals; and not least the satisfaction of her old passion for giving new names to everything, as though this might create the new world in which she longed to wake and find herself – despite all her occupations, Black Jade found that she desperately missed the love, and even the inverted form of support, that Pheasant had used to provide.

But there was no going back. Their relationship, in that way, had ended with his crushing words of accusation. She looked instead, for her help and comfort, to her own household and to her mother.

To Chinghiz, she became closer than ever. At times, as they sat over the chessboard together, they talked, late into the night, about some state difficulty, or about their different childhoods, hers in what he taught her to see as relative freedom in Shansi, his in the stifling and rigorous atmosphere of the palace, where, as he said, he had 'had to create his own freedom in his mind'. He had created, in the end, a mind much like her own: subtle, humorous, courageous and welcoming of challenge.

It was on one of these nights that Black Jade realised, as she bade him good night and watched him leave her with the catlike, dancer's grace that had become quite unconscious, that this was now the man she loved most in the world. The irony of it stung her to a few hard-wrung tears into her pillow; which was lonely.

The depths of Golden Willow's anguish for her eldest daughter's death could be gauged only by the intensity of her stillness for some months following the event. As far as the world might speculate, after this period she put off her grief, as though it might be a selfishness to indulge it further, and began briskly to go about improving the reputation and welfare of her surviving child.

They did not speak of Pheasant's betrayal. There was no need to voice it between them. But there *was* a necessity, Golden Willow saw clearly, to extinguish the foul rumour completely from the minds of any who had been infected by it.

'I have often thought your connection with the church was an excellent thing,' she told Black Jade thoughtfully. 'You should try to keep up your visits to Kan Yeh, you know, even when you are so busy.'

'I have meant to.' Jade was aware of her neglect. 'It is just that I have not felt –' she searched for the exact word – '*innocent* enough, since I came back to Chang-an.'

'Nonsense, the nuns will do you good. And never forget; religion is a great power in the state, and especially among the common people. If you are seen to be a patron of the convents, and to be properly devout, as you have been taught – you will soon find that your detractors have more difficulty in blackening your character.' This was as near as she would come to the unmentionable subject.

Smiling at this unaccustomed sense of the expedient in her mother, Black Jade took her words to heart. She began to visit Kan Yeh again, and found the Abbess and her sisters as welcoming as though she had returned to the cloister. She found that Golden Willow had become Chang-an's most generous patron of the Buddhist faith, and that her tranquil house was now the meeting-place of all the leading scholars and priests.

In order to lighten the mixture, and to spice their arguments, they also welcomed a few of the more intellectual Taoists to their circle. Thus it was that Black Jade met Kuo Shing-jen.

They were in Golden Willow's winter garden, a place where deep, rich colour still magically glowed in the flower-beds, and roses bloomed with smug self-confidence. She had brought the children to visit their grandmother, forgetting that this was one of her days for entertaining her holy men. The house was full of them; Black Jade could hear their voices, loud, eager, travelling up and down the scale of friendly argument, with the great bass of Abbot Hsuan-tsang booming beneath them like water in an underground cavern.

Often, she would take part in the discussions, but today she preferred to remain out of doors with the boys. Her energetic sons would not long tolerate the debate now raging about whether or not the clergy should consent to kowtow to the Emperor. Possibly Bold Tiger, at ten, was old enough to comprehend the tensions that were arising between the churches and the state he would inherit, but it was better for him to be out in the sparkling, frosted air of the Little Snow than earnestly disputing with his elders. She had thought him, on her return, altogether too serious a child, even for a Crown Prince.

Now, the other two had raced off, shrieking their freedom, and here was Bold Tiger, crouching over something he had found in a flower-bed, impervious to the prodigies of flaming leaves around him. Hearing her step, he looked up stormily.

'I hate nature!' he uttered challengingly. 'It's cruel and beastly!'

She bent to see what he looked at; a delicate spider, its silver filigree left behind it, torn and empty, stood motionless, surely not living, its stretched limbs and small body completely transparent.

'It has no blood in it; it has starved to death,' Bold Tiger said accusingly, his brown eyes enormous with pain.

She sighed. It had always been like this with him. Gales of mutinous weeping had been the elegy for every animal that had died within his small compass. His heart was fiercely tender, and no exposition of the balance of nature could comfort it.

'I don't have to tell you that all lives come to an end,' she said gently. 'Perhaps, next time, it will be created higher up the scale of being.'

'Why? Because it has been good?' he demanded, scornful. 'How can a spider be good? Or bad? I don't understand.'

Nor do I, little one, she thought, hugging him, nor do I.

'We must suppose that there are such possibilities – without always expecting to understand them. If your friend has been good, in the way of his kind, he will be rewarded. Isn't that what the Abbot says?'

'Yes, but how can we *know*?' persisted Bold Tiger, prodding his spider kindly, in case it was still incarnate. It wasn't.

'And how,' the solemn intellect pursued, 'do *they* know where to go next time?'

'Who?' his mother asked patiently, wishing his brothers had not disappeared, bent on some devilment of their own. He needed the leavening of their laughter.

'The souls, of course,' the Crown Prince said patiently, waiting.

'Well, no one really knows,' she said, recognising with sympathy one of the unanswered questions of her own childhood. 'But I should think that perhaps it might be like going to sleep in one's bed, at home in the palace – and then waking up next morning somewhere entirely different, and not being able to remember the palace. Do you see?'

Bold Tiger scratched under his coiled and plaited topknot.

'Not really. If you couldn't *remember*, you couldn't *know*, could you? It's no good,' he added gloomily. 'I've heard all the explanations. But it isn't the explanation that matters, not in the end. It's whether or not you *believe* it.' He got to his feet and dusted the soil off his hands. Behind them, in the house, the Abbot was roaring forth, riding yet another hoary controversy to death or victory. She made a note to ask him to talk to the boy again. If only he would not take everything so hard.

Suddenly, to her relief, Bold Tiger's name was howled peremptorily from beyond a screen of damson-coloured trees. His brothers were calling him. She saw the importance of the migration of souls dim in his eyes, and was glad.

'Why don't you go and see what they want?' she suggested.

'Well, if you don't mind.' Bold Tiger grinned and hurtled off, leaving spider, souls and his mother, amused and touched, to find their own answers.

Black Jade looked after him for a moment, ruefully reflecting that he had inherited her own hardihood of mind together with his father's aptitude for suffering – an uncomfortable combination. It might lead him, one day, to become a conscientious ruler, but she would have to give him all the help she could, if he was also to be a happy man.

She walked slowly along the blue-tiled path, trying to see into an unknown future, until a late-blooming rose, a single pale flame on a long, slender stem, captured her attention. She picked it, to save it from the frost, and held it, drinking in its scent.

The young priest came out of the house. He needed the cool simplicity of sunshine to clear the windsurge of words from his head. As he came down the steps to the winter garden, he stopped, arrested by the discovery that he was not alone.

There was a woman there. She stood, very still, in profile, holding a single rose before her face, musing into a private distance; a little puzzled, a little sad, as contained and perfect as a porcelain goddess.

She turned her face and looked at him. Her face, too, was that of a goddess, pure, intrinsically sweet, just dawning into question. As he looked, he felt the beat of something begin in his breast like the hammer-note of a great bell muffled into silence. It struck a deep instinctive warning.

He knew then that, whatever he did, he should not walk down the steps and towards this woman.

Black Jade smiled. They seemed to have been staring at each other too long for anything less.

'Good afternoon,' she called, indicating his freedom of the garden with a wave of her rose. 'Has the discussion finished?'

He thought, ridiculously, that he recognised her voice, though he had never heard it. It claimed his soul with an ease that appalled him. He came to her gravely, as though he were in the temple.

She watched him come. He was a young man of great personal beauty, lightly and finely built beneath his black robe. His face was cut in well-defined planes, but there was a tender look about it, the gift of long, grey eyes and a mouth which, for a man, seemed to give too much away. He looked, she thought, as if he smiled often, but also knew the taste of tears.

She shook her head in self-amazement, censoring the thought. She was confronted with handsome men every day of her life; why ever should she pause to consider this one's eyes or mouth?

'Who are you?' she asked as he reached her, more severely than she had intended.

'My name is Kuo Shing-jen,' he told her, and now she too was confounded by the most alluring voice, surely, she had ever heard – soft but clear, with a persuasive, dramatic authority.

'I am sorry to have disturbed your peace. And, yes, we have talked ourselves to a temporary standstill, at least.' His black robe told her he was a priest and a Taoist. Now that he was close, his physical presence was inappropriately strong for either.

'What a pity you did not come out sooner,' she said lightly, collecting herself. 'My son has just been asking awkward questions about the reincarnation of spiders. He is finding it hard to hold to his faith.'

The priest smiled. 'How old is the boy?'

'He is ten.' She realised that he had no idea who she was. She swayed a little, intoxicated by the spurious freedom of it.

Instantly he offered his arm. 'You must sit down. Perhaps you are ill?'

She sat down, rather quickly, on the low wall beside them. 'No.' She smiled, oddly unembarrassed. 'Not ill. It is only that soon, perhaps, I shall have another son.'

He bowed, made safe and sad by the knowledge. She was married then; it was just as well. He had not noticed the pregnancy, concealed beneath her flaring green gown and fur-lined cloak. Amused, though only at himself, because he had liked to think himself immune to the temptation presented by a beautiful woman, he asked her if she would like him to fetch her something to revive her.

She shook her head automatically, only half hearing him. As he stood before her with his amused, solicitous look, she saw dreamily how well-made he was; the narrow, sashed waist, the straight shoulders, the lustrous blue-black hair, so like her own, curving, uncovered, about the brown sinews of his neck. *Amitabha*! He had spoken again and she had not heard a single word!

'I am sorry.' She passed a hand over her eyes. 'No. No, please – I am quite well now, truly.' Light-headed perhaps, but quite well.

'I was asking if you would tell me who you are,' he said gently.

Ludicrously, passionately, she longed to be no one but her father's daughter. But then, of course, how foolish of her. He was a priest.

'I am the Empress,' she said simply, her voice falling slightly. He smiled slowly and ruefully. His bow was the perfection of grace.

'Of course. How very foolish of me. I should have known.'

'How could you? Unless you had seen me before.'

'To my sorrow,' he said, still, it seemed to her, regaled by some private amusement, 'I have not. I came to Chang-an only recently. I am here to study medicine. My monastery is in Soochow.'

'And will you be with us for long?' she asked, glad that he was obviously not going to apologise further.

'I hope so,' he murmured, held by the unexpected candour of her gaze, noting that he had never before seen eyes which were so green and quite so compelling. 'My invitation, like the resources of your excellent imperial library, is without limit.'

She had opened her mouth to say, with too great a warmth, how very glad she was, when she was rescued from folly by the sudden effluence of noise and motion from within the house. The meeting was over and her mother had come out to welcome her at last, floating through the crowd of saffron robes like a graceful water-bird through lilies. She beamed at both of them.

'Ah, my dear! So you have met Shing-jen? I was saving him for you. He is a most useful visitor. We have talked together on a great many subjects, and it occurred to me that he might be able to do you a certain service, if he would.'

'What kind of service, Honourable Mother?' Black Jade enquired, a shade too brightly. Her mother could read her mind when she liked.

'Oh, I'll leave him to tell you that. I *must* go and speak to the Abbess. If I don't catch her now –' she drifted off, trailing scent and sweetness, unaware that she left her daughter in the throes of a sudden, unbalancing panic that threatened to overturn her.

She struggled to control it, at a loss for words for perhaps the first time in her life, more deeply disturbed by the attraction she felt towards this beautiful stranger than she knew how to deal with, just at the moment.

Miraculously, the Abbot appeared at his elbow, his ruddy face bland with mischief.

'This young man has been cudgelling all our poor brains with his theories, Little Daughter. He has the intellect of the Yellow Emperor himself. But take care; he is also known as an adept at all the arts that make the Taoists infamous! The ladies have hopes that he may be the one to show them the secret of eternal youth!'

Eternal youth; it was almost a description of his own sculptured face. These grey eyes, which now encountered hers with quizzical humour, were surely as young as those of Bold Tiger; except that there was a depth of wisdom in them, and of pain. It was rare, and touching, to see such innocence in the face of a man.

They were gazing at each other. Realising his own part in this, Shing-jen dropped the heavy lids over his tell-tale eyes. Whatever demon of foolishness had visited him, he must not let her see it.

'Your Highness will forgive the ramblings of my old friend,' he said, with a warm smile for the Abbot. 'I am, as I'm sure he means to suggest, a very practical chemist.'

His courtesy restored some of her composure. 'Are you,' she enquired graciously, 'working on any particular project?'

'I'm studying with the master physician, Sun Tsu-Miao. Presently,' he added drily, 'I am examining the effects of cinnabar on the digestion of a number of rats.'

'I see. And do they rediscover their youth and reach rude old age?'

He grinned. 'No. They die, those who ingest a certain amount. It's a pity. The general desire to credit the rosy drug with the power to confer immortality will be *very* difficult to discourage; especially with the court ladies the Abbot mentioned.'

Neither had noticed that the Abbot had slipped away.

'But surely,' she suggested, letting her eyes mesh with his, just for a breath, 'if you prove the mineral to be poison, you are, in fact, offering a long life to those who would otherwise have swallowed it. Knowledge must be preferable over ignorance, even in the vainest of us?'

He smiled into her eyes, and something light-hearted and blessed uncurled within her.

'Exquisite Empress, nothing is ever preferable to a seductive illusion; either to a courtesan or a beggar.'

'Unless, perhaps, a seductive truth?' she murmured, doing nothing to prevent her wayward eyes from returning to his.

He did not reply, but gazed at her as if she were the human representation of *nirvana.* She must keep on talking, or the sky would very probably fall about their ears.

'Have you tried, in aid of the over-adventurous, to discover an antidote for cinnabar?'

'I have, but with small success,' he admitted, with a faint frown that ravished her for no reason other than that it was his. 'But I have a friend who is convinced that its ill-effects can be lessened by consuming quantities of that revolting green vegetable called spinach!'

Her bubbling laugh surprised him. 'I know who that must be! It is Meng Shen, isn't it? I knew him very well when he was a boy. I still wear the perfume he makes for me. I have not seen him for far too long. Tell me how he is.'

'He was working with me in the college of medicine until recently. Now he was gone to Tibet to study the mountain herbs. He always spoke of Your Highness with great affection. I shall miss him. We are good friends, though we argue constantly.'

She nodded. 'His favourite occupation. Has he become a

Taoist, too?'

'No. He calls the Tao the Invisible Path to Nowhere. He is most scathing about religion. He says it is human will which shapes fate.'

'A comforting idea; it is what I would prefer to believe myself. You must bring Meng Shen to me, when he returns. I shall be glad to see him. And now, Shing-jen,' she asked, with an astonishing and newborn shyness, 'will you tell me what it is that my mother thinks you can do for me?'

She had spoken his name; she felt nearer to him.

'It is my dearest wish to help you,' he said softly. His eyes were again the prisoners of hers. A quiver of something that was better not named passed between them.

He hesitated, bent over her. 'It isn't something to discuss here.' The Abbess was bearing down, with a clutch of saffron monks. 'May I call upon you – at some more convenient time?'

The breath ran out of her in unsuitable relief. 'Yes. Yes, please do. I will send to you, by the Abbot.'

He left her then, with his ravishing smile that made her want to get up and follow him to the ends of the earth, or at least to the nearest unoccupied bedchamber. She could not believe this was happening.

Her wits scattered, she was surrounded by robust Buddhist kindness and the tail ends of the afternoon's arguments.

When, after aeons, the company had left, she asked Golden Willow with studied casualness what was the priest's special talent.

Her mother regarded her steadily. 'Well, it's something that, once, I wouldn't even have considered. But he is a remarkable young man, and with a commendable reputation already – did I tell you I used to know his mother? Such a charming women. Yes, Shing-jen has the reputation of a great and good magus. Ah, now don't be alarmed. His powers are *only* for the good. What persuades me that you need him is the fact that he has managed to rid an acquaintance of mine of the evil spirit that was troubling his house –'

'Ah, is that it? Of course.' Her daughter sighed quietly, and the shadows, which had been absent for the last hour, returned to her face.

'Thank you, Mother.' She kissed the soft cheek. 'If you think it is wise, I will ask for his help. You may well have brought me the dearest gift I could wish for.'

'I truly hope so, my dearest child. I shall pray it will be so.'

Oh, it will be so, Black Jade whispered to her heart in a wild premonition of unlooked-for joy. It will be so – even if he should possess no magician's power.

Nearly a month went by.

The young priest, Shing-jen, locked himself up with his rats and concentrated fiercely upon their behaviour. He also subjected himself to many hours of rigorous extra prayers. Sometimes, when his straitened and disciplined mind wandered despite his efforts, he told himself that he had been deluded, arrogant, laughably foolish; the Empress, queen of all women, had naturally not looked at him as he had dreamed she had looked.

But, beneath his self-strictures, he knew very well that she had.

In her jewelled casket of a palace, Black Jade impatiently waited for her child to be born, so that her body could be her own again. Many times, during the long, slothful, wasted hours, half-sleeping over a state paper, she remembered how she had been subject, on that wicked afternoon, to the ludicrous fantasies of a pregnant woman, and that she should be very much ashamed of herself.

She was not.

The baby, obligingly, came early.

Once again it was a boy. This time he was scarcely even a disappointment; Black Jade had not allowed herself to wish for a girl, no longer wanting to tax the disposition of the Gods towards her.

He was a pretty baby, more delicately formed than his brothers. He had, immediately, an endearing tendency to laugh; Welcome assured everyone that it was only wind.

In the middle of the feminine rejoicing which followed his relatively easy birth, during which a sentimentally tearful Welcome showed an alarming propensity to get the wet-nurse rolling drunk, the ageing Lord Shen, the Chief Eunuch, was announced.

Still impressive, still wearing his look of being about to discover some hapless virgin trying to effect a metamorphosis, his stately walk was a little hesitant one, but his magnificent black and gold robes, as one of the young maids remarked, made a wonderful job of keeping him upright.

'His Majesty,' he apprised Chinghiz with proper disdain, 'presents his compliments to the Empress, and proposes to pay a visit to his youngest son. At the hour of the Horse, should this be convenient.'

Chinghiz who sympathised with Lord Shen's contempt for a

master who was reduced to such beggary, treated him to one of his most extensive displays of minutely observed courtesy. Before he left, the old man was seen to smile.

Black Jade, powdered and painted against her will, with her hair combed and her mind in fairly good order, sat up in a jampot of peach and apricot cushions, in a bed-gown of pale, invalid gold which made her look more fragile than she felt. She didn't particularly want to see Pheasant. The rewarding rush of love she felt for the baby was not shared with his father.

He came in quietly, looking rather handsome. One always forgot how much he resembled Shih-min. They exchanged restrained and public greetings, and then Welcome deftly removed the servants, unasked. Pheasant stood beside the cradle, permitting the infant to suck his finger.

He cleared his throat. 'He is small. Is he well?'

'Very well. He is small because he was a little early.'

'And you? You look – glowing. Motherhood always suits you.'

'Thank you.' He was, she supposed correctly, making an attempt at a reconciliation. Knowing him, she had expected it. She had also decided to accept his overture when it was offered. Her more creditable reasons for this were to do with the comfort of the state and the persons about them; another, more important, was to do with Kuo Shing-jen and didn't bear examination.

Pheasant hovered. She did not seem exactly unfriendly; but she still hadn't smiled. Still, her neutral acceptance of his presence was a great advance on the icy self-possession of the council chamber. He felt in his sleeve pocket.

'I have a gift for you.'

This was the test. If she took the box, she also took him.

Black Jade held out her hand. 'How kind.'

They were emeralds. They were fine beyond comparison and costly beyond imagining. They made her think of his father.

'No words can touch them. You are too good.' Her tone was even.

'They are for – another reason – besides the baby.' He needed to put it into words. 'I know I should have spoken before. But you have not been – your manner to me has been rather forbidding during these last months. Frankly, I have not found the courage.' He had found it now; what would it earn him?

'I see.' The lovely voice was pure as a bell. 'But now that I am weakened by childbirth, and confined to my bed, your bravery has returned?'

He heard the irony, but plodded on, determined.

'I'm sorry you wish to see it that way.' He raised his chin, searching for dignity. 'I have wanted to apologise for the outrageous way in which I spoke to you after your sister's death. I regretted it almost immediately, but things had already gone too far between us Black Jade, I ask you now, with the greatest possible humility, to forgive me, if you can.'

She had to smile at last. He would always be the schoolboy in search of a convincing role. He was so absurd standing there, trying to look proud and humble, regal and abject, all at the same time.

Because she had made her decision, the words were easy to say.

'Yes,' she said, still in that hard, clear tone, 'I can forgive you now. There isn't any point in anything else, is there? Come here.' She held out her arms and saw his face transfigure. 'We shall kiss and make up, as good parents should.'

Parents, not lovers.

He took her gratefully into his arms. His kisses, fervent and aching, did not move her. She could not imagine, at this moment, that they would ever do so again. She had awoken that morning, as on so many others during the last drowsing weeks of her pregnancy, wondering how it would be – or was it, perhaps, recalling how it had been, in some dawntide dream – to feel those other lips on hers; cool, innocent, filled with laughter and tears.

Her heart rose as she responded mechanically to her husband's caresses, feverish to please her. She was no longer pregnant. She would regain all her former poetry of form. And then she would see Shing-jen once again.

'I thought I would call him Li Dan,' she mumured softly, into Pheasant's cradling shoulder. 'New Dawn – the symbol of a new beginning.'

He caught her to him in a passion of gratitude.

20

When she could support her morning dreams no longer, Black Jade sent for Shing-jen to come to her.

The meeting-place was her old home in Green Fragrance Court. She went there rarely nowadays, and it was universally understood that when she did so she went alone, except, of course, for her inveterate guardian, Chinghiz.

Now, she wandered about the pleasant rooms, marvelling at the sense of homecoming that never failed. Her servants kept the little house as though she still lived in it. The floors shone with scented wax; the cushions were newly plump; the plants well-watered and flourishing even now, in the eleventh month. An appetising smell of food came from the kitchen, and amber and sandalwood hung on the warm air floating from the glowing coals beneath the *kang* in the various rooms.

She was still often overtaken by sudden tiredness. She had risen and returned to her work too soon after New Dawn's birth. Now she indulged in the luxury of doing absolutely nothing. In a moment, Chinghiz would bring her some soothing tea.

She closed her eyes and allowed her mind to wander in a relaxed and meaningless haze of images. The weight of her daily concerns lifted, leaving her aware only of a receding jumble of incidents – days, people, buildings, maps, plans – that were gradually and insistently edged out by the sweet, piercing song of the caged birds that hung before the windows.

When the birds fell suddenly quiet she opened her eyes.

He was there.

She was surprised at the detail in which she had remembered him: the slender, nervous body, the soft mouth, the grey, discerning eyes, the peculiar delicacy that characterised his movements.

She smiled like a requited child and waved away the bow he offered for courtesy's sake.

'There shall be no ceremony between us. It won't be appropriate if I am to trust you as deeply as I hope to do. Besides,' she added mischievously, 'I understand that you have won your case against His Majesty, and need no longer bend your knees to anything less than a passing deity?'

'Just as you wish.' He returned her smile, thinking how like a small girl she appeared, curled among her cushions.

She made him sit on a stool placed near to her, and they spoke for a time about church matters, the Abbot and his campaigns and his sutras, the needs and excellences of the imperial library, and the health of Golden Willow. When these polite subjects were taken care of, Black Jade rang a small, tinkling hand-bell, and Chinghiz appeared with tea and prawns in batter, cut like butterflies. She noted his close, covert examination of the young priest, but his carved, Tartar mask did not reveal any conclusions he might have reached.

As they drank the rosehip brew and allowed the prawns to melt upon their palates, Jade realised that, with every fluid movement of Shing-jen's blue sleeve, she caught a bitter-sweet note of perfume. It made her think of green herbs and mountain streams, but also of the mystery of temples, by night, in the candles' gleam.

She was trembling. Surely he must see it?

'Tell me a little about yourself, if you will,' she invited, to cover her loss of control. Her cup rattled as she set it down.

He held out dismissive palms. 'I was born in Soochow, of a scholastic family. My parents were often at court. I was the youngest son, perhaps a little my mother's favourite.' He showed no disposition to go on; his self-interest was minimal.

'Why – how did you become a priest?' she asked, clumsily to her own ears. But she needed to know. She wanted to understand everything about him, to comprehend why he should choose the watercourse way and the celibacy of the monastery.

He shrugged. 'I suppose you might say it was my own peculiar bid for the freedom to choose my own destiny – that, at least, is what Meng Shen says it was. I do not see it quite like that myself. There came a point, however, when a choice presented itself.'

'What was the choice, if I am not too inquisitive?'

His sweet smile reassured and captivated her. 'No. Curiosity is part of the charm of a woman. It is an ordinary story. The day came when my father suggested a marriage for me, to a beautiful girl, of excellent family, whom, in fact, I had known and liked as a child.'

'And you refused?'

'The offer made me realise that I did not wish to follow the life of a family man, to care for my wife and my lands, and raise my children, and take my place at court; I miss the children, perhaps, for I am fond of them, but that is all.'

'But the cloister is very far removed from such a life.'

'I followed the Tao. That is where it took me. Nothing could have been simpler.'

'But you mentioned a freedom of choice. Surely there is no freedom in the life of a priest?'

He surveyed her softly, so that she felt his look as a caress.

'What is one looking for – the freedom to choose, or the freedom that comes from having made the right choice?'

Her spirits plummeted. She did not wish him to have made the right choice. He felt the faint change and tried to cheer her, not daring to comprehend it. He longed to touch her, to smooth the childish crease from her forehead.

'We should not be speaking about me,' he said, with that deep, personal concentration that unbalanced her. 'I am here to try to help you. I want to do so, very much.'

Do I also have the freedom to choose, rightly or wrongly? she wondered wildly. Then, sensible again, she governed her voice.

'You know, I think, what I wish you to try to do for me?' She was shy, suddenly, at his knowledge of her deeds.

He knew it. 'We need not discuss the past. The Lady of Jung has told me all I need to know.'

She welcomed his instinct to spare her.

'What will you do? Will there be ceremonies, masses, prayers?'

The priest rose and began to walk about the room.

'A certain amount of ceremony, yes. But please do not look forward to the usual cacophony of drums and cymbals; nor the accompanying stench of putrefying animal carcasses and the more obnoxious chemicals! And there will not be a chorus of admiring acolytes. I am neither a play-acting charlatan nor an alchemistic fantasist. What I do is simple, but extremely efficacious; and I do it alone.'

'That's reassuring,' she said matter-of-factly. 'I've already been the victim of all the other methods. When will you begin?'

He stood before the windows, smoothing the plumage of one of the cage-birds. The light fell on his face, giving it the purity of cut jade.

'I will begin now, if you like. It is not *necessary* that you should see and start to comprehend the power of the magus; but it will give you even greater reassurance if you do.'

'Very well.' Her heart began to drum. 'What must I do?'

His innocent smile was there. 'Nothing.'

'Nothing?'

'You should lie back in comfort, and do nothing at all.'

He was walking behind her couch now, his soft voice steadying her heartbeat, slowing it, telling her she was safe and cherished.

'Try to empty your mind of all that ties it to the earth. Let it flow; let it become a part of the air about you, of the scented air and the bird-song. Let it go free. As it wants to do.'

It was strange, but she had the strongest desire to sleep.

'Let your eyes close if you wish. They will open again, very soon, and you will see many things more clearly.'

Obedient to his gentling voice, she drifted, letting its sound caress her like the warm waves of the childhood river, when she and Rose Bird had played in its silver stream; or like the fingertip fall of blossom on her uplifted face, as she lay in the orchard and dreamed of far-off Chang-an.

Soon, it was she who became the waves, or the blossom; who was floating, weightless because bodiless, a part of the great eternal current of the universe.

It seemed that this was her state for many hours, perhaps for days. Time was no longer important; no longer existed. She knew nothing, was aware of nothing, not even the voice of Shing-jen could reach her. It was the perfection of happiness.

And then she felt that her eyes were opening. They no longer seemed to *be* her eyes, in any physical sense, but some external medium through which she was permitted to look, in her disembodied state, as though she were a reflection looking out through a mirror.

What the eyes showed her was this:

First there was darkness. It was a warm darkness; not dense, but composed paradoxically of a myriad imperceptible points of life. Then there was a bitter-sweet scent, aromatic of mountains and temples, familiar, desired. A cloud seemed to form in the centre of her vision. The darkness went into it and became pure light.

In the midst of the cloud was the form of a man. The cloud rushed into this form and was gone. The man was Shing-jen. He was no longer a monk in a dark blue robe, but a shining, iridescent figure from the legends of the immortals. He towered, preternaturally tall, and he was haloed by a shimmering cloak of kingfisher feathers, peacock feathers, the feathers of pheasants and of the golden oriole. A crown of stars hovered above his head.

His face shone with a fierce and noble purity.

He was the Plumed Man, made out of air and legend, resembling the angels.

Behind his refulgent figure stood a high table where incense burned in a bronze vessel. It held the perfumed heart of the rosewood lianna, sweetest and most ethereal of scents, seductive to man and beloved of the immortals.

The Plumed Man bowed once towards the imprisoned, watching eyes, and turned to the altar.

Upon it lay a jade box.

He opened it and scooped up part of its contents, letting them flow through his fingers in a stream of fine powder. The stream had the glint of pure gold.

He emptied the casket into the brazier.

The flames leaped up in a sudden brilliant, breath-taking aura; rose, vermilion, amber, emerald, indigo.

The aura spread, feeding on itself, expanding beyond the limit of sight.

For a moment it was so exquisite as to be insupportable; then it was fading, falling, folding in upon itself until it was no more than the iridescent brilliance of a man's plumage, glinting in the flames of an altar fire.

And now the eyes must look no longer at the Plumed Man. The flames are dwindling now, their colours dying – all but the gold. The gold is coalescing, burning, moving upward until it is free of the fire, drawing the eyes with it as it moves together, a powdered glitter of a million million facets, until it has gradually assumed, curving and quickening, a new and definable shape. It is the shape of a woman. Still all of gold, her flesh pure gold, her garments of gold, her golden hair streaming in an unfelt wind, she is none the less recognisable as one of the True Ones, golden sylphs among the immortals, whose nurture is air and whose nectar the dew. Their work in the world is to protect children and innocents from evil, and upon certain occasions, responding to the summons of a very great and very good magus, they will undertake to do his bidding on behalf of a more fallible human being.

She swims in the air and it can be seen that she is smiling. She makes a beckoning motion and suddenly the light intensifies and she is surrounded by her sisters. Each alike and yet no two the same, they swirl behind her in the aureate air. The leader holds out her arms with a gesture of infinite compassion. The eyes are Jade's eyes and the gesture is for her.

A brief stab of pain in her brow.

She put up her hand to it for only a moment, and the vision was gone.

She lay on her couch in a room filled with incense. The dying sun was turning every mote to gold.

'Highness?'

Shing-jen was beside her. He was dressed in an indigo gown. His beautiful face registered only concern for her.

She stared up at him, unsure how to give voice to her thoughts.

'Were they real? Were they really here – or have I dreamed them?'

'I can assure you that you have not slept.'

'A vision, then? You have brought me a vision?'

'*I* have brought you nothing. I have merely offered a prayer to the forces which I will hope to enlist in your cause. If they have shown themselves to you, you have been most blessed. And you may be sure, too, that your purpose will be accomplished.'

She believed him. There would be no more ghosts.

A little ball of pain burst inside her head. She gave an involuntary gasp.

'I am sorry. You are in pain.'

'My head. It will pass.'

'If you will allow me. I think I can give you relief.'

He rose and stood at the end of her couch, behind her head.

'Try, if you can, to let the pain go; let my fingers draw it into them. Let it go.'

She was, she was sure, visibly shaken by the wave of desire that shocked her body as his fingertips brushed her skin. She almost cried aloud with the surprise of it. Was this another part of his magic or merely the pent-up accumulation of her own thoughts and dreams, released by his moving hands? She turned her head a little and looked up at him. Seeing his face bent so close to her own, serious with his intent, it was all she could do not to reach up and draw it down to her, so much did she long for his mouth upon hers.

She did nothing, submitting herself to the strokes of his fingers. The pain, which she had all but forgotten, was diminishing, but her head began to swim a little and she found herself moving it slightly, circling in response to the circling of his hands. Her lips parted, her breathing was swifter and shallower. Her eyes shone gloriously into his.

Shing-jen gazed in awe at the face below his. He had known, of course. That morning he had arisen singing. This was the most beautiful woman he would ever see. Her sexuality was an aura that filled the space about them. There was not a man in the universe who would not desire her.

And yet it was not desire which made him, at last, bend and give the answer to her trembling, open lips. It was compassion – compassion for the creature who must live as lonely as himself, set apart by a karma that gave too much and demanded too much in return; compassion for the woman who must be what her husband could not be, and therefore for the woman who was so poorly husbanded.

But if pity began it, passion pushed away pity like the importunate child it is. After the first thirsting, questing kisses, he was no longer the magus, her master, but only a man who wanted a woman with every impulse of mind and body.

When they could bear to let their lips part, he moved round to sit facing her on the couch. He touched her breast tenderly, above her kimono.

'Is it what you want?'

'Yes,' she whispered. She untied the kimono and let it fall from her shoulders. With an exultant cry that was half a groan he sank his mouth upon hers, kissing her with a subtlety that made her weep, taking her breast in his mouth until she too cried out with the pleasure that was like pain until it was taken to its necessary conclusion.

He lifted his head, rose and picked her up in his arms.

'Where is your bed?'

She showed him where it was.

He laid her down and reverently took off the rest of her clothes and his own. He was hard, gilded and shining. Again he became the plumed man for her, something perfect, more than human. Her own amber body gleamed like jewels, floated like clouds, sang like music; he told her so as he touched it into a thousand golden needles of desire; unbearable, exquisite, making her moan and call his name, and spread herself before him like a feast.

When he entered her it seemed at first that they must come to a swift, cataclysmic consummation, a sunburst of unpreventable abandon. She would have welcomed it; she was completely open to him, as willing as a concubine to pleasure him in any way he wished. She arched against him, pressing up to him, driving him deeper into her. He went with her for a while and then began to guide her, taking her up with him into a spiralling vortex of rhythm and joy that was the centre, first of a raging maelstrom as he thrust into her with urgent, furious strokes, later of a great, quiet pool, whose mysterious and compelling currents carried them to a climax whose release was as far beyond the clouds and rain as the existence of those golden visitors of an hour ago was beyond their own.

He knelt and surveyed her. They kissed seriously, like children, with closed lips.

'You have broken your vows,' she said later as she lay against him.

'Yes. But I don't think I stray many steps from the Way by loving you. The union of man and woman is the necessary pattern of the universe.'

'Then you will have no regrets?'

'None. But you know that, really?'

Her smile for him was beautiful. 'Yes. I know. We love each other.'

'Yes.'

It seemed very simple.

*

It was not simple. It was madness, of course.

A marvellous and completely new madness. She was in love with a man whom she had chosen, who had chosen her. They had come together by the sheer force of the attraction between them; no outside authority, parent, Chief Eunuch or Emperor had ordered their union. It was something that did not happen in the Empire of All That Is Under Heaven, except perhaps to the fortunate poor.

It was a love that fed upon itself like fire, as pure and as cleansing. It made the whole world over again for Black Jade, and nothing could have kept her from it.

When Shing-jen was not with her, she saw quite plainly, as though she were a disinterested passer-by, the magnitude of the risk she was taking.

She might already be carrying his child. Pheasant, since the birth of New Dawn, visited her bed regularly. It would be an unworthy thing to bear a child whose fatherhood was in doubt.

There was also the risk of discovery. Upon this subject she was severely lectured by Chinghiz.

'How long do you intend to go on with this?' he enquired grimly, after a whole season had passed in delirium, finding her singing love-songs to her lute and gazing, moon-eyed, into space.

'As long as I can,' she answered deliberately. 'Why? Do you find it too much of a tax on your ingenuity?'

It was unfair. It was Chinghiz who kept her secret, or so he hoped, from the scandal-hungry court. She could not have hoped to hide it from him, even if she had wanted to. She did, however, feel a twinge of something like guilt where he was concerned, which she did not feel at all on Pheasant's account. It was odd and uncomfortable, and she wasn't going to analyse it.

'You know what my life is,' she said, trapping his discouraging eye in a dry, passionate honesty. 'I need this. I need Shing-jen. I need his love, his goodness, his strength – far, far more than I ever needed his power as a magus.'

'But the ghosts *are* gone?' She never spoke of them, but he was almost sure.

'Quite gone. How did you know?'

He grinned. 'You no longer hesitate at corners.'

'I only wish I could tell *how* he did it,' she murmured, smiling the smile that was not for him, and that maddened him, sometimes to anger and often to grief. 'But I can't seem to remember any of it. It is most peculiar.'

'No doubt,' the steward said repressively, reserving his judgment on matters magical. He was grateful to the priest for the effect of whatever it was he had done with his clouds of yellow smoke, even, in a tormented way, for the effect he had on his mistress herself – but he could have wrung his elegant neck for the danger he brought her.

Once again, as he had often done, he tried to show it to her.

'We try, Welcome and I, to shield you from discovery. You don't apparently, care either for your own peril or for ours.' That was mean, but it might hit home. 'Nor do you seem aware, as you used to be, of the enemies who look out so eagerly for just such a lapse as a love affair –'

'Stop this, Chinghiz. You do it every day. My affairs, of love or otherwise, are still my own. And there is no such danger as you insist upon. The Emperor and I are very much closer than we were. And, don't look at me like that! You needn't expect shame – I don't feel any.'

He sighed irritably. 'You may be close to His Majesty. But so are others. Lord Shang, for example, who is no friend of yours. Have you any idea how much time your husband spends in that man's company? He rides with him, hunts with him, drinks with him; he hangs on his sleeve like a paper dragonfly, siphoning up his every word. Do you think that bodes well for you?'

'I know, I know. An Empress must be without sin, or she is liable to find herself without the convenience of her head! But surely, despite the Lord Shangs, you and I are clever enough, between us, to keep mine on my shoulders?' Her look was consciously disarming. Turning from it with real impatience he wished, painfully, that he neither loved her nor even liked her quite so much.

'You should also be warned by what has happened to the Leopard,' he said, as though she had not spoken.

Her suave henchman had at last been caught out in such a vast and blatant scheme of peculation that Pheasant had dismissed him.

'I'm sorry about that,' Black Jade regretted. 'He is a scoundrel, but a very amiable one. I shall miss him.'

'That isn't the point. What your detractors will say is that if the Emperor sees fit to exile your particular friends, he is obviously beginning to turn his face from you.'

'Let them,' she said flatly.

He saw that she wished only to turn her back on the danger,

and his fear for her increased a hundred times.

'That remark,' he flung at her, 'makes you every bit as self-willed and bat-witted as the Leopard ever was.'

He left the room abruptly, without troubling to conceal his anger.

For nearly a year Chinghiz worked to provide Black Jade with alibis. The time came when he could no longer hide the fact that she met with Shing-jen, and he turned his talents to covering up how *often* they met.

The Emperor's connection with Lao-tse, it was said, had deepened her interest in the Tao, and the priest was her tutor. She was also reported to be one of the crowd of women who importuned the handsome magus for the elixir of youth.

'Is that supposed to be an alibi, or a punishment?' she guessed accurately, on hearing this slur on her beauty.

'I thought you had no vanity,' was her servant's sardonic reply.

She shrugged. 'Say what you please. Just try to avoid treason.'

She was so deep in love, he knew with a familiar sinking of his own scarred and faithful heart, that she would still take no care on her own account. She left it all to him; and, because it was all that he could do for her, he did it to the utmost of his expert ability. The priest, too, helped him. There grew between them a quiet confederacy of trust. It was impossible, even if one desired it strongly, not to like Shing-jen.

For what seemed to Chinghiz half a weary lifetime, and to Black Jade a brief, fleeting, concertina-lantern of days, she was entirely engaged by her love. She worked, entertained, and gave herself to her children, her husband or the ministers only to pass the time until she could be with Shing-jen; while her lover and her servant hacked out, smoothed and camouflaged her path, the one beguiling small enemies with his magnetic charm, the other shadowing greater ones with his spider's network, nerve-racked, overworked, and himself increasingly endangered, ill-tempered and aching of heart.

In the end it was Shing-jen himself who brought Black Jade unwillingly back to her senses; as he had known, from the beginning, that he must.

They were in their constant haven, in Green Fragrance Court. The priest stood at the window, looking out. Beyond the archway, one of Chinghiz's guards was pacing, bored and watchful.

Today she was worried, preoccupied, unusually, with her husband. They rarely talked about Pheasant, but he had been behaving oddly with her lately, moody and often unfriendly.

'He was almost discourteous today in front of the council. He hardly spoke to me once, except to clarify some point about hospital supplies. Why should he want to treat me like that?'

Shing-jen came back to her. He held her angry face against him.

'It isn't just that, is it? You wouldn't have cared, last month, last week, perhaps even yesterday.'

Her carefully built righteousness collapsed. 'No,' she said, rubbing her cheek against his breast. 'But there had to come a day, didn't there, when I let myself see what I didn't want to see, because I knew it could do no possible good – that my marriage is a poor, patched and repaired affair, a wretched compromise that can no longer work. Perhaps Pheasant begins to see it too.'

She looked up at him, panting, knowing she had said what should not have been said.

He stroked her hair. 'Finish it,' he told her gently. 'Say it all. At least I can offer that small release.'

'I know it is my own fault, entirely,' she said, calming a little, 'but that makes no difference; makes it worse, I suppose. I thought, when the baby was born, and Pheasant and I came to our – understanding, that I could manage it all; to love you, and still to give him something – the affection I have always had for him; the duty I owe him as Emperor, and the father of my sons. I thought it would be enough. It must have been enough for a long time before I met you. But it isn't. It isn't!' she cried, beginning to weep.

'Hush, my love. Don't.' He sat beside her and kissed her, covering her with his love, until she was quiet again.

'We have never been equals, Pheasant and I,' she said, bent on self-discovery through self-torture. 'Ever since we met I have guided him, and have never been able to respect him as I wanted to, *should* have been able to. And what has it come to? Now, when he sees clearly how much he needs my help – he will still do very little without my advice, though he does lean more on his ministers lately – he increasingly resents my efficiency. And then,' she added with something like shame, 'he accuses me of coldness.' It had been of coldness in the bedchamber that Pheasant had accused her. Shing-jen would sense that, of course. There was only truth between them.

Having listened and thought, he saw that his growing fears were justified. He knew what he had to do.

He did not want to hurt her; but there was no kind way.

He did, however, leave it for a day.

Now he stood again at the window and stared unseeingly at the beginning of autumn's splendour in the trees. It was raining; the end of the monsoon was near. It was a relentless, energetic rain that had the young Tigers running about in it, shouting, and which, if one was a sad and apprehensive adult, destroyed one's own energy and left one limp and resourceless.

She did not hear his sigh, ragged and irrevocable as the fall of a leaf, only the subdued song from the cages.

'Soon,' he said, so tenderly that it would be like a premonition for her, 'I am going to leave you.'

He was there to prevent her wounded cry with his kisses.

She fluttered against him, like the birds, like the useless leaves. He held her till she was quiet, wishing he could suffer her pain as well as his own, which was very great.

'You have known it must come, some day –' He knew that didn't help, now that it *had* come. 'The monastery wants to send me to Tibet, to study with the lamaseries. It will serve as well as another reason to bring us to the break.'

Break: the sound of iron on stone, of harsh waves on a shore, of what would happen to her without him. When he had gone.

'When?' She dragged out the word like a passing bell.

'Soon. A month, perhaps.'

This time he could not stop her cry.

He tasted salt. 'Must you go?' she begged.

'You know I must. We have been too dangerous together.'

Her gaze attacked him, brilliant with possibility. 'Then take me with you!'

'Oh my love! Where could we we go, where we would not be found? We would be disgraced and killed. That is not an end for an Empress.'

'No, no!' she cried excitedly. 'We could leave the boundaries of the Empire – go to India, perhaps? We will take my jewels, enough for a lifetime together. You can work, and study, and I can be your wife. We can build Green Fragrance Court all over again. We'll take Welcome and Chinghiz and –'

He was shaking his head so violently that she was silenced.

'No,' he said with fierce pride. 'I did not come to you to strip you of your crown and your karma, and drag you at my heels through the dust of continents. I said to you once that there is a freedom that comes from exercising the right choice. That is the freedom that is open to us now. It is all we have.'

'Keep your freedom. I don't want it! I don't care for right or wrong. I want you, to be with you!'

'You want us both to cease to be what we are?'

'What do you mean? I am not an Empress; I am a woman who loves you. And you are no priest – or how could you have loved me so well?'

He sighed, a fractured, difficult sound. He wondered what he must say to her, knowing that it would not be the whole truth.

For Kuo Shing-jen, like the Grand Astrologer before him, possessed, when he wished to do so, the gift of prophecy. He had looked into the future of his love and found it absent; looking further, he had discovered the reason for this.

'That is not true,' he said gently. 'The love was a separate thing; a great gift. We must be grateful for it, but we must not destroy it by demanding too much. For it would be destroyed, make no mistake. Can you truly tell me you do not share my sense of that fragility?'

'Oh, I don't know,' she said wretchedly. 'I think not – but what can I do, if you are not with me?'

She looked so miserable that he gathered her close and kissed her white face. 'I am with you,' he said intensely. 'I will always be with you.'

'But you will leave me? In a month or so?' she asked, looking up at him clearly.

'Yes.'

She knew then that she would not change his resolve; nor, perhaps, though she did not altogether understand this, should she try to do so. That being so, Black Jade dried her tears, called up every one of her considerable resources of character and schooled her torn face back to beauty, courage and resolution.

'Then,' she said, winding her arms about Shing-jen and blinding him with the rain-washed aura of her smile, 'We must not waste a single moment of the precious time we have left.'

Their love-making, under sentence, took on a scaring quality unknown even to their previous passion. There were other times when they were joined in such tenderness that Black Jade would come weeping to the climax, and weep for a long time afterwards, already mourning his loss.

He wanted only to bring her happiness. His unselfishness in love, as in life, astounded her. She was surrounded by the gift of him; surprised, enchanted, warmed right through by prodigies of love. In this too, he was a magus.

When they did not make love, they talked. Now, as never

before, he spoke to her of what the Tao meant to him, letting her come to understand that he was, indeed, a true priest, because he thought that this might be of some use to her in helping her to give him up. Following him, she would let him read to her from the Tao-te-Ching, the work of the Li philosopher, Lao-tse. His exposition of its central doctrines – if any body of thought so disposed against all rigid systems could be called doctrine – was the most lucid she had heard.

They argued warmly, with long lacunae when they could not keep from touching each other, about such subjects as *yin* and *yang* or good and evil, or the positive and negative universe. They discussed the nature of the Way, the Tao itself, that mystical mingling of *yin* and *yang* from which all life is received, and from which came the virtues by which Shing-jen had lived his dedicated life, in harmony with the primordial forces of the natural world and of his own unspoiled heart.

One day it was evening before she could come to him. Loud Tiger had a cold and Black Jade had spent the afternoon trying to keep the fretful, active child amused. To her great relief, Young Tiger had brought in his latest gadget, the *camera obscura*, to show his brother, and the two boys became cheerfully obsessed with looking at the world upside-down through its pinhole.

'Mama – you look just like a nice, fat onion,' said her second son flatteringly. 'Your skirts are onion-coloured and your green scarf makes a nice, bright stem, especially if you wind it round your neck *and* your head,' he suggested hopefully.

'Led *be* see!' demanded the invalid, whose bedclothes resembled the plains of Korea. 'Oh yes. *Do* wind it round!'

'No. I think you are quite well enough to do without me, now. I'll send Sweetmeat in; perhaps she will consent to become an onion,' she added cravenly, rescuing the ends of her scarf from sticky fingers.

'Oh, all right,' Loud Tiger agreed. Sweetmeat was notoriously easy to inveigle into all sorts of things.

Their mother left them thankfully, to the sound of the cold-sufferer playing coarse and inventive tunes on his nose.

When she reached Green Fragrance Court it was in candle-light, and he was waiting for her, calm in his black robe, his hands moving on a rope of sandalwood beads.

They embraced and settled in their familiar places, she on the couch, he very close to her on the low stool. He enquired gravely after Loud Tiger.

'He is slightly less troublesome when trapped between sheets.' He saw her give the half proud, half puzzled look of all loving mothers. He wondered when it would occur to her that she had been willing to leave her children for his sake, that she had not even thought of them or their need of her.

But when she was with Shing-jen, there was no room for thought of anyone else. It was not long before, aroused by some chance word or glance, they had moved into the bedroom, clinging together like secretive children themselves.

They made love seriously and carefully at first, every word and look, every touch a new investment both of the complete commitment of their love and of its utter impossibility. They were grave together, their movements gentle. In the end it was not a caress but the burden of agony and longing in her eyes that brought him into her on an impulse of mingled pity and adoration. Soon the agony lay far behind as they swam slowly, somewhere up in the black night among the stars, in that familiar nebula of golden light that was the aura of their passion. They hung together in the heavens like twin planets, incapable of separate thought or sensation, until their gilded calm was overtaken by a sudden, swift blaze that erupted into the ferocity of a meteor. Incandescent, fused, they let themselves be consumed in an explosion of pure joy.

When it was over and they rested, human, on the earth again, they lay lapped in the light of the candles; looking, talking, touching a little, knowing that they were storing up memories.

'You have made me feel like the first woman created, in the arms of the first man.' Her passion now was all gratitude.

Before they could let it carry them on its tide again, he put her gently from him; not far.

'I want to read you something.'

She lay back among the pillows and watched him. She loved him to read to her so that she could look at him like this, telling over the beloved features as a woman new to riches counts her gold.

'This speaks of death, but as a leave-taking, nothing more.' He smiled, to take the shadow from the words.

' "The Master came among us when it was the appointed time; he left us because he followed the Tao. Be content with the moment, therefore, and be willing to follow the Way." ' Shing-jen raised his eyes to hers, his voice soft. ' "The wood is consumed, but the fire burns on; and we do not know when it will come to an end." You are the fire, Black Jade, and have been a part of myself.

I have been the wood for your bright flame; the consummation was most beautiful.'

His words were a prayer for her. She wept in his arms knowing that this was his way of saying goodbye to her. He would leave very soon now. They had agreed that he would not mention the day or the hour of his departure.

'Little Mistress!' They were sundered by an urgent summons from the doorway.

'Yes, Chinghiz, what is it?' Black Jade saw her steward through tears, a brilliant, agitated blur.

'Forgive me, mistress, but there's no time – listen! Kuo Shing-jen must leave at once! He must quit the palace and the city. You are both in great danger. You have been accused of sorcery. At this very moment, Lord Shang is with the Emperor; they are drawing up an edict that will depose Your Highness! It would be exile, imprisonment!'

Black Jade stood paralysed by shock.

Shing-jen, long prepared for this moment, understood at once.

'You're certain I should go now?' he asked Chinghiz quickly. 'Or can I do more for our mistress if I stay?'

'You must go.' The reply was definite. 'If you remain, you will be arrested, probably tortured. She will do better for herself if she doesn't have that to think of. Your absence will make things harder for them. There is a man with a horse outside.'

Their eyes met. Shing-jen nodded, knowing when to trust.

'I'll do as you say. I will let you know where you can reach me.'

He was aware of Black Jade staring confusedly, only beginning, unwillingly, to realise what was happening.

'Not yet. No messenger would be safe. Wait for a while. Now you must hurry. Go now. My man will take you to safety.'

'Shing-jen, no!'

Her cry was like a wound in his side.

She ran to his arms. Their last embrace, recognised and faced after all, was wordless and full of tears. Agonisingly soon, he let her go.

'Today or tomorrow, what does it matter?' he murmured, smiling with her tears on his lips. 'The fire burns on.'

She looked up, seeing again the young man coming towards her in the winter garden. 'The consummation,' she whispered bravely, 'was most beautiful.' Her voice broke.

He laid his hands on her, in love and in blessing, and was gone.

Chinghiz moved out of the shadows into which he had tactfully melted.

'You must think quickly,' he urged her, sensible of necessary cruelty. 'His Majesty may already have signed that decree. You have time for nothing but a frontal assault. You must go to him, now, and accuse your accusers! The chief enemy is Lord Shang; but the man who brought the "evidence" is one of the eunuchs; he swears he has seen yourself and Shing-jen conducting an occult ceremony to bring about the death of a specific subject. They will suggest that the subject was the Emperor. If you are sufficiently strong, you can outface them – they have no real proof, as you must know. But you must go at once, before your husband has come to accustom himself to the idea that any of it might be true. You know how susceptible he is to persuasion, and Lord Shang is a master of persuasion!'

He thought he might have to shake her, but suddenly it was unnecessary. She opened her eyes very wide and seemed to focus newly, as though seeing the world for what it was, after a very different dream.

'Thank you, Chinghiz,' she said steadily. 'He will be safe?'

'You have my word that he will.'

'Very well. Where shall I find the Emperor?'

She had already begun to leave the room.

Pheasant was in his study, seated at his desk. Lord Shang walked the expensive carpet before him and the decree which he had drafted lay between them. The Emperor did not feel well. His head hurt. Events had overtaken him and he was not sure he was doing the right thing.

'Are you absolutely certain of the facts?' he demanded miserably. Lord Shang was rarely wrong; he had come to rely on him heavily, ever since Black Jade had taken to locking herself up with that damnable priest.

'Sorcery! It doesn't seem possible. She has always been so much against that sort of thing. The case of my first Empress, for example –'

Lord Shang had a face like a camel's and a sneer to match.

'Has it never occurred to Your Majesty,' he sniffed, 'that her Highness's professed horror of the black arts might have been no more than a blind, a convenient pose behind which to conceal her own desire for the death of Lady Paulownia?'

'Shang Kuan! You forget yourself. That is nonsense. Nonsense! And as for this latest accusation – I have met the young priest myself and he seemed to me a most pleasant person. And surely the Lady Golden Willow would have nothing to do with anyone of a doubtful reputation? And do you mean to tell me the Abbot Hsuan-tsang would sponsor a sorcerer at court? No, no, it's all –'

'Does Your Majesty now mean to retract?' snapped the camel's mouth.

'What? I haven't signed your damned paper yet, you know!'

'No,' agreed the minister patiently. 'But I have shown you, have I not, that the relations between the Empress and this so-called priest have been malignant to the welfare of the state?'

'We will hear what my wife has to say before we make such statements.'

The camel sighed heavily. 'If Your Majesty would care to look back; how many good men and woman have lost their lives, simply in the interests of Lady Wu becoming the Empress? The Lady Paulownia, of course, and the unfortunate Bright Virtue. And your uncle, the Archduke, and poor Old Integrity. To say nothing of the hordes who have been banished to the ends of the Empire merely for putting themselves in her way.'

'You exaggerate. The reasons were quite different,' Pheasant said; but he was not sure. He had never been sure, now that he thought of it.

'And now,' Lord Shang continued grimly, 'Black Jade has resorted to magic. And why?' He hung his snuffling underlip over the desk, thrusting it under his master's shrinking nose. 'What does this beautiful and accomplished, *clever* woman still want – that she can only gain by sorcery? Ask yourself? What?'

'I've no idea.' It was true. He hadn't.

Lord Shang made a noise that suggested he had found a drinking-fountain. 'The Empress,' he pointed out carefully, 'managed the government of the Empire very efficiently during Your Majesty's own unfortunate absences. Do you not think,' he continued, every word shaken from his muzzle separately, 'that she might well prefer these absences to become – permanent?'

Pheasant looked as though he had been struck with a blunt object.

He had not known his minister had been leading up to *this*.

'That,' he said in a faint voice, 'is a very terrible thing to say.'

'It is, isn't it?' the camel agreed blithely. 'But you see, now don't you, sir, why my decree may be the only way open to you?'

Pheasant clutched at the word 'may'. 'Your proof would have to be water-tight!' He snatched at his dignity. 'And I am by no means disposed towards you in this matter. You should know that.

'The proof will satisfy Your Majesty.'

Pheasant stared at the paper in front of him. He was a very unhappy man.

He jumped when the major-domo came in.

'Your Majesty, the Empress is here.'

'Oh. Yes, well, I don't know that I – Oh! My dear. Here you are!'

'Yes, indeed,' said Black Jade pleasantly, sweeping in busily with Chinghiz behind her. 'I heard that you were not quite yourself and I came to see what I could do. Good evening, Lord Shang.'

The minister acknowledged her as distantly as he judged wise.

Pheasant shifted in his chair, throwing his broad sleeve over the paper on his desk.

'You are misinformed,' he said weakly. 'I have only a slight headache.'

'Slight? Only a slight discomfort? You astonish me. I had heard that you appeared to be going quite out of your mind.'

'What? Who has dared to say such a thing?'

'It's common gossip. Of course I was the last to hear. They say you are about to depose me. On the grounds that, in the little spare time I have, I have taken to witchcraft like your previous spouse.'

Pheasant gasped. He had not expected this.

'I hadn't made up my mind. It isn't signed,' he blurted, the colour of stewed rhubarb.

'Your Majesty,' said Lord Shang sternly, with the aim of getting some backbone back into the jellyfish before him.

'May I sit?' enquired Black Jade politely. 'Thank you. Is *this* the edict? Do you mind if I look at it?'

In an agony of embarrassment, with Lord Shang tutting in the background, the Emperor handed it over.

She read it quickly, then gave it to Chinghiz.

'I see.' He had been right. They were not a moment too soon.

She thought, very quickly, but with perfect clarity.

'It seems my accuser is a man I do not know?'

The minister came forward. 'He is a member of the Imperial household; one of the senior eunuchs.' His voice was without shade.

Black Jade looked at him. 'This man, whom I do not know, is prepared to swear that he witnessed a ceremony in which I and the priest, Kuo Shing-jen, performed acts of sorcery. He goes so far as to state exactly what ceremony it was. Why then, since he was so sure of the evidence of his eyes, did he not go, *at once*, to inform the proper authorities?'

'I imagine,' said Shang coldly, 'that he was afraid. To accuse the Empress is a most serious step.'

'Isn't it?' she agreed sweetly. 'Or perhaps, if this witness saw any ceremony at all, it was an innocent one of praise and prayer? Father Kuo certainly performed many such services for me.' She turned to her husband, accusingly. 'I was not aware that we were spied upon at such times. Indeed, I think it most unlikely that we *were* spied upon.'

Obedient to her inflexion, Chinghiz stepped forward. 'Your Majesty, I can personally guarantee that no one – *no one*, unauthorised by Her Majesty or myself, was present at any such rites. The man you speak of can have seen nothing, nothing at all. He is lying.'

'It is possible,' admitted Pheasant, a little brighter now. 'We shall, of course, examine him again.'

Lord Shang felt the results of months of careful work begin to slip through his grasp. A great deal rested upon the inconstant mind of this impressionable young ruler. He had hoped to have got him to sign the edict before he was faced with the Empress.

'I do not believe,' he said with consummate gravity, 'that such a loyal and experienced servant as this witness would risk his career, perhaps his very life, if he were not quite certain.'

Black Jade challenged his heavy-lidded eye. 'You are calling me a liar, Lord Shang,' she said agreeably. 'That is unwise. Why, I wonder,' she pursued in the same pleasant tone, 'is Chief Minister Shang so eager for my downfall? It seems, on the face of it, unlikely that such an intelligent man would accept this shifty evidence – the word of one man, and produced so long after the event.' She turned gracefully to Pheasant, whose misery came and went in conflicting eddies with every word spoken.

'Could it be because, if you were to depose me, Bold Tiger must also be deposed? And if he is no longer the heir, and my other sons share my disgrace, then Paulownia's adopted son would be recalled from exile to his old status as Crown Prince – to the great delight and untold good fortune of his loving tutor, Chief Minister Shang? And of the rest of the Wang clan, of which he is a faithful adherent?'

The camel's look of loathing told her she was right.

Pheasant did not see it, only the sorrow with which the minister shook his head before kneeling, painfully, in front of him.

'Lord of Ten Thousand Years,' he intoned ominously, 'you will not be the first Emperor, or the last, to be willingly misled by a scheming woman. But I beg of you, listen to the prayers of your faithful servants, throughout the Empire – and *take care for your life* – or that is what she will have!'

Pheasant stared from one to the other, from the white-faced, genuflecting councillor to his comfortable, faintly deploring wife.

Black Jade used the hiatus to straighten the folds of her cloak, which she had thrown on while she and Chinghiz were working out what she must say. Her demeanour ignored vulgar drama.

'You know that I have spoken the truth,' she said quietly, as though she spoke of the price of apples. 'I wish, my husband, that you would ask this minister to leave us. I would like to talk with you alone, if you don't mind.'

Pheasant nodded. His resolution, whatever it had been, had drained away with the queer confidence which Shang had inspired in him. He had only to look at Black Jade, sitting there so quietly and calmly, wholesome, dishevelled, and sanely pretty, to know that there could be not truth in all that rigmarole about black magic.

'You are at liberty to leave us, Lord Shang,' he said, almost normally.

'Your Majesty,' the camel huffed urgently, 'I would implore you –'

Chinghiz demeaned himself so far as to open the door for him. Smiling, he himself followed the minister from the room.

'You will not win so easily,' Lord Shang hissed, knowing his true enemy.

'My dear sir,' advised the elegant steward lightly, 'you were as well to try to fight the stars!'

Inside the study, Black Jade still sat like a mouse, quiet and good, and waited for her husband to speak.

Pheasant coughed, to fill the space.

'This has all been most –' he began. It was a false start. 'I don't really know how to tell you – It all began when – oh, I don't know, Jade. Why did you have to spend so much time with the priest? You know people talk.'

'It wasn't much time, not really,' said Black Jade in a small voice. Only she knew how true that was. Not much time at all.

'You don't have to tell me there's nothing in it,' he began again, his tone overflowing with generosity. 'It was all Shang's idea.'

'Indeed?' Her voiced lacked lustre. She seemed tired now. She sighed softly. 'But you had gone a good way towards believing it, hadn't you?'

'If I have hurt you –'

'If?' She smiled sadly. 'Pheasant, I have warmed your bed, and your heart, I think; I have borne your children, I have given you my love and faithful service since the day you took me from the convent. It was all I wanted. And then, you were ill. And so, in addition to being your wife, and the mother of my sons, and the first lady of the Empire, I took the reins of government for you, and held them until they nearly broke my back. And is this how you repay me?' She was still quiet, all her mind and beauty muted.

He begun to apologise, but she went on as if she did not hear.

'Do you think I have a heart of stone, that you can treat me like this? But perhaps it is what I should expect. It causes me to remember that once you wondered if I were capable of the murder of my own dear sister. Oh my dear, it seems to me that your sickness is a far greater one than we understand; a disease, not only of the body, but of the imagination.'

She finished wearily, hating herself for having used the truth in this way to cloak her own necessity. She looked up now and smiled at him briefly; she would not make him, too, hate himself on her account. It would be only too easy to do. She knew how wide were the helpless swervings of his mind under the influence of magnets held out to it; and hers, she knew, had still the strongest pull of all.

'Black Jade –' He was looking at her like a trapped animal. Suddenly he picked up his edict and tore it violently in two. Then he dropped his head in his hands.

She could not help feeling sorry for him as his shoulders shook with sobs. She thought, I shall never be able to love him again. The weight of the coming years seemed terrible to her. Her victory was ashes in her mouth. It had taken her so far from where she had been, only an hour ago.

Shing-jen, my dearest love, how could you leave me to this?

She went to her husband and put her arms around his shoulders.

'Don't do this,' she said dully. 'It doesn't help. It isn't necessary. All we can do is to try to forget this. And go on as we were before.'

When at last she reeled out of that emotional room and into the clear, cold night air, she leaned for a moment against a pillar, its scarlet dragons writhing dimly in the light of a flare.

'Blessed Kuan Yin,' she breathed, her throat filling with misery, 'What is there left for me now?'

A second's grace and Chinghiz was beside her.

'Come with me.' His voice was calm and detached.

Too tired to question his ordering her, she walked beside him through the gardens, their scents subdued by the cold, their fountains tinkling like crystal, lit by tall, standing torches.

They had all but entered the house before she realised he had taken her back to Green Fragrance Court.

'But why?' Sorrow vied with stupefaction in her tired mind.

'Because you have been happy here. I have something to tell you. I hope there is some happiness in it.'

'What is it?' She was alert again. 'Is it about Shing-jen?'

'He knows about it,' Chinghiz said evasively, standing back for her to cross the threshold before him.

In the soft-coloured room the birds were asleep. She tried vainly not to feel that it was devastatingly empty, would always be so, into the distant recesses of her unwanted old age.

Chinghiz made her sit upon her couch and drink some of the brandy that Welcome liked. He had been going to allow the priest to tell her, but there had not been time. He was glad, for he considered it his due, all things considered. He had guarded the secret; surely he had earned the right to reveal it.

'I have asked Welcome to join us, and one other, whom you will know. But first, I would like to prepare you for what they will tell you.'

'Welcome? What is this mystery? Please, Chinghiz, you can see that I am tired to death. Say what you have to say, and make an end.'

'Very well.' It must be a shock; better a swift one.

'I want you to cast your mind back to the time when the Magnificent Ancestor, Shih-min, was troubled by a prophecy concerning a certain General Wu. Do you remember?'

'Yes. What of it?' She began to feel irritable. She wanted to sleep.

'Do you also recall the exact promise of the prophecy?'

'More or less. What *are* you getting at?'

He knelt beside her, his blue stare very steady and startlingly sincere. It disturbed her.

'I must tell you now that this prediction was a true one; that it was not for the general, but for the one whom it described – the young woman, by the name of Wu, who was already serving in the Emperor's household.'

Her blood was creeping coldly in her veins before he finished – 'A young woman named Wu Chao, known as Black Jade.'

'I don't believe it.'

'You will.' His voice was grim. 'You must. It is your destiny, your karma, you must accept it – and be worthy of it.'

He waited, thought and breath suspended. Had he done well? Was this the spur that was needed to make her control her mourning for the loss of her priest? Or would it prove too much for her, overwhelm her, and produce the catastrophe that could cast her down forever?

Except that, of course, it would not, could not, cast her down.

'You are going to be the first ruling Empress of the Flowery Kingdom,' he said. She heard the jubilation in him then, and for a moment she hated him. She said nothing, only looked into the face she had trusted above all others, and knew that, without doubt, without mercy, without any possibility of escape for her, he spoke the truth.

He went on talking; telling her of the astrologer's visit to her cradle, of Welcome's fall from grace, of his own determination to keep the secret until the time came when she should need it to give her strength. And that he judged that time to have come.

When at last he fell silent, she did not reply at once, but sat quietly, almost somnolently, looking at her folded hands.

'You say that Shing-jen knows of this?' she said eventually.

His mouth twisted. 'He too has the uncomfortable gift of prophecy.'

'And that was why he left me?'

'That is not my business.'

'No? But it was his leaving that has made you speak now, rather than at some later date?'

'Yes.'

'And you think it a kindness?' He could not read her face.

'I hope that you also will come to think so.'

'Perhaps.' Gravely, she tried to smile. 'It was a heavy thing to carry, all these years.'

'I regret only that I must now place the weight on your shoulders.'

'Where, evidently, it belongs. It is hard to realise. You must forgive me if I am a little slow; I am only just beginning to believe you, I think.' He saw with joy a wisp of mischief appear. 'So *this* is the reason why you have been so insufferably superior? I may make you pay for that, my sardonyx!'

'In any coin you care to name!' He welcomed the hardening of her tone.

'I shall think about it. Meanwhile, had you not better prepare something hot and bracing for the Grand Astrologer? He is an old man, and not so well able to sustain a shock as I am.'

He grinned. Of course she had guessed who would come.

'And as for Welcome,' she added wrily, 'I do believe the greatest shock of all is the knowledge that she could have kept the secret for as long as she did.'

'And do you forgive us, for keeping it so long?' he asked, because he had to know.

'For that, yes. For telling me – I don't know. It is too early. I don't know, yet, what I think. Don't talk to me about it, will you, Chinghiz? Not until I ask you. I need time to try to accept it.'

He bowed his head. The weight, after all, had not left him. It had, on the contrary, doubled; the price of his love.

When the astrologer arrived, a little, brisk old man with a sense of humour, she was able to speak sensibly and kindly to him.

Welcome, who tottered in bubbling with guilty tears, she embraced and sent back immediately to bed. Before she went, she insisted upon giving Black Jade the dragon pendant she had played with as a child.

'No. Not yet.' Her mistress smiled, touching her cheek. 'Not until the day when it will be truly mine.'

All that long night she lay awake, trying to believe that such a day would dawn.

21

The following months were strange and bleak. Black Jade rose every morning to the emptiness that was Shing-jen's absence and the odd, astonishing fullness that was the prophecy. She went, quiet and bemused, about her business, worrying her children and dismaying her husband, as, with a slowness that was the complement of her reluctance, she came to some sort of acceptance of the prediction.

'But there is no certainty in me,' she cautioned Chinghiz, who had been waiting, she complained, like a cat at a mousehole, until she should speak of it. 'Prophecies have been mistaken. I have a husband, who is the Emperor, and four sons to follow him. It seems absurd to imagine that I should take the place of any one of them.'

'Not quite absurd.' Chinghiz was not afraid to voice the truth. 'Your husband is not a healthy man.'

She rounded on him. 'In that case I should be the Empress

Dowager, no more. The prophecy offers me the throne in my own right.'

'And that,' Chinghiz swore, 'is what you will have.'

Before she could summon a harsh answer he asked, 'Don't you want it, not at all? I have often thought that you would welcome it.'

She shook her head. 'I don't know,'she said flatly.

It was an honest answer. He had to be content with it.

Pheasant, in penitent mood, set himself to please her.

Lord Shang was exiled, and his family with him; all except his granddaughter, Full of Grace, an attractive child whose quick wits led Black Jade to take her into her own household. She had never liked the law that allowed the innocent to suffer with the guilty. She caught herself with the thought that, one day, she might change it.

As was her nature, she made work her escape from troublesome thoughts. She gradually gave up the small hope of a message reaching her from Shing-jen's Himalayan retreat, though for a long time she could not admit that he was gone from her as surely as the ghosts he had exorcised; as though their love had been, as he had once described the elixir of immortality, no more than a seductive illusion.

Steadily, with the aid of Chinghiz's especial brand of acid and affectionate humour, the energetic demands of her little Tigers, and the renewed dependence of her husband, she began, because she was a healthy and sensible young woman, to take an interest in the future again.

She had only just begun to do so when two events took place which rocked her tentative new foundations. Firstly, her dear friend and surrogate father, Abbot Hsuan-tsang, died, suddenly and surprisingly in the middle of reading one of his precious sutras, his hand falling across the page of illustrated demons, his stout heart stopping with kindly abruptness.

Almost before Black Jade had begun to mourn for the good old man, she was shaken by the second trauma: the shocked realisation that the nausea she had felt as she watched beside the Abbot's catafalque in the incense-heavy temple was not the result of her heart's grief for his premature end but of her stomach's celebration of a new beginning.

Almost exactly nine months after Shing-jen's departure, she would give birth to a child.

'What can I *do*?' she demanded of Chinghiz, pacing her

glowing rooms as though they were a cage. 'I don't know what to feel!'

'What *do* you feel?' Her servitor's interest was faintly malign. Since the priest had gone he had recovered his ebullient wit, with an excess, she considered, of glittering edge.

'Oh – desperate, foolish and enchanted, all at once! This is what I most dreaded; and yet, to have a child of Shing-jen's – ' her eyes misted tenderly.

'If,' remarked the Tartar sardonically, 'it *is* his child.'

Enraged, she threw a vase at him. He caught it easily, raising his brows and grinning at her.

'You are not helping!' she complained, but smiled despite herself.

'What do you think should be done?' He would know, as he always knew such arcane things, what to do about an unwanted child.

He observed her sternly, seeking her true desire.

'About this time,' he said finally, 'you usually begin to pray for a girl.'

'There are times,' she retorted icily, 'when I could find it in me to dislike you.'

'It wouldn't last,' he advised her callously. 'I am *far* too useful. I don't know what you're worrying about,' he added with his most feline smile. 'The Emperor will be delighted!'

Naturally, Pheasant was delighted. He was overjoyed. A child was just what was needed to cement his restored connubial relations. It also removed the nagging doubt with regard to his virility; he could not manage the clouds and rain as frequently as he would like, though Black Jade excited him as much as ever, perhaps even more than before. There was a new elusiveness about her since the episode of the priest; it intrigued him, and offered the kind of sexual challenge he liked. He got out the old manuals, and sent for some new ones from India, complete with quite amazing pictures.

Black Jade accepted his increasingly unusual attentions as her penance from the Gods, and looked forward to the time when her pregnancy would make them impossible.

Pheasant's immodest appetites apart, there followed a period of unusual tranquillity. The removal of Lord Shang had signalled the death throes of the old opposition of the Wang clan and their followers, and Jade now found herself seated very comfortably on the Phoenix Throne. The Son of Heaven relied upon her; the ministers, for the most part, approved of her. There were even times when she could almost imagine herself the figure of the prophecy.

Imagination cost nothing. It was amusing to dream a little. It was true that she would make an excellent ruling Empress. It was, to all intents and purposes, what she had been for the past several months.

But dreams were not realities, and neither were unfulfilled prophecies. Although she supposed that, somewhere in the most distant part of her mind, she had begun to accept the possibility that she might one day rule, she would leave it hidden in those depths. It was no part of her work to assist the Gods; if it was written, as the disciples of that warlike prophet, Mahomet, said, then it would come to pass.

She plunged into a determined effort to build up Pheasant's flagging confidence. He was subject to bouts of depression, when he would be incapable of coherent thought or decision. Disturbed by this, she discussed with the council the possibility of restoring him to himself by means of the ancient rituals of *Feng* and *Shan*.

These rites, performed on the sacred mountain of Taishan in Shantung, were the symbolic statement, before Heaven and his people, of the satisfaction of the Empire with its sovereign. No Son of Heaven would insult his Celestial Father by offering them unless he was convinced of his achievements.

Pheasant was first surprised, then doubtful. He did not feel that he had been spectacularly successful. But when the omens were consulted, they were favourable, and with Lion Guard's help, Pheasant was eventually persuaded. Preparation began for the journey, via Loyang, to the sacred mountain. They would leave shortly before the new year.

Meanwhile Black Jade had a task of her own to perform.

At dawn on a summer day in the season of Great Heat, the miracle happened. She gave birth to a daughter.

'What is she like?' she demanded drowsily, as Chinghiz took the child from Welcome's unwilling hands, and held her as he would hold an antique vase.

'Like you.'

'You know what I mean.'

'Only you. She is like no one else. See for yourself. Look, she has the enchanter's gift. Green eyes.'

Relieved, she dared to gaze at her daughter, and, having gazed, was at once her slave.

'Oh, but she is exquisite! The most perfect baby I have ever had! Her skin is exactly the colour of apricots; and she is so beautifully proportioned already.'

'There you are, you see?' said Chinghiz magniloquently. 'At last, you have got what you wanted.'

'Yes, indeed,' she said, devouring the diminished image of herself with limitless contentment, patently ignoring any claim her servant might make to her production of the prodigy. 'I do believe the Gods have forgiven me my sins at last.'

'Oh, indubitably. But I expect you will find some more to commit, when you are ready.'

'Go away, you insolent man!' She smiled provocatively. 'Tell the Emperor he has a daughter!'

'It will be my pleasure,' he replied, carefully erasing all colour from his voice.

Pheasant surrounded her with the usual boatload of jewels and silks, scrolls and paintings, and the latest Indian manual, for later. Black Jade rested amongst them with the expression of the Buddha at his most beatific. She dressed in a pure, singing red, in a spirit of ecstatic self-congratulation, and was out of bed before she should have been able to stand, lying prone on her face in the temple, giving joyous thanks to the Gods.

It was then, buoyed by gratitude and benzoin incense, that, in the manner of those who have received great gifts, it occurred to her that perhaps this was the turning-point in her existence. Perhaps, after all, the Gods had more to offer her than forgiveness? She determined to make a test of their further wishes. She would confront them on the holy mountain, on Taishan; there, if they had chosen her, they might show it.

The name of the little Princess had been chosen long ago – Taiping, the Restorer of Peace and Tranquillity. Soon, however, with the same inevitability by which her two-year-old brother had become Dawn Tiger, she took her unique place in the family menagerie with the mellifluous and entirely suitable name of Tiger Lily. She had, as Chinghiz pointed out, to cover the fact that he too was besotted by the delicate creature, the complexion, when roused, of the gaudy flower, and the unleashed temper of the fighting cat.

'We shall have to keep Mao-yu's grandchildren away from her cradle,' was his opinion, 'in case she sits on their faces.'

With her new favour with the Gods in mind, Black Jade began to prepare herself, like the rest of the court, for *Feng* and *Shan*.

She wanted to set a precedent. No woman had ever taken part

in the sacrifices. But it seemed to her that since during the *Feng*, the worship of the earth, the spirits who share the offerings are those of previous Empresses, it would be more appropriate if they were served by their own sex. She sent a memo to the Emperor to this effect.

The ministerial debate that followed was long and heated. Many would not hear of feminine sacrifice. Some called it sacrilege.

Little by little, Lion Guard and her other friends talked them round. No woman, they pointed out, had ever run the administration before, or had directed the course of a successful war. They owed Black Jade far more than mere gratitude, and here was the ideal manner in which to honour their debt.

The debt was undeniable. The Empress was invited to plan her part in the ceremonies.

By way of spiritual preparation, she increased her visits to Kan Yeh, spending time in contemplation and debate with the nuns. She did not expect to recapture the innocence of her conscience, but she could offer the Gods a strong will towards it.

The *Feng Shan* procession became a legend in the countryside. Thirty miles of men and horses, carriages and cattle, baggage and banners made its way through the land with the appetite of an invading army which, in many ways, it resembled.

Every duke, general and minister of rank had his family and retinue with him, and expected princely entertainment in the towns through which he travelled. The extravagant cavalcade also contained several foreign ambassadors, including the son of the exhausted Korean despot, the emissary of Japan, and representatives from India, Turkey, Persia, Kashmir and Turkestan. Nothing could have signalled more clearly the present supremacy of the Empire.

For Black Jade, it represented an escape: from her multitude of responsibilities, from the claustrophobia of the palace city, from the need always to think and to plan. She valued every dust-veiled day, thrived on the dreams of every novel night. They were undisturbed nights too, for upon this pilgrimage the Son of Heaven, above all men, must be celibate. Her thoughts, therefore, were free to fly where they would.

The holy mountain was the highest in the northern part of the Empire, rising over 1,500 metres above the Yellow River Valley, crowning a majestic range which spread across 600 kilometres. As they approached the mighty peak, snaking up from the south, every step sustained the illusion that it had sprung straight out of the ground before them. Such magnificence cast an awed silence over the temporal splendour of the imperial cortege.

That night Pheasant kept vigil in the temple of the God of Taishan. He knelt before the blue-painted circle of the altar of Heaven, surrounded by a comforting forest of imperial yellow flags, and prayed with a deadly and humble earnestness that he might indeed be found worthy to make the sacrifice.

In the morning, New Year's Day, the court rose at dawn, robed themselves extravagantly and walked in procession to join him, watched by the range of roseate peaks which leaned in upon them in giant curiosity.

Black Jade was a mere spectator of this ceremony, the *Shan*, the Emperor's worship of Heaven. She stood in veiled anonymity among the ladies of the court, willing him towards confidence and self-respect, as she had done on the day of his accession and many times since.

The worshippers stood in three concentric terraces around the blue altar, the choir and orchestra filling most of the space behind it. The Thousand Scented Incense rose and lulled their senses as the Son of Heaven made his offerings to the God and his ancestors, his slow, reverent movements punctuated by drums and bells. His thanks for the vital gift of a good harvest and other manifold blessings were set down in three Letters Patent, inscribed in gold upon three slender wands of jade. The two which bore the names of his father and grandfather would be put in gold boxes and carried back to the Temple of the Ancestors in Chang-an. The other, which was addressed to the God of Heaven, was placed in a casket of jade beneath the altar. When the long ceremony was over and they were able to be together, Pheasant said hesitantly to his wife, 'I can't believe it; I have been accepted by the God. Right up to the last moment, before I laid the tablet in the casket, I was more than half expecting some terrible mark of disfavour – a fearful storm, perhaps, or even an eclipse.'

Black Jade squeezed his hand beneath the stiff brocade.

'You must learn to think much better of yourself,' she smiled.

'Was I all right? Not too undignified?'

'As dignified as the Yellow Emperor,' she assured him.

After the ceremony they began the ascent to Heaven.

From dawn to dusk the yellow palanquins climbed steadily, following the route which Confucius himself had taken, more than a thousand years ago.

They moved through scenes of unsurpassable beauty. The path

was wide and well-kept, leading through groves of ancient pines, past rocks and monuments inscribed by their predecessors, the enlarged scarlet calligraphy scarring them as though they bled; past the caves of hermits who ran out to meet them; past a hundred shrines and chapels; past the home of a tiger who had been netted only last week; past carved archways standing in sudden grandeur; past the sweet rush of waterfalls, and the swift tinkle and skitter of belled mountain sheep.

The winter evening closed on them quickly. The companion peaks turned slowly from purple through grey to black, outlined against a sunset that heralded the presence of the God in colours of fire and flowers. They watched them change, muting and merging with the passage of the hours, until at last, tired out, they were left in a darkness that breathed with mystery.

The God was very near. They had reached the Halfway Gate to Heaven.

They stayed that night as guests of the Dragon King Temple, and the next morning continued upward. The path gradually narrowed, then became winding stone steps over which the bearers trod warily lest they jolt their precious burdens. Looking upwards to the summit, the white steps appeared to hang before them in the sky, while an infinite distance below, the Wenhe River wound like a single curling hair from the beard of a white barbarian. To the east stood Middle Brook Mountain, a majestic acolyte; to the west lay the Phoenix Range, where the legendary birds had built their eyries.

At dusk they reached the pass to the Gate of Heaven, guarding the path to the summit itself. In a freshening wind they came through a blue and rose gateway and saw the stair before them, leading on upward into the firmament. On the utmost height, upon Jade Emperor Peak, stood the temple where tomorrow's rite would take place.

Weary with exaltation and drugged with too much beauty, they ate quietly in the guest-house, the cinnabar sunset filling the windows, and then slept like children until it was time to get up and watch the dawn.

Black Jade awoke suddenly, as though a voice had called her.

She put on layers of light, warm wool and stole softly out of the house. The guards saluted as she passed, but understood that she wanted no companion.

Her breath gusted before her on the wind that was constant at this height. It was very cold, but the air was exhilarating, like drinking spring water. There was not much light yet, only a heavy, grey-gold blanket of cloud and mist. She walked quickly to the place marked as the ultimate summit.

A giant spur of rock thrust outwards into the void, directly opposite the point on the horizon where the sun would rise. Just now she could see neither sun nor horizon, only a vast curdled and colourless sea of cloud, stretching below, around and above in endless banks of whipped vapour, just beginning to contain the promise of gold. She went out on to the edge of the spur and sat down as, she sensed, was intended.

There was no sense of time, nor of herself, as the Gods conducted for her the daily entertainment that few mortals were ever to appreciate. As the cloud-bank became warm and gilded and the air around her cleared, the mist swirled away as though it had urgent business elsewhere. She became conscious then of many presences. The same golden messengers were here whom Shing-jen had sent her, with the same joy and hope to impart. She could not see them, but she felt their nearness, their never-changing wonder that was akin to hers as the mighty orchestration of colour and shifting shapes began.

First came a mere warning, like an experimental chord or two on a lute, as the horizon made itself known, splitting the sky in a strip of citrus, striking echoes from the cloud above and below. The lemon turned slowly to true gold, solemnly, as though to the purity of flutes. There was a long interlude during which other colours entered, tentative, pale and delicate, the smudged suggestion of heliotrope and blue-grey. The clouds were lifting and clearing, carried on the Dragon King's breath, sweeping clean the deepening horizontal stripe. The sun was a positive presence now, the widening glow of a hidden alchemist's crucible, transfixing the eye with its presence.

And then, like the sudden beat of a drum, slow, regular and a little threatening, the great orb began to lift. Colour burst from it, splashing the cloud and the rock with rose. The horizon revealed itself not as cloud but as sea.

She was looking at the Eastern Sea, the very edge of her universe; a universe of which she, mysteriously, was the centre. She waited, intoxicated, with exultant laughter bubbling in her throat, for the tremendous piece of theatre to conclude.

It came at last with a triumphant fanfare of flame and orpiment, the cloud dividing to unfold a path straight from the heart of the magnificent ball of flame to her feet, so that she sat upon her tiny spur, hanging far out above her disguised and dreamlike world, and almost believed that she could walk into the sun.

It was over. She had taken her gift of knowledge and certainty. She closed her eyes and moved to prostrate herself before the God. Somewhere the golden shapes were singing, in gladness and praise.

She had lain there for a long time when she felt a hesitant touch on her shoulder.

It was Pheasant. He smiled, a little sad in his sacrificial robes. 'I had thought we might watch the sunrise together.'

She rose and shook her head, surprised by the affection she felt for him.

'It has risen without you,' she said.

On the third day the ceremony of *Feng* took place. There was a rumour of excitement among the ranks of courtiers as they waited about the square, yellow-painted altar of the earth. Would the God show his displeasure when a woman offered him sacrifice? They concealed impatience with reverence as the Emperor blessed the offerings, drank the wine and poured the first libation.

The music softened and the incense was filled with flowers. Black Jade came down the steps of the terraces, leading a demure crocodile of consorts and ladies-in-waiting. She wore a coruscating white and gold gown, thick with the wings of phoenixes, and her calm and lovely face was curtained by the twelve strings of pearls depending from her imperial crown. As she walked between the yellow banners, she saw the proud and happy faces of her family and friends on either side; Lion Guard, nodding his approval, all his plans for her justified; the Great Wall, resting his injured leg on a stick, gazing fiercely ahead, his chin working with unsoldierly emotion; her older children, standing with their tutors, Bold Tiger tense with the grandeur of the moment, Young Tiger controlling a sudden giggle and Loud Tiger, alas, grinning widely and irreligiously as she passed, catching the threatening eye of Welcome next to him. Last of all, as she approached the steps to the altar, she saw through her veil of pearls the triumphant Tartar face of Chinghiz, his slanted eyes blazing with pride. Last night they had spoken, briefly, of her new acceptance of her karma, and he had seized and held her by the shoulders in his delight, his blue stare piercing her soul, that only he, of all those present here, had begun to understand.

Her ladies closing like dancers behind her, she ascended the shallow steps to the altar. There she knelt before the spirit tablets of Pheasant's mother and grandmother, and made the oblations of food and wine. The scent and the song arose in clouds about her glittering head, and once again, for the last time, she was aware of the golden guests who blessed her sacrifice, and required, on behalf of their master, a greater one.

Her prostration was again her acceptance. Behind her a soft concerted sigh recognised that she, too, had been accepted.

She was well aware that she rose from the altar much changed. The inward change none but she could truly know. Outwardly, in the eyes of the councillors, the ministers, the priests, she was the first woman whose offering had pleased the God, and her influence and power were increased immeasureably from that moment.

Her destiny was unique and terrifying. She would try with all her strength to be equal to it. She saw that, from this day, she must no longer indulge in dreams that looked back. Before she left Taishan she set down her farewell to those dreams.

> The sun hangs rose and gold above the Eastern
> Sea
> Veiled in cloud as infinite as grief.
> Past and future ... it is here they meet.
> The wind has worn the rock ten thousand years,
> Ten thousand years the river ruled the plain.
> The Dragon of the North still clasps his pinnacle,
> The Phoenix still flashes in the flood,
> But I will wear away ten thousand years
> Before I watch the sunrise with my love.

The imperial couple returned to Chang-an with their popularity much increased. Heaven had approved the dynasty, and the Empire shared its good fortune in various practically acceptable ways, such as grants, amnesties and the foundation of temples.

Black Jade, whom people found quieter than usual, settled swiftly into all her waiting tasks. There was, however, a thorn in her rose-garden; two thorns, to be exact. Pheasant had accepted the services of two young acolytes who had travelled from the outskirts of the Empire to beg to serve him. It was only after they had joined the court that she had learned the names of the favoured pair; they were Stout Heart and Kind Heart, the sons of her childhood's secondary tormenter, Brother Hyena.

'Whatever made you do such a thing? You must have known how I would dislike it!' Jade had demanded, puzzled and disturbed.

Pheasant looked at her mildly. 'It seemed an act of compassion, appropriate to the time, to welcome them back into our family. Their father is dead, and his misdemeanours with him. They are pleasant boys, well-educated. I could not let them waste away their youth on the border; they have committed no crime. And they are your nephews. I thought you would applaud me for it.'

On the surface he was right; she could not fault him. But her instinct lived below the surface, and it reacted warily.

'Perhaps you are right,' was all she said to Pheasant, smiling. 'I don't recall their mother, but let us hope they take after her.'

'They do not, at any rate, remotely resemble hyenas,' smiled her husband drily. 'You will like them. They are good company.'

They were presented to her as she sat in the first spring sunshine, beneath a striped awning, discussing tax relief with a group of junior ministers.

They were attractive boys. Stout Heart even had a look of his grandfather, the General. His bow was studied, his compliments apt.

'Your Highness reminds me of the Goddess of the Lo herself, holding court among her immortals.'

The Empress widened her astonishing green eyes. 'Indeed? I am honoured to make the acquaintance of a gentleman who has had commerce with such a deity.'

Her eldest nephew withstood the laughter good-humouredly. 'I have not had that pleasure,' he said, 'but it could not compare with my present happiness.' His voice was warm; his eyes were not.

And now his brother was making his bow at his side. Kind Heart was plump and loudly dressed. She had seen him look longingly at one of her maids; in that he was his father's son.

'It has always been my dream to meet Your Highness; ever since I was a child. And now the dream has come true.' He beamed about him, including the knot of courtiers in his rich fulfilment.

'I wonder why,' Jade said, attracting his bashful stare. 'I would have thought your childhood view of myself a less than favourite dream.'

'Highness?' He put his hand on his heart. 'Our father taught us to honour you as the flower of our family and the fountain of all good.'

Now she knew her instinct had been right. Their father had hated her, and had brought them up in that hatred. Also to be hypocritical, devious and opportunist, like himself and his brother.

She made them welcome that morning, her friendly, neutral

demeanour including them with her young friends. But when she returned to Chang-an she avoided them, pleading the pressure of work when they called on her. Soon their visits stopped. Chinghiz, deputed to keep an eye on them, reported that they had become the nucleus of a coterie of young bloods surrounding the Emperor in his sociable moods, a group much given to laughter and the company of consorts.

She gave them no further thought until the rumours began. It was her mother, distressed, who brought her the first one.

'My maid told me; she thinks she was *intended* to overhear; two young men in the bazaar – she didn't know them – they spoke of poor Rose Bird's fatherless child, called her filthy names!' Golden Willow was nearly weeping. 'And they said that I had done away with the child, to keep the birth a secret. Black Jade, why would people say such things? And why now? It was all so long ago. If Lotus Bud should hear it, she would be so deeply hurt. And Sage Path would run riot in the streets!'

Rose Bird's children now lived with their grandmother in the pretty house where the holy men still met every week.

'It isn't like you to be naive,' said Black Jade gently.

Golden Willow stared hard at her daughter. Then she nodded. 'No, it isn't. But what can we do about this?' she asked grimly.

'They will overreach themselves; then we shall see,' said the Empress.

It happened very soon.

Black Jade was crackling with anger. Chinghiz gave up his attempt to do her hair in a new style and let her talk.

'To tell his lies to Loud Tiger! Imagine, a child of nine! The boy came to ask me for a string for his bow – he uses them as fast as cash candles – and enquired, in passing, whether it were true that his cousin Lotus Bud was an imperial concubine! Stout Heart had told him that her uncle used her as one. When he asked him what he meant, he just sniggered and told him to forget it.'

'Ah.' Chinghiz examined the turned-up toes of his gilded shoes.

'Look at me,' she ordered. '*Amitabha*! What do you know?'

'Nothing, for certain,' he said quickly. 'But there is a *breadth*, already, to that particular story, that suggests some truth in it.'

'Lotus Bud is a child!'

'She is sixteen. And extremely pretty.' He wished he could spare her.

'She's his niece!'

'Her uncle is in the habit of visiting her unusually often.'

'Chinghiz, she lives with my *mother*!'

'Who is generally out when His Majesty calls.'

Black Jade sat down suddenly. 'Merciful Kuan Yin, can this be true? Pheasant has taken up with a couple of the concubines again; I knew that. But this – this is inconceivable! Surely he wouldn't take advantage of a child like that?'

'The word is that he has. I imagine the Wu boys are the source of the rumour. It may even have been their idea. Their influence tends towards the sensual. I only wish I had known earlier; I learned only an hour ago. I planned to be certain before I spoke to you.'

She rejected her revulsion and made herself think.

'He was always fond of Lotus Bud, even when she was a baby, forever picking her up and letting her scramble all over him. But now, as you say, she is not a child. She is a girl on the verge of womanhood, and very like her mother, for whom you will recall my husband also had a tenderness.' She met his eyes, her own dark with misery. 'I need to know the truth of this. And, whatever the case, I want those boys out of the palace.'

'I'll bring you news as soon as I can.'

She shook her head. 'I know a quicker way.'

That afternoon she visited Pheasant. Stronger and more confident than he had been for some months now, his immediate desire was to make love to her. She suppressed a shudder at the idea, and pretended interest in the illustrated volume of the *Karma Sutra* someone had sent him.

As he reached for her breast, inspired by a blue goddess writhing entwined with a pink god with an elephant's trunk, she put her question to him, her voice dripping with sweetness.

'They say you have introduced our Lotus Bud to the clouds and rain.'

His look of dismay was comic and revealing. 'Do they? Why should they say such a foolish thing?'

'Have you?'

Pheasant sat up and huffily pulled his kimono together.

'I wish you wouldn't listen to gutter talk.'

'The moon is reflected with truth, even in the gutter,' she suggested. 'I would like to know, my lord. I am very fond of Lotus Bud.'

'So am I. Curse it, what do you want me to say? I thought I might make her one of the consorts, that's all. Not as a concubine, but as a protection for *her*. She tells me she doesn't want to marry, and she'd be miserable in a convent.'

'I see. You don't consider Golden Willow sufficient protection?'

'It isn't that.' He sought and found a reason. 'It's that brother of hers. Sage Path is hardly the best example for a young girl. Your mother doesn't seem to be able to control him.'

'He is also your responsibility. You should take a stronger line with him. As for Lotus Bud, don't you think it a little foolish to offer scandalmongers the opportunity of dragging up the old accusation of incest?'

'It isn't – wouldn't be incest! She's your niece, not mine.'

'Technically she is yours too. It is a technical crime.'

'Damnation,' Pheasant swore wretchedly. 'What do you suppose I had better do about it?'

She deduced from this that her husband had indeed relieved his niece of her virginity. She was hurt by it, and she also disliked him for it on Lotus Bud's behalf. He was looking at her like a child or a dog caught out in some small malpractice; he simply did not have the ability, she thought, to distinguish levels of misbehaviour, not when it was his own.

There was no use in making a fuss; it would not improve matters for any of them. 'It will have to finish,' she said clearly. 'You must make up your mind to that.' She left him to think about it.

Pheasant's answer to the problem, by no means a foolish one, was to make Lotus Bud a duchess in her own right, as her mother had been. The rank, and the power it conferred, would place her above the tongue of idle gossip. They would mark the occasion with a public celebration, at which the Empress's affection for her niece would be noticed, together with Pheasant's purely avuncular interest. There would be an archery contest, followed by a banquet given by Golden Willow.

The young Tigers had insisted on charioteering. Archery on its own, they said, was too tame. So Black Jade stood near the narrowest bend on the Chariot Park, holding Dawn Tiger's hand while he jumped up and down like a paper lion-dog on a spring, and talked to Lotus Bud, who was carrying an alert Tiger Lily to the detriment of her pink and blue gauze.

'Well, how do you like your new importance?' she shouted, as they watched the Crown Prince career past, edging out Loud Tiger who was making up for extreme youth with a brutal concentration and blood-curdling equine encouragement. 'Your uncle and I so much want to make you happy.'

Lotus Bud dropped her eyes, colouring. She was Rose Bird all over again, soft, pliable, with the same glowing skin and curving body.

'You have both been very kind.' She did not sound at all happy. 'It is far, far more than I deserve.' Tiger Lily blew some bubbles.

Black Jade understood her trouble. She patted her hand kindly, then absently transferred her own to her daughter's back, in case of wind.

'Nonsense! You deserve very well, of all of us. Be happy, my dear, and enjoy your good fortune. It is a new beginning.' She briefly caressed the shining hair that the baby was using as a bell-rope.

'You make a simply splendid duchess; so tall and so pretty! But I'm afraid there will be *battalions* of young men, queuing to beg for your hand. Are you really so set against marriage?'

Lotus Bud looked about as if hunted.

'No. That is – I can't – ' She floundered, crimson, drawing curious glances from Jade's ladies. 'You don't understand,' she finished, clutching Tiger Lily so tightly that she yelled.

'I do, believe me.' Jade took the child and directed her attention back to the rushing two-wheeled chariots. 'When I married the Emperor,' she said, also watching the race, 'he was not, as you know, the first man I had known. I don't know what the future holds for you – but my advice is to forget the past and enjoy the moment. It is advice,' she added ruefully, 'I often have to give myself. Cheer up, now, there's a good girl. This is your feast day!'

'Yes. Of course,' said Lotus Bud, smiling like an image. She must try for Black Jade's sake to shake off her sadness. She was so kind; she, who had been betrayed. But she wished she had not spoken of marriage. Who would marry her, now, whatever the Empress said? And besides, she loved Pheasant in a way, uncle or not. She was not sure, having no other experience of the feeling, exactly which way it was.

Bold Tiger won the race. It was his third win. His mother disengaged herself from his small brother and went to speak to him.

'My dear, do you think you could bear to let Loud Tiger win, just once? If he doesn't, after trying so furiously, I'm afraid he might burst something; his lungs, or our eardrums probably.'

'Mother! Are you asking me to cheat?'

She sighed. Bold Tiger could be growing into a prig. 'Not at all,' she said sweetly. 'I'm asking you to show the virtue of brotherly love.'

'Oh all right,' he grumbled. 'But you needn't worry. He'll most likely beat me hollow at the butts.'

Loud Tiger won the next race. He arrived at the finish purple-faced and covered in dust, roaring with pride.

'I did it! Mother, did you see? I beat Eldest Brother! I'm the champion! Come on now, and watch me shooting!' He tugged at her hand.

Such unabashed afflatus made her wonder whether she should have let well alone. 'It is not done to boast,' she reminded him. 'You should consider, while you are shooting, what Confucius had to say on the subject.'

Loud Tiger pulled at his topknot. 'What was it?' he asked, deflated.

She said sternly, 'Archery is like the life of a good man. When an archer misses the bull's-eye, he turns to seek his failure in himself.'

'Oh yes, now I remember,' Loud Tiger beamed.

'He was talking,' said Black Jade hopelessly, 'about humility.'

When they reached the wide oblong of grass where the butts were set, they found Young Tiger already there, practising with a new bow he had invented. It had a mechanism, he said, that would ensure a straight shot every time.

'But surely it still all depends on the marksman's eye,' Black Jade said, looking doubtfully at the cumbersome array of splints and chocks at the centre of his bow.

'Well, yes; but I'm trying to eliminate all but human error,' her scientific son explained with generous patience.

The music began, announcing the start of the contest. Black Jade joined Pheasant on the banner-draped dais in the open pavilion opposite the row of targets. The crowd greeted them vocally.

There were six targets. The archers in the opening competition were the three young princes, their cousin Sage Path, and the Wu nephews, whom the Emperor had refused to dismiss, on the grounds that it was impossible to find the source of a piece of gossip. And also, brooded Jade, to repay her for having spoiled his entertainment with Lotus Bud.

She watched as Stout Heart drew his bow, his body perfectly aligned, his thoughts inward, waiting for the flute-player to hit the note that would loose his arrow. The note came; the arrow sped. She saw again the broken breast of a white bird, the arrow vibrating against the golden bars of a cage. She didn't want them here, these sons of her stepbrother. There could never be anything but enmity between the two sides of her family.

'The boy has scored a bull!' cried Pheasant, applauding. He saw her face. 'What's wrong?' She mentioned the sore memory.

Pheasant was annoyed. 'I don't know why you can't forget these old, unkind emotions! Stout Heart is a good lad; I like him. His brother too. You can't go on blaming them for the ancient past.'

'I don't.' She held his eye. 'You know what I *do* blame them for. They are attacking me by attacking the reputation of my mother's side of the family. If you are content with that – '

He moved uneasily. 'They both denied even *hearing* about Rose Bird. Rumour,' he repeated, 'is a hard thing to hunt home.'

'Did you ask them about the other little matter?'

'How could I?' He was losing his temper now. 'You ask too much!'

'Quite. You should, however, take the precaution of removing our nephews, before anything further needs hunting home.'

'Why should I? I find them harmless, amusing and agreeable.'

'Really? *I* find them evil-minded, unctuous and self-seeking.' They smiled brightly at each other, aware of possible eavesdroppers. The argument ended with the arrival of Loud Tiger, who had, as his brother predicted, won his part of the contest and had come to be congratulated. He went on to challenge the champions of the Imperial Company of Archers, who, piqued at such startling ability in a nine-year-old, treated him to some fierce competition. They did not let him win, but were so impressed with his manner of losing that they thumped his small back until it bruised.

Later, as she finished dressing for the banquet, Black Jade remembered the gift she had for Lotus Bud. She refused Chinghiz's offer to be her courier, wanting to reassure the girl before she made her next public appearance.

She found her niece sitting before her mirror in tears. She sent the distressed maid away and handed Lotus Bud some tissues.

'Tell me,' she urged gently. 'You mustn't cry. Your eyes will be red.'

Lotus Bud raised large flooded eyes to the aunt who already knew all there was to know about her. The patient kindness tore her heart.

'Stout Heart was here, a moment ago.'

Pheasant had insisted that the brothers, as family, were invited.

'He called me names.' The soft eyes were ashamed.

'Is that all?'

'No. He said I must ask – my uncle – to raise him to the same rank as myself. He said it was unfair and unfitting that Your Highness's relatives should remain commoners.'

'I seem to have heard that before. What did you reply?'

'I refused. It is not my place to make such requests.' She did not say that, in the case of her refusal, Stout Heart had threatened her with the sexual attentions of both himself and his plump, hot-eyed brother. 'I hate them!' she burst out. 'I hate the way they flatter my uncle, and whisper to him, making him laugh at people who are his friends.'

'Don't worry, child. Pheasant is easily flattered. But why the tears? You seem to have dealt very well with your second cousin.'

'He frightened me,' Lotus Bud stammered. 'Before he left, he twisted my arm and said that if I didn't do what he wished, I would find the consequences very painful.' This was true, he had also pinched her breast, hard, and devoured her lips with his tongue thrust down her throat.

'He is ambitious and cruel,' she said, angry now. 'He intends to rise at court, with my uncle's support. He says our side of the Wu family have had it our way quite long enough.'

'Does he so?' said Black Jade bleakly. 'I am glad you have told me.' She touched the round cheek. 'You have a brave spirit, Lotus Bud. Now I promise you, you have nothing to worry about. He will not be allowed to hurt you again; and he will pay for that nasty mark on your arm. Now, dry your eyes and look inside this box!'

A slave of gratitude, Lotus Bud summoned a waterlogged smile and did as she was told. 'Oh, how beautiful! You shouldn't!'

The necklace was of tiny corals, carved in the likeness of her name; there were earrings to match. It was the perfect complement to her silk-skinned beauty. There were more tears. Then Black Jade showed her, with devastating practicality, how to hide their ravages.

'There,' she cried when she had finished. 'Every inch a duchess. We shall enter the banqueting hall together and there will be an ascending sigh of admiration.'

Lotus Bud smiled passionately. She thought Black Jade the most beautiful woman in the world, and one who outdid the Buddha for loving kindness. Her troubled young heart sank even further beneath the weight of emotion; she regarded herself as lost, and beyond the salvation even of Black Jade.

The small banqueting hall, just big enough for the imperial family and a score or so chosen friends, was a cave of semi-precious stones shimmering in soft light; carpeted, tapestried, a jewelled casket for its jade-and-diamond-studded guests. Lutes breathed; candles gleamed on delicate flesh and superlative stuffs. It was all delightfully intimate; no stiffness, no protocol.

Black Jade and Lotus Bud entered, a little late, glowing like twin lanterns in gold and rose. The room suspired as foretold.

They moved through flower-scented air to their seats at the table facing south. Lotus Bud was placed between the imperial pair.

Behind her, Pheasant leaned towards Jade. 'You look like sisters, of exactly the same age,' he whispered, seizing her hand beneath her muslin sleeve. 'Forgive me?' he said, his eyes burning.

His frequent refrain. She could cheerfully have plunged a knife, had she one handy, into the bulging-eyed dragon over his heart.

'Of course,' she murmured, guileless. 'Sixteen and so lovely; what man would not desire her?' Her lips brushed his ear.

Enchanted, counting himself forgiven, he kept his thigh close to hers whenever he could, and was careful to treat Lotus Bud to a dose of avuncular interest which reduced her to the schoolroom.

The new duchess, though conscious of the honour of her place, would have preferred to be sitting at the east-facing table with her own invited guest, her best friend Sweet Melody, who was batting luxurious eyelashes demurely between Sage Path and Bold Tiger, who had been told to look after her. She saw the three of them laughing together and bit her lip. That was where she belonged, there among her friends, not in her handsome uncle's bed or up here at the head of the table, trying to look like a duchess, and a virginal one at that.

'Little Dumpling,' said her handsome uncle kindly, 'you must hold your chin up. You are our star tonight. Let the past be past,' he added in a whisper, under cover of a dish of baby clams in rose-petal sauce.

She straightened and did her best, picking at the morsels with the ivory chopsticks, carved with her name and the date in gold leaf, which were another keepsake of the occasion. Sage Path caught her eye and grinned, looking wickedly sideways at Sweet Melody. She returned his grin with a wave of her chopsticks, forgetful of her manners. Her brother could always make her feel cheerful, no matter what the circumstances.

And then, suddenly, she wanted to cry again, at the thought of those three, and her cousins and her friends, all young, optimistic and privileged, with long and happy lives before them. Whereas she –

'My dear?'

Black Jade was talking to her.

'– nothing serious. Just a few words, when Pheasant has spoken?'

She nodded. Apparently her uncle was going to make a speech. In her honour. But she had no honour. He above all people should know that. A hysterical giggle threatened; she controlled it and tried to think what she could say in reply to the sentimental nothings that were rolling off the Emperor's caressing and persuasive tongue. She must be calm. She needed some wine. She touched her cup and a servant filled it. Her head was throbbing. He was finishing now. She must be quick. Her sleeve hovered above the winecup; then she lifted and took a few swift gulps. She thought, foolishly, that at least it would cure her headache.

'– and so I give you our toast for this happy occasion – the young and lovely Duchess of Ho-lan, my niece, Lotus Bud.'

She smiled mistily as they all turned towards her, their cups lifted, their faces smiling. Her name rushed at her in an amiable roar, then there was a silence, which she must somehow fill.

She could not get up. A murmur rolled towards her, sympathetic, encouraging. She made a great effort, concentrating all her will on the effort to stand up. There, she had done it. But the will was fading now, could not find or form words, could not make her lips move. She couldn't see properly. Where was Golden Willow? She must tell her, make her understand – There was pain! She cried out.

They saw the red wine arch out over the polished rosewood, and fall. Lotus Bud swayed and crumpled into her chair, her hair streaming over its arm to the ground. Her brother was out of his seat and at her side at once.

He caught her hand and chafed it, shouting her name, angry with fear.

'She does sometimes faint; it must be the excitement – '

It was not the excitement. It was Pheasant who saw first what it was. He went pale and stood very still, his eyes seeking Black Jade's. She read their message and knelt beside the girl's slumped figure, feeling gently for her heart.

She shook her head, her face stark. Next to her, Golden Willow gave a cry and fell back into someone's arms, 'See to her; take her to bed,' Jade ordered. At least she would not also have to face her mother's agony now. She reached behind her, her hand begging blindly for support.

Chinghiz was behind her as always. He lifted her, loving, giving her strength. 'Tell them all to leave,' she said, biting back tears. 'Lotus Bud is dead.'

As the room broke up in disorder, she searched for two faces. When found, they expressed – what she could have expected – only the same horror and pity as the rest.

Later, when Pheasant had left her and gone to mourn guiltily by himself, and she was alone with the watchful Chinghiz, Black Jade stood at her window, gazing through the lattice into the starless dark as though she might find answers blazed across it by a comet.

The doctors had come and gone. They had suspected poison; they would know more tomorrow. Had Lotus Bud eaten anything no one else had sampled? They had thought, and had decided that she had been the only one to touch the baby clams. The dish, of course, had already been washed and put away. She had died almost as her mother had done, except that it had been so mercifully quick. It was like the working-out of some monstrous curse.

Black Jade stood and weighed her good sense against her instinct; her knowledge that she should wait and let others deal with this against the sickening certainty that turned in her stomach – that her nephews had done this horrible thing. They had given the poor child a warning, so that she might live in fear – oh, so briefly – and then they had killed her. Because she had dared to repudiate their threats; because it amused their inherited cruelty; because, dear Gods, through her innocent breast they struck at Golden Willow and herself, against the hated blood of the Sui!

It was not to be borne.

She stood a little longer before the black lozenge of the window, then she turned to the waiting Chinghiz, her mind made up.

'I want the captain of my household guard, here. Now. My father's grandsons have dishonoured the name of his clan. They are to be arrested and executed before I eat this morning.'

Chinghiz looked at her gravely, measuringly. He could find no trace of hysteria. Nevertheless he gave her a little more time, should she wish to make use of it.

'You have considered, of course, that the unhappy young lady may have died naturally, or even taken poison herself?'

His calm voice did not touch her. 'I have considered everything.'

'The palace will be shocked by such swift justice.'

'Let it be shocked. It is the justice that matters.'

'Will you not wait till dawn? Speak to the Emperor, and the ministers of the Board of Punishment?'

'No. Now! Please do as I have asked.'

He thought rapidly. 'It could be said, if anyone wished to harm you in the future, that you have killed your niece because she had been your husband's concubine –'

'– and that I have done away with my nephews to prevent them from making that fact their next item of small talk?' she finished for him drily.

He bowed, unsmiling.

'It doesn't concern me. Such things may be said. I don't know. But I do know that I am right to do this. Go and carry out your orders.' She sighed, the tension suddenly running out of her. 'I find that I am very tired. I should like to sleep now.'

She was asleep, without dreaming, long before the executioner's sword came down.

Chinghiz, having obeyed her faithfully, not without some demur on the part of the captain of the guard, sat up until morning, reflecting on the beginnings of change in his beloved; it was a hardening certainly, but that would not come amiss in the guardian of the Empire.

22

If you know the enemy and know yourself,
You need not fear the outcome of a hundred battles.
If you know yourself but not the enemy,
For every victory gained you will also suffer a defeat.
If you know neither the enemy nor yourself
You will succumb in every battle.

(Sun Tzu, *The Art of War, c.*490 B.C.)

Sorrow ripped ragged the tender membrane of reconciliation that held Black Jade and the Emperor together. Pheasant regretted Lotus Bud furiously and guiltily, and was incensed with Jade for the premature swiftness of her vengeance. She, utterly convinced of its justice, retaliated that he was the one who had made the whole affair possible by his unbridled behaviour.

Into the chasm that opened between them the fickle Gods, as though *Feng Shan* had never been, dropped trouble upon trouble, both personal and general.

The Empire was poor. A massive new Korean campaign had cost them the entire revenue of Hopei, the richest and most populous province, and the health of its octogenarian commander, the Great Wall. In an attempt to meet this, and other heavy commitments to building programmes and administration, they had debased the coinage. This had produced the opposite effect to their wishes and trade was suffering badly.

Their poverty was exacerbated by the onslaught of that most feared and hated enemy, famine; the result of appalling floods in all three of the great river valleys. There followed three disastrous years of successive flood, drought and famine, during which Pheasant tried desperately to feed his starving people and to placate the anger of the Gods.

Such universal anguish drew the unharmonious pair together in duty if not in love; they worked unceasingly throughout this time of trouble, putting the past in its grave and considering only how to deal with the demands of each new day.

It was a time during which each of them grew in stature, Pheasant responding to Black Jade's lead through every point of crisis. When, at last, Heaven relented and sent them back the sun to bless the harvest, they were able to smile at each other again, and to think of their own lives and those of their children.

It occurred to them now, with a wondering sense of the trickery of time, that Bold Tiger, sixteen now, ought to be married. The Crown Prince had a dynasty to continue. They looked about for a suitable bride.

Her name was Lady Firefly. She was small and vivid, with an infectious laugh, and her clan bore one of the Four Surnames. The oracles were consulted and the necessary documents exchanged. Bold Tiger, very conscious of his sixteen-year-old's first whiskers, went nervously to the ceremony of *hsiang-ch'in*, where he would meet Firefly for the first time and see whether he approved his parents' choice. Luckily, being rather a serious boy himself, he was instantly captivated by the lurking suggestion of laughter behind her demure looks; he therefore returned home wearing a golden needle stuck through his knotted hair, the conventional sign of his acceptance, thus saving himself the cost of the two bolts of brocade which were expected to comfort a rejected lady.

Because of the youth of the couple, and because everyone felt the need of a celebration, a certain amount of licence was permitted on the marriage day. It was a winter wedding, and Firefly's friends brought her to him glowing like her namesake through the frosted night, her scarlet palanquin jingling with nuptial bells, and her piquant, mischievous face peering naughtily through the curtains at the torchlit mysteries of the imperial gardens, encouraging her musicians to outrageous gaiety and her pretty, painted escorts to gales of giggling.

At the tiered gates of the Heir's Palace Bold Tiger was waiting for her, surrounded by his brothers and all their friends, with an even larger company of mittened and puffing musicians and several bottles of something alcoholic that tore down their throats like a plough and oxen; this was the result of a recent experiment by Young Tiger to increase the intoxicating content of a liquid by the simple expedient of freezing it, which he did by putting it into the ice-chambers, deep underground, where they kept the sherbet.

The sight of so many nubile maidens coming skippety-hop down the path towards them was too much for the young bloods' party manners. With whoops and yells they raced to extend their welcome far beyond the limits of propriety, raising shrieks and squeals of wicked pleasure from the girls and deploring groans from the grave of Confucius. There was touching and tickling and illicit kissing, and at last even Bold Tiger, who had remained self-consciously in the garlanded archway, trying to look dignified, threw off his better nature and ran to join the others. They opened up before him and he found himself looking into a small, pointed face, with merry black eyes smiling from beneath a slightly tipsy coronet of beaten gold set with rubies.

'Well, won't you help me out?' asked Firefly, thinking firstly that her prince was exceedingly handsome, and secondly that she liked the way his look reassured her amid the happy riot. His eyes spoke only to her, and his lips not at all, as, tongue-tied and (incredibly) sober, he took her from her palanquin and into his house and his heart.

In a bourgeois household, the bride's parents would have accompanied her train, but Firefly's had received an invitation to dine with the Emperor and Black Jade. Youth ruled, and would do things its own way for once.

The master of ceremonies was Sage Path, whose experience in matters of the heart was well known to his cousin. Bold Tiger was not a virgin, but neither had he embraced the pursuit of love with Sage Path's dedicated fervour; this had been even warmer since the loss of the sister he had idolised, and he was constantly reproved by his elders for his excesses. Pheasant had cavilled at this choice of groomsman, but Bold Tiger would have no other and so, tonight, they were at his command.

The unruly crowd was coaxed into some sort of order and entered the palace singing, garlanded with flowers and carrying scarlet candles for good luck. Then there was a dinner of ninety-nine different dishes to be got through; this was somewhat of a strain on the bride and groom, who were not hungry, but most satisfactory to the guests, who were. A good deal more alcohol was consumed and several people made speeches, some of them incoherent. Firefly and Bold Tiger hardly noticed any of it; their only consumption was ocular, of each other, and they said very little.

At last Sage Path clapped his hands and declared it was time to adjourn to the Red Chamber – a rude though literary analogy that set the tone for the rest of the revels. Firefly's troop of girls, their faces shining and their tongues loosened by the wine, swooped on her and bore her away to the master bedroom, their excited voices making an aviary of the gracious halls and courts.

There was just long enough for some necessary repairs to the bride's make-up and general perfection of person, plus a few sweeps of her comb and splashes of her scent bottle and last-minute good wishes and pieces of sweetly ribald advice, before the men were with them again; they came hooting through the festive rooms like a hunt in full cry, drums beating, flutes tooting and viols being violated in their wake. They were by now enormously drunk. Young Tiger was wearing a chamber-pot on his head, his arm around Sage Path, whom he was purporting to support. Loud Tiger, who strictly speaking should not have been there at all, was hiccoughing horribly behind them, and trying to sing a dirty song he didn't really understand.

They calmed down when they reached the nuptial chamber. They had to because now the leaders would perform the Twilight Ceremony which would make their quarry man and wife. Sage Path and Young Tiger stopped and straightened each other's clothing, not that either of them could see straight, and then walked carefully through two ranks of bright-eyed girls who lit their way to the bride with red candles. Behind them came Bold Tiger, admirably steady, his quiet gaze seeking his bride.

She stood in front of the vast flower-strewn bed, trembling very slightly, but smiling so that he should know he was welcome and she was not really afraid.

Everyone was quiet while Sage Path brought them the wedding-cup. They both drank from it, looking at each other shyly over its lip.

Then Bold Tiger's valet and Firefly's maid stepped forward and removed his linen cap and her coronet, and began to undo his sleek topknot and her intricate folds of smooth black hair. When they had done, Sage Path solemnly took a strand of Firefly's silken mane and knotted it with one of Bold Tiger's, which reached his second rib. They were now man and wife.

Because they would also, one day, be Emperor and Empress, there was a few minutes' grace before pandemonium broke loose again. They sipped wine and were civilised and no one looked at the bed. Then began the ragging of the bride.

Firefly had steeled herself to put up with the rude jokes, the vulgar songs and the salacious encouragement. Had she been a poor man's daughter, they might have whipped her to bed with a flail. As it was, she fixed her mind on her bridegroom's handsome face and probable kind heart, and let them get on with it.

Her younger brother-in-law proved to know a great many rude songs. His voice was a battle between that of a sick donkey and a mating crane. There was one jewel she would never forget; it concerned a man who had read *all* the manuals of sensual instruction, and had a very long chorus, with actions, which listed a few of his favourite things – Cat and Mouse in One Hole; Wailing Monkey Embracing a Tree; Hounds on the Ninth day of Autumn; and so on. She began to blush, which made them all very happy. 'It will soon be over,' Bold Tiger whispered, feeling proud and possessive, as well as pleasantly anticipatory.

Next there were rude presents. Firefly received a pair of gilded fish to make her conceive and a nasty-smelling potion with sulphur in it which shrank the vagina and cured frigidity. Bold Tiger got the Deer Horn Potion (deer horn, cedar seeds, cuscuta, schizandra, polygala and boschniakia) which cures failure to erect one's member *and* prevents shrinkage. Having really got down to basics, the male guests (and some of the female ones) became extremely rowdy and began to make improper suggestions. 'Why don't you take Firefly's clothes off so that we can have a treat too…' 'I bet her jade gate is good and tight!' 'How about your jasper column, Bold Tiger? Ready for the Leaping White Tiger, is it?'

Young Tiger, thoroughly imbued with the spirit of the occasion, made a dash for his brother and flung him on the flowery bed, holding him down, while two others got his trousers off. Four girls did the same for Firefly, laying her next to him, her eyes huge with the effort not to cry. Slightly abashed at themselves, the guests fell back after this, leaving the couple, breathing hard, in their crumpled robes and the shreds of their dignity.

Sage Path, who hated a good time to end, leaned over Firefly and lifted her scarlet hem. 'Come on, cousin! Surely I don't have to show you how to do it?'

Suddenly Sage Path was on his back on the floor. He looked up in bewilderment. 'What did you want to do that for?' he demanded of a calm-faced Bold Tiger, who stood, dusting his hands, above him.

'As a sign that the fun is over, cousin,' the Crown Prince said evenly, showing his teeth. 'And now, friends,' he added, indicating the door, 'I thank you for your company, and wish you a fond *goodnight.*'

It was an order.

Bemused, befuddled and still hilarious, they went.

Bold Tiger threw what they had left behind into the waste-paper basket, filled two cups with a fresh, light wine, and returned, smiling and triumphant, to his bride, who had not cried, and who was waiting for him with hope and sweetness.

In the morning they went to present Firefly to his parents, and to his ancestors, in the White Tiger Hall.

It was this quiet ceremony in the cool dark hall, under the loving eyes of his father and mother, who, he thought, no longer loved each other in the way that he and Firefly would love, that the real marriage was made. Bold Tiger contemplated, with a deep humility, the responsibilities that would be his throughout his life, and called on the strong spirit of Shih-min to help him, to guide his thoughts and bless his union with the girl who had given him a night of great happiness, and who now stood, tranquil and certain, beside him, his wife and Crown Princess.

After the sacrifice to the ancestors there was a small reception at which all last night's revellers appeared, suitably sober, some ashen-faced, some chastened, some enviably bright-eyed and sociable.

After the guests had gone, Pheasant invited Black Jade to rest with him in his study, the softly coloured, pleasant room where so much of his life was spent.

They discussed the wedding, the guests, how much they liked Firefly, and the appalling behaviour of their three younger children.

'No punishments, though; not today?' Pheasant pleaded.

'No. Well, perhaps you should have a stern word with Loud Tiger. You haven't seen him. He can hardly lift his head.'

Pheasant looked sheepishly proud, as men do when a son has his first hangover. 'If you like,' he said. Then, made confident by her amiability and the pleasure of the day, he took her from her seat and held her close.

'Weddings,' he murmured, 'and children. They remind me that it is time you and I were begetting another.' He kissed her and did other things that he knew would arouse her. Surprised, she made no objection. When he began to undress her she suggested they move into the bedchamber.

'No,' he said. 'Here. No one will interrupt us.' He moved the dragon-infested chair from behind his desk and seated himself in it.

He patted his knee. 'Come here to me,' he invited.

Pheasant enjoyed the next half-hour, after which he felt virile, young and very cheerful. Black Jade, who felt untidy, tired and rather battered, had enjoyed it somewhat less.

But in some measure, its limits as yet undefined, they were together again. It was by no means the stuff of dreams, but it was something.

The year of respite passed. A bad harvest threatened again. Every resource was strained towards the prevention of millions of deaths by starvation. Everywhere, magistrates were having men beaten for stealing from government granaries. There had been no rains; in Chang-an the air one breathed was filled with the dead-gold dust of the loess that swirled in from the plain.

Pheasant, fearing that Heaven had removed its favour from the T'ang, embarked, as advised by Confucius, on a course of self-correction, in an attempt to be worthy of his mandate. He spent many hours in communion with his ancestors, and many more with his priests. He urged Black Jade to do the same, and would often keep her talking into the night, worrying and harrying his conscience and her own. Already worn out by her days in the conference room, she became exhausted. Pheasant himself became ill again; his heart seemed to beat too fast; he was always tired; he had dizzy spells and aching bones and weakening sight.

The news from abroad did not cheer them. In both Korea and Tibet there were successful revolts against the T'ang occupation. They could afford war less than ever, but they must retaliate or lose face before the world by the economy of retreat.

In the domestic life of the palace, the demon of misrule that had come, uninvited, to Bold Tiger's wedding continued to prevail.

The yellow dust found its way through the closed curtains of Black Jade's palanquin as she travelled, with Welcome muttering and grunting beside her, to her mother's house near the eastern market. She was in a towering rage.

That morning she had found Tiger Lily in tears. Gently questioned, she had said, 'It is because Winter Blossom is crying. She has been crying all night and I can't get her to stop.' Her small face was flushed with worry and ignorance.

'Well, we can't have that, can we, Little Marmoset? Let's go and ask her what's the matter, shall we?'

Tiger Lily had taken her hand and solemnly conducted her to the nursemaid's room. She shook her head wisely.

'She won't tell you, you know. She wouldn't tell me.'

Indeed she would not, for quite some time. Winter Blossom lay sorry and tearstained on the *kang*. A new paroxysm burst out when she saw the Empress, though she scrambled to her feet and managed a soggy bow.

At first she would not speak at all. Then she would not speak with Tiger Lily in the room. So the little Princess was told to go and find her dancing-teacher and departed in dignified dudgeon. She had spent a great deal of energy in sympathy and was now without the reward of satisfied curiosity.

Several sharp minutes later Black Jade had summoned her bearers and left the palace. Golden Willow was not expecting her. Neither was Sage Path.

When she arrived at the pretty, two-storey mansion with its dragon-guttered pagoda roofs and its guardian lion-dogs, she was told that her mother was still in her bedchamber. This was unlike her, but it suited Black Jade's purpose very well. She sent at once for her nephew.

Sage Path entered the room wearing a burnt-orange Arab robe that glittered and showed his chest, and a bemused countenance with black circles round the eyes. He was heavily scented with musk.

'I'm honoured by such an early visit, Exquisite Aunt.' He smiled with the total confidence of the over-handsome.

'I have not come to do you honour, but to exact repayment for the *dishonour* you have done to my household.'

She watched, stone-faced, as stupefaction turned to recognition.

'I intended no such thing.'

'You have taken the virginity of one of my servants.'

He shrugged, his ready smile hovering. 'Oh come! She was willing enough; more than willing.'

'Then why did you not ask to make her your concubine?'

'I have no household; you know that. Besides, she is not of a sufficiently good family.'

'But good enough to have married a husband of her own rank, as is every woman's right, had you not ruined her chances.'

He grinned, scarcely touched. 'Oh, what does it matter? There are a hundred girls like her. First they say "Oh no! How *dare* you suggest it?" Then it is "No. How *could* you?" with a giggle or two. And after half an hour's persuasion it's "Oh yes! Yes. I shouldn't, but you are surely the son of a white tiger and my poor heart is conquered – and, oh dear – I *have*!" '

He was comic but she did not laugh. Winter Blossom's tears had not been comic. She would not let his charade dilute her anger.

'You are evidently too conceited, and too stupid, to comprehend that you have done a despicable thing. You will, however, easily understand this; you are to go to your own apartments in this house, and you are to remain there, under lock and key if necessary, until I send you my permission to leave. You will study the *Lotus Sutra* and write me an essay on its meaning. It should be a long essay, and worthy of the *chin shih* graduate you purport to be. I am ashamed of you before our ancestors.'

He was utterly taken aback.

'But Highness, if you would just let me – '

'That is enough. You are dismissed.' Her tone propelled him.

It was evident that he had gone straight to plead his case with his grandmother, for Golden Willow soon appeared, dressed in a chamber-gown, her grey hair loose and her face anxious.

'My dear child! You should not have had to come here like this. I am ashamed. I have spoilt the boy so that he thinks the whole world is his to take and break. I am sorry. It is only that, since poor Lotus Bud left us, he has seemed more mad than mischievous. I took it for a sign of grief and, well, I have let it go on too long. Let me sit down and get my breath. I'm not absolutely myself today. Dreadful, to stay in bed so long!'

'Of course, Mother. But you're very pale. What is it?'

'Oh, nothing but age, I suppose. I find that, these days, I need more energy than I seem to have.' She gave her sweet smile.

'Then you must rest more. There's no need for you to work so hard. The church will run without your hand to guide it. And as for Sage Path, I really think it is time he left you and became the master of his own household. He needs responsibilities.'

Golden Willow raised both hands in a gesture of fruitlessness.

'Do you think him fit to govern a household? He has no control over himself; how will he exercise it over others?'

Black Jade sighed. 'You are right, as always. I will send him a tutor, while he is confined to his rooms; someone stern and cantankerous, who will stand no nonsense.'

'Very well, dear, but he'll react badly, I'm afraid.'

'We'll see. Now let's forget the horrible boy. It's you I'm concerned about. You don't look at all well. Have you seen a doctor?'

'I'm too old to need doctors. You are not to worry; it is only a little breathlessness. It is to be expected. Now, tell me – what has my granddaughter been doing?'

Golden Willow knew that this was a certain way to distract Black Jade's attention from any other subject. She was satisfied to see her face clear and her body lose its tension as she began to relate the progress of her favourite child.

Bold Tiger waylaid her as she was leaving the map room.

'Mother, something has happened that I think you should know.'

'Walk with me. I'm going to ride to Kan Yeh. Come with me as far as the stables. All the way, if you like.'

'Thank you.' To see her riding through the city was something he enjoyed. It defied centuries of protocol and outraged many people's sense of how a great lady should behave. But her custom of showing her face to the people had, nevertheless, made her the most popular Empress in their history. They worshipped her.

'I would have gone to my father,' he began, 'but you have already taken an interest – it's Sage Path – '

Black Jade released a groan.

'I know.' His face was set; seeing its hard planes, she realised that at seventeen he was already a man. Any lusty boy could make her a grandmother, but it took a man to look so grimly determined.

'Do you remember a girl called Sweet Melody?'

'Of course. She was a great friend of Lotus Bud.'

'Yes. Well, her father has done some rather good work in his prefecture, and has asked if, as his reward, I would take Sweet Melody as one of my consorts. She is a charming girl and I was delighted.' He tensed. 'If only I had taken her right away, as soon as he had spoken,' he said bitterly.

She searched his face, almost sure of what was coming.

He swallowed. He found this difficult. 'Last night my cousin Sage Path escaped from his rooms, and went into the city. There he collected a gang of his hooligan companions and led them to Sweet Melody's home. They broke in, tied the servants, and the others watched while Sage Path raped her. Then the maids were brought in and there was a general orgy.'

For a time Black Jade said nothing, only laid her hand on her son's arm with a sympathetic pressure of her slender fingers. They walked quietly together through the gardens while she came to the decision that must hurt her mother deeply.

Then she said, her lovely voice abrasive, 'I wonder, don't you, at the sheer idiotic foolishness of such an outrage? If he had thought for one second before carrying out such a malicious and destructive scheme, he must surely have seen that it would put an end, forever, to the life he has been leading?'

'Apparently not. I imagine he was concentrating on the pleasure of the moment – and upon that of causing me distress. We have been at odds for some time now; but I never thought it could lead to anything as vicious as this. That poor girl! When I think – '

'Leave it!' snapped Jade, herself too near tears for the excited girl who had sat between her son and her nephew at Lotus Bud's banquet, taking mischievous pleasure in their duel for her attention.

'What will you do?' Bold Tiger would be satisfied with no light punishment. Nor would she.

'Sage Path, what is he?' she asked contemptuously. 'A pretty witless degenerate with his brains between his legs. Waste no more sorrow on him; you won't see him again. I can't give you back Sweet Melody's purity, but I can give you revenge!'

'I'd like to castrate him and make him her slave,' Bold Tiger spat, between his teeth.

'I agree with you. He is worthless. A stain on our honour. But I'm afraid we can't indulge ourselves to that extent. Golden Willow is hopelessly attached to Sage Path. You will have to be satisfied with exile. You may choose where.'

'Forever?'

'Certainly.'

Her son smiled. A small cold smile. She was sorry to see it, sorry his kind, even nature had been jolted in this way.

'Excellent,' he exulted. 'It will kill him. He'd rather die than cease to be the playboy prince of Chang-an!'

Black Jade postponed her visit to the convent with the intention of giving orders for Sage Path's arrest. Before she could do so, a messenger arrived from Golden Willow. His news drove everything else from her mind.

Her mother was very ill; perhaps even dying.

She trembled, her heart hammering under the shock. Why had she not been aware of this before? Her loving instinct should have told her that Golden Willow had not been well for some time. There must have been signs. Why had she not seen them?

She took a dozen officers of her guard with her and rode at the gallop to the Jung mansion.

Arriving, she ordered the soldiers to keep Sage Path, who, as she had expected, was sleeping off his excesses, out of the way. Sick with apprehension, she went to her mother's room.

Golden Willow lay in her bed in the tranquil green and white room which she had not, in the last few days, left before noon, and only then because her sense of duty was stronger than her desire to rest, though not stronger than the need.

She saw at once the self-accusing penitence in her daughter's face and set herself to dispel it.

'Now, you are not to make a fuss, Second Daughter. Matters are as they are because this is how I have wanted them to be. If you are going to tell me that I should have taken more care of my health, or that you have not taken enough care of it, then please save your breath. I've not been ill for very long, thanks to Kuan Yin.'

'But I should have known! You should have told me.' She felt afraid, as she had been as a child when she could not find Golden Willow for some reason.

'Well, I have told you now,' her mother smiled, patting the bedcover. Jade sat beside her and took her hand.

'How do you feel, exactly? Just what is wrong?'

'I believe it is my heart. Dr Sun Tsu-Miao is a little vague; he says we know so little of causes. Funnily enough, I don't feel ill at all, at present; just tired. Which is odd – ' she looked into Black Jade's anxious face, penitent in her turn – 'because Sun tells me I shall probably die very shortly.'

'No! It isn't possible. He can't be right!' Her anguish reached the servants outside the door, who bowed their heads in pity.

'Oh, I think so.' Again the sweet smile. 'No, no, let us not have weeping, my child. Weeping is the one occupation to which I have always thought you singularly unsuited. You may be angry if you must, but please do not display that anger to me. My life has been full of kindness; I am quite content to end it.' She squeezed the hand that was holding hers like a lifeline, and let it go.

'Oh, Mother, how am I to answer you?' Jade tried to smile.

'As you are doing; with a smile. That's better. And now, my dear, will you be so good as to tell me just what my unfortunate grandson has done this time. None of my servants will say anything, but even an invalid knows when one of her household is brought home under armed guard.'

This time her smile, with its lie, was without effort. 'Sage Path was simply being himself, as usual. It isn't important.'

Golden Willow tapped her finger upon the quilt. The skin that covered the long hand was translucent, the veins in dark relief. It had been the wistful beauty of a dead leaf caught by winter light.

'The boy has been in my charge; I would like to hear.'

Jade knew she would persist, and waste her strength. As gently as possible, she told her.

Golden Willow listened without comment. Then she closed her eyes for a few moments.

'What will happen to him?' she asked at last. She would not plead for him. It was no longer possible.

'He will be sent to the provinces.'

Golden Willow poured all her remaining resources into making this easy for her daughter; she would not disgrace her last days by showing the other, more destructive weakness of her heart. She loved Sage Path like a son, and would not stop doing so, no matter how far he fell from grace.

'I will miss him,' she said bravely. 'I will not be the only one. People are fond of him, you know. His personality is so much more attractive than his character.' She would not have long to miss him; there was a consolation in that.

'I will pray for my grandson,' she said. Then, 'May I see him?'

'Of course. He will remain in his quarters. You may see him whenever you wish.'

'Thank you, dear child.' There was so much she had to say to him; so much of the fault had been hers. She had watched Rose Bird spoil him, and had gone on to spoil him further herself. But this was her own burden, not Black Jade's. The price of her love.

'I have so many people to see,' she declared brightly. 'I do wish doctors would not tell one these things; then one would have no necessity to be so *organised*.'

'No one will come unless you wish it.'

'There is duty, dear; and more importantly, love. I want to say goodbye to those I love. It is a natural instinct, once one knows how things are to be. And now,' she said quickly, as Jade's lip quivered, 'I should like to sleep. I feel as though I were at the end of a very exciting day. How odd that is.'

'Mother?' The quiver become uncontrollable.

'Don't worry, little Phoenix, I shall not leave you today.'

Golden Willow was correct. The Gods gave her ample time in which to make all her dispositions, and to try, as she had so often done, to reach the spirit of goodness that she believed to inhabit Sage Path's unplumbed depths. He was extremely attached to her, in his careless way, and she might even have succeeded, had the day not come, too soon for that, when she knew she must send for Black Jade before the daily appointed time of her visit.

It was morning, her favourite time of day. She had greeted it, as always, with a grateful prayer. Now she was sitting up among her pale sea-green pillows, her face very lightly tinted with colour and her hair coiled into a regal coronet. She had never looked old. She did not do so now, only ever more transparent, as though she were slowly melting away like one of the ice-goddesses her grandchildren had made in the imperial park last winter.

Black Jade came, a little dishevelled after her swift ride.

'You look well; you look better!' she discovered in glad surprise.

Golden Willow nodded. 'Sit down and listen, my child. There is something very important I must tell you today.'

Jade gathered her cherry-coloured skirts into a companionable heap on the bed. 'I'm listening.' She had a memory of earlier days when she had been the one beneath the quilts, all ears to hear the tales of the Gods and heroes, as Tiger Lily was now.

'Perhaps I should have told you this before. I don't know. It seemed wisest to me not to speak. It is a burden I have for you – a burden and a holy trust. The greatest there is; but you are very strong, my Black Jade. Strong enough, I think.' She rested.

'Mother.' She knew. She knew without any doubt what it must be. 'You have no need to tell me,' she said quietly. 'I am glad; it must have been a burden for you too. I know about the prophecy. I have known since – before Taishan.' There was no need to mention Shing-jen. Golden Willow had never known, though perhaps she may have suspected it, just how dear that gift of hers had become.

There was a deep sigh. 'Ah? So you knew. Welcome, of

course.' She surveyed the lovely and commanding woman before her. 'I have never seen such strength as yours. Even as a child; such a will, such certainty. Heaven has given you the hardest of destinies, but you have also been given the strength to endure it.'

No, not without you. I can't be alone, Jade wanted to cry, but that was not what Golden Willow deserved. She nodded instead.

'Let us hope so. But what perplexes me is *how* it is all to come about. There is Pheasant, there are my sons; how am I to stand in their place? It is difficult to believe possible.'

'But you do believe it?'

'Sometimes.'

'Don't let it trouble you. Leave it to Heaven.'

'Yes, Mother. That is what I do. It's the only sensible thing *to* do.'

Golden Willow lay back on her pillows, content to have discharged this duty so lightly. She was tired again, very tired.

Black Jade saw the colour drain from her face and was stricken with fear. The appearance of health, she understood, had been a cruel sham. The hand that held hers was as light as snow. She clutched it fast, as though to hold back the melting away of life. Tears, beyond her command, sprang to her eyes. As weak as all those who love deeply, she let them flow as the truth entered her heart.

'There is one other thing –' Golden Willow said, 'not really important; frivolous perhaps, but I would like to go to our ancestors in my old rose-coloured robe, the one with the flowers and the deer embroidered on it. It was your father's favourite; I should like to meet him again, wearing it.'

Scalded by grief, Black Jade grinned back. 'Certainly. But, you know, don't you, that the General will greet you in nothing so fine. He will still be wearing his old army jerkin.'

'I expect so. Do you know, though I never admitted it, that was how I liked him best. He belonged out of doors, your father, and I in the beautiful house he gave me; but I expect we shall manage to meet occasionally, in the palaces and plains of the Western Heaven, just as we did in Wen Shui.'

She smiled with a mischievous happiness that Black Jade had never seen. The feathery hand escaped from hers once more.

Golden Willow turned her face into the pillow.

'Yes, you must sleep now,' her daughter said, tenderly.

She watched until, after perhaps half an hour, the faintest change stole across the pale cheek that lay like milky jade upon the soft sea-green of the pillow; a changing of the light, a distant suggestion of movement, of leaving, like the first, brittle breathing of the thaw.

Then it was over. Golden Willow was gone, leaving the scent of roses.

It was a new and hellish agony, and its expectedness made no difference. Black Jade mourned without sleeping, tossed between her present grief and the host of memories that clamoured out of the past. Chinghiz would not leave her. He knew that she was most terribly bereft, more this time, perhaps, than ever before. The life that had given her life had been taken; she was no longer anyone's child. Her family, now, were those to whom she herself had given birth.

He watched over her, making her eat, sending away those who would trouble her, while she found her difficult way through the loneliness of this particular grief. He ordered her household and comforted her children, doing everything that there was to be done until she should come to herself again.

She was less than half aware of him, quietly creating the time and space that she needed; her self was far away and very private, as she tried to walk a little way with that gentle and compassionate spirit on its journey to find her father. But she thanked him, sensing how it had been, on the day that she finally awoke and allowed her daughter to race in and throw herself upon her chest, kissing and shouting and demanding her love and her time.

The funeral of Golden Willow was the most lavish that Chang-an had seen since that of the late Emperor.

The queue that stretched towards the crimson-covered catafalque in White Tiger Hall was numbered, like the good deeds it witnessed, in thousands. The offered pall of its incense clotted the air long after the cortège set out on the forty-ninth day.

The procession wound through the streets in an ecstasy of music and colour, the scarlet and black of the Wu clan predominating near the coffin, which was carried by the officers of Black Jade's personal guard. The mourners walked behind, wearing the hempen robes prescribed for their rank, followed by the nuns and priests of both churches.

Black Jade, in her phoenix carriage, wept again behind her yellow curtains, remembering two girls, hardly more than children, swaying together up a hillside in Wen Shui.

The day had begun badly. Sage Path, who had somehow

managed to become incapably drunk in his quarters, had refused point blank to put on his white robes and join the procession. The officer who reported it gave his opinion that the young man was overthrown by his grief. Even if this was the case, the insult to his grandmother represented a blasphemous neglect of filial piety. His previous sins had been grave, but this overshadowed them all. Any insult to one's elders was a serious matter, but to dishonour the dead was considered a crime.

When she had left Golden Willow in the little tomb-house, surrounded like a new housewife by her possessions and warmed by the light of a myriad candles, Black Jade returned to the palace and sorrowfully sought an interview with her husband.

Pheasant was tender with her; she looked so young and vulnerable in her white gown. She was still very subdued. They spoke quietly about the funeral and the magnificent response of the city.

It was some time before Black Jade could bring herself to mention Sage Path's defection. When she did, they both kept their revulsion under restraint; this was not a day on which strong feelings might be expressed.

'He must leave us, right away,' Pheasant decided. 'I will have the edict prepared today.'

'Yes.' She was sombre. 'There is one thing more. For my mother's sake – although his crime against Sweet Melody was an outrage of the most appalling kind, I would prefer it not to be mentioned in the decree.'

'I understand you perfectly, my dear. He will be indicted for unfilial conduct and violation of the laws of mourning. It is a greater shame by the laws of convention, but one which will be less discussed among the curious.'

'Thank you. If only – '

'Yes? If there's anything I can do – ?'

'No, it is nothing. Good night, my dear.'

She gave him the fluttering wisp of a smile and left him. She had almost been going to ask for forgiveness for Sage Path. That would be what Golden Willow would have wanted, though she would never have said so. But after all, she couldn't do it. Sage Path would not change his ways. And there was her son's damaged honour to consider. No, it was best left as it was. Weary to the bone, she went back to her rooms, where Chinghiz was waiting with hot wine and a loving silence that was like balm to her sorry spirit.

Several days after Sage Path had set out for the unpleasant

exile that Bold Tiger had chosen for him, the news came that he had hanged himself on the road.

'It will kill him,' his enemy had said. 'He'd rather die than cease to be the playboy prince of Chang-an.'

Now her son looked at Black Jade with a sick recognition of his part in the bleak piece of self-destruction.

'He has always treated the gift of his life too lightly; but I would not for the world have had it end like this. I am to blame.'

'We are both to blame, you and I,' she acknowledged, 'but we should not forget, in the recrimination of regret, that Sage Path was also to blame.'

But the sorrow and futility remained with them, long after Rose Bird's handsome son had descended into the Hell of the Suicides.

There was one more death to sadden them in this year of sadness. Unlike Sage Path's it was an honourable one and was marked with universal homage. The Great Wall had laid down his sword at last. He was eighty-two, with an even greater number of victories behind him. In his last year he had conquered Korea at last, and the vigorous younger men who had helped him to do it were coming home to seek their further fortunes, bringing with them an appreciation of the abilities of the Empress which they had learned from their octogenarian mentor.

Black Jade was glad to have them. The administration needed new blood. Lion Guard was the only minister who was close to her; and he had warned her that his health was failing and he must soon retire. The idea had alarmed her.

'I can't keep you, if you wish to leave me,' she told him regretfully, 'but I must confess that, at the moment, I feel like a citadel whose every bastion has crumbled. Such nakedness is not comfortable.'

Lion Guard, leaning on the slender gold-tipped cane that the younger courtiers aped, thinking its purpose purely fashionable, reassured her with a smile. 'I have been giving thought to just that uncomfortable sensation, Highness. My conclusion is that new clothing can be manufactured very speedily.'

'Ah, but will it have the assured elegance of the old?'

His flawless bow acknowledged the compliment.

'It will if the material is simply placed in your talented hands. Chang-an is racing with new blood,' he said, with an enthusiasm which revealed his real reluctance to leave office, and Your Highness knows you can make any man yours for life with a flick of your delicate eyebrow. Why not make a collection, of the most energetic and talented, and keep them all in one place, where you can draw on their abilities as you please?'

She was interested. 'What had you in mind?'

'An institute of some sort. It doesn't matter what you call it; its real work will be whatever you want it to be, and every man in it will owe his preferment to you personally.'

'A kind of balance, you mean, to the council of ministers?' The council had recently criticised her for excessive expenditure on Golden Willow's funeral. It was not important – they had soon come to heel when she had threatened them with her abdication – but it was the first open criticism they had made of her, and in her weakest moment. She would not forget it.

Lion Guard gave his suave smile. 'I imagine that it would become so.'

When he left her, Black Jade went to stand before the bronze mirror in her study. For the first time, she considered the evils of age. The elegant statesman had told her he was nearing eighty, though he did not look it, or anything like it, nor did he ever look ill. But then, who would suppose that the perfect face before her belonged to a woman of forty-five? It seemed to her that it had scarcely changed since she had left the convent. She thought of Lion Guard's notion of a hothouse of young men, all disposed to be her slaves, and watched it break into a mischievous smile.

And so there was founded the institution of the Scholars of the North Gate, a college for able and ambitious young *chin shih* whose output would be unimpeachably literary, but which would grow to be the Empress's private secretariat, keeping her informed of everything she ought to know and assisting her to deal with it.

They began their work with a series of biographies of clever women, which, though an innocent occupation and long overdue, was not one of which Confucius would have approved.

The palace cheered itself up with further royal weddings. As soon as the mourning period for Golden Willow was completed, Young Tiger, who was beginning to show unwelcome signs of the influence of his dead, decadent cousin, was given a quiet and pleasant girl named New Moon for his primary wife, discreetly followed by six concubines whom he chose himself.

Loud Tiger, much to his utter disgust, was contracted according to Pheasant's wishes to his cousin, the equally noisy Red Poppy, who followed him about with a blissful disregard for his dislike. Happily he was not expected, for a couple of years, to take her to bed, but, as he told anyone who would listen, breakfast was quite bad enough.

The flicker of light-heartedness occasioned by these couplings was short-lived. The Emperor, as though in sympathy with his famine and poverty-stricken land, worn out by continuous drought and flood, descended again into ill-health. His weakness culminated in an attack of such ferocity that Sun Tzu-Miao ordered complete rest. The venerable physician, nearly ninety, also gave him his own life-extending vegetarian diet to follow, as well as a strong decoction of the flowers of the foxglove.

Because he was now eighteen and had impressed them with his intelligence, the ministers felt that the Crown Prince should take his father's place during his convalescence.

Black Jade made no comment on this. Personally, she felt that Bold Tiger was not yet ready for the responsibility, but she did not wish to appear unwilling to give him his chance. The council would guide his hand, and she herself would be thankful for a rest.

Leaving their son to make the best of his opportunity, she packed Pheasant into a comfortable carriage, mobilised the rest of the family and its favourite companions, and set off for the softer air of Loyang.

Though no one had expected it, Bold Tiger's regency was to last for three years. During this period Black Jade stayed close to Pheasant, in Loyang or in the relaxed atmosphere of the Palace of Nine Perfections in the foothills near Chang-an. Although no changes escaped her vigilance or comment, she left the work of the state to her son and his councillors while she tried with all her will to nurse her husband back to health.

She watched him more closely than his doctors, monitoring his food, his sleep and his recreation. She would allow him to do no work. She kept from him all papers that did not expressly need his signature, and would discuss with him only the relative merits of the books and music with which he occupied himself.

Gradually he relaxed and began to look less haunted, though he was still pale and often dizzy or short of breath. Black Jade worried about him desperately. He had passed too near the Yellow Springs for her not to realise that, however she may have held him in contempt in the past, there was still a great deal of affection for him in her heart.

23

One evening Black Jade was sitting with Pheasant on the Peacock Terrace of the summerhouse, tucked away beside an ornamental lake in the palace park; they were talking and languidly playing chess. From behind a grove of willows a solitary flute breathed plaintively of love and loss. It was a blessed mood, and one that they had learned to cherish.

'You are lovelier now,' he told her, watching the fading light fall across her face, 'than you were when I saw you as a boy, and confessed tortured passion to my pillow. It's hard to believe you are the mother of five children.'

She smiled and moved her General. 'Check, you aren't attending.'

'Treacherous.' He pondered the board. 'Tell me,' he said almost shyly, 'do you think we shall have any more children?'

'Why not? I am still young.'

'Yes, but I am not – still strong. My seed must lack vigour.'

She touched his sleeve. 'We have done very well. Our children are strong, intelligent and beautiful, all of them. You have nothing to worry about.'

He sighed. He was ashamed. He was losing his potency, and he was too young for that. The cure preferred by the omniscient manuals was frequent copulation with very young girls, up to ten a night, if possible; the sages did not, unfortunately, explain how, given the nature of the disease, one was to bring oneself to apply the remedy!

Staring broodily across the terrace while Jade plotted his General's demise, Pheasant saw Bold Tiger coming along the lake path. He had recently returned from Chang-an for a well-deserved holiday. He was walking very fast, as if to stern martial music.

'Our son has news for us,' he remarked, regretting the imminent loss of their privacy. 'Not good, I think.'

She looked up. 'He has been in the city all day. He will just have learned about that business of the stolen millet for the Tai-yuan garrison.'

Bold Tiger reached the terrace and ran up the steps with his spare, athletic gait. His brown eyes were hot with knowledge, and his filial bow was perfunctory. 'I have made the most incredible discovery,' he said, panting. 'You won't believe it, either of you.'

'Try us,' his mother suggested, indicating a low cane chair.

He would not sit. 'I don't know how this can have happened. It must be counter to any orders of yours – ' Jade's eye impelled plain speaking. 'It is this – I've just found out that I have two sisters living in the palace city, sisters whom I've never met, whom *no one* has met because they are living virtually as recluses, prisoners almost, hidden away in a small back alley as though they were nobodies!'

Pheasant was frowning, obviously puzzled. Black Jade was trying, unsuccessfully, to think. 'You don't have any idea who I mean, do you?' asked Bold Tiger excitedly. 'These two ladies are, I assure you, royal princesses. My sisters. Your daughters, sir – yours and those of a concubine named Bright Virtue, who was apparently convicted of some crime when I was an infant – ' He stopped. His mother's face was frozen in some unnameable emotion. The Emperor was stricken with obvious shock, tinged with something very much like shame.

Neither spoke. 'I can't believe that either of you knew they were living like this. I had to go to Chinghiz to find out the truth about them. He always knows these things. But even he was unusually vague about them. Precious Virtue and Singing Bird – my sisters; they must be well past the age when a woman expects to take a husband or become a consort, yet no one has done anything for them. How can it have happened?' He was looking at his father.

'My son, you don't know what old sorrows you touch upon here – ' began Pheasant unsteadily.

'What about *their* sorrows? Those two poor girls – what kind of a life have they had, locked up like that? Whatever their mother may have done – I gather she's dead now – there is no justification for this.' His anger almost exhilarated him. He was never happier than when he was the champion of an underdog. Riding his own wave, he failed to notice Pheasant floundering. It was Black Jade who attempted the rescue.

'I'm sorry to hear this, Bold Tiger,' she said firmly. 'It is difficult for you to judge the present situation correctly when you don't know the whole story.' Her calm voice covered a heartbeat like a brass hammer, as the faces of her ghostly tormentors rose up before her in the quiet evening air. 'These girls have, to some extent, been the victims of the law. They were degraded, naturally, when their mother was executed for treason – oh yes; Chinghiz did not tell you that. He left it to us, as was perfectly right.'

'Treason.' Bold Tiger was amazed. 'What treason?'

'Sorcery,' said Black Jade tersely. Pheasant's complexion was the colour of clay. He would be ill again. 'I don't propose to discuss it with you further. It might well satisfy your curiosity, but it would cause your father and myself a great deal of pain.'

'I'm sorry, Mother, but I must insist – '

'You? Insist? By what right?' Black Jade had tensed and sat staring at him. There was no friendship in her stare. 'You forget yourself.'

Bold Tiger withstood her anger, looking miserably and uncertainly back. 'I don't want to be unfilial – but surely, isn't it your duty, Father's duty – ' he turned to the unhappy Pheasant – 'to retrieve this unacceptable situation? Those girls must be married!'

'He is right,' said the Emperor suddenly, dragging his mind away from terrible images of the past. 'It is every woman's right to have a husband. The simple and sorrowful truth, my son, is that we had forgotten these girls.' His voice was heavy, dull as mud. 'They were, and are, reminders of times which we do not care to remember. I am much to blame. I shall see to it that – my daughters – are treated according to their rank.'

'And you will find husbands for them?'

'I will. And now, my boy, it would be a favour to me if you would leave us alone, for the moment.'

'Very well.' Bold Tiger could hardly refuse the sad, courteous request. 'But I wish you would tell me about it. It has been a shock to find them like that, all but kept prisoner – '

'Enough!' Black Jade was on her feet, her eyes blazing with rage. 'Take your clumsy, interfering face out of my sight!'

The Prince stepped back, amazed at the change in her. He had seen her angry, but never like this. This was neither the stern parent of his growing years, nor the impatient, choleric conqueror of the council; she had become alien, a cold monument to a wrath which he could not understand but which laid its icy finger indelibly upon his heart. Again, he weathered it, regarding her with the curiosity reserved for an unknown species. Then he bowed curtly to them both and left. He would ask no more questions here.

'I'm sorry.' Pheasant's murmur reached her from far off. 'This must have been terrible for you. Those dreadful days – '

'May well have returned.' She shook her head to clear it of its attic lumber. 'You must act at once, or we shall be awash in a sea of conjecture. Those girls must be married, right away!'

Pheasant brightened. It was something he could do, some small atonement for the years of ignominy suffered by those who always suffer the most, the innocent. He would visit his daughters, very soon, though he did not say so. He wondered if they would be as lovely as their mother had been. Poor Bright Virtue – it had all been so desperately sad. He had never been certain, at the time, if what Jade had done had been justified in its terrible cruelty. He was not sure now. It was as if a pit had opened at his feet. He looked into it and was afraid for them both.

She read his suffering in his harrowed face. 'Don't,' she said firmly. 'Don't speak of it, or think of it. Or it will make you its captive.'

He nodded, reaching for her hand.

A peacock, one of the spoiled beauties for whom the terrace was named, screamed its unlovely message as if in mockery.

'Nothing has happened,' Black Jade said hardily. 'It all took place a long time ago. We must look to the future. Now, let us think.' Her tone took on a businesslike briskness. 'Whom shall we offer as husbands to your daughters?'

'I don't know.' Pheasant tried to go with her. 'A junior minister? An ambitious young officer?'

'No.'

'No?' Her swiftness surprised him.

'No. The very fact of their marriages will cause a great deal of talk. We cannot prevent that. But if they marry ambitious men, or men of the Four Surnames, they may one day provide a focus for plots, for dissenters. It will be better if each takes some modest young man who will make her happy, and who will be delighted to be the husband of a royal princess without entertaining any idea of rising to that level himself.'

Pheasant sighed. 'It seems an inadequate recompense – but yes, I can see that what you say makes sense.'

'Good. Then why don't I find them husbands among the officers of my guard? They are all the sons of gentlemen and scholars, and are unquestionably loyal.'

'Yes, yes. Do as you please,' he said, suddenly wanting it over and done with, and the hideous bones of the past decently reburied.

'Then it is settled. I'm so glad.' Black Jade touched his cheek, her own equanimity quite restored. 'And, my dear – don't brood and make yourself miserable over this. It will all turn out very well, you'll see. We shall make the girls welcome amongst us, and celebrate their weddings in fine style; and then they will go home with their husbands and we shall hear no more of them.'

*

If the Emperor was satisfied, the Crown Prince was not. When Bold Tiger learned, among other things, the rank of the officers who were to marry his sisters, he presented an accusing countenance across his mother's paper-heaped desk one morning.

Black Jade took one look at him and told him she was in no mood for histrionics.

Her son leaned over the desk, his black eyes devouring her.

'Is that what you think? That my interest in injustice is mere play-acting? Yes. I believe it is possible that you do. Because it isn't one of *your* interests, is it, Mother?'

Ah. So it had only begun, the exhumation.

'Why are you here?' she asked, adding her signature, with its customary flourish, to a grant to a hospital.

With an effort, Bold Tiger put first things first. 'My sisters cannot possibly be contracted to the men you suggest. It would be an incredible loss of face for them.'

She pulled another scroll towards her. 'Have they said so?'

'Of course not. They are overwhelmed by your gracious notice, after so long.' His contempt, her challenge, went unmarked.

'Then I suggest you consult them. It seemed to me they were very happy with the choice. Singing Bird even confided that she thought Captain Chou the handsomest and most gallant man she had ever dreamed of.'

He was taken aback. 'You've spoken to them?'

'Well, naturally. I wanted to know their wishes on the subject.'

'I see.' He took a moment to recoup his anger. 'And I imagine you exposed them to your famous charm – had them grovelling in gratitude at your feet? Do they know, Empress, exactly how their mother died? And why?'

'I suppose,' she said coolly, 'that would depend very much upon the source of their information. If it was the same as yours, I expect they would have shown me just such faces as you do now.'

Her calm infuriated him. The things he had heard about her washed about his horrified mind in a foetid, disgusting soup.

'I have to know!' he cried, his eyes pleading, lacerating. 'You *must* tell me if it is all true!'

She sat back and laid down her brush, carefully, in its holder. 'It appears to me that your mind is already made up.'

'I – no,' he said with difficulty, wondering if he were truthful. 'I have heard so many things; they have shocked me, you understand. You are my mother. To hear such things of you is – unexpected.'

'And yet you seem to have no trouble in believing them.'

'What should I believe?' he asked. 'You won't deny the facts?'

'Indeed no.'

Wretched, he tried to understand her. 'Then, will you explain them? I am your son. I have a right to know your reasons.'

She stood up. 'No, you have not,' she said quietly. 'Nor do I intend to give them to you. As you will discover, during the long and not always simple, not always contented days of your life as a prince and perhaps as an Emperor – one does what one is capable of at the time. If I have regrets, they are my own business, not yours. And now, I really am extremely busy. Why don't you go and visit your half-sisters? I think you will find them content.'

'Perhaps.' His frustration made him sullen. 'But I believe that, first, I will go to see Lion Guard, if he is well enough. Perhaps he will satisfy what you have termed my "curiosity". If you will not?' It was a last appeal.

'I only wish you might,' she answered, her voice low, entirely altered. 'I thought you would have known. Lion Guard died last night. I had the news just after dawn.'

'I'm sorry.' He knew how much her acute and urbane champion had meant to her. He wished, suddenly, that he had not spoken so harshly, had not so easily allowed himself to lose control. It was because he loved her so deeply, and had so much coveted her good opinion, that he had been so unnerved by the discovery of her murderous notion of justice.

'I'm sorry,' he repeated. 'Oh, I wish all this had never happened!' he burst out with loud, resentful regret. 'I wish those girls' damnable neighbours had kept quiet and let things rest as they were.'

Black Jade had just enough patience left to feel a little sympathy for him.

'You are still so very young, in some ways,' she said, trying to smile, to heal his wounds. 'As I was, at the time you want so much to disinter.'

'I don't. I don't! I am sorry!' he cried again. He ran from the room.

Black Jade, just for a moment, laid her tired head on her desk. Lion Guard had died peacefully in his garden. Never had she felt more in need of his ironic wisdom and optimism.

She mourned sincerely for Lion Guard, but she would not mourn for her son's loss of trust in her. That was a problem Bold Tiger must work out for himself. Meanwhile, they both had work to do.

For, despite all her care, and that of a dozen doctors, Pheasant had made no real progress towards good health. He was unable to support the strain of the council chamber, and some of the ministers had begun to speak in terms of his abdication.

Black Jade examined her conscience with scrupulous care. She must not let what was promised for her own destiny affect her attitude to her son. She had so far kept faith with herself; she had done nothing to assist the fulfilment of the prophecy. Nor must she allow Bold Tiger's new doubts of her to intrude upon her judgement. A substantial number of the councillors felt, though they had not discussed it openly before her, that Bold Tiger would, with their guidance and hers, be worthy to hold the mandate. If she disagreed it was on the grounds of her knowledge of his weaknesses, not of prejudice. She was sure of that.

The loudest voice in the abdication faction was that of Princess Constance, Pheasant's sister and the mother of Red Poppy. She claimed that her only concern was for her brother's health, but Jade believed that her genuine wish was to see the next generation on the throne so that the present power of the Empress should be pruned to that of an Empress Dowager, while her own influence was enhanced as the aunt-in-law of the new young Emperor.

Though conscious of the ill-feeling that emanated from the self-assertive Princess, Black Jade put it to the back of her mind. No one took Constance seriously. She was not important. Let her amuse Pheasant if she could, though the Gods alone knew how he managed to find her amusing! At the moment she was busily turning the court upside down with her preparations for the spring festival, her portly figure positively bulging with importance as she harried courtiers and musicians, lantern-makers and boat-builders, butchers and spicers, all with equivalent maximum fuss. Jade, who had somehow found herself working for six of the day's twelve hours again, was glad to leave this task, at least, to her.

On the morning of the festival, however, she woke up pleased with the prospect of an enforced holiday. She exerted herself to look her best, inching into the new, sensuously clinging dress that she had commissioned from Chinghiz by flinging at him a book of Sui verse, with a marker against one of the famous 'Ten Demands' that Sixth Daughter Ting had addressed to her indulgent lover.

> A skirt fashioned of peacock net,
> Red and green, intermingled, contraposed,
> Refulgent as the fish-scaled dragon's brocading;

Clear-cut and luminous, admirably strange;
How coarse or fine, you know, my lord, yourself –
I demand of you, young man, a dress and sash!

The costume was indeed admirably strange, its full gauzy skirt changing colour as it caught and played with the light. Chinghiz, with his artist's eye for detail, had mixed a metallic powder for her eyelids and cheeks, so that they too shone for a second in rose or green as she turned her head.

Constance, it must be admitted, had done her work well. Assisted by perfect spring weather, she had transformed the gardens of the palace into an artificial as well as a natural paradise. The trees were hung with bells and lanterns and wind-chimes, sometimes even with outrageous paper blooms. The small boats on the lake were garlanded with flowers and rowed by little slave boys dressed as the Monkey King's subjects, in fur trousers with long tails. Girl musicians in insubstantial clothing floated across the grass like half-imagined visions. Others spread the Emperor's path with petals as he walked with his wife and his courtiers in the sun and the shade.

They had begun the day with the performance of ancient religious duties. Pheasant, accompanied by his three senior ministers, a white ox and a yellow plough, had gone to the hallowed plot of land outside the southern gate of the city, through which he had welcomed in the spring. He made his offerings in the temple of Shen-nung, the God of the farmers, and then ploughed three furrows while the ministers guided the ox and sowed the seed.

Meanwhile, Black Jade had worshipped with her ladies in the temple of Lei-tsu, the wife of the Yellow Emperor, who had first taught the Flowery People the skill of sericulture. Afterwards they had gone out and picked mulberry leaves and brought them back to the sheds where they tended the silkworms; these would produce the robes that she would embroider for Pheasant to wear at the year's great sacrifices. It was a pleasant ceremony, and there was a good deal of laughing and singing as they moved about the warm sheds, tempting the trays of tiny, sleeping life to wake and take their chosen food.

Now they were free to pass the day in pure amusement. There were songs, dances and charades, performed in a red and gold-striped pavilion by entertainers from the tributary lands. The veiled and saried Indian girls with the enticing but meticulous invitations of their hands and eyes, the lithe golden Sogdians with their green pantaloons and red boots, balancing impudently on rolling balls, and the Cambodian players performing the magical dance-drama about the "Kavalinka", the divine bird of the Buddhist paradise – all these reminded Black Jade of Hsuan-tsang and of the far-off, gilded days when she would sit with Shih-min and listen to his traveller's tales – days of such happiness that it was only by unwilling comparison that she knew she was not happy now.

Outside, on the grass, they watched the imperial household guard, in their scarlet shirts and caps stuck with the feathers of the white pheasant, dance the old favourite "Breaking the Battle Line" without which such occasions were incomplete. This, again, had originally commemorated Shih-min's victories, and seeing it, Jade felt that her own life was similarly moving through the set paces of a familiar dance, and one whose steps she had not written. She wished she could break the form of it, create a new measure of her own to her own rhythm and music. She reflected, as the men whirled and stamped, each man cheering the Emperor as he passed, that fate had seemed to offer her that very possibility, and yet there was no way in which she might stretch out her hand, of her own volition, and take it.

Life was admirably strange.

In the evening there was the inevitable feasting. As it was still warm the imperial family filled one of the prettiest courtyards, lantern-lit and scented with the perfume from dozens of tall vases of flowers. After they had eaten everyone kept their seats and talked to their neighbours, moving after a while to visit other tables, toasting relatives and friends.

Whether it was the strain of so much bonhomie or the tedium of Constance's conversation, Black Jade was uncertain, but after an interminable discussion of the trials the Princess had undergone to provide their day of pleasure, Pheasant suddenly leaned back in his chair and said he thought he would go to bed.

'*Amitabha*! Are you ill? Is it another seizure? I hope not – I should never forgive myself! You should not try to do so much, you know, Elder Brother. Shall I send for a sedan? Here, drink some wine, it will revive you. Oh dear, you do look pale!'

'Don't fuss, Constance, I'm perfectly well; only a little tired.'

Black Jade had already snapped her fingers for the sedan bearers. She never left Pheasant without such transport, though he preferred to walk when he could because it gave others confidence in his ability to recover.

He left without quibbling, pressing her hand in gratitude.

'Now then,' said Constance, shifting her hefty, kaftaned form nearer to Black Jade. 'It's time we had a little talk.'

'Is there something you particularly wish to say, Princess?'

'Indeed there is.' Her plump chin wobbled with sincerity. 'I don't suppose you'll thank me for it, but I'm used to being unpopular with you when I speak my mind.'

'Certainly we agree about very little. But that need not trouble us – we have known it long enough. What do you wish to say?'

Constance got her wind. The dragons on her bosom heaved alarmingly.

'This isn't only my own opinion,' she began, protecting herself, 'The majority of the family agree with me. We think you should persuade Pheasant to give up his duties.' She puffed, as though climbing a hill.

'You mean,' interpreted Black Jade levelly, 'that I should press him to abdicate?'

Constance waved an unexpressive hand. "Abdicate" was not the word she would have chosen; it sounded too much like what it meant.

'He is very ill. He will not improve unless every vestige of care is taken from him.'

'It is already taken from him,' Jade said curtly. 'How do you imagine I spend my days? And Bold Tiger? And the ministers? The care is ours. That is as it should be. But the mandate of Heaven rests with my husband.' She fixed the interfering Princess with a cold and unloving eye. 'Your suggestion is both impudent and treasonable. Kindly do not repeat it, either to me, or, as I hear you have done, to others. Your opinions on this matter are not wanted.'

Constance, outraged, burst into loud, unattractive tears. It was an appalling display for a member of the royal family. Her daughter, Red Poppy, rustling importantly in bright orange satin, chose this dramatic moment to visit her. Her round, pouting mouth became a perfect O as she realised her mother's distress.

'Whatever has happened? Oh do hush, Mother, people are staring! Your Highness, what is the matter with her?'

'She is not getting her own way,' said Black Jade briefly. At this Constance made a lowing noise and threw her sleeve over her face.

'It's something *you* have done, isn't it?' accused Red Poppy. She had all her parent's fearful lack of tact.

'No. It was something she did. She opened that unfortunate

organ, her mouth, when she should have kept it shut.'

'What right have you to speak of her like that? You would not dare do so in front of my uncle!'

Black Jade sighed. This was a truly detestable brat. 'No. Very probably I would not. I should not wish to distress him. But he is not with us. You too, Red Poppy, have too much to say for yourself. Kindly be quiet. And Princess, please try to control yourself. You have worked hard to give us this festival; it is a pity to spoil it for yourself like this.'

Constance subsided into afflicted sniffling. Red Poppy plumped down beside her and murmured comfort in her reddened ear, darting vicious glances at Black Jade.

'That is better. Now, may I offer you both some wine?'

Constance accepted, rather sulkily. Red Poppy shook her head.

'Something more to eat, then? These sweets are delicious.'

'I want no more food or drink of yours,' said the girl with deliberate rudeness, her sharp black eyes snapping.

The taut bow of Jade's patience was loosed, and the arrow sped. Later, how she was to regret its flight!

'Then I shall by no means force it upon you,' she said icily. 'Neither now, nor at any other time. Since it offends you to eat what is prepared for you, you shall not do so in future. Nor need you suffer unwanted company.' She signalled to one of her officers. Two ran up, alert for her command.

'You will escort this young lady to the Peach Tree Court. She is to be seated, alone, in a comfortable chamber. She is to have no servants. You will bring her provisions daily, which she will have the means to cook herself. She will leave when I give my permission. That is all.'

The musicians had never faltered. Only those near at hand had any idea of what was going on at the Empress's table. Their curiosity reached bursting point when they saw Princess Constance give vent to a new paroxysm of tears while Red Poppy stalked away between two guardsmen without a further word for anyone.

The palace was soon agog with the story. There was a certain amount of unkind satisfaction for Red Poppy was not a popular girl. As for her husband Loud Tiger, he was heard to say to his mother when she offered her explanation of his wife's disappearance, 'Merciful Kuan Yin! You can't imagine! A week, two weeks maybe? – without being pursued and persecuted! It's the best present you've ever given me!' The court laughed long and loud over that.

Even Pheasant was forced to smile. Although, for some reason known only to the Gods of family ties, he loved his interfering sister, he had always found Red Poppy a tiresome experience.

One week, two weeks, three, four weeks eventually passed, and still Loud Tiger enjoyed his freedom.

And then it suddenly seemed that the joke was over and Red Poppy should be released, it was hoped to better behaviour.

The officers who had arrested her were sent to fetch her. They found her jailors full of praise; she had been, amazingly, the quietest prisoner they had ever guarded.

As quiet as the grave.

When the officers broke open the sealed door behind which the girl had lived, they were met by the stench of rotting food. There was a great deal of it, neatly piled against a wall. None of it had been cooked. None of it had been eaten.

The Princess Red Poppy, in order to prove herself beyond the government of Black Jade, had starved herself to death.

She knew that she was blamed. It was not so much the terrible mistake of the moment that had found her guilty as the exhumed and accusing witness of history. The woman who had murdered and mutilated her rivals twenty years ago was obviously capable of shutting up a poor, foolish girl to starve. Black Jade saw the bleached bones of Paulownia rattle in late laughter and admitted their hour of triumph.

But that was not the worst of it. The core of her distress was the fact that she also blamed herself. The bewildered members of the family who came to her, ostensibly to offer comfort but seeking in reality their own reassurance, doubled and redoubled her conscience-stricken grief.

The saddest interview was with Constance, who emerged stunned and subdued from her apartments after two days of hysterical weeping.

'I don't understand it,' she kept repeating in a dull monotone. 'You had no reason to kill her. She was only a child. A little too spirited, perhaps, but there was no need to kill her.'

Jade's heart was humbled by the sight of the Princess, her energy gone with her bombast, ashen-faced in her mourning robes. She seemed curiously depleted, as though half her weight had been her confidence in the world she had organised so busily.

'I did not kill her,' Black Jade said gently. 'It was a terrible and unnecessary death, and there are no words to tell you how much I regret the command that was its cause. But it was never my intention to kill her – you must believe that.'

Constance did not seem to have heard her. 'How was it possible? Will you tell me her guards never entered that room? Never spoke to her?'

'It was part of her punishment,' said Black Jade wearily. 'So that she should be forced to contemplate and become a wiser girl. The guards were not at fault. The food was removed every day through the guichet; they thought she was using it.'

Constance passionately shook her head. 'No, no, I don't believe you! You killed her. Her unhappy spirit will return to accuse you, just as those others did, long ago! You are a creature of darkness. Wickedness! I am thankful that soon my poor brother will give place to Bold Tiger and we shall have done with you. Your son was born in the light; your darkness has not touched him. He will not suffer your rule or your cruelty.'

'Where is my motive?' demanded Jade, ignoring the tirade. 'What possible reason could I have had to do away with Red Poppy?'

'People like you don't need reasons. They do what they do simply because they have the power – because they are evil. Your third son did not care for my daughter, did he?' she finished, refuting her own theory. 'As you do not care for me.'

'It is strange.' Black Jade gave her a small, wistful smile. 'When I am accused of something so enormously wicked, and also so foolish – I can think of nothing to say. Only, Constance, that on the grave of my father, it is untrue; and that I can do no more than bend my head before you in abject sorrow for my mistake.'

Constance walked away from her kneeling figure. 'I am leaving this court,' she said. 'I do not suppose I shall return.' For perhaps the first time in her life, she showed a pitiful dignity.

Those who were malicious by nature, noting her departure, wondered if this was what the Empress had desired more than the removal of Red Poppy.

'I didn't love her, but I wouldn't have wanted her to die.' Loud Tiger examined his mother with the puzzlement of a forest inhabitant who comes into the house, and the sophisticated toils of house-dwellers, only when forced. 'Who would have thought she had the grit?'

He, at least, he had been easy to convince. He offered bluff sympathy for her mistake and fled back to his stables, his polo and his hunting, with a sense of lightness that he afterwards realised, with shame, was the absence of his insistent young wife.

His brothers looked at the matter rather differently.

They came together, a grave deputation of two. Beleaguered by their serious faces, Black Jade signalled Chinghiz to remain in the room. Again, she was at a loss for words. All the regrets and apologies under Heaven were too small, ridiculous even. She would not offer them, but waited for her sons to speak.

Bold Tiger began. 'I have just come from my father,' he announced.

'How is he this morning?' Pheasant had taken the tragedy badly. He was desperately sorry for Constance and he would miss her ebullient presence and over-protective affection. Although he had told Jade that he did not think she had intended Red Poppy to die, he thought, nevertheless, that she must bear the blame.

'He says he is considering abdication.'

'I see.'

'He feels his illness will never leave him now, and this accursed business has left him weaker than ever. He has no will to continue as Emperor.'

She was silent. Pheasant had not discussed this with her. That too, apparently, had been too much for him. Or perhaps he had feared that she might try to influence him against such a momentous decision? Well, that was true; she would have tried.

'Mother?' Young Tiger's tone was warmer. 'What do you think?'

She looked at him affectionately. He had simmered down lately. There had been fewer late nights and bawdy companions. New Moon had recently presented him with his first son, and he seemed to take his new duties as a father seriously.

'Surely that is a question for your brother, rather than myself?'

Bold Tiger released a slender smile. 'I would hardly expect my opinion to be valued as highly as yours, Honourable Mother, not by anyone I can think of.'

'It is good of you to acknowledge it.' It was the simple truth, or at least it had been until very recently.

Bold Tiger was getting round to that. 'I am here to solicit that opinion – though I can guess what it will be. It seems to me,' he added before she could speak, 'that it would be as well, in present circumstances, if we were seen to agree.'

'You are telling me that you feel that your father should abdicate,' she said slowly, 'and that, since the unfortunate death of your sister-in-law, my own reputation is a little tarnished, and it would be better for me, therefore, if I were found to be in complete accord with the wishes of the Emperor and the Crown Prince.'

She raised her indigo brows. 'Do I have it correctly?'

Behind her, Chinghiz moved restively.

'If that is how you wish to see it,' responded Bold Tiger with another thin smile. She looked into his carefully set face.

'I dislike your attitude,' she murmured pleasantly, 'though I recognise it clearly for one of my own cast-offs. Do you think we might all sit down and talk about this in a civilised fashion?'

Young Tiger dropped easily into a seat. His brother followed stiffly as though doing the chair a favour.

'Tell me truthfully, Bold Tiger,' Black Jade enquired neutrally, 'do you sincerely believe yourself capable of ruling the Empire?'

'It is what I have been trained, all my life, to do.'

'You are twenty-two years old.'

'I would have the ministers to guide my every step. I have the "Golden Mirror" that Shih-min wrote for my father, and father's own work on government.' There was a hesitation. 'And I would have you.'

'I see.'

Their eyes met. 'Why don't you want this, Mother?' he asked softly. 'You know my father can't go on. Do you want to be Regent? Is that it?'

Young Tiger bit his lip. His brother had spoken the unspeakable.

Black Jade looked away from her firstborn, her green eyes dreaming. What was the truth, now that the turning point was almost reached? If Bold Tiger succeeded she would no longer rule, as she had done for so long, in her husband's place. She would be the Empress Dowager, who owed obedience to her son. Was that what she wanted?

No. Most assuredly, it was not.

'Consider for yourself,' she invited gracefully. 'It seems to me, and might seem to many people, that I am more fitted, by lengthy experience, to be Regent, than you are, by your books and your tutors and a mere three years of semi-office, to be Emperor.' She smiled sunnily at him, shaking his determination to be immune to her.

'My father', he said, tight-lipped, 'was twenty-two when he succeeded.'

'Your father', she stated with delicate precision, 'has had his hand held by a series of ministers, and by myself, since the day he became Crown Prince.'

Bold Tiger drew in his breath and his brother looked at the floor, both embarrassed by such frank comment.

Seeing this, she said, 'Oh, don't think I am criticising the Emperor. He has laboured, with courage, under great difficulties. But can't you see that if you begin in the same way, relying heavily on others, that reliance may become impossible to terminate? Give yourself time, Bold Tiger. And think now, not of your father, but of Shih-min, who said, when he knew he would soon die, that "Nothing is harder to win than an empire; nothing is easier than to lose it." It requires a strong grip to keep it, my son. Do you think that yours is strong enough yet?'

Bold Tiger got up and came across to where she sat. He knelt at her knee and took both her hands in his.

'It would be,' he said, looking at her with Shih-min's eyes and a suggestion of his forceful charm, 'if you would be with me, instead of against me.'

And that, of course, was the nub of it. She wished to rule and was certain that it would be for the best if she did rule; and yet how could she stand against him, her son, of whom she was fiercely proud and whose right it was to take the throne?

She closed her fine, long-boned hands on his. 'Then, if you are so certain, that is how it must be.' She smiled, amused by the sunrise glow of surprise in his face.

'Then you don't mind? You will support me?' His voice rang with gladness. Young Tiger, bewildered by the entire scene, grinned to keep them company.

'Certainly I will. And so will your brother, won't you Second Son? You will be the heir until the Crown Prince is older; how will you like that?'

An expression of comic dismay told them exactly how he would feel.

'We'll think about that when we come to it,' he grunted quickly. 'And now, if you don't mind, we're conducting an experiment to find a more exact value of *pi*. The soldiers are waiting for me.'

'Soldiers?' Young Tiger's preoccupations were always unusual.

'We're going to draw a gigantic circle on the plain where they do manoeuvres. Then we calculate the areas of the largest regular polygon we can get inside it, and the smallest we can fit outside, d'you see?'

'I think so.' Jade was intrigued. 'I might come along and see how you're doing, later. But first, I think I should go and talk to the Emperor. If you would meet me in the Palace of Golden Bells in half an hour, Bold Tiger? We have a lot to discuss.'

Feeling as if he walked on silk cushions, Bold Tiger bowed superbly and left with his arm on his brother's broad shoulder.

'Don't say anything, not for a moment. I want to get used to it,' Black Jade said sombrely to Chinghiz.

'You don't have a great deal of faith in destiny, do you?' Chinghiz remarked, moving sinuously out of the background, which was what everyone thought he occupied on these occasions.

'There may be a considerable difference, don't you think,' she replied spikily, 'between destiny and false prophecy?'

'The impatience of women is the harrow of man,' her servant said piously, his eyes rolling upward.

'One of Confucius' lesser gems?' The tone was sweet-and-sour.

'An observation of my own,' he purred.

'It is all very well to be philosophical, but how will you like being steward to a mere Empress Dowager?'

'I shall weather it with patience,' he announced seraphically. 'And please don't throw anything. We have only the finest Sul porcelain in this room. Do you really intend to give in so easily?' he added smoothly, catching her in mid-grimace.

She sighed. 'When I was in the convent, I had to choose whether to break my vows and return to court, or lead a life that would be unnatural to me. There was no real choice. Now, I must choose between what might become a lifelong separation from my son, and assisting him to perform his rightful duties. Again, I cannot see that there is any real choice. Can you?'

'Put like that – no.'

'I know. You long for true harem intrigue, for plots and stratagems and midnight trysts with dangerous men, or women.'

'As I have said, Little Mistress, I am a very patient man.'

Pheasant was delighted, not to say relieved, at Black Jade's apparent change of heart. He had expected and feared a long wrangle with her about Bold Tiger's youth, inexperience and impulsiveness. Instead she had folded her hands and said demurely, 'You are the Emperor. The decision is yours.' He loved her for it, for saving him a struggle of which he no longer felt capable, and for making things easier for Bold Tiger.

They had come, the three of them, up to the smaller summer palace at the northern end of the imperial park, to think and to plan the future together. Pheasant would not abdicate until he was quite sure that the boy could replace him with a sufficient measure of confidence. They would work together, as a family towards that.

Slowly, as she and Bold Tiger moved closer to each other

again, working and talking together, sometimes with Pheasant, sometimes alone, Black Jade began to see how she might still have a satisfactory rôle to play when he took the throne. He had no intention, she soon realised, of setting her aside. On the contrary, he valued her experience as greatly as the ministers did.

She and he took up their morning rides again, often watching the dawn together like lovers, their horses ambling side by side across the lightening grass. It was a time of day they both loved and they became very companionable by sharing it, speaking very little but glad to be together.

She told him once how she had used to ride like this with Wu Shih-huo, the grandfather he had never known, whom he thought of as the stout companion of his other magnificent grandfather, Shih-min, seeing them engaged in bold, legendary deeds together, in the days before Emperors were reduced to the mere contemplation of "day-to-day detail". He hoped that, in a previous life, he had ridden with them.

'Who knows what brave times might be waiting for you, too?' Jade comforted, sympathising strongly. 'Peace is a blessing that will not necessarily last. There, now – I don't know what I should wish you – continued peace for the sake of the people, or some terrible excitement so that you can take off in your grandfathers' hoofprints!'

'Oh, both! I want everything!' Bold Tiger cried expansively, spreading his arms to embrace the whole future.

'So do I,' she said enigmatically, 'but mine has boundaries.'

He turned and reined close to her. 'There is nothing I will not give you Black Jade,' he said with passionate gratitude. 'I shall begin my reign by showering you with jewels and titles. You are the most beautiful woman in history, and I want the entire universe to know it!'

She blinked. 'I'm overwhelmed.'

He moved away and turned his horse in a little circle, round and round, seized with a sudden ecstatic vision of the future. Laughing, he stood in the stirrups and began to recite the list of her charms, in a mood of lightness and exhilaration that she had not seen since he was a child.

> 'Her eyebrow curves like a willow bough;
> Her teeth are white as jasmine flowers;
> Her hair enfolds her like a cloud;
> Her face is flawless as a face of jade;
> Her body fragrant as the rose;

Her voice is music, her motion dance;
No stronger enchantment under Heaven,
No man who would wish to break it,
For this is the woman who is called Black Jade.'

Tears starred her great eyes as he circled back to her, dropping dashingly from the saddle to kneel at her feet, head bowed to reveal the graceful, muscular curve of his neck. She reached out to caress the shining hair, knotted carelessly at the nape. Suddenly the wish burned in her that this could have been Shih-min's son. None could have been more like him in this intimate, faintly but sweetly shocking moment.

'Thank you, Bold Tiger. I don't think any woman has ever been offered such an extravagant litany.'

'No woman before has ever deserved it,' he said softly. His face was full of happiness.

She wondered, for one blasphemous second, whether any woman had ever fallen in love with her own son.

'Now,' she said, recovering herself, 'you have not given me the latest news of Firefly and the children.'

'Why, Mother,' he smiled, delighted with himself, 'I do believe I have embarrassed you!'

Pheasant was more contented than he had been for a very long time. His greatest pleasure was to see his family together in harmony. He suggested they should send for Tiger Lily and her brothers. 'Let us all enjoy this little time together, before we have to turn to serious matters. We shall pretend we are an ordinary scholar's family, taking our rest in the hills.'

On the morning before the rest of the household were to join them, Chinghiz awoke Black Jade with her usual bowl of jasmine tea. He did not lay out her riding clothes as she had expected, but hovered near her, waiting for her to be fully awake.

He had removed the window-blinds and she struggled to sit up, the sun striking into her eyes.

She protested. 'Chinghiz! That is cruel!'

He watched while she drank the tea and handed him the cup. Then he said quietly, 'It is a cruel morning.'

She looked at him quickly, saw his sorrowful face.

'What is it? Is it the Emperor? Has he been ill in the night?'

He shook his head, wondering how he could tell her. 'No, it isn't the Emperor. His Majesty is well.' Well enough, for a man whose heart is not strong and who has received a blow that has almost caused it to stop beating.

'Who then, or what? Tell me, for the Gods' sake!' She was afraid. It was not like him to take his time in this way. Words usually flooded his lips in a monsoon current; if he had to pick and choose amongst them, it was because he had something very bad to tell her.

'Please,' she begged. 'I must know.'

Uniquely, he sat down near to her upon the bed.

'It is your son,' he said. His voice shook, its brightness all extinguished. 'Bold Tiger.' His extreme gentleness flayed her slowly. 'He is dead, Little Mistress. They found him this morning. In his bed. At first they thought he had overslept. Then – '

'No!' She had begun to breathe very rapidly, staring at him in utter disbelief. 'No. You're talking nonsense! It isn't possible!'

'It is true. I would give my own life if it were not.'

'No,' she cried again. 'I don't believe you. How *can* he be – ?' She began to tremble uncontrollably, her breath tangled in great sobs of panic, of fear, of complete repudiation.

'We don't know yet – the physicians have been summoned from the palace; they will be here soon.' She was reaching out, blind with horror, perhaps for her robe, perhaps for something, anything, that would take away this cup of poison from her. With a small cry of pity and pain, he caught her into his arms and held her, stroking her softly, against the broad warmth of his chest. His heartbeat steadied her a little. She did not move, sensing a far-off comfort that she could not yet have, but wept for as long as she must, wrapped in the protection of his love.

But his arms could not keep her long from the truth she must see for herself. Soon, when she was able, he dressed her and they went quickly to the Prince's bedchambers.

The weeping crowd of servants parted to let them through, their sad murmuring following them into the room where the frankincense was burning to sweeten the path of the departing soul.

Bold Tiger lay on the bed with his eyes closed. He looked beautiful and peaceful and only a little pale.

Black Jade ran to his side and seized his hand. Surely they had been wrong? This was not the appearance of death. She shook his hand. It was cold. She began to chafe it, crying, 'Bring another quilt, and light the fire in the *kang*.'

Chinghiz was beside her. 'It is no use, Little Mistress. He has left us. He has begun his journey.'

'Ridiculous! Look at him!' she shouted, tears starting again at their fool's blindness. 'He is sleeping, can't you see? He is cold. Perhaps he has some sort of chill. We must make him very warm, make the room as hot as an oven, and then he will recover.'

'Mistress, he is no longer breathing,' Chinghiz said finally.

She looked. She searched the fine, sculptured face. Then she flung back the cover and laid her head over Bold Tiger's heart.

It was true. It was true.

Slowly she sat up, rearranging the quilt and laying her son's bronzed arms at his sides. She bent to kiss his lips and his eyes.

Even after this, what her mind had already accepted her heart still refused to recognise. She sat beside him, watching the brave, intelligent face, and waiting. She was unaware either of the murmurous throng that was gathering outside or of the stern marshalling of Chinghiz as he kept them from the door.

Quietly, encouragingly, she began to talk to her son. Wherever he had gone, she told him, it was surely not yet too far to return? There had been cases, she knew, when souls had turned back from their journey. If he had not yet reached the Yellow Springs, could he not seek permission to come back, to continue his young life and his duty? Praying, she entreated him again and again. As she did so, a terrible thought came to her, winding itself into her frightened mind like a serpent in a nightmare; the more she struggled against its seething coils the closer it bound her, rearing its hideous head and glaring into her eyes. It was for her.

This death was for her. The Gods had chosen this, the most cruel way of all, to bring her to the Dragon Throne.

She cried out, at last, in rejection and horror; and then, for a merciful interval, she broke beneath the overwhelming burden, escaping the tyranny of her senses into deep, unconscious darkness.

The doctors said that Bold Tiger must have eaten something that had poisoned him; his abdomen was swollen and his faeces black. Their later analysis confirmed this opinion. He had not cried out, so he must have died very quickly, not even suspecting himself how serious his condition was.

It was hard to believe that anyone would have poisoned him deliberately. He had been universally popular. No suspicion attached to the servants, all of whom had given long and loyal service. His younger brother, Young Tiger, even had he wished (as he assuredly did not) to become the next Emperor, was not yet aware of his father's intention to abdicate.

It seemed, therefore, that the Prince had died a natural death. It was, at least, one so common as to be accepted as natural. The dreadful suddenness of it left the court without breath to suggest anything more sinister.

Black Jade and Pheasant returned to the main palace that night, bringing with them the body of their son to take its place in the Hall of Ancestors. The history of their shared grief was a long and sombre one, but never had they been drawn so close in their extremity as they were now by the death of the son whose birth had cemented their marriage and provided the joyful hope of the entire Empire.

Black Jade, herself sick with mourning, watched helplessly as grieving broke down the remaining resources of Pheasant's strained and suffering heart. She tended him personally, never leaving his side, glad to have something to do with the hands that wanted, with an ancient, senseless instinct, to tear and tear at the yard-long fall of dulled and dishevelled hair that only Chinghiz compelled her to care for.

They could not even mourn as long or as single-heartedly as they would have wished. There were other duties waiting for them.

The ministers spoke of them with grave respect to Black Jade. At last, in response to their whispered urging, she forced herself to turn her own mind, and try to turn her husband's, to the raw necessity of naming the next heir to the throne.

During one of the long nights when she could not sleep but sat up with him, dry-eyed and brooding above a Go board where the pieces never moved, Chinghiz said to his mistress (for there was nothing he could not say), 'The woman who murdered the Empress Paulownia and her friend, and who starved Red Poppy, could also be capable of killing her own son, if she wished to rule. Bright Phoenix, they are starting to say that you wish to rule.'

She smiled briefly at his even note. 'Gossip excites them; it is more interesting than grief. And perhaps they are right.' Her voice rose. 'Perhaps my son's death is a punishment.' Her eyes were wide open with lack of sleep and with the new vision of horror she was making for herself. 'My temperament is such that my hand strikes, and afterwards I am sorry for it. It was so, in a lesser way, with Red Poppy, as it was with Paulownia. I should have considered the girl's stubborn nature before choosing such a punishment. It seems clear to me now,' she sighed, devoid of all hope, 'Bold Tiger's death is a recompense for the old sin, and the new; and a sign to me that I will not escape my karma.'

Chinghiz brought her wine. It was not a time to offer the solace of touch. 'I understand the Gods no more than you,' he said gently, 'but it seems to me that Heaven has chosen you because you are worthy of the mandate. There is no other possibility.'

'You think so? Then must my second son die also, to satisfy those determined Gods?'

24

Youthful folly has success.
It is not I who seek the young fool.
The young fool seeks me.
At the first oracle I informed him.
If he asks two or three times, it is importunity.
If he importunes, I give him no information.
Perseverance furthers.

(The hexagram Meng, 'Youthful Folly', the *I Ching*)

Young Tiger had succeeded to the crown of the Heir Apparent with considerable reluctance. Shocked by the death of his brother, he threw himself into his new duties with a sober determination, saying goodbye, for the present, to science, and settling himself to catch up on his lesser knowledge of statecraft.

He was eager and cooperative in the council chamber, impressing ministers with his ready intelligence and his startling, though not always convenient, gift of total recall.

When Black Jade suggested that the best method of learning about government was to study its history, she found that she had set the seed of a new obsession. The water-clocks languished, the value of *pi* remained at 3·1415926, the solid star globes and armillary spheres were not consulted; Young Tiger had immersed himself in history to the tip of his topknot. He was soon engaged, with devouring enthusiasm, upon his own appreciation of the later Han dynasty, which he hoped would become a definitive volume.

He found Black Jade an unfailing support. She was never too busy to answer his questions or talk things through with him. He was not aware that she took an equal interest in his physical welfare; his health was monitored and his food tasted at her command. It was not a very strong defence against the possible malice of Heaven, but it was all she could do to protect him.

On a summer afternoon, about a year after Young Tiger's promotion, he arrived in the Inner Palace to find his mother playing a game of courtyard chess with Tiger Lily, Dawn Tiger and their friends. They were making a lot of noise, and by no means keeping to the squares which, as living chessmen, they were supposed to occupy. Black Jade, naturally, was one of the generals; Tiger Lily, fiercely competitive, was her opponent.

'It's all right, I'm in check just now,' Black Jade called as the Prince approached. She came towards him flushed and smiling, looking very little older, today, than his twelve-year-old sister.

'I'm sorry to interrupt your game. I wanted to talk to you.'

She pushed back some stray pieces of hair and peered at him closely. There was trouble in his calm, clever face.

'Of course. Wait a moment.' She looked round for a substitute. 'Dancing Oriole, will you play general for me?'

A very pretty girl of about seventeen bowed and moved to the square Jade had occupied. Young Tiger took appreciative note of her sweet face and delicious figure. She caught his interested gaze and blushed charmingly. He would seek her out later.

'She looks a little delicate for the field of battle,' he observed.

Black Jade smiled. 'Do you like her? She is one of my maids. But her father is only an eighth rank official; she is not quite suitable to be your concubine.'

He shook his head. 'It was an idle comment.' And he had not come here to make idle comments, nor to ask idle questions.

Black Jade led him to the small courtyard outside her study. It was the most secluded retreat in the palace, paved with deep blue tiles and shaded from the hot summer sun by fig and orange trees. They sat beside the white marble fountain which was presided over by its own private divinity, a graceful image of the Water Goddess, Shen Nu, who lived on the mountain of Wu Shan where she enticed mortal heroes into a transient embrace amid its swirling mists and falling waters. Her symbol was the rainbow and her power was to give abundant fertility to every form of life. She was the ancestress of all the imperial clans, and was both loved and feared for her vital giving or withholding of the precious element of water. Black Jade was very fond of her. She touched the slender statue and smiled at her son.

'You already have her blessing. Three sons, all healthy babies!'

'Yes, I've been very lucky.'

He did not respond to her smile. He seemed tense and nervous, which was most unlike him. She offered iced sherbet; he refused, tapping his fingers on the carved balustrade of the fountain.

'Well then, perhaps you should tell me why you are here?'

'I will. Give me a little time. It's rather difficult.' He smiled now; the sort of smile one gives the tooth-puller.

'Do not worry – you know I will help if I can,' she encouraged.

'Yes. Well, it's a little delicate – '

She waited, projecting an aura of bright receptivity.

Young Tiger cleared his throat. 'I have recently been told something very unpleasant. You may already know of it. Indeed – ' he lifted his chin and directly searched her face – 'perhaps you are the only person who knows the truth of it.'

'Don't make mysteries, Young Tiger; it is too hot.'

'Very well.' He marshalled his courage. He hoped she wouldn't be angry with him, or distressed. He would rather be cut in half than hurt her. 'My informant was a friend of mine who had his information from his mother, who is now dead. She was once a lady-in-waiting to my – to your sister, Rose Bird. She told him that I am not your son but your nephew; that I was born to your sister at the same time as a son of your own who died at birth, and that I was smuggled into the palace to take his place.' He finished in a swift gabble, stunned by his own daring.

'Good heavens!' Jade was more severely stunned.

'Yes. Well, you can imagine why I found it difficult to repeat.'

He looked both deprecating and immensely relieved.

'Indeed I can. But I'm not sure *why* you found it necessary to repeat such an injurious piece of nonsense. It doesn't only reflect upon myself – it dishonours the dead. I'm surprised at you.'

'I'm sorry. I hadn't thought of that.' He resembled Pheasant as he floundered. 'I just wanted to find out – ' Too late, he saw her face change. His voice died.

'Are you telling me,' Black Jade said softly, her hands holding on to each other in her lap, 'that you wish to ask me if there is any *truth* in this venomous slander?'

Young Tiger bent his head, his expression reminiscent of the slaughterhouse. 'I'm sorry,' he repeated. 'I suppose it has been rather crude of me.' He met her eyes again, shrugging faintly. 'I had to know, that's all. After all, how could I become Emperor, if – '

She interrupted him flatly, her small body stiffening with anger. 'Did your loose-tongued friend hazard any guess as to who your father might have been, or is that still a matter for conjecture?'

His face burned. He was utterly miserable. 'The Emperor. That was not changed.'

'I see.' She was spitting like her pride of panthers now.

'You would make a treacherous liar of my sister, a lecher of your father, and a bastard of yourself! I hope it makes you content! Where am I in all this? Did I play the whoremistress, to bring my sister to my husband's bed?'

'No! Please, Mother, don't. I beg you, don't be so – I didn't mean to upset you like this. I should not have spoken. I'm sorry!'

He rubbed his hand across his forehead, pressing his knuckles against it, devastated by her anger and even more by the hurt he knew to be fuelling it. He knelt before her, dropping his head.

'I'm a clumsy fool. Forgive me! I can't bear it if you won't.'

Black Jade dashed an angry hand across her eyes. 'Yes, you are,' she agreed wholeheartedly. 'Now please go away. And tell your informative friend it might be better if he were to leave court for a while. I wouldn't like to think he was anywhere in my vicinity.'

'Very well. Anything! Only please say you accept my apology?'

She looked at him wanly, pushing back the intrusive tendrils of her hair. He saw that they were damp and his heart smote him so that he almost wept himself. She seemed so small and woebegone. Hating himself, he gazed up at her, his brown eyes soliciting forgiveness with a passion previously shown only for a lunar eclipse or the wars of Sui Yang-ti.

'Oh yes. I acquit you of the desire to cause distress,' she said dejectedly. 'But that can't alter the effect, can it?'

He would have said more, tried to undo what he had done, but she waved him away. She wanted to be alone.

When he had gone she remained for a long time, blindly contemplating the image of the Water Goddess with eyes that saw only the past.

After this, Young Tiger found that his relations with his mother became serenely businesslike. Without seeming outwardly very much changed towards him, she succeeded in keeping him at arm's length. It was not difficult, for Young Tiger was the victim of an embarrassment of unfathomable depths. Very soon he asked if he might visit Chang-an for a time, so that he could try his hand at solo government with the skeleton cabinet that remained there permanently. Pheasant was loath to let him go, but Black Jade persuaded him that it would be a good thing for the boy.

'He will learn to think more clearly, without help, when he is alone,' she said, expressing a hope that was deeper than the Emperor could know.

Perhaps the Crown Prince's absence would put an end to any further retelling of the old story about his birth. She hoped so. Chinghiz, however, considered it vital to discover how far it was current. They could only suppose its purpose to be aimed against herself. There was no reason why Young Tiger should not inherit the throne whoever his mother was; the Emperor might name any of his sons as his heir, even that of his lowest concubine. But if Black Jade were not his mother, she could not take on the power of the Empress Dowager, but would be reduced to a nothing, a relict who would do best to shave her head and retire to a convent. Perhaps, already, there were those who liked this prognosis of her future; men who perhaps wished themselves to wield the chief influence over Young Tiger when he became Emperor.

Black Jade sent a request to the inquisitive Scholars of the North Gate to discover who were her son's friends and what they whispered to him. Here in Loyang, Chinghiz would perform a similar service. For the sake of protecting Young Tiger, that innocent and enthusiastic spirit, from the consequences of his unenviable position in life, she would turn two capitals into a circus for spies.

The separation went well. In Chang-an, the ministers reported, Young Tiger acquitted himself with merit. His private life, they hinted, might leave a little to desire. He had become over-fond of women and wine and once again sought the company of his old night-time companions; but his conduct in the council chamber was exemplary.

Black Jade wrote letters praising his achievements and gently criticising his trips over the tiles. He replied politely and briefly, begging her pardon for disappointing her. He continued to lead his life exactly as he pleased. The chief intimates of both his nocturnal pleasures and his daily conferences, the North Gate informed her, were two of his half-brothers by consorts, and one of the younger ministers.

Pheasant, pleased with his son's progress, was happy to allow him a few small excesses. He was shaping well, that was the main thing. It was good to be able to relax, to know that the Empire was still in good hands, despite the tragic loss of Bold Tiger. For himself, he was content to spend his last years or months – he could not know which – surrounded by the energy and laughter of his younger children and their schoolfellows. He spent as much time as he could with Loud Tiger, joining in the gentler of that muscular young man's pursuits and finding that the noisy, disaster-prone child had grown into an uncommonly sweet-natured and affectionate adult.

Black Jade valued this period in their lives, all the more because of Pheasant's precarious health which taught them to cherish every moment of happiness.

The person most gifted in the art of creating such moments was Tiger Lily. A born impresario, she stage-managed the lives of everyone around her into one long succession of pleasures. Although, now thirteen, she was the youngest of Jade's children, she had the strongest will of them all. In league with her adoring brother, Dawn Tiger, who for her sake still lived in the Inner Palace, she ensured that her parents never lacked entertainment.

'If I hadn't been born a princess,' she had once sworn, when she was eight, 'I should have been a dancing-girl – or a soldier – or a travelling musician.' She had never seen any reason why being a princess should impede her progress in these desirable professions, and was therefore a dedicated dancer, an excellent archer and a superb lutanist and singer.

These were not the only ways in which she resembled her mother. When the state courier from Tibet visited the court, he was ravished by the sight of this tiny, exquisite reproduction of the Empress. The ruler of his country, the T'san Pu, was presently suing for an end to the border wars between himself and the Empire. He had expressed his good intentions with exotic gifts and the proposal that the Princess Tiger Lily should travel to Lhasa to marry him. The enchanted emissary, who was fond of very young girls, foresaw nights of supreme pleasure for his fortunate master.

'Well, what do you say, Little Pearl?' Pheasant enquired of his daughter. 'Should you like to marry a king and live in the high Himalayas?'

Tiger Lily wrinkled her perfect nose. 'No, Father, I should not. I have read the letters of Princess Wen Cheng, who married the T'san Pu in my grandfather's time. She says the Tibetans are wild men, covered in hair, who paint themselves with red ochre! She spent most of her time improving their looks and manners but nevertheless I shouldn't care to risk it.'

'Would you not? Well, perhaps I can sympathise,' chuckled Pheasant. 'But what shall we say to the Tibetan Ambassador? We don't want to offend him just now, or we shall have another war on our hands.'

'I don't know. I'll think about it,' promised Tiger Lily soberly.

The next afternoon she assembled her family in her private courtyard and treated them to tea and cakes she had made herself. The sugary figures of men and horses melted in the mouth, if, that is, they had not crumbled in the hand.

'It's really very simple,' the hostess said, licking her fingers with aplomb. 'I wonder we didn't think of it right away. You have probably all forgotten that I am, in fact, a nun.'

'*Amitabha*!' They had indeed forgotten. Tiger Lily had been enrolled at Kan Yeh as a hostage to good fortune after Golden Willow had died, an innocent young soul dedicated in place of the one that had gone to the Western Heaven. Her vows had been light ones, involving little more than a promise to say her prayers regularly and to attend certain services. But the girl was right; just now these vows could be put to good use.

'The only trouble is,' detected Dawn Tiger thoughtfully, 'the envoy is *here*. And he will s-stay here for some t-time. He can *see* that my sister is not a nun – from her hoydenish be-behaviour if from nothing else!'

Tiger Lily grinned and threw her crumbs at him. 'If you like I'll put on a grey robe and go into Kan Yeh until he has gone. But I *won't* shave my head, not if the rest of the universe were clamouring at our borders!'

'No, indeed,' agreed Black Jade, admiring the black silky tail beneath her daughter's perky green cap. 'But perhaps you need not go quite so far as Kan Yeh.'

Everyone turned to her.

'You are rather cramped in this courtyard,' she deplored, 'especially when you try to cram half the palace into it as you so often do. Don't you agree, my lord? Shall we give Tiger Lily a little more space in which to grow?'

'I'd be delighted to,' laughed Pheasant, 'if I had the least idea what you are suggesting!'

'I propose that we should build her a convent of her own – here, in the palace grounds. Then no one can say she is not a properly dedicated nun!'

Dawn Tiger roared with laughter, the Princess clapped her hands in delight and the Emperor looked doubtful.

'I hardly think – ' he began.

'Why not? Surely we may do as we please? It is only natural that we should wish to keep our child as near to us as possible, even if she has taken her vows. Who can criticise the idea?'

'Someone will, you may depend upon it,' sighed Pheasant. 'But you are right, Black Jade, it is our own business. Let us do it. At least it will solve the problem of the marriage offers that are bound to keep cropping up from now on.'

'Marvellous! My own convent!' Tiger Lily was thrilled. 'It will be a fairy palace! And dearest, most Honourable Father – when I must have a husband, you'll let me choose him for myself, won't you?'

'I will think about it,' the Emperor promised gravely.

Tiger Lily's convent was the talking point of the year. It was, as she had promised, a diminutive palace, full of architectural novelty. Externally it was very simple, with the same quiet appeal as the Taoist temples which perched upon mountain crags all over the Empire. Its entrance was a single flight of marble steps leading to a red-painted colonnade carved with flowers, its single roof unspectacular, though prettily tiled in blue.

Inside, where the curious would not be permitted to trespass, it was a gallery of ten thousand delights. The golden wood floors were covered in silk carpets from all over the eastern world, and the walls with tapestries and paintings and cartoons of Tiger Lily's favourite stories; Mu-lan, the girl soldier, marched across her bedroom with her ignorant male comrades, looking unsurprisingly like the Princess herself. The elegant rooms were filled with exotica from every tributary land; in every one shone the lucency of jade and the glint of gold, and there was the scent of sandalwood and the green glow of living foliage.

Tiger Lily had been very strict with the *feng shui*. Every door and window was wide enough to admit an army of *Ch'i*, the good spirits who enter a house, as they do a human body, by its openings. There were no acute angles or blank walls to impede their movement. Her favourite chairs faced the door so that she could properly play hostess to these benevolent visitors, and knowing they were fond of wind chimes she hung these near every current of air.

The most important part of her new home was, of course, the temple. This was dedicated to Kuan Yin and housed a growing number of fine carvings of the Buddhas, sent from India. The new young Abbess of Kan Yeh offered the service of dedication, and the nuns were Tiger Lily's frequent visitors.

The court did not know quite what to make of it. It was an odd situation, certainly, but not an unseemly one. Both the Princess and her mother were genuinely devout, having followed the supreme example of Golden Willow in giving their patronage to the churches. What little criticism there was soon ceased. The Tibetan envoy returned to his mountains, to tell his master regretfully what he had missed.

After a particularly pleasant and uncomplicated summer the Emperor had another stroke. He thought he sensed the approach of death and Young Tiger was recalled to Loyang and appointed co-Regent with Black Jade. The young man was glad to be among his family again and his immediate grasp of affairs demonstrated how well he had learned from his advisors in Chang-an. He spent much of his spare time with Pheasant, reading to him or mulling over the less strenuous daily concerns. It was his father, therefore, who first noticed the change in him.

'I'm worried about the boy,' he confided, puzzled, to Black Jade. 'He has become a model Heir Apparent, but there is a tension beneath his ease of manner that I don't understand. And although he has obviously missed his family, he seems loath to discuss with me anything which involves you; have you any idea why? Have you quarrelled with him over something?'

'No,' she said. 'Perhaps he objected to some of my reproving letters – nothing to get excited about, just the usual young man's tricks. Too many bright nights; the wrong girls.'

But it was not that, or at least she did not think so. A small shadow hovered over her, warning, irritating. She waved it away.

Pheasant sighed. 'What a trial it is, as well as a pleasure, to have children. I wish I might be here to see how they will all turn out.'

She reached for his hand and squeezed it. 'You will watch them from your ancestral throne. I too, one hopes.'

'Yes, but – ' he smiled – 'I have been wondering – why not find out a little on account? There is a new astrologer at court, a Taoist, a man who has travelled in India and Persia. I thought perhaps – '

She was laughing. 'I know. I've not met him yet, but he has told Tiger Lily she will marry a soldier. She's thrilled, of course!'

'Is she indeed? It seems a little extreme to refuse the T'san Pu and look forward to a common soldier.'

'I don't suppose he will be at all common. Would it set your mind at rest to see this man, or one of the other astologers?' She would see him first herself to make sure he was the sort of person who had the sense not to tell the Emperor what he would not wish to hear.

But this proved unnecessary. 'Ah, no. I think I have done with the future. It will soon have done with me. Perhaps I am a coward, but – *you* see him, will you, my dear? I want to know neither the length of my days, which he will exaggerate, nor the unfortunate extent of my children's troubles, which he will minimise.'

'His reputation suggests he simply tells the truth,' said Jade. She thought that perhaps she *would* give the man an interview. She would speak only of her sons; nothing of herself.

Young Tiger came to her late one evening, as she relaxed on the cool veranda of her bedroom. He was flushed and his words were a little slurred as he excused himself for such an unaccustomed appearance.

'You see I needed the wine – to give me courage!' he announced, steadying himself on the trunk of a potted magnolia.

'Courage?' She raised her brows. 'Whatever for?'

He grinned, slightly askew. 'Have plenty of courage us'lly. Kill a tiger, soon as look at it. But you, Mother – you're something diff'rent. I'm not sure how to deal with you.'

She looked, not unkindly, into his bleary, troubled eyes, and counselled, 'You should think of me as a more domesticated breed of tiger, my dear; not lethal, but not to be trifled with either. Now, perhaps, if you don't mind, we might go indoors. I think those guards at the end of the colonnade have been roused to quite a high enough level of curiosity already.'

She rose and led the way so that he had to follow her. Inside, she called for Welcome and black tea, very strong, very hot.

'Well, whatever next!' the old nurse demanded, puffing mightily. 'If I were you, Young Master, I should stick my head in a basin of cold water. I'll fetch one, if you like?'

'That won't be nec – I won't need one, thank you.' He drank the tea, screwing up his face at its bitterness.

'Thank you, Welcome. You may go to bed now. Chinghiz will bring anything else I may need.'

Welcome grunted, viewing Young Tiger with disapproval. 'You won't find wisdom at the bottom of a wine-jug, Second Son – only a sore head. And serve you right!' she ended triumphantly, shuffling huffily off to her couch at the foot of Black Jade's bed.

'And now, my son, kindly explain yourself.'

'Yes. If I can. You are going to be angry, I know. You see – it's the same thing as before. The same old, evil, unbearable thing. I know I have already received my answer, but I have to ask you again. Mother – am I truly your son?'

She caught her breath, not in surprise, more in recognition of what had been waiting in her mind ever since Pheasant had mentioned the boy's discomfort about her. It had had to be this again; it was the only thing it could be. She thought, too, that she knew why.

She took her time. When she said quietly, 'You know, don't you, that you are offering me a grave insult? To say nothing of the injury; to be stricken twice with the same arrow is something no poor victim expects.'

'I'm sorry. Oh, damnation!' He pressed his balled fist into his brow. 'What can I say? I *have* to know, especially now that we're officially yoked together like two oxen.'

'You ask me again because you have been told that Rose Bird's child has now died; and you are now asking yourself if any other child ever existed, except for yourself?'

He gave her a startled glance. 'Yes. How did you know?'

She sighed. 'It is not difficult to surmise.' She continued, 'But there is no reason for you to have asked the question once again; not on your own initiative. You already had my answer. Who has caused you to think again, and to make enquiries about my sister's child?'

He shook his head. He would not tell her. He was loyal to his friends. As Emperor, he would not regret such loyalties.

She did not press him. She already knew. It took little imagination to realise that the two young half-brothers, sons of concubines, and the rising minister who were his most frequent companions had an interest in his future being untrammelled by the influence of an Empress Dowager. Why, she wondered, with pity tinged with contempt, could he not see that for himself?

'Very well, if you think you owe these sage advisers more than you owe to me.' She tried to sound dry and incisive, to keep the pain out of her voice. She did not want him to know how deeply he was hurting her.

'It isn't that! You know it isn't!' he cried desperately.

'No? What then?'

He was lacerated by the glacial tone. 'It is need, pure and simple. I *need* to know if I am yours!'

'Why? You are the Emperor's son; you appear to be sure of that, at least. As such, the throne is yours. Why bother about the rest?'

'You are saying this to hurt me.'

She laughed, not steadily. 'Am I not justified?'

'I don't know.' He leaned against the silk-covered wall, his face like that of a condemned man.

'And if I tell you – again? That I am your mother. Will you be satisfied? Or will the question still eat away your sleep?'

He shook his head, mute and staring.

'Because there is nothing else; only my word.' She turned the point of the arrow once more, in her own breast as well as his. 'No one else would know, except Chinghiz, except Welcome – and they, as you know, would say whatever I wanted them to say. My sister is dead; so is her child. Your father would have been told nothing. So. There you have it. My word. Nothing else.'

Young Tiger was weeping, his hands clutching the wall behind him.

'My poor son. You have ravelled yourself a net that will trap you no tigers; only yourself.'

His eyes burned, his tears were hot. He reached out his hand to her, groping for what he had lost. 'Help me, Black Jade!'

'I have tried.' Her voice was small now, small and despondent. 'But you still haven't told me. *Why* all this? Such sadness, such hurt – when the throne is yours already.'

'Stop it! Stop! You are cruel and you know it. It isn't the throne. I never wanted it! It is you! I want you. I want to be your son. I love you, Mother! Does that mean nothing to you?'

'Oh yes.' She repulsed the soft desire to crumple up and weep in his arms. It would no doubt have satisfied him – for the moment. But she knew now that he was a lute upon which any master might play. It was a competition she did not intend to enter. 'Yes, it means a great deal to me. I am glad to hear you say it, for I must admit you have made me doubt it. I wish you would go now, Young Tiger. Go to bed, and sleep if you can. I am very tired. Your father is ill. I need all my strength to care for him. I have no reserves for these emotional tornados. I wish you good night.'

'So you won't help me?' he said dully, coming away from the wall.

She gasped in pain and unbelief. 'I can do no more!' she shouted then, her patience and her taut spirit exhausted.

Young Tiger studied her with a face that was like his father's, not hers; fine-boned and delicate, its expressions uncertain and changeable, like his mind. Again he put out his hands, as though begging. They were long, slender hands with thin, square-ended fingers, a musician's hands; like hers.

She turned away from him, calling for Chinghiz, and left the room. He would have to find his answers in himself.

Young Tiger remained, staring after her and then at his own supplicant's hands. He turned them over once or twice, then dropped them to his sides, as if, after all, they did not belong to him.

The next morning he stood beside Black Jade in the council chamber, impeccably neat, his conversation bright and precise and his judgement apparently unimpaired by lack of sleep or of satisfaction from her.

The fortune-teller Ming Chung-yen cut a striking figure. Very tall and of indeterminable age, he had a long, humorous face and the spare, sinewy body of the man who spends most of his life on horseback or on foot. His skin was tanned to the colour of old boots and his eyes were creased at the corners by many winds. Over his dark red robe he wore the hide of a tiger slain in its prime, its marmalade stripes arguing with his own multicoloured beard. His brown feet were in thonged sandals and he carried a likely-looking gnarled staff. He did not bow, so he was presumably a priest.

Black Jade offered him a seat and some refreshment. He accepted the wine and ignored the food. She asked him about his travels.

'Recently I have come from Tibet. For much of the way I was with some soldiers returning from the border.' He drank deep and the light of the professional storyteller entered his sharp, far-sighted eye. 'Our path took us up mountainsides where we often had to cut our steps into the stone; across raging torrents upon bridges as insubstantial as a spider's web; climbing heights which squeezed the breath from our ribs as we staggered towards the summit; but we were hardy, and there was always a temple to take us in and mend us at the end of the day.' Now his gaze narrowed its focus and rested on her. 'In one of these, August Lady of Jade, a shrine of the Taoists which clings to an impossible crag and shares its perch with eagles, I was desired by one of the priests, if I should come this way, to give you a message.'

She felt very still. She seemed to have been waiting an age for him to continue.

'Please,' she said softly, without breathing, 'will you give it to me?'

Ming drank again. 'Of course. The holy sage said to me that, if Your Highness would be so gracious, you might turn to the fifth poem on the scroll that he once gave you, the one on the scented cedarwood paper with the rose-quartz handles. The poem itself is his message.'

She inclined her head with the generous grace, he thought, of a woman who knows herself beloved. Ming's curiosity was great, but he knew better than to spoil his chance of employment by any attempt, however subtle, to indulge it.

'You have my gratitude for acting as a courier. Your travels must have been most interesting. I look forward to hearing more about them. The Emperor, too, loves to hear travellers' tales.'

His stories, she knew, would be highly coloured and embellished with a wealth of exotic and terrifying incident. His recital must wait, however, until he and she had done their business together.

She explained what it was that she wanted him to do.

'I shall need a little time in which to observe the princes closely. I shall want to be absolutely certain before I speak.'

'That is understood. You will have the run of the palace for as long as necessary.' She smiled. 'But kindly do not extend any more of your revelations to my daughter. I feel strongly that it is happier if parents alone know of their children's fate. The knowledge of the future is a great burden,' she added soberly.

'As Your Highness wishes.' He was not surprised. He knew something of her own history in respect of his calling. His profession operated in a smaller arena than was generally known.

Black Jade walked quickly, taking only Welcome, through the gardens to Green Fragrance Court. The cedarwood scroll was in the little desk where she kept the books Shing-jen had given her.

Her heart was beating like a green girl's. She was swept through with joy that he should think of her after so long. There was also sadness, as there was in the hours when he still claimed her thoughts, when the night was too long or when she was solitary, here, in the rooms they had shared together.

She took up the scroll, struck with the wondering sense that he too had held it in his hands. That consciousness brought with it the memory, almost the sensation of his touch; his fingers light upon her neck, his lips in her hair, as she read again the verse he had sent to her across the mountains of the years.

The poem had been written by Wu-ti, Emperor of the Liang dynasty, a hundred years ago.

Who says that it's by my desire,
This separation, this living so far from you?
My robe still smells of the perfume that you wore;
My hands still hold the letter that you sent.
Round my waist I wear a double sash;
I dream that it binds us both with the same heart's knot.
Did you know that people hide their love,
Like a flower that seems too precious to be picked?

It was agonisingly sweet to give in to such pure tears. She sank down on the chaise and closed her eyes, repeating the words again, feeling them enter her breast.

Much later, when it was growing dark and Welcome was tired of waiting, she came into the room carrying a woollen shawl. She checked at the sight of her mistress, sitting all alone in the twilight, with a tangled scroll in her lap.

'Why, I'm sorry, Little Phoenix; I would have come to you before, but I could have sworn that you had someone with you,' she fussed.

'Don't disturb yourself, old friend,' said Black Jade, her whole being imbued with a rare and joyous tranquillity. 'There was someone; but he is gone now.'

Ming Chung-yen had been a member of the court for nearly three weeks. He had entertained the entire imperial family with his tales of travel and adventure, and he had told many fortunes, keeping strictly within the limits Black Jade had imposed.

On the afternoon when he came to her and told her all that she wanted to know, she gave him a new plum-coloured robe and ten bolts of silk, which would probably carry him all the way to India, where he was now bound, like a prince.

'I wonder,' the Empress asked him with a touching shyness, 'if it is possible that you will climb again to the monastery up on the impossible crag?'

He shook his head. 'I would gladly go there again, for Your Highness's sweet sake. But,' he spoke delicately, 'the holy priest who made me his courier will no longer be there.'

A sigh escaped her, a breath as faint as a dying perfume.

'Ah. Then, do you – would you know where he has gone?'

'He will have gone into India, as I do myself.' Ming smiled with deep kindness. 'It may be, therefore, that we shall meet again.

India is very vast – but the net of coincidence spreads even wider than the continents.' Green eyes – how lovely they were – thanked him for his hopefulness.

'Then I too have a message, if you should ever encounter him. It is similar to the one you brought me. Ask the holy father, if you will, to turn to the fifth line of the seventh poem in the silk scroll with the crystal handles, and to read on.'

'I shall not forget.'

She knew she should not ask the question that leaped in her, but whatever the reply, it must bring Shing-jen closer to her.

'Tell me, Ming Chung-yen, when you looked into the face of the priest, what did you see for him?'

The seer's eyes crinkled appreciatively. 'What I would be glad to see for myself: a long and peaceful life, spent in contemplation of the Tao; enough travel to keep the mind alert; and a quiet ending in a place of great beauty.'

'Thank you. I am glad.' She knew that she did not have to ask him whether she would ever see her lover again in this life.

They talked for a while of the matters that concerned her, then Ming left her. He would start for Chang-an at the end of the week.

The lines that Shing-jen would almost certainly never read began:

> I turn back and look at the empty room;
> For a moment I almost think I see you there.
> One parting, but ten thousand regrets –

Tiger Lily had arranged one of her entertainments. It was for her family and her enormous gang of friends and took place in the Hall of Pleasant Laughter.

The programme consisted largely of foreign dance and music; Loyang was becoming almost as cosmopolitan as Chang-an.

Tiger Lily sat beside her parents in the low-lit hall, making indiscreet comments on both performance and performers.

'That Sogdian girl, the one with the snakes – quite sumptuously sensual, isn't she? Well, she is also known to weave those hypnotic hips before, or should I say *beneath*, Captain Jai Hung of the guard!' Or, of the energetic offering of the beautiful twin boys from Paekche, 'Actually, it's an old fertility dance from Greece, *not* so suitable, when you think of what they say about those two – '

'Such remarks are not clever, First Daughter; they are merely crass and unladylike.' Black Jade was genuinely annoyed with her.

Tiger Lily grinned. 'Sorry. It's the atmosphere. All this sex – it begins to affect one after a dozen rehearsals.'

During the next song, a ululating affair from a Kashmiri girl with huge, sad eyes above her veil, the Princess disappeared. They waited indulgently to see her take the stage herself, an opportunity she could never resist.

There was a brief recital by the young ladies of the academy of music. These gifted pupils, whose status was on a level with that of imperial concubines, set the standards of popular music, teaching the upper-class courtesans of the city, from whom their songs passed to the lips of their customers and thence to the rest of the world. They sang 'The Willow Tree' and 'North of the Wall,' an affecting ballad of love and war.

After this the stage went dark except for a ring of light at the centre front. A slow, insistent drumbeat began, joined by a martial encouragement of horns and gongs. A single small figure came into the ring of lamplight, waving a sword and uttering warlike cries. It was, of course, Tiger Lily, her green eyes glinting wickedly beneath a scarlet turban stuck with kingfisher feathers. She wore a long tunic of purple brocade, clasped with jewelled and jade-hung belts; the ceremonial uniform of a general of the imperial army. Her dance, which she seemed to have made up herself, was ferocious and, because she was solitary and so diminutive, endearingly comic. The audience loved it.

When the show was over and the Princess had rejoined them, Pheasant took pleasure in teasing her. 'I see you haven't neglected to award yourself an impressive number of medals.' He set swinging the line of jade plaques at her belts. 'But you are no general, my child. What are you playing at? This is hardly a suitable costume for my daughter!'

Tiger Lily nodded, with her bewitching gamine grin. 'No. Then do you suppose it might be suitable for a son-in-law?'

Black Jade, at her husband's side, gave a gurgle of laughter.

'It seems our daughter is trying to tell us something.'

Tiger Lily tapped her red-booted foot. 'But have I succeeded?'

Pheasant was bemused. 'You wish to be married? Is that what all this is about? So soon?'

'I shall be fifteen next year.'

'Well then, we shall have to think about it,' he smiled.

'That is what you said *last* year. Now I would like you to do more than merely think. But he must be a soldier. And I must like the look of him. A great deal.'

'It would surprise me greatly,' said Black Jade shrewdly, 'if you had not already someone in mind. Am I right?'

Tiger Lily was not given to blushes. 'You might be.'

'I see. We have to guess, is that it?'

'Honourable Mother! You know that the young ladies of the palace are not supposed to have social contact with the officers.'

'Yes,' agreed Jade grimly. 'And I also know about the picnics in the countryside, the roadside seats at military reviews, and the secret tea-parties in the convent. You shall tell us whom you have chosen, Little Tigress, and then we shall see.'

Three days later, a Captain Bold-hand asked if he might see the Empress. Black Jade received him in Shen Nu's courtyard, beneath the dark green spread of the giant fig tree.

She had to admit, right away, that the young officer was very handsome, almost excessively so. He was tall and he held himself as though he set a high value on every inch. He wore the scarlet summer shirt and white pheasant feathers of the Emperor's guard and a short, ceremonial sword. He had the bold, proud face of the northern races, the bones prominent, the skin a deep olive. He was sleek and oiled and perfumed, self-satisfied as a cat.

As he rose from a perfectly respectful bow, Jade saw him look at her frankly, as a man looks at a woman, and find her more than satisfactory. His eyes were warmly brown, with the glitter that proclaimed his awareness of his own attractions.

How on earth, she wondered, had her spoiled little daughter, without her knowledge, come to develop the precocious appetite that could appreciate a man like this?

Ruefully, she asked him to sit.

He introduced himself and they spoke of his home in Shansi. He came from a distinguished family of scholar-gentry who had given loyal service to each of the T'ang emperors.

After these polite preliminaries Black Jade asked thoughtfully, 'Are you an ambitious man, Captain?'

She watched him swiftly calculate the best answer.

'As I am bound to be, if I want to bring honour to His Majesty's service and to my clan.' He smiled, showing white teeth.

'No more than that?' she challenged lightly.

'Should there be more, Highness?' He betrayed innocent puzzlement.

She frowned slightly. 'Why, for instance, did you wish to see me?'

He looked at his boots, as if in some discomfort, or possibly admiring his reflection in their high polish. Then he lifted a frank, warm gaze.

'Well, to tell the truth, Her Highness the Taiping Princess asked me to present myself to you.'

She nodded. 'And how many times have you been in my daughter's company?'

'I have seen the Princess on a number of occasions.'

'Alone?'

'Your Highness?'

'Oh come now, Captain; you know why you are here.'

The frank smile reappeared, with a certain relief. 'It is not my place to speak, Luminous Sovereign.'

'No, nor mine,' sighed Black Jade. She really did not much like this young man, handsome and charming as he was. But he had taught her something about Tiger Lily; the girl was right, it was time she was married. And if this was the husband she wanted –

'I suggest that you ask to see the Emperor,' she told Bold-hand. 'Perhaps he may tell you something to your advantage. You may go now – oh, and remember one thing, will you?'

'Your Highness?'

'Do not be in too much of a hurry to climb. It always looks so much better if one appears to be the recipient of good luck, rather than the engineer of too much good management.'

His smile, intended to leave a lasting impression of its brilliance, became uncertain. His moustaches wobbled.

Ah well, Jade thought, as he marched away rather fast, there is plenty of time. She will probably tire of him before it comes to a wedding. I should, in a night! But then, I am no longer fifteen, thanks be to the Gods! And when I was, she mused, how much less sophisticated I was than my gifted little daughter.

Pheasant found, after due inspection, that the young Captain was an altogether delightful person. He sounded almost hurt when Jade remarked that she thought he carried an overload of charm.

'The lad is bound to be eager to please,' he defended.

'So you will consider him, then, for Tiger Lily?'

'In another year perhaps. I think so. But they must not continue to meet as they have been doing. It isn't seemly. I shall send the boy away for a while, to earn his badges.'

This satisfied Black Jade, though it did not at all please the impatient Princess, who at once set up an elaborate courier service with her absent suitor.

'You don't really want me to marry him, do you, Mother?' she accused, gloomily looking in the mirror. In another year she would be old!

'He would not have been my choice. And perhaps, in a year, he may not be yours.' She looked into the polished bronze at the cross, lovely self-image and caressed Tiger Lily's tumble of night-black hair. 'But I wanted, above all, to give you a *choice* in this matter. Choice, my child, is the most valuable element in our lives. It is extremely scarce.'

Chinghiz had brought startling news.

'The astrologer Ming has been found, dead, on the road outside Chang-an. He's said to have been killed by bandits. His luggage was missing and his horse had gone.'

'Oh, Chinghiz, I wouldn't have had that happen for the world! Such a splendid man. But why would anyone kill a priest? They couldn't have expected him to be carrying anything of worth.' She recollected. 'It must have been the silk I gave him. I didn't consider the perils of the road when I wished to reward him.'

'No, Little Mistress. Astrologer Ming presented your silk to the Hung-fu Monastery, in memory of Hsuan-Tsang. He took only one horse and a single servant boy.'

'Was the boy killed too?'

'No. And that is what makes this death so interesting.'

'It is a sad death, Chinghiz. Sometimes you can be a little too detached! I liked the astrologer.'

'I liked him myself – don't mistake me. What is interesting is the message that came to me from that servant boy. He is not dead. I chose him for his quick wits.'

'*You* chose him?'

'Certainly. I had divined that your interest in Ming was more than usually benevolent.'

She nodded her thanks.

'The boy says they were attacked by a dozen or so armed men; well-dressed. He thought they were probably soldiers out of uniform; they carried themselves well and the ambush was disciplined. He was clubbed on the head and played dead, knowing he couldn't help Ming against so many. They threw him into the ditch and rode off, leaving his master dying from a chest-wound. He lived long enough to be sure the boy had learned the number of a certain verse of poetry, and the name of the person to whom, if ever possible, it should be addressed.'

There were tears in Black Jade's eyes. 'They have been good servants, both of them. Is the boy here?'

'He is with friends of mine in Chang-an. He will be safe.'

'Then you do not believe the attackers were brigands?'

'No. Ming made himself an enemy; someone who stole his records as well as his life.'

Their eyes met. 'They would find very little' she said, 'names and dates – in some cases, not even these were recorded.'

'Ming was known to have spent a number of private hours with you,' Chinghiz replied. 'Who could have been so troubled by that circumstance that he would commit such a crime?'

'I'm sure you will discover that very soon.'

Meanwhile, she too would ask questions of the only person who, to her own private knowledge – at least she had thought it was private – might have considered the hapless fortune-teller an enemy.

'Did you want to speak to me about something particular, Mother? Or am I simply your chosen companion for your ride? It is, as they say, an honour that, lately, I had not looked for.'

They were riding across the open grassland of the game park. Black Jade had told her small escort to remain fifty yards behind.

'Your tone is very dry, Young Tiger. Yes, I wanted to see you, and I do not wish us to be overheard.'

'Indeed? I apologise. For my tone.' He kept his eyes on his horse's neck.

She paced him exactly, her hands resting quietly on the reins. Her mount was a grandson of the dearly loved Snow Prince, as pure a white but with a streak of mischief of which his grandsire would not have approved.

'Well, Honourable Mother?' Young Tiger was tense.

'Only a simple question. You will easily recall the astrologer, Ming, who was with us for some time. He was very much the fashion amongst you young people.'

Her son stiffened. 'I remember. What of him?'

'He was found dead some days ago, on the road to Chang-an.'

'He was unfortunate. What bearing does this have on our conversation?'

'Only that I thought you might know how he came by his death.' Her voice was casual, deceptively gentle.

'I?' The syllable was injected with amazement. 'Why should I?'

'Because I think you have been spying on me, my son. I think you know what Ming told me concerning your future.'

'How should I know? I didn't even know you had consulted him. What are you trying to do to me, Mother?' He had quickened their pace without noticing. She slowed and he reined to match her.

'What has he said, then, your precious astrologer? Why should I care so much? Has he promised me imminent death, that I should want to bring him to his own? You would think,' he added on a note of high-pitched scorn, 'that he would have had the sense not to travel, since he must surely have been aware of what awaited him!'

'Astrologers never make predictions for themselves,' she said mechanically. 'Young Tiger, *do* you know what he told me? Shall I repeat it – or is it unnecessary?'

'I must have made it quite clear,' he said rapidly, 'I have no idea!'

'Then you will be intrigued. Perhaps more than that. Ming had studied your features and those of your brothers, at my request. His conclusion was that you did not have the physiognomy – nor does your horoscope suggest it – of the one who will succeed to the throne. He said that Loud Tiger resembled his grandfather and would share some of his good fortune, but that New Dawn would be the most fortunate of all.'

'Damn his impudence!' Young Tiger exploded. He turned on her savagely. 'And what use, I wonder, will you make of this prediction? You ask if I know how he died. Well, now I ask you why it was that you should commission this charlatan to belie my heritage?' He lashed his horse with his whip and slewed it round to face her, his shoulders heaving with the energy of his anger.

'Could it be,' he demanded bitterly, darting a gloved hand to catch her wrist, 'because *I am not your son*?' He drew a long breath over coals. 'Because you wish only your sons to rule? Or even – ' there was an obscenity in his eyes – 'as some are saying, that you think to rule yourself when my father is dead – and *that is why you murdered my brother*?'

'No!' Her cry would have brought tears to stones. 'You *cannot* think so! Oh, where have you gone, my son, that is so far away from me, and from the truth?'

'The truth!' he spat contemptuously. 'What do you know about the truth? And as you say, what can I know of it? But I tell you, Black Jade, if you have committed even one of the things of which the whispering walls of the palace accuse you – then to have substituted your sister's child for your own, only to betray me when I came to the throne, would have been a mere half-hour's distraction for you.'

Her head was reeling. She clung to the reins. She wondered if he could be a little mad, driven by his obsession.

'This is nonsense, all nonsense,' she pleaded, concentrating her will on the effort to remain in the saddle. 'Please, my son – for you *are* my son – tell me you will put these nightmares away from you, and look to the future and your duty to the throne.'

He shook his head; a tear rolled from the corner of his eye.

'Ah, you are so very beautiful; your voice pours perfumed oil – but it will not serve to heal the wounds you have made.' He glared at her, a furnace of rage and hurt. 'I can't believe you! I won't trust you.' He whispered now, his words catching on thorns, 'I don't care any more, how you try to ruin me. I won't let you do it, do you hear me? I am my father's son and that makes me fit to rule. I don't know if I am yours.' He turned suddenly and headed off at an angle across the grass. His parting words flew back at her as she struggled to control her surprised stallion.

'But I hope I am not! By all the Gods, I hope I am not!'

Behind her the little knot of courtiers watched him go; then they hurried towards her as she slumped on her horse's neck.

Certain now that Young Tiger had had Ming killed, Black Jade began to fear some dreadful, irrational consequence of his obsession. In order to keep him under close observation, she persuaded a reluctant Pheasant to commission an investigation of the murder.

'But you'll find nothing against the boy, nothing,' he was confident.

'May the Buddha grant that it proves so,' Black Jade replied. She wished that she could tell him the whole of this trouble, but it was impossible; to learn of Young Tiger's suspicions of her would distress him and make him ill. It might even, she was forced to recognise, sow the same suspicions in himself, for father and son were alike in their susceptibility to doubt.

No, it was enough for Pheasant to be concerned lest the Crown Prince's name be stained with the scandal of murder. She would suffer alone this strange pain that struck at the very roots of her womanhood. It was an agony she had not expected, had not imagined to exist; that a son of hers could hate and fear where he had loved so well. She longed for the tragic rift between herself and Young Tiger to be healed, for the future to take back its bitter offerings.

She ordered the Vice-Chancellor not to hurry his investigation.

After several months of active service north of the Wall, Tiger Lily's handsome Captain returned, covered in medals and glory. She and her father were overjoyed at his success and Black Jade felt it would be curmudgeonly of her to react differently. She therefore bestowed her smiles upon the hero with the rest, and made only a token protest when her daughter begged that the wedding be celebrated right away.

'Little Pigeon, are you sure?' she asked wistfully, as she duly admired the designs Tiger Lily had brought for various exotic costumes she might wear for the ceremonies. 'A husband has to last for such a very long time.'

'You mean, bitter-sweet Mother, that I was not a child who kept my toys for long,' the Princess deduced with an adult smile. 'Yes, I am sure. I have waited a year for him; doesn't that prove how sure I am?'

'It is an indication,' Jade admitted. 'Nevertheless, it is now the time to consider, very seriously, whether you really want this marriage, or if you would not be well advised to wait until you are a little older?'

'A little wiser, you mean, a little less bold, less wild, less alive? No, I don't want to wait. I want Bold-hand, and I want him now!'

Black Jade sighed. 'You must not mind my small doubts. They exist only because I so much want you to be happy.'

'I will be. I promise!' The small face radiated the truth of it. 'Goodness, we could do with a wedding to cheer things up in the palace. Everyone is so gloomy lately. If only that grim minister would hurry up and clear Young Tiger's name.'

'You know nothing about the matter,' said Jade repressively.

'Only because no one will *tell* me anything,' Tiger Lily complained. 'Not even Chinghiz. And my father looked sick when I mentioned it.'

'Then I hope it has taught you that you must not mention it again.'

'I hate mysteries! Especially in the family.'

'I don't wish to discuss this any further.' Black Jade's face was frozen in distaste.

For once, Tiger Lily did as she was told.

The wedding took place on the fourth day of the beginning of autumn, when the heat was still balmy but not intense, and the clear indigo nights held the warm scents of the day in their embrace.

It was a day of pure and unrestrained rejoicing, for everyone loved the ebullient little Princess and was captivated by the spectacle of her evident happiness.

It was also a day to remember. No mere sedate and

conventional family visitations were to precede the tying of these electric tresses. Tiger Lily and her hero had planned something unusual to amuse themselves and their guests.

In the morning the palace awoke to the sound of horns and trumpets blowing the 'call to battle'. Hurrying into their best clothes they sent the servants running to investigate. Upon every door they found the announcement that a mighty confrontation was to take place in the imperial park between the Forces of the Green Dragon and the Army of the White Tiger. Supporters' favours would be sold at the Gate of the Dark Warrior.

Pheasant came, beaming, into Jade's chamber as she finished dressing.

'What is our young genius up to this time?' he wondered with paternal indulgence. 'It seems she will turn even her own marriage into a general entertainment.' He fastened her three diamond bracelets.

'She said something to me about an old-fashioned Taoist wedding,' Black Jade recollected. 'I might have known she didn't have temples and priests and hours of prayer in mind. It is to be the battle of the sexes, fought out on our field before they even reach the marriage-bed. I do hope they won't use real swords!'

They did not. They used flowers.

It seemed, as they stepped from their palanquins at the specified gate to the park, that every flower in the province must have been picked to decorate this day. Ropes of flowers lined their route through an ecstatically flower-flourishing crowd, who pelted them with sugared rose-leaves, providently retrieved by a grovel of small boys in their wake. Then, enthroned, with cheers, upon a floral dais beneath a floribund canopy, they proceeded to the royal review of the troops.

They trotted up daintily on their superbly-trained horses, coming in from both sides of the field, a man and a woman meeting together in front of the dais and crossing their long lances, blunted and entwined with roses. The bride's riders wore green silk habits and carried the standard of the Green Dragon, the symbol of the feminine principle that once, long ago, had been male; the Captain's contingent, magnificently masculine in white brocade breeches and tall white boots, displayed their bronzed chests beneath the banner of the White Tiger, which, equally, had once signified *yin* rather than *yang*. The reasons for the exchange were lost in antiquity, but were somehow satisfactory in their suggestion of a mingling of the sexes.

The young cavaliers wove and swerved with dazzling skill,

Tiger Lily's veridian virgins almost as able as Bold-hand's war-hardened band. There was a moment that, later, Black Jade would remember with a stab of unblunted pain, as Young Tiger surprisingly entered, under a white banner, to dip his lance before his mother's throne. Their eyes met and she saw that the challenge in his was no fanciful play with flowers, but real, and merciless, and for her.

Before she had recovered from that cold regard the youthful commanders were presenting themselves; to the west Bold-hand, splendid upon his midnight stallion harnessed with glowing white blooms, while Tiger Lily tossed him her challenge from her little white Arab, smothered, like her own perfect person, in a wealth of greenery which was mostly emeralds.

The armies ranged themselves, banners fluttering, at a distance of two hundred yards apart. At a signal from the generals Pheasant raised his hand. A trumpet sounded, and he brought it down. At the drop of the yellow sleeve, the flowery battle commenced.

It was not so much a battle as a rout. The garlanded warriors racketed towards each other, carolling merrily, waving their staves and urging their horses, green wildfire upon silken snowstorm. They met and engaged, each seeking an opposite and stabbing or swiping in a hail of bouncing blossoms as they tried to unseat the enemy. If you did fall off, you were counted as a prisoner and brought back, loaded in chains of flowers, to the dais.

Jade recognised, even in the considerable uproar, the belling of a rutting stag that announced Loud Tiger's personal triumph, and was pleased to award him the prize of his victory – an imperial yellow garland, what else? – when he brought in his giggling captive, a robust young lady who had managed to black his eye before she was down.

Gradually, in this pleasant manner, the field diminished, until only the fiercest and most dedicated fighters remained. A parley was held, and it was decided to attack afresh, and to fight to the death, and so have done.

The dozen or so cavaliers on each side went into a huddle of snorts and gurgles and stifled shrieks. They then reformed their skeleton ranks and Pheasant obliged again with the signal to charge.

It was not fair. Everyone said so. On the other hand it was excellent strategy, though not perhaps up to the level of the great Sun Tzu. The little battalions thundered towards the centre, their beaten cohorts and frenzied spectators roaring them on; they met and circled, seeking the right chance, the perfect timing for the stunning stroke. Then, what was this? The gorgeous green girls stood up in their stirrups and leaned near to their would-be ravishers, unabashed and unafraid, the light of battle in their eyes, its strength in their sinuous arms, as they moved expertly in upon their expectant opponents whose weapons were already rising, then neatly reversed their lances (whose roses all seemed to have collected at the shaft end) – and tickled the hapless White Tigers under their delicate armpits!

What a fall was there! The hardened horsemen collapsed like so many drunken babies, falling off their embarrassed mounts in a welter of blushes and roses, giggling hysterically and begging for mercy. Cruel as eagles, their heartless victors closed upon them, ravaging their exposed bodies to the torture of a thousand very small cuts – they had neglected the courtesy, extended by the Tigers themselves, of removing the thorns from the roses.

It was all over – an ignominious defeat for the *yang*. Bold-hand and his bleeding belligerents were rounded up and chained with daisies, then brought to the Emperor for judgement.

Pheasant, who had never laughed so much in all his life, deliberated for a moment with a solemn face before announcing gravely that the worst sentence he could think of was that the conquered Captain should be married forthwith to his victorious daughter.

After everyone had had a rest and changed their clothes, the ceremony of the tying of the knot took place, setting the seal on these martial nuptuals, in the flower-festooned reception hall of the bride and groom's new apartments. Hearts were still high, but the extravagant mood gave way to a period of grace during the simple, beautiful ceremony.

Not only the women shed sentimental tears as Tiger Lily disembarked from the scarlet and gold palanquin which brought her into their midst. Her wedding-dress, based breathtakingly upon the costume of a team of Persian dancers she had recently seen, was made up of a series of red gauze veils, dusted with powdered gold which seemed to have fallen from the coronet which circled her coiled and jewelled hair. She looked transcendently happy and very slightly demonic as her green eyes collected those of the crowd through the scarlet chiffon that floated before her face, accepting their adulation with a wicked, winking glint.

Black Jade, herself shining like an idol in a gilded creation that appeared to be made of the mingled beams of the sun and moon, gave the sign, when the soft ceremonial was over, for the carrying away of the bride. She caught a last lingering look passing between the soldier and his prize, and read the promise in it, the impatience and the young hunger. A wave of envy surprised her by its strength. To combat it she thought determinedly of a naked girl wrapped in a red quilt, slung like a bale of goods across a eunuch's shoulder, to be opened by her master like a desirable present.

In the bedroom, while the fireworks and the music clamoured and cracked outside the windows, Tiger Lily gave herself voluptuously to the pleasure of disposing of her tiresome virginity. It was something she had wanted to do for a very long time.

Beside her golden glowing body, which had told him how long, Bold-hand leaned, feasting his eyes and stroking her into an agony of impatience.

'We have waited a long time,' she suggested, touching him shyly.

'That was not my wish.'

'I wanted it; you know that. But I was afraid of what my mother would say if she found out.'

'Not your father?'

'No.'

'No. On reflection, I see it. Black Jade is a formidable woman. I would not like to have her for my enemy.'

'Then you had better take *very* good care of me,' said Tiger Lily.

Tiger Lily was barely married and settled with her soldier in the exotic new apartments from which they rarely emerged, when Black Jade was forced to turn her back on all such pleasant domestic matters. After the successful conclusion of a meeting of the Extraordinary Committee on Education, Vice-Chancellor Pale Flame asked if he might have a private word with her.

Pale Flame, whose name indicated that he had not, at birth, been expected to survive, was very tall, very thin and as strong as whipcord. His features expressed nobility of character but offered little hope of laughter. Nor would he offer it now.

'Your Highness,' he rose from the kowtow without wasting words on the usual exaggerated compliments, 'I have a report from the committee which has been looking into the affairs of the Crown Prince. It pains me deeply to have to say that its findings are of a delicate and serious nature.'

She needed to sit down. She waved the Vice-Chancellor also to a seat.

'To deal firstly with the case of the unfortunate fortune-teller, Ming Chung-yen: it has been established that Young Tiger was indeed responsible for the death of this man.'

Black Jade drew in a long, cold breath. 'Please continue.'

'Among our early investigations of the Prince's habits, friends, entertainments and so forth, we interviewed a young woman named Dancing Oriole, who has served Your Highness as an attendant – '

'Why, yes. A pretty girl. I haven't seen her for some time. There are so many girls at court, and their duties change so often.'

Pale Flame nodded gravely. 'Well, it seems that this Dancing Oriole has been having sexual relations with Young Tiger – hardly an appropriate liaison, though in itself no great matter.'

In a flash of visual memory she saw a sweet-faced girl run to take her place on the chess-court, blushing as she caught the appreciative eye of the Heir Apparent.

'It was sensed, when she was questioned,' the thin man continued, sitting up very straight on his stool as though to make up for the crooked behaviour he must describe, 'that there was something more to this relationship. The girl is very young and does not dissemble well. It was soon learned that, urged to it by the Prince, it was she who arranged for the astrologer to be killed on the road; she has a cousin in His Highness's guard. She wept most bitterly as she confessed to this. I do not think it is congenial to her nature to do such things. One might term her a victim of passion.' He uttered this with the dry deliberation of an entomologist discovering a rogue species.

'Poor child,' Black Jade said. 'She was, I think, more the victim of her heartless lover than of her own love.'

Pale Flame raised narrow brows and forbore to comment.

'Leaving this unsavoury matter, I will pass to the one which gives greater cause for concern. August Highness, on the evening of the sixth day of the Beginning of Autumn, we entered the stables of the Prince's residence in the eastern palace. Our enquiries had led us to expect what we found – that is, a very large armoury of illicit weapons; swords, crossbows, cutlasses, staves, maces, quarrels, and perhaps four hundred suits of armour.' He paused, to allow the intimation to reach her.

'If my son has collected such a store,' she said at once, 'he must have in mind some possible use for it. Whatever his reasons,' she added unhappily, 'he has broken the law.'

'The law is designed to protect an Heir Apparent against the promptings of evil counsel and his own worse nature. I fear that, in Young Tiger's case, it has sadly failed.'

'Evidently. Is there more?'

'Only that certain of the Prince's close companions are known to have aided him in gathering this cache. Their opinions upon the matter of the imperial succession are known to be – equivocal.'

'Who are they?'

He handed her the list. It was headed by the three men of whom she had already been warned – the rising young minister, who would find his rise most abruptly cut off, and Young Tiger's two half-brothers, who would not now increase their fortunes at his expense.

Black Jade read it through, then quelled the impulse to run from the room like a hysterical schoolgirl and instead quietly expressed her thanks to the minister for the thoroughness of his committee's work.

Pale Flame gave her a moment's grace. 'We are very distressed Gracious Empress, to be the bearers of such sad news. We have asked Kuan Yin, in the Hall of the Ancestors, to have compassion on the suffering it must cause you.'

The harsh lines of his face had softened. She thought, as she managed to smile his dismissal, that he must, after all, be rather a kind man.

Pheasant would not believe the evidence. When at last, by the sheer overwhelming amount of it, he was compelled to do so, he said he did not care; nothing should happen to his beloved son. If Young Tiger was really guilty of the devastating things of which they accused him, he must have been misguided by his friends. It did not signify. Nothing should change. He would show true imperial magnanimity; he would pardon and forgive his errant heir, and all would be well again.

'There is clear proof of conspiracy against the throne,' Pale Flame reasoned, with carefully concealed impatience. 'There cannot, according to the law, be a pardon.'

The Emperor stared at him. 'I refuse to say anything more about it,' he said firmly. 'I am ill. I shall go to my chamber.'

He shut himself in his private rooms and refused to see his ministers. It was left to Black Jade to bring him to understand clearly what it was that Young Tiger had done.

'Pale Flame is right. We cannot pardon him, however much we might wish to do so. He has committed treason.'

'How do you know? I see no proof of that. He has said that he simply felt insecure, that the astrologer Ming had said he would not come to the throne and he feared that this might be on account of some armed rebellion – by one of the other princes or some dissatisfied duke. The Gods know how often such things have happened! I believe him, Jade. Why can't you? I don't know how you can harden your heart like this.' Then he saw that she was weeping.

'I haven't. Do you think I don't remember what it used to be like? When Young Tiger was a boy, so full of curiosity and so sure of himself. Don't you think I have asked myself, time and time again, how he could ever have become the closed, suspicious, hostile creature he is now?'

Pheasant smiled wistfully. 'I do know,' he said hesitantly, 'What he has made you suffer through his fears about his birth.'

She gasped. 'How long have you known?'

'Oh, weeks, months, what does it matter? I usually get to hear of things, sooner or later; somebody tells me, just before they become common knowledge.'

She wept freely now. 'I didn't want you to worry.'

'That isn't important. But don't you see – this fear must be Young Tiger's chief reason for his "treasonable" collecting of arms? He must have expected a day when you would use your power to take the throne from him, and raise a "true" son in his place.'

'Yes. That must be true. But it isn't what matters. Because Young Tiger can't possibly hold the mandate, not after this. It isn't whether his actions were inspired by fear or malice that counts – it is what they made him do; it is the kind of young man he has become. He will not make an Emperor.'

Pheasant shook his head. All this was making him very tired. He moved to his day-bed and lay down, depressed. He had no strength to combat her words or her wishes, hers or those of anyone else. He knew that he would not be able to save his son.

'I love the boy,' he said softly. 'Try to make them treat him kindly, and like the true prince he was born. And most of all, I beg of you, my dear – please, somehow, before it becomes too late and they send him away from us – find a way to make him *know* that he is your son!'

She kept her promise. Her last interview with Young Tiger would be seared on her heart until her death-day. She could see how it would be, what his mood was, as soon as she entered the room in his palace where he was now a prisoner.

'Have you come to gloat, Black Jade? You must be well satisfied.'

'No. I am not satisfied.' It took courage to meet the blaze of hatred in his face. 'And I will not be, until you have accepted that everything you have done has been for nothing, for the sake of a venomous lie. I tell you once more – I will say it as many times as are necessary to make you believe it – you are the true son of my body. I carried you within me, and I loved you from the moment you were born. I love you now. All the evil that is present in your life comes from having doubted it.'

The burning mask did not alter. She scarcely recognised him.

'I want you to go away from here and not to return,' he said slowly and heavily as though the words were frozen to the roof of his mouth. 'I do not believe you. I think you have been a murderer far more often than I.' He saw her crumple and almost fall as he repeated that appalling accusation. He smiled, a wavering and abstracted grimace. 'As for evil – all the evil in my life has come from you. By the Buddha, if you don't leave me now, Black Jade, I swear I'll do you harm!'

There was no doubt that he meant it; he looked like a man gone wild in the wilderness. She was drenched with pity for him. The wilderness was real, it was here among the sharp knives and the whispering galleries of the palace, and its savagery had been too strong for him.

She put out her hand. 'No, you won't hurt me. You love me also. I know that you do.'

'Get out! Get out of here and leave me in peace! You have come here to torture me. I can't believe you. You killed my brother! You will kill me! I hate you, Mother!'

She turned and fled then, for she could bear no more. There was nothing she could do for Young Tiger. He would not let her help him. And for herself, she needed to be alone, to hide from the world for a while in a place of safe and blessed silence, like her son.

Young Tiger was convicted by his judges of having been involved in a conspiracy to rebellion. He was degraded to the status of a commoner and sent to prison in Chang-an.

In Loyang, according to custom, the vast store of arms and armour which he and his exiled fellows had garnered was publicly burned in the market-place at the Bridge of the Ford of Heaven. This invited the citizens to contemplate the catholic appetite of the law, which will embrace the highest prince of the blood with as much enthusiasm as the lowest felon.

Shortly after this dismal scene, the court itself transferred to Chang-an. Young Tiger was then removed to a place of permanent exile, from which his father never ceased to hope that he might one day be allowed to return.

25

It was not an auspicious time for the ascent of a new Crown Prince, especially if, as in the case of Loud Tiger, no one (including himself) had ever expected or hoped for his accession.

'Do I have to?' he boomed with consummate dismay, when told of his fortune. 'Why not Dawn Tiger?'

'Your brother is five years younger. Don't worry. You'll do very well if you listen to your advisors,' Pheasant encouraged. He was sorry for the boy, for he was simple and affectionate and the sophistry of the court had completely passed him by. His life was led out of doors with young men of similarly uncomplex natures.

'It's not exactly the best of times, is it?' the new heir gloomed. 'A new war with Tibet – Tiger Lily should have married the T'san Pu and civilised the brute! The Turks on the prowl again – these increasing raids are a disaster we can't afford. And as for our hanging on in Korea, well, where *is* the money to come from?'

Black Jade chuckled. The last money-making scheme anyone had thought of had been the sale of manure from the imperial stables. It was popular, but hardly the salvation of the royal purse, and revenue, at the moment, was very low.

She did not by any means despair of Loud Tiger. He did not have his dead brother's natural flair for administration but neither was he capable of Young Tiger's neurotic fears. He was very attached to both herself and Pheasant, and would follow their lead as closely as they could wish.

'We had better find him a wife,' Pheasant decided, 'an intelligent girl, a little older than himself – someone to keep him steady.'

Their choice fell on the daughter of a minister who was a member of the powerful Wei clan of the north-west province of Kuan-chun, whose friendship as keepers of the border was vital to the throne. Lady Heavenly Pearl herself was beautiful, accomplished and spoke modestly when interviewed. Her manners were perfect and her conversation restrained.

'I like her,' announced the prospective bridegroom after their first decorous meeting at one of Black Jade's ministerial tea-parties. 'She's as far away as you can get from Red Poppy!'

And so, for the first year or so of their marriage, it seemed. But when, after a bare nine months, Heavenly Pearl presented her husband with his first son, she abandoned the modest airs of her girlhood with a will and took on those of greater consequence, bustling about the palace in a managing manner reminiscent, to Loud Tiger's growing alarm, not of his late unlamented wife but of his deplorable ex-mother-in-law, the Princess Constance.

Black Jade, noting with disfavour that wherever she went, Heavenly Pearl was likely to be there before her, arranging chairs or running shrewd eyes down lists, remarked to her son that his wife was becoming a little tedious, and should be told as much.

'*Amitabha*!' Loud Tiger rolled his eyes. 'You tell her, then, Mother, not I! She doesn't take kindly to criticism!'

From which the Empress deduced that the unlucky Prince was again the victim of a strong-minded wife. She sighed. She had thought Heavenly Pearl ideal at first. Ah well, they would just have to find a way to make an Emperor out of Loud Tiger without also making one of his busy young wife.

However, this was the least of her cares. At present all her strength was bent upon Pheasant. Since their return to Chang-an he had suffered a grave relapse, in spirit as much as in body. He felt the loss of his older sons deeply and constantly, praying daily for Bold Tiger's spirit which was no doubtless tranquil in the Western Heaven, and for poor misguided Young Tiger, who had originally not wanted to be an Emperor much more than he had himself.

He brooded unhappily upon the nature of their fates, which had brought the palace so far from the Way. Black Jade assured him that harmony had already returned with Loud Tiger's accession and with the birth of his little son, but Pheasant could not feel this to be true. All his instincts pointed him towards a time of darkness. Perhaps it was only that the time was drawing near, later than he had any right to expect, for his own death; but perhaps he sensed some other dark night, not his own.

In the spring, confident that he would improve there, Black Jade persuaded him to move to his favourite summer palace in Loyang. Gradually some of her determined optimism caught his wavering spirit and he began to please her by making plans again, to behave, as he put it to himself, as though he were already immortal.

As she warmed to the task of teaching another son to govern it became clear to Jade, and to Pale Flame with whom she had established a relationship founded on mutual respect, that Loud Tiger was unlikely to be capable of taking any important decision on his own account for some time. He was willing, but his mind was woolly and undisciplined. He was unable to concentrate for long and would race off at any entertaining tangent rather than pursue the mundane matter in hand. He was only happy when he escaped the council rooms and got back to his horses, his dogs and the men who understood them.

Black Jade shared her doubts with Pheasant.

'What he knows, he has learned by rote. He is incapable of logical thought. He always looks to others for his answer.'

'Poor lad! He should have been born a farmer or one of my huntsmen, whose only necessity is to look after the animals and pray for good weather.'

'Maybe so, but one day he will have the responsibility for the welfare of those farmers across the whole Empire. A foolish Emperor is as hard a curse as bad weather.'

'He will have your own good sense to guide him.'

'A household cannot have two masters,' she said abruptly.

'No, but it must have a good steward as well as a master. You will be Loud Tiger's steward, as Chinghiz is yours.'

'I don't look forward to the prospect.'

Loud Tiger's own attitude was even less acceptable. When exhorted to try to learn how to fulfil his role, he would say such things as "An Emperor has to do very little, as I see it. He has as many ministers as hairs on his head, all devoted to giving him advice."

'If you plan to let your ministers govern for you, you will soon find yourself their puppet,' Jade said sharply.

Loud Tiger shrugged good-naturedly. 'Oh no. If they get out of hand I can always demote them, or even kill them off, to give the others a good example.'

'That,' said his mother grimly, 'is about the least intelligent idea you have yet expressed; which gives me very little hope for the future of the Empire.'

Loud Tiger looked after her departing figure and scratched his head. 'It is only what every Emperor has done, all except Father anyway,' he muttered in a haze of puzzlement. He wished he was better equipped to please her, but he never really understood exactly what she wanted of him.

The Emperor had remained for so long in the summer palace, enjoying its peace and submitting to the ministrations of his doctors, that the council thought it would be wise for him to make an appearance in the city in order to put an end to a current unpleasant rumour.

'Are you sure you should do this?' Black Jade worried. 'It is winter now and very cold. Surely, if the citizens need to assure themselves that you are still alive, they could send up a deputation to visit you here?'

'No, I must go back to them. They won't believe I am well unless they see me on my feet. I am quite up to it, truly.'

But strangely, from that day his health began to fade. The dizzy spells returned, and the blurred vision. And he was tired, always so tired. He slept through most of the day now, though at night he woke with chest pains and laboured breathing. Black Jade, nursing him for longer hours than ever before, flatly refused to let him return to the main palace.

'It is something I must do,' he insisted, his eyes restless. 'The people must know they still have an Emperor. What use am I to them if all I can do is lie here?'

'At least,' she begged, 'wait until you are a little better.'

But he would not hear of it. He made the short journey to the Palace City in the sparkling cold of the Little Snow. Layered in quilted wool and carried in an open palanquin, he was met by a welcoming crowd at the Bridge of the Ford of Heaven. They cheered his return, he thought sombrely, with as willing a voice as they had cheered the conflagration of Young Tiger's fears and hopes.

The thought inspired him to offer a general amnesty to all convicted criminals except those who were guilty of treason. He determined to proclaim it himself from the great tower of the city's southern gate.

The Great Snow was now with them and it lived up to its name. On the morning of the proclamation Loyang lay somnolent under a deep white quilt; the air tingled and rang with the sound of hammers as the banners were erected in the square before the south gate.

Chinghiz reported that Pheasant had experienced some difficulty in rising; he had had an uncomfortable night and his breathing was erratic. Black Jade dressed quickly and hurried to his apartments.

She found Pheasant, weighed down by his ceremonial dragon robe in winter black, practising the declamation. His voice was not strong. Certainly it would not be heard across the vast space before the gate tower.

'To please me – do not make the attempt,' she entreated. 'You will have other opportunities. Let this one pass. It would be better, would it not, to appear when you are well?'

'I am quite well, really, my dear. It is just that the cold keeps catching in my throat.'

'No, you are *not* well, and if you go out in the snow you will be worse. You must not take such a foolish risk!'

He would not listen but had himself carried to the stables, intending, if he could, to ride through the city.

His horse was brought, but the effort to straddle it proved too much for him and he fell back, gasping for breath. Even now he refused Black Jade's desperate plea to abandon the attempt, and sent a message to the waiting populace that as many of them as possible were to come to the White Tiger Hall to listen to him read the proclamation from the throne.

He did so, in a voice that was as steady as he could make it. He was assured that it had carried to the back of the hall. When he had finished he felt far weaker than he had expected – it was not as though he had done anything but *talk*! The doctor who seemed to be always at his shoulder felt all his pulses and then insisted that he did not move.

A day-bed was brought and placed in the anteroom of the hall, where Black Jade sat next to him and held his hand, her heart beating raggedly with the knowledge that, this time, he was very ill indeed.

Stoves were brought and the windows were hung with heavy layers of brocade, so that the room had to be lit with lamps and candles like a shrine. The worried ministers and distressed servants melted away as Black Jade dismissed them, leaving only the conclave of physicians hovering in the next room.

'Are we alone, my dearest wife? Our surroundings are strange, but I must confess I like the atmosphere. All this light; it is like a festival! And how it suits you. You look so young and lovely. Do you remember the first time we were alone together, when I was a boy – that time I found you in Green Fragrance Court, when I was so frightened of my brother Tai?'

She stroked his hand. 'I remember.'

'You were so kind. You seemed so much older than I was. You have always seemed so in the ways of the spirit and the mind;

though in body I now feel ashamed before you.'

She bent to kiss him quickly. 'Don't say foolish things. We have known each other too long to notice which is spirit and which is body. It is the love that matters, nothing else.' She would try to give him what small gifts she could, for she sensed that they might well be the last she would give. If Pheasant was dying at last she would make sure that he died in the certainty of her love. And if that love was not, and perhaps never had been, of the kind that he wanted or had thought it was, he had not known that and now would never know. This at least was work she had done well. And then, too, she *had* loved him in so many ways, as a mother, as a friend, as a willing concubine. It was her own tragedy, perhaps never his, that she had always remained herself, detached, separate from him, and had never known that mingling and expanding of *yin* and *yang* that had created the harmony she had experienced with the two men she had wholly and unselfishly loved.

Pheasant was watching her. 'You have been the only strength I have had, you know that.'

She shook her head at the past tense, a kind deceit. 'You say that because you feel rather weak today. It will pass.'

'Insubstantial,' he smiled. 'That is how I feel. I wish it were otherwise. There are a hundred things I want to say to you.'

'Say them tomorrow,' she said, tucking the wolfskin around him.

'Yes, I think I will sleep for a while now.'

She watched him as he slept. She would not leave him, but took brief refreshment where she was, now and then calling for one of the doctors to reassure her that he was no worse.

Pheasant did not wake until the evening, when he sent first for his secretary whom he despatched to his study, and then for Pale Flame, his first minister.

'You are going to give him your will?' asked Black Jade. 'Are you sure it is necessary, so late?'

'Yes, my bird. There is the need.'

She felt a sudden chill of desolation, as though he were already gone.

'Please don't look so woebegone,' he said. 'It deceives me into thinking you a child who will be alone and friendless in the world, when I know very well you are nothing of the kind.' His smile summoned hers in return, but at that moment she felt just as he had described, small, discouraged and alone.

The Chancellor arrived and the Emperor presented him with

his will and with the power to continue the government.

The contents of the will were, naturally, known to Black Jade. It decreed that the Crown Prince was to ascend the throne before his father's coffin, so that there could be no discontinuity in the dynasty of the T'ang. It also ordered the young Emperor to refer all important matters of state, civil or military, to his mother, the Empress Dowager, for her binding decision. This had the approval of the council.

When Pale Flame had gone Pheasant leaned back on his pillows with a satisfied air. He looked suddenly younger and much of the strain had left his eyes. He asked Jade to send for wine and a little food. She did so, then gave the servants leave and fed him herself.

He sighed contentedly. 'This is very enjoyable. It is rather like the picnics we used to have, when we would stay out too late because it was so warm and the night so beautiful, and they would bring us lamps, and the fireflies would come out.'

She nodded, her eyes soft. 'And sometimes we would lie out under the stars until dawn, and then have to come in with stiffened bodies and crumpled robes – and the old men whispered disapproval behind their fans.'

'Shall we do that again, when summer comes,' he said, enjoying the fantasy, 'perhaps on the summit of Taishan – and watch the dawn come up together, after all?'

'Yes, let us do that,' she said gently, seeing his lids grow heavy.

'An Emperor should visit Taishan as often as he can. It gives him strength. I was well after we returned from there. Will you read to me about it, my love? Read to me how the Yellow Emperor called the spirits together. I want to drift into sleep on the sound of your voice.'

'Very well.' She gave a swift message to a physician and the book was brought. She made Pheasant more comfortable and gave him a few more sips of wine, warmed in her hands before one of the charcoal stoves.

'Listen then, and let your mind take flight. "Upon Jade Emperor Peak, the Yellow Emperor ordered all the spirits of the mountain to assemble to do him homage. His appearance was magnificent beyond all imagining; his bright face shone, light streamed from his golden robes. He drove upon the mountain in an ivory chariot drawn by six terrible dragons. The Wind God ran ahead of him and swept his path; the Rain God sprinkled the dust at his wheels. Wolves and tigers loped beside him, tamed by the enchantment of his presence. The concourse of spirits ran behind him, serpents streaking between their feet, a flight of phoenixes flashing overhead. He cried aloud to Heaven, exulting in the glory, and Heaven answered him with laughter and with joy. When he reached the summit – " ' She looked up to see whether Pheasant was still listening, for this was his favourite part.

He was not. In the same soft manner as his father had done, he had ceased, at last, to hear her voice.

She wept then, as she had never thought she would weep, for all the time they had shared together, for the misunderstandings there had been between them, and most of all for the fragile spirit of the man who had wanted to be so much more than his present incarnation had equipped him to be, and who had spent his life, as his father had done joyfully and his son would do unwillingly, in the long shadow of the Yellow Emperor.

PART THREE
Autumn Fires

26

To secure ourselves against defeat
Lies in our own hands,
But the opportunity of defeating the enemy
Is provided by the enemy himself.

(*The Art of War*, Sun Tzu)

'You are the Empress Dowager. You have a fool for a son. The government is in your hands. If you can keep it, you need never lose it.'

They were alone in her study. Chinghiz stood before her with his arms raised, exulting like some ecstatic war-god, blue fire shooting from his eyes and blue devilment issuing from his lips.

'You might at least,' Black Jade snapped, 'allow me time to mourn.'

'There *is* no time.' He knelt at her couch and looked keenly into her face. 'How deep is your mourning, my mistress?'

She slapped his face. A scarlet line spread across the finely chiselled cheekbone. He rose and turned his back on her. 'How deep?'

She stopped her anger. What good could it do?

'You know,' she said with difficulty. 'You know that I was not always able to love him. That at times he inspired me with contempt. That at times he – feared me. But we have been friends, lovers, the parents of children. Do you think I feel no pain, now that he lies before the altar of his ancestors? And if sometimes his weakness demeaned him as Emperor, won't you also count his strengths, his abiding kindness, his true concern for his people and for all of us here in the palace?' There were tears on her cheeks.

'I am not interested in seeing you weep over the past,' the steward said cruelly, folding his white linen sleeves, 'but in taking stock for the future. You are a woman. Alone. The Son of Heaven no longer stands like an invincible army at your back. Alone. And with a prophecy to fulfil.'

'Are you so eager to be the power behind the throne?'

He touched his slanting cheekbone as though she had slapped it again.

'Not the power,' he said smiling. 'Perhaps, a little, the inspiration.'

She did not reply. He fetched wine and offered it to her, her chance to make peace. She took it and drank once. Her own white sleeve fell against his. She thought, with the shocking irrelevance that occurs at times of death, that he was beautiful.

'Yes,' she whispered, 'you will always be that. I am glad', she added in recompense for her blow, 'that I have you so close to me. You should not say I am alone.'

Rewarded, he let his eyes fence with hers for another sweet, dangerous second. The danger was all his and he knew how to measure it so that the peril did not outweigh the delight. Then he rose and swept her with him into the future.

'You are alone only in that you have reached a paramount position of power. You can't doubt that Heaven is working for you now.' He counted the signs of celestial favour on tapering, vermilion-tipped fingers. 'His late Majesty has made it clear that he wishes his son to trust to your judgement. Pale Flame has publicly made himself your champion in submitting to the council that you should rule until the coronation; the other ministers will follow him.'

'And so they should,' she returned with asperity. 'Woman or not, they have been thankful enough for my abilities all these years.'

'Happily, the common desire of ministers of state, where there is good government, is for continuity. In addition,' he raised a sapphire-encircled forefinger, 'Loud Tiger himself is more than eager to leave the Empire in your hands.'

'That is because,' Jade grimaced, 'he knows next to nothing about statecraft, dislikes what he does know, and cares only for his interminable sports, his livestock, and his sportive, lively wife.'

'Heavenly Pearl,' brooded Chinghiz, his teeth grinding the words. 'She, I fancy, may be the only dissenting voice in the chorus encouraging her husband to do as he pleases and leave government to those who understand it.'

As usual, he was right.

At the end of Loud Tiger's first month of nominal rule, Pale Flame asked if he might discuss his progress with Black Jade. In the cabinet changes that had accompanied the accession, the minister had become President of the Secretariat, an office which would give even further scope for his outstanding talents.

They spoke together in the map-room after a rather contentious debate on the number of troops they might safely pull out of Korea and Tibet. Jade had wanted to bring home as many as possible to their families, but the council were more cautious.

Her loudest opponent had been Lord Wei, the father of the new Empress, whom Loud Tiger had raised to the rank of first minister without consulting anyone. It had not been a popular move.

'I advised His Majesty against the appointment but he was not inclined to listen,' Pale Flame deplored.

'Had I known of his intention, I would have prevented it myself,' Jade agreed. 'It is a clumsy stroke to show such favouritism so early in the reign. And it has always been accepted that such honours must be earned. Lord Wei has done nothing whatever to deserve his position.'

'Even less, one might think, than the son of His Majesty's wet-nurse, whom he has just made a fifth grade official.'

Black Jade groaned. 'The boy is behaving like an idiot. He will make a mockery of himself if he continues like this. Have you no influence over him? You were his tutor for long enough.'

'That is just the trouble,' the dry voice regretted. 'Now that he is no longer committed to obeying me he makes it clear that he wants none of my advice. He appears to feel,' he added glumly, 'that his best counsellor is the Empress.'

'That girl!' Jade shook her head. 'She is at least intelligent, I'll grant her that. But she is no politician; how could she be? This is the road to disaster. But leave it to me, Pale Flame. I will speak to my son.'

She chose her opportunity with care. A hawking party, in which a great many courtiers took part, was a sufficiently public though unofficial milieu.

They rode out into the park in a noisy family party with the rest of the court straggling behind. The men carried their hawks on their wrists, their tail bells jingling in gold and jade, their yellow stares masked in leather and silk. The austringers followed the women, bearing the weight of their birds. The great giants, the eagles, the sakers, the Greenland gyrfalcons, sat jealously on their keepers' pommels, their terrible power only just concealed. Black Jade, Tiger Lily, and the young Empress carried their own birds in this way. Close behind the imperial cluster, their disciplined presence, as always, notably felt, was a company of Black Jade's impeccable guards, their crimson shirts figured with the same night-black falcon that bided its hour of victory beneath her caressing hand.

'Where is Bold-hand – I don't see him?' Jade enquired of her daughter, who was riding next to her in a fetching outfit of emerald suede dyed with alum, matched by the hood of her 'skylark yellow' goshawk.

Tiger Lily shrugged. 'I haven't the least idea. We don't live in one another's sleeves,' she said testily. Then, 'What *do* you think of Lord Wei's little entourage? A trifle pretentious, would you say?'

The Emperor's father-in-law was riding, a little ahead, between his daughter and Loud Tiger. Escorting them, in a self-conscious pack that was neither guard nor simple attendance, was a group of gentlemen with fierce northern faces and bristling whiskers, dressed in their clan colours of blue and puce. They did not carry bows like Black Jade's spotless archers, but their swords were very evident in new embroidered sheaths.

'He evidently feels that the court is a dangerous place,' the Empress Dowager suggested brightly.

Tiger Lily chuckled. 'I feel sure he will discover, to his cost, that he is right to think so.'

'What are you two hatching?' called Dawn Tiger cheerfully from his sister's side, a position he was delighted to regain. They had been inseparable since their nursery days, and he had been a lost soul since her marriage.

'Nothing has been hatched here, except hawks,' his mother assured him pleasantly. 'But, if you watch, you will see that they will be more than equal to the task of humbling over-reaching clansmen.'

'Ah, I w-wondered if you w-would do anything about them.' Dawn Tiger fixed her with a speculative eye. 'Just promise me one thing, m-mother. If, by any chance, or m-mischance, or simple stratagem, I sh-should ever, by the grace of Heaven, become Emperor – just let me k-know exactly what you want me not to do – and I won't do it!'

For answer, Black Jade lifted her black hawk and it shook its bells at him, thinking its blind waiting over. Dawn Tiger laughed aloud and swept her a low bow from the saddle. He was joking, she thought; but only just.

They had reached the stretch of carefully kept countryside where the game could be taken; rabbits and pheasants in the forested borderland, heron, crane, geese and other waterfowl in the irrigated heath. The huntsmen and austringers dismounted and the grooms ran to take their horses while they received their orders from the Emperor.

Loud Tiger was in his element. His decisive thunder soon had everyone in their place and knowing what to do. Normally, he would fly his bird first, but he had offered that courtesy to Lord Wei as an honoured guest and welcome relative.

The sport was particularly good that day. Lord Wei's white goshawk took several brace of pheasant, and half a warren of coneys; the Emperor's Manchurian falcon disposed, elegantly, of a fine heron and a welter of waterbirds; Heavenly Pearl, sharp and fastidious in ice-blue satin with puce linings, sent her clouded goshawk speckling into space to return, time after time, with the swiftest kills of all, much to the disgust of Tiger Lily whose yellow bird was feeling liverish and was letting her down.

To general surprise, Black Jade did not loose her falcon, but kept the great, long-winged aristocrat quiet on her saddle, slowly and constantly stroking its ink-dark plumage and giving it the occasional scratch beneath the weighty, blue-lustred wings which was what it liked best of all.

Lord Wei, as etiquette insisted, abandoned the game for a space and trotted through the green and gold scrub to pay his respects to the Empress Dowager. Heavenly Pearl came with him, her little smiling face full of little pointed teeth. Noticing their movement, Dawn Tiger, who had been watching his mother all morning without reward, whistled a few well-worn private notes which fell, not far off, on his sister's ear. Their glances locking, they reined in to satisfy their curiosity.

'That is a wicked-looking creature you have there,' Heavenly Pearl was saying as they drew up beside the ravishing figure in the Wu colours, winking at the sun in a ransom of rubies.

'He is not so pretty as your little dappled lady,' Black Jade agreed, admiring the 'clouded' grey and white mingling of feathers that gave the goshawk its name. 'But he is quite exceptionally successful. He has very rarely failed to take his prey.'

'My lady is no laggard either,' the Empress smiled. 'Shall we have a bet on them; ten pieces of embroidered silk as a forfeit if either should fail?'

Black Jade continued to smooth her falcon's feathers. 'Why not? And if neither fails?'

Heavenly Pearl's smile narrowed. 'Oh, they will not disappoint us. In any contest there must be a loser.'

'In that case,' suggested Jade, looking very much amused, 'Perhaps we should try a wider range of skills? Will you join us?' she demanded of her flanking offspring, who nodded their consent.

'Then surely we are two clearly separate sides,' Lord Wei said suavely, the square black brackets above his opaque brown eyes disappearing into his magenta cap. 'His Majesty is riding this way. Let us wait and solicit his aid for the Wei.'

'Then let it be, for the purposes of the contest, Wei against Wu,' said Tiger Lily charmingly, dimpling at the gem-encrusted minister.

'And m-may the best clan win!' exhorted Dawn Tiger with a certain amount of mischief.

The Emperor arrived, breathless, and was told what was afoot. Heavenly Pearl was to let fly first, as Black Jade had been the one to enlarge the action.

The gamekeepers sent up a pheasant, swooping ungainly towards the sky and freedom. Its dream was over on the instant and it was returned, a sodden mass of soft, still pulsing plumage, its breastbone crushed in the honed, efficient, feminine bill. Hawk and huntress cooed together, both visibly preening.

'Your Majesty, will you be next?' Black Jade invited Loud Tiger courteously.

'A pleasure, but Heavenly Pearl's hard to beat,' bellowed the Emperor affectionately.

'Perhaps h-he should try *beating* her more often,' murmured Dawn Tiger to his sister behind Jade's spear-straight back. The resulting ill-mannered laughter went up with Loud Tiger's brave white falcon, a prized tribute from Manchuria. It met its mark, one of the keeper's favourite white pheasants, which he had been saving especially for his idolised master, in a sudden airborne flurry, like a miniature snowstorm. Heavenly Pearl had opened her hands to clap, and her father to congratulate, when out of nowhere at all a vast black shadow engulfed the plummeting snowfall and winged on swift, scything pinions to its home. Black Jade, unnoticed by the sky-gazing sportsmen, had loosed, at last, her great black falcon.

The black-eyed bird sat now, as though in her lap, its catch decently disposed of, its alert gaze, cock-headed, asking if that were all there was to do. She left it unhooded; it would not hurt her; she had trained it since it was taken from its fledgeling nest. It sat, unwinking, its ruby collar coruscating, its demonic jet eye misprising all but her. If a bird could be said to love, then this one loved.

'Alas,' uttered its mistress detachedly. 'What very appalling behaviour. I must offer my apologies. But sometimes,' she turned a regretful face towards her son, 'even an Emperor among birds, such as yours, can come to grief in bad company.'

There were gasps of delayed horror and dawning comprehension. She had done this on purpose.

Everyone knew it. No one spoke it. Neither Lord Wei nor his daughter wished to seem to understand the insult to themselves. Tiger Lily and her brother knew they would have Jade to deal with if they uttered a syllable. Loud Tiger had simply no idea what she had meant.

But Black Jade had not finished the lesson. 'It was too bad of you,' she told the black culprit, straightening a ruffled quill or two. 'It was hard on him,' she explained to the slightly dazed assembly, her smile fashioned of clotted cream, and broken glass, 'to smell the blood around him, and not to be used according to his nature. You must forgive him. I'm sure my other son can erase this unfortunate moment from our memories, with the help of his own well-schooled bird. Dawn Tiger, if you will favour us?'

'At your charming command,' said Dawn Tiger, trying to keep a straight face. He sent his grey goshawk into the smiling sky as the gamekeeper released a small flock of pigeons. Its trick was to take two, holding one, cleanly killed, in its talons as it swooped for another, then swerved to bring both home.

'No. N-not to me,' Dawn Tiger informed it as it landed on his outstretched gauntlet, dripping blood and dropping the plump, warm bodies neatly on to his horse's neck. 'You should take them to my lady mother; she has earned them.'

'Why, thank you, my son. How dutiful you are,' Black Jade teased him, her own eyes reflecting the laughter in his.

'Well now, how shall we say the contest stands?' she asked innocently, looking round the little circle.

'Oh, I think we should call it a w-washout, don't you, Heavenly Pearl?' solicited Dawn Tiger, enjoying himself. 'Or w-would you like to admit victory to the W-Wu?'

'On this occasion, perhaps,' agreed the Empress, her little teeth showing in what might have been a smile.

'Oh, let's forget it; it has all been among friends,' Loud Tiger blared optimistically. 'I'm hungry. Let's go and eat.'

He rode off, trailing his dispirited co-contestants.

Behind them the accumulated laughter exploded, startling the dozing birds.

'Gods! If even my poor brother can't w-work out *that* exquisite analogy, he is a c-clod of oafish loam!' Dawn Tiger cried, weeping with mirth.

'The Wei clan understands,' said Tiger Lily. 'Look how they're dragging their tails! All that tinselly self-confidence has quite gone. Well done, Mother!'

Black Jade sat still for a moment, wondering if, perhaps she had gone a little too far. It was no great matter if she had. The Wei must be shown that it was not they who would stand at Loud Tiger's shoulder.

Loud Tiger, however, was not the man to show them. When his wife explained to him the combined advice and threat that Black Jade had extended so elegantly, he did not intend to accept either.

He came to her in the nearest thing she had ever seen to a thoroughly bad temper, and complained bitterly of the way she had treated his wife and her father.

'I'm sorry you feel the way you do about Lord Wei's appointment,' he said thunderously, his eyes on the air behind her left ear. 'But the Emperor's father-in-law should have a position of some dignity. Heavenly Pearl is most offended,' he added bleakly.

'Is she indeed? Does she, I wonder, suppose a provincial prefect to be capable, not only of the *dignity*, but also of the considerable specialised, and specially learned, ability of a first minister?'

'Yes, she does!' the Emperor shouted mutinously. 'And so do I!' Heavenly Pearl had demanded that he stand up for himself, had accused him of being frightened of his mother, had reminded him that it was he, after all, who was actually the Emperor.

'So much so that I intend to make him the President of the Chancellery. What do you think of that?' He finished on a wavering note of determination and the fear at which his wife had sneered.

'Not very much,' replied Black Jade acidly. 'Nor, I imagine, will the members of the council. I strongly advise against it.'

Heavenly Pearl had told him what he should say to this.

'I don't believe, Honourable Mother,' he attempted imperial loftiness, 'that the appointment of the Chancellor is a matter of state such as my father intended you should advise me upon.'

'Do you not?' Her patience was in tatters. 'Then by all means give it to your father-in-law, simply because he is your father-in-law! Raise all your ministers from the ranks of the peasants of you like! Listen to your ignorant little idiot of a wife and ignore the counsel of men who have been educated solely in order to give it to you! Go your own way, my son – and see what a sorry state you will have created. Good day to you!'

She swept out with cold magnificence, leaving Loud Tiger shivering in the breeze of her anger. He was amazed at his own audacity. He was afraid of her; Heavenly Pearl was quite right. He was really very sorry about that. He had never been afraid when they were all children. He wondered, dismally, why things had to change. Still – he brightened – he had done as Heavenly Pearl had wanted. Now he could make Lord Wei the Chancellor. He liked Lord Wei, who seemed to credit him with far more intelligence than anyone else did.

During the next few days he canvassed the support of the coterie of younger courtiers and junior ministers who were his friends, with the aim of Lord Wei's elevation.

Later that week, Pale Flame again sought out Black Jade. His long face was like a graveyard.

'Highness – His Majesty will take no advice. He informed the council this morning of his firm intention concerning Lord Wei. On behalf of my colleagues, I remonstrated with him. His answer was this – "What is there to prevent me from doing as I like? By the Buddha, Lord President, there is nothing to stop me from handing over the entire Empire to my father-in-law, if I wish! Your wretched opinion is of no account." '

Black Jade closed her eyes, ashamed of her son.

There was a full, deep silence. Two sighs fell into it.

At last Black Jade raised her head and met Pale Flame's harassed gaze. She spoke formally, knowing her words would be repeated verbatim to the council. 'The divine office of Emperor, filled so magnificently by his grandfather, Shih-min, and held so bravely by his father, has affected the empty head of this foolish boy as though it were nothing more than the captaincy of a class of schoolboys. His words, like his deeds, are unworthy of an Emperor of the T'ang. I fear that will always be the case.'

She watched the minister comprehend her meaning. The stern lines of his face tensed, as though their muscles contemplated exhausting work. He smiled briefly and nodded. He was her man.

She felt the wings of the prophecy brush the still air above them. She shivered, accepting their chill salute.

Quietly, they went together into the council chamber.

The next morning, after he had breakfasted, Loud Tiger was respectfully requested, on behalf of the Empress Dowager, to attend an audience in the Great Hall of Audience near the south gate of the Palace City. He went rather doubtfully, thinking of his last meeting with his mother.

'Cheer up,' Heavenly Pearl encouraged him from the unravelled silk cocoon of their bed. 'They must be expecting a huge crowd, to fill that vast chamber. Black Jade can't mean you any harm; she would never cause you to lose face before such an assembly. She has probably thought better of her attitude and wishes to be in your favour; she has arranged some spectacular surprise for you.'

This, at least, was true.

Loud Tiger, much cheered, dressed in one of his most sumptuous dragon robes, in winter black embroidered with green scales and red flames. He arrived at the Great Hall, entering at the back, and spoke amiably to the courtiers who flanked his path. Inside, on the dais, he found Black Jade already seated in state next to an empty throne. She too was formally dressed, wrapped in a black phoenix robe figured in scarlet and showered with diamonds as though she had been in snow. She greeted him pleasantly and he sat down beside her, unaccountably nervous again.

He looked about the hall. The whole court seemed to be here, their politely inscrutable faces no doubt masking avid curiosity. The room was bordered with a scalloping of the palace guard, a very sizable contingent.

Loud Tiger leaned towards Black Jade, smiling, unsure.

'Now, won't you tell me why you have gathered us all here? Is there something I don't know? Some reason to celebrate?'

Her answering smile was brief and seasonal. 'I believe so, Your Majesty. I am not sure that you will agree with me.' She met his eyes, finding bewilderment and a dawning alarm.

'I wish you would just tell me, and be done with it,' he muttered.

'Matters will become very clear.'

Turning away from him with a sense of pity she did not show, she lifted a hand towards the captain of the guard. Instantly a dozen officers stepped smartly forward and stood on either side of the throne. Pale Flame came forward from the front rank of the courtiers. With him were his new vice-president, Lord Liu, recently promoted from the North Gate, and General Wu-ting, known as the Thunderbolt, on furlough from the wars.

Loud Tiger groped for comprehension, looking dumbly from one stern, regretful face to another. He began to feel a churning in his bowels. If only someone would speak!

Ah. That old gargoyle Pale Flame was going to put him out of his misery. It was certain, now, that nothing pleasant was about to occur, not if that canting devil had anything to do with it.

Pale Flame strode up on to the dais. He made the formal obeisances, first to the Emperor, then to the Empress Dowager, then impudently half-turned, without seeking permission, to face the court. Loud Tiger squinted at Black Jade, but she did not appear to be offended by this rudeness. Great Heaven, the man was going to make some sort of speech! He leaned forward, frowning, but Pale Flame had already begun –

'By order of Her Serene Majesty, the Empress Dowager, it has been decreed that you, Li Che, known as Loud Tiger, have been considered unfit to continue to rule the great and glorious Empire of the T'ang. You are, therefore, deposed from the throne as of this moment. You will be known henceforward by the title of Prince of Lu Ling.' The dry voice finished, hanging in the breathy, frosted air on a wave of excited tension.

Loud Tiger came to his feet, looking furiously at Pale Flame, then, more accurately, at Black Jade. 'You can't do this!' he bellowed. 'What right have you? Why should you?'

Black Jade replied with a calm dignity that pointed up his disarray.

'Did you not, in front of witnesses, declare your intention to give away the Empire to your father-in-law, Lord Wei?'

'Oh, don't be – that is ridiculous!'

'It may be. But it is also a treasonable sugestion.'

'It *can't* be!' Loud Tiger roared incredulously. 'How can the Emperor commit treason?'

'By failing in his duty to his people, and to the sacred mandate. As you have done. My son, I am very sorry.' She nodded to the guards.

'What are you – But you can't – Mother you know I didn't really *mean* what I said about Lord Wei! I was angry with Pale Flame – he was being insolent and –'

'Your excuses are not dignified,' rapped his mother. 'Nor are they of any consequence to us. You have been deposed. Kindly do us the honour to step down.'

The guardsmen were standing gravely on either side of him. Black Jade was waiting with an implacable courtesy. Quite suddenly he wanted to weep. He must not do that, not in front of all these people, all of whom had claimed to be his friends, his loyal subjects. Oh sweet Buddha, what would Heavenly Pearl say to him now? She would never forgive this loss of face, of throne and fortune – everything she had wanted so much, everything he had loved giving to her.

He groaned, the quietest sound he had ever made, then stepped down from the throne without looking again at any of them.

He went away between the silent rows of guardsmen. They would take him to his old rooms in his father's palace, where he would live with his curtailed household and his furious, pregnant, wife.

All over the Great Hall, after the Emperor had gone, men looked at each other without appearing to do so. No one asked leave to speak. When the sound of marching boots had died away, the Empress Dowager rose and addressed them with a melancholy gravity, the diamonds shone like tears upon her brilliant gown.

'My lords, this is a sorrowful day for all of us. We shall go now and pray in the Temple of the Ancestors, seeking their guidance and reassurance in our trouble.'

There was a reverent murmur of assent. But she had not yet made any move to leave. They looked at her, seeing sadness, great beauty and a loneliness which each man wished he might assuage.

'I have,' she said, her voice grey and level, 'one last son to offer to Heaven.'

27

A household cannot have two masters.
(Chinese proverb)

New Dawn was proclaimed the Emperor.

The understanding between Black Jade and this youngest and most philosophical of her sons was perfect. His was to be a purely nominal sovereignty. The title of Son of Heaven had passed to him, but the mandate had not. It hung, somewhere in abeyance, between himself and the Empress Dowager, leaving him nothing but hollow ceremonial. Not a single voice was raised in protest.

Black Jade herself, after the act, was astonished at the ease with which she had carried out what could only be described, however indelicately, as a *coup d'état*.

'Why should there be protest?' carolled an ecstatic Chinghiz, airing his latest inspirational garment of carnation raised velvet, spangled with vulgar gold and lapis lazuli. 'The people are content. The Empire is at peace within its walls. For many years you have deserved our gratitude as a wise judge and a shrewd politician. Why should anyone wish to change your government for the ascendancy of one ignorant young man or another?'

'Why? Because I am a woman. Because when I was a fifth grade concubine, and Pheasant wished to make me his Empress, the price of my success was accounted in men's lives and livelihoods. It is a matter of some wonder to me – whether or not one believes in prophecy – that the same concubine, albeit rather more exalted, can pull down the Son of Heaven from his throne and enlist the aid of these same sort of men as those who lost their lives as her supporters.'

It was true. Despite the prophecy, she was chastened by a sudden wonder at the simplicity of its working out.

'Little Mistress,' declared her servant with his most impressive sweeping bow, 'you have become indispensable to us.'

She looked affectionately at the handsome, still slightly outrageous though very distinguished figure of the man who composed the tenor of her days. He was now the only one in whom she confided with a lack of reserve that she did not share with either Dawn Tiger or her daughter, close though she was to both of them.

'You also have become indispensable, my Chinghiz,' she told him softly, watching his eyes slant in azure pleasure. 'Your position in the palace is now enviable. There must be many who would like to be in your place. I have no doubt you know who they are, and how to guard against them?'

She received a smile which appreciated her good sense.

'How much more, then,' she continued, smiling into the wide eyes whose exceptional colour could almost cause pain, 'must I be on guard. It seems to me, as I look about the court, that there are several men who, given the necessary encouragement, would find it very easy to dispense with this exalted concubine. I was thinking of Pheasant's uncles, the T'ang princes, for example.'

Chinghiz lowered his courtesan's lashes. 'If Your Majesty were to remain content with things as they are, then I have no doubt the princes would also be content.'

She laughed. How well he understood her.

'Ah, my dear friend, in some ways you are more to me than any other man could be. No, as you guess, I am not content. Not yet.'

He nodded his cloth-of-gold turban, its jewels glaring and winking.

'You wish to consider, Flower of the Lotus, how far you might travel towards that enviable state?'

'Not how far,' she whispered, her lips curving, 'but how *soon*!'

He threw up his hands. His golden, muscular arms praised Heaven.

'Thanks be to all the Gods! At last you have consented to recognise your karma.'

'Perhaps. But don't rejoice too soon, my cockerel! We have some distance to travel yet.'

*

Black Jade began her regency with an act of grace. It contained a great many popular favours, in terms of amnesties and tax relief, and the longed-for order for thousands of soldiers to return to tend the altars of their starving ancestors.

'We are not', she told the council, 'a military nation. We can surely guard our borders without a standing army.' On that basis, against some demur, she shortened the terms of all military service and raised jaded army morale with a series of bonuses. It was important that the officers should be personally loyal to her.

To counteract the still unacceptable degree of corruption in the overstrained provincial administration, a new branch of the Censorate was instituted, to be recruited at grassroots level.

The title of the reign – the only name by which the Emperor is known to his people – was to be *Wen Ming*. Brilliant Creativity, suggesting the flowering of art and scholarship, and a general regeneration which the two sovereigns wished to encourage.

In an orgy of festive re-titling, the graceful city of Loyang became an earthly symbol of the celestial residence of the Queen Mother of the Western Heaven. Renamed Shendu, the Holy City, it presided over a secretariat called the Terrace of the Male Phoenix, a Chancellery in the Tower of the Female Phoenix, an imperial library on the Unicorn Terrace, and a Cabinet office mischievously entitled the 'Terrace of the North Pole'. There were a whole bouquet of floral nicknames for solemn masculine agencies, and pretty ones for dreary state offices. Black Jade sat in the midst of the embarrassment of beauty like a jewel in a navel, well content with her amusement.

There were two pieces of bad news.

Old Arsenic, the general she had despatched to guard Young Tiger, had returned, exhausted, from Szechwan, begging to see her.

His face was livid and he was trembling.

'Why are you here, General? Is there some rebellion, despite your precautions? Is my son well?'

Old Arsenic looked wretched. 'No, Majesty. I wish it were that.'

'Then please speak.'

But he stood with his head bowed, not daring to look at her. He was, she saw, ashamed. Unreasonably, she began to feel fear.

'What is it, General? Quickly, please!'

'The Prince, Young Tiger,' he said despairingly at last, 'is dead.'

'Great Heaven!'

She gasped and clutched at her breast, groping for the back of the seat behind her. Pain struck her with the unexpected ferocity of a wild animal's attack. 'I'm sorry – I – what did you say?'

He saw nothing but her eyes, a wide green sea of pain, rippling with shock. He knew then that he had mistaken her. He could not speak.

Black Jade put out her hand to him. She was dizzy. She couldn't see the man. Young Tiger – her son – her foolish, fearful boy who had repudiated her, who had been afraid of her!

The reaching hand entreated. 'How,' she managed to ask, the room turning, 'did he die? If it is true,' she added, on a sudden insane surge of hope.

The General swallowed, his furrowed face as vulnerable as a child's.

'It is to my sorrow, Your Majesty, that the noble Prince has hanged himself –'

'No! I *won't* believe it!' Her cry made him, simply, wish to go and do the same.

Chinghiz, never far off, had glided in and stood close to her now, the clear planes of his face standing out stark with anger for what had hurt her. He forced wine through her lips, which she could not keep from trembling. 'I am not cold,' she said foolishly, breaking his heart. He longed for this accursed bearer of ill tidings to leave them, so that he might comfort her in his arms.

'How did this happen?' he demanded urgently.

The General pulled himself together, glad (if that was the word) to be dealing with a man (if that was the term).

'I am somewhat confused, my lord –'

'For the God's sake, man – just tell me how and why it happened!'

'When I arrived at the prince's prison – I mean – his house,' he floundered, exciting Chinghiz to white rage. 'It seemed to me that it was not readily defensible. Bearing in mind Her Majesty's instructions, I insisted that His Highness should move, so that I could protect him more easily. I chose a stout building and posted a strong guard.'

'In other words,' said the steward crisply, 'you imprisoned him.'

'His Highness was made very comfortable,' the General claimed hopelessly. 'But he disliked the change. And he also seemed to take my presence amiss, taking it into his head that Her Majesty had sent me to spy on him.' He turned sadly to the shaking figure in the chair; she seemed, to his broken man's fantasy, to be encircled by the bright robes of her furious protector.

'Young Tiger said, Honoured Lady, that whatever he did or did not do, I would report to you that he planned some evil, because –' he halted, begging the Gods for help – 'because that was what you wanted to hear. He repeated this on several occasions. I'm afraid,' he finished on a note of desperate compassion, 'that the young Prince was no longer himself.'

She shook her head and did not speak.

'So, General, you imprisoned the Prince, and then threatened him?' asked the silky voice of the eunuch.

'Heaven forgive you, sir! There were no threats.' He kept his eyes cast down. They were running with tears.

'Then why,' persisted the voice, 'did he hang himself?'

'I think, my lord, that his mind had become unbalanced by his own fears.'

'That would not be surprising, when you had thrown him into jail and then terrified him with your talk of rebellion and plot! You were sent to protect Young Tiger, General, not to harry him to his death!'

'Sir! Majesty!' The commander dropped to the floor and began to beat his head upon the ground. Still clinging to the tiles, he looked up at Black Jade with such mingled fear and disgrace that Chinghiz knew he had guessed correctly. This man had taken her for a monster.

She saw it too and cried out savagely, a single incoherent wail of utter denial. While he caught her, reeling in the darkness that assailed her, he called sharply for the guard to come and take the wretched creature from her sight.

She did not, as she might have done, try to extract a useless vengeance by sending Old Arsenic to the headsman. She took away his rank and titles and let him go free, unable to kill a man who had thought, however mistakenly and hideously, that he was doing his duty to her. Chinghiz applauded this, but for the more pragmatic reason that the man was one of the forces' favourite commanders, and Black Jade would always need their goodwill.

Young Tiger was given a state funeral, his misdeeds forgotten.

As she knelt, in her white garments, before his spirit tablet, and gazed in patient agony at the young, unmarked features of the portrait on the temple wall, she tried to reach his departed ghost before it descended to the Hell of the Suicides.

'You know, my son, what my punishment must be; to live forever with the knowledge that it was I, however unwittingly, who brought about your death. And such a death! If only you had taken more courage, you might have lived. You will know by now that it was never my desire that you should suffer, as you know, too, that I am your mother. You should not have doubted me, Young Tiger. That doubt was the root of all your sorrows. Now, you will be able to forgive me, and to understand that I wanted you only to find your own way to self-knowledge, for it was this that you lacked, rather than any knowledge of me. Pray for me, my son, as I shall pray for you. I cannot believe that the Holy Mother will allow you to stay long in that sad place. I will beg, every day, that your reincarnation is swift and honourable.'

It was evidently the season of irony in Heaven, for the next item of news was precisely the event which her shepherding of Young Tiger had been designed to prevent.

A rebellion of some size had broken out in the city of Yang Chou at the confluence of the Yangtse River with the Grand Canal. Surprise was immediately cancelled by instant recognition of the reasons for unrest. The city was the home of a number of high officials exiled for corruption. Disgraced, without influence, they were normally too wary of further punishment to indulge in treason, but the recent change of government and their ignorance of its exact strength had emboldened them to this extreme attempt to repair their fortunes.

Its original aim was purported to be the reinstatement of Loud Tiger and it was led, regrettably, by a grandson of the Great Wall, one Early Warning Li, and his brother. This Li usurped the governorship of Yang Chou and announced himself as the saviour of the Empire. The rebellion began to spread; not far, but enough to make the War Ministry send 300,000 troops to crush it. When the imperial advance made his capture of Loyang an impossibility, the intrepid 'Grand General' set up an impostor who resembled the dead Young Tiger, claiming that he had escaped from exile and would take the throne. This was a great relief to Loud Tiger, who had feared and disliked being the object of a revolt.

Black Jade's main preoccupation was not with rebels, but closer to home. What, in view of the existence of the uprising, was the attitude of the older leaders of the T'ang clan? Especially that of Pheasant's uncles, Prince Han and Prince Lu, both men of great personal influence. She knew that they were not her supporters, although they had never spoken out against her. But would they use their territorial overlordship to join the rebels?

Several of her informants thought that they might. She had

invited her nephew Bold Fortune, younger brother to the nephews executed for the murder of Lotus Bud, to court, to take the place of the dead Sage Path. He and his cousin, Rich Talent, had behaved with exemplary virtue and loyalty, eager to expunge the disgrace to the Wu clan, and had been promoted to the mysteries of the North Gate. Rich Talent was now certain that the growing ascendency of the Wu clan was provoking a backlash on the part of the princes, who feared that she would indeed take the throne entirely from Dawn Tiger.

His advice was somewhat stringent. 'Kill them, Majesty. It would be wise; if they think you plan to do away with their dynasty, they may well attempt to assassinate you.'

'This is true, Rich Talent,' she allowed. 'But rather than murdering my late husband's relatives in cold blood, I would prefer to put your findings to the council.'

The ministers were divided. Several of the younger men were in favour of executing the princes before they became a danger to the throne in its present occupation, but those in the higher grades, led by Pale Flame, were strongly against such Tartar tactics.

Black Jade looked at them sceptically. She had learned something very interesting, recently, about Pale Flame.

'Could it be, Chancellor,' she asked him pleasantly, 'that you have a certain sympathy with the princes, and perhaps even with the rebels themselves? I am told – though – *you* did not volunteer the information – that one of their leaders is a nephew of yours.'

Pale Flame guttered visibly. 'I have not sought to conceal it, Majesty. To my shame, it is true. But it has no bearing on my reluctance to put innocent men to death.'

'Their hands may be innocent, as yet,' Jade said firmly, 'but I am assured that their intentions are not.'

The thin minister looked unhappy. 'Majesty, forgive me; they have seen you hold the reins of government – incomparably – for the late Emperor and two of his sons. Now they watch as you raise temples to your ancestors. Their fears are understandable. All they require is reassurance that Your Majesty does not intend to usurp the throne.'

So! He had declared himself. He was not, any more, her man. It was a pity – he was quite the cleverest man in the cabinet. But this time he was wrong.

'Do you seriously think it would be acceptable to have bloody revolution in the streets of Loyang? And that these reactionary old men should set one of my sons upon the throne as their puppet? Really, you try my patience!'

Pale Flame met her icy glare equably. 'Your Majesty must do as she thinks fit. But I must beg to be excused any further discussion of these matters.'

She would lose face if she ordered him to stay. It was a rift she had expected, but a serious one. The result was that her husband's uncles kept their heads and were issued with grave admonitions to loyalty. Black Jade was aware of having made a more threatening enemy in Pale Flame. She would need to discover just how far the enmity would take him.

The revolt was giving more trouble than they had anticipated. Some of the early clashes had gone against them while the imperial army was still not fully manned. A council meeting was called to discuss the situation.

To Black Jade's surprise, Pale Flame was not only present but obviously intended to take a leading role. He described the rebel successes in gloomy terms as the destruction of harmony and the probable beginning of a disastrous civil war.

'The Son of Heaven is of age; but he does not govern. This, and only this, is why a man of no account, such as the despicable grandson of the honoured Great Wall, is able to raise up so much opposition.' He paused and directed an unctuous kowtow towards the throne. 'If the Empress Dowager will return the government to the Emperor, a return to peace would follow. There would not even be any need for further reprisals against the rebels.'

It was an open challenge. Before Black Jade could speak, one of the censors pressed forward, a young man whose face shone with indignation.

'Pale Flame was the Emperor's tutor. He has always been entrusted with the highest authority. He owes everything to Her Majesty. Yet, it seems, he has no wish to punish the rebels, and he talks of Her Majesty giving up the government!' His excited eyes swept the room. 'I can't speak for the rest of you, but I for one find his attitude decidedly suspicious! Just where, I wonder, *does* the Chancellor's loyalty lie?'

They were silent, but several heads nodded; as many others shook vehemently. 'That is something we shall find out as soon as we may,' Black Jade said calmly. Then, turning to the grim-faced first minister, she said with gentle regret, 'You have been very foolish, Pale Flame. You have surprised and distressed me. Please consider yourself under arrest.'

He surveyed the soft-seeming, beautiful woman with a dry

appreciation.

'Very well, Majesty – but I am guilty of nothing but loyalty to the Emperor.'

The debate as to whether or not the Chancellor would have come out in support of his rebellious nephew exercised the tongues of the court for some time. His close friends and colleagues firmly denied the possibility. One of them, a well-known army commander known as the Terror of the Turks, sent Black Jade a memorial declaring the utter impossibility of such a slur. It was Chinghiz who eventually supplied the evidence of his true treachery.

'It was such a simple plan, Little Mistress, and might easily have caused you some inconvenience – though little more than that. The court and the army are too loyal for there to have been any lasting ill-effects. You recall the day you were to visit the shrines of the Buddhas in the Lung-men caves?'

'And it rained, so I did not go? What of it?'

'That rain was Heaven-sent. I learned of their plan from a loyal army officer whom Pale Flame had tried to win over. He intended to capture you inside the caves, while there was no one but priests and nuns to protect you. He had gathered a large enough band of malcontents to overpower the guard outside. You would have been imprisoned and Pale Flame was to set up his government in the name of the Emperor.'

She was shocked. 'I had no idea it had gone so far with him. The worst of it is that he was once such an upright man. Perhaps,' she mused, 'in a manner of speaking, he still is. If he is truly convinced that a woman's rule means the dissolution of harmony –'

'Then he must suffer the consequences,' said Chinghiz grimly. He had no time for sympathy with her enemies.

Despite a certain amount of passionate protest from those who remained incredulous of his guilt, Pale Flame was indicted and sentenced by the tribunal of censors. He was beheaded in the market-place, the most degrading of deaths for a man of rank.

'A traitor's death,' shrugged Chinghiz when Black Jade showed a continued tendency to pity the defective Chancellor.

But she had been badly shaken. 'How many more agree with him?' she brooded. 'I must know, for certain, whom I may trust.'

However, in less than four months the rebellion was snuffed out. It had contained the seeds of its own failure, having fallen into internecine factions and failure to make a coherent attack. For a time, nevertheless, Black Jade's sleep was disturbed by dreams of what might have been if the rebels and the conspirators within the palace had ever joined forces.

She ordered the seneschal to summon the entire court. Then, wearing her bleakest black robe, jet-embroidered, with Shih-min's emeralds as her sole ornament, she appeared before them in the same hall in which she had dismissed Loud Tiger.

Speaking from the throne, she let them know her mood at once.

'Is there anyone here who considers I am in any way at fault in the eyes of the Empire?'

There was a bewildered murmur of negatives.

'I am glad that is understood.' She glared at them. 'You will know how far I assisted the late Emperor in his lifetime, taking all the care of the state on my own shoulders, learning good government from the ministers, unstinting with my time and effort. The peace of the realm is the result of my labour. When the late Emperor died he bequeathed his powers to me. I did not consider my own wishes, but continued to be your good guardian. As for most of you here today, you have received your rank and titles, your work and good fortune from me. And yet,' her voice became colder still, 'you will have noticed that all the authors of this recent treason have been high-ranking ministers or generals. Why should such as these, such as *you*, be so inimical to me? Pale Flame, a great statesman, who had been honoured to receive my husband's Will; General Li, the grandson of one of our best-loved heroes; that other general, so much respected for his taming of the Turks – all great men and so recognised. Why should they have shown me such hostility after my long service to the Empire? Can there be any acceptable reason for such ingratitude?'

She paused and let her gaze travel the hall, jade cool and unforgiving. Her voice was charged with contempt as she continued, 'However eminent and powerful these men have been, I have been able, as you have seen, to destroy them.'

Another pause, for their consideration of this fact.

'If any of you gentlemen feel that you might manage to fulfil their treasonable aims more successfully than they have done, I invite you to make the attempt. If not, then you will serve me with the respect which you owe me, and be saved from making yourselves the laughing-stock of the Empire.'

She had done with them. In the bruised hush that followed, they bowed their chastened heads as if before a blade.

This was as it should be. For let them make no mistake; from this day forward their heads would be of no more account to her than those of the flowers she was about to cut in her courtyard, where she would try for a blessed hour to forget the very existence of those rows of awed and sycophantic faces.

Suddenly her anger died. Its place was filled by pure exhilaration. Chinghiz was right. She was at one with her karma now. She was the sovereign in all but name and had declared herself as such.

She surveyed the bent, submissive heads once more and laughed aloud, a shocking, brilliant and unmistakably cheerful sound, as she left them dumbfounded and set out for the haven of her heart's tranquillity in Green Fragrance Court.

'It is time to begin,' she told Chinghiz one morning as he took advantage of Welcome's slight indisposition to brush Black Jade's hair.

'Yes. Very soon, you will take the throne you are promised.'

'Yes.' She put her head back, dreaming. His hands were so gentle. 'And one day, when I am very old, one of my sons will take it back.'

'But first, while you are still young enough to enjoy it, you will fulfil the destiny whose prediction set you apart from the hour of your birth. In whose light, and shadow, you have grown.'

The even, languid strokes of the brush could not keep thought at bay for long. She sat up straight, frowning.

'And when I take it, how will I hold it? We may have spread the T'ang princes over all eight directions, but who is to say they won't try again to raise rebellions in their prefectures? They will never accept me, never – a woman, and not even a Li! And even those tamed ministers think that to set a woman on the Dragon Throne is to fly in the face of nature!'

'History is against you, I admit. The throne, by its nature, is *yang*; the supreme power of woman is *yin*, and its unnatural ascendancy will destroy all harmony. Yet Heaven has chosen you, and presumably has the answer to this paradox.'

'It seems to me,' Jade said, for she had thought about it a great deal, 'that *my* best answer lies in doing what I must do very, very slowly – so gradually, in fact, that by the time the crown imperial is placed upon my head, no one will really notice that it has not been there for many seasons.'

'I agree. There must be no shock of novelty.'

'I need time,' she pursued, 'and I need help. More institutions like the North Gate, which I can rely upon absolutely.'

Chinghiz twisted the long strands of her hair into two fanciful wings and pinned them with bright enamelled butterflies to point the effect. 'What you must have,' he advised with a calculated nonchalance, 'is a reign of terror.'

Black Jade smiled. 'Is that what we want? Perhaps. An intelligence system that works quickly and efficiently, in which there are no rebels, no conspirators. A new system, employing new men. Not the scholar-official families and the members of the great clans, but *any* man who can prove his ability and enterprise, and whose *only* path to success depends on his loyalty to me. Certainly, such men will be less delicate in their handling of the situations they will find than the gentleman who does not like to disgrace another of his kind.'

At first they placed their 'new men' in the Censorate and the Board of Punishment, giving them positions of semi-importance that often had the desired effect of causing some elderly official to resign rather than work with anyone who was not a graduate. In many cases this was easily understandable; there was, for example, the hopeful ruffian who used to sell hot cakes in the southern market, who had come to Chinghiz with information about a junior minister who had not confessed his part in Pale Flame's conspiracy.

Black Jade decided to reward him by making him one of the new 'itinerant generals' whose business it was to comb the Empire for rebelliousness and stamp it out where found.

At the end of his interview he seemed loath to remove himself.

'A hundred thousand thanks, Beloved Majesty,' he said thickly, grovelling with enthusiasm before the dais where Black Jade sat, with Chinghiz, formidable in his black and scarlet, in his place behind her shoulder.

'But I wonder – ' the rascal pursued.

What more? 'Go on.' She wished to be rid of him. His smell had overpowered several incense burners.

'Precious Queen – it seems to me this job is much the same as that of a censor. Do you think you could see your way to making me one of those? I would then be such a mighty fellow that people would queue up to inform on each other!'

'A censor,' she told him firmly, 'must be a *chin shih* graduate.' She rattled a paper at him. 'It says here that you cannot read. Do please get up! And stand back a little.'

The fortunate cake-seller obeyed, grinning apologetically with a selection of blackened teeth, posted in his red maw like untended tombstones. He was a very large man indeed.

'Leopards can't read either, Majesty – but no one fears them any the less for that!'

Black Jade laughed, sensing a sympathetic tremor in Chinghiz.

'Oh, very well! Why not? You shall be a censor. After all, you needed no formal education to sniff out the rebel whose head you saw roll in your market square.'

The new official's gratitude resembled the moving of mountains. His thanks were liberally laced with spit.

'If I might ask one more favour, Exalted Excellence –'

'More? Perhaps you would care to become the Crown Prince?'

His rude laughter was horrible with teeth. 'Nothing like that, Mighty Empress. It's just that I'd like to offer you a box of my cakes, by way of appreciation. It's a small thing, I know – but they are very good cakes.'

The Empress, her lips trembling, was graciously pleased to accept.

When the unlettered censor had gone she fanned herself vigorously and demanded more incense. But the cakes were indeed, as she discovered when the sight of them proved too great a temptation, very good ones.

'Leopards,' she said to Chinghiz, licking her fingers. 'That reminds me of our own poor Leopard. If only he were still here; he would be in his element. All the same,' she added, 'we can't have too much of this sort of thing. There had better be a special examination for all those below the eighth grade who apply for posts – not too difficult – just enough to prevent our having to employ too many leopards!'

The most talked-about institution in Loyang was the Prosecutor's Office, the *Shujengtai.* It was moved to new quarters in the tower of the Gate of the Beautiful View. It was not long before some wag pointed out that the same written characters, pronounced differently, also meant the Gate of the Law's Conclusion. The latter title came to be more appropriate as time passed.

The credit for this was due to three of the 'new men' produced by the wider recruiting system. They were 'investigative judges' with exceptional powers of detection, trial and punishment. Judge Soh was an ex-informer who became an 'itinerant general' like the cake-seller, and soon established an unparalleled record for extracting confessions from his suspects. Judge Chou had been a grade three secretary in the office of the council, with a reputable background in law and a useful appreciation of ministerial requirements and tolerances. Working with Judge Lai, a disgraced official who had escaped a sentence for curruption by turning informer, he opened a training college for the network's recruits, where they soon learned to be as efficient as Judge Soh.

All three made it their secondary business to see that the Empress Dowager was not distressed by any discovery of the exact methods by which they managed to be so superbly productive of results. Her Exquisite Majesty was concerned that their work should, in the main, discourage any further notions of revolt; their private boast was that, by the time they had finished with him, a suspect would not even dare to breath the word 'conspiracy', nor indeed, in most cases, any other.

It was decided that it would be sensible to lessen the likelihood of further attempts on the throne by the removal of Loud Tiger from Loyang. Black Jade would be sorry to see him leave. They had got on quite well together after he had accepted the fact of his deposition.

'*I* don't really mind so very much,' he had admitted to her once. 'It is Heavenly Pearl who really feels the disgrace more strongly. She did make such a beautiful Empress. And she is so much better with people than I am – well, courtiers anyway. Such a charming manner!'

Black Jade had remembered something she had heard about a blind god of love – the Greeks, wasn't it?

Now she realised, as the family gathered to say farewell to him, that he was trying, rather unsuccessfully, to conceal his own eagerness to leave. He was going to a pleasant mountain town in Hopei province, where he would be well-guarded and would be able to lead the outdoor life he loved.

'I'm sorry you must go,' she said affectionately. 'But you will enjoy Fang Chou, and the air will be good for the children.'

'And free of conspiratorial whispering,' Loud Tiger suggested, as quietly as he could. 'Don't worry, I have no desire to be trapped into Young Tiger's tragic net. I'll be glad to go; I was beginning to look over my shoulder whenever I was inside the palace. Every time I meet one of my grand-uncles I shy off like a startled deer. I shall enjoy being myself again, in Hopei. As for Heavenly Pearl,' he said, watching his wife's bright, spitting-cat face as she and Tiger Lily engaged in a spiked conversation, 'she will get used to it, in time. She will soon make life over as she wants it to be.'

'Yes. Well, perhaps you will make sure she confines her attentions to her own "court" and does not meddle with ours?'

'Of course!' he belled, unembarrassed. 'And Mother – if you ever hear that *I* am plotting rebellion, remember this; that after all

I have seen and experienced in my short life, my only remaining interest is in a pleasant, uncomplicated survival!'

Black Jade chuckled. 'I'm not sure that remark is the height of courtesy, but I do know what you mean. And I'm sorry for it,' she added, brushing his sleeve with her hand. 'May the Gods guard you, Loud Tiger, until we meet again.

28

A few weeks after Loud Tiger's departure the resulting area of silence was filled with a visitor for Black Jade. Small, sparkling, voluble as a rookery and enduring as a hundred-year egg, Lady Hero had come down from her hills to see that all was well with her friend.

'You look pale,' she criticised, wagging a handful of jewellery.

'I'm tired, that's all. You are the best tonic I could have.'

'You work too hard. You should allow yourself more pleasure. Not that you look anything less than absurdly lovely – you never do. Look at me,' she sighed. 'Over seventy, and it's beginning to show that nearly every day of it has been spent out of doors. I have a hide like my old saddle and the complexion of a pickled walnut! I suppose I might even do something about it while I am here.' An innocent remark that was to lead in very unexpected directions.

One of Black Jade's ladies-in-waiting, the Princess Golden Fortune, a vivacious middle-aged matron with a penchant for mild misdemeanour, had, it seemed, discovered a source of astonishingly revivifying cosmetics. She would be only too glad to introduce Lady Hero to their purveyer.

'Who is it? Some monk, I suppose?' Hero wrinkled her brown nose. Monks had not figured largely in her satisfactory life.

'Far from it.' Golden Fortune blushed like a girl. 'Feng Hsiao-pao is as far from being a monk as I from the Hare in the Moon. He is – well, he is almost indescribable.' Her small round eyes lit up. 'Why don't you come and see for yourself, both of you? He performs in the market-place nearly everyday.'

'Performs?' said Black Jade.

'He is an exponent of the martial arts, a very distinguished one. He is worth seeing, I assure you. And he is also,' she added sighing, 'quite the most magnificent man it has ever been my pleasure to set eyes upon.'

Lady Hero grinned reminiscently. Her late husband had been a very well-made man. 'Then let us see him by all means!' She warmed to the idea. 'We'll go on a private expedition, in a plain palanquin, just the three of us, and watch the show. It will do you good,' she insisted as Black Jade looked dubious. 'I don't suppose you've seen an honest piece of male flesh for quite some time!'

'*Amitabha!* We shall be quite ridiculous! A party of elderly schoolgirls, escaping from our governesses!'

'Precisely,' said Hero firmly. 'Won't it be fun?'

In the end they went in two plain palanquins because Tiger Lily got wind of it and insisted on joining them. She travelled with Golden Fortune, and any citizen who was curious as to the latest palace gossip had only to run alongside them for five minutes to stop with his eyes bulging.

In the other conveyance, a serviceable dark blue sedan belonged to Welcome (who was most put out at being left behind), Black Jade confided to Hero her plans for an imperial future. To her surprise and relief, they were accepted as calmly as if they had been the butcher's bill.

'I have thought that you would be Empress, ever since that old prediction of Shih-min's that he made such a fuss about, going through the Wu clan with a fine tooth-comb! I wonder you didn't think of it yourselves – or perhaps you did?'

'No. I knew nothing of my own karma then.'

'And if my brother ever thought of it, he kept it to himself. I am glad for you, my dear. You will make a superb sovereign.'

'You don't care that the mandate will pass from the Li to the Wu?'

'Gods, no! An intelligent woman is better than a fool of a man, for my task; especially if it is one that matters. How will you do it? Nothing military, I suppose?' She sounded regretful. 'No. Something subtle and feminine.'

Black Jade smiled. 'I am already doing what is necessary. I am making myself daily, hourly, more indispensable.'

Hero understood. For a time they discussed the tactics of indispensability with the gravity of veteran commanders. Then Jade wanted to stop and buy plants in the Green Market, amazing the stall-keepers as she removed her veil and presented her well-known flawless features above her undistinguished rust cape.

Lost Dog Square was unusually crowded. Jade's bearers, also in plain clothes, had difficulty in thrusting their way to the front. In the end Hero stripped off a forgotten pair of earrings to bribe them a place to the side of the raised square stage, with its curtained booth behind, where the contests would take place.

Hero shivered. 'How odd to be without one's jewellery! I feel quite cold.'

'At least it won't be stolen. Dare we get out, do you think?'

'But of course! Why else are we dressed like peasants?'

They descended and the sedans were put behind the bannered booth.

'On my soul, their stink is as powerful as their noise!' Hero found.

Nonetheless, as Jade stepped into the sweating, scented, cheerfully screaming mass, she experienced a paradoxical sense of freedom. Standing between Hero and Tiger Lily, she was jostled and shoved from all sides as the spectators began to settle themselves down for the fight. Behind her, catching sight of her face inside the brown hood, a friendly individual with a single tooth and powerful, garlic-and-ginger breath, offered her a swig of his 'dragon-piss' liquor.

'Er – no, thank you,' she said nicely. 'I – I've taken a vow.'

The contest began. There were several bouts of stave-play, such as her half-brothers had enjoyed in Wen Shui. There was a very fat pair of oiled wrestlers from Japan who spent most of the bout trying to hug each other to death. There were some very young boys who fought in fours, skipping and hopping and tripping each other with their skinny long legs like fighting crickets. There were two very pretty boys, wearing a great deal of make-up, who emerged from their fight without a smear or a tear or anything much more than a smack on the face, wearing each other's kimonos. There were Indian wrestlers, who were dark brown and very quick. There were a pair of *kurung* from Malaya, with curly hair and jet-black bodies. And so on.

At last the ring was empty and there was an interval of pleasantly sensual music on drums and oboes.

'Whoever he is, he knows how to keep us waiting,' muttered Hero, who was becoming slightly cramped. They were, by now, sitting cross-legged in the dust like everyone else.

A man passed by, selling cushions. They were small and hard, but Tiger Lily bought some. She also bought some roasted nuts, some crystallised plums and a small flag with a phoenix on it.

'Heaven above! I hadn't thought. Feng! It's the character for a phoenix. How novel!' Golden Fortune was vastly amused. 'Imagine, Your Maj – my dear friend, sharing your symbolic life with a musclebound adventurer who has charmed the clothes off more women than you possess jade ornaments!'

'Oh, so he is no longer indescribable,' was Jade's dry comment.

Certainly he no longer remained so, for all at once the music ceased and the scarlet and cyclamen curtains at the back of the stage were flung back. A man strode to the centre of the ring; a giant of a man, in a vast purple cloak which swirled about him as he moved, arms raised to accept the almost hysterical welcome of the screaming, adulatory crowd. He returned to the centre and lowered his arms, waiting for the noise to subside.

Like any callow girl from the provinces, Black Jade stared. He was the biggest man she had ever seen, overwhelming in his immediate animal presence. The purple cloak must have been two yards long. Beneath it his skin was darkly golden, the muscles of his broad chest glistening with oil. He lifted a hand and a henchman removed the cloak. He was indeed magnificent – it was the only word. His body was perfectly proportioned and brought to the peak of its development; there was no hint of excess flesh, no bulkiness of extra muscle, nothing that was not necessary and beautiful.

'Great Heaven! What a great and glorious gift to these old eyes!' cried Hero simply, feasting them.

'Hush,' said Tiger Lily. She was concentrating.

Black Jade said nothing.

Feng was wearing a loincloth of clouded leopardskin and a barbarically large phoenix pendant which he removed and gave to the henchman. He flexed his arms and looked out over the crowd, smiling as they roared at him. His head was shaved and nobly shaped, its ovoid dome shining, deep gold like the rest. His face brought to mind the portrait Jade had once seen of one of the great Uighur warlords, high-boned, proud and superbly confident. It contained the possibilities, she thought, of both brutality and gentleness. An intriguing face, full-lipped, the eyes hooded above the wide cheekbones, a glint of gold in the well-shaped ears. His smile, dramatically arrogant as he swaggered for the crowd, was also warmly embracing in recognition of their worship, and contained an odd gratitude.

His opponent appeared, a very large, very dark-skinned Turk who was evidently also a favourite, though his welcome was less vociferous than Feng's. He carried more flesh, but probably not more weight. They were of an age, perhaps thirty-five.

It was a long flight and a satisfying one. There was, it seemed, a great deal of money resting on its outcome. Tiger Lily, an inveterate gambler, learned that the odds were slightly in Feng's favour and bet twelve taels of silver on him, which she unkindly despatched one of the bearers to fetch.

Jade had watched her brothers and the stableboys fight when she was a child, and had seen a number of polite bouts between guardsmen at the palace, but she had witnessed nothing like this. It excited and frightened her in roughly equal proportions. The two men moved according to their own mysterious rules – sometimes murderers, strangling or twisting near to breaking-point, sometimes dancers, speeding light-footed away from each other with only their eyes still interlocked. Their dialogue was like that of disputing lovers, she thought, tantalising, involved, ecstatic, intermittently independent.

It was over. Feng had won as they had known he must. The crowd went wild with delight. He was their darling, their own, their pride! The phoenix flags waved deliriously and a shower of flowers began to descend on the stage. Laughing, he caught some of them, holding an armful while his purple cloak was restored to him. He walked to the front of the ring, his skin glowing beneath the sweat, his smile as fresh as a child's. He began to throw the flowers back, choosing his targets with a careful eye – a pretty servant girl, a buxom housekeeper, a violet-eyed hostess from the tea-room. All were caught and kissed mistily, pressed to hearts and crushed in bosoms, until he had only one left.

He looked round again, taking his time, his head on one side, considering who might be worthy, perhaps even who might return the favour with an even greater one, later that night.

'Me! Me!' muttered Tiger Lily, too loudly for Jade's peace of mind.

'Remember who you are,' she ordered softly.

The scarlet flower landed in her lap.

Startled, she found that Feng had dropped to one knee and was staring in puzzlement into her face. The man beside him murmured something and his eyes widened. Then they became amused.

She picked up the bloom and nodded, smiling the pleasant court smile she kept for her ministers. The man was, after all, only a common entertainer, however proficient in his art.

'We must go,' she said suddenly, rising to her feet.

'What about the face-cream?' asked Tiger Lily. 'For Lady Hero.'

'What do you mean?'

'Had you forgotten?' carolled Golden Fortune. 'It is why we came. Feng Hsiao-pao is a man of many occupations. One of them is mixing those marvellous cosmetics I was talking about.'

'Not now,' said Jade hastily. They had already gone too far in their foolish adventure. 'You can send for him later, if you wish.'

When the Princess Tiger Lily sent for Feng Hsiao-pao, he found his route deflected to the palace of the Empress Dowager.

She received him in the small anteroom off her study, furnished with a few chosen treasures in marble and jade and the usual profusion of flowering plants. Saffron and aloeswood hung on the air. Chinghiz was unobtrusively preparing nine-dragon tea, sent from the famous tea-house in Canton.

The doors opened. Black Jade was again taken aback by the sheer physical presence of the man who entered. Feng was wearing the purple cloak, thrown back from his superlative shoulders over a kind of barbaric breastplate of interlaced gold thongs and thin, Arabian trousers in a deep indigo. His arms were bare except for a string of heavy gold bracelets, and the phoenix and pendant was on his breast. His expression, though perfectly respectful, bore traces of the faint amusement she had last seen in it.

He salaamed deeply in the Iranian fashion, a more graceful and sensual movement than the kowtow.

'You are welcome, Feng Hsiao-pao, even if you do not stoop to the three kneelings and thc three knockings.' Her tone was dry.

'It is not the custom among my people,' he said quietly. He looked straight into her face, reacquainting himself with the beauty that had stunned him in the moment of his triumph in the market-place. It had been that face, not his second's whispered words, which had made him believe she was the Empress.

She was sitting, half lying, propped on her elbow on one of the long chaises shc favoured. Her green dress was low-necked and her gauzy scarf had slipped from her shoulders. Her body was slender, perfectly balanced, completely at her command.

'What people are those?' she enquired in a voice like sherbet, cool and with a suggestion of sharpness.

'I am from Serindia, from Khotan.' It was one of the four oasis towns in north Tibet which had paid tribute to Shih-min but had since been lost in the border wars; a lovely and civilised place.

'Khotan,' she repeated, 'where the caravans rest on the Great Silk Road to Persia. Your tribute was in that exquisite white jade they say is made out of moonlight.'

'If Your Majesty wishes,' he said politely, 'it will be my pleasure to send for some of it.'

'You are most kind. And will you also offer moonlight jade to my daughter?' she enquired silkily.

He smiled. His teeth were white and even. It was a very attractive smile. 'The white jade is incomparable; therefore I should suggest it only in conjunction with your own unsurpassable beauty.' He had seen the Princess, also, in the market-place. She had looked at him without shame, as other women did. She was lovely enough, and, in his unerring judgement, would have the appetite in bed of a little cat in heat. He might well have been disposed to gratify it had he not, as he supposed he had, been prevented.

Now, faced with this extraordinary woman – complex, powerful and, he discovered, quite urgently desirable – his plans began to change.

She withstood his scrutiny, suddenly aware of what he was thinking. A spark of anger was born but died beneath an appraisal whose honesty also muffled her breathing, making it a little unsteady.

She realised that she, too, was staring.

She laughed, to cover her discomfort. 'You must forgive me. You are somewhat of an exotic. And then, it is satisfying to stare at someone occasionally, being so much subjected to it myself.'

'I am delighted to be stared at. But I hope there is some other way in which I might serve Your Majesty?' His voice was very deep, with a slight intriguing break in it. Always susceptible to the music of voices, its rough and smooth timbre struck an automatic response in her.

'I'm not sure. I believe my daughter wished to consult you upon a matter of cosmetics? It seems, forgive me, a strange art for one of your profession.'

'I have many professions. I have travelled a great deal, and have interested myself in all forms of entertainment. It was the pursuit of the drama, in many countries, that introduced me to the methods of caring for the skin. But I can have nothing to teach Your Highness in this respect.'

'Perhaps not,' she acknowledge. 'What else, then, do you offer us in Loyang?'

His derisive-sweet smile returned. 'At present, as perhaps you are aware, I am an impresario of the martial arts.' She was looking, he noticed, at her servant, an extremely grand and very good-looking man (not, surely, a eunuch?) who was pouring tea with an air of matchless disdain. 'You may leave us, Chinghiz,' she said when he had finished.

Chinghiz, resentfully reading this upstart giant's tiresome mind, was thoughtful enough of his mistress's safety to release into the room, as he left it, one of the larger and shorter-tempered of Mao-yu's house-trained grandchildren.

Feng held out a seducing hand at once. 'Your attendant does not trust me,' he smiled. The panther fawned on his hand.

'*She* evidently does,' said Jade sardonically, 'which rather ruins the effect which Chinghiz intended, I think, to convey. I believe that you will not expect to be received by my daughter,' she ambushed bracingly, 'and, since we are already enjoying our tea-party, you may as well amuse me for a while. Tell me about your other professions, Feng Hsiao-pao.' She did not, she realised, want him to leave,

'Oh, I have tried most things that a gentleman may do – and several that he may not. I am writing, in what spare moments I have, a treatise on architecture in your Empire and the lands in which I have travelled. It is my ambition, one day, to build something fine, something exceptional – a monument for my grandchildren. A temple, perhaps, or even a palace.'

She ignored the ambition, for the moment. 'And have you many of them?' she murmured kindly. 'Grandchildren, I mean.'

'I haven't the faintest notion,' he said charmingly. 'I have not,' he informed her, knowing it was what she wished to know, 'as yet chosen a wife or any regular consorts. My life-style is not conducive to domestic harmony.'

'Perhaps not. Tell me more about Khotan. Who are your family? Do you hail from a race of giants, or are you the exception?'

He laughed huskily, enjoying her teasing, though she had taken care to keep laughter severely out of her voice. 'Always an exception,' he agreed, 'though not in that respect. My father was two yards high, and so are six brothers. He was a Khan, one of the ruling family in Khotan. We had an excellent education, a great deal more liberal than your Confucian strait-jackets, and our home, though not nearly so extensive as your palace, was a house of great cultivation, filled with fine music and beautiful objects.'

'And your mother?' asked Jade, her curiosity further piqued.

He smiled, his strong fingers deep in the fur at the back of the panther's neck. The animal rubbed her polished black face against his knee, her yellow eyes hazed with adoration. 'My lady mother was well-born and a Buddhist nun. She was serving in the temple when my father found her.' The smile became a grin again. 'He was taking part in a friendly border raid at the time. I believe it was love at first sight – ' He stopped and looked deliberately into her eyes. 'Do you believe in such strong emotions, Exquisite Empress?'

'I have no reason to disbelieve, since I have read of them so frequently,' she said, disturbed by that candid gaze which was asking other questions than the one he had spoken. She continued quickly, denying herself any interest in those questions or in his demanding eyes, in the strength of his beautiful body, in the evident attractions of his curious, travelled mind. 'What took you away from such a paradise? Another border raid?'

He shook his head. 'I was simply born restless.'

'I can see that. You stand on one spot, but nothing about you is still. Roam the room, if you must. Or perhaps you would prefer to walk with me in the courtyard?' She knew she should let him go, now, before she began to listen to her assaulted senses, to admit his effect on her whether she willed it or not.

'The courtyard,' he mused, as though it needed thought. 'If that is where you truly wish to go.' The panther purred shamelessly.

She dared not ask him what he meant. She thought, suddenly, that she was not going to be able to rise to her feet; her limbs simply would not obey her. She gazed at him, admissions pouring in from all sides till she was swamped in her guilty desire.

'You have, after all,' he murmured, with that blinding invitation of a smile, 'a peculiarly rich choice.'

Yes, Yes, by the Gods, I have, she thought then. The freedom of it exploded slowly within her head, making her light and exhilarated as though she had drunk a far headier potion than dragon-leaf tea. I am the Empress! Her madness progressed, sweeping through her in a wildfire of irresponsible happiness. I have so much power – surely I have the power to take what I want, what I *need*, from this man? But how, she wondered next, am I to manage it?

'Is something amusing Your Majesty?' Feng had moved a little closer to her couch. He surveyed her quizzically with folded arms.

'Yes, it is.'

'Will you share the joke with me?' His eyes were waiting.

'I believe I will,' she murmured. 'I am pondering a new and interesting problem of imperial protocol.'

He shook his head regretfully, his face as innocent as that of a scrubbed boy. 'Then I'm afraid I am useless to you. Protocol, of any kind, was never one of my interests.'

She saw that he understood, perfectly, her dilemma. He was

playing with her, just as his hand was idly tempting the velveted claws of the cat. Very well! She would give his monstrous arrogance no further help. If he wished to find himself in her bed – and Kuan Yin aid her, she hoped he did – he must find his own way to it!

He was stroking his chin in an imitation of sagelike wisdom. 'I believe I *might* have some intimation of your problem,' he said gravely. 'I knew a duchess, once, who perhaps shared it.' He captured her gaze again and his voice fell to a pleasurable growl. 'It was her romantic fate to fall in love with her steward. She saw that he returned her affection but could not bring herself to speak of it, though she knew that he must not do so.' He hesitated.

'And how did they solve the problem?'

'Protocol did permit him to challenge her to a game of chess – in which the prize should be the wish of the winner's heart, written in verse and handed to the loser.'

'Who won?' asked Black Jade directly.

His lazy-lidded look was openly amused. 'Ah – I wonder which you would prefer? The lady – to satisfy your own competitive spirit? Or the gentleman, because, despite that spirit, that is how you feel matters should be between a man and a woman?'

Caressed by his eyes, she said, 'If I had won, I should have been truly magnanimous. I should have written: "The dearest wish of my heart is that your own should come to pass." '

His deep laughter rewarded her logic.

'An excellent solution! They have neither spoken any unseemly words nor broken the sacred bounds of protocol.'

'But they understood each other.' She looked up at him beneath lowered lashes, a girl's trick she had almost forgotten.

'They understood each other very well,' he agreed. His own eyes were no longer innocent or full of laughter, but contained an intentness of purpose which told her frankly of his desire, and of his knowledge of hers, and his intention to satisfy them both as soon as might be.

'We may dispense, then,' Jade said demurely, 'with the chess game?'

He threw back his head exultantly. Then he held out his hand. She stood up, not steadily, and went to him.

He caught her by the shoulders and held her away from him so that he could look his fill at her face in this moment of his triumph. The signs of her hunger were there, in the parted lips, in the green eyes slumbrous with the thought behind them, in the rise and fall of her breasts, in the slight trembling of her whole frame that she was trying to control.

He swung her up into his arms so that he could kiss her, sinking his mouth on hers with a firm possessiveness. She moved her lips against his, exploring their shape, matching their persuasion; and then with a suddenness that sent its unequivocal message straight to the roots of his manhood, her mouth was open and softening under his, her sweet saliva welcoming his thrusting tongue, her hands caressing his head in swift, feverish little sweeps, her whole body became limp and heavy with wanting him. He raised his head. Her glorious eyes blazed at him, promising the mating of two white tigers – something legendary in the lists of love. He saw the willingness in her and was able to wonder at it for perhaps one full second – and then he too was carried away on a tide as pure and forceful as the dragons of the wind. They kissed like desperate lovers who might be torn apart at any moment, rather than experienced amorists who had just met. Something of their childhood sang in both of them as they looked seriously into each other's transfigured faces – the boy who had built his palaces in the desert sands, and the girl who had dreamed of freedom in Wen Shui.

When he carried her into the bedchamber they were quiet for a time. He undressed her as unobtrusively as Welcome might have done, then sat beside her while his eyes paid homage to her naked beauty. Now that he saw her it was as though he looked upon something already familiar to him, familiar and unbearably precious. The thought came to him then, before they had even set out on their road together, that if he were ever to lose her he would also lose his mind. It frightened him, he who had taken every woman he wanted since he was a boy of fourteen, to be so humbled, so spellbound by this one woman's body. It was not (the unregarded critic in his brain told him) even a perfect body, though it must have been so until a very few years ago. And if the amber flesh was a little softer, the delicate bones a little more pronounced than they had been, there was still a sweetness of line and perfection of balance that spoke as closely to his heart as to the clamouring in his blood. It was an experience he had never encountered, to feel so much a part of a woman before his flesh had even entered hers. He was softened by it, and strangely renewed. He did not touch her for a while, only gazed at her as she lay against the pillows watching him with those enormous, jade-lit eyes.

At last he touched one finger to her thigh, a promise of his swift return, then rose to remove his clothes. A small sigh escaped her when he stood before her in his magnificence of line and muscle.

She smiled at herself. She was undoubtedly the single most powerful woman in the world – and yet the sight of this splendid male animal could bring her to the same state as any lustful peasant girl who let her lover mount her in the hot field with the dust for a bed. Well, so much the better! Heaven knew she had starved long enough. She held out her arms and he came to her.

'Tell me,' she whispered as he stretched his length beside her and began to cover her umber flesh with his own darker glow, 'was there really ever a duchess, and an intrepid steward?'

'There must have been,' he smiled, his lips tracing her breast, 'many, many times since Heaven and earth were separated.

But never before a man such as this. She ran her delighted hands along the bronze undulations of skin and muscle, lost in lust and aesthetic pleasure. She wanted him to come into her, her body cried out for it, but she also wanted to continue in the simple exploration of his physical perfection. It was as though she were invited to open herself to a creature out of mythology, or to the smooth convolutions of one of the great images of the Buddha in her cave cathedral at Longmen. The Weaver Maid herself must have sent him to her, in the compassion learned from her own long months without love.

A sudden sweet and fiery pain in her breast restored her fully to the moment. Feng had begun to travel her body with as thorough an appreciation and curiosity as he had shown her Empire. He made it clear that he did not now wish her to participate; she was to lie still and allow him to explore her.

He stretched her arms above her head and let his lips amble down one of them, nuzzling into her armpit, catching the faint, sweet scent of her sweat mixed with Meng Shen's perfume. He moved upward to her ear, his tongue flickering like a sensitive serpent's while his fingers teased her nipples into coral. She moaned a little and moved beneath him, her arms encircling him instinctively, her thighs open. At once he moved away from her, leaving her throbbing and bereft, then knelt and turned her over. With exquisite slowness his mouth moved down her backbone, lingering mischievously like a boy who knows he is wanted at home, until he reached its base. He still did not permit her to move but undertook the longer odyssey of both her extended legs, with particular and agonising attention to the soles of her feet and the back of every single toe. A light kiss upon the dreadfully aroused flesh of her thigh; then nothing.

Black Jade lay obediently motionless and waiting. Still there was nothing. She could scarcely even hear him breathing. She raised her head and looked at him over her shoulder. He was sitting peaceful, with his arms around his knees, contemplating the country he had travelled with the satisfaction of one who is just about to commit the view to brush and ink.

'What now, then?' she demanded acidly. 'Do you put on your clothes and go home, on the understanding that if I want any more I may apply in the market-place?'

Feng roared with laughter and she found herself the right way up and pinned beneath him, receiving a mouthful of kisses and roars.

'Does it annoy you so much, my tigress, that I don't perform by the book?'

'Not at all. I've never known a man who did.'

'And you have known how many men?'

'That is an insolent question,' she informed the laughter that shook him still.

He rolled to one side and leaned on an elbow, lazily stroking her hip and flank. The colour of his skin was like the burnt sugar into which the children had liked her to dip peeled cumquats.

'It is relevant,' he said gently, 'if only to your present appetite. I intend no insult – how could I? You are the summit of all I could ever hope to enjoy. But it would be a pity, wouldn't it, to spoil our first pleasure together with too much haste?'

He was right. She had gone hungry too long and now the feast had made her greedy.

He began then to court her seriously, still taking his time and letting her take hers too, so that when at last she received him it was the perfect moment – a new beginning and a long way to go.

Though he was very careful with her, she was awed and a little afraid at the revelation of his strength. He kept his weight from her with expert consideration, but even the sight and the sensation of one long, large, liquid amber thigh covering hers was enough to cause an odd flutter of archaic fear in her. This was a man who could kill her with one hand. It was a foolish thought and she put it away from her. At that moment he looked into her face and entered her, and there was no further possibility of any thought at all.

At first he was tender, his lips in the dark jungle of her hair, his hands clasping her to him, his rhythm restrained and seeking. Then, when she began to cry out and move beneath him, he rose on his arms and threw back his head, his eyes half-closed, golden and dreaming in his warlord's face, a temple mystic who has achieved communication with his God. He circled in her like a man who approaches the truth with sureness, taking her with him so that she lost all sense of herself. She no longer knew his body from her own and no longer wished to. She was cloud and he the rain and each was necessary to the other.

When she descended from the heights she found it hard to believe that she had been carried to that bright and distant peak by this man of whom she knew nothing, except that he was the essence of all that was wonderfully animal and that he could make her laugh.

When she looked at him, out of eyes that made him think of grass under showers, she saw that, for him, it had been nothing new. A marvel, yes; but one he had known he could accomplish. For herself, she realised that there was still much to learn, that the conjunction of each new man and woman offers a new infinity of possibilities. The knowledge gave her back her youth with both hands.

Like Shih-min, Feng was a man who exulted in the power of his sensuality, but he was also, like Shing-jen, a priest of the senses, who knew how to find the Way in the joining of *yin* and *yang* in flesh. Black Jade was more than content for him to be her teacher.

29

'You can have no idea of what you are doing!' Chinghiz did not attempt to disguise his disapproval. 'You have never, in your entire life, had anything to do with a man of this type.' He tugged ferociously at the hem of her dress, as though he would like to nail it to the floor and so insure her good behaviour.

Her annoyance fought with some small embarrassment. 'Emperors, generals, clergymen,' she listed. 'All of them, except Shing-jen, men whose conduct was circumscribed by their position in society. Can't you see that to know a man like Feng is a revelation to me? He has no preconceived notions about the world, is bound by no onerous duty. But he is as much a gentleman as you are yourself,' she added spikily, 'and it will *not* please me should you choose to forget it in his company.'

'Your every wish is, of course, my command,' Chinghiz replied with the lifeless courtesy of an automaton. He began, having done with her dress, to punish her hair.

'He is well-born,' she continued in a grumbling tone, 'and you know that Khotan is celebrated for its articulate citizens as much as for the quality of its gemstones.'

'His mind may be of coral and his manners as smooth as polished lapis lazuli; he may play the lute like a God, and speak with the tongue of the Yellow Emperor – he is nevertheless a market-place adventurer who makes a living by showing off his physical prowess and making fools of silly women!'

'Chinghiz!' He stopped brushing, warned by the tension in her shoulders. 'We have never really quarrelled. It would be a pity if we were to do so now.' Her tone was frosted with mica.

He sighed. 'Tell me, then. I am willing to learn. What charms does the Serindian hold for you, apart from those which are obvious?'

'Gods! Why must you be so miserable? I would have thought you would be glad to see me happy!'

'Yes. So would I. Odd, isn't it?' The mobile lips twisted queerly, as though he were in pain. 'There. You are dressed. Go and meet your lover, if that is what you have planned to do.'

'You know very well I am going to discuss the re-allotment of the grain stores with the council.'

He bowed. 'And after?' He needed to know where she might be at any specified time.

She laughed. 'We are going to play polo, or *Ta ch'in* as Feng calls it. It will be a suitable opportunity for his informal introduction to the palace. I have arranged a match between the most athletic of my ladies and the gentlemen of the court. Feng will lead their team. He is, of course, a considerable champion, since the game originated in his part of the world. Why don't you come and watch? Or will you join the courtiers' team?'

Chinghiz discovered a plethora of necessary tasks.

Black Jade had already offended the rigid Confucianism of her elderly ministers by her tendency to organise events in which all ages and sexes mingled freely, the only qualification being their enthusiasm. In bringing into the palace a man last seen on the wrestler's stage, she was offering them a hard pill to swallow. As it became obvious that the new, outsize presence amongst them was a permanent fixture, the criticism became irritatingly common.

Black Jade decided to tackle the problem head on. 'Before my government decides that you are the epitome of all evil,' she told her lover, 'I intend to give you a status that will confound criticism.'

'Compassionate Heaven! You'll not make a knock-kneed *minister* out of me?' Feng spoke as though naming a loathed insect.

'No.' She sighed, anticipating his next reaction. 'I want you to take Buddhist orders. I have decided to make you the Abbot of the White Horse Monastery.'

He groaned, but she saw that his interest was engaged. The White Horse was the oldest and most revered monastic foundation in the Empire. It had been endowed by the early pilgrims who had travelled into India and brought back the first Buddhist texts to the Middle Kingdom.

'The temple and cloisters are very beautiful, but they are old and need some attention,' Jade tempted. 'That, at least, is easily within the competence. Think,' she added virtuously, 'how pleased your mother would be.'

'I think not,' he said. 'She would be fearful, as I am, that I would be temperamentally incapable of fulfilling my responsibilities to the order.'

'Perhaps,' Jade suggested hopefully, 'the spirit of the place will improve your nature.'

'I doubt it. And I give you warning – if you are disappointed, later, do not altogether blame me.'

'You underrate yourself, I am sure. You will make a splendid Abbot. You will need a new name for your ordination. What shall it be?'

He reached for her and began to open the buttons she had fastened in honour of the church. 'You must choose; I am your creation.'

She thought for a while, then laughed. 'How about Huai-i – Embracing Righteousness? It seems eminently suitable to your present change of status, in both senses.'

'Don't underestimate your subjects' sense of irony,' he warned.

'I don't. It will amuse them. Where are we going?' He had risen effortlessly with her half-naked body in his arms, but was not taking the direction of the bedchamber.

'For a swim,' he grinned, carrying her to the door leading to the open pool where the Emperor Yang-ti had sported with his concubines. 'I want to make love to you in the water. Since I am to be such a thoroughly reformed individual, I may as well begin the process of purification right away!'

Eventually Feng became reconciled to his approaching holiness. The monastery was a very rich foundation and its monks were widely famous scholars. If it was not precisely lively in its present ambiance, he would be able to alter that when he began to enrol his own new novices. He began to take an enthusiastic interest in its future.

Others expressed doubts.

'If my mistress has temporarily taken leave of her senses,' was Chinghiz's abrasive comment, 'it is surely not necessary to proclaim the fact to the ends of the Empire?'

Hero, who had remained at court as a fascinated observer of her friend's romance, chuckled, and jangled in sympathetic amusement. 'Dearest girl – no one who has met Master Feng, or even heard of him, would ever believe that he has been so suddenly illumined with the light of Gautama; but then, happily, so few of your subjects are aware of his delightful existence that it won't matter a jot!'

Welcome said doubtfully, 'He will look very well in the Abbot's robes, Little Phoenix – but won't he want to keep taking them off?'

The rest of that conversation was ribald. Welcome approved wholeheartedly of Feng, who tickled her and called her a wicked old woman, and who had made her beloved charge happier than she had been for many years – for which she would forgive him much. She was also greatly diverted by Chinghiz's obvious jealousy of the man and was not above teasing him about it, which earned her some very nasty moments and a forced abstinence from plum brandy.

When Feng moved into the White Horse Monastery, to the horror of half the clergy and the delight of the citizens (who foresaw some entertainment from it), he was already accustomed to being pointed out and accosted as one of the physical wonders of the capital, together with its more fabulous works of architecture. Now he was to become Loyang's most beloved and scandalous legend.

One morning, Black Jade determined to visit the monastery herself, to see how her lover was settling into his new home and eminence. As she often did, she went, in her red and black palanquin, by way of the Green Market, eager to add to her gardens. Hero was with her and they were escorted by a detachment of her guard.

The plant market was part of the teeming, clamorous complex of the western market, whose sprawling, vulgar riot held far more appeal for both women than its genteel eastern counterpart near the Palace City. It was colourful, exciting and slightly dangerous, being the centre for all foreign merchandise, for the sellers of silk and the dealers in drugs. It was always voluble with argument and often sparked with steel when some barbarian thought himself cheated. It was the precise social opposite of the court and Black Jade loved it for that.

The only unfortunate thing about the market was that, to reach it, one must first pass through the square where malefactors were publicly punished. It might contain anything from a few half-starved wretches bent under the weight of the cangue and the shame of the unkind messages nailed above them, to a dangling corpse covered in flies and surrounded by its weeping descendants. Today, unhappily, there was something rather special.

It was the noise that made them aware of it above the general hubbub, a high-pitched, ululating sound, constant, agonised and without hope.

'An animal must have escaped, half-slaughtered, from the butchers' bazaar,' was Hero's opinion. 'It is quite remarkably hideous! Like the sounds one imagines to inhabit the Tongue-cutting Hell!' She raised her voice. 'Bearer! What *is* that appalling sound?'

One of the guards moved close and addressed the curtains.

'It's some poor devil in torment; don't look out, Majesty, Highness.'

'I suppose I shouldn't,' Hero said, 'But it is so *extreme*. I'm sorry, Jade my child, I absolutely *have* to know what it is!'

She extended a sunburnt hand and the curtain jingled aside.

'Oh, sweet Heaven!' The erstwhile conqueror of the city reeled back, white and sick, her bracelets quivering in shocked sympathy.

'What is it?'

'Don't look! It's disgusting! Only a fiend could do such a thing to a human being. It is past bearing!'

Black Jade was already leaning out. 'They are executing *my* justice,' she said firmly, seeking whatever terrible thing it was. 'Oh, merciful Kuan Yin! This can't be possible! Bearers! Stop at once!' There had not been far to look. She would never forget what she saw.

On the raised stone platform reserved for the most evil of criminals a stone *kang* had been built, its hot coals smoking in the sunlight. On top of its compact cubic structure at about chest height, was an iron plate, also, naturally, very hot. On top of this was placed the upper half of a man.

Neatly sliced in two at the waist, his black blood still sizzling like hot oil on the plate, his arms moving in a pantomime of unspeakable agony, his eyes stretched wide, their sense gone, his mouth open and making that terrible sound, he still, horribly and most blasphemously, lived.

For just a few seconds Black Jade allowed herself to give in to the nausea in her belly. Then she shook her head as Hero tried to prevent her and stepped down from her vehicle, pushing back the veil that swathed her wide-brimmed hat.

There was a wash of noise as the Empress Dowager was recognised, and then an uneasy silence except for the one uncanny sound which every one of the thousand people within earshot wished they might deny.

Her white face quite without expression, Black Jade gave the order to the captain of her guard. 'Kill him. Cleanly.'

She did not look as the inhuman misery ended. Suddenly the dreadful noise had ceased, and the shamed silence with it.

She turned to face the executioner, a shambling figure in funereal white, his features obscured by a scarlet mask, rising from the kowtow.

'Who gave the order for this abomination?'

The big man hung his head. 'It was Judge Lai, Gracious Majesty.'

For a second her eyes widened in shock. 'Thank you. If you receive further orders of a similar nature, you are to consider them countermanded by myself; or you will suffer the same fate. Is that understood?'

'It is, Your Compassionate Majesty.'

The crowd moved back out of her way as she returned to the haven of the palanquin, too subdued to make much of her as they usually did.

Without further speech, she and Hero were carried, sombrely, to the Green Market.

'Would you prefer to go home – or straight to the monastery?' asked Hero at last, breaking their appalled silence.

'No. I need the beauty and sanity of green things just now. Hero, how can such things be done, in my name, and I know nothing of them?' But she knew the answer herself; she had given too much power to the leopards among her servitors. She had thought that she needed them, and perhaps she did. But if a man must be despatched for his crimes, she would see to it that he was at least despatched decently, in the time-honoured ways, not made a plaything for the cruelty of madmen. Judge Lai. She must meet him. She shivered.

In the relative peace of the Green Market she rested her outraged eyes on the healing miracle of growing and flourishing herbage; the deep green of trees that still concealed the mystery of their northern forests among their dark branches; the brighter gloss of the sacred fig beneath which Buddha sat, entranced; the pale, milky shoots of some papyrus stranger from the banks of the Nile, fighting for their life in the colder climate of Loyang. And everywhere the sight and scent of flowers, their colours, natural and unnatural, making the head swim and the heart sigh. Suddenly, their ears were savaged with strange sounds for the second time that morning.

This time it was a comfortingly ordinary, if extremely loud, hullaballoo, such as is made by a great many very young men up to their private entertainment. There was roaring and singing and the whooping encouragement of horses. There was also the sound of indignant shouting, uncontrollable laughter and an awful lot of expensive-sounding breakages. The ironmongers' bazaar and the china stalls seemed to have entered into unhappy conjunction.

Even as the head gardener rose to his feet in perturbation, a small local tornado swept down upon his hapless tables and trays, pots and pergolas and a whole paradise of vegetable life was sacrificed to the running feet of a group of terrified Taoist monks, their habits clutched about their vitals as they tried to escape the mounted pursuit of an enthusiastic gang of hooligans in saffron robes, who were almost helpless with unkind laughter as they took swipes at the undefended topknots of their quarry with long, curved scimitars and screams of blood-curdling intent. Each one was large, athletic and bald as a brass button. They too were monks, and it was dreadfully obvious to Black Jade – as she stared, her eyes on stalks, at their uproarious leader, who demonstrated a stunningly superior skill by riding circles round his chosen victim till he had him petrified, and then lopping off the signature of his order in a single precise and horribly close stroke – to which of her capital's myriad monasteries they belonged.

She sat as though hypnotised, her teacup halfway to her lips, as Feng rode riotously roughshod over everything in his path, his purple cloak flying and the startled populace darting from under the hooves of his great white stallion. He was singing a Buddhist hymn, interspersed with gulping carols of laughter, and his excited novices galloped after him, thrilled with this unexpected religious experience they were having. Feng did not, of course, notice Black Jade. Practically no one did. It was understandable.

The unfortunate Taoists, their black gowns draggled and torn, were herded along a path marked by alarm and accident into the end of the punishment square nearest the devastated plant market. Unable to help herself, Jade followed, with Hero in her wake.

The horsemen had stopped hounding and circling and were drawn up nicely, facing the woebegone captives, who were now queuing up to have their heads forcibly shaved. Jade heard Feng, in the pleasant, purring growl that so aroused her senses, offer them the choice, as a civilised man and an Abbot, of losing either their hair or their heads. They all chose the former.

'What are you going to do?' asked Hero, in a very low tone, for her. She was, quite simply, overwhelmed by the moment.

Jade dug her nails into her palms to stop a cowardly desire to sit down on a broken stall and burst into unimperial tears.

'I don't know,' she said, shaking her head over and over. 'I just don't know. He's like some elemental demon; how does one begin to control a creature like that?'

Lady Hero, for once, could offer no advice.

Chinghiz was furious. He stalked her chamber, not much less of an elemental than the disgraceful man who was the subject of his peroration. He had never shown her so much anger.

'You *cannot* consider continuing with this relationship! You must have learned, after today's escapade, that you are in thrall to a mischievous child. Let him go, I beg you, before he drags your dignity in the dust with that of his ancestors.'

She said nothing.

'Look at me, at least,' he entreated.

'If I'd wanted a lecture, I'd have sent for the senior librarian,' she said pettishly.

He eyed her coldly. 'When does he visit you next?'

'That is none of your business.' Her cheeks flamed.

'It is the business of every sensible man in the Empire when the Empress acts like a madwoman,' he said crudely.

'You are insolent. Please go away. I wish to be alone.'

'When is he coming here?' Chinghiz insisted.

'Tonight! At the hour of the Pig. Now are you satisfied? And I'll thank you to be absent when Master Feng arrives.'

'I will be absent, if you promise to give him *his* leave permanently.'

She looked at him with dislike, feeling cornered and foolish, knowing him to be right according to the dictates of common sense.

'I will speak to him about today's – activities. Now, *will* you go! I'm sick of the sight of your disapproving face!'

'I shall be delighted to take it elsewhere,' he said stiffly, flint-eyed and superb. 'I had intended to spend the evening smoothing down ruffled feathers in the monastery, and among the elders of the churches. And then there is Judge Lai to be placated.'

'Judge Lai?' Her mind reverted with a shock. 'Why ever do you say so?'

'Because,' he continued implacably, 'although you may not care for some of his methods, he is quite the most formidably efficient legalist we have had in our dynasty. The man you so much pitied was one of the leaders of the Fang Chou rebellion. He had been hiding out in the hills. He had killed a number of men in several different ways, each more cruel than its predecessor. I'll describe them if you wish – and you may expend more of your pity.'

'I do not wish my reign to be known for the inhumanity of its way with criminals,' she said coldly.

'Reign?' His brows flew up in derision. 'If you continue as you are doing at present, there will be no danger at all of your ever coming to reign!' Having enjoyed this parting shot, he departed on his errands of diplomacy.

When Feng arrived, somewhat late, exuding brandy and bonhomie, he was surprised to find his mistress in a very ill mood. No one had told him that she had been a witness of his afternoon's amusement. He did not, however, seem especially concerned when he found out.

'Oh, that,' he said lazily, relaxing beside her on the day-bed she had not invited him to share. He took up the ends of her hair.

'We were just teaching those insolent Taoists a lesson. They are altogether above themselves since the late Emperor decided they were part of his clan.' He began to pull her towards him, not hard, by the shining rope. She resisted.

'What's the matter? Surely a small thing like that doesn't annoy you? Where's your sense of humour? You should have seen them –' he chuckled – 'scared to death, almost pissing themselves with fear!'

'I did see them. I thought your behaviour was unforgivable, and so utterly childish. I was ashamed. To think that I had made you the Abbot of that great house – to have you destroy its good name in one petty episode of foolhardy swaggering –'

'– Hold hard! I don't like the sound of this. It's uncommonly like the tongue-baiting of my old schoolmasters. Not a pretty thing in a woman, whoever she may be!' He seized her hair again and pulled her closer until she was lying across his lap, held still by the tension of the hank wound about his arm. He pulled it a little, grinning cheerfully into her upturned, furious face.

'I think you must be punished for that. Not only Judge Lai knows how to inflict delicate torture.'

'There are guards outside,' she said, aware that his hand was introducing itself to thc traitorous flesh beneath her light robe.

'Call them,' he said, untying all her ribbons in swift succession. 'I suppose they are accustomed to find you nearly naked?' he added suavely, pulling her captive hair so that she was forced to turn over in his lap. 'Now then, my exquisite vermilion bird – either you agree to come into the bedroom with me right away, or I shall remove your delicious silk trousers and call the guard myself. Which is it to be?'

'Great Heaven, Chinghiz was right – you *are* a monstrous child,' she said, half in wonder, half disgust – and self-disgust at that, as her glowing body offered the child its woman's responses.

'He does not like me, your Chinghiz. But it doesn't matter. He's a good watchdog. Have you made up your mind? Ah yes –' his hands assured themselves, relaxing their hold on her hair at last. 'It seems that you have. We must not quarrel,' he murmured, pulling her close. 'The world outside our bed and our conversation has no real meaning for us. If it pleases you, my glistening jewel in the lotus, I will become more temperate in my behaviour – though not, as you are about to discover, in my punishment. It will be very long and very delicate. And you will cry out for it to finish!'

He was able, in the hours that followed and the night that came after, to keep his word most thoroughly.

In the morning, Black Jade found it very difficult indeed to put up with Chinghiz's expression of superior distaste.

She would keep her lover, because she must. He was the return of all her youth; he made her spirit sing. She *could* not give him up. Neither, however, would she lend herself to his excesses. She must not be seen to condone his eccentric behaviour.

She made this clear, both to her ministers and to Feng himself, on the day that he displayed his uncontrollable arrogance to the Vice-Presidents of the Chancellery who happened to be in his path. Having brushed the offended minister aside like a peasant, he was astonished when the vice-president ordered the guards to secure him and slap his face. Bristling at the insult, all his humour gone, he strode on to the council chamber to complain to Jade of his treatment.

He could not know that she welcomed the opportunity. She saw his temper as soon as he entered the room, ignoring the protests of the guards, who trailed after him, shamefaced.

Black Jade, seated on the Phoenix Throne she favoured, was discussing the erection, mooted by a keen junior official, of a kind of public letter-box for the receipt of information, practical suggestions, and guarded criticism of the government. It would, the young man thought, encourage the people to feel themselves important to their Emperor, and to keep a firm eye upon their neighbour's business – always a useful trait.

'Why not? It has been done before,' Black Jade continued, her smooth discursive tone unaltered, her imperious eye stopping the oncoming giant in his tracks. 'Let us make the box a thing of beauty – in bronze; an urn or a large vase. It shall have mouths open to four directions, marked according to their uses. Have a model made up and bring it to me. Excuse me, Honourable Ministers. It appears that Master Feng has something of importance to relate. Well, sir? We are not accustomed to be interrupted.'

Feng bowed quickly. His anger had evaporated, but only a little. He was surprised at her cold, impersonal tone, echoing an equally detached and disinterested gaze.

'My apologies for the inconvenience. But perhaps I might provide an opportunity for Your Grace to remind her "honourable ministers" of the respect due to the Abbot of our leading monastery. The Vice-President of the Chancellery has just offered me an unforgivable insult. First, he made no effort to stand out of my path when he saw that I was in a hurry; then, when I brushed past him, he caused my face to be slapped. I demand redress.'

She could feel, rather than see, the curl of amused satisfaction that writhed inside the shut, serious mouths of the ministers. The vice-president was not the only one to have suffered the arrogance of the Abbot.

She let a long pause go by, keeping her unblinking gaze, cool and remote, on the restless figure in the purple cloak.

Then she said quietly, her low, beautiful voice carrying to every part of the room, 'It seems to me, Abbot Huai-i, that it would be more convenient for you if, in future, you were to enter and leave the palace by the north gate, rather than using the same path as my most respected ministers. Then there will be no possibility of such an unfortunate event being repeated.'

She nodded a clear, curt dismissal.

Feng, sensing the ministers' elation, knew that he had badly misjudged his time. Worse, he had misjudged Black Jade. The woman who had just turned away from him as if he were of no more consequence than the servant who was showing him to the door was not the willing mistress with whom he shared the deep enchantment of the senses; she was the Empress Dowager, and she was letting him know it.

After this, he began to use the north gate. Nor did he complain to her again, in public of his treatment at court.

The ministers, on the other hand, heartened by Black Jade's discretion in the matter of her lover, did complain, with increasing confidence and frequency, about the antisocial activities of the gigantic Abbot and his flying cavalry of raucous novices. At last Feng, irritated by the flights of stinging petitions buzzing in a constant cloud about Jade's desk, cooled the ministers' ardour by having one of them beaten half to death for his over-enthusiastic criticism. The complaints did not stop, but it was obvious, in spite of them, that the ministers were prepared to accept the existence and status of Feng as a mildly unpleasant corollary of the good government dispensed by Black Jade. This being so, she could begin to accelerate the process by which that government would become hers under Heaven.

'I have been distressed, lately, to hear a great deal that is unsavoury about the Gate of the Beautiful View.' Black Jade addressed Bold Fortune, who had struck up a close friendship with Judge Lai, the prosecutor whose reputation was growing daily more sinister. Since the great bronze urn had been set up in the public audience hall near the gates of the Palace City, the strong arm of the law had been seriously strained by overwork.

'There is a balance here, as in all things,' Bold Fortune assured her. 'Though I have to admit that my friend Lai has become known as "Deathshead" among the criminal fraternity, the court is equally well-served by Judge Hsu, who came to it with the reputation of never once having ordered a man to be flogged, let alone executed. His intriguing arguments allow many prisoners to escape even Lai's intricate web.'

'An enlightening example of *yin* and *yang*,' murmured Chinghiz, tongue in smooth cheek. 'One man he wasn't able to save,' he added informatively. 'The news came half an hour ago – an accusation had been placed in the urn, stating that a certain official had sold arms to Early Warning Li. The man was found guilty and will be executed.'

He hesitated. 'Who was he?' asked Jade, to satisfy him.

He raised a quizzical brow. 'The man who invented the urn. There is a saying, among the western barbarians,' he pronounced gravely, looking at no one in particular, 'that those who live by the sword will die by the sword. Rather apt, in this case.'

Both Bold Fortune and his cousin Rich Talent laughed extravagantly at this excellent jest of fate. Black Jade, her servant was pleased to note, did not.

When they were alone again, just the two of them, she said passionately, 'I shall dismiss them all – all the leopards and the jackals, Deathshead Lai and the inventors of urns. When they have done their necessary work. When I am secure. I shall keep the gold and throw away the dross.'

The imperial family was celebrating a rather unusual occasion. It had to do with the latest of Black Jade's novel attempts to solve what her children referred to, privately, as The Problem of Feng. Calling for her brother the Emperor on her way to the Dowager's Palace, Tiger Lily summed it up between dimples.

'There is simply no way of making that man respectable. You can dress him as an Abbot; you can even *address* him as one; it makes no difference. Feng is an adventurer and a renegade from society, and however much he may adore Black Jade, that is what he will always be. Personally,' she added, rather too casually, 'I like him that way. He's like one of our panthers, but not so tame.'

Dawn Tiger deplored the sensual droop of her eyelids. 'I should l-leave him alone, if I were you,' he advised. 'You w-wouldn't want to cross staves with M-Mother over *that* sort of thing.'

'Why? Whatever do you mean, Little Brother?' The vivid little face was scrubbed clean by innocence. Her grin spoiled the effect.

'You know very w-well,' the Emperor frowned. 'You're jealous. You always have been. You had a fancy for Feng yourself.'

'And I would have had him, if I hadn't been silly enough to let her see him first,' his sister regretted without malice. 'Time, however,' she added mischievously, 'is on my side. They are bound to part one day, don't you think? And then –'

'Then you h-had better take to your convent, and stay there, rather than planning a-any little a-affairs of the h-heart. I say it only because I don't w-want to see you make a fool of yourself.'

'I know.' She stroked his neck beneath his dark blue cap and nibbled his ear in the sisterly fashion that scandalised his servants.

'You are my fairy guardian, and will protect me from myself.'

'So you won't f-flirt with F-Feng at this ridiculous levée?'

'No. I will be a vision of chastity, and keep close to my husband, which, these days, amounts to the same thing.'

He looked at her with grave affection. 'I am sorry you have not been happy with Bold-hand.'

'You needn't be,' said Tiger Lily cheerfully, smoothing the aquamarine taffeta over her tiny hips. 'I manage to make myself perfectly content without his assistance.'

'You are incorrigible.'

'Probably. I take after Mother. Shall we go to the palace? Will you wear a formal crown?'

'No. I shall be present as a member of the f-family, not as the E-Emperor. Indeed,' he smiled soberly. 'I don't th-think I shall be present a-anywhere as the E-Emperor, very soon.'

'I know.' The Princess regarded him closely. 'Don't you mind? If it were me, I should never allow it to happen.' Her tone was fierce.

'No. But, luckily for us all, I am not like you-you. And no – I don't m-mind. Not really. I don't h-have the a-abilities of a Son of H-Heaven. And I h-have seen her rule us and care for us a-all my life. I cannot conceive it o-otherwise. I am content,' he finished with simple humility.

'If only *I* were a man,' said Tiger Lily darkly.

When they arrived on Black Jade's manicured lawns the celebration was in full swing. There was an air of faintly religious gaiety, provided partly by the music and partly by the presence of a great many monks in saffron robes. Some of the younger ones, it is sad to relate, also wore jewellery.

The Empress Dowager and the Abbot of the White Horse Monastery held court in an elegant pavilion made entirely of scarlet paper, layered and cut into the fantastic shapes of phoenixes and horses. An honoured guest was General Bold-hand, Tiger Lily's misprised husband. He was dressed magnificently in his best uniform, and he did not look comfortable. This was nothing to do with the fact that some of his buttons were rather tight; it was the nature of the occasion that distressed him, though he tried hard to conceal this. He had just, by a deed of adoption, become the son of the redoubtable Abbot, who stood airing his teeth beside him, clapping him heartily on the shoulder every now and then to show his appreciation.

Dawn Tiger and his sister came forward to congratulate them both.

'Dear Father-in-law,' murmured the little Princess, dropping into a filial bow, both hands on one curved thigh, her lashes emulating the wings of humming birds at feed, 'what a singular honour has touched our house!'

'Yes, isn't it?' Feng agreed, his deep brown eyes glinting yellow with laughter.

'Bold-hand has been very civil about this,' Jade approved to her daughter a few minutes later, when Tiger Lily was teasing her by looking too openly amused.

'What choice has he?' shrugged Tiger Lily. 'Besides, he has always wanted to be a general. The uniform suits him, though I must say he is getting a little too fat.'

'Connubial contentment, no doubt?' said Black Jade with a hint of irony. Bold-hand's absences from his first wife's bed were as well-known in the palace as Tiger Lily's own peccadilloes among his handsome officers.

'I hope that is not intended as criticism, Mother?' she enquired silkily, surveying Feng's exotic length in its brilliant robes.

'Alas, how could it be?' Jade sighed. 'I should love to be able to send you about your marital duty, my darling, spoiled and beautiful child – but I believe I may have forfeited that right.'

They smiled at each other in mutual amusement and affection, green eyes reflecting the same exquisite face, tinged with self-knowledge on one side and with self-will on the other.

'Dawn Tiger just remarked that your Abbot is like an untamed great cat,' Tiger Lily said thoughtfully. 'I think he is right. How will you tame him, Black Jade? For you will have to tame him, or let him go. It is the way with cats.'

'I have managed quite creditably with Mao-yu and her numerous descendants,' said Jade imperturbably. 'As long as they are well-fed and wholly occupied, they do well enough in captivity. And a great deal depends, does it not,' she said dreamily, catching Feng's longing eye across the flower-strewn floor of the pavilion, 'on the nature of the captivity?'

'Ah, yes. You have made him your slave,' said Tiger Lily lightly. 'But such dangerous beasts have been known to turn on their owners.'

'You mistake me. I am not his owner.' Her mother's voice was cool. 'Nor is he mine. You need not, I think, concern yourself about our relationship. It thrives, I assure you.'

'Then I am happy for you. Both of you.' Tiger Lily spoke the plain truth. But it did not prevent her from wondering just how it would be to lie in the strong arms of her feral new father-in-law.

In the matter of occupying the captive, Black Jade had been gifted with an inspiration. For some time she had wanted to commission the building of a *Ming T'ang*, a Hall of Light, a modern reconstruction of the ceremonial temple of the ancient and revered dynasty of Chou. The problem was that no one had any clear idea what the early *Ming T'ang* had looked like. Its structure had been debated by architects and antiquarians over three reigns without any satisfactory plans ever having been drawn. Without any expectation of results, Black Jade had mentioned the subject to her lover. To her surprise Feng was immediately entranced by the notion. He knew of the existence of the Chou temple and already held several ideas as to its probable form.

'If you will give me a drawing-office and some good designers and engineers, I'll build you the wonder of the Empire! It will be the most astonishing edifice the world has ever seen! The immortals will flock to inhabit it, and the Gods themselves will envy the Empress whose name it will sing down the dynasties!'

'Do you really think you could?'

'Ah. You don't yet trust me. You think I care for nothing but the cruder sensations of life – our own delightful flights apart. Well, you are wrong. I can be serious when it pleases me. Give me what I need, and I will prove it to you. It will be a gift, a pledge of love that will make us legendary.'

Today she was going to give him what he wanted. She knew, because she was coming to know *him*, that he would not disgrace her – not in this.

She called him over to her, her eyes bright with pleasure.

'I have something for you. I kept it until today.'

'Something more? The day is already rich with gifts.' His eyes boldly suggested others that they might soon exchange alone.

They had been together for many months but such looks still had the power to quicken her pulse. She smiled quickly, 'Not yet,' and took a little box from the sandalwood stool at her knee.

He took it from her. 'What is this?' It contained an elaborate gilded key.

'It unlocks your own chambers in the North Gate. You will find assembled there the men you need, the architects and the engineers, the best in the Empire – to build your *Ming T'ang*.'

He stared at her, his bold face for once without artifice or irony. She had given him the dream he had treasured as a child, and with it her trust and a further proof of her love.

With an instinct of pure gratitude, he fell at her feet and

knocked his great head three times before her. 'My Empress bestows her gifts like Heaven itself,' he said. Everyone present was touched, many quite unwillingly, by his obvious sincerity.

The court was even more impressed when the plans for the new temple were completed more quickly than any of them would have believed possible after the years of altercation. After some slight delay caused by historians who wished to see the *Ming T'ang* rise upon its former site in the southern suburbs, a more convenient one was agreed upon, inside the Palace grounds, near the south gate. An old audience hall was destroyed to accommodate it and the construction work began at once, with Feng in sole charge. Black Jade was gratified when both scholars and artisans praised him as a master-builder with whom they were proud to work. Together with the hundreds of affronted peasants, assorted citizens and Taoist brethren whom he had formerly enjoyed tormenting, the Empress Dowager heaved a sigh of relief to see him so utterly engrossed in his work.

With her restless lover safely occupied, Black Jade decided that the wheels of Empire were now running smoothly enough for her to make a preparatory test of the political climate in the event of her taking the throne.

The method she chose was a conventional one, beloved of the Chinese; that of appearing to do the exact opposite of what one was, in fact, about to do.

It would involve the assistance of Dawn Tiger. Taking a cartload of gifts for her three grandsons, Black Jade paid her son a familial visit, including Welcome, who loved to see the babies, and the four maids (now her most confidential attendants) whom she had first known when all of them were little more than children in Green Fragrance Court. She kept them about her to remind her of those days.

The Emperor and his favourite consort, Lady Lotus Face, were playing with their children in the Court of Happy Laughter. Dawn Tiger welcomed her with his peculiarly sweet and open smile and gave her the kowtow of filial respect. Lotus Face followed him, beaming. She was a tall, handsome girl whose air of confidence came from the knowledge that her clan were large in lands and power and that the young Emperor loved her dearly. Black Jade liked her for her obvious dedication to him, and because the girl had given birth to her own favourite grandson, the plump two-year-old Little Dragon, who was now staggering with great determination at the heels of his older brothers who were pretending to be horses; his attempts at a gallop were comic and endearing. When he saw Black Jade he gave a whoop of delight and ran, at a fast wobble, to throw himself upon her, certain of his welcome.

Winded, Jade extracted sweets from her sleeve pocket and distributed them to the whole stable. When they had galloped off again, with appreciative snorts and whinnies, she indicated that she would like to be alone with Dawn Tiger.

They went into his study and sat down amid the swooning scent of benzoin. She explained why she had come.

'Your majesty, I feel that the moment has come for me to restore to you the powers and the tasks I have undertaken on your behalf.'

For a moment Dawn Tiger looked seriously shocked. Then, because he had always had an instinctive understanding of her, his face cleared and he smiled again.

'Ah, so the time has come?' he said, offering her his best *samshu*, the rice-wine she liked. 'I thought we had almost reached it. What will you do, offer me back the throne in an edict, so that I may refuse it gracefully – and finally?'

She sipped from the marble cup, looking gravely at him over it.

'Unless you wish to accept it,' she suggested lightly. 'You are, after all, the Son of Heaven.'

He shook his head, still smiling. 'Let us not play games, Black Jade. I am no Son of Heaven. Heaven desires a daughter for a change. It is a good change. I have never wished it to be otherwise. I think you know that.'

'I believe I do.'

'It is your karma to take the mandate. Neither I nor my brother would ever stand in your way.'

'You have my thanks,' she said humbly. 'It has been such a strange story. I know that what I shall do will be what Heaven wishes. And yet, I dislike having to take what is yours.'

'Oh Mother, can't you see that I long to give it?' he asked warmly. 'It has been a thankless task for me, and a humiliating one – I have been a simple ceremonial object; I have ploughed the first furrow, I have offered the sacrifices. I have greeted each season at its city gate. I pay homage to Heaven and to the ancestors, and I live my life according to the imperial calendar. But it has all been a hollow mockery! While I have acted out the ceremonies, like a shadow puppet in a booth, you have done the work of the Emperor. I cannot tell you how happy it will make me to give it all over to you.'

'Then I am glad,' was all she said. He knelt and rested his forehead on her knee while she stroked his dark head.

After a while he looked up and surprised the brightness of tears in her eyes. He thought how lovely she still was. There was a sheen to her skin that rivalled that of Lotus Face, who was scarcely twenty. If that was what the Mad Monk had done for her, his powers must be as improbable as rumour made them. But perhaps it was nothing to do with the Serindian giant, only with her own large spirit, which could welcome and encompass all the complexities and responsibilities that he had most loathed and feared.

He rose and went across to an ebony chest which stood against a wall. He opened it and drew out shining folds of vermilion cloth. He shook it out and held it up for her to see. It was an exceptionally beautiful summer robe, in a light brocade with gold leaf entwined in its silken threads. It was embroidered all over with the five-toed dragons which were an Emperor's personal emblem.

'I had it made for you, a long time ago,' he said. 'Will you do me the honour to accept it?'

It was a delicate gesture, and typical of his sensitive instinct where others were concerned. He would allow no clumsiness in this moment. It was their own private experience, a graceful expression of a unique relationship which would remain unaffected by the changes to come.

'I thank you with all my heart, Dawn Tiger,' Black Jade said quietly. Then, with a glint of humour which he understood with deep affection, 'You have given me what, I believe, I have always wanted most in the world.'

He nodded. He had, or would very soon have, given her the world itself. All under Heaven – which he did not want.

30

When the Emperor declined, publicly and irrevocably, to govern his empire, the majority of his courtiers and officials thought he had proved himself a poor thing by his refusal, and were quite content to go on being ruled by Black Jade.

One day Bold Fortune demanded to see Black Jade on a matter of the utmost importance. He had been told she was occupied but he insisted. Something of his excitement communicated itself to Chinghiz, whose business it was to prevent interruptions when his mistress was with her lover. He said he would see what he could do.

Bold Fortune waited in the court outside his aunt's study, where he sat beneath the fig tree and tried to calm himself by contemplating the statue of the divine Shen Nu, whose affinity with water was entirely appropriate to his mission.

After some time Black Jade appeared, wearing a loose robe in a cloudy green colour and accompanied by the Abbot. Although they did not touch each other both exuded sensuous satisfaction, together with the impression, edged and delicious, that it might turn again at any moment to ravenous hunger.

Feng's exaggerated masculinity had its usual stultifying effect on Bold Fortune, who admired him tremendously. He lost much of his own hard-practised swagger in the face of the master's splendid assurance.

'Well, Younger Brother,' Feng growled in greeting. 'I trust your business is sufficiently pressing to merit disturbing us?'

Bold Fortune bowed nervously. 'I hope you will think so.'

'Then tell us,' commanded Black Jade lazily, sinking down on the bench that surrounded the wide bole of the fig tree. She looked at Feng who had thrown himself down beside the fountain, regretful at this separation of their flesh that had just been so meltingly joined. Even satisfied, her body ached for him.

Bold Fortune surveyed them with envy and pleasure. What was between them seemed a tangible thing, filling the air about them with a strange charge, as though the Black Dragon of the Thunder were always with them.

'Is there some problem with our ancestral temple?' Jade asked, swinging her foot as if she could not care less. Her nephew had almost completed the building of the Wu temple, but there had been difficulties, largely owing to Feng's wholesale theft of his masons for work on the *Ming T'ang*.

'No. No problems. Much the opposite.' Black Jade straightened her slumbrous posture, catching his note of triumph. 'I will be brief. Gracious Majesty, a great gift has been delivered into my hands.' His voice shook and trembled on the last word. 'You will recall the miraculous tortoise encountered by the ancient Emperor Yu?'

They nodded. The ancient Emperor had been sitting on the bank of the Lo River, brooding upon the hardships of government, when a giant tortoise had clambered out of the water and presented its broad shell for his scrutiny. Inscribed upon it were the mystical characters from which the intelligent monarch was able to derive the gift of written language.

'You don't tell me we have had a return of the venerable beast?' enquired Feng, with a mighty yawn which concealed his interest.

'Not quite! But it's something almost as good. It was brought to me early this morning by one of the river fishermen. A stone. Covered in ancient characters! I took it to the North Gate and let the antiquarians have a look at it.' He paused, enjoying their growing anticipation.

'What did they find?' Black Jade encouraged.

'A recipe for turtle soup?' suggested the irreligious Abbot.

For once, Bold Fortune ignored his idol, his eyes fixed steadily on his beautiful aunt. 'It is a prophecy,' he said.

He saw her stiffen slightly. 'These are its words. "A sage mother shall come to rule mankind, and her reign shall bring eternal prosperity." ' Breathless, he waited for her response.

Her smile was a slow and lovely thing, its illumination spreading to all four corners of the court. He felt blessed by it and looked shyly at the ground, dazzled.

'I am impatient to see it. You must send for it at once. You have done very well in this, Bold Fortune. You have my thanks.'

'I did nothing,' he protested, flushing with pleasure. 'It was the fisherman who found it.'

The stone was the wonder of the universe. It was proclaimed to the ends of the Empire, and everywhere the people rejoiced to know that Heaven had at last made itself clear on the subject of the mandate. Women especially rejoiced, feeling themselves suddenly more valuable. If they gave birth to daughters they did not hang their heads because they had 'lowered the roof', but tilted their chins and spoke ringingly of Black Jade.

Jade herself was ecstatic; she had weathered a year of criticism and treachery without flinching at the tempering it had given her, and the Goddess of the Lo had sent her her reward.

In Loyang the citizens shared the joy of their Empress as she solemnly led the whole court to the Altar of Heaven in the southern quarter, to give thanks for the modern miracle. The holy stone itself was given the title of the *Pao-t'u*, the 'Precious Design' of Heaven. The languid summer waters of the Lo were declared sacred. Any further fishing, naturally, was prohibited. The ultimate catch had been taken.

Black Jade added to her list of titles that of Sage Mother, the

Divine Sovereign, as suggested by the stone. She was particularly pleased with the word 'sovereign', which denotes supreme rule without stipulating the sex of the ruler.

On a wave of euphoria she began to plan a splendid ceremony for the proper veneration of the stone. She would display herself in a semi-divine aspect as the object of the prophecy. The proceedings would be a prodigy of beauty and holiness.

'Then you shall hold it in the *Ming T'ang*,' cried Feng when she spoke of it.

'It is finished? Truly? When may I see it?' He had not allowed her near his own private miracle for many months, wanting to show her it whole and perfected.

'Soon. It will be your gift to Heaven, this magnificent celebration in my unparalleled colossus of a building!'

'Yes – I should like that. The two of us together, enshrined forever in the holy stone and the temple that guards it.'

Feng found himself wanting to weep. His eyes burned with preventing it. His love for her was also a colossus, over whose ever-increasing proportions he had no control. It was almost an insanity within him. He knew it, but could do nothing to alter it. Now he seized her with swift possessiveness.

'Soon you will be the people's Goddess,' he muttered, his mouth close to hers. 'But first you are mine; woman first, then Goddess.'

It was true, even more true after the three years they had now been together. He could arouse her instantly; not even a touch was needed. He would come into a room and look at her, his heavy lids veiling the heat in his eyes, and she would feel herself become liquid with wanting him. If he did not look at her, it was worse. And if he paid attention to any other woman it was a knife in her heart. He did so very rarely. She knew that, by now, he was all hers.

She fell on her knees and raised her hands to him, moving them until she had his jade stalk cupped between them. She took it in her mouth, stroking, worshipping, sucking the strength of his *yang* into her, pushing her swollen breasts against his thighs.

He stood, accepting her homage, glorying in his power to exact it from her, until it became painful not to allow himself to explode and fill her throat with his precious seed. He bent and gently picked her up. Her robe was undone and her body naked beneath it. He set her upon the tip of his stalk, feeling her warm wetness welcoming him. He pushed into her, settling her down upon him, very deep, his hands under her buttocks moving her sensuously to give them both intense pleasure. Her perfume surrounded him, shaken from the silken fall of her hair. They kissed, she moaned a little, almost at her zenith. He slowed her, making her concentrate on their kissing, on the flicker of his eyelash on her cheek, on his dark, demanding eyes as he told her that they were each other's completion, that they would always create perfection together. Soon he allowed her to release her *yin*, feeling that little contraction of the cinnabar gate that caused a resurgence in him, holding her even closer as she shuddered and buried her exalted face in his shoulder. Woman first, and then Empress.

They lay in the peace that follows love and made their plans for the ceremonies which would bring rejoicing to the Black-haired People and would marry them in private delight.

A decree was sent out; every individual of any prominence in every province was to attend the festival, noblemen, prefects, the military, officials of all the eight grades. No one was left out.

There was a saying among the people that one must modify one's plans according to the circumstances, a heartfelt necessity for a nation of farmers subject to the celestial puzzle of alternating drought and floods. And now that necessity introduced its impartial presence to the palace.

'Majesty – there is regrettable news.' The Minister for War was apologetic. He had been forced to intrude upon the Empress when she was still taking her early morning tea.

Black Jade waved him to a seat. He did not take it but stood looking serious and embarrassed. No sixth sense came to her aid.

'It is at a most inconvenient time for Your Majesty – but there is rebellion in Shantung. Young Wolf Li, the governor of Po Chou, has formed an allegiance with several other Li princes and is marching on Chi Nan with five thousand men!'

She could hardly believe it. At the worst possible time. She controlled her furious disappointment, her mind already engaging with the problem.

'And just how did these princes manage to recruit so many so quickly? By issuing a false decree?'

'Yes, Majesty. They claim to have the Emperor's personal decree, and have also issued a private one which states –' He hesitated.

Black Jade tapped her foot.

'– which states that your Luminous Excellence intends to destroy the imperial family completely, and to set her own in its place.'

'It does not, I imagine, mention that I have given birth to four Li princes myself,' she said. 'And what steps have you taken so far?'

'There are fifteen thousand troops on alert and ready to march as soon as the commanding officer is named.'

She did not need to deliberate. There was one general who would die a thousand times to prove his loyalty, and to make amends, if he could, for the one great mistake of his life.

'Send Old Arsenic. And tell him that this is not a time to be lenient.' Knowingly or otherwise, the General had caused the death of her son, Young Tiger. Now he would pay for it with the blood of five thousand rebels, including that of most of Shih-min's and Pheasant's remaining relatives.

The General made a more adequate recompense. Among those defeated and finally executed were two half-brothers of Shih-min, the Princess Constance, two sons of Pheasant by concubines, and, most tragically, two sons of Young Tiger who sought to avenge their father by helping the rebels. The strangest defection was that of Bold-hand, Tiger Lily's estranged husband.

After the rigours of the revolution and the sorrow of its aftermath, it was an immense relief to return to the preparations for the festive ceremonies of the worship of the stone and the inauguration of the *Ming T'ang*. Black Jade decided to hold two separate celebrations, as the nature of the *Pao-t'u* made it an irreverence to combine its veneration with that of any other deity.

The ceremony of the stone took place in the season of Little Cold, just after the winter solstice when the yellow earth was freshened and chastened by the monsoon winds and rain.

The court made its way in solemn procession from the south gate of the Palace City along the broad boulevards furred with a light, sunlit snowfall, and down to the banks of the Lo River where an altar had been set up for the occasion. The column was led by Black Jade, going most gorgeously in a black satin dragon robe, gloriously gilded and embroidered, and covered with the beautifully fashioned skin of a white tiger, the great symbol of male sexuality and power, as opposed to the female emblem, the green dragon. Even as these two completed and complemented each other, she wished to say to her people, did the woman Black Jade complete and complement the sacred office of Emperor. Green Dragon should mate and mingle with White Tiger and follow the Tao in perfect harmony.

Demonstrating his own acceptance of this future marriage of

imperial *yin* and *yang* was Dawn Tiger, who, although still carrying the titles of the Emperor, was content to ride, and ultimately to walk, behind his mother.

When everyone who could manage it had crowded near to the riverside altar, they saw that the simple stone table formed the background for an unprecedented display of the Empire's most valuable treasures.

Many were recent gifts or tribute from beyond the borders, rare vases from ancient dynasties, astonishing jewels from Khotan. There were birds and animals; a white goshawk from Silla, a pair of trained elephants from Champa. Here were silver-cased swords and engraved suits of armour; there were heaps of coins and urns of incense, bright bolts of cloth and unknown flowering plants whose brilliant blooming shamed the snow. There was a choir of black-skinned monks to sing the praises of the stone. There were drums and trumpets, bells and stone chimes, flutes and lutes and plangent, tingling zithers.

Above all there was the imperial regalia, laid out on the scarlet altar cloth for all to marvel at; the hidden, ancient jades, heavy and dense with the mysteries of time and sacred usage.

Most revered was the emblem of Heaven. This was the *pi*, a plain jade disc with a circle cut out of its centre. It symbolised the *yang*, the positive, the principle of light, man himself under Heaven. The emblem of earth was the *tsung*, a squared cylinder of jade whose interior was hollowed into a womblike circle to represent the *yin*, the dark, the negative; woman.

At the front of the altar lay the *Pao-t'u* and next to it the sceptre of the Son of Heaven, a green stem of jade as dark as obsidian.

Black Jade walked towards the altar with a dramatic grace that stated her awareness of the moment. She stood before it thoughtfully, green eyes resting on green jades, then she folded to the ground in the kowtow to Heaven which was the signal that the ceremony had begun.

The service was reverent and most beautiful. The music offered gems to hang in the air, and the worship of the stone, based upon the ancient rites of the golden age of the Middle Kingdom, the dynasty during which the art of government was perfected by the beatified Duke Wu of Chou, was an affecting and uplifting liturgy. But what would remain in the memory, long after all the pomp had become a mere impression of noise and colour and motion, was the still figure who had lain, a personal sacrifice, before the altar, and then had risen in her black robes, her white tiger-skin, to offer food to the Gods. She had been served by no acolytes; her son had not come near her. No one had approached the altar save her. She had separated herself from all of them, cut off because she was the chosen of Heaven. No one who had seen that ceremony would go home that day with any doubt of it.

If the rites of the *Pao-t'u* had been the dedication of Black Jade to the Gods, subsequent festivities were completely given over to the glory and honour of man. The New Year was normally a time of mayhem and madness; this year it would reach a peak of inspired insanity that would satisfy even Feng's appetite for grandeur and spectacle. Traditionally a family celebration, it was of great spiritual power, when the proper observation of the rites would influence the fortunes of the coming year.

Like every household throughout the Empire, the imperial family met together just before midnight on New Year's Eve in the intimate Hall of the Heart's Content, in the Emperor's private apartments. Black Jade was attended by Feng, Bold Fortune and Rich Talent and their wives, and a pensive Tiger Lily, still very much subdued by the loss of her husband in the recent revolution.

The first duty must be performed in the open air. This was the rite whereby the Gods of Heaven and earth were thanked for their care during the year that had ended. Dawn Tiger at the head, they formed a procession and walked to the Court of Singing Clouds, where an altar stood, lonely in the light of flickering candles. Incense filled the air.

Dawn Tiger, acting for once as the family patriarch rather than the high priest of a whole nation, gave the prayers of thanks with solemn dignity and made the offerings of food and wine.

Now there were the lesser Gods to be considered. These were the household Gods who guarded the home against evil spirits; they were stationed at the paths outside a house, at its gates and its doors, in all its courts and, most imperatively, in the kitchen; this was the domain of Tsao Wang, who was especially feared by children, for he leaves the house on New Year's Eve, the lips of his portrait liberally sweetened, to make his annual report to Heaven on the conduct of those in his charge.

The guardian Gods were thanked, with a special military salute reserved for the keepers of the gate, who were none other than Shih-min's two grizzled generals whose alarming portraits Jade had first seen on her entry into the city of Chang-an so many years ago. They had now been universally promoted to be the spiritual janitors of the Empire. Little Dragon was especially fond of them because they had been real soldiers and he had often been told the tales of their valour.

Now it was time to go to the Hall of the Ancestors, the chamber which is the heart of the house, for it holds its history and its reputation in the portraits which cover its walls, and its soul burns in the candles standing on its altars.

Tonight the ancestors rejoiced with the living, enjoying the contemplation of the feast that was set before them and the good appetite of the generations who had seated themselves about the long table in the centre of the hall. As she had often done before, Black Jade would eat her meat with the bright eyes of her two Emperors upon her, the glow of the candles lending them a strange half-life. She saw Feng look closely at Shih-min's martial features, and with less interest at Pheasant's benevolent face. It had not occurred to her to wonder if either might be insulted by the presence of her lover. Well, it was too late now; she could hardly ask Feng to take his meal in the courtyard.

The time just before eating was known as the Mending of Quarrels. If anyone had displeased or contended with any relative, he must now make reparation. There was a subdued fifteen minutes while the children went dutifully round, kowtowing to their seniors and apologising to each other for slights and misdemeanours throughout the year.

'I am sorry, New Song, that I broke your cricket-cage.'

'And I regret sincerely, Little Dragon, that I let out your best fighting cricket.'

'I am sorry,' whispered Feng, close to Jade's ear, 'that I have not enjoyed the clouds and rain with you nine times each day of the year.'

'Nine may be the luckiest number,' she murmured, 'but I think in this case it might have led to serious debility.'

'The manuals all say that a man needs up to ten women every night. The Yellow Emperor slept with twelve thousand, and *he* became an immortal.'

'Ten different women – not the same one ten times!'

'You *are* ten different women.' His breath invited her and she felt her loins melt.

'This is not a proper conversation for the moment. Kindly be quiet, or talk to Lady Liu; *decently*, though!'

As he turned away, grinning, her attention was taken by an altercation that had broken out between Tiger Lily and Bold Fortune who was standing up and glaring at her, his chest heaving.

'*Amitabha!*' cried Jade severely. 'What are you thinking of? Is this the time to quarrel? Tell me the trouble at once.'

'The Princess accuses me of a dishonourable act,' declared Bold Fortune, evidently very much annoyed.

'I was merely enquiring; I made no accusation,' drawled Tiger Lily, who could be maddening when she wanted to be.

'She asked whether *I* had "arranged" for the holy stone to be found in the river! It is the greatest insult I have ever been offered. I demand an apology!'

Black Jade's heart mistimed. 'Since my daughter has spoken, the question must now be answered. *Did* you arrange it?' He would deny it, even if it were true. It was strange, but the question had never once occurred to her. She had taken the *Pao-t'u* in the same spirit as her prophecy.

Bold Fortune stopped his righteous quivering and faced her calmly. 'No, Gracious Aunt and Empress, I did not arrange it. There is no need for such dishonesty on the part of men when the Gods themselves are the guardians of someone's destiny. If anyone "arranged" that the stone should be found, it must surely have been the Lo Consort herself!' Fu-fei, the Lo Consort, was the generous Goddess of the river, an empress among spirits whose interest in the fortunes of humanity might well lead her to champion a woman such as Black Jade.

'Daughter, you have been most ungracious. You shame yourself before our ancestors.'

Tiger Lily rose, chastened, and came to kowtow before her mother. To bring shame to one's ancestors was the gravest of all sins. She knew that, for once, she had gone too far. Quailing inwardly at Jade's unloving expression, she presented herself before her cousin.

'Bold Fortune, I am greatly sorry for what I have said. I beg you most earnestly to accept my humble apology.' She fell gracefully to the ground and knocked her head twice.

'Please stand up. Of course you are forgiven, dearest friend and cousin,' he beamed, pleased, now that his anger was over, to be the centre of attention. 'And see,' he added, 'the incense clock is close upon the exact hour of the Rat.'

They all turned their eyes to the flat face of the tile engraved with the divisions of the hours; the measured trail of incense which led from hour to hour had burnt away to midnight.

'Happy New Year!' they all cried, forgetting the quarrel. The children were kissed and the adults bowed like bamboo in a wind.

'This will be your year of triumph,' whispered Dawn Tiger

softly to Black Jade. Her eyes filled at this sign of his unselfishness. She was particularly affectionate to him for the rest of the night. She saw that her nephew noted this and did not look pleased. So then, his expectations were growing in the good compost from the Ever-Glorious River?

It was time now to fall to the feasting. The cooks had excelled themselves, sensing, as good servants do, the unspoken premonition that this was going to be an extraordinary year.

The adults were traditionally supposed to stay up until dawn, when Heaven and earth would be greeted again and their blessings asked for another twelve months. But sleep was needed for tomorrow's festivities, and after an hour or so's soft conversation they soon followed the children to bed, heaping themselves with furs as they crossed starlit courts in snow that fell like feathers past their bright faces – from which, one might believe in the white light, the year's passing had removed every trace of adverse experience.

The night had kept some of its magic for the morning, the sun replacing starlight upon a city whose indigo mystery had been changed by its shaman's hand to an alert silver sparkle. The noise of its awakening reached Jade before Chinghiz could call her. Beside her, Feng slept as though sleep were the only form of life, his long body thrown across her bed exactly as he had fallen last night, drugged with wine and contentment. She lost her small hand on his upflung arm for a caressing instant, then left him to sleep until the last moment, while she went to keep the peace between Welcome and the steward, who enjoyed their feast-day arguments almost as much as the occasions themselves.

They dressed her in the dark blue robe of the Empress and set the crown, with its twelve strings of falling pearls, upon her own coronet of blue-black hair.

'Loop back the pearls somehow. Welcome. I want the people to see me today.' This was done and she pronounced herself satisfied with her looks, though Chinghiz, as always, wanted to paint her face to a more dramatic effect.

'It isn't necessary. I shall be so happy that my face will shine! You will see.'

Before leaving the palace, she held a brief private interview with the Chief Astrologer. When she reappeared the promised shining was already apparent. She had waited a very long time – almost a lifetime, it sometimes seemed – but this year, 690, would bring an end to the waiting.

Feng now came to wish her good morning and to admire and be admired. He wore a scarlet tunic over gold breeches and a black cloak with a gold lining. His skull gleamed with scented oil and his white teeth, always his best ornament, flashed their pleasure in conjunction with his black, appreciative eyes. He nuzzled a warm kiss into Black Jade's palm, so as not to disturb Chinghiz's artistry, and then they were ready to depart for the *Ming T'ang*.

'Remember, it is all for you, only for you,' he told her as he helped her into open sedan she had chosen to ride in. 'It is my gift to you, the emblem and reconstruction of the love I bear you.'

She smiled and watched him mount his white horse, tossing back the cloak to dazzle the populace with the lining. She noticed that others smiled too, as they took their place at the head of the grand procession. She was glad; she wanted her lover to be popular. It seemed that the court was now prepared to forgive him for the depredations of his monastery-full of worldly and over-energetic young monks upon the neighbouring countryside. After all, many of them were the sons of ministers.

If the progress to the Holy River had been as noisy and jubilant as its pious nature had permitted, the approach to the *Ming T'ang* was made through a city gone mad. Everyone was in the streets, including the four generations of his relatives, his horses, his dogs, his servants, and his singing birds on their long leashes vying for airspace with a million brilliant kites in the shapes of dragons, butterflies, bats, tortoises, magpies, peonies, cranes, lotuses and the twelve animals of the zodiac – all in continued danger from the fusillade of fireworks that welcomed the birth of the year. The noise was tremendous, swelling and booming in waves as Black Jade moved slowly through it; Loyang had forgotten its manners for once and was in full-bellied, ear-splitting cry, bellowing like a cattle-market and beating about the ears of its beloved Empress its cries of blessing and wishes of good fortune.

It is not very far to the *Ming T'ang*, but Jade felt as though it had been some broad isthmus which she had swum unaided. When she reached the corner that would turn upon the temple her mind was already so bruised by the people's affection that she was in no condition for the shock which struck her.

The breath raced from her body as they set down her sedan. The *Ming T'ang* stood before her in all its impossible glory, too much for the eyes to encompass or the mind to comprehend. It shone, it sang, it tingled and jangled with colour, glittered with gold. It curved and aspired and leaped and curvetted, holding up its hundred thousand gilded fingers to the Gods in a dance of exultation.

Feng swung from his horse and helped her from the palanquin. She scarcely saw him, hardly knew she had moved. Her eyes were fixed and wide; her only communication was with the *Ming T'ang*. It rose 294 feet in three stories, two rectangular and the upper circular, in the form of a pagoda. Tens of thousands of men had built it, whole forests had been brought from the mountains to support it. The ground floor, covering an area of 300 square feet, formed a square whose sides were painted red, black, green and white, respecting each season as did the Emperor's mantles. The twelve sides of the central tier represented the zodiac and displayed the characters for each lunar month. It raised a circular projecting roof supported by nine iron pillars in the form of writhing dragons, from which reared the top floor, whose rounded wall was painted with the twenty-four constellations and upheld a splendid cerulean blue dome, the emblem of Heaven. Triumphant upon its summit was a great golden phoenix, the sign of the Empress, supreme in the firmament. Black Jade lifted up her arms to it in a gesture of wonder and acknowledgment. Watching her, the crowd murmured in ecstacy, proudly sharing her appreciation, and Feng, with his instinctive mastery of the moment of grace, flung his colossal figure at her feet and performed an athlete's kowtow, telling all the world that this was his offering to her.

Pandemonium reigned as they mounted the shallow steps and entered the gilded scarlet doors.

Within, the lower hall was candle-lit and richly scented. Black Jade looked about her in admiration, seeing that the whole structure of the building was internal, supported by gigantic, exquisitely carved wooden pillars, ten handspans around, soaring from the ground up to the roof and carrying the subsidiary beams and buttresses. Feng had said it had needed a thousand men to drag one of them from its forest home.

The walls were painted with vivid scenes of life and work in every month of the year and in all parts of the Empire.

Gazing upward, the eye was captured by detail after detail of loving sculpture on beams and trusses; the Monkey King darted out from the vast central trunk to snatch a golden peach from a carved branch; an angelic immortal rested in a niche, unaware of the clutch of ducklings who were about to invade her peace. Everywhere were rare and precious objects; ancient scrolls and delicate reliquaries, chests of jewelled and scented wood, a gold incense-burner mysteriously made in concentric spheres of filigree work, exuding an aromatic cloud that was a subtle and refreshing reminder of pine trees and falling water. And all about them were the serene smiles of the Buddhas, often reclining, always relaxed and benevolent; here too was a lovely porcelain image of Kuan Yin, in a robe of turquoise starred with gold, holding her vase of the healing dew of Heaven and the willow twig that speaks of her tears for mankind.

A figure which she did not recognise caught Jade's attention.

'Which Bodhisattva is that?' she asked Feng, close behind her.

'Ah, that is something, and someone, very special. It is an image of the Buddha Maitreya. It is from Khotan.' This was the Buddha who is yet to come, who will rule over the earth in a last incarnation as a Bodhisattva. attaining the perfection of Buddhahood for himself and lasting peace for humanity. It was represented by a slender seated figure, wearing the jewels and decorated headdress of an Indian goddess.

'Are you certain? I have never heard of a *female* Maitreya!'

'No? Well, I assure you, there is at least one sutra about her.'

'Which one?' Jade must have read a thousand sutras during her year in Kan Yeh, and as many since, but never one which referred to a feminine Maitreya. The usual image was of a slack-bellied laughing figure, fat, indulgent and male. She was intrigued.

'I'll bring it to you one day,' he said. 'I think you will find it more than interesting.'

She realised that he was full of suppressed excitement and that it was not, for the moment, related to the *Ming T'ang*. Now, however, they were joined by the ministers and clerics whom Jade had invited to the ceremony, and she had to forget the subject of Maitreya for the present.

When the guests had admired the hall extravagantly, the imperial party trooped out into the morning again. The crowds were still vociferous, but had been cordoned off to give plenty of privacy.

Black Jade herself carried out the sacrifice, with Dawn Tiger as her first assistant and the boy New Song, the Crown Prince, as second assistant. It was Jade and not the Emperor who carried the jade sceptre which had been shown to the people at the Lo Ceremony. Her hand shook when it first touched its coolness.

The feasting, even more than that in the hall of the ancestors on the previous night, was notable not only for its delicate flavours and witty conversation but for the sensation of the diners that they were watched by unnumbered pairs of eyes. They were perfectly comfortable in this feeling, especially when the Abbot

Embracing Righteousness recounted to them the history and magnitude of the jewels, gathered in handfuls from the tribute chests, which now winked in the sockets of ten thousand Buddhas, five thousand dragons, five hundred tigers, a myriad monkeys, streams of fish and flights of fowl, and in the hearts of painted flowers and the hilts of candelabra. It was decided, Jade could not remember afterwards by whom, that they should give the hall the alternative name of the Palace of the Ten Thousand Divine Appearances.

For the rest of the fortnight of public holiday, while her people became one with their children and played games, ate sweets and avoided all possible responsibilities, Black Jade let herself be seen about the city in the guise of their loving, indulgent mother, smiling at their pranks and content in their happiness. Sometimes the Emperor was at her side; more often he remained in his family courtyards, keeping the feast in a private fashion. Jade joined them as often as she could, for she enjoyed being a grandmother, and Dawn Tiger was the only one of her sons with whom she had always enjoyed an uncomplicated and wholly loving relationship. His mind was as clear to her as water and as pure. He cared very little, if he cared at all, that she was about to receive the mandate of Heaven. If anything, he would be relieved when at last it was accomplished. It did not, as in the cases of her first two sons, prevent him from loving her.

31

It was at the beginning of the summer, when the palace was brilliant with flowers and the gardens shrieked with sun-happy birds and beasts, that Feng brought her the *Great Cloud Sutra.*

She was beside a lake, standing with brushes and inkstones before a sandalwood desk, beneath a canopy of white lawn that floated softly with every breeze. The sun had passed its zenith and the sky was silver-blue and hot. Maids and musicians were dotted about the grass under bright paper parasols. The air hummed with lute-strumming and muted conversation.

Feng crossed the green acreage with his long, easy stride, the light wind blowing his gauze shirt and breeches against his beautiful body, so that when Jade looked up and saw him she wanted him at once. She had recently begun to marvel at how this could still be; also to be grateful for it.

He held the silk scroll very carefully. It was old and precious.

'I am sorry to interrupt your work, but the time has come for you to see this. I had to send for it, from Khotan. And then I wished the White Horse elders to examine it. We are agreed, they and I, about the message it contains. It is quite extraordinary, and, I think, of great importance to you. Will you read it?'

She held out her arms and he placed the scroll gently in them.

'Must I read it now?'

'Yes,' he said with unusual gravity. 'You must.'

She sighed. 'I was working on some new characters that I have invented – simple ones, which everyone will understand, to take the place of several that have become so complex that only the *chin shih* scholars can use them. A language should inform the people, not keep them in ignorance.'

'Yes, yes, but that will keep. Please, my heart's song, do as I ask, because I ask you.'

She smiled into his eyes and led him to a pile of rugs and pillows beneath the white canopy, leaning close to him while he unrolled the beginning of the scroll for her.

'The *Great Cloud Sutra*,' she read. 'It is the one you promised me on New Year's Day. The one in which Maitreya is a woman?'

He kissed her lightly on the side of her head. His perfume aroused her. She carried his hand to her breast, but he shook his head. 'I will leave you to read. I'm going to play polo.'

'If you must, beloved.' She knew he could never be still while she read; he needed an outlet for the excitement that ran through him and into her own nervous system, making her eager to begin.

Nevertheless she watched him stride away, loving his perfectly unconscious grace of movement, wanting to read, yet longing for the night that would bring him back to her.

She made herself concentrate. Soon it was no effort. Her eyes raced through the characters and the scroll lay untidily disposed over the cushions. She had become so involved with it that she did not bother to wind it back upon its jade spool.

Maitreya, the expected one, the saviour who will return in the last period of the Dharma to purify the corruption of the earth and begin the Age of Gold, was here personified as a great woman who would be born seven hundred years after the death of the Buddha Gautama, and who would become the supreme ruler of an empire to which all other kingdoms would bend their necks. Reading, Black Jade felt a stirring of intense emotion. She knew, long before she had finished the sutra, what message Feng intended it to hold for her.

The words were beautiful, their promise a glory.

When Maitreya came to be the Queen-Goddess of all the world, 'The harvests will be bountiful, there will be joy without limit. The people will flourish, free of sickness, free from sorrow; from anxiety, fears and disasters, free. All her neighbouring rulers will offer allegiance, and all her subjects will kowtow to the Woman as the successor to the Dragon Throne. After she has taken the Tao, the world will be awed and submit before her.'

'Yes,' she whispered, as once, long ago, she had cried out, exalted.

'Yes. Yes. Yes!'

The working nucleus of older and more scholastic monks of the White Horse Monastery produced a commentary upon the *Great Cloud Sutra* which induced a ripple of almost hysterical reaction centring in Loyang and radiating to the borders of the Empire and beyond. The people's pleasure in the conclusions that were drawn, and their conviction of the rightness of these conclusions, were the result of the fortuitous combination of everyman's desire for a hero, a saviour, a God-made-man, and the personal charisma of the woman who had guided them for so many years. Woman-made-God would do very well.

To encourage the spreading of the commentary Black Jade announced that she would found a Great Cloud Temple in every large town. This earned her the worshipful gratitude of the church for her patronage, and of the people who felt their security enhanced by the identification of their Sage Mother with the faith that nurtured them. They began to believe in the *Great Cloud Sutra.*

She knew, of course, that she was not a Goddess, not the Maitreya.

Perhaps the educated among the people knew it too, though the peasants did not. What was important was that they *wanted* to believe. If she was Maitreya, she must become the ruling Empress; and they wanted her to become the ruling Empress. Their accord had brought about the moment. The publication of the sutra had been her last step towards the throne.

The Empire was in her hand. The rest would be mere form and custom.

And she owed it all to the inspiration of her magnificent Feng. She had not experienced such sustained happiness since she had first fallen in love with Shih-min. In many ways, Feng was her first lover's opposite; he lived from day to day at the highest pitch he could strike, careless of all responsibility except in his love for her and, briefly, in whatever enterprise might catch his passing interest. He had brought a life to her body that was so intense that it transcended itself, giving new and ardent strength to every endeavour. Let others dwell on his faults, his arrogance, his mischief, his contempt for authority – for her he held the key to the Garden of the Immortals.

The first sign that she should commission her coronation robes was in the conventional form of a petition from a censor begging that the dynasty be changed. Following good form, she rejected it.

The petition reappeared, bearing the 60,000 most important signatures in the land, while a cheerful mob demonstrated in its favour at the gates of the Forbidden City.

Again, it received a modest refusal.

Now, the Emperor himself took his steps in the formal dance in which they were engaged. He sent Black Jade a request that he might change his family name to Wu, so that he might have the honour to belong to the dynasty that had eclipsed the T'ang.

His wish was granted; he was, after all, his mother's heir.

After this there were several favourable portents. A flock of vermilion birds, symbols of good fortune, were seen swooping joyously about the Dragon Throne. A phoenix, Black Jade's personal emblem, the heavenly creature which appeared only to mark the birth of a sage or a prophet, was reported flying above the imperial park. Witnesses swore it had perched for a full minute upon the eaves of the palace. Chinghiz remarked astringently that upon the evening of the fifth day of the ninth month it had been seen by a dozen persons, but by the same time on the next evening nearly a thousand had claimed sight of it.

'Faith,' said his Little Mistress, well pleased, 'is a remarkable thing.'

The next time the petition was presented, with Dawn Tiger's name at the head of the list, Black Jade wrote upon it the single word: 'Approved'.

Four days after the flight of the phoenix the decree went out – the T'ang dynasty was abolished and the dynasty of Chou would take its place. Black Jade had chosen this name in memory of the golden age of the chivalrous Duke of Chou, the 'perfect gentleman' of Confucius. His family name had been Wu, and she would adopt him as her ancestor just as the Li clan had adopted the Old Philosopher, Lao-tse. It was an impeccable choice, for the intelligent Duke had been personally responsible for the entire system of government and administration which had guided the Flowery Kingdom for two thousand years. To invoke his name was to call down blessings from an approving Heaven.

On the twenty-first day of the eighth month, in the season of White Dew, Black Jade put on the imperial robes of an Emperor and showed herself to the people upon the balcony of the great tower of the Heaven Gate. She announced the change of dynasty in her own voice, its confident tones ringing with a joy that reached out to everyone present, so that the many-coloured wheatfield that lay prostrate before the wind of her coming was murmurous with pleasure, as though birds were trapped in it. When she had finished speaking they arose from their kowtows – blue, indigo, violet, scarlet, rose, emerald, turquoise – every courtier and officer in a new gown, to herald her reign with as loud an utterance as has ever been known to man.

'Black Jade! Black Jade! Black Jade!'

Three days later, Dawn Tiger abdicated, very quietly, once more to become the Imperial Heir. Black Jade put on the dragon robes again; this time she would also wear the crown.

When they had finished dressing her, when Chinghiz had given the last twitch to the dark sapphire silk and had added the last tiny brush-stroke to her deep blue brows, the four maids who had been with her since her entry to the palace held up the long bronze mirror so that she could see herself.

'Your Majesty is the most beautiful thing upon the earth,' whispered Sweetmeat, blushing at her own daring.

'Like the Queen of the Western Heaven, come down to live amongst us unworthy mortals,' fantasised Silver Bell, soft-voiced.

They crowded, murmuring, about the gilded image in the polished bronze, fluttering, admiring, breathless and suddenly shy.

And when she looked at the woman they showed to her, gleaming softly in the midnight gown, her face transfigured with a happiness that no man, not one of those who had loved her, could have given her, only the strong will of Heaven, she felt that she could only agree with them. That woman was far more than herself.

'Thank you,' she said, her low voice throbbing a little. 'Thank you all for your love and your loyalty. We have waited a long time, all of us, for this day.'

Feng came into the room, resplendent in the ceremonial robes of the Duke of O'Kuo, glittering with gold and the emerald eyes of an embroidered mythology of monsters. He had been raised to the nobility in company with every male member of the Wu family, twenty-three in all. He would not be close to her today; it would not have been fitting; but he had come to make his obeisance before her, to lay himself at her feet and swear his love and his allegiance until death.

When he rose to his knees she came to help him up herself, her hands touching him before the eyes of her servants. She thought she heard Chinghiz sigh as she did so, and it was not a sentimental sigh. He cared no more for the Duke of O'Kuo than he had for the prize-fighter or the Abbot of the White Horse Monastery.

Feng left her then, their eyes exchanging promises for the night. It was almost time for them to take her to the throne-room.

The servants seemed to be hanging back. The maids looked from one to the other, their faces tear-stained with joy and tension. Yarrow pushed Welcome forward, her lined face scarlet with suppressed excitement.

'What is it?' Black Jade asked. 'Is something wrong?'

'No. But there is something still to be completed,' Chinghiz answered her, his handsome face suddenly regaining all its young faun's humour.

She waited, knowing better than to hurry them. They loved their private dramas even better than the public ones.

'Please sit down, Little Mistress,' Welcome ordered, sniffing uncontrollably. She wiped her eyes on the sleeve of her new silver-grey dress and jacket.

Sometimes, Black Jade thought with a rush of affection, one forgot how old she was. The day might well be too much for her.

'Welcome! You must not weep,' she said lovingly. 'This is a time to be joyful. I want to hear you singing, as you always do when we are happy – or even scolding me, if you will. But don't cry, I entreat you. It is not good for you.'

Welcome straightened her face and her gown at once. Then she assumed an expression of deep importance while the others ranged themselves in a semi-circle before their mistress.

'What is this?' Black Jade was intrigued. 'Are you going to make a speech?' If so, it would doubtless be the first of many that day.

They were all smiling, as though at a beloved child. Chinghiz was shaking his head and laughing at her.

It came to her then, like the flash of a firework, just as her old nurse put her hand into her sleeve pocket, kneeling at her feet.

The tears started before Welcome had even drawn out the little medallion, made of cheap bronze, a gaudy gimcrack thing with its cracked enamel and its uneven, linked chain. She gave a little cry, like a woman receiving the body of her lover, and reached out her hand to clutch at the dragon pendant.

She rose and lifted Welcome to her feet, put her arms about her and wept unashamedly on her cushioned shoulder; the child from Wen Shui overwhelmed with love and joy and the rightness of promised dreams come true.

'Dearest friend, thank you from my heart! It is more important to me than any crown could be. Now I truly believe I am the Empress!'

Standing back a little, the better to observe what was also the crowning moment of his own dedicated life, Chinghiz murmured, as if to himself, 'Yes, it is true; the consummation is upon us. At last!' He spoke with a savage, shuddering exultation.

She turned to him now; she had been conscious, ever since he had awoken her with that fierce blue light streaming from his eyes, had coaxed and gentled her through the motions she must perform, had bathed and oiled and scented her body, his hands whispering about her like the wings of dragonflies, had dressed her and perfected her, with an intensity of purpose that had almost unsettled her, that this day was his as much as it was hers – his, and no other man's. It was right that she should say it aloud, though he knew it as well as she.

She motioned the others to go and repair their tear-streaked faces and stood alone with him, past and present vibrating in her like the purring of her great cats.

'You know, don't you, my Chinghiz,' she began, her voice catching, 'that the deepest thanks are yours. Over all the years you have been, I think, the better part of me. We have sung, nearly always, to the same music. I could not say that,' she raised her face to his, 'of any other man I have known. Stay with me, always. We make our newest beginning today. We have made so many together.' She laughed, her hand reaching to touch his slanted cheek. 'Do you remember the first?'

Chinghiz caught the hand and carried it to his lips, knowing she had given him licence. Pain and pleasure made him giddy.

'Indeed I do,' he said. 'Ours is a relationship which began with the leap of a tiger. It was a uniquely auspicious omen. How could the future have been anything but glorious after that?'

They looked at each other for a long space, in affection, collusion and mutual congratulation, and in the universal sadness that was always a visitor to their most serious moments.

'Come, Little Mistress,' he said steadily at last. 'It is time for you to receive the mandate of Heaven. But first,' he added in the old laconic tone, 'perhaps I had better make good the damage to your face. Try, please, *not* to indulge in any more tears!'

They took her to the hall where the throne was waiting.

The vast, crimson-beamed chamber was packed tight with every degree of nobleman and minister, all half-drunk with incense and expectation.

Facing them at the north end, isolated on its high dais, remote, dreaming and magnificent, stood the Dragon Throne.

There was a hush as Black Jade entered by the south door, moving through the coloured ranks, clothed in her beauty and the sacred hour.

The first minister came forward to usher her to the throne, then fell back as she began to ascend the steps, her face distant and entranced. She felt the world drop away behind her as might a bird in flight, a phoenix or an immortal. There was music; she did not know if it was real. There were strange swirling clouds which might have been aromatics but seemed imbued with higher, stronger presences which were moved by pleasure, even by triumph. They had come to her, here, even as they had been with her on Taishan. The watchers, their breath stopped, saw her smile like a Goddess as she turned to them before the throne.

The mandate was truly hers. She knew it in this Heaven-given moment, as surely as she knew the weight of the crown she wore.

She stepped backward, feeling the gilded ebony behind her, then seated herself and listened as the deep sigh of acceptance of the Black-haired People went up into the scented clouds.

They brought her the sceptre and the sacred jades, and the Chief Minister read the proclamation which told the universe who she was.

'Wu Tser t'ien, Sheng-shen Huang-ti.' The Empress Wu, Patterned after Heaven, Holy and Divine Sovereign.

Black Jade, daughter of Wu shih-huo.

The prophecy was fulfilled. Green Dragon had become White Tiger.

Epilogue

For those who would like to know – Wu Chao's (Black Jade's) reign as Empress was as eventful as her earlier life had been. Her government continued to be astute and efficient, and her grateful ministers supported her through several abortive attempts on the part of the Wu or the Li to replace her with one of her sons.

Her private life remained the enjoyable scandal of the court, though the turbulent Feng overreached himself at last by burning down the *Ming T'ang* in a passion of jealousy when his mistress turned to a new lover. This was Meng Shen, once the boy she had taught at Kan Yeh. He had become a calm, witty and eminently sensible man, a physician and scholar, who was to keep her affection as long as she lived. His good sense could not prevent her from indulging in other less wise liaisons, however, notably with the Chang brothers, a pair of young court butterflies whose outrageous behaviour and rapacious family turned the court upside down. With deep regret, the ministers persuaded the Empress's third son (Loud Tiger) that the time had come for her to abdicate.

Defeated only by the fact that she was eighty years old and in poor health, she consented to retire gracefully to the Dowager's Palace, from where she cast an ironic eye over the chaotic webs of intrigue in which her children struggled thereafter. When at last a single strong figure prevailed, it was her favourite grandson, 'Little Dragon', who was to carry the Dragon Throne of the T'ang to the apex of its glory, a fitting heir to Li Shih-min and to the astonishing woman who, alone of her sex, has ever held the mandate of Heaven.

Chronology

Age of B.J.	A.D.	
	625	Black Jade is born in Wen Shui.
13	638	Her father dies and she enters the palace in Chang An.
17	642	She becomes the favourite concubine of Emperor Li Shih Min.
18	643	She befriends Pheasant who shortly becomes Crown Prince.
24	649	Li Shih Min dies.
25	650	Black Jade spends a year in the convent of Kan Yeh.
26	651	She returns to the court. Lotus Bud born.
27	652	Shc becomes the new Emperor, Pheasant's concubine.
28	653	Her first son, Bold Tiger is born.
29	654	A second son, Young Tiger, is born.
30	655	Birth and death of her baby daughter. Suspicion of Empress.
31	656	Despite machinations of her enemies, Black Jade becomes Pheasant's Empress Consort.
32	657	Ex-Empress Paulownia convicted of sorcery. Black Jade has her executed. Loud Tiger, the third son, is born.
32	657	Haunted by her victims, Black Jade removes to Loyang for a year.
33	658	Death of Old Integrity.
34	659	Death of Archduke Wuchi.
35	660	Pheasant's first illness.
36	661	Black Jade conducts war with Korea. Death of Rose Bird, Black Jade's sister.
37	662	Dawn Tiger, her fourth son is born. Black Jade falls in love with Shing-jen the Taoist priest.

38	663	He is accused of sorcery and has to leave the capital.
39	664	Birth of Tiger Lily, her long-awaited daughter.
40	665	Truce in Korea.
41	666	Imperial visit to Taishan.
42	667	Lotus Bud dies at 16.
		Three years of famine.
44	669	Bold Tiger marries at 16.
45	670	Golden Willow dies, Black Jade's mother, also Sage Path and Great Wall.
46	671	Young Tiger marries at 17; Bold Tiger at 14 contracted to Red Poppy; Pheasant ill again.
47	672	Loyang becomes the permanent capital of the Empire.
	672-5	Bold Tiger is Regent.
50	675	Black Jade causes death of daughter-in-law, Red Poppy.
		Bold Tiger dies at 22. Young Tiger becomes Crown Prince at 21, tormented by rumour that he is not Black Jade's son.
52	677	War with Tibet. Tiger Lily's convent built when she is 13.
54	679	Young Tiger murders Ming the Astrologer.
		Tiger Lily meets Bold-hand at 15.
55	680	Tiger Lily's marriage at 16. Young Tiger is exiled. Loud Tiger becomes Crown Prince at 23.
58	683	Pheasant dies. Loud Tiger becomes nominal Emperor at 26 under Black Jade's guidance.
59	684	Loud Tiger desposed at 27. Dawn Tiger replaces him.
		T'ang rebellion put down. 'Reign of Terror'.
60	685	Black Jade falls in love with Feng. Makes him Abbot of White Horse Monastery.
61	686	The Stone of Prophecy discovered. Black Jade moves towards throne.
63	688	Revolt of Tang Princes crushed.
65	690	Black Jade ascends the Dragon Throne.